The heart of the eternal

By

Nuredhel

Chapter 1: A wise choice of action

The great chamber was quiet, only the slow trickle of water over rock could be heard and everybody present tried to stand still, not make a sound. The pool in the middle of the room was crystal clear, the water almost impossibly pure and cold and the raised dais in the middle was lighted by one single ray of moonlight from above. This was the one night of this century when the moonlight would hit the dais and it was a sacred night to every race within this realm. Everywhere around the pool people were gathered, all wearing the same white cloaks and all being caught in a sensation of awe and peace. This room was a sanctuary, and it had been for ages countless. The walls were natural but here and there small carvings had been made, depicting the gods and their powers and the entire room was rather dark. The only light came from that beam of moon light but all there could see rather well in spite of it. The water reflected the pale light rather well.

The dais held a throne, very simple and not at all very elaborate but nobody dared to look at it or its inhabitant. She sat there with her eyes closed, naked and covered with her long bluish hair. She wore no jewellery, no adornments and her skin was unmarred and perfect. She did look like a young maiden on the cusp of womanhood but everybody knew she was ancient. A power older than any of the ones present on this day. The girl on the dais opened her eyes, they were pale blue and piercing and she started to chant. The water around the dais became milky, lost its transparency and it seemed to almost boil along the edge of the pool. Then it fell quiet and she got up, walked down the few steps towards the water and stepped in. It should have been deep, way over her head but it wasn't, it just reached her calves and she stopped and raised her arms. "Hear ye, I am here, I am ready, I will see."

A tall figure on the edge of the pool bowed deeply. "So it shall be, tell us o lady of the moon, who is chosen. Who is it that fate watches and favours? Whose future will be decided today?"

The girl stood there like a perfect image of unspoiled beauty, her hair so long it dragged behind her and she had the long elegant limbs of her race and the delicate features. But she also radiated strength and power and nobody would ever dare to question her right to change destiny itself. All bowed to her will, mortal and immortal, kings and pawns. She smiled slowly. "Hear me brothers and sisters, the gods have spoken to me, Dih'rien of the first walkers, and told me the name of the one in their favour."

She raised a hand and pointed at one of those gathered there, a very tall figure that stood in the middle of the crowd. "Step forth brother, the will of the gods cannot be denied"

The figure seemed to shiver if only for a moment, then he did step forth. "I will not question the will of the gods"

He dropped the cloak and was as naked as the girl, they all were. The cloak was all that covered their flesh. He was very tall, even for one of his race and if the girl was a picture of perfect feminine grace he was the epitome of masculine elegance and strength, the body looked as if it was carved by an artist and he moved with the unrestrained elegance of a predator. Only a few scars did mar this tall male and he seemed to extrude raw power and majesty. His hair reached his knees, it was unbound and he wore no jewels, just as the girl. Nobody was allowed to carry any sign of status or wealth while in this most holy of caves, here all were equal. His skin was rather dark, like oiled leather and his hair a deep colour of gold, like a ripe field of wheat. He was as beautiful as the girl, just in a more ragged way. He walked forth and stopped at the edge of the pool. "Step forth Ahravan and do not fear"

He swallowed visibly and took a tentative step into the pool. He didn't sink, his feet found solid ground where there should have been none and he walked slowly across the pool, towards her. Everybody knew that if a person who was wicked and dark of soul and mind stepped inn he or she

4

would fall to the bottom and drown. The girl was almost as tall as him, which was rather odd considering that he was the tallest person of the crowd. She cocked her head. "Ahravan, son of Nirhaen, are you ready to hear the words of the gods?"

He nodded, his head held low in respect and nervous reverence. "I am o high one!"

She smiled and laid her hand on his head, closed her eyes. To be the one called forth thus was a tremendous honour but one with a somewhat bitter taste, you didn't always like what was being told and whence the prophecy was heard it couldn't be undone. What was said would happen, one way or the other. He was shivering from head to toe and everybody there were silent, you could have heard a leaf fall. She opened her eyes again, a tender expression on her face. "Assembled, listen to my words and remember them, this is the prophecy, this will be, and nobody, mortal or immortal must stand in its way!"

The crowd mumbled as one. "Nobody!"

She took his hands, held them loosely in her own. "The gods have spoken and their will is clear. You will send some of your best men to the mountains, in the valley where the winds meet they will find a girl, she has the mark of the gods in her skin. She has seen few summers but is no child and her soul is carrying a rare gift of which she is unaware. Use the crystal of truth and the mark will be visible, placed at the back of her neck. That girl must be brought to you and you will take her as your spouse and her presence will cause great change, and her gifts will flourish. What was lost so long ago may be found through her and our future secured. Go now, and make it so, the gods have spoken"

The male gasped and his eyes revealed his shock and confusion but he nodded. "The gods have spoken, so it will be, so it must be!"

The girl bent a little closer, placed a swift kiss on his forehead. "Go, and be blessed. I see great joy which will come because of this"

He didn't answer, he just bowed deeply and turned around, walked back with slow steps, everybody could see that it had upset him though. The girl climbed up onto the dais again and the light from the moon suddenly disappeared, as if it had never been there. The dais seemed to disappear as well and the crowd started to chant slowly and in a whisper as they all made their way to the entrance. The tall male stood there, looking a bit helpless, he seemed to breathe with some difficulty. Then he pulled the cloak back on, almost clumsily before he joined the rest. It was said, it would be done. That didn't mean that he in any way loved the idea. The valley where the winds met, that could only mean one thing, his future spouse was human.

The sharp autumn wind did bite her bare skin and she pulled her shawl tighter around her, the huge net on her back was heavy but she was used to hard work and proud of her strength. It was filled with dry grass and she fought her way up the steep slope and found the narrow path where she could take a few deep breaths of air before walking on. Her father came up onto the path behind her and he smiled and looked pleased. "Just three more loads left, then this field is done"

She grinned and started walking, this area was so steep and full of cliffs they had to gather the hay for their sheep using a sickle and such nets. It was the only way for they couldn't even swing a sling blade where it was steepest. They had used to harvest a field a little to the west of this but it was almost vertical and they had to tie themselves onto ropes when doing something there. The land wasn't very fertile at all and sheep and goats were their main source of wealth, if one could use that word. Here every straw had to be harvested and gathered for the coming winter and the survival of the herd depended upon it. The farms lower down towards the valley bottom kept cattle and they were way more wealthy and much better off but Ulfar had always been stubborn and he had made it there. The farm was small and the buildings rather tiny but it were all well-made and he knew how to farm this land, even if the fertility of the area he owned was very bad. They could farm grass and some vegetables and everything else they needed they had to trade for, exchanging it with wool and cheese. The barn was placed in one of the very few spots on the property which was relatively flat. It wasn't large but it was already filled with hay and the building which housed the animals was next to it and all of their animals were inside. They had thirty ewes and some goats, one pig and some chickens and geese and that was it. It was all that this little piece of the land could feed.

They emptied the nets into the barn and Ulfar sat down, took a sip of water and the girl got one too, the sun was sharp and even if it was cold there you could feel its sting. She pulled her braid back and straightened her skirt, it was a bit short and rather worn and she felt very self-conscious about this. Ulfar sighed and petted her knee. "Come on, we need to get the last loads back here, it will rain tomorrow "

Wenja smiled and grasped the net, it was woven from the thin hairs of the goats and weighed next to nothing, her mother Sina had made them and she was an expert at this type of weaving. She even made fishnets. The path back to the field wasn't long, the whole property was large but they only harvested the fields closest to the farm itself. Those had the best growth conditions and thus they could keep the best hay for the winter when the sheep had to be fed each day. Ulfar was a bit quiet this day, his usually merry whistling absent and Wenja knew that something was wrong, but she didn't ask him and she knew that he wouldn't tell her unless he wanted to. So she held her mouth shut and tried to be efficient. It would be dark soon and they had to be done by then, not only was the terrain in itself dangerous in the darkness but the area did house dangerous beasts like wolves, mountains cats and the so called wraith wolves which were huge canines which hunted not in a pack but as solitary beasts. They got the last hay in and she saw that the sun did set into the skies, he was right, it would rain the next day for sure. The farm house was small, it was cramped already and Sina was on her way with their next babe, which was why she wasn't allowed to go outside and help with the hay. The rules there were strict, a woman couldn't leave the house when she was pregnant for it could make the spirits jealous of her and make her lose the baby or even worse, make the baby weak or sick.

Sina sat by the bench with her knitting pins and she was busy trying to fix one of Ulfar's sweaters, she was a good wife and mother and Wenja loved her dearly. Halda lay in her bed and Wenja cringed, the rasping breath had been there for months now and it didn't get any better, not even by a bit. The local wise woman, Luda, had given them herbs which were to be burned and the smoke inhaled but it had only eased the girl's breath for a few days. Wenja went over to sit by Halda's side, the girl smiled and held up a small embroidered patch of cloth. "Look, isn't it pretty?"

Wenja smiled and stroked Halda's hair. "It is very pretty, you will make a good embroiderer sister"

Farkur was busy repairing some tools, he was eight and a bit of a rascal and his brother Surun sat at his feet, wailing because he wasn't allowed to play with the knife. He was only three so it was no wonder. Their sister Idah at five was trying to knit some socks but the result didn't really look that much like a sock at all, more like a pouch of some kind. Here everybody had to pull their weight if they were to survive and Wenja swallowed her feeling if despair. Halda was thirteen, a very thin and reed like girl with a very pretty face and a wonderful voice but she had been confined to this bed for a long time now. She had slipped and fallen down one of the very steep canyons and broken her back and her legs were paralyzed. She couldn't even sit in bed and Sina had to help her relieve herself and even wash the girl each day. Her hands were agile enough and Halda did make her contribution to the household by embroidering and knitting and even making beautiful braided ribbons for clothes and to tie back hair with.

Wenja felt so sorry for Halda, she would never get married and never see a better future for she was not going to survive the winter. Luda had said so much, the girl's lungs were weakening and sometimes she would cough for hours. It broke Wenja's heart but there was nothing they could do, nothing at all. They were too poor to buy medicine and the nearest real healer was weeks away. Luda was wise in her own ways but she couldn't cure this and she didn't try to fool them by giving them false hope. She was straight forward and even Halda knew the truth, this autumn would be her last unless a miracle happened.

Ulfar helped Sina prepare some food, it wasn't much they had. Just some porridge made from wild wheat, some dried apples and some mutton. The meat had been dried and salted and was hard and looked like black wood but they were grateful for what they had. They drank some sheep milk and Sina moaned as the baby kicked her rather hard. She would be due in just a month now and Wenja wondered how they were gonna make it with one more mouth to feed. When Surun was born Sina had had very little milk and the boy had grown very slowly, he was still small for his age and he didn't really speak, there seemed to be something wrong with him. Wenja knew that the local women despised Sina, the reason was that she was of a rather poor family who didn't own land and just worked for others and still Ulfar had fallen in love with her and married her. Ulfar wasn't rich, far from it but he was still better than Sina in the eyes of the village and thus everybody looked at Sina with suspicion. Surun didn't look like Ulfar, he was dark and his eyes almond shaped and many of the local gossip makers said that Sina had been unfaithful and slept with another man to have a baby that dark. Ulfar was blond and tall and even though his back was bent from hard work many thought that he was handsome.

Wenja wasn't really Ulfar and Sina's daughter, she was the daughter of Ulfar's sister Rutha who had left the valley and married a man from the coast. She had been gone for years and when she returned she had carried Wenja on her back and worn clothes nobody there had seen the likes off. She had worn a richly embroidered cape, long flowing skirts and a white blouse. The women had been jealous in spite of the fact that Rutha had been a widow, her husband lost at sea. Wenja had been a year old then and Rutha died when she was two, it was something in her stomach, something which grew and ate her from the inside. Ulfar did adopt Wenja and Sina and he loved her like their own flesh and blood. Wenja didn't look like the villagers at all, she was taller than the other women there, and her body more slender too. Her hair was dark auburn red of colour and her eyes bright green with a hint of grey and she was of those who has skin like porcelain with not even a freckle. Ulfar was worried because of Wenja, he knew that she was smarter than the other village girls and now that she had passed eighteen she was more than ready for marriage but who deserved his little princess? None of the villagers, that was for darn sure. They would regard her as a ewe, used for breeding and hard work and that sparkle in her eyes would die out forever.

Sina made sure that everybody got some food, even Halda, she was only thirty years of age but looked older, her hair grey and thin and her skin wrinkled. She had four children and the fifth on the way but she had given birth to many more than that. She usually carried one baby a year but few of them had survived, losing infants was normal there and it had worn her out. Wenja knew that she had lost some pregnancies too and that had been extra hard on her. The only good thing about it was that she didn't have to go to the village and face the vicious rumours more than once a year when they celebrated the winter solstice. Most women there had lost more children than they had seen grow up and it was just accepted, it was the way it always had been. Ulfar put his cup down and sighed. "Dagar came to me today, again!"

Sina swallowed, her hand trembling a bit. "And?"

Her husband tried to smile but his eyes were dark. "He wants the fields love, and he wants them bad. He thinks there may be ore underneath our land"

Wenja felt her throat tighten. "Is there pa?"

Ulfar shrugged. "I don't know, I am a sheep farmer, not a miner. But he says that he can find it and he has offered me gold for the farm."

Sina looked down. "You didn't accept"

Ulfar shook his head. "No, this land has belonged to my family for many generations, we are older than Dagar and his kin and our claim to this land indisputable. Even he knows that. But he tried to tempt me, even though I have told him it doesn't work"

Sina sighed. "Gold doesn't last, without the farm, where would we go? We cannot be like the thralls, homeless and wandering about, looking for work and scraps of food"

Ulfar sent her a sad smile, her family was among those who had been regarded as nothing but filth. Owning land meant status there, being without a home meant that you were nobody.

But even with gold they couldn't buy another farm, good farms were expensive and he was too old to buy land and build a new house and get new livestock. No, they had to stay and he had to ward off Dagar. He was the wealthiest man of the village and the most ruthless one, he seemed to be aiming to buy all the land in the area and become like a small king. Nobody liked him but many did fear him, some said that accidents had happened to those who had refused his generous offers.

10

Sina rubbed her belly. "Has he mentioned Mjorr again?"

Ulfar nodded and his face got hard. Mjorr was Dagar's son and he was twenty two years of age and a terrible man the way this valley saw it. He didn't leave any woman alone if she was attractive and rumours said that he had sired many bastards in the nearby valleys. It was a terrible shame but Dagar didn't scold the young man at all, he seemed to believe that this did prove his son's manliness and strength. "He told me that Mjorr is ready to give three cows for her"

Sina scoffed. "Three cows? Is he insane? We don't sell our children and only three? Our little treasure here is worth three hundred cows"

Wenja grinned and blushed, she was glad Ulfar said no to all these attempts Mjorr did at marrying her. He had asked several times and was getting more and more bothersome. That very summer he had tried to drag Wenja in behind the old temple when they visited the village to trade and it hadn't been hard to guess what he had wanted to do. He had tried to get inn under her skirts and she had grasped a fat pile of cow shit and smeared it into his face as she cried out for help. Mjorr was used to the girls fawning up to him but Wenja saw through him. If she married him he would cheat on her and leave her and probably treat her without even an ounce of respect. Ulfar leaned over and ruffled her hair. "I told him to go packing, my daughter is not some cow for sale, not something to mount and then forget."

Wenja made a grimace. "He cannot have liked that"

Ulfar shrugged. "No, he didn't, but I don't care. Not even Hodan likes him and I heard Bagir tell that he refused Dagar entrance to a ceremony last week, claiming that he was impure. I bet that Adrai and her little school of gossipers loved that"

Bagir was a local herder and he was extremely skilled with the sheep. He and Ulfar had been friends since childhood and Wenja liked Bagir, he was very smart and cunning and he didn't like Dagar at all. He was said to have let two of Dagar's best rams drown in a flash flood two years ago. Wenja chewed her meat slowly, it was hard on her teeth but she didn't care, at least she got food. When everybody was done eating they put the children to bed, they shared one bed and Wenja shared bed with Halda.

The three beds they did have were small and short and hard and Wenja was glad she was tired most of the time, then at least she did sleep.

The next morning came with sleet and wind and Ulfar did go outside to feed the sheep, the last two years many sheep had died in this valley because of a new plant which spread like wildfire and for once Dagar was smart for he paid a copper coin to everyone who managed to keep it away from their land. The seeds did poison the sheep and cattle and the chief had agreed upon the plan. Karkar was the chosen leader of this valley, a very wise elderly man with a large family and a very powerful wife who always had something rather crass to tell Dagar whenever they met. And she did despise Mjorr and didn't stop telling the young girls that a pretty face meant nothing unless the interior was just as fair. Karkar had a man working for him, his name was Marhan and he was a former soldier and very large and strong. The sole reason why Dagar hadn't openly tried to seize power was said to be Marhan for even though Dagar had some thugs working for him as well they were valley boys and they had rarely ever held a sword.

Sina was preparing wool to make felt and Wenja helped her, it was hard work which required hot water and soap and they had been boiling soap earlier that autumn and Sina had some bars laying in a shelf, prepared with perfume. Sigunn, Karkar's wife wanted to buy it and Wenja knew it was out of pity and compassion. The soap wasn't that good, but it was at least able to make things clean and Sigunn had money and she wasn't of those who hated Sina for having married her way up in life. By buying her soap she showed support and the other women of the village wouldn't dare to go against her since she was the chief's wife and high priestess of the local temple. Sina and Wenja were half done with the bone breaking work when there was a knock on the door, Sina did look nervous right away, she wasn't used to strangers and she was wet and her clothes worn thin. Wenja opened, it was Sigunn and she smiled and bowed her head. "The gods bless this house, my oh my Sina, you look like a balloon"

Sina sighed with relief, Sigunn wasn't dangerous, far from it and the woman placed a small basket on the table. "I have come for the lovely soap of yours Sina, and I brought some snacks for the children."

Farkur did grin from one ear to the other as Sigunn gave him a piece of rock candy and Idah curtsied as a real woman. Surun got some too and started wailing for more right away. Halda got a large lump and thanked with a wide grin and shining eyes. Sigunn got the bars and put them into her cloak, she did look half drenched and Sina tilted her head. "It is a long way up here from the valley in such nasty weather."

Wenja knew what her mother did mean, Sigunn hadn't come all this way for just some soap. She opened the basket and took out some bread, a bottle of wine and some packets wrapped in linen. "I thought about you and your delicate condition, I know you have little food but this ought to strengthen you dear"

Sina blushed. "That is too much, just the wine…"

Sigunn shook her finger. "No protests little one, you need it. You are right, it is a long way to go, but I had to come here, I have some news which cannot wait"

Sina blinked and sat down, slowly. Her intuition told her it was bad. "Yes?"

Sigunn opened one of the packets, it was a sort of cheese Wenja hadn't seen before, it looked creamy and soft and the elderly woman cut a large piece out of it and handed it to Sina. "Try this dear, it will do you good"

Sina took the piece gently but her eyes were large. "Tell me, what is wrong?"

Sigunn sighed. "Mjorr, cursed be his bones, that is what's wrong. He is furious, and he has sworn that he will marry Wenja, with or without Ulfar's consent"

Sina gaped and Wenja felt cold all the way inside, like there was a cold claw grasping at her guts. "No, that isn't possible? He cannot do that?"

Sigunn nodded. "I am afraid he is desperate and stupid enough to force the girl, so Wenja, stay here. Do not leave the farm unless your father or Bagir is with you. If Mjorr has his way with you the laws demand that you get married, be it with or without your consent and blessing"

Wenja almost panted, rape was the ultimate sin among their people, and few would even use the word. The mere idea of being forced into a marriage thus made her shiver to the bone. Sina was hoarse. "He cannot truly believe that he can get away with such a crime? His father is powerful yes, but he isn't the high priest"

Sigunn nodded. "Mjorr thinks that his father can fix anything on his behalf. I fear that he already has. Wenja here is too beautiful for her own good that is the sad thing"

Wenja swallowed. "There is nobody in the village I like, and nobody I want to marry"

Sigunn smiled gently. "I know sweetheart, but you have come of age and I fear that Mjorr wouldn't stop even if you were betrothed to someone. He wants you, and he wants you bad. And a man who is used to get what he wants is a very dangerous thing indeed. "

Sina groaned. "Oh by the goddess, I am so grateful you warned us Sigunn. What are we to do?"

The woman laid a hand on Wenja's, the hand was warm and worn. "Keep her safe, and when summer comes go south, into the larger valleys. Seek out the markets, I am sure a maiden as fair as Wenja can find a good husband there, someone who cares and knows how to take care of a woman. The men here are no good, no, forget about them"

Sina giggled and Wenja tried to smile. Staying indoors the entire winter, it would be tough but doable, if the alternative was to be forced into becoming Mjorr's wife. Sigunn took some coloured yarn out of her basket and walked over to Halda, "Here dear, some nice things for you, one day you will embroider the gowns of every bride in this valley for sure"

Halda blushed and took the yarn with trembling hands, Wenja saw that her hands were shivering more than they had previously and she felt a terrible feeling of sorrow building up inside. Sina ate some cheese and had some wine and Sigunn grasped the bag again. "I must take my leave of you so I return before it gets dark, but remember my words. I fear that Wenja may not be safe from that idiot, even as a wife to another man. That lad is not right in the head you know, his mother should have smothered him with his diapers"

14

Sina nodded. "He is an only son that is too bad. He has been allowed to roam free for too long"

Sigunn pulled her cloak on again. "Yes, and his sister is living in his shadow completely. The poor lass is a mere shadow of a person"

Wenja made a grimace. She had seen Mjorr's sister Prina, she was a thin pale girl with blonde hair and a pair of enormous eyes which always looked terrified. Dagar didn't care about his daughter, he rarely mentioned her at all and she received no love from him. She was a burden, a mistake. Dagar's wife had died two years after Prina was born and Dagar had never remarried for if he did he would have to stay true to his wife and he didn't care that much about that notion at all. He was almost as bad as his son, and everybody knew that rather well.

Ulfar did return from the barn when Sigunn had left and Sina told him everything, he sat down and made a grimace. "That is bad, that is very bad. Wenja, you know of the cave with the old drawings?"

Wenja nodded. "Yes, it is high in the mountains, by the dark lake?"

Ulfar smiled, it was a very thin smile. "One can live there, and only I and Bagir know of it. I showed it to him years ago. If it comes to it I will send him there with you and you will be safe. It will be a cold winter for sure but Mjorr won't find you"

Wenja closed her eyes. A winter alone, in a cold dark cave, away from everyone she loved, away from the light. No, she wouldn't make it, that was too much to ask for. "I cannot do that father, please, I…I would die"

Sina nodded in despair. "She is right, it is too dangerous. We can keep her safe, tell Bagir to keep an eye on our farm, ask him…ask him for a dog."

Ulfar stroked his beard. "You are wise wife of mine, a dog, yes. Mjorr cannot trick a dog, it may warn us if someone comes here with ill intent"

He got up. "I will go to Bagir now, I can reach his hut and get back before it becomes too dark"

He grasped his hat and cloak and took off and Wenja swallowed the taste of bile. If only Mjorr could go and drown in a bog or something like that. Sina was nervous and Wenja even more so and when Ulfar did return very late both had gone to bed. Ulfar had borrowed a dog from Bagir, a very large black long haired one with kind eyes and a set of very impressive teeth. "This is Bjarkad, he is very kind but will guard our house!"

Ulfar did go to bed too and the lights were blown out. Wenja lay there shivering, what sort of future would she face now? She was going to have to watch her every step until she got so old and ugly nobody would want her. It wasn't a life, it was like being a prisoner and she just prayed that they could go to the markets early the next summer, so she could get away with her honour intact.

The next day's Wenja had to stay in the house, at all times. She didn't even go to the sheep barn to help Ulfar feed the animals as she usually did. Instead Farkur helped him and Surun was wailing constantly since he couldn't stand to be away from his big brother. Sina did take it with some acceptance, she never complained about anything, even when she really ought to. There was plenty of work to do and Wenja was never bored but she had a constant feeling of dread at the back of her mind, what if Mjorr decided to attack? He did have friends who were just as stupid and brutish as himself and not even Dagar was able to control them. The dog was a blessing, he was a good watchdog and would bark whenever he did notice that anything did move in the area around the farm. Ulfar did praise the dog each time that happened and gave it treats. Then Bagir dropped by on his way to the village with some hides, the man was dark and thin and his face tanned and worn by sun and wind but he had a sparkle in his eyes and he was smiling all the time. But this time his smile was absent and his eyes were dark, he kicked the snow off his shoes and petted the dog which wagged its tail in ecstatic joy.

"I have seen Mjorr, the other day. He was wandering around by the dam, I didn't ask him what he was doing there but he did look like a thundercloud"

Ulfar scoffed. "That lad looks as if he has tried to suck on a sour apple for too long, why can't he realize that my daughter isn't for him?"

Bagir shrugged. "She resists him, that makes her irresistible in the eyes of a man like that. I know the type, he isn't right in the head, not by a longshot."

Sina did heat some water and gave Bagir some tea, the man did thank her with a small grin. Ulfar leaned his chin into his hands. "We can only hope that the paths south open early next spring, so we can go to the markets. If Wenja goes somewhere else I hope he will forget about her"

Bagir sort of mumbled. "I wouldn't count on it, that incident with the cow dung did sting his pride. No woman has ever fought back you know"

Ulfar scoffed. "And whose fault is that? The villagers raise their daughters to be meek and tame and then they complain about their wives being boring and dumb?"

He petted Wenja on her shoulder. "I am proud to say that my Wenja is capable of thinking on her own"

Bagir nodded and snickered. "She would be too strong for a man like Mjorr, he would fear her and a man like that hates what he fears. He can never marry a strong woman, he would end up murdering her."

Ulfar had a hard expression upon his face. "I trust that you can keep an eye on us?"

Bagir nodded. "I surely will, the snow is coming and tracks can be seen from afar. I know your way of walking Ulfar, if I see any strange tracks I will let you know!"

Sina did look relieved but Wenja felt nervous still. How could anyone be that spoiled and mad? Bagir sighed. "There are rumours spreading throughout the village, Dagar is getting tired of Mjorr causing problems. Dagar want to increase his influence through the valleys and he can't when his son is causing one scandal after the other, they say Dagar is negotiating a marriage to the daughter of one of the valley chieftains south of here"

Ulfar sighed deeply. "If only that was true, then my daughter would be safe"

Bagir let out a small growl. "No, she wouldn't. Mjorr is determined Ulfar, he wants her, if only to humiliate her, make her unattractive to others."

Ulfar looked down. "I know, it breaks my heart to keep her trapped inside of this small house but there is no other way."

Bagir nodded. "Stay strong, the gods are with those who don't break. One day Mjorr will meet his destiny, do not doubt that"

Sina rocked Surun on her knee. "If that only could happen soon"

Bagir did leave and now snow was starting to fall, the area was very pretty but the cold was an enemy and they always feared that the winter would be too long, that their storages would run out before the warmth returned. Wenja stayed indoors, weaved and knitted and tried to keep herself occupied and Ulfar had more than enough work with the sheep. The pig was ruining his small home so Ulfar had to rebuild it and Farkur helped him. The boy was going to become a very strong man one day, and a capable one too for he wasn't afraid of working hard. A week went by and then one morning Bjarkad acted in a funny way, the dog was whining and hiding under the house and refused to come out. Ulfar had to drag him out and then the dog spewed and there was blood in it. Sina was terrified it could be something which was contagious but Ulfar didn't think so. It had come too fast.

The dog was laying in front of the hearth shivering and whimpering and in obvious agony and then it spewed more blood and they just knew it, it was dying. Ulfar was shocked, what could this be? The dog had been perfectly healthy the day before and it had to be some sort of injury. Before noon the dog died and Ulfar knew that Bagir would mourn him, the dogs meant the world to that man. He went to tell Bagir and the herder did come with Ulfar when he returned. The two men did cut the dog open and Wenja had never seen that expression on her father's face before. He was furious and scared at the same time and Bagir was fuming. Sina was massaging Halda's legs and she turned her head, her eyes told Wenja that she realized that something was very wrong. "What was it?"

Bagir swallowed hard. "A most terrible trick hunters used in the old days, when they hunted wolves. They would boil the rib of a lamb and sharpen it in both ends, bend it and put it inside of a small piece of meat and leave it for the wolves and when they ate the piece of meat it would thaw in their gut and the rib would straighten itself out again and pierce its guts"

Sina gasped and Ulfar cussed, Surun made huge eyes, he wasn't used to his father using such strong words. "Mjorr was behind this, mark my words. He was afraid of the dog."

Bagir sighed "I have no more dogs to spare, I am sorry. I don't know what to do, but I can stay here if you like. I just need a place to sleep in the hay"

Ulfar smiled, a grateful expression on his face. "Bless you friend, that would be wonderful, with two men present the bastard will find an attack less tempting."

Farkur was pulling at Ulfar's coat. "I am a man too, three men!"

Farkur did ruffle his son's hair. "Yes, you are a man too, of course you are. Three brave warriors, that ought to keep the women safe now wouldn't it?"

Farkur did look very proud and he did hold his head up high, he was beaming with it.

They buried the poor dog and Wenja knew that whoever did it was capable of doing even worse things, a dog was very precious up there. The farms couldn't make it without good dogs protecting the herds and the worth of a watchdog could be greater than the worth of a good horse.

Bagir would go down to the village every now and then and he did listen to the gossip and kept his eyes open and one evening he did return and his eyes were wide and he was almost panting. It was obvious that he had seen something very strange and Wenja did think that he looked a bit like a hunting dog which has caught an interesting scent. The family gathered by the table and Bagir stared at Ulfar. "Strangers have arrived at the village, travellers from afar. They are emissaries from the Ath'ir"

Ulfar gasped. "What? Are you kidding me?"

Bagir shook his head. "No, it is a group from what I have been told and they have a lot of wagons and everything but that was left in the village down by the lake, the road here is too narrow for such. There are at least five of them here now, and three are of the eternal"

Sina gaped and Wenja had to swallow, the eternal, she had never even seen one of those before. Ulfar frowned. "What are they doing here? Our protectors does usually stay on the plains?"

Bagir grinned. "Oh, that is where it becomes interesting, you see, there is a sort of prophecy and they have come because of it. There is someone they need to find"

Sina frowned and Halda did lift herself as much as she could. "Who?"

Bagir shrugged. "A maiden, with a mark at the back of her neck. They demand that every unwed woman is gathered by the temple tomorrow, to be checked"

Sina did look a bit suspicious. "Why? What do they want with this maid?"

Bagir snickered. "She is to get married to the Ath'ir"

Ulfar did look as if the moon had fallen down. "Are you serious?"

Bagir nodded and stretched. "Oh yes, and the mark is invisible to the naked eye so it can be anyone!"

Wenja wetted her lips. "Oh, what if it is Prina? She is unwed, and young. Or Solfi, she is pretty"

Sina scoffed. "If it is Solfi then pity be with the Ath'ir for she is a despicable one"

Wenja blinked. "Does that mean that I have to go to the village?"

Bagir nodded. "Yes, every unwed maiden has to go. It is an order, and we cannot go against the will of the protectors. But worry not, there will be people everywhere and we will be with you, nobody is gonna try something funny in the middle of a crowd"

Halda sighed. "I cannot go"

Sina stroked her hair. "No sweetheart, I am so sorry. This is so sad"

Wenja tried to cheer her sister up. "You know, I can tell you all about it when I return"

Halda nodded slowly. "Do that"

She turned her head to Bagir. "Did you see them, the eternal? Are they as pretty as people say they are?"

Bagir nodded. "Yes, like gods, but I only saw them from afar"

Wenja felt a knot in her gut, one part of her wanted to go, desperately. She had never seen anyone of that mysterious race and she had wanted to, ever since she was a kid. The other part of her was terrified, what if Mjorr did try something after all? But they had to obey, everybody knew that the Ath'ir and his warriors was what kept the mountain region safe from terrible monsters and it was a pact as old as time itself. The gods favoured those who did honour the eternal.

Ulfar sighed deeply. "Then we'll go early in the morning, before dawn. And we will bring our spears and our knives and you Wenja will carry my sword"

Wenja swallowed hard, she had learned how to stab and strike with that sword but nothing more. Sina tried to smile. "It will be good for you dear, to get out of here again. Stay with your father and Bagir, it will be fine"

Wenja sent her mother a forced grin, it didn't feel like it would be fine, it felt like it would be a very stupid thing to do. But they had to go, everybody knew of her and refusing the call would be to throw shame upon their name. Was seeing the eternal really worth the risk? Only time would tell.

The next morning Sina woke her up very early and they got dressed with the warmest clothes they had. Bagir carried his spear and Ulfar had some long knives and Sina did slip Wenja a small knife she normally used for cutting threads. It was tiny enough to hide in a sleeve and Wenja did attach it to her tunic before pulling her jacket on. Sina did look nervous, she was wringing her hands and hugged Ulfar when they were to leave. "Watch her well beloved"

Ulfar nodded. "I will, do not worry my sunlight"

Wenja did pull the cowl of the cape up over her head and then they started the long walk down to the valley. It was very steep to begin with and Bagir had made a sort of railing many places, ropes tied to trees and rocks and Wenja knew every rock there but now there was snow and it was treacherous. The heavy skirts made it hard to walk but she bit her teeth together and endured, it wasn't all that cold yet so she didn't have to worry about frostbite. As the path became less difficult she saw the lights from the village in the distance, like far away stars. The small gathering of houses wasn't large but she had never been outside of this valley and to her it was grand. The entire village seemed to be awake and she heard dogs barking and voices from afar. Bagir nodded at her. "Stay close to us girl, do not leave us under any circumstance"

Wenja nodded and they walked on, the village was not at all that large but now everybody were outside and they gathered by the temple. Wenja gasped, some horses stood tied to the tethering poles and she had never seen animals like those, she hadn't even believed that a horse could get that large and that beautiful. They were sleek long legged animals with wide heads and large nostrils and all were silvery grey, like polished steel. The tack was rather simple but adorned with silver thread and sparkling beads and the horses did look as if they could run for days without becoming exhausted. Ulfar let out a sigh of sheer admiration, only the chief and Dagar did own a horse there, and those animals were small and long haired and looked like sheep compared with these aristocratic beauties.

Wenja saw Hodan by the temple gate, he did look very excited and she remembered that the eternal were so much closer to the gods than any human could ever hope to be. To him this had to be like being visited by the very deities themselves and he was almost in tears. The power of the eternal did hold their realm safe and Wenja didn't think that any there had ever met one of this mysterious people before. Hodan did clear his voice. "My herd, listen to me, bring them all forth, all the maidens who never have known a man."

There weren't that many girls in this village who weren't married, just five not including Wenja and she did see that Mjorr and Dagar stood at the back of the crowd, looking pissed off. The girls did step forth and Wenja got a firm nod from Ulfar. "I will be watching you"

She swallowed her fear and stepped forth, she stood there among the others and they formed a line. The other girls were giggling and blushing and they appeared to like the idea of becoming the wife of the Ath'ir. Wenja didn't care, she just wanted this over with so she could return to her home and the safety of the well-known timber walls. Prina was there too, she was pale and her eyes even more enormous than before and Wenja saw that her hands were shaking. Hodar did raise his arms. "Welcome the emissaries of our great lord and protector. "

Four figures did emerge from within the temple and three of them were very tall indeed, over a head taller than even Karkar. Wenja had to gasp, they were beyond beautiful, they were angelic. So filled with youth and life and yet their eyes spoke of oceans of time. One of them was dressed like a warrior with armour and two swords across his back but the

22

two others wore very elaborate robes in some material Wenja had never seen. It was shimmering and seemingly very soft and she wondered how that had been woven. The thread had to be so thin it was barely visible. The two in the robes were rather fair skinned with long silvery hair and blue eyes, the warrior had skin as dark as a winter night and his hair was a deep deep blue, almost indigo. The eyes were amber coloured and he was both stunning and scary at the same time. Beside them was a human, a very handsome man who wore a very nice jacket and some elaborate jewellery which identified him as the one in charge of this part of the realm. Everybody were silent, staring at the three with huge eyes and one of them bowed his head gently. "Good people of this village, we have come in peace and in hope of connecting our peoples even tighter than before. Our great leader has been given a prophecy, a maid from this valley is to be his new bride"

One of the men there did look a bit suspicious. "Do you expect us to just hand over our womenfolk to strangers?"

The emissary shook his head. "No, of course not. If the girl doesn't want to come with us we will not force her. But there will be great benefits for her family if she does."

Some other voice was heard from the crowd. "Such as?"

The tall blonde smiled, a very gentle smile. "The family will be given a hundred pieces of gold, fifty cows and ten gold arm rings, And also ten good broodmares and hundred rolls of good cloth."

The crowd fell silent, it was a bloody fortune, not even Dagar was that rich. Everybody just stared with their jaws almost hitting their chests. The other emissary lifted his hands and gestured towards the girls. "You need to pull your cowls down, and bare your neck. Do not worry, this will only take a few seconds"

The human opened a small box and took out a large flat crystal, it did glow faintly and he handed it over to the tall eternal with obvious reverence. Hodan appeared to be close to tears from sheer religious joy. The girls had fallen silent too, they appeared to have understood the severity of this now. Everybody was staring and many hoped that their relative would be the chosen one. The first girl was Solfi, she appeared to be pretty confident and convinced that she would be the one even before she was tested. Her face did look triumphant already and the tall eternal lifted the crystal and held it over her exposed neck, let the light hit the skin. He held it there for a while but nothing happened and he lowered the crystal again. "She is not the one"

Solfi did look pissed. "Are you sure that thing is working? It could be defective?"

The tall eternal shook his head. "No little one, it is not"

He just moved on to the next girl in line, it was Prina and she did look terribly nervous. She had bared her thin neck and both the eternal did stare at her and Wenja saw pity in their eyes. The crystal didn't reveal anything and Wenja did see that Dagar looked disappointed. Perhaps he had hoped that his daughter would collect this huge prize. The next girl was the daughter of the village blacksmith and she was used to working hard, short and stocky and her hands were stained black from the work at the forge. She did look rather humble as she bared her neck and everybody held their breaths. There was nothing and now there was just Wenja and two more girls left. Wenja saw that the daughter of one of the cattle breeders was tested and there was nothing there. Now it was just her and one more girl and she held her breath as the tall emissary stopped behind her. She had pulled her long hair to the side and her jacket was pulled down. Everybody held their breaths, Wenja had never been one of them and few did believe that she could have any chance now.

The emissary did lift the crystal and at first nothing happened, then all of a sudden glowing signs seemed to appear on her skin, as if drawn onto it with fluorescent ink and the emissary let out a small yelp. "Behold, the chosen one is found, the gods have spoken!"

The crowd gaped, then some shouted. "She is cheating, check her again, it cannot be her!"

Wenja did shake, it couldn't be true, she couldn't be the one? It was impossible. Ulfar did look stunned and Bagir did stare at her with awe, then he did raise the spear. The eternal did shake their head. "There can be no cheating, the crystal speaks the truth. She is the one, and nobody can deny this"

Hodan nodded and raised his arms. "Order, the voice of the sacred has been heard, Wenja is the one they came for"

There was a roar of anger coming from the crowd and suddenly Dagar rushed forth. "Do not dare to tell us that this…feckin' whore…is the chosen one!"

The two eternal did stare at the man and their eyes had gotten hard. "She is to be titled as Eth'ir from now on human, and the village is blessed to have raised her"

Mjorr did push his way through the crowd, he carried a short sword and there was madness in his eyes. He was aiming for Wenja but didn't make it that far, a hand shot out from seemingly nowhere and he was grasped in a terrible grip which almost crushed his arm. Mjorr did let out a shriek of agony and the tall warrior did pick the sword out of his hand as if the man was a kid playing with a toy he wasn't allowed to touch. Wenja felt faint, dizzy. It wasn't true, no, it wasn't real. The emissary bowed to her. "My name is Ehbrial, this is Khirhien, we are the advisors of the Ath'ir. We are honoured to meet you"

The dark skinned one bowed his head, he had tossed Mjorr back into the crowd as if the human was a mere ball of wool, close to weightless. "I am Rhawan, the Si'ish of the Ath'ir. I am honoured to serve you my lady"

Wenja whimpered, Ulfar and Bagir came over and Ulfar took her hand, he didn't appear to have words. Ehbrial smiled and the human emissary walked over and took the crystal, put it back in the box. "I am Thokan, I serve the Ath'ir and I am very honoured that the Eth'ir is from my part of this realm"

Wenja couldn't think, was this true after all? There was still angry murmurs coming from the crowd and Khirhien raised a hand. "The mighty Ath'ir will also reward this valley for having raised his bride, you will be given all the wheat you need for the next ten years and every household will receive ten gold coins, one each year"

Suddenly the mood changed drastically, now they were cheering and Wenja felt embarrassed, how greedy they all were. Ulfar was a bit pale. "Oh high one, must she do this?"

Ehbrial shook his head. "We do not force people, it would be against the will of the gods. She can choose freely"

Wenja felt that her legs were about to give way underneath her but she stared at Ulfar and Bagir and knew that the wealth promised could change everything. Ulfar swallowed. "If she chooses to do this it must be of her own will. We do not sell our children, and I will not let her leave if you cannot promise that she will be treated well"

Rhawan went down on one knee, he was so tall he still almost was of the same height as Ulfar. "I give you my word, the Ath'ir will treat her like the treasure she is, no harm will ever come to her and she will never be beaten nor starve. I swear this"

Hodan had stood there the whole time and he appeared to be overwhelmed. He was a very strict man but Wenja had liked him in spite of it for he was always fair. He swallowed again and again. "What blessings for our small humble community, such wonderful blessings"

Ulfar did look shocked still and Bagir was fidgeting with his belt. "Wenja, this is up to you, we can make it you know, without all that wealth."

She took a deep breath, stared at the inhumanly beautiful faces. "I know so little about you eternal, but they say you have healers who can heal almost any disease?"

Khirhien nodded. "Yes, our healers are blessed, and we do have one in our group as a matter of fact. Ahnriel is a very skilled one"

Wenja swallowed hard, marrying one of the eternal? Having to go to bed with someone that wonderfully beautiful and terrifying? Being his wife, bearing the children of someone that far above her? It was impossible and yet she had caught a sliver of hope, one she refused to let go of. "I will do it, I will come with you but only if you agree to heal my sister"

Ulfar gasped. "Wenja…"

The eternal didn't seem to be shocked by her determination, they just smiled. "We will gladly help, what ails your sister?"

Ulfar was hoarse. "She fell down a canyon two years ago, her legs are paralyzed and now…her lungs are failing"

Rhawan was frowning. "That is serious, and may not heal but I am sure that Ahnriel can heal her sick lungs and give her more strength. "

Ulfar let out a small wail. "Even that would be wonderful, a true miracle"

Wenja saw that her father was close to tears, the money and everything would make him a man of importance and the family would never have to starve again. Wenja felt that her decision was made, and her will adamant. She would not go back on it now, no matter what the future would bring, it would be worth it. She could save her family and then she didn't care about her own fate. Ehbrial put a hand on her shoulder. "Our leader will surely open his heart to such courage and such love. He will be blessed by your pure soul"

Rhawan grinned. "I will ride and get Ahnriel right away, we have to leave tomorrow so this night will be your last one at home little one"

Wenja swallowed hard, Bagir embraced her. "Our brave girl, you have the courage of a lioness"

The dark skinned eternal did mount one of the horses with a fleeting movement and galloped off and Wenja still felt dizzy. Thokan bowed his head. "Your family will be revered by us all from now on, do not worry young one."

Ulfar swallowed visibly. "My daughter, the wife of the Ath'ir. I cannot believe it"

Ehbrial smiled gently, he did seem like a genuinely good person and Wenja did notice that neither of them did stare at her worn clothes and her poor appearance. "I am sure it is well deserved"

Bagir made a gesture. "My lords, there is one thing you ought to know. The young man who stormed forth and Rhawan threw away, he is a bad one. He has been trying to convince Ulfar here to let him marry Wenja for a long time but he is a nasty piece of...a promiscuous scoundrel. Ulfar has declined and Mjorr is very dangerous, he may try to harm her knowing she will become the bride of someone else"

Thokan did frown. "Oh no, that is bad, but we are armed and the escort is large too. She will be safe, and I doubt that this Mjorr will dare to travel all the way to the plains?"

Ulfar took a deep breath. "I cannot say for sure, he is mad and spoiled and like Bagir said, if he cannot have her he may think that nobody should"

Wenja whimpered, she remembered the insane expression on Mjorr's face, he had wanted to kill her, she was sure of it. Khirhien crossed his arms over his chest. "We will keep our eyes open then, this human sound like someone who has lost his sanity a long time ago"

Bagir frowned. "He should have been strangled with his own umbilical cord when he was pushed out of his mother, that would have been better for everyone"

Hodan sort of herded them into the temple where it was warm and Wenja was still cold, why she didn't know. She stared at the two tall eternal, they were more than a foot taller than any other male she had seen and she saw that their bodies were slender and elegant and yet extremely powerful. What would it be like to be bedded by someone like that? Were they like human men in that regard or were they different? She forced herself to breathe, it would not help her if she did panic now.

Before long they heard hooves and the dark skinned one returned with another tall cloaked figure behind him. It was a female and she was gorgeous, but very exotic. There were drawings all over her face and her eyes were violet while her hair had an odd tone of grass green. She did look vigorous, and she smiled and appeared to be very glad to see Wenja. "So this is the one, such exquisite beauty!"

Wenja had to blush, she felt like an eclipse compared with this female but she did notice one thing though. The female wore a sort of tightly fitted tunic made from leather with a soft wool shirt under and she had very little shapes. There were hardly any breasts to speak off and she appeared to be boyish in shape in general. Wenja had very nice breasts and a narrow waist too and she felt much more womanly than this eternal, in spite of Ahnriel's obvious beauty. "So, your sister is ill?"

Wenja nodded. "Yes, please help her"

Ahnriel smiled and patted Wenja's back. "I will do my best. We brought extra horses"

They walked outside and Wenja saw two stocky dun horses next to the large long legged ones, they seemed to be calm beasts and Rhawan gestured towards them. "Ulfar, Bagir, you may take these, they are yours to keep"

Bagir was blinking in disbelief and Ulfar took the reins with obvious reverence. He had never believed that he ever would own a horse. Wenja hesitated and Rhawan rode over to her and pulled her up, placed her in front of him in the saddle. "It is my duty to keep you safe precious one, don't be afraid, I will not let you fall and neither will Silverwing"

Ulfar made his horse move forth. "It is a very steep path, are you sure your horses can do it?"

Rhawan nodded. "Yes, our steeds can handle any terrain. Don't worry, it will be fine"

Wenja had never sat on a horse before and the ground was terrifyingly far below and it went so fast. The horses were trotting and she saw that Thokan and the two other emissaries were to stay behind. She felt the warmth from Rhawan's body and he felt safe, like a solid wall built to protect you. She had a strong feeling that Mjorr would have to come up with a very devious plan indeed if he was to get through this eternal. The way he moved did reveal that he was a skilled fighter, and extremely dangerous.

Chapter 2: A tale of friendship and loss

The path was covered with snow now but it didn't matter that much to these eternal and their huge steeds, the two horses Bagir and Ulfar had been given were just as capable of handling the snow and the trip back to the farm was done in just a couple of hours. The horses had no problems with the steep parts of the path, they did barely slow down at all and Wenja sat there and felt as if she was flying up the ragged terrain. She saw that the riders did lean forth a bit and they let the horses have their heads all the time and neither of the animals did hesitate, not even once. Ulfar was grinning but his face did reveal some confusion. "Honoured ones, pardon me for asking but we are poor and our house is small, we have no beds big enough for your kind"

Rhawan just snickered. "But you have a barn? We can sleep in the hay, and the horses have blankets and can stay outdoors for the night"

Bagir did lift an eyebrow" My lord, that is…"

Rhawan grinned, "Beneath us? Not at all, I am a warrior, I have slept in far worse places, believe me"

They reached the farm and Sina did open the door, alarmed by the sound of hooves and strange voices. She gaped and ran back inside, suddenly terrified of the tall strangers. Ulfar got off the horse and Rhawan and Bagir went to take care of the animals while Ahnriel followed Ulfar and Wenja inside. Sina was hiding in a corner, in obvious shame of the poverty which was very visible. Halda lay in her bed and you could hear her laboured breathing from afar. Ulfar embraced Sina who still looked petrified. "My light, this is Ahnriel, she is of the eternal.

She can heal, and she will try to help Halda. Wenja is the chosen one, we will be given such gifts "

Sina just whimpered and stared at Ahnriel who pulled off her cloak and smiled, she didn't appear to be shocked by the condition of the house at all. Farkur, Idah and Surun sat in the corner, cramped together like mice in a trap, staring with wide eyes at the strange woman. Ahnriel nodded at Sina. "Your family is greatly blessed and our leader will show his gratitude by gifting you with all you need to live a good life"

She went over to the bed and Halda did look stunned, her eyes were huge and Wenja sat down next to her. "Don't be afraid sister, she will help you breathe better"

Halda swallowed. "She is so pretty, is she real?"

Ahnriel smiled and took the girls hand, sat down next to her too. "I am real yes little one, and I am very glad I am here for I am sure I can help you, at least make it easier for you to breathe."

Halda smiled, she did look so shy but at the same time she suddenly had hope in her eyes. "That would be nice"

Sina stood there and appeared to be in complete disbelief still, Ulfar held her gently. The door opened and Bagir and Rhawan entered, the room was suddenly overfilled or so it felt for Rhawan had such a presence and his head did touch the roof in a few places. Ahnriel smiled at the dark skinned one and Rhawan bowed his head to Sina and the children. Farkur was staring with huge eyes at the swords the warrior now removed and leaned up against the wall. Ahnriel leaned over Halda and laid a hand on her chest, very gently and then she started to chant something, it sounded very sweet and soft and yet there was power in her voice and her eyes started to glow slightly. Halda gasped and Sina did look very nervous. Rhawan smiled at her. "Do not worry good woman, this will not hurt at all, it just feels warm"

Halda squeaked. "It does mother, it feels…good"

Ahnriel was chanting louder and her entire body was glowing, her hands seemed to hold onto something incredibly bright and strong and she seemed to be pushing herself hard. They heard that Halda was breathing easier already and Ahnriel did let go for a moment. "Can you help her sit up for a moment? I need to check her back, I have a suspicion"

Sina rushed over and she and Ulfar did lift Halda's upper body up so she was leaning forward. Ahnriel did pull the thin gown up and Wenja stared at her sister's pale and skinny back, there were no muscles left at all, just bone. Ahnriel swore and then she let a hand glide down the back, they saw how uneven the spine had become. "She didn't break her back completely, but several of the bones are misaligned. I may be able to fix this but that will hurt"

Ulfar gasped. "Will she be okay again then?"

Ahnriel tilted her head. "She may, but it will take years before she is as strong as she ought to be, it will take a lot to retrain her body"

Sina bit her lower lip. "Do it, please?"

Ahnriel nodded. "It may not work, I warn you, but I will try and do my very best."

Halda nodded. "I am not afraid, it hurt a lot to begin with, I can handle it"

Ahnriel did stroke the greasy unwashed hair. "I am sure you can, you are such a brave little girl"

The eternal did lean forward with both hands on the spine, she chanted but this time the chant was different, not so gentle, more demanding, like a general shouting orders. Wenja didn't understand a single syllable but she realized that these were words of power, of immense power. Halda let out a shriek and they all saw how the body suddenly twisted and shook and it did look unnatural and disturbing. Sina was sobbing and Idah and Farkur looked terrified. Surun did look more curious than scared, he was too young to understand this. Ahnriel did struggle, they saw it. Her body was tense and her expression one of intense concentration and focus. Sweat was flowing off her skin and Halda was writhing, Ulfar and Bagir had to really use strength to hold her still. It seemed as if it lasted forever but finally the green haired woman let go and she sighed and looked fatigued. "It is done, now it is up to the gods"

They could see that the back was straight again and Halda was gasping for air, the feeling had to be extremely strange.

Sina sat down and embraced her daughter and Wenja saw that Halda was smiling and she was breathing normally. It was all worth it now, that moment made it all worth it. She couldn't have cared less about herself when she knew that her sister would be healthy again. Sina was sobbing with relief and joy and she grasped Ahnriel's hands and kissed them in reverence. Ahnriel did look a bit embarrassed but Rhawan smiled. "I am very glad it worked, but there is a long path ahead of her now."

Ulfar smiled and there were tears in his eyes. "We will walk it with her, we cannot thank you enough"

Ahnriel did blush and then she got up. Rhawan went outside and came back inn with a bottle and a small sack. He placed the bottle on the table and opened the sack, there was some cheese and a large bread and he smiled. "We would like to share a meal with you, there isn't much we have but at least there is a small taste for everybody"

Sina got efficient, she cleared the table and found some cups and everybody did get a place even though it got a bit crowded. Farkur was still staring at Rhawan and Idah was fascinated by Ahnriel's hair. Wenja felt as if she was in some sort of odd dream, this was wonderful and yet…She couldn't help but being a bit afraid too, she would have to leave it all behind and she had never been outside of the valley. And now she was to travel to the plains? She knew that it was a long way to go, a very long way. They would be travelling for weeks and perhaps even months. Rhawan cut the cheese and it was sweet and fatty and Farkur did gobble up his piece as if he never had seen food before. Sina scolded him for being a bit too eager but Rhawan laughed and ruffled the lad's hair. "He is growing, a lad his age needs his food"

The bottle contained wine and Wenja got a little, she had never tasted wine before and the fruity taste did surprise her. She realized that she would have to get used to wine for Ahnriel said that wine was being drunk at every special occasion and it was normally rather strong too. Sina was practical, she was gathering up Wenja's belongings and the small bag she put things into told everyone that the girl didn't own much at all. Rhawan was smiling. "You will be travelling by carriage, we have several ready by the lake. You will have several people dedicated to teaching you everything you will need to know and you will be given clothes and things according to your new status"

Wenja had to blush, she had always wanted pretty gowns for what girl didn't? Ahnriel giggled. "You are so rare little one, that hair of yours, does it come from your mother's side?"

Ulfar shook his head. "Wenja's mother was my sister, she was a widow and died here when Wenja was just two, we adopted her. But the hair comes from Wenja's father. He was a redhead"

Ahnriel nodded. "Our Ath'ir will adore it, he is very fond of beauty"

Wenja didn't feel beautiful at all; the girls of the village were prettier than her in the eyes of the mountain people. Halda got some cheese too and she was weeping, she felt her legs again, they hurt but Ahnriel said that it would pass. She would have to start slowly but by the spring there was a good chance that she would be able to leave the bed. Wenja was very curious but she wasn't sure if she was allowed to express this. Girls were supposed to be quiet and demure and Rhawan saw her expression and saved her from the situation. "So, I bet you have many questions little one, ask away. We are here to answer them"

Wenja looked at Ulfar who nodded, it was alright. She took a deep breath. "I know so little about you eternal, only that you protect the mountain realms"

Rhawan smiled gently and placed Idah next to himself, she had been sitting on his knee, playing with his long braid. "Well, there are a lot of things you need to know then. First of all, only you humans call us eternal, we ourselves call us elves. There are several tribes but they are divided into twelve clans each with the responsibility for an area of the plains. Our Ath'ir is the leader of all the twelve clans, their war leader, the one who makes sure that everybody knows what to do at all times"

She swallowed. "So he is a warrior?"

Rhawan nodded with pride. "The very best there is, that is why he was chosen to lead."

Sina held Surun, the boy was trying to reach Ahnriel's hair to chew on it. "Tell us more about him please"

Rhawan bowed his head. "Of course, I will tell you all I can. His name is Ahravan and he is older than me, he has seen many wars and many great battles of old"

Wenja had to whisper the name, Ahravan, as if she was to taste it. So that was the name of the one who would be her husband. It felt strange. Rhawan did continue. "I am his Si'ish, that means bond brother, we are not related by blood but are sworn to each other. He saved my life once and I his and thus we look out for each other."

Ulfar did nod. "I have heard of that yes, an ancient custom"

Rhawan smiled back. "Yes, I am the person he trusts the most so he sent me to make sure that his new bride makes it to the plains safe."

Sina frowned. "You said new bride, has he been married before?"

Rhawan nodded. "Yes, once. It was centuries ago and it was to a mortal woman like Wenja here."

Bagir tilted his head. "So, he is a widower?"

Rhawan did chuckle. "Yes, the way you see it. But that marriage wasn't a happy one at all"

Sina looked surprised. "Oh? What went wrong?"

Rhawan sighed. "The woman was a gift, from a local human leader and Ahravan couldn't refuse to accept her out of fear of insulting the giver. She was a very vain person you see, extremely fond of the new title and a bit too aware of her heightened status. She didn't act like a very wise person at all."

Sina made a grimace "I have heard of women like that, but he was…he was kind to her?"

Rhawan nodded. "Yes, he did care about her, even when she acted as if she was the ruler of the whole land. She died after many years and he did mourn her, even though she had been rather despicable at best"

Wenja looked down, a man capable of mourning even a bad person? That was making her feel a bit better. Rhawan petted Wenja's hand over the table. "Ahravan is a good man Wenja, don't worry. He will treat you with all due respect"

Bagir was fidgeting with the table knife. "The monsters, are they around still? I know that the twelve clans keep them from entering the mountain land but some say that the beasts are gone and that we don't need protection any longer"

Rhawan sent the man a wry grin. "I have heard that too, but unfortunately they are still around. Pouring down from the north every now and then, spreading havoc. We fought some huge packs last year. If they reach the mountains of the inland there will be no stopping them I am afraid so we keep our eyes open and have sentinels out at all times"

Wenja swallowed. "You say monsters, but what sort of creatures are they?"

Rhawan sighed, "There are little kettles here so maybe that is better spared for another time?"

Ulfar nodded, he knew what the eternal meant. The kids shouldn't hear about this. Bagir shrugged. "I have heard a lot, I can imagine that only superior warriors are able to fight them"

Ahnriel smiled and waved her fingers at Surun who was sucking on his thumb. "Yes, there are both humans and elves in the twelve clans though, we work together as one. The people of the plains are a hardy bunch and they are expert fighters too. That is needed yes"

Ulfar looked down. "We would be in trouble without the protection now wouldn't we?"

Rhawan smiled, a swift grin, almost apologetic. "Yes, we have met many humans who think that they don't need us nor the pact between our races but that attitude usually ends the moment they face their first beasts."

Bagir chuckled. "I can imagine that. We had a man in the village some years ago, huge burly guy, and very sure that he was the strongest one there. But unfortunately he ran into two bears and we had to come and help him out of a tree. He wasn't so brave after all"

Rhawan laughed out loud, he had a very soft and deep laugher and Wenja could imagine that he was a good singer. They said that the eternal had voices like angels and she did believe that now. Ahnriel sighed and stretched herself. "The gifts will be brought to you when we reach the lake, and I think that we will add some gold for you are by the great goddess not wealthy. And with a new little one on the way…"

Sina was blushing and looked down. "Yes"

Ahnriel did look at Surun. "He is adorable, but there is something wrong with him, I am sure you have seen that?"

Sina nodded. "Yes, he is…slow"

Ahnriel tilted her head. "Yes, and unfortunately there is nothing I can do about that for it isn't an injury but the result of you not having enough food while carrying him and being tired and worn down. The new little one on the other hand will be strong and healthy. "

Sina blinked. "Oh thank the gods, I have been so worried. Is it?"

Ahnriel smiled. "It is a girl"

Sina did look relieved, girls were less rambunctious and demanding than a boy and could help her with her work. Ulfar swallowed. "Will Surun ever be normal?"

Ahnriel shook her head. "No, he will always be small and weak but his mind isn't too damaged, he is smart but he needs more time than others to understand fully. I suggest that you let him become a herder, that is simple work but one he can do even if he isn't that large and strong"

Bagir grinned. "He will be like me, the terror of every mother looking for a son in law with status and power"

Everybody laughed and Wenja felt how her heart seemed to swell with love, her family meant the world to her and now she had saved them, but would have to leave them behind. Rhawan stared at her. "Is there anything else you want to know little one?"

She blushed. "Yes…how…what does he look like?"

Rhawan grinned. "He is taller than me believe it or not, and his skin is dark but not as dark as mine. His hair is like gold though, and his eyes green, like a meadow in summer"

Wenja looked down, taller than Rhawan? How was that even possible? Ahnriel giggled. "He is beautiful, you will have a husband who is good to look at"

Sina giggled too and her eyes were shining, she appeared to have gotten her joy of life back. Rhawan got up and almost banged his head on the roof. "It is getting late and we will leave you now and see if we can get some sleep."

Ulfar nodded and walked out to show them the way to the hay barn and Wenja sat there and felt so strange. It was like any other evening and yet not. It was her last one in this home. She didn't want to cry but she felt tears forming in her eyes and Sina embraced her. "There there Wenja, do not cry. You have saved us all child."

Wenja tried to smile. "I know but…leaving you will be terrible"

Sina put her hands on Wenja's shoulders. "I know, and I don't want to let my girl go, but it is time for you to become so much more than a sheep farmer's daughter. I can let you go now, knowing that your future will be a bright one. I will see you leave knowing that you will be safe, I'd rather never see you again but know you are happy than fear that Mjorr will ruin your life completely."

Wenja shuddered. "Mjorr. Rhawan did just throw him into the crowd, like he was a ragdoll. I don't think Mjorr will dare to do anything nasty again"

Sina sighed and embraced her again "Let us pray that this is true."

Wenja went to bed next to Halda who had fallen asleep already, exhausted by all the new impressions. She did feel the familiar scent of her sister and the house and tried to make sure that she would remember it forever. She was so tired and yet it was hard to relax enough to sleep, she was writhing about for a long time before she finally succumbed to her body's need for rest. Her last thought was in wonder, why had she been chosen for such an honour?

The next morning came with clear skies and freezing cold and Wenja felt how her throat almost closed up, she felt terrible but at the same time, she would be safe and her family would become rich and safe too. They prepared her in silence. She ate and hugged her siblings one last time. Idah and Farkur wept but Surun did just suck his thumb and tried to squirm his way out of her grip. She had been given Ulfar's cloak in addition to her own and she tried to not cry. Ahnriel did saddle the horses and Rhawan stood there waiting for her. She hugged Ulfar and he kissed her forehead and blessed her and Sina held her tight and whispered that she was very proud of Wenja and that her husband surely would adore someone that kind hearted and bright of spirit. She hugged Halda who wept and Bagir squeezed her hand and tried to smile. "If that husband of yours ever treat you with anything but the outmost kindness and gentleness tell him that I will hunt him down"

Wenja had to grin. "I will"

Sina dried some tears. "Be blessed my daughter, bear him strong children and love them well"

Wenja blushed, she knew what one had to do to have children and the mere idea made her cringe a bit. Rhawan lifted her onto the horse and jumped up behind her, she felt numb, as if she was in some sort of shock. She waved her hand at Ulfar and Sina and Bagir did grin and threw her a kiss. Wenja choked a sob as Rhawan turned Silverwind and let the horse trot slowly down the slopes with Ahnriel just behind him. Wenja did hide her face against the fur cloak the eternal did wear, he put an arm around her and whispered into her ear. "Do not cry little one, nothing bad will happen to you henceforth. I give you my word"

She closed her eyes and let the movements of the horse rock her into a state of half sleep, it was better than to think that she now was about to leave behind everything she had ever known and loved.

The path was long and now they weren't heading for the village but for the road leading to the lake further down the valley. Wenja had just seen it from a distance and only in summer and now it was like watching an entirely new place. She felt cold still so Rhawan wrapped his own cloak around her and he felt like a furnace so she got warm rather fast. The horses were steady on their feet and before long she was busy studying the landscape. When they reached the road the other emissaries were already there, waiting for them and Wenja found that odd but she didn't ask. They rode rather fast down this way wider and better path and she had never moved so fast in her entire life. She was terrified to begin with but then she realized that the horses wouldn't fall and she started to relax and enjoy the scenery. The snow covered the landscape and transformed it into a very beautiful sight and here and there they passed small barns and other buildings meant for the herds. Rhawan rode in the middle of the group and he had his swords hanging on his horse and could reach them within the blink of an eye if he had to.

"There will be many waiting for you, everyone is very eager to meet the one chosen for our Ath'ir."

Wenja just blushed and felt embarrassed, she was still wearing her out worn dress and cloaks with more holes than fabric. The village by the lake was way larger than the one she came from, it was at least twice its size with three times more people and she had never met any of them. She felt herself tense up as they approached the gates and she saw that a row of covered wagons stood lined up just inside of the gates. Many large horses were relaxing in a paddock and she saw many people clad in good clothes scurrying around. She hid her face against Rhawan's chest, felt silly for doing it for it was what a child would do but she couldn't help it at all. Many came towards them when they saw the riders and Khirhien and Ehbrial did raise their arms and let out some shrill sounds which sounded almost triumphant. Wenja whimpered and Rhawan laid an arm around her, in a very protective manner. Thokan was grinning from one ear to the other. "Everybody, she has been found and she is a jewel among women but she isn't that used to strangers so please, leave her alone and give her time and room to adapt"

Khirhien did jump off his horse and he made the crowd disperse with a sharp word, then Rhawan did dismount and helped Wenja down. She felt her legs shake and she was trembling like a leaf in a storm. What was she going to do and say? The horses were taken away and Rhawan took her hand and the others sort of shielded her as they walked towards one of the huge wagons, it was made from timber and tarp and it looked solid. Rhawan smiled. "This will be your home during the journey."

Wenja nodded and the door at the back of the wagon opened, a young woman with dark hair and huge blue eyes did peek out and she smiled from ear to ear. "Oh wonderful, here she is, we are ready for her"

Rhawan petted Wenja on her back. "Wenja, this is Sefa, Sefa, this is Wenja. She is very shy and not used to people so be kind to her"

Sefa was wearing a very pretty dress with a sort of huge apron on top of it and she had a belt tied around her waist and her hair was braided back and adorned with small sea shells. It did look very pretty and Wenja swallowed hard and had to look down, she had lost her voice or so it felt. Sefa cocked her head. "Oh my dear Goddess, you look like…Ah, you are so pretty dear but you are too thin, and your hair? It is a disaster! Come, come, we will make you pretty in no time"

Wenja was hauled up the short stairs and into the wagon and it was surprisingly roomy. There were some closets and a huge bed at the end of it and several females sat there, smiling and staring at her. Wenja whimpered and tried to turn around to run but Sefa grasped her and hugged her, the woman did smell of lavender and roses and the scent did calm Wenja down, for some reason. "Whoa, easy there, we don't bite at all, as a matter of fact we are all very nice, and we are here to help you"

Wenja tried to speak but it became a sort of squeak. Sefa sighed. "You are truly a village girl, not used to seeing anyone except your family. By every deity known to mankind, you are gonna face the shock of a lifetime then"

She turned Wenja towards the females gathered there. "I will introduce everyone, so listen up"

She pointed at an elderly woman with some grey strands in her brown hair and a very gentle face with some strange tattoos in pale blue along her cheekbones and on her chin. The woman wore a very elaborately embroidered dress, some high boots made from fur and a headdress which did look absolutely ridiculous but probably was a traditional sort of thing. "This is Theka, she is gonna be your chambermaid and help you get dressed, help you bathe and so on. If there is anything you need just let her know."

The next female there was one of the eternal, she was fair skinned and her hair the colour of sunflowers, she was very pretty and wore a dress of thick blue velvet. Wenja felt rather inferior just by looking at her. "Nefhriel, she will teach you all you need to know about the elves and their customs. There is a lot to learn I fear"

Nefhriel did bow her head gracefully. "I am honoured to serve the new Eth'ir"

Then another female got up and she was huge, and stocky and her skin was dark. She had thick hair the structure of a horse's mane and it was black and coarse and the woman did have tusks and a very broad body with huge muscles. She bowed her head and Sefa grinned. "That is

Floth'bha, she is a half orc and she will be your body guard when Rhawan isn't near. Nobody get past her with ill intent"

Wenja did believe that, the half orc had several knives in her belt and a huge axe too and she looked as if she could break a man in half with just a flick of her wrist. The last one was a tiny woman with a stocky body and a round face surrounded by thick braids in a very odd tone of strawberry blonde. She had sideburns which were carefully braided and wore enough jewellery to break the back of a horse, or so it seemed. Sefa giggled. "This is Imh, she is a dwarf and she is your personal cook from now on. She'll put meat on those bones before you even know it"

Imh raced forth and bowed politely, she appeared to be very maternal and she smacked her lips together and looked at Wenja with narrow eyes "Too skinny, way too skinny, not good at all."

She smacked Wenja over the rear and the girl winced. "I have meal ready, just wait here, soon there will be warm food"

Imh raced out of the wagon and Wenja could just blink, a dwarf? And a half orc? It was a bit too much, she felt faint and had to sit down. Theka shook her head. "Food first, then a bath. The bath house is prepared to receive you, I bet your skin is dying to get massaged, and your hair needs a proper wash."

Wenja swallowed. A bath? That did sound heavenly, she hadn't bathed in months. Sefa sat down next to her. "I am gonna be your constant companion, the one to help you adapt. I was born and raised with the twelve clans so I know all that there is to know. "

Wenja managed to nod. She felt as if her head was spinning, constantly. Sefa pointed at the walls and the closets. "We have filled the wagon with things you will need, clothes and stuff. And you will be given so much more when we arrive at Ohtanar"

Wenja frowned. "Ohtanar?"

Sefa grinned widely. "Yes, the capital of the twelve clans, it is moving you see, they move it with the herds, about once a month. We will reach it when it is placed by the River of wild steeds."

Wenja had no idea of what Sefa was talking, she had never even seen a map of this land and she felt like an idiot. "How long will it take us to get there?"

Sefa shrugged. "We spent the autumn travelling to get here but the route back will be a different one since Ohtanar has moved. I guess at least between two or three months if everything goes smoothly?"

Wenja closed her eyes. "Two or three months? That is…"

Sefa smiled. "A long time but you will not have time to be bored, believe me. We have so many things to teach you"

The door opened again and Imh and some other females did stand outside of it carrying several trays with covered bowls. Sefa and Nefhriel did grasp the trays and placed them on the bed and Imh grinned widely before she shut the door. "Enjoy little one, there will be more before the night falls"

Wenja stared at the trays, they were large and the number of bowls large too. Sefa started removing the lids and she saw that two of the bowls did contain some sort of ale. It did smell rather funny and she cringed. Sefa chuckled. "You will get used to it, dwarven ale is the best really, it does smell to high heavens but the taste is great. Trust me"

The bowls did contains stew, some sort of white substance Sefa called rice pudding and also sauce and boiled vegetables and pieces of cheese and fruit mixed together. Wenja didn't even know where to start, and how to eat this. Nefhriel did open a cupboard and took out some plates and some metal spoons. They were elegantly formed and Wenja hadn't even seen spoons made from metal before. Sefa sat down next to her. "Just fill you plate with whatever you like, I recommend the stew first, it is rather heavy so it will fill you up good"

The stew was delicious and suddenly she found herself stuffing her face as if she had been starving for weeks. The feeling of food in her stomach, it was wonderful. The ale was bitter but the taste very refreshing and she liked it. When Sefa removed the plate Wenja felt as if she was about to burst and Theka shook her head in disbelief. "You have been malnourished for a long time dear heart, but you won't have to starve now. You will learn how to eat properly when your hunger has been satiated"

Wenja did blush, she had been stuffing herself like a mad and it wasn't very ladylike at all. Sefa sighed. "You will need some rest and then I will take you to the bathhouse."

Wenja felt drowsy and she couldn't believe that she from now on could eat all that she wanted. "That is great, I feel tired"

Theka nodded. "No wonder, poor little one, being uprooted like that and taken away from your kin. How many summers have you seen?"

Wenja blushed again. "Eighteen, I think"

Theka shook her head and stroked Wenja's hair. "Barely more than a child, but the gods have spoken. So, rest now and I will go and prepare everything"

Wenja swallowed. "Will I be alone here, in this wagon?"

Sefa shook her head. "No, I will sleep here with you every night, you are not to be left alone. I understand that there has been some sort of problems back at the village you come from? I heard Thokan mention a mad man?"

Wenja had seen that Thokan had stood outside of the wagon, discussing something with Rhawan and she nodded. "Yes, a local man, he wanted to marry me but father wouldn't let him and he tried to kill me when I was declared to be the chosen one"

Sefa clicked her tongue. "Aii, not good, but you are safe here. We have many warriors with us and you should not be afraid. Rest now, there will be new clothes soon"

Wenja did lay down, the bed was wide and warm and soft too and she had never lain in anything that luxurious in all her life. The blankets were made from wool and some were furs so silky she couldn't believe it. Sefa did tuck her inn and smiled, stroking her hair. "I will wake you up in a few hours"

Wenja wasn't so sure she could sleep now but before many minutes were gone she was fast asleep and Sefa sighed and looked down at her with some amount of pity. The girl was so innocent, so naïve and she was probably a capable worker but now she would face a whole new world. Sefa hoped that this wouldn't break her but make her stronger. She went outside and sat down on the stairs, Rhawan sauntered by and stopped, greeting Sefa with a small smirk. "So, what do you think?"

Sefa shrugged. "She is as vulnerable as roses on a frosty night Rhawan, such a beautiful soul but so unprepared for what she is to face."

Rhawan nodded. "I know, she is exquisite but knows way too little about the world. You will have to teach her well"

Sefa grinned. "Oh I will, I will start tonight already. But the things Thokan spoke off, the mad man?"

Rhawan did grunt. "Oh yes, the piece of scum. We will leave already tomorrow morning, just to put some space between us and that piece of worthless shit. I will stay close at all times Sefa and should he show up rest assure that it will be the very last thing that he does. The gifts for her family have been sent already and the people I sent off with it will return tonight. "

Sefa mumbled. "Bless you Rhawan, I have seen my fair share of jealous men convinced of their own right to rule and possess. It is never pretty"

Rhawan nodded slowly. "Human males are so primitive, I cannot understand them at all"

Sefa had to snicker. "Oh you are not the only one, believe me."

Rhawan did lean onto the wagon. "We have sent the gifts for her family, and those for the village too. I have rarely seen such poverty, I am sure that Ahravan will love spoiling her, she has lived such a hard life until now"

Sefa crossed her legs. "Really, she deserves it. I can see how she has toiled, her hands are worn and her shoulders wide"

Rhawan smiled. "I better go and check on the horses, everything has to be ready at first sunlight."

Sefa just waved her hand and he left, she sat there and sighed. Teaching Wenja the things she needed to know would be tough indeed. She hadn't said anything about it but her main job was to prepare the girl for her life as a married woman, if Sefa knew these valley dwellers right the girl could be completely ignorant when it came to the facts of life and what sex really was. She would most likely know the basics, having seen animals mate, but there was so much more to it when it came to people and she feared that the girl could be of those who had been taught that her place was on her back under her husband and that she ought to be passive and frigid. If that was the case Sefa would have a monumental task ahead of her, no doubt about that. She went back inside, Wenja was fast asleep so she laid down too, to rest and prepare herself for the task ahead. Wenja had probably never had real friends and that was something which could be exploited.

Wenja slept for three hours, then Sefa woke her up and made her put on a new cloak and some warm boots before they went to the bath house. Only larger villages had such a thing, and Wenja had only heard of them but never really learned what a bathhouse was. The building was built on the edge of the village and there was some distance to the other houses. It was a wide building made from notched lumber and it was solid with several hearths and some large containers which held water. There were ovens beneath the containers and the water was being kept warm at all times. Several large tubs carved from rock were placed on the floor and some screens put up around them so people could have some privacy. Wenja gasped as she entered. The hearths had been lighted early that morning and the room was very warm, steam filled it and Sefa took her over to a small room where she was told to get undressed. Wenja hesitated, she had never been naked with anyone else present and she sort of refused until Sefa too got rid of her clothes. Nefhriel and Theka were already there and both had taken off their dresses and walked around in their shifts. Wenja felt terribly self-conscious and Sefa sighed and grasped her hand. "Don't look like a lamb being hauled off to the slaughter, nobody is gonna harm you, and don't be so shy. Bodies are natural, we all have one you know!"

Wenja whimpered and Sefa sort of pushed her into one of the small rooms, the tub was ready and filled with warm water and it was perfumed! The scent of lavender and soap rather strong. Wenja blinked, she saw that Nefhriel and Theka were waiting on the other side of the screen and she felt a little better with only Sefa there. She stepped into the tub, very carefully and Sefa tilted her head. "You have a wonderful body dear, such an elegant shape but Imh is right, you are too thin."

Wenja gasped for the water was rather hot but it felt good too, it did most definitely bring the heat back into her bones. She sat down and Sefa did pour water into her hair. Now the two others did enter the small room and Nefhriel started massaging her scalp with soaps and Theka rubbed her skin clean while Sefa did file her nails and removed hard skin. Wenja

46

felt like a price horse before an auction and Nefhriel did make her stand up after a while. The elf did smear some sort of pinkish ointment onto Wenja's skin under her arms and in her groin and the girl did blush furiously. Sefa nodded. "It is needed dear, it removes hair, it is a tradition."

It did sting a bit and Wenja was glad when she could sit down again. The ointment was washed off and now she was as hairless as the day she was born, it made her cringe a bit. Then her hair was washed yet again and they put oils in it and combed it and Sefa did even cut it a little. Nefhriel did cock her head. "Your hair is very lovely, such a rare colour. Have you ever cut it?"

Wenja shook her head. "No, never"

Theka grinned. "Good, when you reach the capital it will be like satin, believe me"

They rubbed her skin with something which smelled good and then she was taken out of the small room and shoved into another room. Theka was ready with some clothes and Wenja got utterly confused right away. She had never worn smallclothes before and the items Theka did lift off the bench were so thin and elegant and they were embroidered and so lovely. Theka smiled. "You have never worn anything under your skirts now have you? These are underpants, you wear them closest to your skin"

Wenja put them on, they were so light and the fabric so incredibly soft. Suddenly she felt a bit silly, and very feminine somehow. The next thing she was handed was a small shirt with no sleeves and it had a ribbon sewn into it underneath the breasts and it could be tightened. Wenja stood there and let the women dress her like a doll, she felt like crying for when had she ever worn anything that lovely? A sort of shift went over the underpants and then she had to put on a thin gown with long sleeves and the real dress went on top of that. It was deep green with a very lovely pattern of embroidered vines along the chest line and the skirt. She got a belt made from light brown leather and Sefa did braid her hair and when they were done she got a set of long stockings pulled on, they were attached to the thigh with ribbons and she got the boots back on and could leave. She felt like a new person and Sefa did smile. "You

look like a noble woman now dear, and soon you will outshine everyone.
"

Wenja tried to smile, moving with that many clothes on felt odd and she had to turn around to really see how the dress looked. Theka did smile. "You will get used to it, this is a very simple gown."

She got her cloak on and they returned to the wagon and Theka and Nefhriel did bid her a good evening. Imh had already been there leaving more food, bread and cheese this time and a jug of wine and Wenja did moan. If she was to eat that much she would end up looking like a overfed dog before they reached their destination. Sefa sat down with her after having showed her the closets and what they contained. Wenja couldn't imagine that everything was hers. Sefa smiled and did show her also some jewellery which was hers to have and some very nice combs to hold her hair up. They did eat a little and Sefa did sit down on the bed with her legs crossed and tilted her head. "I bet there are many things you wonder about, do not be afraid to ask. There is no thing called a silly question from now on"

Wenja swallowed hard. "Do you know him, Ahravan?"

Sefa nodded. "Yes, I do know him rather well. He is very kind, a bit quiet and not a very cheerful person but there isn't a mean bone in him"

Wenja looked down, her fingers fidgeting with her sleeve. "I am…I am a bit scared!"

Sefa sighed. "That is understandable but consider this, being the wife of an elf does bring great benefits for you, also physically"

Wenja frowned. "Ha? How come?"

Sefa snickered. "You will live much longer than otherwise, at least as long as you are still intimate."

Wenja went beet red and Sefa sort of sighed. "Listen, there is no shame in enjoying the joys of the flesh, whenever you join he will share a little of his strength with you. It is a blessing Wenja, and one I do hope you will be able to enjoy fully"

Wenja sort of squeaked. "I…What if…what if he doesn't like me?"

Sefa did pull her shawl tighter around herself. "Oh he will, believe me. For some reason elven males do find female humans irresistible. It has to do something with our body shape, we have real breasts and hips and an elves female will only have breasts when she is pregnant or nursing."

Wenja gaped. "Is that true?"

Sefa nodded with a wry grin. "Oh yes, to them a human female is very alluring, you don't have to worry at all Wenja, he will desire you"

Wenja cringed. "I…"

Sefa ignored the small squeak and tilted her head. "I bet your mother has lost children right?"

Wenja nodded. "Yes, several, some at birth and two lived for a few months but died suddenly"

Sefa took her hand. "Wenja, what if I told you that this never will happen to you? That you never will face that grief?"

Wenja looked shocked, and confused. "How is that possible?"

Sefa made a grimace. "You see, there is no such thing as a half elf, other races can produce hybrids but elves cannot. A child born of a human mother and an elven father will be an elf, a child born of an elven mother and a human father will be human"

Wenja blinked, a strange feeling of relief rushed through her. "Is that true?"

Sefa nodded. "Yes, very true. So any child you give him will be eternal as you put it. Marriages between male elves and female humans aren't that unusual"

Wenja frowned, her face revealed her curiosity, this was so new to her. "But the other way around?"

Sefa shrugged. "Not unheard off but very rare, few elven females will risk bearing children they one day will have to watch die from old age"

Wenja nodded. "I understand that"

Sefa sent Wenja a wry grin. "Also, eternal or elves can control their bodies way better than humans, you won't have to bear any children before you are good and ready for it. He will be able to decide whether or not his seed will be fertile."

Wenja blushed again, she felt both hot and cold, the very idea of that sort of thing…

Sefa leaned against the wall of the wagon, her expression a bit roguish. "Many women do wish for an elven husband, they are way better than human males in almost every way, but few dare to take that step though. Even with the effect of slowed aging you will one day become old and he will still be young and beautiful."

Wenja swallowed. "How much older than normal can one become in that way?"

Sefa shrugged. "Depends on the individual, but it isn't unusual to live for at least three hundred years. I have heard of one who lived until she was four hundred but I am not so sure that it is true."

Wenja gasped. "Three hundred? How old did his first wife get?"

Sefa looked down. "Only one hundred and eighty. Ahravan did care you see, but he didn't love her and he tried to avoid bedding her. And thus she got old faster than if they had been in love"

Wenja swallowed. "That must be a cruel fate, knowing that you may live for so much longer but then your husband denies you that privilege"

Sefa stared at Wenja and her eyes were hard. "Yes, but know this, none of the eternal would ever use that as a punishment, or to control someone. His wife was a despicable person nobody truly liked and he tried, he truly tried to change her and make her see the errors of her ways but he failed to do it. She was just…terrible"

Wenja nodded. "I see, but…do one have to be married to an elf to get the benefits so to speak?"

Sefa took a deep breath. "No, if you sleep with elves often enough you will have the same effect. So the unbound males are very sought after"

Wenja sort of stared. "That sounds…"

Sefa scoffed. "Like there is no moral left? As if everybody is terribly depraved?"

Wenja looked down. "Yes, in the village…the rules are so strict. People cannot touch anyone they aren't wedded to, and you cannot do it unless you are wedded"

Sefa sighed and rearranged her dress a bit. "Wenja, listen. This is the first lesson of many, and a shocking one for sure but listen carefully. The twelve clans are a very different people from what you are used to and their culture is extremely different. Forget everything you have learned, this will be like starting a new life"

Wenja swallowed and Sefa handed her a cup of wine. "Here, to strengthen yourself."

The girl took the cup and drained it. "Thank you"

Sefa did look like a teacher now and her eyes were calm. "First of all, the clans do not regard sex as anything which is shameful or to be hidden. They are very open about it and it is natural to them, like eating and drinking. Most of the eternal are more attracted to the soul than the body so gender doesn't mean that much. They regard the sharing of one's bodies as something good, something which gives life meaning"

Wenja swallowed. "I…see"

Sefa smiled. "Nobody will take advantage of someone, or try to force a person into doing something they doesn't want. You don't have to be afraid of the males of the clans Wenja, they may express admiration but nobody will touch you."

Wenja sort of blinked. "Even if they do find human females attractive?"

Sefa nodded. "Yes, believe me. The people of the clan's respect each other, that is more than one can say about the people of the valleys right?"

Wenja nodded, she remembered the tales of girls who had bedded someone without being wed and the scandal that always caused. Sefa tilted her head. "I have bedded many of the eternal Wenja, and believe me, you have something to look forward to"

Wenja gasped. "You have? Oh Gods, I…"

Sefa smiled and nodded. "It is never anything but amazing, and I have reaped the benefits, I am way older than I look."

Wenja felt herself blushing again. "Is…Is there a difference between the eternal and humans? Physically?"

Sefa stretched her legs. "No, not really. They are just much prettier, usually rather well-endowed too. But they do have better control of their bodies just as I mentioned and they can last quite a while, and they are able to continue even if they have come"

Wenja did look a bit confused and Sefa did roll her eyes. "You are really very innocent aren't you? A human male can usually not start at it again right away, he has to rest."

Wenja felt like a beet, her face was stiff. "A-alright"

Sefa smiled, there was mischief in her smile. "So, then there is another small difference, they do usually come hard, and a lot. And they feel the pleasure much stronger than us humans, it can make them pass out. There are also a couple of other differences but we can talk about those later, when you are more comfortable."

Wenja felt confused again but she sort of understood too, she wasn't stupid and with just one room she had often heard her parents in bed together. It had made her disgusted to begin with but now she wasn't so sure anymore. She had to giggle and look down and Sefa did grasp her hand. "So you have nothing to fear Wenja, Ahravan is as gorgeous as they come and he will be very patient with you, don't worry"

Wenja could just blush and hide her face, the things Sefa said had brought some strange images into her head. Sefa sighed. "It is getting late and we have to leave early tomorrow. Let's get to bed now and we can continue this little chat then"

Wenja had slept already and wasn't really ready for bed but somehow she felt tired and she let Sefa help her out of the dress and they crawled into the bed. Wenja couldn't really believe it, the day had sort of flown by her because there had been so many new things. She pulled the covers over herself and then she closed her eyes and fell asleep, overwhelmed by it all. Sefa did sigh and tried to sleep too, there was so much Wenja needed to learn, it would be a monumental task for sure.

As the village and the camp slept a tiny figure came crawling towards the gate, it was covered with a thick horse blanket and it hesitated, stared at the gate. The figure was shivering, and then it sort of gathered itself and walked forward, slowly and with obvious fear. It stopped by one of the wagons, the one carrying provisions and it did crawl up swiftly and disappeared into the darkness. Not a sound was heard and the snow did cover up the tracks rather fast.

The morning sun did rise above the mountains and with it came a flurry of activity, there were people running everywhere and the camp was being transformed. The emissaries did bid the inhabitants of the village goodbye and left them with a very generous sum of money and the ones in charge of the wagons did scurry around like squirrels, preparing the horses. Wenja was sitting in the door staring at the commotion, she would stay in the wagon and Sefa would stay there with her. The other females did ride but since Wenja never had learned that art she was allowed to sit in the relative comfort of the wagon. The thing had springs and was very well built too.

The horses were hitched up to the wagons, the riders did mount and soon they were heading out of the gates and onto the road. Here it was a real road and the wagons were made for this sort of terrain. Wenja sat on the bed, it was not exactly a very easy way to travel for the wagon did bounce and shake but it was better than riding and Sefa tried to teach her the words to a local song as they drove along. The driver and another man sat on top of the wagon and Wenja did pity them, it had to be terribly cold. Wenja smiled but she felt a bit uncertain still. "The language, is it the one the eternal use?"

Sefa nodded. "It is indeed, that reminds me, do you speak any other language than this one, the language of the inner valleys?"

Wenja shook her head. "Ah, no? "

Sefa sighed. "Too bad, most of us do speak it well but some don't, I know that Ahravan doesn't. He knows a few words and phrases but not much I am afraid"

Wenja sort of shrunk. "He won't be able to understand me?"

Sefa tried to put on an optimistic face. "Don't worry, I will teach you the common speech of the plains and the elven language too. You will be able to communicate whence we get there."

The dark haired woman found a deck of cards. "Ahravan does enjoy games, I will try to teach you his favourite ones, so you can play them."

Wenja wasn't used to games but she nodded and gathered her wits, this could get interesting. The day went smoothly with no problems, they stopped a few times to let the horses drink and the road was relatively flat so the speed was good. The snow wasn't that deep so they didn't have to put skis on the wagon wheels and as the sun started to fall towards the horizon they gathered on a small meadow by the river. They had gotten to lower terrain after all for here there was little snow and the river was open and not frozen. Wenja was helped out of the wagon to stretch her legs, she felt as if she had been shaken up like a kids toy. Sefa did tell her a little about this area of the valley when there was a commotion coming from one of the wagons, they heard a scream and someone was shouting and Rhawan was there immediately, like he had materialized out of thin air. Sefa stood in front of Wenja and the man driving the wagon came forth, dragging someone behind him. "This one hid in the wagon, does anyone recognize her?"

Rhawan stared and Wenja did gasp, it was Prina. She was shaking all over and blue around the lips and Wenja couldn't believe it. "Prina? What are you doing here?!"

Rhawan went over. "She isn't dangerous, just a village girl."

The one driving the wagon did let go but he did still look suspicious. "What is she doing in my wagon, stealing?"

Prina was sobbing and she dropped to her knees in front of Wenja. "Please, don't send me back, they will kill me"

Rhawan looked puzzled and he put his sword back in its sheath. "What are you talking about girl, who wants to kill you?"

Prina wailed, she did look absolutely terrified. "My father, and…and…the others. I…Have to hide, I cannot go back"

Wenja saw that Prina was shaking and she didn't wear very solid clothes, just her ordinary dress and a horse blanket. It wasn't enough to keep anyone warm, that was for darn sure. Wenja took her hand and the others there did disperse, a girl was not anything exciting. "What is wrong Prina, what is happening?"

Prina gasped and she stared at Wenja with those enormous eyes, they were filled with despair. "I…They want me to marry some man father owes money to, to forge an alliance, he is a terrible old troll. And…"

Rhawan growled. "That is awful, forcing a young child into such a situation"

Wenja just sighed "Rhawan, she is Mjorr's sister"

The dark skinned eternal gaped and then his face became very sinister. "I bet that family has got some lose screws then, treating a girl thus"

Wenja caressed Prina's hair. "So you fled to avoid that?"

Prina was shaking. "Yes, and…I am with child"

Wenja just gaped, staring at Prina who hung her head low, almost panting. "What?"

Rhawan sat down onto his haunches and he did look terribly upset, so did Sefa. "You shouldn't be out here then, you are frozen girl. You need to get warm again, fast"

Wenja saw how Prina shuddered and she remembered the gossip of the village. Prina was one nobody bothered to even look at, because of her brother and father. Who would risk the wrath of Dagar showing any interest in Prina. Wenja laid a hand on Prina's cheek. "Prina look at me, I will not let them take you, you are safe here. We will soon be far away from the valleys"

Prina wailed. "Oh bless you, I can be your slave, just…don't let them find me!"

Wenja swallowed. "Prina, nobody has ever spoken a word about you having an admirer, who was it?"

Her voice was soft and Prina cringed, as if she had been hit. "I…I cannot tell you"

Rhawan sneered. "Cannot or dare not? We will protect you, you are under the protection of the Ath'ir now"

Prina hid her face in her long unkempt hair. "Mjorr"

The words were barely audible but Wenja and Rhawan heard and the dark skinned elf jumped to his feet, his eyes shooting lightening. Wenja felt sick, nauseous. How was that even possible? Prina gasped for air. "He…he was drunk, and he…he came to the barn, I was milking and he…He said nobody wanted me anyhow so he was gonna show me what I was missing and I wanted to scream but he almost strangled me and…I was sure I was gonna die"

Sefa had heard and she had tears in her eyes. "Get her into the wagon, now. And get Ahnriel, she needs a healer."

Rhawan lifted Prina up and they put her on the bed and Wenja felt as if the fear she had felt for Mjorr was being replaced by something much stronger, a sort of burning gnawing wrath. Rhawan was saying something in his own language which made Sefa cringe, it had to be bad. Prina was just wailing and shaking and Ahnriel did burst into the wagon. She shooed Rhawan out and then she did examine Prina very quickly and with great care. "She isn't lying, she is more than two months on the way, it won't show for yet a couple of weeks but she was smart to flee now"

Sefa sort of growled. "Was she damaged?"

Ahnriel did wash her hands in a basin. "Yes, there were tears, they have healed now but there is scaring. The bastard was brutal"

Prina was still weeping and Wenja grasped her hand. "We have to hide her, to keep her safe. Can we do that? "

Sefa sat down and nodded. "Yes, we can camouflage her rather well. There is this group of religious people who cover their heads in dense veils, only their eyes are visible. We can use nut juice to make her skin look darker and her hair can be dyed too. We will make her look unrecognizable."

Wenja tried to smile. "Hear that? Nobody will recognize you, you will be safe"

Prina just gasped and Sefa sighed. "I will tell Imh that we need extra food, and get a proper dress and other clothes. From hereon she isn't to leave the carriage unless all of us are present."

Wenja nodded and held Prina's hand. It was so thin and frail it felt like holding the hand of a child. She couldn't even imagine what sort of hell the poor girl had been through, violated by her own brother and now with child as a result of that. It was horrible. Rhawan did stick his head into the wagon. "I will ask for more of the men to stand guard tonight and if Mjorr or someone else of that family does show up he will be punished according to the crime"

He closed the door and Wenja stared at Sefa. "What does that mean?"

Sefa was a bit pale. "To the twelve clans there is no worse crime than rape, it is worse than murder in their eyes. So if a person does commit such a crime and is caught there is only one possible outcome and that is death, but it will happen in the same manner as the crime"

Wenja felt dizzy. "Are you…you cannot be serious?"

Sefa sighed. "I am, that person will be raped until he dies from the loss of blood. If it takes too long they will strangle the person slowly, as he is being used the same way he used his victim. It is cruel but the clans see it as just"

Wenja swallowed hard. Raped to death, that was a terrible fate but somehow she felt that it would have been very fitting if Mjorr was to suffer that way.

Chapter 3: Life is an open road

'

The great camp was on the move and the line of wagons and sleds was very long. Huge mules and oxen were hitched up to the largest ones, the sleds made to transport the parts to the large huts. They were made from thick felt sewn into rectangular pieces which were three meters tall and six meters long. You needed several to build just one of these great huts and they were made with a very elegant sort of hoop and hook system which enabled the handlers to erect the hut in a very short time in spite of the weight and the large size. The huts were held up by a sort of T shaped wooden bar with hooks attached to the top which was the bottom of the T which was turned upside down. The walls would be double and the inner layer wasn't that thick and more elaborate and often woven in lovely colours and patterns. The outer layer was usually grey or white and rather rough and about four inches thick to keep the cold out. As a result the huts required a lot of wagons to be moved and you usually had to fill at least two large ones with just the outer and inner layer of the wall. The huts were round and inside of the hut there were more T shaped bars and they were used to separate the huts into separate rooms. The walls were thin and usually almost veil like and they didn't stop the warmth from entering every nook and cranny. The ovens were very valuable with a dwarven design, made from metal and rock and they were heavy but whence they got warm they could keep the hut warm for days and they could be taken apart and moved rather easily.

The greatest move was the hut which belonged to the Ath'ir, not because he wanted a larger hut than the others but it was tradition. The hut of the Ath'ir was the one where all the more important meetings would be held and it had to be large to room that many people and he was given way more personal space than most others there. The Ath'ir was a humble person and everybody knew that he would have been perfectly happy with one of the small felt tents the other warriors lived in. The enormous herds of cattle sheep and horses followed the caravan, each warrior usually owned at least ten horses and the families had between fifty and a hundred sheep and at least five cows and bulls so the herds had to move often to avoid starvation. They moved in an ancient rhythm they had followed from before time was counted and it was the sun which dictated it. They moved around the vast inland area which consisted of mountains and valleys and in the winter they sought the east side of the mountains where there was little precipitation and thus little snow. The west side of the mountains was great in summer for the region was very lush and fertile because of much rain and the herds could fatten themselves up rather fast and the tribes had done this every year. There were twelve regions and they spent from a couple of weeks to several months in each one and the camp did move slowly. With the sleds and wagons and all the livestock the speed was at a crawl and the kids were running around playing as the group moved forth.

The twelve clans did consist of both humans and elves and the races did live together in a very symbiotic relationship, both capable of things the other can't. There were also a group of dwarves travelling with the clans, they were smiths and carpenters and they fixed the ovens and did also help the elves find water when it was a drought. The dwarves could sense water moving through the bedrock and knew where to dig and how deep, and they never missed. The chief was riding with his group of elite warriors, they did keep a keen eye on the surroundings for even though there were no enemies there who would dare to attack such a huge group one could never be too sure that wolves or other predators didn't try to snatch a sheep or a calf.. The winter was a peaceful time, the monsters did rarely show up when it was cold and thus they had time to do other things but someone would always be alert nonetheless. One could never be too sure and nobody dared to take any chances.

The terrain was not as flat as some perhaps would guess, the horizon was flat enough but the landscape had small pits and valleys and here and there rivers had cut into the terrain and created canyons, large and small. They knew every rock in their land and how to cross the rivers and avoid problems but that didn't mean that it went smoothly all the time. The wagons in special were vulnerable and the dwarves would run from wagon to wagon checking the wheel rims before they were to cross a river. The rocks could make the wheel burst and then they stood there in cold water and had to fix it before anyone could move an inch further.

The moving of the camp was tiresome but they regarded it as a very joyful event for they would be heading for fresh pastures and new scenery and the women who were riding on the sleds and wagons would sing and chat while the males tried their best to impress.

This autumn had been special, the Ath'ir had sent his Si'ish off to find the girl who was foretold to be his bride and everybody were very excited. The humans had never met his previous wife and they had just heard the tale of her but the elves were after all immortal and many of them remembered her and they crossed their fingers and hoped that this new wife of his would be a better person.

Ahravan was riding his favourite horse, a giant stallion he had been given when it was a foal since the previous owner had been foretold that the horse would kill him if he kept it. No inhabitant of the plains would ever just kill a horse and so he gave the animal to the Ath'ir who accepted gracefully. The horse wasn't the normal silvery or golden colour but raven black with a golden shine to the coat and the mane and tail was golden, Ahravan had named the horse Ayr'esh which meant Swordblade and the stallion was very brave and capable of running for hours at top speed but nobody else was allowed to ride him and he would throw anyone who tried. Ahravan did stare at the horizon, they would soon make camp for the night, in two days they would arrive at the designated camp site and they used the same sites each year and knew the way to them like the back of their own hands. The year had been a good one, the livestock had grown fat and strong and most of the females had given birth too. The herd was their wealth and there had been many babies born too, it was a good sign.

The cold wind did tell the tall elf that the weather was turning and he made a grimace, it meant that it would be rather cold and he was a bit worried for the youngest members of the clans. They would be wrapped up in sheep hides and put in the warmest spots of the tents but still there was a certain danger.

He waved an arm and the front riders sent a man back, Ahravan saw that it was one of the human warriors, a lean and elegant man known as Sehvar and he grinned and pushed his cowl back. "My lord?"

Ahravan pointed at the greying skies. "I don't like those clouds, how far away is the first campsite?"

There were several potential campsites along the route and the man spat and made a grimace. "Half an hour, maybe one if the wind picks up"

Ahravan nodded. "Good, we will make camp there. Send the gatherers out and tell everybody to prepare"

The gatherers were young men and women who had been given the task of finding fuel for the camp fires. The plains were rather open with little trees, just a small groove here and there and they were sacred so nobody would ever fell a tree. Instead the huge caravan did burn cow dung and the gatherers did spread out with huge sacks and started to gather dung from last year. The piles could be found everywhere and by now they were bone dry and would burn rather well. It was a sort of competition, the youngsters were trying to be the one who gathered the most sacks and they were running around like a pack of bunnies. Ahravan had to grin, he had once been among them but that was a very long time ago now. They saw the camp site now, it was a flat little plain shielded by a tall cliff and Ahravan let out a sigh of relief. He was a war chief but the people did regard him as their leader also when there were no wars or battles to be fought and he felt the responsibility all the time. He hated to lose anyone, and even if the humans did die of old age he didn't want anyone to leave this world too early. They had lost two hunters this summer, both had been surprised by a flash flood and drowned when they were fishing in a canyon river and Ahravan had been furious for days.

The camp site was easy to prepare, they just set up simple tents now and built fires in the fire pits which had been covered the last time they had come this way. It was a swift job to clear them out and soon fires were burning and tents erected all over the place.

Ahravan made sure that the wagons were placed alongside each other to form a wall which shielded the camp from the wind and he erected a tent of his own. He missed Rhawan, they would often share a tent and Ahravan had felt lonely ever since Rhawan left. They had rarely been apart since they swore to be blood brothers. Rhawan was perhaps a rather reckless person who was a bit too impulsive at times but he was able to handle danger very well for he was a quick thinker and Ahravan knew that it was a good trait to have. Ahravan preferred to analyse a situation before he did anything and that could be wise but also dangerous. The two of them did complete each other and they were extremely close. Ahravan did trust Rhawan with his life and that was the reason he had sent his Si'ish off to get that girl. Rhawan would be able to determine what sort of person she was and thus warn Ahravan if there was something he needed to be aware of.

Ahravan sat down by his small fire and warmed some water, he was fond of tea like all of them were and prepared it very strong and sweet. Honey was one of the things they did get form the humans of the inland mountains and it was very precious. He knew that he used his fair share of the jars they got each autumn and he had to grin, he had a sweet tooth and couldn't deny it. He wrapped his thick cloak around himself and stared into the flames, normally Rhawan would keep him entertained with silly stories and endless bragging about his latest conquests and Ahravan sighed. The seer had really caused a lot of uproar, he hadn't really wanted to get married again and least of all to a human being, he just knew that he was going to have to change a lot in order to be able to live with that girl and he didn't like change at all. He still remembered Safya, she had been a gift and he had tried to be grateful but he had seen through her right away. Her father had loved her, beyond doubt, and she was a very spoiled person already when she came to him. Some humans did seem to be unable to really see what sort of flaws they offspring had and Ahravan had tried to love Safya but failed.

She had been a very tall woman with thick black locks and dark eyes and a lot of passion too, normally he would have loved that in a woman but she was passionate in the wrong manner. Her tribe had very little to do with the twelve clans and they had a very different view on life and

62

that had caused problems from day one. Safya had been furious when she discovered how close he and Rhawan were and she was constantly accusing him of being unfaithful. He had tried to explain their lifestyle to her but she refused to listen and many had been angry at her. To her two males living together was a sign of sin for sure and Ahravan had been rather tired of her constant complains.

In the beginning she did her duty in bed with a sort of fake show of submission and he hated it, she pretended to be pious and chaste and in reality she was rather insatiable. But she would never confess to liking it, no way, she always acted as if it was a huge sacrifice to go to bed with him and Ahravan had grown tired of her before two years had gone by. She tried to ruin the relationship between him and Rhawan and she did almost attack any female who dared to speak to him. Ahravan had figured out that the best way to deal with her was to simply buy her off, gifts usually made her as sweet as a pit of honey for a couple of days and then he would escape the sour nagging and that was extremely precious. He gave her jewellery and nice gowns and whatever and thus he did keep her happy most of the time but he felt miserable. It wasn't a marriage, it was…he couldn't even describe it and he was feeling relieved when she started to age. It was not a very nice manner of thinking but he couldn't help it. He refused to lay with her and he did know that she did try to seduce several of the other elven males of the clans but they refused, knowing what she was after. When she died he did bury her with all the right rituals and he felt more relieved than ever before.

Safya had wanted to give him an heir and he had seen how she was with the kids of others and he had refused to impregnate her, he didn't tell her that elves can do that and neither did the others. She was treating children like accessories and he had seen her hit a kid who ruffled her dress. So he lived with her constant nagging and knew that she would have raised a son or daughter to be on her side completely. In some ways he felt sorry for her for she saw having kids as her main purpose in life but there was no way he would want an heir with a mother like that. The title of Ath'ir wasn't hereditary and she just couldn't understand that, she believed that any son she bore him also would be Ath'ir. So her world was rather small and her understanding of it even smaller.

Ahravan was very nervous when he considered this new woman who was to become his wife, she came from an area of the inland mountains which was very isolated and also very old fashioned. People in there were ruled by superstition and an utter lack of true knowledge and Ahravan was afraid that she would be like Safya. If she was of simple birth then she could be a person who never would be able to adapt and he knew that the seer had said that great joy would follow but he did doubt that. He stared into the flames again, he couldn't disobey the gods, but he had rarely felt less tempted to follow their orders. The people of the inland highlands were a group of blockheads the way he saw it, they seemed to think that everything which didn't include toil and misery was sinful and what sort of life was that. Alright, they didn't live for that long but then they should really embrace that tiny sliver of life they did get. Safya had been so shocked by the fact that the twelve clans saw it as completely fine to have many bed partners and even partners of the same gender. The fact that several couples lived together was also something she tried to put an end to but no matter what she did the members of the clans just laughed at her and told her that this was how it was done there and if she didn't like it then she didn't have to sneak around spying on others. Ahravan made a grimace and took a sip of the tea, she had just been the type to interfere with everything, even his orders. She obviously believed that she knew all there is to know about fighting enemies but Ahravan had been forced to ban her from the council meetings for she went ballistic when the other war leaders refused to listen to her. It wasn't that fact that she was a female and a human being, it was the fact that she tried to give orders when she had no authority to do so, and bad ones too.

He had to snicker, the times he had to carry her out of the hut, kicking and screaming, it had been humiliating also for him for among his kin a marriage was like a dance, you did cooperate, you didn't try to cause problems for the other part of the relationship. There had been some good moments, all had not been bad but when he looked at it in retrospective the whole thing had been a disaster from one end to the other. He did want a family, and someone special to love but he had no idea of what the price of that would be. He and Rhawan had been the thing he had put his faith in and he was afraid that this new woman would disturb their deep friendship. Ahravan was about to find his bedroll and go to sleep when he heard some disturbing sounds from the other side of the camp, it was screams and shouts and he got back onto his feet within the blink of an eye and ran off. The screaming continued and it was a child which did most of it. Ahravan did feel his heart sink, something had to be very wrong when there was such commotion.

What he saw made him gasp and grasp his blade, a tiny girl sat pressed up against the cliff and in front of her Ahravan saw a giant snake, it was thicker than the girl and the head was hovering high above the terrified child. The others there were afraid to get nearer in fear of making the terrible creature attack and Ahravan swore. It was a sort of snake which was very rare but also feared. It lived deep in the sand and it was blind but hunted by following vibrations. The wide flat head was moving from one side to the other and it was trying to find the child but the girl had stopped screaming and sat as still as a mouse. The children there were trained well and knew how to behave and she was petrified but able to think in spite of that.

Ahravan saw that the snake was rather skinny, it had probably gone into winter hibernation in the dunes around the cliff and now the activity had awakened it. He was thinking fast, bent down and grasped some small rocks and he gestured towards the child. The clans had a sort of sign language they used when hunting and even the children knew it. The girl nodded and Ahravan threw a rock at the cliff some meters away from her, the snake immediately turned its huge head around and the jaws opened, this snake didn't have fangs like normal ones. Instead it had hundreds of needle like teeth placed in several rows and the bite was said to be so terrible the pain alone killed. The poison was terrible too and made the flesh dissolve and Ahravan threw a second rock and judged the speed of the snake. It was rather sluggish and he gestured to a couple of the elves who had gathered there, in shock and fear. Nobody dared to move out of fear of triggering the snake and Ahravan signed a swift order. Nobody hesitated, they followed his order right away and started stomping their feet against the ground, in a heavy rhythm. The snake turned around, the vibrations came from all over and it got confused, not knowing where to strike and where to go. Ahravan took a deep breath, then he ran forth, swift as a wind with light steps and he knew that the beast wouldn't notice his presence before it was too late. His sword was very sharp and made from the best steel, he had worked on keeping the edge razor like and he did jump towards the snake with a powerful leap and brought the blade down with all his strength. The blade did pierce the body right underneath the head and he cut it almost in half. His momentum tore the blade lose again and he landed on his feet, bringing the sword back up for a new attack. The snake was letting out some ghastly hissing sounds and it was writhing and trembling. The tall elf ran past it, making a sweeping cut and now he did finish the cut and the head fell off. The body collapsed into tremors and he grasped the kid and ran out of the danger zone. The blood of this snake was very hot and acidic and could seriously scald you if it hit your skin.

The body fell silent and he shook the blood of his blade and delivered the kid to her hysterical mother, the warriors gathered and many came to pat his back or squeeze his hand. "Such a great idea, you confused it"

One of the dwarves stood there and nodded his head, Ahravan smiled and felt that he in fact was a bit shaken. He hadn't noticed when it all happened. "Yes, they are very sensible so too many feet at once should have an effect"

He turned to the warriors. "Check on the horses and cattle, where there is one there could be more, and place a row of bonfires around the perimeter."

He took a deep breath, if Rhawan had been there he would have insisted on them both getting royally drunk to celebrate the victory and then Rhawan would probably go out seeking someone to bed if Ahravan didn't want to lay with him and Ahravan would have been alone again. He saw that the kid was unharmed but scared still and went over to the healer to ask him to give the kid something which would enable her to sleep without getting nightmares.

Afterwards he returned to the tent and sat down to have some more tea before bed. As an elf he didn't have to sleep that often but the march towards the next goal was tiring even for one as strong as him and he needed the sleep now. He drank a little, got rid of his jacket and jerkin and laid down in his bedroll wearing just his thin inner pants and a tunic.

66

The bedroll was made from thick furs which had been treated so they were silky soft and still very warm and you could keep warm even when it was very cold. Before long he was fast asleep and the entire camp was quiet. Some were guards and stayed awake but most of the clans slept through the night, they needed their rest.

Ahravan was dreaming and it was a good dream, he was riding over the wide plains on his large horse and there were nothing holding them back, it felt like flying over the grass. It was the freedom he always had loved, the open landscape and the knowledge that it all was for him to explore. Then the dream changed, he was suddenly in a cave and there was a pool in it, like in the sacred cave of the seer. The cave was lighted by fat lamps carved into the very wall itself and it looked like a very old place. He was there and yet not, as if he was just a spirit watching a scene from the realm of the soul. Then he saw someone approaching the pool, it was a woman and she was naked, just covered with long hair in a most amazing tone of auburn and red and it looked like dark flames against her skin. She was staring at the ground in front of her as she walked forth and her movements were very slow, as if she was afraid. Ahravan saw that she was human, rather tall and very elegant with lovely curves in all the right places. He wondered why he was dreaming this and he couldn't take his eyes off her. She was truly gorgeous and he wondered if she was real or just a phantom of his mind. The hair was very rare, he had never seen anyone with that sort of colour before and her eyes appeared to be green and grey in a strange and very enticing union. She walked into the water and it reached her waist, she was wetting her hair and then it looked as if it became blood as it reached the water, it was a bizarre sight for it was impossible. The water turned red all around her and she turned around and he could have sworn that she was looking straight at him. "Remember this, the love of one, the blood of two, the power of three, the promise of four"

The dream changed again, abruptly! He gasped and opened his eyes, feeling confused and slightly startled. It was getting light so he got up and started to redress and reroll his bed. The camp was being packed away again and he found some food and then he got his horse and mounted, still remembering that strange and ominous dream. What in the name of every deity had the meaning been?

Wenja and Sefa had managed to calm down Prina with the help of Nefhriel and some cups of soothing tea, now Wenja helped Sefa wash the girl with some water heated over a fire and they were shocked by how much grime they managed to get off her skin. No wonder why Prina did look so greyish, she was very filthy. Her hair was dirty too and Sefa was cussing like mad as she struggled to get the grease out of the thin locks. Prina was clearly malnourished and Imh had been ordered to prepare some really heavy food for her. Wenja had never imagined that Prina could be that abused but now she did see that the men of the family had put all the hard work onto her. She had been working more than anyone else and done the work of several grown women. Wenja saw that Prina's hands were filled with scars and hard skin and it had cracked in several places and her back was already a bit bent. Sefa was clicking her tongue as she tried to scour the last dirt out of the poor girl's skin. "You are so filthy I bet a mine worker would be way cleaner, did you never bathe?"

Prina was hanging her head. "No, I wasn't allowed to, the warm water was for father and Mjorr!"

Sefa almost growled. "Why am I not surprised? But that ends now, you will never become a goddamn work slave again"

She grasped a pair of scissors. "Your hair is damaged beyond repair, I need to cut it"

Prina just nodded and Sefa did make a swift job of the thin locks. "With good food you will get much nicer hair when it grows back out."

Prina just stood there, apathetic and broken and Wenja did still have a hard time understanding how it was possible. Mjorr had raped his own sister, that was a sin so great Wenja was unable to really wrap her head around it. The rules against incest were terribly strict in the valleys, you were not allowed to marry any person who was related to you and it meant that people sharing a common great great ancestor couldn't marry, and if they were related closer than that it was seen as a great sin. That meant that most had to leave the valleys to find a spouse but it was worth it for in the ancient days many had married their cousins and the result had been that many were born ill or retarded and disease was frequent.

Prina just stood there and Sefa did rub ointment onto the skin and then they found some clothes Prina could use. They even found a sort of head veil which covered most of the head but not the face and they added a normal veil which hid the lower half of it. Imh came with a kettle and it was a sort of soup, boiled on marrow and vegetables and it did smell very good. Imh filled a bowl and handed it over to Prina who just stared at it, she did look flabbergasted. Imh nodded firmly. "Yes, it is for you girl, eat!"

Prina was given a spoon and ate slowly, Wenja did see that she was missing several teeth and cringed, Prina did look like an old woman. Sefa whispered to Wenja as Prina tried to eat. "How old is she really?"

Wenja swallowed hard. "She is sixteen"

Sefa let out a small gasp. "Are you kidding me?"

Wenja shook her head. "No, I am serious. She has worked herself halfway into an early grave. I thought I was working hard but it is nothing compared with what she has endured."

Sefa growled. "A good thing we are on the move, I will ask if we can continue driving for the next days. We have many spare horses and the men can switch between driving and sleeping. We need to get as much space between ourselves and her family as possible."

Wenja nodded. "They are gonna be furious for sure, and I think Mjorr is capable of murder."

Sefa tilted her head. "I hear you, we will let the dogs lose, they can keep watch. "

Wenja had seen some very large long legged dogs in one of the wagons and the animals had looked fierce and strong. Sefa sighed and crossed her arms over her chest. "When we reach Ohtanar I bet that Ahravan will be mighty shocked by all of this, but the clans have many warriors and they know the plains like the back of their hand. They won't let anyone near who isn't welcome and someone like Mjorr is most likely to get lost before he gets near the city anyhow."

Prina cringed each time the name was mentioned and Wenja wondered what would happen to the girl, it was unlikely that she would be able to overcome the trauma she had been through. Sefa prepared the wagon for the night and she told the guards to keep an extra keen eye open and Rhawan did volunteer to sleep on the roof of the wagon with the wagon driver. Prina was placed between Wenja and Sefa and the girl was trembling most of the night and there wasn't much sleep to be had for anyone. In the morning they left very early and Imh did cook in the wagon, there was a sort of container you could put coal into and it was large enough for a small kettle. Imh made tea and then porridge and she almost forced Prina to eat two portions. Theka and Nefhriel did travel with the wagon this day but Floth'bha did ride with the guards. She rode a massive mule and Wenja hoped that the mere sight of the half orc would deter anyone trying to do something silly.

The road was very good and Rhawan had confirmed that they would continue for a few days with few stops, just to get as far away as possible. It would be hard but it was needed. They passed a couple of villages now and Wenja was curious but also shy, she peeked out of the wagon and saw that the people here wore clothes slightly different from the ones in her own village. Here the colours were more vivid and the valley was less steep and there were grapes planted in the valley side which tilted to the south. Rhawan said that they grew grapes and made wine there and he did even buy a bottle from a local man. He and one of the other guards did taste it with Sefa and Theka and the two women did cringe and spit and the guard called it horse piss. Rhawan did drink it with a grin, Wenja couldn't believe that the eternal was able to swallow that filth for it did stink!

Prina was terrified of Rhawan and Nefhriel and she did almost piss herself when Floth'bha did stop by to introduce herself. Wenja had believed that she was naïve with a very narrow horizon but she saw that she wasn't so bad after all. Her parents had taught her much in spite of being simple farmers and Prina had not been allowed to learn anything. Theka did sort of interview the girl and found that her lack of knowledge was shocking. They followed a river now and the guards did buy some fish from the locals and Imh promised to transform it into something delicious. Theka and Sefa started to teach Wenja and Prina some of the language of the plains and to their shock Prina was like a sponge and learned very fast. Wenja struggled a lot more but the skinny girl did understand the nuances of the language immediately and Theka said that she would have been a very wise person already if she had been born into another family. Nefhriel did promise that she would teach them how to read and write too and that made Wenja a bit nervous. She had never even touched a pen.

The wagons kept moving that night, slowly but steadily and they stopped a few times to change horses but for no longer than half an hour. Rhawan and some of the fastest riders did ride back in their own tracks to check that they weren't being followed and Wenja and Prina started to get used to the many people who followed them. There were wagon drivers and guards and men who cared for the horses and a cook who made the food for the group. He was a human, a very fat man with a kind face and slanted eyes and a soft voice. Wenja liked him for he treated her as an equal. The guards did show her great reverence and she felt so silly when they bowed for her. Prina did cover herself whenever she had to leave the wagon, they did use a chamber pot if they needed to relieve themselves at night but Wenja hated it so she made sure that she had done all such things before it got dark.

Sefa did keep their minds occupied with card games and she and Theka were good teachers. Nefhriel too tried to teach them things and Wenja started to realize that the elves were very different from humans in more ways than she had known before. Since Wenja was to marry one of the eternal Nefhriel was explaining a lot about their culture and the girl was a bit shocked to learn that it was believed to be a bad omen if a bride was untouched, it could mean that she was of a cold nature and that the marriage would be a very platonic one. She was also shocked when she was being told that the elves had several grades of marriage. Since she was human her marriage to Ahravan wouldn't be regarded as a full marriage, she would die eventually and leave him as a widower. But there was also a sort of non-binding temporary marriage which could last from a single day to many centuries and some marriages did include more than two individuals. It all made her head spin, and then Nefhriel told her that since her children would be full elves if Ahravan fathered them they would grow much more slowly than a human child and not reach full maturity before they were between forty and seventy years of age. That made Wenja feel a bit odd, she risked dying of old age before her children, if she got any, had even reached adulthood.

The next days were tough on everyone, they reached a rather steep valley which lead down towards a lake and the road was bad and a bit dangerous. They couldn't stay in the wagon here and had to walk and Rhawan did walk with them and Floth'bha did protect their back. She wore her axe all the time and the guards were very efficient too, circling the wagons and always being on the lookout. They reached the lake and there they had to rest for a whole day, the horses were tired and had to eat and here there was no snow yet. It was warmer too and Wenja was glad she could shed the heavy coat.

Theka was very adamant, she would make sure that Wenja and Prina did learn how to write and provided them with white smooth inner bark from some local trees. Nefhriel and Sefa did help them and Wenja did feel fantastic when she finally managed to understand the connection between the letters and the sounds and the words. The alphabet they used was invented by the elves and it was elaborate and very beautiful but difficult. The girls had to practice on the basic shapes for hours and Wenja didn't have time to miss her family at all but at night the longing would return with full force and she was suddenly glad she had family she could miss. Prina was thawing up, it was as if she was throwing a shroud off herself and her true personality did slowly emerge from under it. Wenja did find that she in fact liked Prina, the girl was very clever and Imh was force feeding her every second hour. Prina was afraid she would get fat if the dwarf didn't stop demanding that she ate bone marrow and other fatty foods every day.

But the food and the attention and the feeling of security did something to both of them, Wenja too loosened up and now she would smile at Rhawan and even try to joke. She was learning the language too but that did take time. She was no linguist, that was very obvious. She often made mistakes which made the entire wagon erupt into laughter and Wenja got this strange warm feeling in her chest, these women were her friends and they cared about her and she found that she cared about them too. She started to know them, Theka was a widow and her husband had died twenty years ago in a terrible snowstorm. She had two children and both were at Ohtanar. Sefa was unwed and had quite a reputation for being a mischievous little rascal who loved to play pranks on others and she and Rhawan were obviously very good friends. Nefhriel was also unwed but she had someone back home who was waiting for her and she was just keeping him waiting for her final answer to torture the poor male. She believed that it shouldn't be too easy to get a yes. Wenja learned that a true marriage between elves did involve a sort of bonding of spirits which was unbreakable and eternal and it would make them into two pieces of a unity for sure.

Theka did tell the two girls a lot about the history of the realm and Wenja was feeling more and more curious about the monsters but nobody seemed to be willing to tell much, only that they came from the mountains to the far north and that they were extremely dangerous and hard to kill. The valleys were getting wider and the mountains less tall and ragged and Wenja felt that she was entering a new world every day. She saw so much she never had even imagined. One day they drove through a forest with trees so tall she was sure they would touch the skies and they were enormous in circumference, so large a wagon could have fitted inside of the trunk. She saw people wearing odd clothes, new breeds of cattle and houses which were built in strange new ways. Prina did already speak the common language very well and she did even dare to speak to locals when they stopped. She wore the veil and they had dyed her skin darker with nut juice and she had gained some weight too so it was very unlikely that anyone who saw her would think that she was some runaway village girl. The cape and the veil made many believe that she was some sort of holy person for there were a few groups of believers who would leave their families behind and go into the service of their gods and they always covered themselves thus.

Prina started to suffer from morning sickness and Wenja didn't envy her this, she was miserable for hours every day and Imh was almost torturing the poor girl and making her eat so much food she felt stuffed like a sausage. But Wenja too did experience changes now that she was being fed well and she felt how she got more energy and how her body slowly got more shapes. Her bosom got more ample and her hips weren't just bone anymore, she did heal from her previous lack of good nutrition rather well.

The group did catch the attention of many on their way, they passed by several villages and farms and although most were very friendly Wenja did see a few people who were not. It was the elves in special who caused these kinds of reactions and she had a hard time understanding why anyone would act thus? Some even spat and left when they saw the eternal and a few did signs which were supposed to ward off evil. Sefa explained that many humans believed that elves did get their eternal lives from somehow draining humans of theirs and others did believe that elves stole human babies and transformed them to elves since they couldn't have children themselves. That made both her and Prina scoff and Prina wondered why on earth anyone would believe that the eternal were unable to breed?

Rhawan was sitting there with them playing cards and he answered rather wryly that it was believed that since the elven males were prettier than most human females they couldn't really be males, that they were lacking certain masculine traits.

Sefa started to laugh so bad she almost spurted tea all over the table and then Nefhriel told them all about the time she and some other elves had been sent off to a city to the south to buy some rare herbs and while they were there the mayor were treating them all as if they were female, believing that this was the truth. In the end one of the warriors had been sick and tired of being referred to as "lass" or "her" and he had just pulled down his pants at the dinner table and confirmed that yes, he was indeed male and no, he didn't miss anything, rather the opposite.

But Nefhriel did also explain that the superstition some believed in had caused problems, people had accused them of stealing children and come searching for them when the truth was that the kids had gotten lost and died and others had believed that elves could make you sick. These days such reactions were rare but they did still happen. Rhawan wasn't worried about these things, he worried more about the fact that they travelled with many wagons and good horses and that could tempt thieves and highwaymen, even with this large escort. Since elves were rarely seen in the highlands few were aware of the fact that they are superior fighters and he was worried that some idiot could try to attack them. Floth'bha did just snicker and pet her axe, she promised that if some dimwit did give into temptation then she would make sure that the person forever more would have to squat like a girl in order to pee. Rhawan cringed and told them that Floth'bha once had castrated a male orc who had tried to get a wee bit too familiar with a friend of hers. Wenja didn't doubt that, at all.

Floth'bha was a sort of enigma for she never spoke that much about herself and although she was a very cheerful person she could be terrifying as well. Wenja sensed a great darkness in the half orc and she did understand that some of this was because she had suffered a lot in her youth. Half orcs were rare, and most of the time they weren't accepted by neither humans nor orcs. Her mother had been human and although Floth'bha never said anything it was common knowledge within the clans that she was the result of rape. It had been a terrible burden to bare and Floth'bha had become a warrior, just to prevent this from happening to others.

Imh told them a lot about the dwarves and Wenja did find their conversations most enjoyable, the small woman had a very peculiar sense of humour and tried to teach Wenja some words of her own language. It did usually end with the girl feeling as if she had somehow managed to turn her own tongue into a knot! But the language was very interesting since the way you pronounced some words changed their meaning completely and Wenja did make some blunders which made Imh curl over in wild laughter. When she was caught having referred to the man who drove the wagon as "the one wearing a shrubbery" she decided that she had had enough and concentrated on the common speech instead. She could learn dwarfish later on, when she had the time.

They had been on the road for a few weeks when they entered the first real obstacle on the way, it was a river and it was very wide and deep and they had to use ferries to cross. The ferries were huge flat bottomed barges which were attached to a strong cable stretched from one side of the river to the other and you moved the ferry by turning a sort of mechanism which pulled it forth. The mechanism was placed on land and were being powered by four huge horses and the ferryman was grinning from one ear to the other when he saw the huge number of people, horses and wagons. Rhawan had brought lots of money and he did pay the man very well but crossing took the entire day since the ferry could transport only one wagon and a couple of horses at a time and it didn't exactly race across the water.

Wenja did feel nervous when it was their turn to cross, she saw that the ferry was very solid and well-made so there was little danger but she had never seen that much water before. It made her feel dizzy and Prina was afraid that there could be monsters in it. Why nobody knew but somebody had probably scared the girl with tales of strange creatures. Rhawan did make sure that some of the guards crossed with each wagon, nobody was left behind unguarded and when the last wagon and the last horses had crossed it was getting dark. The ferryman bowed deeply and shook Rhawan's hand. The payment ought to keep his family fed for most of the winter and the man was obviously very grateful. He cleared his voice and pulled the tall eternal aside. "I wish to warn you my lord, you transport great wealth and I know for a fact that there are some men of a somewhat shady reputation living in the next village. Stay here until the morrow, and don't stop there. They may try to rob you, or worse"

Rhawan took a deep breath and his eyes got narrow. "I thank you for the warning good man, and may the blessings of every God be with you and your kin"

The ferryman appeared to be almost weeping with gratitude hearing this for many believed that a blessing from one of the eternal would ensure that you would have a good and long life. Rhawan turned around and sighed, that meant that they would have to be very careful indeed. The smaller villages did usually house only honest hardworking people but when the villages grew people didn't need to work to stay alive and some did seek easier ways to make a living. He told the other riders of the news and they all agreed that staying by the river was smart, he didn't want to upset the women but told Sefa who snorted and responded by finding her throwing knives and attaching them to her waist. Floth'bha was told as well and she swore she would sleep under the wagon for the next nights, just to protect Wenja and Prina. Floth'bha had taken a particular liking to Prina and acted a lot like a very protective older sister and Prina did like the half orc too. She felt safe when Floth'bha was close by and since they both had suffered a lot they had a sort of connection between them which was hard to explain but definitely strong.

The next morning came with sour wind and sleet and it meant that it would be a rough day, the wagons were prepared and checked and the horses hitched up and off they went. The roads here were very good for there were several large villages in this area and they transported a lot of goods south so some stretches were even covered with cobblestone. The village the ferryman had spoken off was indeed rather large and it had a wall built around it and even a mote. You had to go through it since the road did split it in half and now Rhawan did organize the caravan in a new manner. There were two riders by each wagon, and two riding in between the wagons and the rest did ride in front of the wagon train or at the back. Floth'bha was riding in front and he did take up the rear and they were told to keep going no matter what. The wagons were covered with thick tarp and the ones holding their provisions were guarded by a dog each. Wenja and Prina were told to stay in the wagon and Sefa and Theka did sit on the roof wearing rather raggedy clothing. Nefhriel was riding, dressed as a warrior with her hair braided back tightly and a double blade at her side. The weapon did require great skill and Nefhriel did reveal that she was a warrior too, not just a teacher.

The village was rather rich, the houses large and well-kept and the streets were relatively clean and well cared for with few holes and bumps. Some people were scurrying along and few bothered with even looking at the wagons and the riders, that caravans did pass through this place was common and since the village saw much trade the inhabitants were used to seeing both elves and dwarves.

They had reached the gate on the opposite side when they heard an odd sound, it was a sort of shriek and it made the elves turn their heads in confusion. Rhawan did gesture for the others to go on, he turned his horse and rode towards the source of the sound, it was heard again and he couldn't identify it. It had to be a sort of animal but what? The sound came from a small square and he rode into it, with his blades ready. There was a small crowd there but the people did look scared and he saw why. A huge brute of a man was causing the commotion, he was obviously trying to sell the animal which was tethered to the well and the crowd were too afraid of him to just leave. Rhawan cussed, he felt faint for a few seconds, what he saw was sacrilege. These creatures were sacred and no elf would ever dare to lay hands on one. It was a Zahar, and it was obviously abused and starved. Rhawan did almost lose his cools there and then but he managed to rein in his wrath and tried to estimate the situation, the way Ahravan would have done. The Zahar was a stallion and it was not yet fully grown, but already it was taller than most horses and the long legs with cloven hooves were covered with mud and deep cuts from a whip. It was wearing a halter and a cruel bit which had cut into its mouth and the animal was desperate, the piercing yellow eyes wide open. How a human had managed to catch one was beyond Rhawan's understanding but this had to end, now!

The Zahar was snow white with stripes of grey and the mane and tail was also grey in a slightly darker tone. The horns on its head hadn't fully developed yet and the lack of canines told Rhawan that it couldn't be more than a handful of years old. He raised his voice, making it calm and almost indifferent. "Excuse me, what a peculiar animal, where did you come by it?"

The man did notice the elf and sent Rhawan a fat grin. "Oh it is rare ye see, I found it trapped in a canyon, a rockslide had sealed it off"

Rhawan hid a grimace, that made sense, no human being would be able to catch a Zahar if it was free to run. "Is it for sale?"

The man extended his arms. "Of course, if you can tame the beast. Do not remove the bit, without it the thing will attack"

Rhawan sensed the magic within the piece of steel, it was probably spells laid into it and he reached out to the Zahar with his mind. These were magical beings, and they could communicate with elves the way they did with their closest friends. The Zahar was terrified, it was hurting and it was angry. Rhawan did whisper soothing words through the mind bond as he dismounted and walked towards the animal. "How much do you want?"

The man grinned, Rhawan had to hide his gaze since he otherwise would reveal just how pissed off he was. "Twenty gold, not a shilling less."

Rhawan pressed his lips together and sent a friendly smile to the people assembled there. "Go home good people, there is nothing more to see here"

Most did listen and obey, most of them with obvious relief. He sensed that they had disliked this but that the man was someone they all feared. Rhawan walked around the Zahar and saw that it was skinny and the coat matted and covered with dirt and blood. He knew what he had to do. "I think it looks a bit thin?"

He kept his voice indifferent and the man nodded. "Didn't want the oats I gave it, stupid nag!"

Rhawan felt a need to roll his eyes, the man didn't even know what sort of animal this was. Zahars are omnivorous and prefer meat over grass, if eating something other than meat they will often try to find fruit and vegetables or even nuts but rarely grass and never things like oats and stuff. He saw that the Zahar was following him with its gaze and the man started to look a bit nervous. The eternal was almost a head taller than him and very wide shouldered and he did move without even a sound. Rhawan did send the man a grin but it was an ominous one and his eyes were dark. "Know what, that is a Zahar, a sacred animal. You have committed sacrilege and broken the laws of the Gods. The punishment for such atrocious crimes is death"

The man tried to intimidate Rhawan by leaning forward, frowning. "How would I know? Buy it or get lost"

Rhawan smiled still, but the smile was becoming a sneer. "Know who I am? I am the Si'ish of the Ath'ir, I am his hand and his blade. The laws of the realm are very clear, and you have just pissed on them."

The man swore and attacked, used to the fact that his great bulk gave him an advantage but this time he was acting foolishly. The elf just spun around and pulled one of his slender daggers with lightning speed. As the human tried to punch him he just slid underneath the movement and thrust the dagger in under the man's lower jaw where it penetrated the oral cavity and the palate and entered the brain with a sickening thud. He pulled the blade free and the man just fell, dropped dead like a brick made from lead. The people who were still there just gaped and the elf shook the blood of the dagger before sheathing it again. He turned to the people. "This man has broken the laws given us by the Gods, and he has been punished for this."

One of the men there did step forward, he was a tiny guy with a thin moustache and a wrinkled and sun worn face, he did bow his head with his hat in his hand. "Good sir, this man… he was the scourge of this village, a brute and a criminal and no tears will be shed on his behalf. But he has two brothers, and they are almost as bad, I can guarantee you that they will seek vengeance for this, no matter what he did"

Rhawan made a grimace. "I see, but I fear them not, go home, speak of this to everyone. Nobody is above the laws of the gods!"

The man bowed deeply and the crowd scattered, he walked over to the Zahar and managed to get the halter off it. The animal shook its head and he sighed when he saw the marks from the whip. "Oh my beautiful one, what am I to do with you?"

The Zahar rubbed its nose against his chest and he stroked the head gently. "Follow me, and we will help you heal"

The animal snorted and nodded its head and greeted his horse with a short whinny. Rhawan mounted and the Zahar did follow him willingly, it would require a lot of attention and help before it was fully healed. He saw that it was limping and stiff and he swore that he would do whatever he could to help it regain its health.

He caught up with the caravan some farthings away from the village and the elves just stared, then they all let out a wailing sound and appeared to be very shocked by what they saw. Rhawan stopped his horse. "We do not stop tonight, we have to keep moving. A very bad human had captured this Zahar and I killed him as was my right and duty. But he has brothers and I fear that they will try to avenge him, even if he did break the law"

Floth'bha was baring her teeth. "I will not let anyone get near us, I know spells"

As a half orc Floth'bha had some inherent magic and it was very primitive and not very strong compared with that of elves but it was efficient since it usually was less elegant and more brutal. Rhawan stared over at Nefhriel. "Could you add some magic as well? I must focus on the poor creature, it needs help urgently."

One of the wagons was of the roof less type and they used it to transport tents and some kitchen equipment. Now that was transferred to one of the other wagons and they stopped and helped the Zahar jump up into the wagon. The guards gathered straw and moss and made a bed for it and the animal did sigh with relief and did lay down immediately. They covered the sides of the wagon with tarp and as they moved on Rhawan sat down with it and tried to transfer as much healing energy into it as he could.

Wenja was shocked when Sefa told her of the incident, she hadn't even peeked out of the wagon as it passed through the village and the danger of an attack made her stomach knot. They had many guards and they all knew how to fight but she was still getting nervous. Nefhriel and Floth'bha did disappear into the woods and Rhawan did give orders to everybody. The caravan did move forth rather fast, they didn't spare the horses and the small stops they did make during the night were just to switch the tired horses with rested ones. Wenja did sleep rather well in spite of it all, she had gotten so used to the movement of the wagon she didn't actually notice it anymore and she was also used to sleeping with Sefa by her side.

The morning light came with mist and they entered a wide valley with a flat bottom and Rhawan was a bit worried. The road was very good there but the area surrounding it was rather swampy and they couldn't leave the road at all. The wagons would sink or get stuck if they did and he would have preferred to spread them more out. As it was that was impossible and he ordered the drivers to arm themselves and he also placed archers on the wagon roofs. The problem here was that there seemed to be a parallel road to this one and it was narrow and hardly more than a cattle track but it was a real road and if someone did use it they could potentially get ahead of the caravan since a rider could travel so much faster than a long line of wagons. The Zahar was getting better, the healing energy had been accepted and the animal was healing fast but it was still weak. One of the hunters had ridden off and returned with a small deer and the Zahar had devoured half the animal with glee. The strange cat like eyes were calm and mild when one of the elves were nearby but it sneered if a human got too close to the wagon it laid in.

They tried to keep a brisk pace and the drivers were glad the valley was relatively flat, the horses didn't have to really spend much strength on pulling the wagons. The few guards who weren't riding sat in one of the smaller wagons and kept an eye on the surroundings. Rhawan had mounted his horse and he had his blades ready at his side at all times. They had put many miles between them and the village but he didn't doubt that the men he had been warned about would try to cause them problems, the question was just when and where.

He doubted that they were patient, and he did also doubt that they were smart. If they were anything like their brother they would be brutish and stupid and convinced of their own superiority and the strength that comes from numbers. As the day passed they got closer to where the valley did narrow down and it ended in a rather narrow canyon. It was a perfect spot for an ambush and he did use his elven skills to communicate with nature itself and the things he felt in return told of disturbance. He stopped the front wagon when they had a mile left before they reached the canyon and told the driver that he ought to pretend as if he had problems with a wheel. Rhawan gestured to the guards and Nefhriel did show herself in the bushes. "I ride ahead"

He knew that he was putting himself in harm's way but he was very confident and Nefhriel and Floth'bha would also be there, like hidden shadows. The half orc was huge but she was just as good at hiding as any elf and the mere sight of her ought to startle even the most tenacious human. The road did narrow down and it became less even too, the steep sides of the canyon was to blame for that, each spring rocks would come loose and sometimes they did harm the road and there were few present to make repairs. Other things were more important than fixing a damaged road in the middle of spring when the fields had to be prepared. Rhawan knew that there were someone there, probably hiding among the large rocks which formed the scree on both sides of the road. He pretended as if naught was wrong and rode slowly. These men he had been warned about were after all just human, they didn't have any magic and he had fought humans before, he didn't fear them.

Rhawan suddenly realized that these men were more vicious than he had expected, they were perhaps not the sharpest tools in the shed but

82

they did fight like mercenaries, like the barbarians from the isles to the west. His horse did stumble with a groan and Rhawan did barely have time to get out of the saddle before the animal fell. The elf was a bit shocked, he hadn't really thought of the possibility of them felling his horse to get to him. It wasn't what people normally would do since horses were expensive. These brutes on the other hand did clearly think differently and he cussed as he dodged a crossbow bolt which hissed straight by his head. He had his swords ready and was on the move within the blink of an eye and he knew that the bolt had come from somewhere to his left, and above him.

He disappeared into the scree with the elegance of a weasel and moved so fast no human would be able to copy him. But no matter how fast he was, he groaned as another bolt sliced through his flesh just above the hip and he knew that there were two crossbows there, one on each side of the canyon. He broke off the bolt with a gasp and whistled, a thin birdlike sound which to Nefhriel and Floth'bha was a clear warning. He just hoped that they would be able to take the bow man on the other side down fast. Another bolt came flying and shattered against the rocks and he made a stiff grin, these guys were careful, they didn't dare to face him in hand to hand combat, cowards.

He sniffed, his nose was almost as sensitive as that of a dog and he could smell them, there were at least three on this side of the canyon, maybe four. He had no idea of how many there were on the other side, the wind was going in the wrong direction for that. He did sneak forward but it did go slowly since he had to keep himself covered the whole time, then he heard something very welcome, a hoarse roar of fear from the scree on the other side and then the sound of steel against flesh. Floth'bha was hollering. "Two here, a bowman and some inbred looser"

Rhawan grinned, now he didn't have to think about covering his back anymore, he could move forwards much more freely without being pinned down from both sides and he picked up his pace. The scree was a good place to hide, with lots of nooks and crannies but that also meant that it was easy to move forward without getting seen and he had sort of established where the attackers were. They were probably trying to move too now that the ones on the other side were gone and he stopped and listened with uneven intervals. They were still there, he could hear them, sometimes a foot would slip on a rock, a sleeve would brush against a bush. He on the other side made no sounds whatsoever and he did slide forth between the rocks effortlessly. The bolt did hurt like hell but he had been trained to ignore pain until he could deal with it safely. He saw the first one, a smaller man wearing rather good wool clothes and a hood made from tarp. He didn't look like a wealthy person but he wasn't really poor and he was carrying a crossbow and a quiver filled with bolts. The man did look as if he was about to piss himself and Rhawan did sneer. This man had killed a good horse and put a bolt in him and he didn't accept that.

Rhawan did slide around a huge boulder without a sound and plunged his dagger into the man's neck just below the skull. The man didn't even have time to squeak, he stiffened, the body jerked a few times and then he went limp and Rhawan did lower him to the ground, without a sound. The other men were near and Rhawan did listen carefully. He heard heavy breathing and felt the scent of fear and also sweat, ale and grease. He heard a faint whistling sound and knew that Nefhriel and Floth'bha were right behind him.

He got up on top of a boulder and took a peek around, he saw the other men right away. They were huddling up against a boulder which formed almost a small cave and he saw the family similarity with the one who had tortured the Zahar right away. All three were large men, and rather hairy and he had to snicker to himself. The similarity between these men and some huge monkeys he once had seen was striking.

He stayed out of sight and waited, they probably knew that the archer was gone now and they had to rely on their skills with a blade. He saw that two of them had swords, rather short stubby weapons more alike a cutlass than a broad sword and he saw that the weapons were old and worn. The third of them carried an axe and it wasn't much to brag about. It was perhaps perfect for chopping up wood but it was not made for use in battle. The head of the axe was too heavy and the wooden handle too long. A skilled axe wielder would be able to use it well nonetheless but this man was no warrior and Rhawan did see that the three men were slightly overweight and all had the same floating features and bad skin. A whistle came from the left and Rhawan did signal back, it was Floth'bha and she signalled that she was ready to attack. Another whistle came from the right and Rhawan smiled, all three of them were there and he signalled that the two women were to show themselves when he did but it was his fight.

Rhawan did pull both of his blades and took a deep breath. He jumped up onto a rock and the three men flinched at the sight, they grasped their weapons and Rhawan sent them a nasty grin. He was angry now and he knew that the beauty of the eternal sometimes made humans ignore the fact that they are superior warriors. "So, it wasn't enough that one of your wretched kin did capture and torture a sacred beast, you have killed a good horse and you tried to kill me too, I see that common sense and wisdom has fled the petty excuse you have for a brain"

The men let out a roar to encourage themselves but then Floth'bha showed up on another rock, baring her impressive teeth and Nefhriel was showing herself on the other side, wielding a short bow and she was aiming for the three men.

Rhawan almost growled. "So, I will give you the chance to fight for your honour, but expect no pardon, you have signed your own death sentence now humans!"

The men stared at Floth'bha with disbelief and Rhawan did to his disbelief see that one of them was confident enough to leer at Nefhriel. The audacity made him gape, and when the man grinned at the elf and perched his lips as if in a kiss Rhawan did snap. That sort of disrespect was just ghastly. It would not be tolerated by his people at all and he jumped down and attacked. His first move was a very nasty one, he was going to let these men suffer and he did slide along the ground and his first cut was a very low one. He cut the leg out from underneath the man with the axe and he fell with a howl of shock and agony and the blood was spurting from the stump. The other two yelled and charged forth and he kicked one of them between the legs so he crumbled to the ground with a hoarse shriek and the other got an elven steel blade straight through his chest.

Rhawan did swing the other blade and did decapitate the one on the ground clutching his aching balls, then he plunged his blade through the skull of the axe man. It was just done out of rage, the man was already dying from blood loss. Floth'bha grinned but she did look disappointed. "You should have left some for me"

Rhawan nodded. "It was just three sister, no match for a fighter of your calibre. We will need your strength again later for sure"

Floth'bha did grin and nod and Nefhriel stared at him. "You are hurt"

Rhawan nodded. "A bolt, but it isn't a serious injury, I hope."

Nefhriel did look as if she doubted his words and Floth'bha did check the scree, she just ran from one rock to the other with a sort of brutal elegance. She returned after just a few minutes. "They were no more than six in all, I see some horses tethered in a Holt of trees a farthing from here. I'll go get them."

Rhawan sighed. "Yes, bring them along. I fear that this isn't over yet."

Nefhriel did frown. "What do you mean? We killed them?"

Rhawan sent her a sort of tired grin. "Yes, I know, but they have friends for sure, and such brutes does often leave an impression on the ones of an equally weak mind. "

The she elf rolled her eyes. "Oh, typical, so someone may try to avenge them? That is just silly!"

Rhawan nodded. "Yes, it is. But if this area really harbour those who spits on the laws of the realm I wouldn't regard it as impossible. These humans make their own laws and rules and they are often very hard to understand."

Nefhriel scoffed. "Humans are hard to understand, and that is that. Period! They are such…odd creatures"

Rhawan sighed and walked over the rocks back to where his horse fell. He felt a sting of rage yet again, he had been fond of that animal and to the elves a horse was a family member. He wished that he could have let those men suffer much longer than they had. He removed the tack and then they pulled the body out of the road and covered it with branches. Rhawan felt depressed and angry and Nefhriel did let him mount one of the horses the men had left behind, they rode back to the caravan and Sefa did approach them and she did gape. "They killed your horse Rhawan?!"

The dark elf nodded and jumped off the horse he had taken with a groan, the wound was starting to hurt now and he tried to smile. "Get Ahnriel, I need her help"

Sefa did run off and Nefhriel and Floth'bha did take the horses and tethered them to one of the wagons. Ehbrial and Thokan did ride over to Rhawan and both did look nervous. "So, what are we to do now?"

Rhawan made a grimace. "We will continue, do not let this hinder us."

Ehbrial looked down. "We can shorten the path a little, if we use the old dwarven roads."

Rhawan sighed and tried to ignore the pain but the wound was throbbing and he hissed and hoped that Ahnriel could fix it fast. "Yes, but only if they are maintained. There ought to be someone who knows what condition they are in. But you are right, it will save us many days of travel, check the maps"

Ehbrial did grin and took off and Ahnriel did appear and she was waving her hand at Rhawan. "Come, the wagon is ready, I don't want to do anything out in the open"

Rhawan followed her to the house wagon, careful not to reveal the severity of his injury, he was rather proud and didn't want the others there to know of his weakness. Wenja and Sefa were already in there and Ahnriel did smile at them. "We need to use this wagon for a few moments, it is the only one with a decent bed"

She grasped some extra sheets and threw them onto it and Rhawan did hesitate. Wenja stared at the blood on his clothes and she was pale. "Is he hurt?"

Ahnriel nodded. "Yes, but I will fix it. Off with them rags Rhawan"

Rhawan did moan but pulled off his jacket and tunic and kicked off his boots. The injury hurt more by the minute now and he allowed her to lay him down on the bed. Wenja stood by the door gaping and Sefa did seem to enjoy herself. Rhawan bare chested was a sight to behold. The healer did touch the remaining piece of bolt and wiggled it around a bit, it made Rhawan hiss and groan and she grasped a knife and cut away his pants, then she pulled them off him and he sighed and laid an arm over his face, he didn't want to look at the injury. Wenja just stood there, gaping even wider. She had never seen a naked man before other than her baby brothers and this was…different. She couldn't pull her eyes away from his mid-section and Sefa giggled. "Oh yes, he is a sight to behold. Just feast your eyes on that Wenja, it is good for you. When you become a wedded woman you will get used to that sight for sure"

The bolt sat lodged in his flesh and it had caused a lot of bleeding and swelling too and Ahnriel was swearing. "You have moved way too much with that thing in you, it is nasty"

She found a bottle of something and Rhawan saw it and let out a deep groan. "Oh have mercy on me Ahnriel, can't you just heal it?"

The healer shook her head and the green braids were shaking. "No, I need to disinfect the wound whence the bolt is out, and this will do the trick"

Rhawan just sighed and Wenja tried to avoid staring at his manly parts, the wound was so nasty she couldn't bear to look at it at all. "What is that?"

Ahnriel did grasp a set of thongs, she felt the skin and tried to determine how deeply the bolt was lodged. "It is a strong disinfectant, it takes away any impurities or poisons but it has a sting to it, I cannot lie"

Rhawan growled. "Sting? Try burn! Like hellfire!"

Ahnriel did grasp the bolt shaft with the thongs and then she pulled, rather swiftly and Rhawan let out a howl of agony and blood gushed from the wound. Ahnriel did wipe it off with a rather calm expression but Wenja felt as if she was about to pass out, she felt so sorry for Rhawan, it had to hurt terribly. Then Ahnriel did uncork the bottle and poured from it into the wound and they heard a sizzling sound and it did bubble and hiss. Rhawan did go stiff, his body arching and he let out a keen and bit his teeth together, so hard it almost broke them. "The goddess damn you woman, you could have…warned me!"

Ahnriel did shake her head. "That would have been no good, you would have tensed up. Look, the wound is clean now"

She wiped fluids from it and Rhawan was panting. "Oh you owe me, you owe me so much…"

Ahnriel did giggle. "I know, but you will have to wait for a few days, you need to recover first"

88

Sefa snickered. "Hear that Rhawan? You have something to look forward to"

Wenja did frown, what were they talking about? Sefa did nudge Wenja in her flank. "She'll bed him, when he is good and well again!"

Wenja did blush. "Oh, I…see"

Ahnriel did find a needle and some extremely thin thread and then she put some stiches in him, he didn't even flinch as she sewed him up and then she smeared a sort of thick cream over the wound and wrapped a bandage around his hips. "Two inches to the left and down and it would have gotten stuck in your pelvic bone, that would have been way worse. This was just a flesh wound so quit whining"

Rhawan was growling. "I am not…Whining!"

Ahnriel giggled and finished the job. "Alright, you can get dressed again, it is no good spoiling Wenja here"

Rhawan just scoffed. "As if that is possible, Ahravan is larger than me, in every manner!"

Sefa had to laugh. "Hear that Wenja? Your future husband is a stud, I bet he will bring you immense joy"

Wenja felt her face burn and she had to turn around, oh gods, that was information she didn't need, at all. Sefa did look rather smug and Rhawan did manage to get his clothes back on, he sighed and pulled his boots on. "I think we may rethink our original plan, we have to reach the plains as fast as we can, I don't want to spend more time in the valleys than absolutely necessary."

Sefa tilted her head. "Really? But how are we to travel faster? "

Rhawan did get up and Ahnriel did remove the soiled sheets and took them with her, the wagon was already moving again and Wenja saw that they had reached the canyon. Here they had to slow down since the road was narrow and uneven. "We may have to use the old dwarf roads"

Sefa did look rather surprised. "Really? I have only heard of them"

Wenja did sit down, she still felt a bit bothered for Rhawan was so very present at the moment, she couldn't help but thinking about what she just had seen. "We hope that they are useable still, they should be for they were well made"

Wenja swallowed. "What are they?"

Rhawan smiled and cringed as he sat down, the wound was obviously painful still. "Tunnels through the mountains. As we reach the outer mountains you will see that the mountains become very steep walls of rock, like vertical barriers. And they are very long, dividing the valleys from each other for many hundred miles in each direction. But the cliffs are very narrow and thus the dwarves did dig into them ages ago, and made tunnels which shortened the passage between the valleys with several days."

Sefa looked excited. "Oh, I wonder if we can use them, it must be scary, going through the rock itself"

Rhawan grinned. "The tunnels are large Sefa, several wagons can travel through them side by side, and they used to be very safe but I don't think that they are that much in use anymore. The trade from this part of the valleys have diminished over the years"

Sefa nodded. "Yes, we can find them?"

Rhawan nodded. "We have maps, I have told Ehbrial to find some, I will go now and see if we can plan the route more in detail"

Wenja shuddered, tunnels? That made her think of the few mining shafts which had been made by the villagers, looking for copper. They were black and narrow and terrifying and they had always reminded her of hungry maws, eager to devour anything which came within their reach. Sefa sent him a grin. "Let us know when you have made the decision, I have heard a lot about them, and that they are quite a marvel"

Rhawan bowed his head to them and opened the door. "I will"

Wenja turned to Sefa and the dark haired woman did see the questions in her eyes. She smiled at the redhead and took her hand. "Do not worry, the roads will be safe. They will not enter them unless they are. "

Wenja bit her teeth together. "Oh, I don't worry about that, I trust everyone here. How could I not? But…"

Sefa had to raise an eyebrow in a gesture of mock surprise. "There is something else you need to learn more about is there not?"

Wenja sighed and look down. "I had never seen a naked man before…"

Sefa sort of scoffed and pulled her legs up underneath her. "I sort of guessed that yes, but you do know the differences don't you?"

Wenja blushed deeply, feeling the need to hide in her hair, as she used to do as a child. "Yes, I have seen my brother's bathe, but never an adult"

Sefa sighed. "Wenja, it is natural. He didn't have anything other men doesn't have, yes, he is rather generously gifted but that is normal for his kind."

Wenja felt herself shiver, a wee bit. "Oh gods, I cannot imagine..."

Sefa stroked her hair, gently, like a mother would. "You are truly such an innocent person, I am telling you this sweet one, don't worry about that. There is nothing to fear at all"

Wenja hung her head. "I have heard tales of the opposite!"

Sefa almost sneered. "Ah dogshit, forget about those tales. They are lies, we have bodies Wenja, and those bodies were meant to bring us joy, in every manner possible. I can assure you that you will look back upon this conversation in a few weeks' time and wonder how on earth you could be so ignorant"

Wenja felt how her cheeks were burning. "I am scared!"

Sefa did give her a bear hug. "Don't be, Ahravan is nothing but kind and generous and he will take so good care of you"

Wenja felt silly, and yet she felt that she had to know. "What if he doesn't like me?"

Sefa scoffed and crossed her arms over her chest. "Wenja, you have never looked at yourself in a mirror have you? I can guarantee you, he will fall head over heels the moment he lays his gaze upon you. To an elven male you are a treat, a temptation with huge bold letters. He will adore you"

Wenja did take a deep breath. "The wedding itself, how...I know so little..."

Sefa smiled. "It is just fair that you are taught our customs, to give you time to prepare. The wedding will last for no less than three days."

Wenja gaped. "Three days?!"

Sefa nodded solemnly. "Yes, it is a lot of pomp and circumstance you see, rituals which has to be followed and I can guarantee, you will not have time to be bored."

Wenja swallowed hard, three days? A wedding feast back home lasted for one day at the most and even though it was a grand event and filled with joy and good cheer nobody could afford anything really large. "So, what will happen?"

Sefa did push herself up against the wall and found a comfortable position, Wenja did the same, a bit hesitantly. "The first part of the wedding starts at sunrise, you will both be dressed in your finery and the shaman of the tribe local to the area will bless you. Then there will be gifts given and there will be a feast. You will do some dancing and some other rituals will be followed as well but we can get back to them later on. This first night you will sleep in the same tent but he will not be allowed to touch you, yet. "

Wenja frowned. "Really?"

Sefa nodded. "Yes, during these three days you are to be regarded as betrothed, not yet wed. He can't lay with you until the final night."

Wenja swallowed. "Ah…alright, but then what happens the next day?"

Sefa sighed. "You will travel, to a sacred grove. There the shaman will take you through even more rituals and there is a sacred pool in which you have to bathe. Then you will be kept separate for the night, and both of you will fast and only drink water until the next morning."

Wenja started to realize that this wedding thing was very complicated. "Does everybody have to go through all that to get wedded?"

Her voice did reveal her confusion and Sefa shook her head. "No, well, most of it is rather mandatory but it will be more elaborate since Ahravan is the Ath'ir. The last day starts with prayers and offerings, then you will be blessed again and there will be yet another feast. When the moon rises you will be taken to the sacred tree and spend the night there."

Wenja frowned again. "The sacred tree? What is that?"

Sefa made a gesture. "An enormous oak, so old that not even the elves are sure of its age. It is hollow you see and there is a room inside of it, that is where newlyweds spend the wedding night, it is a blessed spot"

Wenja had to blush yet again. "A room inside of a tree?"

Sefa used her hand to sort of draw in the air. "Yes, it is rather large and there is a heating pit in there which keeps the room warm and comfortable, many fat lamps and of course a bed"

Wenja did feel nervous again, it was still weeks ahead of her but still, she couldn't help but think of it. She missed Sina now, and the rest of her family. With them at her side she had felt strong but now she was adrift and she had no things with which to anchor herself. She felt lost. Sefa giggled. "The bed often shocks those who are unprepared for it is no ordinary bed. It is a pit filled with fine sand and it is covered with the softest furs imaginable. It is like sleeping in a cloud"

Wenja had to blink. "Sand?"

Sefa giggled. "I know, sands gets everywhere now doesn't it? But not the sand from that pit, it is very safe."

Wenja felt embarrassed but at least she knew a little more about what she was to face. It did help, but not all that much. She was still feeling very confused and very nervous.

Rhawan had entered one of the wagons where Ehbrial and Khirhien sat with Thokan and a couple of the guards. They were studying the maps and Ehbrial did smile at Rhawan. "We think we have discovered a possible route which will take us to the plains a bit earlier"

Rhawan sat down by the small table and Ehbrial pulled out a map. "See? We can use these old tunnels here"

Rhawan stared at the map, he saw that they had marked the tunnels and he frowned and let his finger follow the thin line which showed the path they had to take in order to use them. "This may be tough? Can we be sure that the tunnels are open?"

Khirhien shrugged. "No. but the chances are that they are. They were made to last remember? And it will save us two weeks if not more"

Rhawan made a grimace and stared at the map. "Alright, but the roads could be terrible and I don't like all the rivers!"

Ehbrial nodded. "Neither does I but we have the equipment we need and with the recent events we do have to go faster. We need to get back to the clans, I don't trust these humans as far as I can throw them!"

Rhawan mumbled. "You are not alone brother. Well, we will try the dwarf roads then, I bet Imh will be thrilled by that decision."

Thokan grinned. "Our beloved chef will be our guide for sure. I bet she knows everything which is to know about those tunnels."

Rhawan nodded. "I will go and check on the Zahar, we need to turn north when we reach the next valley"

Thokan nodded and the dark elf did leave the wagon and ran back to the one with the Zahar. The animal was getting better but it was still weak and it made a soft sound when it saw him and he petted it reverently and gave it some dried meat to chew on. He hoped that it would recuperate completely soon. He mourned the loss of his horse, there were other good horses in the herd of riding horses they had brought and he picked out a dark auburn coloured mare. She was brave and obedient and a bit playful and the rich colour did remind him of Wenja. She had blushed so deeply when she saw him in the nude and that made him stop and think for a moment. To an elf nudity was something very natural and something they saw almost every day but he knew that humans were rather different. She hadn't seen anyone undressed before? That was a bit of a shock but he had to grin. Ahravan would have to work really hard to get inn under that one's skin, that was for sure. It would be a tough job but he was sure that Ahravan could do it, and make her trust him completely. Rhawan swallowed, he had to admit that he was a wee bit jealous of Ahravan, Wenja was gorgeous and he would have been sorely tempted if she hadn't been for his Si'ish. But he and Ahravan were very close and they shared everything so maybe one day he too could hope to enjoy her charms? He doubted that the idea would thrill her as of yet but who knew, people did change over time and the culture Wenja was about to meet was very different from the one she had been raised in. It would probably set her free like never before. At least they could hope that it would.

Chapter 4: Deep deep down...

Wenja and Prina had to suffer through yet some lessons in the common tongue as Nefhriel and the others decided that the stretch of road which lead down towards the next valley was boring and that the girls ought to study instead of admiring the scenery. Prina was already rather fluent in the common tongue, she had a bit of an accent but her vocabulary was growing with every day and she would bother the drivers and guards with questions whenever they stopped. She was like a sponge, sucking up new knowledge every day. Wenja on the other hand did struggle and it seemed to be harder and harder for her to concentrate. There was simply too much going on and she was having a hard time overcoming her feeling of being homesick. The chance of her ever returning to her place of birth was slim, and she had no idea of whether or not she ever would see her family again. That made her depressed.

Nefhriel and Theka did wash their hair each day and put oils and stuff in it which made it shiny and soft and the food had a very visible effect on them both. Prina did look healthy for the first time since she was a mere babe and Wenja was stunned to see that Prina in fact was very pretty. But she was starting to show, just a wee bit but it was enough to give her secret away if anyone saw her and she often refused to leave the wagon if there were strangers nearby.

Wenja too had put on weight and she felt good physically, but her mind was having problems. She was lagging behind when it came to the languages and Nefhriel did try to teach her other things, like the most common customs of the twelve clans but it seemed as if she didn't want to listen. She was missing her family way too much and even though the women assigned to her were becoming her best friends ever they didn't fill the gap left by her parents and siblings. These valleys were far more fertile than the one she came from, the forests were dense and vigorous and she had never seen trees that large. The farms were rich too, with large buildings and she was stunned by the sight of sheep and cows way larger than the ones her father kept. Writing was very hard, she would sit in the wagon staring at the many wonders outside and she forgot what she was supposed to do and her thoughts just drifted away.

The thing she thought of the most was the fact that she was to get married, she couldn't escape it. She knew that many of the girls in her village would get married off to someone they didn't know beforehand but they wouldn't leave the valley. And they would have their families close by, even after they were wed. Wenja felt as if she was about to leave the world and enter a new and alien one and she kept praying that she would be strong enough to cope with it. She remembered the many times Sina had been pregnant, and the births too. She and the other kids were always shooed away but they didn't go far and even from the barn they had heard how Sina was screaming. Ulfar had always sacrificed a lamb, praying the Gods to spare his wife and Wenja knew of many who had died in childbed. The very idea of such an end scared her to the bone and she felt that the fears grew with each passing day.

Prina didn't seem to be scared though, she acted a bit oddly at times, as if she tried to forget about the whole thing and denied that she was with child. Nefhriel tried to talk to her several times but it didn't help and Prina seemed to ignore every piece of advice she was given. Sefa thought it was because of the way the baby had been made, Prina didn't want to be reminded of it, at all. The road they now followed was not used that much and they had to travel at a slower pace, Wenja had often left the wagon and gone to look at the Zahar and the animal seemed to accept her, which was odd for it didn't normally like humans nearby. It would growl at Prina and Thokan couldn't even go near the wagon it was inn. Now they saw what Rhawan had meant when he said that the mountains of this region did resemble vertical walls. Wenja felt dizzy for they were so tall they disappeared into the skies and smooth like a dance floor which had been flipped into a vertical position. The valleys had flat bottoms but gentle slopes too towards where the mountains met the ground and she saw screes and huge boulders which had come lose and fallen down. She often felt as if the huge wall of rock would crumble and crush them and she refused to look in that direction. The mere idea of them going through all that rock was insane.

Rhawan did explain that they would have to cross through five of those long narrow mountains, and it would save them much time but it would be tough. Imh had been thrilled when she was told of this new route and she was riding in the front wagon, giving the driver some advice Wenja suspected that he'd rather be without. But after a week of driving they reached the first tunnel and Wenja had to gape when she saw it. The road turned towards the mountain side and disappeared into it underneath the spread legs of a giant statue. It did look a bit like Imh and the dwarrowdam did explain that all the tunnels had a female statue guarding the entrance. The dwarves were very peculiar when it came to gender roles, a woman's place was in the home but that gave her immense power for everything indoors were her domain then. She could decide whether or not her husband should be allowed to leave the house and if he could bring his weapons or not. The female dwarves were in charge of the society and held in extremely high regard so by placing a female statue there the dwarves did signal that this was safe and something useful and reliable.

An old man lived right by the entrance in a sort of hut, he was bent and worn and he appeared to be rather poor too. He approached them and seemed to be a bit shocked by the sight of the caravan. "My lords, ladies, none have used this road for at least twenty summers"

Rhawan did dismount and he looked at the entrance, the tunnel looked as if it had been hewed the day before. "I guessed that, but it is safe still?"

The old man nodded. "Yes, worry not, it will last until the mountains themselves do crumble and fall. There is just one thing…"

Rhawan tilted his head. "Yes?"

The old man sort of grimaced and scratched his head. "I am no longer young, but I did pass through, some fifteen years ago. I could still walk well back then, I used to guide people through you see"

Rhawan was just waiting and the man sighed and lowered his gaze. "I saw something odd in one of the side tunnels, a crack of some kind. But it didn't look natural, more as if the rock had been split apart on purpose. And I felt a strange smell too"

Rhawan did frown. "Do explain?"

The man made a gesture. "It did smell as if a billy goat had been living in an outhouse, for a long time"

Rhawan waved his hand at Ehbrial. "Trolls, what do you think?"

Ehbrial nodded sternly. "Yes, most certainly. Has the road been used since then?"

The old man shook his head. "No, nobody has been through since, I was the last one. The roads to the east are more popular these days, the trade has changed and this tunnel is no longer needed"

Rhawan stared at the old man and his eyes were calm. "Well, we do need it now. We are many and we are armed so it shouldn't be a problem, not really"

The old man winced. "But if there are trolls?"

Rhawan smiled at him. "Trolls are not that dangerous, not if you know how to deal with them and we do."

The man tilted his head and he stared at the long row of wagons and riders with curiosity. "Well, may the gods protect you then, but why are you here? So many, and of the eternal?"

Rhawan did flip a coin over at the old man who took it with obvious reverence. "Oh. Thank you my lord"

"We are on our way back to the plains, transporting the new Eth'ir"

The man bowed his head and placed his hands on his chest in a gesture of blessing. "Then may her days be many and filled with joy and her nights be peaceful and fertile"

Rhawan just grinned and gave the man yet another coin, he did look as if he needed it. Rhawan did shout to the drivers. "You will need to check the brakes before we enter, the tunnels aren't completely flat and there can be parts which are rather steep."

Everybody did go over the wagons carefully and Wenja did stare out of the window, the tunnel did look like a gate in a wall and that made her feel a bit better but not all that much. After a short while they were ready and the first wagons started entering the tunnel, they attached torches to the wagons and Rhawan made them aware of a very special feature built into the tunnel. Along the side there was a narrow groove and it was filled with some sort of liquid. He touched it with the torch and the liquid caught fire and suddenly they had a glowing line following the wall of the tunnel.

It didn't give much light but enough for them to see and the floor was rather rough and made it easy for the horses to get a good footing. Wenja did not look out of the wagon as they entered the tunnel, she tried to keep herself occupied with some embroidery and Imh had come to join her. The female dwarf was very cheerful and Theka did ask her if she ever had used these roads through the mountains. Imh did confirm that she had, but not this particular one, and it was many decades ago but most of these tunnels were made to be very similar to each other and she was sure that it would be easy to reach the other side of the mountain now. She did explain the workings of the huge lifts to them too, the dwarves had built lifts where they couldn't build tunnels and they had been a feat of great ingenuity and skills. The lifts were not in use these days for the dwarves didn't live in these parts of the realm anymore, they had moved to the south east and had huge cities in the mighty mountain ranges there.

Wenja did find the things Imh told her fascinating, Imh was a widow and that meant that she was very free and that was the reason why she was living with the twelve clans. A dwarf woman was not allowed to travel when she was in her fertile years, the ability to breed was crucial to a race where the number of females was so low and the birth rate very slow. To have many children was to be of high status and Imh could declare with pride that she had four, and several grandchildren too.

She had been wife to a very powerful leader and now she was free to explore and enjoy her golden years. A dwarf could live for as much as four hundred years and the females often got even older than that so she would have at least a century where she could gather wisdom she then would transfer to her offspring.

The tunnel was very flat and so wide the wagons could have been driven three abreast without problems but Rhawan did order them into a row and placed riders ahead and behind and also at the sides. It would take them two days to get through and Wenja felt sick when she heard that. Two days in there? Without any sunlight? The Zahar had recovered now and it wasn't resting in the wagon anymore, it was running along with the horses and didn't look as if would leave them just yet. Rhawan was a bit curious as to why but the animal appeared to like them and it was still a bit on the skinny side so perhaps it saw an opportunity to get fed instead of hunting for itself.

The rumble of the wagon wheels got terribly loud in the tunnel and Wenja was rather sure that she would have a headache before long but after a while she sort of got used to the whole situation and she forgot to listen. Nefhriel was drawing some sketches of the dresses the women of the twelve clans used and Wenja was shocked for this sort of clothing was new to her. The women would wear pants under the dress and it would only reach her knees and have a split in front and in the back which enabled her to ride. Wenja was gradually realizing that she had to learn how to ride and the idea made her cringe. The horses were so huge and she had grown up being taught that women never should ride astride for it was indecent.

Rhawan did sometimes rest in their wagon, he was constantly riding along the caravan, keeping an eye on everything and Sefa was obviously flirting with him every time and he replied in the same manner. Wenja was blushing each time she caught them playing this little game of theirs and Sefa seemed to enjoy teasing her thus.

They had travelled for most of the day when Rhawan ordered a stop, the horses needed a break for the rock was hard on their legs and they needed drink and food. There were watering troughs placed with even intervals along the tunnel and the water was fresh and cold and came from subterranean rivers but they had to bring feed themselves and luckily they had hay enough for all the animals. They would rest there for the night and Rhawan did come to the wagon, he had brought a flagon of wine and Sefa found some cups and she did also find a small crate which contained something which looked a bit like pieces of coloured glass. She handed one over to Wenja. "Taste this, it is very good"

Wenja did hesitate, it didn't look like food at all but Sefa did put one in her mouth and appeared to be sucking it and Wenja took a green one and put it in her mouth. It was very sweet and the taste just wonderful, like something clean and fresh and yet powerful and Sefa giggled. "It is very expensive so just one, suck it slowly so it lasts"

Rhawan too did take one and Sefa did pour some wine. Wenja felt that the strange candy left a sort of tingling feeling in her mouth and it was very pleasant. "What is it?" "

Rhawan sat down on the bed and poured himself some wine. "It is a substance which comes from the far south. One of the clans do go there in the summers and they bring some back each year when the clans meet for the winter camp."

He grinned. "They call it Star drops but it doesn't have anything to do with the stars. It comes from some insects"

Wenja swallowed hard. "Insects?!"

She suddenly wondered if it was such a good idea to eat this after all but the taste was just so wonderful and it got better all the time. Rhawan nodded and sipped at his wine. "Yes, a sort of aphids, they are huge, like the palm of my hand and they suck the juices out of a particular plant. It grows only in a very secluded valley and it is quite toxic but the aphids do tolerate the poison and they excrete the sugary parts of the juice at night. In the morning the drops have hardened and the locals gather them underneath the plants."

Wenja bit her lower lip not to gag. "Oh Gods, it is…dung?"

Rhawan nodded. "You could of course call it that, but we chose to see it otherwise. If you put it in wine it will sweeten it a lot and on its own it tastes good and it also has some effects left from the poison"

Wenja felt a bit sick. "It does?"

Rhawan nodded. "Yes, it removes inhibitions, takes away fear. It is very useful at times, the warriors often have some before they ride into battle"

Wenja had to swallow some wine. "You have…odd customs!"

Rhawan grinned widely and his eyes were shining. "Oh, but that is nothing, wait until you get familiarized with the cuisine of the River clan, it made me back off when I first encountered it but now I have no problems with it at all"

Sefa scoffed. "Oh gods, you are so brave Rhawan, I have never managed to eat their traditional dishes at all. It makes my stomach crawl"

Wenja felt a bit dizzy and she realized that the candy indeed had some rather strange properties. "So what sort of food are we talking about?"

Sefa let out a snort. "Food? We are talking about a test of courage here, I wouldn't call it food at all. I would rather starve to death and that is the goddamn truth!"

Rhawan laughed, a soft and somewhat lazy sound. "Oh but they eat it almost every day dear, of course it is food."

Wenja was getting curious and she leaned forth. "So what is it then? Fish?"

Rhawan nodded. "Among other things, the river is sacred to them and they eat everything in it, and by that I mean everything. Even the grass growing on the rocks is edible, I once tasted wine made from it and that tasted like a mixture of turpentine and old horse sweat but they love it"

Sefa cringed and Wenja sort of giggled, he did have a way with words. "The main course is of course fish, served in every conceivable manner. Then we have oysters and other shellfish, roe and fish sperm and..."

Sefa interrupted him. "If someone of that tribe does invite you for a drink and serve something which looks like milk, don't drink it!"

Wenja gasped for air. "Ah eeewwww!"

Rhawan did continue. "The shellfish are often boiled or salted and it isn't too bad really. The same can be said about the oysters and the shells, most of that is served raw. But the fish, oh by every deity, they have some very interesting methods of preserving it!"

Wenja found a more comfortable position. "Do tell me, please"

Rhawan nodded and drank more wine. He appeared to be very relaxed and Wenja did understand that Sefa found him charming, for he was. "Well, the most common dish they serve is the one I have gotten used to, believe it or not. The river has a sort of eel living in it and they can be as long as thirty feet but they are very slim and look nasty too"

Sefa was rolling her eyes. "That is just the first name, I saw one once and I almost pissed myself, it was ghastly, like some goddamn...monster"

Rhawan giggled. "Oh yes, the teeth are impressive, they use them for sewing needles and stuff. Anyhow, they skin the eels, the hide is very thick and makes excellent leather and then they take this huge jar and fill it with a sort of wine, some grass from the river, some gallons of broth made from boiling the bone marrow of a cow or an ox and then they add a lot of spices, the gods alone knows which ones by the way. The skinned eel is laid into the jar minus its head and tail and they put the lid on the jar and leave it in there for a few months."

Wenja just gaped. "A few months?! Are you kidding me? That sounds like…"

Sefa did nod. "The recipe for food poisoning, but believe me, nobody has died from it, yet"

Rhawan did grin again. "The eel is ready when it falls apart, and the taste is in fact not bad, sweet and a bit tangy but good. You have to get used to it but whence you have it is no big deal"

Sefa grinned. "Yes, I saw you eat some once, you were wolfing it down!"

Wenja frowned. "So that is how they prepare fish?"

Rhawan did nod. "That is one method yes, but they do salt and dry them also, or bake them into wads of clay and bury them in the ground for a year. That dish is one I do not recommend at all for it smells like piss and looks like…I don't know."

Sefa bit her lower lip. "It looks like mucus, you can always tell when they have opened a clay packet of such fish for the entire camp stinks of it for days."

Rhawan nodded vigorously and filled his cup again. "Ahravan wanted that dish banned from the main camp but they didn't obey, it is too precious to them. I think I rather kiss an orc than eat that filth"

Sefa did giggle. "And I bet that you are too proud to be able to eat such fish"

Rhawan tilted his head, there was a devil dancing in his eyes. "Oh, that bet is on dear, just you wait and see when we get back"

Sefa made a swift gesture. "Then it is a deal, if I win, what do I get?"

Rhawan raised an eyebrow. "Whatever you wish for, you know I deliver, always"

Wenja realized that this was more than just flirting and she felt herself blush yet again. Sefa did crawl closer to him and she was licking her lips. "And what if I lose?"

Rhawan did stare at her and Wenja saw that his eyes were rather dark. "How about as many kisses as I wish for? But I want to check the goods before I agree on the bet"

Sefa did giggle and she crawled even closer to Rhawan and before Wenja had time to ask what they were doing Sefa was sitting across Rhawan's lap facing him and she did kiss him, with obvious hunger.

Wenja had to gasp, the two of them seemed to have forgotten all about her and she wondered what she was to do now? She felt odd still and some part of her felt curious. She had never seen anyone kiss like that before, her parents did kiss every now and then but with their mouths closed and very fast. This was so different and Rhawan looked as if he had his tongue in Sefa's mouth? Wenja did blush and turned around, staring at the wall instead. Sefa did giggle. "Oh Wenja, don't be so prudish, watch and learn"

Wenja felt her heart beating like a drum in her chest, this was wrong and yet so terribly enticing and she saw that Rhawan had put a hand in under Sefa's skirts and he was moving it. Sefa did moan and closed her eyes and Rhawan started to kiss her neck and the other hand was busy with her bodice. Wenja saw that Sefa was rubbing herself against his hand, looking as if she really enjoyed it and Rhawan was breathing hard and his eyes were so very dark now. Wenja saw that Sefa did fidget with his belt buckle and that was when she had had enough, she got up and fled out of the wagon, trying desperately to control herself. She felt her hands tremble and she had to be the most wretched person in the whole world for she felt as if she wanted to be in Sefa's place. She wanted to touch Rhawan, to feel him touching her and she remembered how she had used to help Ulfar with the sheep. Each autumn she had watched as the ram did mount the ewes and sometimes she had felt this strange tingling in her body. She had never told anyone for she somehow knew that it was something she wasn't supposed to talk about but now she felt it again, just so much much stronger. She felt her heartbeat all through her body and in special down between her legs and she whimpered and ran until she found a sort of alcove a bit away from the wagons. The horses were tethered there and she pressed herself against the cold rock and tried to force herself to calm down. The wagon wasn't far away, and she

104

whimpered as she saw that it had started to move on its springs, in a rather vigorous rhythm.

The other wagons were placed in two rows and this was the one at the back of the rows so nobody saw what was going on, or at least Wenja hoped nobody did. The others were eating, gathered by a fire pit and Wenja felt her heart beating like thunder in her ears but she couldn't help it. She slowly walked back to the wagon, it felt horrible but it was stronger than her own will. She put a foot in the wheel closest by the window and lifted herself up, peeking in through the rough glass. Sefa was on her back on the bed and Rhawan was on top of her, he held himself up on his elbows and his pants were down by his knees from what Wenja could see. Sefa had her skirts around her waist and her legs were wrapped firmly around Rhawan's hips, pulling him tightly to her. She was grasping onto his shoulders with her hands and arms and Wenja could hear that they both were moaning rather loudly. She gasped and did cling onto the wheel with an iron grip, Sefa was tossing her head back with an expression of something which resembled agony on her face and Rhawan's face was hidden in his thick blue hair but she could hear him making some deep almost growling sounds.

Wenja's eyes were drawn to his hips, saw how his muscular rear moved with a sort of primeval rhythm and the wagon did sway a little with each thrust, the springs were taking quite a beating now and so was the bed for it was creaking. His skin did glisten with sweat and Sefa did move her legs out of the way, grasped onto his butt instead of his shoulders and she appeared to be clawing at his skin for he tossed his head back and hissed and then he started moving even faster and harder and Wenja saw that Sefa arched back against the bed, pressing a hand over her mouth to stifle what could only be a scream. Rhawan did lose the rhythm, he sort of stiffened up and then he thrust one last time and arched, head thrown back and face contorted by bliss. Wenja heard him growl Sefa's name several times and he shuddered visibly, so did Sefa too.

Wenja let go, ran back to the alcove, almost in tears from shame and shock and a sense of disbelief. She had peeped at them, she was shameless! Oh by every god there was, she shouldn't have accepted that piece of the accursed candy, never! But the images felt as if they were glued to her mind and she felt like weeping but couldn't. Her body was trembling, her heart beat like a drum in her chest and she felt something warm and wet spreading between her legs. She was such a whore, why would she feel thus if she wasn't? She wanted it, she wanted to have what Sefa had, to feel those strong calloused hands touching her skin, making her writhe and moan. Rhawan had said that Ahravan was handsome and gentle, that he would be kind to her and treat her well. Wenja imagined herself laying like that, with a male on top of her, with skin not as dark as Rhawan's and hair like gold and suddenly the thought of getting married didn't seem so terrible after all. Would he kiss her the way Rhawan had kissed Sefa? Put his hand up under her skirts, making her moan? Wenja leaned against the rock again, eyes closed and her breath fast and shuddering. She felt how her inner thighs felt slick and wet and she had to rub them together and then something just snapped. It felt good, it felt so good she no longer could control herself. She spun around, facing the wall and pressed herself against it, felt how the uneven surface seemed to mould itself after her body and she whimpered and rubbed herself against it. The warmth filled her, every cell and every nerve and she remembered how Rhawan's perfect rear had moved, tensing and relaxing, tensing and relaxing. With a gasp she spread her legs and pushed against a protruding piece of rock and her legs felt as if they were about to give in underneath her but an insane feeling of sheer pleasure exploded through her body and she bit her lip not to scream. She was clinging to the cold rock as her body fought its way through her very first release and she felt warm liquid running down her legs and everything exploded into white light and a feeling of relief stronger than anything she had ever experienced before.

When she was able to gather her senses again she felt as if she was flying and at the same time she was so terribly heavy and relaxed and she squeaked and didn't know what to think or feel. Was this something bad? Had she done something terrible? The storm in her body had calmed down, she felt extremely well and if this was what Sefa had felt back in the wagon there was no wonder she had looked the way she did. Wenja cringed, she was slick and wet and tender in funny places and had this really been normal? She sort of waddled off to the wagon where they kept the spare clothes and the troths they used for washing. She saw nobody there so she got inside and found a clean petticoat and a dry skirt and then she changed without daring to look at herself. She washed off with a cloth and cold water and the mere touch felt strange, almost electric. She was so very sensitive now, and it made her cringe but some part of her didn't feel any shame at all. It had felt wonderful so how could it be wrong?

She waited for a few moments, combed through her hair, found some of the perfume Theka used and put some of it on her wrists and on the skirt and then she left the wagon and headed back to her own. Sefa was sitting in the door, looking very smug and happy and Rhawan was nowhere to be seen. Wenja couldn't look at Sefa, she had watched the other woman lay with Rhawan, how could she ever talk to Sefa again without remembering that? Sefa tilted her head. "You left faster than a racehorse leaves the starting line, did we awaken you?"

Wenja swallowed. "Awaken?"

Sefa nodded. "Yes, your lust, I could feel that you were nearby you know, did you like what you saw?"

Wenja yipped, staring at Sefa with huge eyes, how could she have… "You know?"

Sefa nodded. "Of course I know, there is little light here and the window is not very large but your shadow was rather visible still"

Wenja just wished that the ground could open up and swallow her whole, she let out a sob and wanted to turn around and run but Sefa grasped her hand. "No girl, don't flee. I am here to teach you remember? And now I have taught you something new, did you like watching us?"

Wenja felt like a wretch, her head bowed deeply in shame. "Yes"

Sefa smiled widely. "See? That wasn't so hard to confess now was it? Wonderful, that was just what we had hoped for. You are perfectly normal Wenja, don't worry. And now you know what your body wishes for too, and what you can look forwards to. "

Wenja let out a keen, she felt so exposed, so naked and Sefa gave her a quick hug. "Ahravan will have a bride who knows her own body, who knows what she likes and what she needs. And I will make sure that this is what he gets. Did it arouse you?"

Wenja had to nod, remembering the wonderful and oh so irresistible feeling which had hijacked her body so completely. "That is excellent, did you touch yourself? There is no shame in that young one, as a matter of fact it would be very good if you did, it shows that you are normal"

Wenja gasped and tried to find the words. "Uh, I…I rubbed myself against…and I felt…"

Sefa gaped, then she laughed and there was sheer joy in her eyes, "Oh sweetheart, by the Goddess herself, did you come?! That is wonderful"

Wenja tried to remember how to breathe. "I…I think…I…"

Sefa hugged her again. "How fantastic, then we know you aren't frigid, and when Ahravan does claim your maidenhead I am quite sure that you will scream with joy and not in pain at all."

Wenja had to sit down, the mental image she got…it made her stomach churn again but this time the feeling was different, it wasn't as much fear as it was a sort of tingling anticipation. Sefa did stroke her hair. "Listen, from now on I want you to touch yourself every night, do you hear me? Find out what you like, where it feels good to be touched. Learn how to love your body and the joy it can give you"

Wenja swallowed. "And that wouldn't be…wrong?"

Her voice was thin and Sefa shook her head. "No, absolutely not. Quite the opposite. See it as your gift to your future husband, that he is given a bride who knows what she wants and can tell him how to please her."

Wenja blushed again. "Back home they wanted the girls to be ignorant?"

Sefa sort of snorted, hard! She sounded like a horse. "Oh that bullshit is just something you have to forget about. Do you know why they want their brides to be clueless?"

Wenja frowned and shook her head. "No?"

Sefa grinned, a rather vicious grin. "Because then they won't have to worry about being exposed as terrible lovers. It takes the pressure away from them, they can just fuck and be done with it and doesn't have to care about her at all, she can be in agony and they won't mind as long as they can stick their cock into something alive."

Wenja gasped from Sefa's harsh words and the dark haired girl did look stern. "The eternal are very different, believe me. To them the pleasure of their partner comes first, then their own. Ahravan will worship you, every night you wish for it."

Wenja did blush and Sefa sighed. "If you need some advice just come to me, I have plenty to give and I don't mind letting you watch again, Rhawan is wonderful and he can truly make a girl mad with need."

Wenja had to giggle. "I sort of saw that yes"

Sefa smiled. "Good, now you know that it isn't anything to fear, when you go to bed now think about your wedding, and how you will entice and arouse your husband."

Wenja felt the need to hide her face again, not sure if she really wanted to think about that at all, just yet. Sefa got up and patted her on the head. "I have of course changed the bedding, so the bed is clean. I suggest you get some rest for according to Rhawan the next part of the journey may be a bit more demanding"

Wenja did nod and she felt almost relieved when Sefa did go to join the others. She didn't want to talk about this anymore and she made sure that her appearance was normal before she went to find Imh and got a portion of her excellent stew. Afterwards she returned to the wagon to find Prina there, she had been talking with one of the guards and they had discussed the different ways wool was being treated and Prina was very excited for she had learned that the clans would mix other types of fibre into the wool to make different types of cloth and she was dying to test that out. Prina was glad to be there, glad to have been offered this chance to escape but Wenja was in the opposite situation and she wasn't so sure that she was any better off now than she had been earlier that day.

She was very quiet as Prina enthusiastic told about the new things she had learned and if her friend had been more observant she would have noticed for sure but as it was she didn't. They went to bed and Prina fell asleep right away, her mind was opening up more and more as she started to realize what freedom she had gained. She was becoming a very sweet and very charming personality and everybody had started to like her.

Wenja wished that she too could be that open and naïve but she didn't have it in her. Perhaps it was because Prina had lived such a terrible life before, when Wenja had been poor but loved.

The next day the wagons were placed in a long line again and the front riders returned and told of a bridge. That made Rhawan tense up visibly and he rode ahead and was gone for a while. Wenja saw that the drivers too did look nervous and Imh who sat there helping the girls with some stitches grinned widely. "The bridges are not very wide usually, and they have no rail."

Prina did look puzzled. "Are there rivers in here?"

Imh giggled. "Yes, and other things too. I think this one spans a gorge"

Rhawan did return, he was shouting orders and they started to reorganize the row of wagons. The lightest wagons were to cross first with the loose horses and the heaviest stuff was to cross the last. The road was heading downhill now, not at a very steep angle but it was steep enough and the drivers used the brakes rather much to control the wagons. Wenja and Prina did leave the house wagon and walked next to it, they were entering a cave and it was so gigantic they couldn't see the roof at all. Ahead of them was a huge open space, flat and even and it was shaped almost like the half of a circle. From the middle of it a narrow bridge stretched over what looked like just darkness and it reached a similar half circle on the other side. The stretch didn't look very large at first, but then they got closer and now Wenja did see how truly enormous this place was. The entire cave was light by some odd crystals protruding from the walls, they did throw a very faint light over the flat area and Wenja was feeling oddly exposed. She suddenly had a sense of fear and Imh chuckled. "The fear of open spaces, my people are familiar with that. There is grandeur in these mountains young one, and nobody would expect it"

As they drove down onto the flat space they saw that the ground had been covered with elaborate carvings, not very deep but they were clearly depictions of figures and Wenja wondered what they were. The bridge was not as narrow as they had thought to begin with but it was seemingly fragile, like a thin pen laid over a gap between two tall desks and Wenja had no idea of how deep this gorge was. Prina was pale and stayed close to Imh and Rhawan was riding around, checking the wagons. Nefhriel came walking over and she smiled at them. "Nobody rides in the wagons as they crosses, only the driver. And everyone walks over before the wagons start to cross"

Wenja swallowed hard. "How deep is this gorge?"

Nefhriel shrugged. "Nobody knows, it may be bottomless"

Imh laughed. "Oh dear, there is a bottom down there, somewhere. Be sure of that, but it is a very long way down. The very rock itself has split here and there are some other gorges just like this one which haven't been explored even by my kin"

Rhawan did wave his arms at them. "Come on, everyone, cross now"

Wenja gathered her courage and they started to walk, staying in the middle of the bridge. If they didn't look to the side it wasn't too bad, the bridge was wider than a normal road and perfectly smooth but how was it built and how had it withstood the ravages of time so well? Nefhriel smiled at her. "The dwarves knows rock the way we elves knows trees. The things they build last, for ages."

The bridge was way longer than anticipated, the gorge almost a mile wide and Wenja felt a need to run as fast as she could to reach the safe other side but she managed to keep the need at bay. Prina was shivering as they reached the flat plain and Nefhriel was calming her down with soothing words. Now the horses were being herded over and the animals didn't need much time, the Zahar did run with them and the horses didn't mind the odd animal at all. When the people and the horses were over the first wagons were driven across the bridge, the house wagon as among the first since it was rather light and Rhawan was organizing the wagons into a new order as they reached the other side. The road would tilt downwards even more from now and so they put more horses onto the heavy ones. Wenja was relieved to see that all the wagons made it across without any problems, the bridge was more than sturdy enough for them but Rhawan didn't like to take any chances.

They had a short break before they drove on and Imh had managed to make a rather tasty meal. Here the tunnel looked less refined than on the other side and it was less wide so Rhawan did reduce the distance between the wagons and he did also order the riders to stay by their sides at all time. Wenja remembered what the old man had said and she was curious. Ulfar had used trolls to scare the kids with when they were small and Wenja had not really believed in trolls for many years. She was too old for that. She sat down in the wagon after the meal and then she asked Sefa and Theka if they had seen trolls? None of them had but Nefhriel had and she told Wenja that trolls were creatures which lived deep within the mountains and they were rather primitive and not very smart but they weren't evil. They were just like animals, if someone bothered them they could react violently but otherwise they were rather peaceful. They ate small animals and insects and mushrooms and could get extremely old but they weren't immortal, they just lived very slowly.

Imh too knew a lot about trolls for the dwarves would often encounter them when building their mines and cities and she told that it was seen as wise to be kind to the trolls and leave them alone. Rhawan did check in on them and Ahnriel rode by too, wanting to check in on Prina. She was worried that the girl would suffer from her fear of heights and darkness. The guards were on high alert now, they had reached the area the old man had spoken off and if there had been trolls there fifteen years ago there was a good chance they were still there. They had driven down a very steep area with curved slightly when they heard a shout and the caravan stopped. Rhawan did ride ahead and Wenja and the others felt a bit nervous, what was this?

Rhawan did ride fast and the first wagon was at the bottom of the hill, the road would be flat for some miles ahead and then the tunnel would rise again. But there was something in the road ahead and the driver hadn't dared to go on. Rhawan did whistle and Ehbrial did ride up to him. "Tell me what you see"

Ehbrial swallowed hard. "A troll?"

Rhawan nodded. "Yes, in the middle of the tunnel, with the light on. Something is wrong"

The narrow groove with the burning liquid had continued on this side of the gorge and the light was rather strong, it looked as if the liquid was more potent here. Rhawan did dismount and he did draw his swords, Ehbrial did follow him and the tall silver haired eternal was armed with an axe and a shield with sharp edges. They moved forwards very slowly and saw that it was indeed a troll and it was very large. This had to be an old male and the creature appeared to be sitting in the middle of the road, leaning forwards with its legs slightly spread and its arms hanging loosely down. The head was hanging too and as they got closer Rhawan slowed down and sneezed. A most horrible stench reached their noses and Ehbrial almost gagged. "Oh sweet Goddess, this is terrible"

Rhawan had to blink, the smell was so ghastly it did burn their eyes and as they approached the troll they did see that it was alive, in spite of the death scent. It moved its head slowly and Rhawan did hold his blades ready, he had no idea of what this could be. The troll was covered with a sort of greyish crust, and it had cracked many places and let puss ooze out of the cracks and what looked like fungi was spreading all over the cracks. This was one dying creature and Rhawan was shocked and also confused. What sort of disease could kill a troll?

The creature grunted, its small red eyes covered with fungi too and it was apparently blind for the pupil was almost gone. It waved its head slowly, the mouth was half open and they saw that it didn't have any teeth and the tongue seemed to have fallen off. Rhawan swallowed hard, the thing was in agony, and it would yet take it days to die, if not weeks. He reached out to it with his mind, trolls have very simple thoughts and were like animals and he managed to get in touch with it rather easily and what he saw made him stagger back with shock and pity. "They were a whole tribe, warriors, females and cubs. Perhaps fifty of them in all. He is the last one, they have all died"

Ehbrial gasped. "What happened?"

Rhawan sighed. "They found something deep in the mountain, some sort of pretty rock and it cracked open. And then they all got ill and started to die. He was the strongest one, I think he tried to make it to the surface, thinking that the sunlight may burn away the disease"

Ehbrial did look worried. "Can it be dangerous to us as well?"

Rhawan shook his head. "No, I don't think so. I think this is something only trolls are susceptible to."

Ehbrial weighed his axe with his hands, he did look uncertain. "Well, we have to do something, it cannot just sit there, it is blocking the road."

Rhawan was about to answer when they saw that Ahnriel walked closer to them and Wenja was with her. Rhawan did look confused. "What are you doing here?"

Ahnriel sighed. "Wenja insisted, she says she feels something strange, and it comes from the troll"

Wenja had been standing by the wagon, waiting with the others when she suddenly felt an odd surge of energy rushing through her, she felt as if she was hearing someone calling her name from afar and she felt an almost irresistible urge to go forth and seek the reason why they had stopped. She started walking and Nefhriel did grasp her arm. "What are you doing?"

Wenja swallowed hard. "I…I have to go, I don't know why, but I hear…I hear something…"

Nefhriel did frown. "What are you talking about?"

Wenja did shiver. "I don't know, I don't understand."

Ahnriel did swerve by, attracted to the raised voices and she did look concerned. "Is she feeling unwell?"

Wenja tried to shake the feeling away. "No, I…I have to go, I have to see what this is about, it is important, believe me!"

Nefhriel did look a bit stunned and Ahnriel nodded. "Alright, I can go with you, but I am in charge, understand?"

Wenja nodded. "That is alright, but I have to go, now!"

Ahnriel did grasp her by the hand and they did run along the wagons. Wenja did gasp when she saw the figure sitting on the rock floor, and she slowed down. She felt it again, the odd voice, just out of range of her hearing.

Rhawan did frown and he still held his sword ready. "Really? What?"

Wenja tried to gather her senses, to calm down. "Oh, there is a voice, I think it is coming from that thing…oh Gods, what is wrong with it?"

Rhawan shrugged. "Some sort of disease, it is almost dead"

Wenja had never seen anything this ghastly, or disgusting, but she did feel pity. The troll was suffering, she could almost feel its agony and she took a deep breath and stared at Rhawan. "I don't understand, there is something here, something strong but…I cannot really grasp it, I don't understand…"

114

Rhawan turned to Ahnriel. "Could she be a psychic?"

Ahnriel shrugged. "I have no idea, but we can try a mind link, it may work. At least it will enable her to hear, I hope"

Wenja just stared at them and Ahnriel did sigh. "We can help you, if you want to let us?"

Wenja nodded and Ahnriel did place a hand on her shoulder while Rhawan did touch the other one and Wenja let out a shrill cry and her legs seemed to give way under her. Suddenly she was staring at something which wasn't a troll at all, she saw a figure of pure light, and it was flaming and writhing around, clawing at something which seemed to restrain it. Two glowing eyes were staring at her and now she did hear the voice clearly, it was shouting in a tongue she didn't understand but judging by the shocked expressions on the faces of the two eternal they did. The voice howled and shrieked and then the glowing figure just disappeared and Wenja did collapse into Rhawan's arms. Ahnriel was almost panting. "Did you hear that?"

He nodded, his eyes wide with shock. "Yes, and I saw! A fire spirit, trapped within flesh. How did that happen?"

Ahnriel shrugged and petted Wenja's cheeks, she appeared to be almost unconscious. "I have no clue, but the things it said, how does that make sense?"

Rhawan sighed and helped Ahnriel carry Wenja back to the house wagon, the troll was dead now and Ehbrial was getting some horses so they could drag the carcass out of the way. "I am afraid it makes sense, it makes so much sense it is almost too much"

Ahnriel frowned. "What do you mean?"

The blue haired elf held Wenja tightly to him, why did she see this? Was there something extraordinary about her after all? "You don't remember the time when the monsters first arrived do you?"

Ahnriel shook her head. "No, I don't. I wasn't born back then, few of us were"

Rhawan did smile, but the smile was sort of stiff. "Neither was I but I have heard the tales. The beasts don't come from this world Ahnriel, and the first wave of attackers almost wiped out the entire population of the realm. Only a few brave souls managed to stop the onslaught"

Ahnriel nodded and her eyes were distant. "I have heard the tales yes. The gate was closed off and our world saved. "

The tall male did smile and he hoisted Wenja a little higher towards his shoulder, she was trembling still. "Yes, but as I am sure you know the gate wasn't completely shut, sometimes it will still open for a brief moment of time and allow new horrors access to our world and we have to fight them off, as is our duty."

Ahnriel swallowed visibly. "The thing the spirit said…"

Rhawan took a deep breath. "The gate may be closed completely, but only by the hand of one born twice"

Ahnriel closed her eyes. "The one who is the key, the one who is chosen"

Rhawan saw that Sefa ran towards them, obviously worried and he smiled at Ahnriel. "We don't tell them what we know, I have no idea of why Wenja saw this, if it is a coincidence or something more"

Ahnriel nodded slowly. "Yes, if she is among the gifted we will find out, sooner or later. "

Sefa stopped. "What happened?"

Wenja sort of groaned. "Oh my head, I saw…I saw something and it was beautiful but I didn't understand what it was saying"

Sefa helped them manhandle her and they put her down on the bed. "What did I see? Please, I need to know?"

Ahnriel and Nefhriel did sit down on the bed as Rhawan had to return to his work. "You saw a fire spirit, a free soul which never has been born into a body. They can possess living creatures and some are malicious while others try to help. The one you saw was probably a benign one, but it fled the moment the troll died, it wasn't bound to it anymore."

Wenja frowned. "Why would a fire spirit possess a troll?"

Ahnriel stroked her hair. "It is strange but it is said that fire spirits are drawn to trolls for some reason, it could be that they come from within the earth and that trolls are the first living beings they encounter. "

Wenja moaned. "My head hurts, and I feel so tired"

Ahnriel did pet her hand. "I will get you something for your head and I will let you sleep afterwards"

116

Sefa did stop Ahnriel on the outside of the wagon. "What did really happen? Is she a seer?"

Ahnriel did make a grimace. "I haven't got a clue, but she is a very pure soul, and spirits are drawn to such."

Sefa sighed. "She is indeed pure, and her heart is larger than it ought to be. Is she gonna be alright?"

Ahnriel nodded. "I cannot see why not? She just saw something few humans are prepared to see"

Ahnriel did bring some medicine back and Wenja did fall asleep right away, her body felt heavy and strange and Sefa and Theka did stay by her side. The caravan was moving yet again and in a few hours they would leave this tunnel.

Back at Wenja's home things had changed a lot over the last weeks since she left, Ulfar had bought more equipment and more land and he had gotten food and clothes for his family. More so, they had hope again and it had changed their mood and made them more optimistic. When the summer came they would move, Ulfar had bought a much larger house at an abandoned farm close to the valley floor and with that additional land he would become among the largest land owners in the area. Now people did show him respect and he was treated as someone of great importance. It felt good and yet it was strange in some ways for it did show just how much wealth influenced the way people acted.

Sina was due any day now and she was confined to the bed and Ulfar was worried about her health. She had regained much strength due to the better food but he would have preferred that she got even stronger before the baby was due. The village had been oddly quiet for a few weeks now and Ulfar hadn't seen Dagar nor Mjorr for a week at least. Then one morning Sigunn did visit them, carrying things like wine and baby clothes but in reality she was bearing some rather grim news which Sina shouldn't be allowed to hear. Everybody knew that Prina had gone missing and at first the village believed that she had gone outside for some reason and gotten lost in the winter storms. It wouldn't be the first time that happened, it could of course be that she was depressed since she wasn't the chosen one and that too was acceptable. Then some traveller said that he had seen someone who could be her heading for the camp of the eternal the day they left and apparently Dagar had put two and two together and gotten four.

Sigunn said that Dagar and Mjorr had left and that they were going to find Prina again to punish her for having run away and Ulfar didn't for a second doubt that Mjorr also wanted to get even with Wenja. They needed to warn everyone but how? Mjorr and Dagar were many days ahead of them already and even with horses they couldn't catch up with them. That was when Bagir did make his suggestion. The mountains were like a round island in the middle of the flat plains and if Wenja and the eternal had been heading westwards the clans would move north and then follow the edge of the mountains southwards again on the other side, towards the winter grazing grounds. If someone crossed the mountains heading eastwards they could meet the clans and at first Ulfar did protest for the mountains to the east were much wilder and more dangerous than the ones to the west. Few did cross them and the last area was known as the spine and was seen as a range nobody should try to get across.

Bagir volunteered, he knew the mountains and he also knew that he could get across and then ride north and intercept the clans, possibly before Dagar and Mjorr could catch up with them. Ulfar did protest but Bagir was very steadfast and refused to budge and in the end Ulfar gave inn. He did fear for his daughter and he knew that if anyone could do this is was Bagir. He was a son of the mountains and more than capable of crossing, even in the middle of the winter. He was given all the equipment he needed and two strong mountain horses and he left early in the morning, very adamant that he would be able to warn everyone that Dagar and Mjorr were up to no good.

Wenja did sleep for quite a while and when she did wake up they were out of the tunnels and heading down the valley toward the next part of the old dwarf road. She felt dizzy still and her head was hammering, but more than that she was confused. What had she really seen? Her wold had been rather simple up to then, what you did see was what you believed in, her father had been rather adamant there. Many of the villagers had been terribly superstitious and couldn't do anything without safeguarding themselves with countless rituals and Ulfar said that it was both time consuming and silly. Wenja had been brought up to be rational, when some of the old herders said they had seen monsters or fairies high up in the mountains Ulfar would laugh and blame the sightings on bears and too much beer and when the old women whispered about curses and dark magic he scoffed and told Wenja that superstition was the comfort of the ones who didn't even try to understand the world around them.

But she had seen a spirit, did that mean that she was a seer? She hoped not, they had tales in the village of a woman who had been gifted and she had drowned herself in a lake, because she couldn't stand it anymore. The valley they had entered was rather narrow and there weren't any settlements there, just the road and a river and some huge open clearings which did look very nice even now in winter.

The hunters did leave them for a while and returned with a couple of deer they had shot and the chef and Imh did start working on the meat right away. Wenja felt restless, and she was also a bit bored for she didn't want to study again and she longed for some fresh air. She sat on the stairs of the wagon and looked out at the forest as they drove along the road and Rhawan did ride up to her and he smiled. "You look as if you need to go for a quick ride, it will cheer you up"

Wenja did look at him, the horse he rode was very tall and she hadn't forgotten how scared she had been when she last sat on a horse but he was right, she needed something new to think about. She nodded. "Alright, if you promise it is safe"

Rhawan did grin. "Yes, I would never let you fall, you know that by now"

She got up and he bent down from the horse and lifted her up by her waist, placed her in front of him and she let out a small yip as she was forced to sit astride the horse. The saddles these eternal used were not like the saddles the villagers had, they were made from some sort of soft material and there was nothing hard on them at all, it was all just a sort of pillow with straps attached to it. Wenja did grasp onto the front of it and Rhawan did chuckle. "Our traditional saddles are way better than the ones the humans use, both for the rider and the horse"

He made the mare trot and then he let her gallop and at first Wenja was terrified because of the speed but then she managed to relax and it became rather exciting. The landscape was very pretty and Rhawan started to tell her the names of the things they saw in his own language and she tried to copy it with variable luck. He did ride around in wide circles, showing her strange trees, animal tracks and other interesting things and Wenja did find that she liked this. She turned to him, her eyes shining with curiosity. "They say there are other animals out there on the plains than here in the mountains?"

Rhawan chuckled. "They are right, the fauna is very different and so is the flora by the way"

He had to explain those two words to her and Wenja did listen as he told her about the huge herds of antelope and the rare but very dangerous spear noses which were almost blind but able to run as fast as a horse. It was fascinating and she got a better image of the land which would become her home soon, it started to fascinate her. Rhawan did tell her of the giant animals with long trunks which sometimes could be seen by the watering holes and how they were to be left alone for they were smart like people and never forgot. He told her about the large flightless birds which used to hide in the dense bushes and were absolutely delicious to eat and the fat fish which lived in the small lakes. He did love his land and she sensed that very well, it was in his voice.

Wenja started to like this a lot, she was leaning back against him and she laughed when he reached out to the side and snatched a few berries from a bush. They were very large and deep blue and he showed them to her. "These berries doesn't taste like anything at all, but they make very good paint and if you make wine from them it tastes very nice."

Wenja nodded. "So, when I get there and get married, what am I to do?"

Rhawan did frown. "What do you mean?"

Wenja felt a bit stupid. "What are my duties, my chores? I must certainly do something to earn a living? Your Ath'ir cannot possibly wish for a lazy wife?"

Rhawan managed to hide his mild shock. "You will be the Eth'ir Wenja, you do not need to do anything unless you wish to. But the women usually sew, or herd the animals or hunt smaller animals. And make things, like pottery and jewellery."

Wenja bit her lower lip. She hadn't thought about that concept yet, that she was to become one of great status, that she in fact would be like a queen. "Do they weave?"

Rhawan nodded. "Yes, weaving is held in high regard among my people, it is a very useful skill"

Wenja smiled. "That is good, I like weaving"

Rhawan did point towards the river. "See those birds over there?"

Wenja nodded. "They are pretty, such a nice colour"

The birds were wading in the shallows on long spindly legs and they had a very brightly coloured plume, sharp green. "They are sacred, nobody is allowed to hunt them except once a decade. The Ath'ir is allowed to fell one on a sacred day, and only a male. The feathers are woven into a sort of headband, which is to be worn when the clans gather for council."

She swallowed. "Can you tell me more? About…Ahravan?"

Her voice was a bit thin and Rhawan did pity her. There wasn't much chance of her getting any time with Ahravan before the wedding, she would be thrown out into the deep end right away. "Of course, but where do I start?"

Wenja tried to remain calm. "His habits, does he have any habits he doesn't want to break?"

Rhawan chuckled. "Yes, understand this Wenja, we elves are not prone to change, and if we do change rest assure it is something we don't do easily, nor fast. You humans can turn around and become someone new almost without even hesitating but our personalities are set whence we have matured."

Wenja turned her head around. "So you don't like changes at all?"

Rhawan did make a grimace. "Oh but we do, we just…we prefer to know of them beforehand. Ahravan is very smart and he is coping with sudden changes rather well but whence in private? Not so much."

He took a deep breath. "Right, there are some habits of his you ought to know about. First of all, if he is reading don't disturb him. Nothing will happen if you do but his mood may be a wee bit…dark. Second, he isn't truly alive until he has had his morning tea. If you make sure that it is ready and very strong he will worship you endlessly"

Wenja tilted her head. "You do drink tea? We do too, but I don't think you will like the one we use!"

Rhawan steered the horse around a fallen tree. "Oh? What sort of tea do you drink?"

Wenja shrugged. "The leaves of Isha bushes, that is that bush over there, with the dark green leaves"

Rhawan scoffed. "Oh by the Goddess, they are bitter as fuck…sorry, very bitter"

Wenja nodded. "Yes, we use honey in it, but it is said to be good for one's stomach"

The dark skinned eternal made a smirk. "Perhaps, but we wouldn't drink that if we got paid for it, it is horrible?"

Wenja giggled. "Yes, but we don't have wine"

Rhawan sighed. "Too bad, you will learn to like wine, we have some very nice types"

Wenja had to turn around again. "What types? I have only heard of wine made from grapes?"

Rhawan laughed. "But you can make wine from just about anything, I once tasted wine made from the flowers of dandelions. It wasn't too bad"

She frowned. "Really? Then it is sad father doesn't know that, some of the pastures we own are covered with dandelions in spring. It could make buckets and buckets of wine for sure"

They rode down a small hill and back onto the road next to the wagons. Wenja sort of wriggled a bit, she was still curious. "But Ahravan, does he have other habits?"

Rhawan did let the horse walk next to the house wagon. "Well, of course, you may not think of it as habits though. He likes to bathe, in fact he often jokes that he must have been meant to be born as a fish. And he is awfully ticklish, under his armpits."

Wenja had to giggle. "Really?"

Rhawan nodded. "Yes, and he hates to wear sweaty clothes, the washers are kept busy whenever he is around."

Wenja swallowed again. "So he likes to keep himself clean?"

122

Rhawan did smile. "We all do, a person who isn't fond of cleaning up is someone we won't trust."

Wenja thought of the coldest winters, when they couldn't bathe at all but washed in front of the hearth, in a small bucket of lukewarm water. After a few weeks you didn't feel the smell anymore but she was rather sure that they all had been stinking rather badly at some times. "But how do you bathe? Is there rivers and lakes everywhere?"

Rhawan laughed. "No, we have tubs, portable ones. And we heat water too, it is rather easy. I bet that you will be used to having a bath every day."

Wenja sighed, that did sound heavenly. Rhawan did lift her down off the mare and she landed safely on the stairs of the wagon. "You look so much better already, Ahravan will fall for you for sure, head over heels"

Wenja blushed and went back inside, there was a big chance that dinner was ready soon and she felt a bit better. The headache was gone and she was in fact rather hungry. Some food would be nice now and she was looking forward to seeing what Imh had conjured up. She had to ask the dwarrowdam for her recipes one day, the use of spices was not what Wenja was used to but the food was always excellent and packed with flavour.

Rhawan did ride along the caravan, his face a bit tense and he let the horse gallop ahead of everyone. He passed Floth'bha and Ehbrial and didn't even stop to say hi to Thokan. He rode for a good fifteen minutes until he reached a small lake, there he dismounted and ran down to the shore. He was way ahead of everybody and all alone and he sat down on a rock, trying to calm himself down. Riding for almost an hour with her soft and yet firm derriere pressed against him had caused some unwanted reactions. He was glad he had chosen a pair of really tight pants that day for she hadn't noticed and he had managed to keep the conversation normal too. She hadn't noticed that he was in dire straits.

He would have to find Sefa later that evening, or perhaps Nefhriel or Ahnriel but he couldn't really wait that long. Wenja was just temptation incarnate, her smell, the silky hair, the shape of her... He had been so tempted but he knew she would be scared if he made a move on her, and possibly very offended too, and not to forget confused. He tried to think of something else but it was impossible, he was too aroused and he gave in to it. He got his pants out of the way and gasped with relief as the tight fabric no longer restrained him. It wasn't often that he had to do this but he was no stranger to it. He wondered what it would have been like if she had been an experienced woman, if she would have let him take her, there on the horse? He could almost see it, her laying forward over the neck of the steed, with her skirts lifted and him entering her from behind. The mere thought was enough, two quick strokes and the world turned into white light as he came, muffling a groan with his hand. Oh goddess, he was mad to think about her thus but he couldn't help it. He shivered as he spilled onto the ground and the pleasure made him lightheaded and almost drowsy. This had helped a bit but he needed someone's touch soon, or else he would go insane. Yes, he would visit Sefa that night, there was no way around it.

Out on the plains the clans were approaching the next main camp site, everybody were relieved that the city could be placed in one spot for a few weeks and the kids and youths were busy leading the animals to the best pastures. This camp site was old, they had used it for centuries and everybody knew where each tent had to be raised and where the different other buildings ought to be too. It was an age old routine and nobody went idle for very long. Corrals were made for the riding horses, made out of sharp poles and rope, the ovens were assembled and tested and placed inside of the tents before the walls were erected. Things had a certain rhythm, a sort of age old order which couldn't be broken. Since everybody knew what to do and when raising the tents and buildings were done in a surprisingly short amount of time, when the last stragglers arrived the main tents were already in place and the fire pits dug open again. Some hauled water, others went to find fuel and some went around and made sure that the camp site in fact was safe. Every rock and root was being flipped to make sure that there weren't snakes or scorpions or even worse critters hanging around.

The bath tents were put up, the healers got their tents finished and then everybody found their designated place and settled down. It was a chaos but an orderly one and the atmosphere was a good one, they were tired

124

from the long trek and now they looked forward to resting and regaining their strength. Ahravan was helping the ones who took care of the horses, he was putting up fences and helping them sorting out the animals they would need while in camp. The others were released to run free for as long as they stayed there. It was a job he had done thousands of times before and yet it always held the same joy for him. This night he would sleep in a decent bed again, and before that he would have a good meal and an even better bath. The dust of the journey had made his skin prickle for the last days. The girl who had been attacked by the huge snake had recovered well and was okay and they had checked every camp site extra carefully before they decided where to rest. This site was a good one for a long stay, there was a river close by, a lake too and a groove of old trees not far from the site. The trees were sacred but there were berries growing there and mushrooms and some animals were drawn to the place too. It would be some good weeks for sure.

Ahravan finished the job and entered his tent, the dividing walls were already put up and the roof was being pulled on too, it was made from very dense felt and on top of that was a layer of water proof tarp. The ovens were in place and lit and Ahravan sighed with a sense of relief and smiled to himself. This would be so good.

He found clean clothes and left the dirty ones in a hamper for the cleaners and then he walked off to the bath tent. Normally he got a tub brought into his tent so he could bathe in private but that never happened on the first day of a stay. People were just too busy to heat water for just one bath and carry it from the heaters to the tent. The heaters were a dwarven invention, huge metal containers which could be placed over a fire and the water could be brought to a boil very fast. The bath tent was almost as large as his and there were many separate rooms, very small with just room for a bath tub and a chair on which to lay one's clothes. The tubs were made from a sort of watertight leather stretched over a thin frame made from some very strong wooden spokes. It did look a bit like a canoe, with the leather on the inside instead of the outside and they could be taken apart easily. Ahravan had a real tub, a metal one but that was not unpacked yet.

He entered a room and one of the servants did fill the tub with warm water and left soap and towels. Ahravan slid into the tub very gently and closed his eyes with bliss. This was what he had been longing for, probably for at least a week! He just relaxed for a while and then he washed his hair thoroughly and rubbed himself with soap, everywhere. The elves were very careful with their hygiene and not without reason, the beasts which ravaged the lands had a very acute sense of smell and nobody wants to be an easy target. He wiped the last water off his body with the towels and felt like a new person, the warmth had done him good. He stared down at his own torso, he had gained a few more scars since the last time he was here but they would vanish in time, scars never lasted very long on his kind. He did have tattoos, several of them, made in a very striking blue colour which really stood out against his dark skin. An ordinary tattoo would fade within a few decades but these would last as long as he did. They were made with the use of magic and they had been terribly painful but he was proud of them.

He got the clean clothes on and left the bath tent, some of the youngsters were digging latrines, also an important part of the camp life. They usually dug at least five long trenches which got covered with boards they had brought with them. A bench with holes were placed across the trench at the end and then it got moved forwards as the trench filled up and earth was shoved inn over it from the end. It was a very smart system.

He sat down to eat, someone had prepared a huge kettle of stew and he was hungry so he ate until he felt almost ready to burst, then he talked to the guards to organize them and determine in which order the men should be on duty and when he returned to his tent everything was in order. The bed was ready and he smiled and sat down on it. The bed was unusual, it was made from a huge frame which could be taken apart and the bottom was ropes. It formed a sort of box and the matrasses were put down into it. The matrasses were made from a thick fabric filled with straw and hair and moss and down and they were covered with several layers of sheets and blankets. It was both comfortable and very warm and he pulled off his socks and clothes. He normally slept in the nude and let a hand run over the top layer, silky furs which felt just wonderful against his skin.

He rolled into the bed and pulled the top layer of furs over him, felt how his body started to relax. He needed a good night sleep and squirmed a bit just to enjoy the feeling of being pleasantly warm.

Here on the plains the summers could be brutally hot and the winters equally cold and he remembered nightmarish ones when they lost almost half of their livestock and many of the humans of the tribe did perish. It was usually the very young and the very old which died and it was always such a terrible thing. This winter looked as if it would become a rather gentle one and he was glad, but he also wondered what it would bring. Rhawan would return to him in a few weeks, with his new wife to be and Ahravan couldn't help but think about it. What would she be like? It was a very pressing question but one he wouldn't find an answer to before she did arrive in the flesh and he closed his eyes and let his mind drift off to sleep. He needed that now, and before long he was lost to the world.

The next morning one could have believed that the city had been there forever, people were scurrying around doing their business and Ahravan got dressed and felt good. He was whistling as he found his boots and sat down by his table to enjoy a quick meal. The servants had left him with bread, tea, some wine and then a huge chunk of cheese and some jam. It was simple food but good and he ate with a good appetite. This day the sun was in fact out and the wind wasn't too bad so the temperature was nice. He walked outside after having braided his hair and he smiled and nodded at everybody he knew.

He was heading towards the paddocks, he had some horses he wanted to check in on and he saw that Laupir was standing next to one of the saddle racks, trying to untangle a huge pile of reins. Laupir was human and one of the best horsemen of the clans, he had grown up on horseback and knew everything there is to know about horses and then some. Ahravan did bow his head in greeting and Laupir smiled but made a grimace and pointed at the mess. "The next time we do move we have to make sure that the ropes and reins are sorted out beforehand and tied into neat knots. This is a nightmare!"

Ahravan saw that most of the reins were twisted together and it looked a bit like a huge bush. "The apprentices did this?"

Laupir nodded. "Oh yes, the kids. I know that they don't know any better but by the Goddess, I want to warm their behinds!"

Ahravan chuckled. "Leave the job to them, it ought to teach them a small lesson. So, what do you think?"

Laupir scratched his head. "The mares?"

Ahravan nodded and Laupir put down the work, the tangle was just horrible and the tall elf didn't exactly envy the poor souls who had to fix this. The man shrugged, Laupir was a very tall man but he was way shorter than Ahravan and he had a very slender build. Some said that Laupir looked as if the first real gust of wind would carry him away but there was strength in him, the wiry springy kind. He had shaved most of his head but kept a pony tail at the back of his skull and he had lots of tattoos. Laupir was known as the best horseman of the clans if you didn't add the elves to the equation and that gave immense status, because of that Laupir was very important and had a lot to say and he was popular too. Ahravan liked him a lot, he had a lot of very good qualities and he was honest. Laupir was more likely to cut off his own legs than tell a lie and he was just like most men of the clans, he was rather quiet, a man of very few words. "You want my honest opinion and I have to admit it, breeding the two dun ones was a mistake"

Ahravan had a herd of brood mares and he had bought a few more that spring, just to replace a couple of mares who had been very old and died the last winter. "Are you saying that they are no good?"

Laupir nodded. "The tall one has thrown her foal for sure, she was pregnant but she isn't pregnant any more or else you can call me a dwarf and the other one? She looks like a balloon on legs and she isn't due for yet five months. Something is wrong with her"

Ahravan sighed. "Right, can the tall one be used for riding?"

Laupir tilted his head from one side to the other, he was grimacing. "She moves with the smoothness of a lame camel my liege, riding her is like riding…well, I don't even know what to compare her with"

Ahravan looked down, the mare was very tall and he had hoped to breed some large foal out of her, large steeds were needed when they were fighting. "Alright, you can remove her from the herd of pregnant

128

mares and add her to the herd of loose horses but make sure she isn't being impregnated again before spring, and with only my best stud"

Laupir grinned. "Sure thing. The other one?"

Ahravan was thinking. "Put her in a corral on her own, close to the camp and keep an eye on her. It would be too bad if we lost yet another foal. If she does lose it though, sell her, I have no use for a sick mare"

Laupir gave him a swift nod and then he looked at the Ath'ir with a curious expression upon his face. "So, you are truly getting married again?"

Ahravan had to make a swift grimace, he didn't like being reminded of this. "Yes, I am. So I have a task for you"

Laupir smiled. "I am all ears"

Ahravan made a gesture. "The woman I am to wed comes from the high valleys, they don't have much horses there. There is a great chance that she doesn't even know how to ride. I want you to find the horses I am to gift to her as a wedding present."

Laupir did all of a sudden look very eager. "That is an honour my liege, so, what do you want?"

Ahravan took a deep breath. "Five good broodmares, of the best bloodlines. Five geldings, the best hackneys you can find. Three ponies of a gentle disposition and one or two stallions, also top notch and not of the same bloodlines as my own. I would also like to gift her with at least three mares for riding and a Da'ifh"

The last made Laupir raise an eyebrow. "Ahravan, that will be tough. A Da'ifh is rare, and costly. I will have to send messages far and wide to find one suitable for a woman"

Ahravan nodded. "I know, but you will be given free hands. I want my wife to be safe, and such an animal will protect her with its life. "

Laupir chuckled. "Well, if she doesn't love you after having received such generous gifts then she is a fool. I will see what I can do!"

Ahravan smiled and petted Laupir on his back. He knew of very few breeders of Da'ifh's and the animals were extremely costly and held in high regard. He didn't own one and none others in the twelve clans did either but he felt that the girl he was to receive would need some extra protection. A Da'ifh wasn't supposed to be ridden, it was a stallion which was trained to fight, to kill and to keep its owner safe. It would follow its owner and keep any attackers at bay as the person rode to safety. The Da'ifh's were of a very rare breed of horse, they were huge and rather stocky compared with a riding horse, not very fast but with terrible strength and they would fight until the bitter end if they had to.

Ahravan walked back to his tent, some men were arguing very loudly and he stopped, both me stared at the ground and one of them did place his hand over his heart. "Ath'ir, our apologies, but we need your wisdom"

Ahravan sighed. "I will give what is mine to provide, so, what is the problem?"

The youngest of the men sort of scoffed. "He has stolen seven of my goats, that is the problem!"

The other man shook his head. "I haven't stolen anything, they have just wandered off and joined my herd, you ought to keep an eye on them!"

Ahravan rolled his eyes. "Seven goats? You are arguing like this because of just seven goats? Please, just get them back into the right herd and make sure that the goats are looked well after, end of discussion!"

The one who claimed that his goats had been stolen sort of grimaced. "But my liege, he has milked them! I want compensation for the milk"

Ahravan rolled his eyes once more. "Right, give him half a wheel of cheese and I don't want to hear more about this, alright? I have way more important things to think about"

Both men bowed their heads and Ahravan swore under his breath as he entered his tent. This was one of the things he didn't like about humans, their tendency to quarrel about everything and nothing and that at the same time. Their minds didn't work at the same level as that of his race, their perception so much shorter. Ten years was a very long time to them, to him ten years was a blink of an eye. Two other elves were waiting for him in the room set aside for meetings, both were female and he bowed politely. "Dairhen, Shirhiel, I am glad you could come"

Both smiled. Dairhen was a very elegant female with white blond hair as long as she was. She wore a very elaborate dress made from braided sickles of leather in different colours and she had painted her forehead with intricate patterns of blue and green. Shirhiel was shorter and dark of skin and hair, her hair was divided into hundreds of thin braids and they were so dense she had shaped them into some rather strange forms. It looked as if she was carrying a small tree on her head. She wore a very simple gown made from wool and her arms were covered with rings. Dairhen took his hand and she cocked her head, smiling wryly. "So, you need to prepare for the arrival of the Eth'ir, and provide her with everything she will need"

Ahravan nodded. "Yes, clothes, shoes, equipment of every sort"

Shirhiel giggled. "Well, we will do our best, but remember, we don't have her measurements so the clothes will have to wait for her arrival. But we can gather fabrics and we can also get her the other things she will need. Some clothes doesn't need to be made to size, and then there is jewellery and hair ornaments and such"

Ahravan swallowed. "Yes, let's talk about that. I will give you free hands here, ask the dwarves if they can create some elegant and not to gaudy things."

The two women stared at each other and smiled simultaneously. "Yes, that is a good choice, we will do that. We will gather the best fabric available in multiple colours"

Dairhen bowed deeply. "Within a week from her arrival we will have everything ready for her, fitted and sewn according to her colours and style"

Ahravan let out a small sigh. "Wonderful"

The two left and he sat down, thinking about the upcoming event. He would no longer be alone, that had been the greatest problem when he was married last time. The woman he had been wed to had been clingy and jealous and he had felt as if she was trying to choke him. He just prayed that this girl was different. Being the Ath'ir did mean that he had to do a lot of work, even paper work. He had to keep an eye on the soldiers and their equipment, make sure that the weapons were ready at all times and receive reports from all over the area regarding possible threats. It had been quiet for quite a while now and he hoped that it would last. When he had finished the day's chores he was hungry again and had some food before he went to help the warriors train the new recruits. Some young men and women did try to join the ranks each year and the training was very hard and had to be. Very few did make it to the end, most quit or were found to be lacking in one way or the other. One should perhaps expect that the warriors all were elves but that was far from the truth, about one third of the warriors were human, one third elves and one third dwarves. The attacks did require different types of soldiers and all the three races had some sort of advantage they could use.

Ahravan knew that the recruits this year were predominately human, the elves didn't have any youths at the right age now and neither did the dwarves. But he had high hopes for many of the young ones and some could become very good fighters in time. He did change into some better clothes and went off to the training ground. Some of his officers were ready and he stopped and stared at the gathered group. They had twenty recruits in all and everyone did kneel when they saw him. He smiled and picked up a fencing staff from a rack, walked down to the flat area where the training was done. Here the ground was soft since every rock had been removed and even in the coldest of winters training was rarely dropped. They had to be able to fight, no matter what.

He spun the staff, staring at the group. Out of twenty two or perhaps three would become warriors of the clans, the rest would be fighters alright, but they wouldn't be a part of the elite group dedicated to fighting the monsters. That was only for the very best of the best and he pointed at one of the young men, a slender but wiry fellow with short brown hair and the tattoo of a rearing horse across his back. "Ersha, show me what you have learned"

Ersha placed his hand over his heart with a bow and went over to pick up a staff, he did carefully choose one fitting his strength and reach and Ahravan did find a starting position. He was there to evaluate but also teach and he was an expert at seeing the flaws of these young ones before they manifested themselves as bad habits.

Ersha did attack, a very swift and elegant thrust with the staff which would have knocked the air out of a human opponent but Ahravan did just slide out of the way and blocked the staff with his own. Ersha did recover like an expert but Ahravan had already seen a problem, and he touched Ersha's shoulder with his staff as a sign that the fight was to stop.

132

Ersha did move into a rest position and Ahravan addressed the group. "Did you see what he did wrong here?"

The other young students did frown, they hadn't seen any flaws with the seemingly perfect manoeuvre and Ahravan smiled. "It wasn't large but it was there, let me demonstrate"

The officers made sure that everybody saw and he did copy Ersha's move, just much slower. "See? It should be visible now!"

One of the other recruits did light up like a torch. "I saw it, I saw it, it was his foot!"

Ahravan nodded and pointed at the youngster. "Indeed it was, as he thrust forward he put his weight on the right foot and forgot his left one, if he had to say jump backwards he would have lost his balance and he would have stumbled. A good observation. Now, everybody. Grab a staff and try to copy our moves, once with the flaw and once done with the left foot ready for a swift move"

Everybody obeyed and he smiled as he saw the realization dawning on their faces, this was the best part of teaching. Not all got it right the first time but after a few trials they all moved the right way and the officers did not need to correct them anymore. Ahravan was standing there considering maybe showing them some new moves when he heard the sound of hooves and shouting. He turned around to see that three riders were heading towards the training grounds and he did recognize their clothing and hairstyle as typical for the local tribes of the area. There were small non nomadic or semi nomadic tribes on the plains which didn't belong to the twelve clans and these looked as if they belonged to one of those. A tribe which moved around within a relatively small area, farming sheep.

The three riders stopped their stocky horses and dismounted, all three of them bowed very deeply as he approached them and he saw that neither of them were warriors. They were equipped as herders and he placed his hand over his heart in a gesture of greeting. The three looked as if they were a bit overwhelmed by being in the presence of so many elves but the oldest one did gather his courage and spoke. "Ath'ir, we have come to ask for aid, we fear that something terrible may have happened to one of our villages"

Ahravan frowned. "Something terrible?"

The man nodded,, his eyes on the ground. "Yes, nobody has seen anyone from that village for more than two weeks and one of the herders did ride in that direction to check things out but he saw a huge flock of ravens and didn't dare to ride further."

Ahravan knew that some of the tribes saw ravens as a bad omen and feared the birds, he shook his head at this superstition. "You fear that they may be dead?"

The man nodded. "We usually keep in contact, two weeks is a long time o honoured one!"

Ahravan had to agree, now in winter contact between the villages would be more sparse but two weeks? And ravens? He took a deep breath. "I will go with you and check this out."

The three did look very relieved and they all bowed their head in gratitude. Ahravan did miss Rhawan now, and he sighed and raised an arm, got the attention of the officers. "Gather twenty of the best, and make it fast. We will ride hard so make sure their horses are ready for it"

He turned to the three. "Wait here, we will gear up and be ready in a short time"

He ran to the hut and found other clothes, put on his light leather armour and a thick cloak and he wondered what this could mean, if they were lucky the village in question had just deemed the weather to be too harsh for travelling but he somehow knew that it would be too good to be true.

He returned to the three and saw that twenty of his best riders were ready, with their horses at hand and he was handed the reins of his stallion by one of the officers. The three men did look nervous, a man came with three of the elven bred horses for them to ride back and they were almost twice the height of the sturdy plain horses they had arrived on. "Worry not, these horses will not let you fall off."

The three men tried to look grateful but they had problems reaching the stirrups and one of the warriors decided to help them and simply tossed each man onto the horse like they were dolls. Ahravan smiled. "You will show us the way then, and do not worry, these horses can run for an entire day without feeling fatigue. "

The three nodded and the horses started to run and before long the group was heading out onto the plains at great speed. Ahravan was thinking as he rode, he and the horse were like one being and he let the stallion have his head and he just concentrated upon riding well. The smaller villages were never large, the land couldn't support larger permanent settlements and the largest permanent city he knew of lay far to the south at the border of the southern mountains and it was a city built by the ancient order of mages. These days they were gone but others had taken over the city and now it was a place of knowledge and culture. Most of the villages contained perhaps three or four families and the number of people were rarely over forty. This part of the plains were wind swept and the snow didn't stay long, they could ride fast and he knew that the horses enjoyed this, being able to stretch out.

The warriors did chat a bit as they rode and the three men were clinging onto their horses with a bit of worry on their faces. The elven bred horses were ridden without a bit of any kind and most didn't even have a halter on so the three probably felt a bit helpless. As the sun reached zenith they rode into a very shallow valley with a narrow river and the three pointed up ahead. "The village is behind that ridge"

Ahravan nodded and the group rode on, there was a sort of path there but it hadn't been used in a while and Ahravan did already know that something was very wrong. There hadn't been any fresh tracks in the snow there, no sheep, no cattle. He looked up. Some ravens did in deed hover over the village and as they rode over the ridge he felt his heart sink. There were four huts there, made the same way as his. No smoke could be seen rising from them, and there were nobody to be seen anywhere. Some dark shapes could be seen in the snow between the huts and some ravens did take to the wing as the riders got closer. The three men were wailing, all looked terrified and Ahravan sighed and pulled his sword. This could be anything. He didn't stop his horse until he reached the first hut, there he did dismount and told the others to circle and look for dangers. The three men remained on their horses, too scared to dare to dismount.

The dark shapes were dogs, all dead and covered with snow and the animals seemed to have fallen down as if shot. This told Ahravan that whatever had happened most likely happened during the night. There were no sign of the sheep and the cattle the village made a living from and he made sure that two of the other elven warriors were by his side as he carefully did approach the entrance to the first hut. These huts were made with a sort of extended hallway in front of the entrance, it kept the cold air out and the thick felt which served as a door was frozen stiff. He pushed it aside with his sword, Chelan and Orthur were right behind him and he pushed aside the lighter fabric which was the door into the hut itself. It was rather dark in there but light did seep down from the opening in the roof and Ahravan did feel faint as he saw what the hut contained. He had to swallow hard. The hut was ice cold and the bodies were covered with a thick layer of frost, the people did look as if they had died very suddenly, without a warning at all. A man sat by the small table, his head rested in a bowl of stew and he had the wooden spoon in his hand still. Two children lay on the floor, one of them clutching a doll and the face had an expression of sudden terror. A woman sat in the bed, a nursing baby in her arms, still attached to her bared breast.

Chelan did gasp. "It looks as if they just…died?!"

Ahravan nodded with a small growl. "People never just die! There is always a reason for it."

He moved around, there were seven people in the hut in all and they were all frozen solid. They had been dead for a while. Something had killed them but what? Humans were susceptible to plague but no plague killed this fast? And where had the livestock gone? If the owners had died the sheep in special would have sought out the herds of the other villages nearby. He took a closer look at everything, nobody had reacted, they had all died within seconds of each other, dark magic?

The hairs stood up at the back of his neck and he squeezed the hilt of his blade, no, magic was something very few could hope to master and he would have sensed it. It always left a sort of stain, something in the air like a barely noticeable stench. Orthur did wave a hand. "Over here, look"

He stood by the hearth and Ahravan did walk over, the fire had died out a long time ago but there was something odd in the ashes. It looked like small golden lumps of something, like round pebbles? Marbles?

Ahravan got a terrible suspicion and ran over to the table. He grasped the dead man and tilted the body backwards so he landed on the floor with a thud, legs in the air. He saw that neither of the people there wore shoes, the floor was covered with felt except around the hearth and he brushed the frost off the frozen feet with hammering heart. It was almost invisible, a small puncture wound, barely the size of a pinhead. Chelan and Orthur saw it and their eyes got large. "What in the name of the Goddess?"

Ahravan swallowed hard. "Check them all for such wounds, fast!"

He ran out of the hut and into the next one. There were ten people in there, including two old women and all had died in their beds. The last hut was empty, it was a storage room and he ran back to the first hut. Chelan did swallow and his eyes were huge still "They all had a wound like that, some more than one"

Ahravan bit his lower lip. "Right, get a fire going. "

Chelan did frown. "Why?"

Ahravan did sheath his blade. "Because all this must be burned!"

He walked outside and stared at the three men who had warned them of this. "They are all dead, as you guessed. And this village must be burned to the very ground itself and not even the ashes must be touched until two winters have passed"

The oldest of the three did frown. "What? Why?!"

Ahravan pointed at the huts. "I know what killed them, and it is a terrible enemy, one I never thought I would see again"

He didn't say anything more and a couple of the warriors did put torches to the huts. In spite of the cold the felt did burn since it contained a lot of greasy oils. He saw that the three were a bit in disbelief still and he tilted his head. "The sheep and the cattle has fled, probably eastwards. You may find them near the lake, the animals have instincts which are meant to protect them."

The huts did burn rather well now, the heat made steam rise and the smoke did paint a grey streak across the skies. This could be seen from many miles in every direction. Ahravan was about to whistle for his horse when a sound could be heard from the third hut. It had contained just three dead people, a young woman and two men and they had been weaving as they died. It was a sort of shrill scream which couldn't have come from any human throat and Ahravan did spin around and pulled his blade again, with a swift movement. The hut was burning vigorously and the flames were clawing towards the darkened skies, the heat was almost unbearable so close. The front of the hut collapsed in a cloud of sparks and then something shot out of the inferno, something tiny and extremely fast. The three men screamed like women and Ahravan let out a small roar and sprang into action. The creature did look a bit like a very narrow centipede, and it wasn't much longer than his foot but it had a tail like a scorpion and two large pinchers at the front and it was lightning fast.

The elf did jump out of its way and bored the blade through the body with a hiss of disgust. The creature shrieked again and writhed on the blade for a while, it was smouldering and Ahravan grasped a torch from one of the warriors and made sure that the thing did burn into ashes. The three men were pale and Ahravan did clean his blade in a tuft of dry grass. "What…what was that?"

Ahravan straightened himself up again. "A beast I haven't seen in centuries. They came with the monsters, back when the beasts first appeared. I had thought that they were extinct by now"

The oldest of the three was shivering. "Was it…an insect?"

Ahravan shook his head. "No, a sort of demon. Things do not need to be large to be deadly, and this thing killed everyone here before it laid its eggs in the hearths. When the spring thaw arrives the eggs would hatch and the spawn would have fed upon the dead bodies"

The three men turned green and Ahravan stared at the burning huts. Was this just a coincidence? There hadn't been any sightings of this kind for many generations of men so where had this one been hiding all that time? He knew that these monsters could hibernate, they had seen that before but for many hundred years? No, that was impossible. He turned to the three men. "Listen, I will give you a very important task, if this beasts is just one of many, returning to the lands, then you need to warn everyone"

The three nodded, still trembling slightly" Yes"

Ahravan felt cold to the marrow, and it had nothing to do with the temperature of the air. "Find every village, every tribe and tell them that they must find as much wild Chirach root as possible, dry it in the hearth and ground it up into a powder, spread it around the camps and villages in a circle, with no holes in it. And place some fists of it under the floor, rub the dogs with it, wear some in clothes. It is the one thing which repels the horrors"

The oldest of the three did nod, his eyes still very wide. "Oh, we will do as we are told, but…how did it kill so many? So fast?"

Ahravan did sigh. "They are extremely fast, and they can make themselves almost invisible. But they are not dangerous in daylight, then they can be seen. It is inside of the huts they are a threat and out in the dark nights."

The three swallowed visibly and Ahravan nodded. "They do fear fire, and can be killed. Ride now, you can keep the horses and if anyone sees anything like this let us know, immediately"

The three bowed their heads and turned their horses and Ahravan stared at the burning huts. He hoped that this one had been the last survivor, a relic from a past long gone. But he feared that he was wrong. Somehow he felt that this had been a harbinger of something way worse which was to come and he waited until the huts and the dead were reduced to ashes. The fire had killed the eggs and he was glad the three herders had been smart enough to seek his advice. If they hadn't then this scourge could have spread. Each of these little terrors could lay hundreds of eggs and he remembered having burned large villages back in the past. The stench of burning flesh still haunted his nostrils and they had even found people who were still alive but being eaten from the inside by that terrible spawn. He had given those poor souls a swift death before they were burned, it was the only way. Nobody could save those who had been infected while being alive.

The poison the beasts did use to kill did sometimes just paralyze, and nobody knew why. But it could be that some people were almost immune to the poison and thus survived the first effects of it. The warriors did stand there, waiting for his orders and he frowned and took a deep breath. "Ride out, warn people. The three rode eastwards, ride north and west, the south is probably safe until further notice, these monsters never liked the summer heat"

The warriors did split into groups and rode off and Ahravan did mount his horse and stared at Chelan and Orthur. "You follow me back to the city, we need to teach the recruits what to do if they encounter anything like this. And I want more scouts sent out, I have a very bad feeling about this"

Both warriors did bow their heads and they spurred their horses and rode hard back, Ahravan did think about Rhawan, wherever his Si'ish were, he hoped that he didn't have to struggle with something like this.

Chapter 5:Of darkness born

A small group of men were heading down the valleys, they were six in all and wore good clothes, rode fine horses. To most they seemed like men travelling in order to do business but the truth was very different. The two front riders were seemingly doing this for the same reason, they were heading off to punish that goddamn little whore for having run away and ruined the plan her father had made. Dagar didn't see further than that, but Mjorr had more things on his mind. When they caught up with those goddamn eternal he would make sure that this Ath'ir or whatever he was never would want to touch Wenja with a ten foot pole. That bitch was gonna pay for having rejected him, when he was done with her he would let the other men have their way with the whore and then he would cut her up so bad not even her own mother would have recognized her. And Prina, that little piece of shit. She was gonna die, and that before Dagar could figure out his little secret.

Mjorr had been no stranger to rape, he had forced himself onto many women over the last years and Dagar had covered it up, never scolding him even once, even bragging about his son's virility. But this? Dagar would kill him if he found out that Mjorr had fucked his own sister, the laws against such were absolute. If it became known Mjorr would have ruined the family name for ages to come. So the best thing would be to make sure that Prina never got the chance to speak, not that Dagar would believe that little runt but who knew? Mjorr didn't like taking chances, so he had already hired people who would make sure that Prina was gone from this world before he and Dagar arrived.

Mjorr had contacts and he had sent some people he met ahead of them, he just hoped that they wouldn't be delayed in any manner for timing was of the essence. He knew that the men were former mercenaries and very experienced and eager to get some money since they were getting too old for war now but this should be easy enough for hardened veterans and mercenaries rarely had any scruples at all. He had already managed to slow his own group down a couple of times. Once by making his horse go lame and the other time by pretending to be ill for a whole day. Now he had no more excuses left but he felt confident. Finding that goddamn city couldn't be all that tough, there were people living on the plains and where there are people money does talk. Dagar was just angry because Prina had run away, the deal he had been close to sealing with the master of one of the villages further down the valleys would have made him rather rich even compared with before and Prina had been the price for the deal. Mjorr didn't doubt that Dagar would kill her but Mjorr wanted the bitch to suffer. They were weeks behind the caravan but Mjorr didn't care. They would reach the city eventually and then he would have his vengeance. It was a very sweet idea and he was not scared of the eternal. They were large alright, and inhumanly pretty to look at but otherwise from that? He had no respect for them, anyone looking that beautiful had to prefer having someone ramming their ass instead of taking a woman. Mjorr was humming to himself as they rode along. Dagar had found four huge burly guys who acted as body guards and they all were capable of murdering their own mother if the payment was good. Mjorr felt safe, and rather content. Things would move in his direction for sure, the gods had always favoured him, or so he did think.

The caravan had reached the second tunnel and this one wasn't even guarded, the entrance almost hidden by bushes and shrubs and the road leading up to it almost gone due to heavy rain and a minor landslide. They had to haul rocks out of the way and make use of some rather primitive boards made from logs to get the wagons into it. But they managed without breaking any wheels or anything and the tunnel was just as nice as the last one. And exactly similar to it, with one exception. This wasn't so long, they would get through in a couple of hours and the next one would be just a short drive away whence they got through. Rhawan sent some of the riders ahead to check if there were any sort of obstacles in the way and he felt rather optimistic now. They were moving along very fast.

Wenja and Theka and Imh were in the wagon, entertaining themselves with some card games and Imh were teaching them a new one. It was very intricate and it did demand that you were able to bluff a lot. Wenja did struggle in the beginning and Imh won every round until Theka suddenly saw the light and understood the system. Then it became a struggle between the two of them with Wenja as a passive competitor. Imh did grin from one ear to the other. "This game is very popular among dwarves, so be warned. Do never play twelve fingers against a dwarf unless you want to lose everything you have. I have seen that many times."

Wenja frowned, back in the village such games were not allowed, the old said it was a trick of evil and that it would ruin people. "You have?"

Imh nodded and placed a card on the table, the clue to this was to always have cards of a higher value than your opponent and the one who ended up with the highest card at the end won. "One of our kings, Dulrun of Blackgorge lost his entire kingdom, his wife and his favourite war pig, it was the loss of the pig which made him most upset."

Theka giggled and Wenja had to look at Imh with a frown. "He mourned his pig?"

Imh nodded vigorously and saw that Theka had thrown a card of similar value to the one she had thrown, her grin was as wide as her face. "Oh yes, that clan rode great boars to war you see, armoured beasts. And he did love that goddamn boar as if it was his own flesh and blood. He went to war over it"

Wenja had to gape "What?!"

Imh had a wry glimpse in her eyes. "Oh yes he did, I kid you not. He did find out that the one who won the boar from him had turned it into stew, and that was a terrible insult. So to war he went and he lost with bravado but avenged his boar. They say he had the balls of his enemy tied to his belt when he made his last stand"

Wenja paled and Theka scoffed. "Oh my, well, that is vengeance for sure."

Imh giggled and placed her last card on the table. "And I won, be glad we aren't playing for money, I would have made you poorer than a goblin"

Theka laughed. "Believe me, I am, glad that is"

Wenja leaned back against the wall. "When we get there, and I get…married, he…he cannot…"

Theka frowned. "He cannot what?"

Wenja swallowed. "Back home, there was this one man who married a girl from the village, and after a couple of years he sent her back home with nothing, and kept the son she had given him. "

Imh rolled her eyes. "Humans!! They say orcs are barbarians but believe me, not even an orc would dispose of his wife like that, sending her packing? Hrmph. A dwarrowdam would take the manhood of a male who treated her thus, we are very good with knives you see. And elves? Once he has spoken the vows you are safe little one, he will never abandon you for as long as you are alive. Believe me, there is nothing to fear."

Wenja let out a sigh, managed to smile. "Yes, it is just…this is new to me, and everything…I cannot understand it all, yet"

Theka did grasp her hand. "I know dear heart, but you will see that this is a good thing, a thing of blessing. Your life will be so much better than before. "

Wenja did smile to herself, a small shy smile. "Yes, a blessing"

Prina and Sefa did enter the wagon, Sefa had found some herbs which Prina had to make tea from every day to fight the morning sickness and Wenja knew that Prina still pretended to just suffer from an upset stomach. She didn't want to accept the truth yet and Sefa was almost in despair already. She knew that if Prina was to remain healthy and have a safe birth she would have to come to terms with this soon.

The wagons did use two hours and when they saw daylight again it was getting dark so they decided to wait until the morning before they entered the third tunnel. It could in fact be seen from the exit of the second one and the road heading towards it was in fact very nice. This very narrow valley was uninhabited, it was closed off at both ends and thus sealed and here only wildlife did roam. The animals weren't afraid of people at all since they probably never had seen a human being and they soon discovered that although it was cute and endearing that deer came over to sniff their horses some of the animals were less welcome.

144

They had made camp for the night when it became clear that the valley was home to an unusually large population of red squirrels and the lights did attract the little rascals. Before long they were overrun with squirrels who were the carriers of an insatiable curiosity and more energy than a herd of toddlers. The squirrels were everywhere, they even found a way to enter the wagons and the horses were being covered with squirrels which were gnawing at the mane and tail to get hair they could use to insulate their nests. The warriors had to stand guard to prevent the horses from looking as if they all had mange come the morrow.

Wenja had never seen squirrels before, they didn't live in the high valleys so she found them to be extremely cute and tried to touch them but Sefa told her not to. Squirrels could carry disease and they did also bite if they felt threatened. Some deer came and tried to eat the hay the horses were supposed to have and Rhawan did run for his hide trying to get away from a pissed off skunk he accidentally disturbed. The valley was rather warm and that too brought a new problem, a sort of insect which preferred a rather high temperature and could become extremely bothersome. In the end everybody slept in the wagons with the windows shut and the doors closed and Wenja had to fight a feeling of this being creepy when she heard squirrels scampering all over the wagon when she tried to sleep. Prina and Sefa did sleep rather well in spite of the racket but Wenja had a very tough night.

The next morning they had to repair some harnesses for the squirrels had gnawed upon several of the leather straps and one of the guards had forgotten to put the lid back on a half full barrel of ale and now the ground was covered with squirrels, dead drunk! The next tunnel was easy to enter since the entrance was at the same height as the valley floor, they just drove straight inn but it was steep whence they got in there and nobody were to sit in the wagons since the floors were a bit slippery. The drivers had the breaks on the whole time and Wenja was glad they were used to the tunnels by now. This one didn't have any artificial lights and they had to rely on torches and some of the horses became skittish and nervous due to this. But this tunnel too was very short and they were through before midday, now they were way lower than before and the valley they had entered was wide and flat with a lake in it and a couple of villages. The next two tunnels were few days away, and they were close so Rhawan was confident that they would be able to get through them both within two days, three tops. The last one would take down to the level of the plains and then there would be perhaps a week or two of travel over the plains to catch up with the city. Wenja loved travelling now but somehow she also looked forward to the journey's end. She was getting tired.

Rhawan had started to act rather funny when she was near, it seemed as if he tried to avoid her and that made Wenja a bit confused and also hurt for she did like Rhawan and trusted him too. He would often disappear with Sefa or Nefhriel and Wenja blushed when she thought about the things he probably did to them. Sefa had told Wenja to learn about her own body and her own desires but Wenja hadn't dared to, besides, she had gotten her moon days and they had lasted longer than normal. Wenja wasn't regular at all and she didn't bleed much either but Sefa told her that this would change now that she suddenly got proper food again. Back at home she had only used some old rags but the women she travelled with showed her how to use some sorts of pads made from thin fabric stuffed with a very soft and absorbent moss. Wenja had been terribly embarrassed when she told Sefa of her problem but Sefa didn't even raise an eyebrow and had the needed things prepared right away so the embarrassment didn't last long. She also got a tea she could drink to avoid her cramps and she got very jealous when she was being told that elven females never had to worry about this problem at all.

The valley was lovely even if it was winter, the lake had frozen over and some of the guards did entertain themselves with skidding around on it when they had a brief stop. Wenja was used to ice but she had never seen such a huge lake and she was stunned to see that the locals did drill through the ice to fish. Rhawan did push forth, he was getting more and more eager to return to Ahravan and they didn't stop at the villages at all. Some people did approach them to try to sell things but he did send them off. Some even asked if they could buy horses from the group of extra animals but the Zahar would almost attack if any humans got too close and Rhawan knew that the animal probably never would forgive what it had been through. Frostfoot didn't trust humans at all, except Wenja who could pet him and scratch him without any problems.

The next tunnel was placed almost in the middle of a small village and it was well taken care off. This one was in use and there were people travelling through it almost every week. They decided to enter in the morning and the caravan did stop close to the opening for the night. There was a bathhouse not far from the tunnel and they were welcomed to use it, the owner didn't get that many guests for as he said, the locals were a filthy bunch of idiots who suffered from water phobia and saw bathing as something you did after you were born, when you got married and when you were to be buried. Wenja did very much look forward to a proper bath again, she had finished the moon days now and felt in need of getting clean and the women did occupy the bath and made the most out of the hot water and the soap. This bathhouse had a very nice soap and is smelled of roses and Wenja just loved it. It was so smooth against the skin and she had to remember her mother's soaps which didn't foam and felt as if you were trying to rub yourself with a piece of cold hard rock. Sefa and Theka had returned to the wagon to find clean clothes and Nefhriel was still in the tub, scrubbing herself vigorously. She claimed that she felt as if she had been taking a bath in lard and Wenja was laughing as she started to rub herself dry. Her hair had gotten both thick and shiny now and she could see how her body had changed. She stood there with the towel hanging from her arm, admiring how her breasts now were perkier than before and how her skin did glow instead of looking grey and dirty. She suddenly felt that someone was looking at her and she looked up, startled. It was Rhawan and he stood there blinking, his mouth half open and his eyes dark. Wenja didn't move, she felt a sudden urge to cover herself up but she couldn't, it felt as if she was paralyzed.

Rhawan just stared, he was only wearing boots and pants and had some clothes gathered in his hand, he had probably believed that the women were done bathing since Sefa and Theka had returned to the wagon. Wenja felt herself blush, the look in his eyes… He wasn't leering at her, it wasn't anything like the way Mjorr had been acting. But the look in his eyes, it was burning and it made her legs feel weak and that odd warm feeling did suddenly appear again and sank downwards, heading towards that area between her legs. Wenja did gasp and saw that her nipples had gone hard and she felt a sudden urge but didn't know what it was about. Rhawan did turn around, swiftly, like a ghost and was gone and Nefhriel got out of the tub and sighed. "He has fallen for you Wenja."

Wenja swallowed. "No, that cannot be true? He is…he just lusts after me…that is all"

Nefhriel shook her head. "No, I have had him often enough lately and it is you he thinks about when he peaks. He cannot hide that for me, we are both elves."

Wenja felt confused, Rhawan…Rhawan had fallen for her? But… Nefhriel smiled, a very soft smile. "You know that we do see such things differently than you humans? Don't despair, he and Ahravan are bond brothers, as one. If you can find it in your heart to make room for one more then Ahravan will most likely be more than willing to share you with Rhawan. Then nobody will be unhappy"

Wenja let out a squeak. Two husbands?! By ever god! But she knew of many men who had two wives so why not really? And suddenly a small part of her started to like the idea, she knew Rhawan and she trusted him with her life. Ahravan on the other hand was a stranger, one she hadn't even met yet. With Rhawan there she felt that perhaps she would be less afraid, less on her own. She suddenly remembered what she had seen that night in the tunnel and felt herself blush all the way up to the roots of her hair. Nefhriel chuckled. "Get dried off sweetie, I am sure this will be alright as soon as you get settled in."

Wenja had to hide her face. "But…will everybody…how…"

Nefhriel did place a hand on her shoulder. "Wenja, I bet most of the people of Ohtanar already expect Ahravan to share you with his Si'ish. They would be more surprised if he don't than if he does."

Wenja felt embarrassed and silly but she had to giggle. "I didn't expect him to…to like me"

Nefhriel tilted her head. "No? But you are special Wenja, not only beautiful on the outside but yours is a light so incredibly pure. We elves sense that, and yes, we all are drawn to such souls. Believe me, Ahravan will be just as smitten as Rhawan, rather fast."

148

Sefa and Theka did burst in through the door, in a cloud of steam. "We just saw Rhawan running towards the last wagons, bent over with a funny gait."

Nefhriel did giggle. "Oh, he saw Wenja here, in all her naked glory. No wonder he had an odd posture then, he is probably sporting the boner of a lifetime"

Wenja blushed again, even deeper and Sefa giggled. "Great, then there will be little sleep tonight, you or me?"

Nefhriel threw her head back. "You, I had him last night and I am still sore. He can be a bit too vigorous at times!"

Sefa made a grimace "Aii, you are right there. He has overdone himself lately, I bet he has been yearning for you Wenja since we met you"

Wenja had to giggle but her face was still burning. "I guess…I guess I ought to be grateful…that you are here I mean. That you can…take care of him"

Sefa placed the clothes she had gotten on a chair. "Believe me, it is no sacrifice. We'd gladly do it, he is amazing and just you wait and see, I bet both he and Ahravan will have you screaming for more before you know it"

Wenja did put the clothes on, she bit her lower lip and tried to come to terms with the idea. Two husbands, and both of the eternal? She was either a very lucky woman or she was about to get into very deep water indeed.

That night was rather peaceful, they had guards around the wagons in case someone felt the urge to try and steal some of their equipment and Wenja did sleep rather well. She was clean and warm and Imh had as usual outdone herself when cooking dinner. The next morning came with a terribly cold wind, snow flying horizontally and very low temperature. Wenja was suddenly looking forwards to entering the tunnel, there they wouldn't notice any of that. Rhawan did make sure that the drivers were ready and that the guards had bought some supplies for the last stretch of the journey. Imh had raided the local market and bought all the best vegetables and meat and paid more than well for it so she guessed that she would be more than welcome if she ever was to return to this place.

This tunnel did have lighting and in fact it was equipped with not just one but two lines of oil filled basins.

Wenja had been thinking a lot, the suggestions Nefhriel had made had been a bit shocking but the more she thought about it, the more she found that she accepted the idea. But she was still nervous, she had only heard good things about Ahravan but would she like him? And would he like her? That was yet to be seen.

The tunnel was very wide and well maintained but it was very obvious that it was cold now for there was ice some places and some icicles hung from the roof here and there. The front riders did knock them down and made sure that it wasn't any dangers connected with the ice. Wenja and Sefa were sitting on the back of the wagon, the dark haired girl was trying to teach Wenja more of the different languages but Wenja's mind was somewhere else. The wagon was one of the more heavy ones and it took eight horses to pull it and the driver was an expert, he knew exactly how to get the best out of every horse and they kept a bit of a distance between the wagons. Frostfoot was running along with the lose horses, the Zahar hadn't left them yet and it was a bit odd but nobody tried to shoo the animal away. A Zahar was intelligent, if it wanted to follow the caravan then be it. Floth'bha rode by, she was riding her huge mule as always and smiled at Wenja. Being in charge of the Eth'ir's safety was a great honour and one she did take very seriously. The tunnel was rather long but it was relatively flat all the way with a few ups and downs and neither were steep. They were heading up one of the slight inclines when they heard a shout from the front and the wagon's stopped.

Sefa got up on her feet. "What is happening?"

There was a sound of shouts, then horses whinnying and sudden screams and Floth'bha came rushing back, she was always armed and now she threw herself off her mule and landed by the wagon with the grace of a huge cat. She almost growled. "Get back inside, I think we are being attacked!"

Sefa gaped. "Inside of a tunnel?!"

Floth'bha nodded and unsheathed her blades, she carried a heavy short sword and had an axe on her back and the half orc was strong enough to wield both weapons with terrifying power. There were more shouts and

150

screams and the driver hit the brakes and locked the wheels, he was getting pale. Floth'bha yelled to him. "Do not go down from the roof, stay up there!"

Now there were noise coming also from the back of the caravan and Imh came running and jumped into the wagon. "Gnomes, we are being attacked by gnomes"

Sefa did stare with huge eyes and Wenja gasped. "Gnomes?!"

Imh nodded and found a frying pan in one of the cupboards. "Nasty little critters, I absolutely hate them"

Sefa growled. "No shit, they stink, and they steal anything which isn't bolted down"

Wenja hadn't even seen a gnome before and she blinked and stared at the others, not really knowing what to think or do. There was still screams being herd and horses were whinnying, there was a fight going on for sure. They heard Floth'bha roar and she was spinning around, obviously using her blades for all that they were worth. Then the wagon started shaking and they heard that something was trying to pry the door open. Floth'bha did smash into the door with her sword and they heard a shriek. The calls and shouts got closer and now they heard a lot of shrill cries which resembled war cries. Imh shook her head. "Darn it, they are cowards on their own but gather them up and they will attack anything if they think it can bring them something useful. Gnomes are mad about gold"

Wenja stared. "Gold?!"

Imh nodded and held the frying pan like a battle axe. "Yes, everything shiny really, they are nuts about it. I have no idea why for they don't use the gold for anything, not even jewellery. It just lays there in their dens, in piles."

There was a splintering sound and one of the two small windows shattered. An arm reached in through it, waving around as if to find something to grasp onto and Imh grunted and swung the pan with all her might. A dwarf is strong, very strong. And the females no less so than the males, in fact some dwarrowdams are stronger than the males and Imh had worked all her life. The pan hit the arm and crushed it against the wall. They heard an infernal shriek of agony and the arm was dragged back, it looked a bit like a piece of sausage, no bones at all. Wenja was staring and Sefa sort of growled. "If any of them make it inside then make sure they don't bite you. They can have all sorts of diseases"

Floth'bha was dancing around the carriage, slaying gnomes with the elegance of a fighting bull and suddenly they heard a sort of howling sound and the Zahar came running and joined in the battle. The animal was kicking and biting and killed gnomes like a professional and Sefa did throw a swift glance outside. It was obvious that their carriage was the one which got attacked by the majority of the gnomes and the warriors came running towards it now, the gnomes were being pushed back.

Rhawan came rushing and joined Floth'bha and still the gnomes kept coming at them. It was bizarre really. Sefa frowned. "I have never heard of gnomes being this tenacious before? What is it that they are trying to achieve?"

The door suddenly flew open and a short thin creature with a rather large head and a strange sort of armour tried to push its way inside, wielding what would be defined as a letter opener by any other species. Wenja shrieked and before she even had time to think she did kick the thing straight between the short legs and sent it flying back outside with a loud shriek. Imh slammed the door shut and placed a chair in front of it, locking it. Sefa did grin widely. "Brilliant Wenja, that was extraordinary. Good to see that you have got it in you!!"

Wenja just panted, she had not been thinking at all and just acted and it felt good, having done her share. The horses were kicking whenever a gnome went too close and the hollering and screaming seemed to gradually diminish. There weren't that much noise anymore. After a short while there was relative silence and there was a knock on the door. Sefa opened and Rhawan entered, he had blood all over and he did look terrible but wasn't hurt and he smiled, his eyes were shining. "We are done, there isn't one gnome left. I just wonder why they attacked us. The villagers didn't mention gnomes at all"

Imh sort of shrugged. "They move around you know, could be that they are trying to build a new nest in here somewhere. "

Rhawan sighed. "Yes, that would explain a lot but the drive of these things? If they face resistance they will normally just scoot off. I have never seen gnomes fight like that before, some even wore armour."

Sefa scoffed. "Armour, that is an exaggeration for sure, more like cardboard and string!"

Rhawan nodded and took a look at the shattered window. "Yes, but they were trying to fight, and they did continue until all of them were slain. That is not normal"

Imh tilted her head. "You are right, not normal at all. Absolutely not. So, what could it be?"

Rhawan shrugged. "I have no idea, they don't speak the common language and none of them surrendered."

Floth'bha stuck her head inn through the door. "The men are ready to move on, none of the horses are hurt and the wagons are okay too"

Rhawan smiled. "Fine, give the order to move out. We need to get out of here fast."

He petted Wenja on her shoulder. "I saw that flying gnome, impressive"

He winked at her and then he left and the driver started to prepare the wagon for departure. Wenja sat down and she felt confused. The gnomes had been so small, they barely reached her knees and yet they had attacked? Imh too looked a bit shocked and Sefa sat down and looked as if she didn't quite believe her own eyes. The wagons started moving again, the guards did clear the way and Wenja saw that the ground was covered with dead gnomes. They had been fighting like crazy so what was all of this really about? The tunnel was heading downwards at a very gentle angle now and the drivers were shouting to each other, discussing the incident. They did have some of the guards ride behind the caravan too now, just to make sure nothing caught up with them and Rhawan was riding back and forth, shouting orders quite often. They reached the light again after a couple of hours, the attack had slowed them down and Wenja was glad when they reached the exit. She suddenly felt very trapped inside of the mountain. The exit was close to a river and they had to cross but the water wasn't deep and it wasn't frozen over yet so it was rather easy. The only thing which happened was that one of the horses pulling one of the supplies wagons lost a shoe and they had to stop and replace it. One of the drivers did throw off a couple of dead gnomes which still were clinging to the wagon and Wenja saw them and cringed. Even dead they did look absurd and she shook her head in disbelief of the strange attire they wore. It was as if a kid had seen a warrior once and tried to make a replica of his armour. This valley was flat at the bottom like the previous one and the river was wide and flowed slowly. There were huge Holts of trees everywhere and Wenja had never seen the type before. They were very tall with many thick branches and even if the branches were naked now she could see that the trees were beautiful.

Rhawan did notice her interest and jumped onto the wagon, he made her sit on the steps with him and he pointed at the trees. "These are Mhala trees, they are very precious for their nuts are delicious and plentiful and the flowers smell divine and can be collected and turned into perfume."

Wenja stared at the naked branches, she hadn't seen trees that tall before. "How do the flowers look?"

Rhawan grinned. "The trees with dark bark are female, their flowers are tiny and bright blue, like…sapphires. The trees with smoother lighter bark are male, their flowers are huge and produce so much pollen and they fall down after a while and are being collected. The flowers are golden, and very pretty"

Wenja did wet her lips. "Mother…mother did have a small bottle of perfume, she never used it but we were allowed to smell it sometimes, and it did smell so good. But that was made from roses I think"

Rhawan nodded. "Roses are cheaper yes, the perfume made here is expensive."

Wenja pointed at another type of tree, more gnarly looking with fewer branches and way darker thicker bark. "What is that tree?"

Rhawan tilted his head. "Dhuner is the name of that type of tree. The wood is extremely hard and excellent for carving stuff and making tools. The berries are poisonous though and so is the inner layer of bark. They have to be dried for a year before anyone can do anything with them."

The valley did house a few farms and Wenja did stare at the large cows and the strange sheep. They were large and their legs were short and the wool dark on their faces and legs. The road was well used here and Wenja smiled and listened to the elf who told her about the way people of this area farmed the land. Here and there the south tilting fields were used for growing grapes and she did also see fruit trees and bushes. The convoy did stop once in a village since they needed some nails in case more horses dropped a shoe and Wenja saw that the women there wore very colourful clothing. And everything was embroidered, with very intricate patterns and the more embroideries the better or so it seemed for even the socks were covered with patterns. Prina did buy a pair of socks from an nice old woman, Theka had given her some coins and the girl was so fascinated by the colours. Theka did tell her that it was normal for a woman there to start embroidering her burial shroud the day she got married, just in case and it would usually take at least a year to embroider something that large.

The next and last tunnel after the outer valleys was heading due west and it too was at ground level. They didn't have to leave the valley floor to enter it. The river had grown very wide and very slow running and there were strange things built in it. Wenja had no idea of what they were until Floth'bha told her it was scaffolds made to support fishing nets which were strung across the river once a year. A type of fish would be heading up river towards the lakes and then people could catch them by the score and store them for later. Wenja saw huge cow like animals which had curved flat horns and they didn't have much of an udder , she was a bit puzzled until Sefa explained that they were buffalos and that they were used by those who couldn't afford a horse. Wenja learned something new all the time.

This tunnel wasn't used as much as the last one and the entrance was worn and rocky but they got inside without any accidents. This was the very last tunnel and Wenja was glad it was for she was tired of them. This one was steep, and it wasn't straight as the others, instead it was formed like a corkscrew and headed downwards and the drivers did slow down a lot. They put some special pieces of wood onto the brakes to make them stronger and more effective and Rhawan did make sure that the distance between the wagons was great. Here they could afford no mistakes. The tunnel was rather narrow and one guard rode by each wagon and the rest in front or at the back. Nefhriel and Ahnriel were riding at the front now and Wenja and Sefa were in the wagon. The wagons had to carry torches again and the light was sparse and flickering. Wenja was very relieved that this was the end of the tunnel travelling, now there were just this stretch left and then the plains would appear. The tunnel would take them down to the level of the plains themselves and it was rather long but it was way better than the alternative.

Crossing the mountains in winter was no easy task and Bagir hadn't expected it to be an easy task, but he had to do it none the less. The valleys were snow covered now and the passes were probably not open at all. He would have to find his way through the maze of low valleys and he feared that he would be held back by the weather and the snow. This winter seemed to be one with little snow and still that meant several feet of it even on even ground. He had two good horses and switched between them but even with their help he didn't manage more than ten miles a day, at the most. He had to find places to rest for the night and he had to find food for the horses too. Luckily he had money now and could buy hay and a shelter but there weren't that many settlements on this side of the mountains. It was in the rain shade of the large mountain range and here the valleys were not suitable for farming. Some sheep herders did live here but they were few and far apart and he also knew that some small communities lived there and they made a living from hunting and gathering. Some of the species of animal which lived in there had very valuable fur and he had seen the price which were set for those pelts. It was nearly enough to buy a good horse.

Bagir had been riding for almost two weeks and he had managed to get through the worst part of the journey, or rather, what used to be the worst part. Now the valleys were tilting towards the east and there ought to be little snow there but he found that this was wrong. There were huge drifts of snow and it was heavy and wet. This wasn't normal and he realized that the journey would be even harder than he had anticipated. He got stuck several times and had to turn around to look for alternative routes and one dark evening he found himself in a small village of hunters placed close to a very steep mountainside. The rocks did loom over the few huts and he realized that they had placed the village there on

156

purpose. The huge cliff did allow avalanches to pass over them and thus the place was safe, although it didn't look that way at all.

He was welcomed by the inhabitants who were shocked to receive visitors at this time of the year, it could be months upon months when they didn't see any strangers at all and any news from the outer valleys were more than appreciated. He did tell as much as he could, there weren't that much which happened from year to year but he could at least share some information and it was welcome. The village consisted of just three families and they were poor but had what they needed to make a living there. He knew that a storm was coming and it would be bad so he was glad he had found some shelter there. The leader of the small clan was a man well into his sixties, he was bent and worn and his left arm was amputated below his elbow, terrible scars did mar his face and Bagir did realize that this one had seen war. The injuries weren't the type you get in an accident for sure.

As the night fell the men gathered around the hearth and the old man chewed on some local roots and spat into the flames. The juices coloured the spit red and they did also have a soothing effect. Bagir didn't like those roots for they were very bitter and you became dependent upon them after a while but many used them in the high valleys, to stave off hunger and the weariness of long hard days. The old man's name was Hayas and he was the father and grandfather of most of the people gathered there, he had five sons and two daughters and they were all there with their spouses and kids. Bagir had lost count of the children for they did all look pretty much the same, dark hair and eyes and a sprite like temper and he knew that this was a very strong family for sure. They were closely knit and could survive even in this harsh environment.

Hayas did sigh. "You are travelling towards the plains? It is risky business in the best of years, this year it is almost suicidal. There has to be something really important compelling you to risk your life thus"

Bagir nodded. "It is, I have to reach the city of the twelve clans before some evil minded idiot does"

Hayas squinted, the smoke from the hearth made everybody's eyes water. "An evil minded idiot?"

Bagir made a grimace. "Aye, a rapist and abuser of women, an oath breaker and evil doer. He was after the daughter of my best friend and when she got engaged to someone out there he went berserk and now he is on his way to avenge what he regards as an insult"

Hayas wetted his lips. "This evil doer, does he have a name?"

Bagir noticed the tense atmosphere within the room, some of the women were staring at him and he felt a bit nervous. "Yes, he is Mjorr"

One of the women there let out a piercing wail and Hayas closed his eyes for a moment, when he opened them they were blazing. "Two summers ago a group of hunters met a young man further west, they were travelling to trade some pelts and among them was one of my granddaughters. She was going with the hunters to seek the healer who lives by the lake of eternal ice. She had some problems with her…monthly curse, and the women here couldn't help her at all"

Bagir felt that his face had turned stiff, like a piece of cardboard. "She was how old?"

Hayas nodded at the others there, they had gathered tightly. Many of the men did look absolutely furious and Bagir had already understood why. Hayas was almost growling. "Thirteen. She matured faster than normal for some reason, most women here doesn't start to bleed until they are at least seventeen but she got her curses when she was eleven, way way to young. Her mind was that of a child still"

Bagir held his breath, he had heard of such cases, a child trapped in the body of woman, not able to understand its implications. "He raped her"

His voice was flat and Hayas nodded. "Yes, lured her away from the others with some excuse no adult would have fallen for, and had his way with her. "

Bagir swallowed. "I am so very sorry, he tried to do the same to my friend's daughter, doesn't take no for an answer that one. "

Hayas was staring into the embers of the hearth. "She died, he had made use of her…in manners no man is supposed to. She was torn apart and got an infection, nobody managed to save her."

Bagir clenched his teeth together. "Then you know why I must get across the mountains at this time of the year, I have to warn my friend's daughter that Mjorr is heading her way"

Hayas nodded and gestured towards one of the young men there, he could be in his early twenties and had a very gentle face with some odd tattoos along his cheekbones and above his eyebrows. The hair was very long and pitch black and he had filed his teeth too. It did look a bit alien and had to have been painful. "We understand, Igkhan here is poor Ubha's brother, he swore to avenge her."

Bagir stared at the young man, there was strength in his gaze, and determination. "You are entitled to your vengeance young one, I will not stand in your way"

Igkhan smiled, the sharp front teeth made him resemble a wild cat and now Bagir realized what the tattoos were about, they were an attempt at mimicking the markings a lynx has in its face. "I will follow you Bagir, you are a man of honour, and two travels faster than one. I know the mountains and I have been to the plains too. I can find the best path for sure"

Bagir had to smile. "I am very thankful, you are right, two is way better than one. These mountains are not safe for one man travelling alone"

Igkhan nodded slowly. "They are hardly safe for two neither but two sets of eyes do see better than one. We leave when the storm sets"

Bagir felt relieved, he had felt lonely and he kind of liked this young man, the mountain folk were hardy and tough and also, they knew how to fight. He sent the hunter a grin. "Wonderful, what weapons do you have?"

Igkhan tilted his head. "I am an archer and I am very good with long knives too."

Hayas was chuckling. "Don't listen to him, he is not very good, he is superb. And give him a slingshot and he can hit anything. We use metal balls you see, they kill the hares but won't pierce the skin and damage the hide"

Bagir got curious. "Metal balls?"

Hayas nodded. "Oh yes, let me see here"

He rummaged through his pockets and found a shiny ball the size of a large marble, it was so smooth and even and Bagir had to gape. "It is perfect, but…where do you get them?"

The mountain folk were skilful and good with their hands but they were no smiths, there were no ore there and nobody knew how to dig for bog ore. Hayas was grinning widely, he was missing many teeth but still it did make him look very charming. Bagir understood how this man could have so many descendants. "A cave in the mountains north of here. I think the dwarves had a city here eons ago, and there were several chests left there with these balls. We take good care of them and don't waste even one, they are precious for we have just so many but with a good slingshot they are better than arrows."

Bagir stared at the ball, what in the name of every God did the dwarves use these balls for? They were made from good steel and valuable. Hayas did scratch his beard. "They say the dwarves used these under things which were heavy, to make them move easier. Like doors and stuff"

Bagir frowned. Ball bearings? He had heard of the technique but he had never seen it in use, the dwarves were for sure superior to any other race when it came to technology. Too bad they preferred to stay hidden and that they didn't share their knowledge unless they absolutely had to. "That may very well be, they are smart"

Hayas nodded and hid the ball again. "We have not seen any dwarfs here for centuries, but we are glad they left the balls behind, they are very useful."

Bagir turned to Igkhan. "How much time do we need to get to the plains?"

The young hunter sort of frowned. "Hard to tell, three weeks I think, if we are lucky. There are dangers we have to be very aware of"

Bagir pulled his cloak tighter around himself. "Like?"

Igkhan shrugged. "Orcs? There has been some increased activity among the orcs of late, some tribes are hostile and something is happening for sure"

Hayas nodded solemnly. "Yes, they are upset for some reason, more aggressive than before."

160

Bagir had never met an orc before and knew that they were normally very aggressive but honest, and they followed a very strict code of conduct. "What could cause that?"

Hayas sighed. "Rumours say that one of their leaders are dead, it had shattered the balance of power within the tribes. Now every male will want to rise in rank and that means that the peace will be disturbed."

Bagir felt a bit nervous. "Do we have to worry?"

Igkhan shook his head. "No, not really. We are just two humans and not worth bothering with, if we avoid getting involved in any battles we should be okay. They don't see us humans as worthy opponents and will avoid us. They think humans are weak and that it is contagious"

Bagir had to scoff. "Really?"

Hayas nodded with a wry smirk. "Oh yes, orcs are all about strength you know, and courage. Weak babies are killed at birth, and they won't take care of a wounded warrior if he didn't fight bravely. It is barbaric in our eyes but I understand them. They live in areas where weakness means death, it has to be that way or they will all die. "

Bagir sighed. "Yes, I do understand."

Hayas patted him on the back. "But worry not, for now you are safe here and we would love to hear the tales of the lower valleys. The women will bring us some ale soon and there will be food too, we don't have much but we love to share"

Bagir bowed his head. "I am very grateful my friend"

Hayas smiled. "If you can show my grandson here to vengeance we owe you. No, don't worry. A new face is welcome and your tales will be worth way more than some ale and meat"

Bagir felt grateful, these people had very little and yet they shared whatever they had with others. He found a better position on the rugs and prepared to tell some of the long tales he had grown up with, he knew that they were unknown to these people.

The descent to the plains was tough, way worse than Wenja had anticipated. She had sort of imagined that the valleys and the mountains were sloping gently towards the plains and that it wasn't at all very steep down to where the mountain range met the huge plain. She was wrong.

The valleys did end up high in the mountainsides and she had seen valleys like that before, her father had called them hanging valleys and it looked as if the mountain area had been pushed up sometime long ago by a giant hand and rivers which had been flowing onto the plains did now form huge waterfalls before they reached their old riverbed. She knew why the tunnel was needed now, it was way safer than the other paths. Rhawan told of roads and paths so steep that people had to tie themselves to strong ropes before they tried to enter and the path they had used to enter the mountains so much further south had been rather steep too. The wagons had been purchased on the other side of the step as this area was called. Now they could bring everything with them to Ohtanar and that was good, it had been expensive. The tunnel was slippery and on the last leg of the trip they attached some horses also to the back of each wagon, just to help breaking the wagons down.

The Zahar was running around and looked excited and Wenja realized that it knew where they were heading. It did make the odd animal excited for some reason. Prina was very scared and had to be comforted by Theka and Wenja did draw a huge sigh of relief when they finally reached the end of the tunnel. Here the ground was rather flat but the plains were not what she had expected them to be. She had never seen the horizon like that, so wide and so open and she suddenly felt exposed, why she didn't know.

Sefa did giggle. "I know what you feel, it is normal. You will get used to it, don't worry dear"

Wenja saw that the plains did consist of rolling hills and Holts of forest and wide stretches of high grasses. It was pretty and here there were no snow at all, just ochre winter grass and the dull green colour of some conifers. The other trees were bare and she tried to imagine this land in the splendour of spring, it had to be wonderful. Rhawan did hum a very sweet tune as he rode along the line of wagons to check that everybody was alright and he did look happy. The horses were let lose to graze and the wagons were checked for damages, some wagon wheels had to be changed for they had been cracked by the strain and the guards were working to get the work done. They would rest there for the rest of this day and the night and Wenja was fascinated by the strangeness of this landscape. Flocks of birds did hover over the Holts here and there and it was as if she felt a sort of melancholy from the land itself. Why she didn't know. She raised her hand to give her eyes some shade as she tried to spot the mountains on the other side of the plains but she saw naught, just a slightly curved line where the skies met the earth. Sefa petted her on her shoulder. "Ah Wenja, I know what you are trying to do, but the other side of the great plains is so far away, we can travel for months before you can see that area"

Wenja had to swallow, that far?

Rhawan sauntered by, he had a piece of dried meat in his hand and was gnawing at it with glee. "This land is where we belong Wenja, what we love and where our hearts lie. It is wonderful and I do look forwards to showing you its wonders."

She nodded slowly, she could understand the freedom of this place for here nothing kept you trapped, or so it did seem at least. "Are the plains like this all over?"

He shook his head. "No, some places it is very flat, and boring. And there are lakes and rivers and areas with just gravel and some places with lots of small cliffs. To the west there are some areas of mountains but it isn't as large as the inland area, and it is surrounded by the plains. You will learn about it as we go, I promise you"

Floth'bha and some of the others had gathered some braziers from the wagons and were heating them up and Imh was running around in a fit of panic, trying to find the ingredients for a gravy she wanted to try with the venison they were having for dinner.

Wenja suddenly felt very good, safe. This was no longer strangers but her friends and she realized that she didn't miss her family quite that much any longer

But she couldn't help thinking about them, would her sister have gotten any better by now? Weeks had passed by since she left and Ahnriel had said that there would be change although a slow one. She missed Sina and her father and everything really. But she felt that she had changed a lot already, she knew so much more now and had learned a lot. The night started to fall over the land and she had to stare at a sky filled with stars and they were so much brighter than she had ever seen them before and the sky itself so vast. She had to stare and blink and remembered how the mountains had shaded the skies, she had never seen most of these constellations before.

Sefa walked over with a cup of wine, she was smiling. "It is pretty yes?"

Wenja nodded and took the cup. "Yes, very. So, what is the occasion? Wine this late?"

Sefa cocked her head. "No more tunnels, I don't know about you but I don't like the idea of travelling beneath the earth: I am a child of the plains, remember that"

Wenja sat down in the dry stiff grass, it was hard to believe that the horses found any nutrition in it but they did eat it with glee. "I know, so, is there something I have to be aware of here? I mean, like dangerous animals and things like that?"

Sefa sighed and sat down next to her. "Of course, there is danger everywhere, I bet you had some things you had to look out for back home too right?"

Wenja nodded and sipped at the wine, it was very sweet and good. "Yes, wolves and bears and snakes too, in the summer that is"

Sefa made a grimace. "There aren't bears here on the plains, but wolves are a problem at times. They don't attack people though, just young horses. Snakes are not that uncommon but only one species of snake is dangerous. They hide in the sand and they are very large but rare, extremely so. I bet you'll never encounter one of them, ever"

Wenja treasured the sweet aftertaste. "So, other things?"

Sefa leaned back. "Oh, yes. Well, there are some huge cats which can be pretty dangerous if you come across them while they have cubs or a fresh kill. And near the rivers there are these huge stocky animals which are stupid as a brick but very aggressive with huge jaws and teeth. They keep the rivers from getting overgrown with water grasses but they are very dangerous when annoyed and also unpredictable. We stay clear of them"

Wenja liked to hear about such things, new animals and plants. The world was so much larger than she had ever imagined and she took a deep breath and felt strangely relaxed and happy. "So, they are useless?"

Sefa scoffed. "Wenja, no creature is useless, they do a good job preventing floods and problems with the rivers. But their meat is inedible and stinks, they do have thick skin though, it makes excellent leather. And their teeth can be carved into all sorts of stuff, even small statues and cutlery and such"

Wenja tried to imagine such a beast and couldn't, Sefa giggled. "A friend of mine has a toy made from such a tooth. It is very nice, and realistic"

Wenja frowned. "A toy?"

Somehow she understood that Sefa was talking about something very different from the toys the kids were using. "Yes, a very nice carved cock, just the right size for her too. She swears she wouldn't have made it without that thing"

Wenja gasped and went beet red. She had a feeling that this had become a natural condition for her of lately. "Uh…"

Sefa petted her hand. "My friend is alone, not seeing anyone and she is a bit shy so she takes her joy where she can find it, and if you cannot get the real thing then a good dildo is the best substitute"

Wenja bit her lower lip and tried not to look too shocked. Rhawan came sauntering by and he was carrying a small bottle and was humming. He stopped and bowed his head politely. "So, you two ladies look very jolly, care to share what the mirth is about?"

Sefa cocked her head. "Oh we were just discussing my friend Etha's ivory cock, Wenja have never heard of toys before"

Rhawan coughed, then he sprayed a thin mist of wine over his surroundings. "The God's curse you woman, a small warning perhaps?"

Sefa shrugged. "Oh you know me Rhawan, no reason to hide the truth now is there. We all enjoy a good tumble and if there aren't any males available then even I know how to deal with that"

Rhawan rolled his eyes. "Forgive me for not being too shocked by that piece of information, yes, I do know you Sefa"

She smiled widely and tilted her head. "Speaking of fun, are you alone tonight?"

Rhawan sighed and sat down, he raised an eyebrow. "As a matter of fact I am, Nefhriel is busy and Ahnriel…well, she isn't available at the moment."

Sefa got a hungry expression on her face. "Excellent, I was wondering if you could help me teach Wenja here a wee bit more?"

Rhawan did almost gape. "Ah, really, uh, what?"

Sefa did pout and pulled her knees up. "You do know how to use your tongue, way better than most?"

Rhawan let out a small gasp of air, he was blinking. "Seriously? Are you nuts woman?"

Sefa shook her head and Wenja frowned. "His tongue? I don't understand?"

Rhawan was blinking, if he hadn't had such dark almost black skin he would have been blushing intensely. "Uh…well…."

Sefa held up her hand and spread her fingers, then she put the hand to her mouth and let her tongue move back and forth between her two middle fingers, with a wicked grin. Rhawan turned away and moaned and Wenja got even more confused. "What?"

Sefa giggled and lifted and eyebrow in a very suggestive manner. "A finger is good, a cock is better but a tongue is the best, at least for starters that is"

Wenja suddenly realized what Sefa was talking about and her eyes got huge. "Ah oh Gods!"

Sefa nodded. "You usually say something in that manner yes, at least if he knows what he is doing, and Rhawan does"

Wenja was gaping and Rhawan was staring down into the ground. He was swallowing hard, over and over again. "Sefa, do you really want to do this?"

Sefa nodded. "Yes goddamn it, Ahravan sent me to teach her remember? And I am gonna do just that, don't you agree with me when I say that he deserves a bride who is ready for him?"

Rhawan sighed, "Yes, he does. And she does too, she should go to him with joy, not fear."

Sefa giggled again. "Then we have a deal, come to the wagon later when things get quiet. I will make sure that everything is ready"

166

Wenja stared at Sefa. "I am not so sure that…"

Sefa tilted her head, her eyes were stern. "You don't think it is appropriate to watch right? Don't worry, we don't mind. You should see the huge spring feast which is held each time the great mother tree blooms. It is wild!"

Wenja frowned. "A spring feast?"

Sefa nodded. "There is a mother tree in every one of the sacred grooves and there are many of them, spread all over the plains. The trees don't bloom every year though, some does bloom only once a century or even more rarely so it is a reason to celebrate when they do. The trees are sacred, arriving at a groove when a mother tree blooms is a very good sign indeed. "

Wenja saw that Rhawan got on his legs again and walked off, he did have a peculiar gait. "So, they have a feast?"

Sefa nodded. "Yes, with wine and song and dance and it is a rite of fertility involved in it too. It usually ends with everybody fucking like mad rabbits. I had just come of age when I participated in my first spring feast and I lost my maidenhood that night, I think I counted to seven when the night was over. "

Wenja blinked. "Uh seven what?"

Sefa rolled her eyes. "Seven males, I had had seven males in me that night, and I was limping for days afterwards but it had been amazing. I will never forget it!"

Wenja sort of coughed. "Oh gods, seven…I see"

Sefa turned towards her. "Listen, I have said it before and I will say it again, the twelve clans don't view these sorts of things the way other does. If it brings joy it is a good thing, no questions asked. I was younger than you are now when I started enjoying these gifts and I have never looked back. As a matter of fact, a person who haven't lost their virginity at the age of eighteen is seen as a very sad thing, and possibly flawed in some ways. They think it is a bad omen, that this person will remain alone and childless"

Wenja knew she was eighteen, she had to blush. "But…you don't have any children do you?"

Sefa shook her head. "No, not yet. I want some but not yet, I am so active I will remain young for many years still and I have to find a male who is willing to put a bread in my oven"

Wenja stared at her friend. "Don't you have to get married to have kids?!"

Her voice was a bit shocked and Sefa scoffed. "Heck no! Alright, the male I chose will have to help me raise the kid naturally but I don't want to get tied up to one male, absolutely not. Why taste just one piece of meat when there is so much available? I want to taste it all, and believe me, I intend to"

Wenja swallowed. "I…see. Well, I intend to stay faithful, we don't screw around where I am from"

Sefa sort of grinned, a very wicked smirk. "Oh and you will be for sure, just remember that a pair of sworn brother's share everything"

Wenja glared at Sefa. "That doesn't mean that they will share me"

Sefa leaned over on her elbow. "Oh but it will. Ahravan will be the one to take you first for sure but after that? When you are well and good broken inn? I bet there won't be long before you have Rhawan in you too, as often as you like"

Wenja had to look away, she swallowed. "I…"

Sefa purred. "Oh come on girl, you like the idea right?"

Wenja had to lower her head in shame. "I..I sort of do, I know Rhawan, I don't know Ahravan, yet"

Sefa caressed her arm. "See? Every woman of the clans will envy you, two gorgeous males to keep you satisfied in every conceivable manner and to take care of you. I am jealous already"

She sat up and sighed. "But there is one thing which makes me a bit worried though"

Wenja frowned . "What?"

Sefa grasped a straw of dry grass and started tearing it apart, one small piece at a time. "Prina, she is learning a lot and fast but she fails where you succeed. I haven't managed to teach her anything about this sort of thing and I fear for her sanity when she reaches the camp. She is pretty Wenja, in fact she has become beautiful and the males will be all over

168

her, wooing for her attention. She needs to change before that happens or she will lock herself up in a tent and never venture outside again"

Wenja sighed, Sefa was right, of course she was right. Prina did learn the languages and the customs much more easily than she did herself but she was shying away from everything which had anything to do with sex or males at all. It wasn't just her background, it was the tragedy which had befallen her and Wenja doubted that Prina ever would be able to overcome the trauma. She doubted that Prina would allow a man to touch her again, ever. "You are right, but she is with child, she has to think about that first and foremost"

Sefa sighed. "Theka tells me that Prina still is ignoring that fact, she pretends as if she is alright, as if nothing of it ever happened and she refuses to acknowledge the fact that she is pregnant. This may end in a disaster"

Wenja bit her lower lip. "I pity her"

Sefa nodded. "So do we all dear, but she has to wake up and face the realities soon. This cannot continue much longer. Yes she was raped and yes, the rapist was her own brother but she has to think about her baby. It may be normal after all, we don't know that yet and if Mjorr ever crosses our path again Ahravan will kill him"

Wenja closed her eyes. "When you said that the punishment for rape was death, did you mean it, the rest I mean?"

Sefa nodded. "Of course I meant it!"

Wenja cringed. "So someone will...do that to him?"

Sefa sent Wenja a very cold glance. "Most certainly, but it will not be a male, if he raped a girl then a woman will wear a sort of attachable cock and fuck him with it, and it will be made to cause agony and injury."

Wenja got pale and Sefa almost sneered. "Usually it is one of the female shamans who does this, and yes, it has been done. It isn't often mind you but we don't show any mercy for such beasts"

Wenja swallowed hard, she felt the taste of bile in her mouth. "Have you seen it?"

Sefa nodded. "Once, when I was twelve. They caught an orc who had raped several women, he survived for most of the day, they heard his screams for miles away but in the end they strangled him. Then they threw the body in the river, it was well deserved"

Wenja realized that this people had very strict rules in spite of their seemingly carefree lifestyle. "So, what else can you get punished for?"

Sefa sort of grimaced. "Horse theft. If you steal a horse you have to pay the owner back twice the value of the horse, even if it is returned hale and healthy. If you don't have any sort of wealth they will flog you, one strike for each Igh the horse is worth"

Wenja had learned that Igh was the sort of measurement of value out there. It wasn't a physical thing but used to estimate wealth. A horse was worth fifty Igh if it was a common hack, a hundred if it was a good stallion. She had to cringe. "And what else?"

Sefa stretched her long legs. "If you kill someone you will be forced to leave the twelve clans forever and you are no longer protected by the Ath'ir and the laws. Anyone can kill you and nobody will punish them. A man who beats his wife or kids will be forced to leave for ten years, twice that many if there is permanent damage. A woman who beats her husband or children will suffer the same punishment. Theft is punished with flogging, or a walk of shame"

Wenja frowned. "Walk of shame?"

Sefa nodded. "You will be stripped down to your skin, smeared with manure and have to walk around the camp four times while you call out the nature of your crime."

Wenja had to scoff. "That sounds terrible"

Sefa nodded. "Yes, and we have very little crime, thanks to that. Our people follow the laws, and it is good that way"

Wenja had to agree. "But what are we to do about Prina?"

Sefa sighed and pulled her knees up, laid her arms around them. "I have no idea, Theka has agreed upon staying with her most of the time, and she is a wise old woman but I doubt that she will be able to get through to Prina"

Wenja bit her lower lip. "But the baby, it will be born, how will she react then?"

Sefa shrugged again and looked down. "That would be anybody's guess, but children are greatly appreciated within the twelve clans. If she cannot take care of it someone else will adopt it beyond any doubt"

Wenja sort of frowned. "Really? Even if the parents were siblings?"

Sefa nodded. "It isn't the kid's fault, and like I said, the baby could be perfectly fine. Even kids with disabilities are taken very well care of"

Wenja remembered something and cringed, Sefa saw it. "What?"

Wenja sighed, a very deep sigh. "One of the women in the village had a baby two years ago, it wasn't…right. They drowned it in a water barrel, said it was a demon"

Sefa gasped. "Oh Gods, nobody would do that to a child here, even if the baby was born malformed. The gods decide when to call someone back to them, humans shouldn't interfere with that"

Wenja managed to smile, she remembered all the tales she had heard from Sigunn and Sina, and realized that the people she would become a part of were way more welcoming and understanding than her own. Sefa did pat her knee. "We can just pray that Prina does get over it, eventually. She will live a very lonely life is she doesn't."

Wenja nodded slowly, Prina had been very lonely before too but here, among such free and open minded people she would be an outcast if she didn't thaw up a lot. What could be done about that?

Sefa got up and brushed some grass from her dress, she sent Wenja a grin. "And now, off for a quick wash before bedtime. "

Wenja did make a grimace. She remembered the things Sefa had said to Rhawan. She got up and felt a bit nervous. "Do you really mean to go through with what you suggested?"

Sefa nodded. "Heck yes, you do need to learn Wenja, there is so much more to this than just fucking, you will see"

She gathered her skirts and walked off towards the wagons with her head held high and Wenja in tow. Wenja felt embarrassed, she remembered the situation in the tunnel and she remembered what they had said about Rhawan, that he had fallen for her. It felt…it was exciting in a way but also a bit worrisome. And now this, well, Sefa had probably her orders and Wenja was curious, she had to admit that. The wagon was empty and Sefa made one of the men bring some warm water and she found some cloth in one of the closets and a bowl. She was obviously excited and Wenja wondered what she was planning on doing. The hot water was poured into the bowl and Sefa grinned. "Go ahead, wash yourself."

Wenja frowned. "Why?"

Sefa rolled her eyes. "If you like what you see I bet Rhawan will be glad to show you how it is done"

Wenja gasped and she almost dropped the cloth. "Ah…"

Sefa sighed and took her hand. "Listen, he won't go too far, you will remain a virgin until your husband decides to deflower you, but that doesn't mean that you shouldn't have a taste of pleasure first."

Wenja felt her skin burn. "I thought I was just gonna watch"

Sefa nodded. "To start with yes, but you need to see to learn little one, me just explaining stuff won't really be enough. Have you done what I told you to do?"

Wenja shook her head, it hadn't felt right, at all. Sefa closed her eyes and she did look a bit exasperated. "Right, but you truly should. Anyway, from now on I think we have to take a more hands on approach to this, quite literally."

Wenja was trembling and Sefa pointed at the bowl again. "So go ahead, wash yourself."

Wenja did obey, with trembling hands and Sefa helped her get into her night gown, which was rather prudish and didn't show much at all. Sefa kept her long petticoat on and washed too, very thoroughly and then she grinned. "I do sometimes use perfume down there but I won't this time. Rhawan prefer the natural scents, most do as a matter of fact."

She sat down on the bed and Wenja sat down too, a bit reluctantly. "I will show you what to do Wenja, and how to enjoy it. Don't be shy, it is all very natural and gives such great joy."

Wenja did remember that feeling she had gotten when she watched Sefa and Rhawan fuck in the wagon, and suddenly she longed for it again, to feel it rush through her body.

The camp had fallen quiet now, the guards were taking their rounds and the horses were tethered and the bon fires put out. Sefa did look impatient and she grinned when they heard footsteps outside of the wagon. Prina was sleeping in one of the other wagons now with Theka and Imh and Wenja was glad, she was rather sure that the girl would have gotten a serious shock if she had been there to see this. Rhawan did enter, he had braided his hair and he wore a long loose tunic and a pair of doeskin pants which did look rather old and worn. He swallowed as he entered the room and his smile was a bit stiff, his eyes were flickering back and forth and Wenja realized that he was nervous.

Sefa did get up and poured some wine into a cup, she handed it over to him and he did take it and emptied it in one go, he almost belched and put his hand over his mouth with an expression of slight embarrassment. Sefa did take some wine too, but not as much and she did savour the taste. Wenja felt a knot in her gut, she had no idea of how to react. Sefa sat down on the bed again and her grin was very wry. "So, shall we?"

Rhawan blinked and he bit his lower lip. "Just like that?"

His voice was a bit hoarse and Sefa giggled. "Yes, just like that. It isn't as if you are known to be reluctant now are you? "

Rhawan still hesitated and Sefa rolled her eyes. "Right, okay, come here"

She moved until she was sitting on the edge of the bed and then she gestured for Rhawan to come closer. "On your knees"

Rhawan obeyed, he got down on his knees in front of her and Sefa did look very pleased. "So, Wenja, pay attention"

Sefa did spread her legs and then she lifted her petticoat a bit. Rhawan took a deep breath and then he leaned forth and disappeared underneath the fabric. Sefa raised an eyebrow. "He isn't this shy normally, believe me!"

Wenja felt her heart beating hard, she felt so terribly embarrassed and wished she was miles away and yet…she knew she had to learn. Back at home she had believed that sex was something very straight forward, that it was something men did enjoy and women had to endure and that everybody did it the same way. She had understood now that it was way more to it than that, but like Sefa said, seeing is believing. Rhawan was obviously busy and Sefa did lean back now, and pulled her petticoat up so it laid around her waist. Wenja had seen Sefa naked a lot of times by now, they had bathed together and she had no problems watching other females being undressed, it didn't bother her at all. But this…it sent her into a frenetic bout of blushing yet again, she realized what Sefa had meant by saying that Rhawan had a wicked tongue for he was obviously good at this. Sefa was breathing hard already and moaning and she reached down and laid a hand on his head, gently sliding it through his hair. "Oh by the Goddess, just like that…"

Wenja stared with huge eyes, Rhawan was holding onto Sefa's thighs, very gently but with some force so she wouldn't move and Wenja understood why this made Sefa act the way she did. It had to feel…She couldn't quite explain it, but strong, very strong. Considering how sensitive Wenja knew she was down there it was no wonder that Sefa was gasping if she was the same way. And Wenja was starting to understand that this was common for all women. Sefa was panting and tossing her head back and forth, writhing as Rhawan obviously unleashed all his expertise. Rhawan too was breathing rather heavily now and Wenja hoped that Sefa would allow him some pleasure too, and not claim it all for herself.

Sefa turned her head and Wenja saw that her eyes were glassy and dark. "This could be the main course but also just an appetizer, remember that. For some it is enough, for others it will just tease and arouse."

Wenja tried to nod, but the sight, oh Gods, it made that odd heavy feeling return to her and with it a sense of hunger she now recognized. Sefa was moaning and arching, her eyes hooded and close to closing. "I am…close"

Rhawan seemed to be sucking now and Wenja felt like a pervert but she couldn't tear her eyes away from what she saw, not at all. Then Sefa tensed up, an odd sound came from her throat and she closed her eyes, her face contorted by pleasure and Rhawan let out a growl and continued and Wenja saw that Sefa was shuddering all over, and she was keening. Wenja remembered the feeling she had had and her body was aching, she felt her pulse beating like a drum down there and she knew she was wet already. Oh Gods, she had had no idea that watching something like this could make you feel thus, so needy for something she yet hadn't experienced. Sefa stopped shuddering and sat up slowly, her eyes still

174

glazed and distant and she had a silly grin on her face. "Thank you Rhawan, that was wonderful"

Rhawan grinned, he did look as if he had way more self-confidence now and he tilted his head. "You are most welcome, so, what now?"

Sefa sat up all the way and sighed in bliss. "Now it is Wenja's turn, if you feel up for it dear?"

Wenja yelped, she just stared at Sefa. "Me? But…"

Sefa tilted her head. "You are aroused, I can see it and you are breathing funny. Don't worry so much, just enjoy it. He will do exactly what he did to me, nothing more"

Wenja stared at Rhawan and he looked down but his eyes were very dark and he was almost panting. "I'd love to do it Wenja, believe me. I do so much want to show you real pleasure, please let me"

Wenja hesitated, the mere idea…But she somehow realized that there were no way around this, she had to learn and her body was craving something now, and she would find no peace until that craving was heard. She nodded, slowly and with obvious nervousness and Sefa grinned widely. "Excellent girl, sit as I did"

Wenja did slide herself closer to the edge of the bed and hesitated for a moment, then she pulled her nightgown up and spread her legs slowly. Rhawan made a sound deep within his throat, it sounded like growling and his eyes got even darker. Wenja got a bit nervous, had she unleashed something which couldn't be controlled? Would she regret this? He was staring at her feminine area and he did shiver a bit. Sefa grinned. "Go for it, just be gentle, I bet she won't last very long this first time"

Wenja squealed as she felt warm hands on her knees, Rhawan did lean in and placed a soft kiss on each knee, whispering something which sounded very soothing and gentle and she felt herself tremble, part in nervousness and part out of an odd feeling of anticipation. Then Rhawan spread her legs a bit more and Sefa took her shoulder and made her lay down on the bed and told her to relax. Rhawan kept placing tiny butterfly kisses up along Wenja's inner thighs and she gasped and felt terribly warm all of a sudden, like there was an open hearth next to her, fully ablaze. Sefa took her hand. "Don't think dear, feel"

Wenja tried not to hold her breath, to relax and just ease into it but it was darn hard, she was sure she was trembling so hard the entire wagon was shaking. Then he kissed her mound and Wenja had to let out a loud gasp as she suddenly felt something warm and slick and slightly firm slide down between her folds and ending up on her bud, giving it a slight push. She sobbed, she was seeing stars, suddenly she felt nothing except that exquisite feeling of his tongue, caressing her clit with expert rhythm. It was too much, it was overwhelming and her body was twitching from the stimulation, and yet she craved more, so much more. "R...Rhawan..."

She didn't recognize her own voice and he just caressed her thigh as an answer, didn't stop even for a second. She was glad that the odd ointment they had smeared her with the first day she was with the group had removed her hairs, they hadn't come back and she was as smooth and silky as she had been the day she was born. That felt good, she felt clean and she already knew that elves didn't have any body hair so she guessed that it was all natural for him. His tongue was so slick and warm and did such amazing things with her, exploring and teasing and she was moaning and trying to press herself up into him. Sefa was chuckling, and caressed her hand. "That good ha? I don't doubt it, he is outdoing himself right now"

Wenja couldn't answer, it felt as if every muscle in her body was about to explode and she arched back with a loud keen as the world exploded into white light and pleasure surged through her, so strong it stole her breath away. She was hovering, feeling how muscles she hadn't even known she had were caught in spasms and it sent wave after wave of ecstasy through her body. When she started to come back to her own senses Rhawan was kissing her knee lovingly and he was sending her a very pleased smile. "You have such fire little one, such passion. I am honoured to have watched it come undone."

Wenja blushed, somehow it was a bit embarrassing and yet not, she trusted Sefa and she trusted Rhawan and it had been wonderful. She felt that this had been even better than the experience in the tunnel, so much more profound. Sefa grinned and petted Wenja's hand. "You were so lovely in rapture dear, Ahravan will be more than pleased with you."

Wenja felt a bit dizzy and she giggled, couldn't stop. She had no idea why she felt so silly right now. Sefa slid to the edge of the bed again. "And now Rhawan, your reward"

Rhawan got up, slowly and he was obviously very aroused for the loose pants were tented and stretched. Sefa turned her head to Wenja. "This is also so you may learn, remember what you see. We can return the favour so to speak"

She grasped the drawstring which held Rhawan's pants up and untied it, let the garment fall and Wenja let out a gasp. She had seen Rhawan naked before, but he hadn't been aroused back then and now she was staring at something which looked very different from the flaccid member she had seen back then. How in the name of every God could that fit inside of someone? She was staring with eyes like tea cups and Sefa laughed out loud. "Oh Wenja, it is really very apparent that you never have seen a good cock before. Enjoy the treat"

Rhawan was breathing hard again and Wenja saw that the whole thing twitched ever so slightly and that it did look rock solid. She kept staring and Sefa slid a bit closer and out her hands, placed them on Rhawan's hips. "Watch and learn, Ahravan will love it if you do this to him"

Then Sefa leaned forth and kissed the tip of Rhawan's cock and he hissed and closed his eyes, Wenja had to swallow hard. Then Sefa licked it, slowly and deliberately and Rhawan moaned and shivered and Wenja blinked, he did react very strongly, was that normal? Did this really feel that good? The next thing Sefa did made Wenja cringe, she opened her mouth and took the whole thing into it and started to bob her head back and forth and Rhawan gasped and closed his eyes, his expression one of almost agony. It was apparent that Sefa used her tongue and sucked too and Rhawan keened and tried to stand still, he was sweating and Wenja felt an odd wave of warmth rush through her again. Seeing him like that did something to her, something almost painfully arousing. Sefa continued and Rhawan whimpered and groaned and then he laid a hand on her head. "Stop, I am close…I need…"

Sefa giggled and let go and Wenja saw that the whole member was dripping wet and she couldn't believe that Sefa had managed to have all of that inside of her mouth? Sefa saw her expression and giggled. "You learn how to control your gag reflex after a while, and I have a good throat."

Wenja cringed, her throat? Had that huge thick thing gone all the way into Sefa's throat? Oh Gods! But Rhawan had obviously liked it a lot and Sefa cocked her head. "The males absolutely love this, it feels wonderful for them"

Rhawan was still trembling. "Please!"

Sefa nodded and got up, she turned around and winked at Wenja. "He prefers to come inside of his partner, not over her, but that is a personal preference. You can of course continue and swallow when he peaks but that is a lesson for later"

Wenja was still just sitting there, staring with huge eyes. Her body had reawakened or so it felt and seeing that huge thing did strange things to her. It was so large, and a bit scary looking too and yet her body didn't seem to agree with her thoughts, she felt her pulse again and that wet feeling. Sefa got up on her knees on the bed and arched her back with her legs spread and Wenja realized that Rhawan was about to take her, like a horse mounts a mare. It sent a shiver through her and she whimpered. Sefa grinned. "Aroused again? Don't worry, it is alright."

With Sefa on all four on the bed she was in the right height for Rhawan to reach without having to crouch and Wenja did see that he was trembling, his eyes black and she heard how fast he was breathing. She realized that he probably was beside himself with need.

Rhawan grunted and grasped Sefa's hips and used a hand to steer himself straight and Wenja gasped, she sat so close she could see everything in detail, how that thick hard member slid into Sefa and it didn't seem to hurt her at all, as a matter of fact Sefa let out a loud moan which was so filled with sheer lust and pleasure it made Wenja shiver. Rhawan too moaned and closed his eyes and he started to thrust rather vigorously, Wenja saw that he slid back and forth, slick with Sefa's juices and since his skin was so dark and Sefa was pale it was such a contrast and made Wenja see every little detail. It made her ache, she had to press her own thighs together and she craved it again, that feeling of ultimate surrender, of absolute bliss. Sefa gasped and made grimaces with each thrust. "Wenja…touch…touch yourself…"

The words came as gasps and Wenja couldn't resist. She let a hand slide down and found wetness and slickness and when she found that by now oversensitive little bundle of nerves there was no way back. She had to rub it like Rhawan had done with his tongue and Sefa tensed up and screamed and Wenja knew she was coming, Rhawan stopped moving, he just heaved for air and then he roared and shuddered, grasping onto Sefa so hard she had to get bruises. Hearing them, seeing them, it was too much and Wenja screamed too as it rushed through her for the third time in her life. She arched, legs trembling and her body felt as if everything suddenly had become slick and warm. Her nipples were hard and her nether lips felt swollen and right now she couldn't think about anything except what she just had seen. She tried to imagine herself there, on all four with Rhawan's cock buried deep within her and that mere thought sent her into yet another frenzy. She writhed as new waves raced through her and she felt how warm liquid did flow from her, squeezed out by the contractions within.

Rhawan leaned onto Sefa for a while, obviously exhausted and he caught his breath again and smiled, kissed the back of her neck gently. "Thank you Sefa, I needed that. You are wonderful as always."

Sefa giggled and got up, walked over to where the bowl of water still stood. Wenja did see that her inner thighs were wet and slick and there were drops of something white and obviously very sticky there. A salty strange smell filled the air and Wenja felt that she was blushing still, it had been so intimate and yet…it had been beautiful and she felt moved somehow. They had showed her their most vulnerable moments and she ought to be very grateful. And she felt wonderful, she couldn't deny it. Her body was at ease like never before and she giggled as aftershocks did rush through her. Sefa did wash herself thoroughly and Wenja saw that Rhawan still was very large but not hard anymore and he got a cloth and cleaned himself too, before pulling his pants back on. Sefa winked at him. "Thank you dear, Wenja has most certainly learned a lot tonight"

Wenja had to blush and nod and Rhawan sighed. "That is great, I cannot wait for us to return to Ohtanar though, if we don't hurry I will lose every ounce of self-control and have her, before her intended husband does"

Wenja gasped and Sefa just chuckled. "Oh don't worry Rhawan, I will guard her virtue like a hawk."

Rhawan just scoffed and straightened his tunic and Sefa got a devilish expression within her eyes. "But we do need more practice, next time I think Wenja can learn how to touch you"

Rhawan stopped and stared at Sefa, eyes huge and Wenja did see that in the slight darkness of the wagon they did glow, a soft glow like that of distant fireflies. "Are you nuts? If she touches me…"

Sefa giggled. "You will come all over her, I know. But she has to get used to that too, if you two hunks are to share her she's better get used to a lot we haven't even mentioned yet"

Rhawan rolled his eyes and groaned and evacuated the wagon, Sefa was chuckling. "Oh he loves the idea, he is just a bit overwhelmed by it, that is all"

Wenja looked down. "Won't Ahravan become jealous?"

Sefa shook her head. "Not a bit, I bet that word isn't even in his vocabulary."

Wenja found a cloth and washed too, she was over sensitive and tender and it felt strange but she couldn't regret this, she felt way too good. Sefa found a night gown and changed the sheets, she was grinning. "We will both sleep well tonight, by every God he is good."

Wenja looked down. "It doesn't hurt at all? He was so…large"

Sefa scoffed. "No, it feels just wonderful, like you are whole and filled and it is just right. I have to admit that the first time can be a bit uncomfortable but whence your body adapts there is no feeling quite like it"

Wenja slid in under the covers as Sefa finished making the bed. "I hear you"

Sefa got into the bed too, grinning . "And do you believe me?"

Wenja nodded, staring at the other woman. "I do, now"

Sefa blew out the lamp on her side. "Great, and now, let us sleep. This does most certainly make you tired"

Wenja had to agree, as soon as it became dark she was out like a candle and didn't even dream anything.

Chapter 6: The devil you know...

Ahravan had sent a lot of riders out to warn the tribes of the new danger, he was rather worried and couldn't help but miss Rhawan, he felt alone. Oh he had been the Ath'ir long before he even met Rhawan but that was a long time ago and he had grown accustomed to Rhawan's presence and support. Standing alone now felt strange and almost unnatural. He had his officers and brave warriors but it would have felt so much better if Rhawan had been there. He wondered when his Si'ish would return, and how things would become afterwards. He just prayed that the woman Rhawan had been sent to fetch was a decent person, he had had enough of dramatic womenfolk and if she was anything like his previous wife he would try to get rid of her somehow. The oracle said that great joy would come from this but he had his doubts still.

The fact that these small monsters had been sighted again was a cause for concern, he had thought that they were extinct and long gone but apparently some had survived the passage of time. Had that poor little village been an exception or would they have to prepare for more cases like this? He was feeling weary as he walked to the hut where the lead shaman lived, she was an elderly human with a somewhat dark attitude and a sarcastic view upon life but she was good at what she was doing and her connection with the world of spirits was undeniable. She was skinning a rabbit as he entered the hut and she gave him a swift glance and spat into the flames of her oven. "So, our great leader does honour this poor wretch with his presence, what do I owe the joy of this visit?"

Her voice was sharp and if you didn't know her you would think that she was trying to insult him, Ahravan did know her though and it was all just a way of testing people, of seeing how they would react. "I have come to seek your advice wise one"

She scoffed. "Advice, ha, advice is like crabs these days, freely shared and not at all welcome."

Ahravan had to grin, the eternal didn't have that problem, only the humans who didn't shave. "I wouldn't say that, I would welcome your knowledge"

She laid down the half skinned rabbit and tilted her head. "So, what is it that you want to know oh great one?"

The sarcasm in her voice could have made smaller men angry but Ahravan just grinned. "There has been a sighting of stinging demons again, a small village. Everybody dead"

She froze and her eyes told of disbelief. "Really? You burned everything I hope?"

He nodded. "Of course, no spawn could survive that blaze"

She sat down and pulled her shawl over her shoulders. "I don't like this Ahravan, no, I don't like this at all. I need to speak to the spirits, this has to mean something"

Ahravan frowned. "Are you sure?"

She nodded and grasped a small drum, it was round and flat and strange symbols were drawn onto the stretched leather. She found some pieces of bone in her pouch and laid them on the drum, then she started to chant and Ahravan shut up. She had to do this without being disturbed. She started to bang the underside of the drum and the bones were dancing over the leather, moving from symbol to symbol, her eyes were glittering in the darkness. Ahravan knew that she had some gifts his people didn't, elves do rarely die and to them the other side is something incomprehensible. Humans do die eventually and they had a steady faith in the afterlife and so she could tell him things he never would be able to see for himself.

She kept banging the drum, and he knew that she could read a lot out of the way the bones moved and how they landed, her eyes were distant and yet keen and after a while she stopped and laid the drum down, she tilted her head. "Be aware Ahravan, danger is coming. I can see it clearly, the spirits are upset. Darkness is coming, the gate is no longer closed"

He swallowed hard. "Are you serious?"

She nodded and put the bones back into the pouch, her movements were those of a young person, swift and precise. "Yes, more beasts will come, prepare."

He felt his heart speeding up." Is there anything we can do?"

She stared at him. "Yes, remember the dream, that is all the spirits said. And wait, when the time is right it is right. Not before."

He frowned. "I am afraid that doesn't tell me much at all."

She cocked her head. "Oh but it does, sooner or later you will understand. Go now, I feel that danger is nearer than you can imagine and it is a mundane one, not one created by the forces of darkness at all"

Ahravan felt confused. "What?"

She sighed. "The evil of men, you will see it soon, first hand."

She turned her back to him and he knew that this meant that she was done talking for now, he had to bow his head in respect and he left the cabin, feeling somewhat confused. Laupir was waiting for him outside of the hut, the man was holding a colt by the reins and he was petting the horse. Ahravan tilted his head. "Is that the son of Ayr'esh?"

Laupir grinned. "Aye, his first of last year. I am starting the training today, and I am having great expectations. Dhai is gonna be a good steed for sure"

Ahravan petted the colt too, he wasn't as tall as his sire and the temper seemed to be a more gentle one. "Have you managed to get hold of a Da'ith?"

Laupir nodded. "I sent a raven off to the south, to one I know and asked for them to send their best northwards. The answer was promising, they have one available and they will send it to you, as a tribute."

Ahravan smiled, he was looking forwards to this. "Excellent, if we are in luck it will arrive before my bride does"

Laupir smiled. "Probably. I know the riders from those tribes, they ride like the wind and their horses needs little rest at all."

Ahravan still felt worried, the evil of men? What had the shaman meant by that?

He went off to train some of the recruits and then he took a long ride around the camp with some of his riders. Some of the herders had

184

complained about a pack of wolves which was too bold for their own good and he ordered that the best guard dogs were set to watch the herds of sheep. The cattle could look after themselves, the long horned cows were aggressive and pity upon the wolf which believed that it could get a calf easily. It would end up skewered by sharp horns. The area hadn't much snow and the little that was had blown into drifts along the hills and the grass was still edible so the animals had plenty to feed upon. It was a good thing, he remembered winters when the herds had starved and summers when the heat had driven the animals mad. That evening there was a feast in honour of one of the gods the tribes did worship and everybody was cheerful and the wine did flow freely. Ahravan sat there and felt melancholic, he missed Rhawan again and didn't feel like he could contribute to the merriment. Word games were popular among the tribes and clans and usually one person would start and try to explain a word or expression just by body movements, the one who got it right had to continue and soon everybody were roaring with laughter. Ahravan did sigh and knew he had to be present for yet a few hours, it was his duty and he felt that he was getting a slight headache. When the music finally died down and the party goers did return to their huts Ahravan was drunk and felt miserable, he stumbled back to his own tent and fell onto the bed, missing Rhawan intensely and feeling very insecure when it came to the future.

Mjorr and Dagar had been travelling fast and they had reached one of the larger cities by now. It lay along the trading route and Mjorr was fascinated by it, he had never been this far from his home before and he was staring at everything with huge eyes. Dagar didn't like that, it told everybody that his son was new there and that was unwise. He told Mjorr to stay calm and pretend as if everything he saw was well known for him already. They weren't there to trade and they just passed through the city on their way. But many tried to talk to them still and Dagar knew how to deal with tenacious salesmen, he got rid of them one after the other. Mjorr was staring at the women in the streets, most were married and well above their youth but there were fair maidens too and also some women Dagar knew were whores. You could easily tell for they wore their hair in a particular manner and their gowns were too low cut to be decent. Mjorr was leering at them and Dagar felt a sting of anger, his son was a red blooded male but that didn't mean that he should think with his pecker instead of his head. It was unwise to let the contents of his pants point the way, but Mjorr did that all the time and Dagar had started to grow a bit tired of it. He was not that much better than his son when it came to sheer lust but he did know the meaning of the word discretion and he could control himself. Mjorr had little or no self-restraint when it came to females and Dagar was getting worried.

He had often had to cover up when Dagar had gone too far and either raped a girl or begotten a bastard somewhere but now he was starting to see just how out of control Mjorr really was. The lad was leering at the females they passed by, even those Dagar would categorize as darn ugly. He was staring to learn a lot about his son these days that he didn't appreciate at all. Dagar was a businessman, he was hard and played a tough game and there was no room for compassion or softness in his heart but he did love his son and heir like every man should and he was starting to feel some doubt. Had he been too soft on the lad?

Dagar didn't care about his daughter at all, she was there, that was all but the fact that she had run off had infuriated him since it made him look bad and ruined the chance of creating a good business connection. His honour dictated that he had to punish her, and to do that he had to find her. It irked him that they hadn't caught up with those goddamn eternal yet and he swallowed the doubt and the little voice in his head which claimed that perhaps that was for the best. He had seen those overly tall and overly pretty creatures and he wasn't an idiot, he knew power when he saw it, rather well as a matter of fact. So if they were to succeed they would have to be careful and play their game well, and be discrete and stealthy. Mjorr was everything but, everyone with eyes would notice the way he behaved and remember it too and Dagar was contemplating sending Mjorr back home but they didn't have enough men to escort him and lately the lad hadn't been very obedient at all. He would most likely just follow from a distance. Dagar didn't know of the men Mjorr had sent ahead of them and that was good for if he had then Mjorr would have experienced discipline first hand. Dagar had never laid a hand on his son

186

but something like that would have earned the lad a good spanking, beyond any doubt. Even if he was a grown man by now.

Mjorr was enjoying the sights, wolf whistling at some of the girls they rode by, making obscene gestures towards the less than honourable females they saw and having a good time. He was rather sure that the men he had hired were getting closer to the caravan and that they were ready to get rid of that goddamn cunt. He should have killed her himself, hid her somewhere. That would have been easy now in the winter and if she was found come the thaw nobody would think it was anything else than an accident. He was angry at himself for she hadn't been that good at all, he had had way better many times.

But travelling was fun and interesting and he found that he forgot about their goal rather often, he wished that he could return to these cities when they were done, there was so much to see there and so much pussy to fuck and he was sure he would be very popular there. He had money, he had power and he was young and rather handsome too, oh yes, the females would flock around him. He grinned to himself, they had stayed at an inn some nights ago and he had given his father the one room they had been able to rent, he had slept in the hay and he hadn't been alone. A few gold coins had ensured that the stable master's daughter and her friend had spent some hours with him and if he had been a bit rough with them, well, who cared? They were whores, it wasn't as if he had taken their virtue or anything and if getting fucked in the ass went against their principles he didn't care. That way he wouldn't risk any more bastards. He knew he had some but he didn't care, they were nothing he cared about. Some day he would have to marry of course to have a legitimate heir but that was far ahead in the future. He bet his father would chose a bride for him but the old man would have to reconsider that, he would pick a spouse when he was good and ready, not before. And that had to be a woman of exceptional beauty, chaste and rich and obedient. Yes, preferably some noble woman, he was sure he would be able to increase their wealth and influence enough for the nobility to accept them.

Mjorr was daydreaming and they rode out of the city gates and Dagar was getting a bit tired. He wasn't young anymore and spending day after day on horseback was taking its toll of him, he felt it in his bones and he ached in places he normally wouldn't ache at all. It was the price to pay for all this but he didn't like it, he had always been strong and vigorous and being reminded of his age wasn't funny at all. He stayed straight and rode well but he knew that it would get worse, way worse. The valley they were in was rather steep and the roads treacherous so they had to ride carefully and here and there they had to stop to remove snow and ice from the horses hooves. Dagar did this himself but Mjorr let one of the men do it for him, he didn't even dismount and Dagar knew he had spoiled the lad. They were rich and they had influence but that didn't mean that you could sit on your arse and do nothing and that was just what Mjorr intended to do. Dagar was sad he only had one son, if he had had more the competition would have shaped them into strong men, hard men. Mjorr was too used to getting away with everything he did and Dagar had been too proud to see how he had allowed the boy's flaws to become a real problem. When they got back home he would have to change things, a lot.

When the group reached the large lake known as Aivarhat Mjorr had started to become bored again, there were few people travelling at this time of the year and he had started to feel a bit strange. They stopped to rest the horses and that was when Mjorr got the first taste of what karma was all about. He had to take a piss and got off his horse and sauntered over to the bushes by the road. Normally he wasn't shy at all but he didn't want to flash the men they had brought since they could get jealous of his endowment. In truth Mjorr wasn't that well-endowed at all but nobody had ever dared to tell him that. He got his pride out of his pants and relaxed and that was when it hit, a piercing burning pain unlike anything he had ever felt before. He yelped and stared down, the joy of his life was sore and a bit red and was that puss?

Mjorr cussed, so bad it was a miracle he didn't spontaneously combust there and then. He had caught some sort of venereal disease from those two cunts! Fuck it. He couldn't tell his dad for then Dagar would blow a fuse and demand to know what he had done to get sick. He finished peeing while moaning and whimpering, it felt like he was pissing fire! There had to be something he could do to get rid of this? He would ask the men, they had been around and he bet that they had experienced something like this. But not his dad, no way. Mjorr tucked himself back inn, shivering and sweating and he just hoped that it wouldn't get any worse than this. Perhaps some good brandy would cure it? Yes for sure, that would fix just about anything, Dagar did have a bottle in his saddle bags. Come the nightfall he would help himself to some, then the problem would be solved.

The morning after a feast used to be very peaceful, in fact it was strange if anyone got up and out of bed before noon. Ahravan woke up to the feeling of having a head made of lead and a tongue covered with cotton, or at least that was how it felt. He cussed and sat up, his head was spinning and he felt a bit nauseous. He had tossed back too many goblets of wine last night, that was for darn sure. He could drink a lot and he often did too but this? Oh by the Gods, he had downed several bottles. What had gotten into him? Except the wine that is? He wobbled over to where he kept his washing equipment and poured some cold water into a bowl before washing his face. It did sting a bit since the water was at freezing temperature but it did refresh him and he washed his entire body thoroughly, not just his face. It did help a lot, then he got redressed and found some drinking water and forced himself to drink as much as he could before he prepared for the day. There would be no training this day, most of the young ones were in no shape to train and he was pretty sure that this also was true for the more mature warriors.

He found some cheese and bread and sat down to eat, the cheese was the soft almost buttery kind he was very fond off and he enjoyed the slightly nutty flavour. The twelve clans did make many types of cheese, from a sort made from goat milk which was stored for years and so hard you needed a good knife to even carve tiny slices out of it to a type which was so soft it was almost like sour cream in texture. But all were delicious and he had to think about that one time when they had visited some tribe living to the far south and it made him cringe. They too ate cheese, lots and lots of cheese and their speciality was a type which had smelled like old unwashed socks and underwear and the taste had been even worse, but they loved it so it had to be something you had to get used to. He was planning on going for a ride, just to clear his head, the weather was nice now with a clear sky and no wind so he was rather sure that it would cure his headache rather fast. He had several good riding horses beside Ayr'esh and he wanted to take his favourite mare for a ride. She was a very nice dapple grey with a muscular rear and an elegant build and she was the fastest horse he owned, at least over shorter distances. Ahravan was thinking about Greyflower and a trip to the nearest river as he got his cloak and boots on, sunny weather didn't mean warm on this time of the year and you had to dress well. He attached his sword and his two long knives to his belt and found the short rider's bow he always carried if he was out on his own.

The camp was relatively quiet still as he emerged from his hut, some kids were running around playing and squealing and some of the elderly humans had gathered by some tables to chat and play a board game. It was rather complicated and you needed both dice, some very elaborately carved figurines and more than a hundred small balls in four different colours. Ahravan loved that game but he had never been any good at it, there were just too many possible moves and the rules were numerous as well. He was heading towards the corral where the riding horses were and he stopped by the tent where they kept the saddles and tack, he owned several very good and valuable saddles and his people were extremely conscious about the tack the horses wore. They would never make a horse wear tack which could harm them in any way and most of the elves rode without a bit, just a halter and some simple reins. He had seen way too many horses with sores and injuries from ill fitted saddles and also animals with their gums and mouths torn by sharp bits so in this city any damage to a horse was regarded as just as bad as damage to a person and it would be punished accordingly.

Greyflower was a very ticklish mare and she didn't like to wear a saddle at all so he usually rode her with just a pad and a girdle, she accepted that but nothing more elaborate and he was humming as he strolled towards the corral.

He had started to open the gate when a call was heard and he turned around and stared, one of the citizens came running towards him, obviously upset and he now saw that some people were gathering near one of the huts on the outskirts of the city. He closed the gate and tilted

190

his head, the person who approached him was an elf, a rather spindly looking fellow with very long blond hair and soft brown eyes. Ahravan didn't remember his name but knew that this one made a living embroidering leather and cloth and designing carpets. The male stopped and he was heaving for air. "Ath'ir, I apologize for interrupting, but my children…they have gone missing…"

Ahravan frowned. "Missing?"

The male nodded. "They weren't in their beds this morning"

Ahravan hung the saddle pad on the fence. "How many are they and how old?"

The elf swallowed hard, there was fear in his eyes. "It is my youngest daughter and my son, she is twelve and he is fifteen"

Ahravan felt a sting of worry, a twelve years old elf is the equivalent to a four year old human and fifteen was a five year old. They were very young indeed. "Tell me more"

The elf nodded. "I have two more daughters but they are adults, and they have their own hut. Both the children were fast asleep when my wife and I returned from the feast and we sent the baby sitter back home. But they were both gone when we woke up, oh Gods!"

Ahravan tried to think, two kids of that age couldn't have gotten far and someone had to have seen them? "Is there someone they could have gone to visit? A friend perhaps? A relative?"

The male shook his head. "We have already checked, nobody has seen them"

Ahravan followed the elf back to the group, a weeping female was in the centre of it and he realized that this was the wife of the male. She did look terrified and Ahravan walked over. "What were they wearing?"

The female sobbed. "They had taken their coats and boots, but nothing else. Oh Gods, please, find my children!"

Ahravan saw that several of his warriors were approaching them, curious and alarmed and he sighed. They would need to organize a search party. "Children will often be impulsive, there isn't something they have seen recently which they would seek out? Somewhere you have been? Children that young doesn't think very far you know"

The father was thinking and the mother blinked and then she gasped. "The small holt east of here, we were there three days ago to pick nuts, it could be that they wanted to return to that place for there were some very playful squirrels there and they said they wanted to go back and play some more"

Ahravan snapped his fingers. "There we have it, they have probably gone off to find the squirrels then, and they don't have a perception of distance at that age."

The father did look relieved. "They cannot have gotten far"

Ahravan shook his head. "No, find a horse and we will ride out now, I bet we will find them rather fast"

Some of the warriors did join them and Ahravan rode Greyflower and let the father borrow one of his other horses, a tall brown gelding. The Holt was an hour's ride away and Ahravan felt pretty confident that they would find the two rather easily. They would be cold and tired and probably scared too but there shouldn't be too many dangers out there at this time of the year and nobody had seen wolves or other predators this close to the camp. The wind had removed what little snow there had been so there were no tracks to follow but they spread out and rode slowly and Ahravan saw that the father was swearing to himself. "What is bothering you my friend?"

The male shook his head. "I drank too much last night, as did my wife too. We were drunk, if we had stayed sober we would have woken up when the kids tried to get dressed"

Ahravan sighed deeply. "Don't think about that, children are often very good at sneaking away when the parents least of all expect it. I did sneak out of my parents hut when I was just ten and they found me playing in the dog pen, my mother had been awake and working on an embroidery the whole time."

They rode at a steady pace over the frozen plain and the riders made sure that every bush and every rock was examined, even the snowdrifts were checked for footprints but there wasn't anything to be seen. Ahravan started to get a bit confused, they hadn't seen anything yet and by now they should have caught up with the kids. Had he been wrong in his assumption? Had the children taken a different path after all?

192

The father looked worried again and Ahravan stood up on the horse's back to get a better over view of the surroundings. He saw nothing and the Holt was already visible in the distance. The last stretch was completely flat and there were nothing to be seen at all, just untouched grass.

The male was urging his horse on. "Fheliel will murder me if something has happened to them, it was I who convinced her that it was alright to have some more wine"

Ahravan shook his head again. "Listen, you cannot blame yourself Erabhan, it isn't your fault. Children are rather rambunctious at that age"

Erabhan did sent him a look filled with despair and the other riders were circling them, looking for tracks. One of the warriors came over, he reined in his horse and bowed his head. "My lord, there are no tracks here, the snow is pristine. Even if they strayed off course we would have seen some tracks by now"

Ahravan took a deep breath and Erabhan let out a thin wail of despair. "Pick two swift riders, ride to the Holt and check it, then return to us, I feel we may be looking in the wrong place"

The rider did nod and turned the horse and he took off with two others at his heels. Ahravan wheeled Greyflower around and the father was grey faced and trembling. "Is there somewhere else they could have gone? Some place they would be attracted to?"

The male shook his head. "Not that I know off, but…"

He fell silent for a few seconds, then he went even paler than before. "Oh Gods, the baby sitter, she took them to the river a week ago, to wash clothes. They could have been heading in that direction?"

Ahravan took a deep breath, the river wasn't ice covered yet and very dangerous. "Let's ride, everybody, ride hard"

He spurred the mare and she took off like an arrow from a good bow, the powerful hind legs did drive the animal up to an insane speed. Ahravan rode to the camp again, there he switched to another horse, a long legged colt and Erabhan caught up with him just as he got in the saddle. Ahravan did shout orders, he sent riders out in every direction and they were to check the entire area around the city for fresh tracks, he didn't trust that the kids had been that predictable after all and as he rode towards the river he felt a knot of fear in his gut. He was rather sure that this would end badly.

The river wasn't that far from the camp, and it was wide and the current strong but it wasn't very deep, you could easily ride across it without any problems but a small child didn't stand a chance if it fell in. The women had found a perfect place for washing, it was an area with smooth rocks which tilted at a very low angle into the water and here and there were loose rocks where you could sit or hang your laundry. Some baskets were left there and also some long hard pieces of wood which were used as a tool to get the filth out of the clothes. Some buckets of soap did also stand there where they had been left and Ahravan did dismount and started to walk around. He was the first to arrive and there were no signs there of anyone having visited the place since the day before. He saw no fresh foot prints in the sand along the river's edge and he ran along it for a while. He was getting more and more confused, where could the children be? The camp was surely searched by now, not a basket or mat unturned and even the tents where kids had no business being were being examined. And they were not by the river? Erabhan did weep by now, he was shaking and Ahravan tried to understand, he had never been a father and he had never experienced the loss of a family member in such a manner but if something had happened to Rhawan he would become very affected indeed. "They are not here, they must have taken off in some other direction"

Erabhan shook his head. "But why, and where to? There is just the plain, nothing which can tempt a child?"

Ahravan was grimacing, he tried to imagine being a toddler, new to the world and infinitely curious. The children of the twelve clans were trustful and fearless, they were used to being looked after and didn't fear anything really. It was a dangerous thing in some manners but being innocent is one of the glories of being a child. Ahravan did mount again. "Ride back, comfort your wife. Nobody will rest until they are found."

Erabhan sobbed. "I have lost them, I know I have lost them"

Ahravan didn't quite know what to say. "I am sure we will find them, how far could they have gotten?"

194

He kicked the horse into a trot and started making circles around the washing site, just to check that the kids hadn't reached the river somewhere else. He rode for a long time but saw nothing and when he did return to the city there were people everywhere. Many had ridden out to help in the search while others were just waiting for news and many were worried. There were many children in the city and the parents were naturally afraid that something similar would happen to their little ones. The day did slide by with the speed of a slug, everybody was on edge, waiting for some sort of news and when the sun set the atmosphere was one of despair. Nothing had been seen and Ahravan was starting to feel that this was something way different from what he had first believed. The children couldn't have gotten that far off on their own? Or could they?

It was dark when one of the scouts rode into camp on a horse which was close to collapsing with fatigue, the rider dismounted and his eyes were wild. "I have seen something, a camp fire I think, by the cliffs north of the Wolf's pond. And I think I heard screams"

Ahravan was on his feet. "You are alone?"

The rider nodded, he was a young human and didn't carry any weapons. "Yes my lord, had I ridden with anyone I would have investigated. But I deemed it more wise to ride back here for backup"

Ahravan patted him on his back. "A very wise decision indeed!"

He turned around, waved his hand. "Gather all my best warriors, and bring my horse"

Erabhan came running. "I am going too"

Ahravan laid his hands on the male's shoulders. "I wouldn't think that this is wise my friend, if something…"

Erabhan grasped Ahravan's collar with both hands, the eyes were wild. "I have to know! You cannot stop me from coming along"

Ahravan sighed. "Right, I know but do as you are being told."

Erabhan nodded and one of the warriors came running with Ayr'esh. The huge stallion was pawing the ground and Ahravan mounted swiftly. He saw that the lad had been given another very fast horse, a white stallion by the name of Windseeker who belonged to Rhawan. What he wouldn't have given to have his Si'ish by his side now. By now there were almost fifty riders gathered and the youth looked excited but also nervous. "It is a long ride my lord"

Ahravan sent him a swift smile. "I know, but we can ride fast even in darkness, just hang on"

He let the great warhorse speed forth and the others followed him like one. Reaching that cliff would take hours, even at this speed.

They left their horses by a small groove of bushes, the animals were well trained and wouldn't whinny and Ahravan ordered the lad to stay with the animals, he had a nagging feeling within his guts, this was not boding well. They saw the camp fire, it was a distance away and looked like a deranged firefly from where they were. The warriors were skilled and experienced and Ahravan turned to them. "I will move closer, you follow. If this is something which require that we make our presence known I will hoot like a burrowing owl, got it?"

They all nodded and Erabhan was trembling. "What is this?"

Ahravan swallowed hard. "I do not know, yet. But if someone were screaming we should investigate, so, be quiet and if this is just some innocent travellers we won't even let them know we were here"

He moved forth, as an elf he had excellent night vision and he had no problems finding his way. He heard voices, laughter even. He cocked his head, the voices were male and human and he closed his eyes, concentrated. Some horses were tied not far from the camp, small sturdy animals and he could smell them. He walked over to a huge rock, peeked forth from behind it. It was five humans and they were poorly clad and he could smell sweat and smoke and meat gone bad. These were men without a tribe, probably outlaws and he felt a sting of anger. Then he heard something which made him freeze, it was a sort of whimper and it was coming from the other side of the camp. He knew his men were behind him and he did sneak forth with the speed and stealth of a huge cat.

The camp was a simple one, just a fire and some bedrolls and not even a real tent. He heard movements and more whimpers and he did crouch down beside a bush. The light was very bad there but he saw. A man was laying there and Ahravan saw only his legs and his butt for his upper

196

body was hidden behind a rock. But that butt was moving in a very tell-tale manner and Ahravan could barely make out the shape of something underneath the man. He could smell blood now and seed and fear, heard the sound of flesh smashing into flesh and heard the man grunt and pant. Ahravan felt cold to the core, this couldn't be true? No, this…this wasn't real. He got up, slowly, moved closer so he could confirm what he otherwise wouldn't wish to see at all.

The rock shielded him, the man couldn't see in the dark the way an elf does and what Ahravan saw almost made him reveal his whereabouts, much against his own will. The small body was almost entirely covered by the man's bulk, and Ahravan saw the naked skin which looked like snow in the darkness. The child was on its stomach, and the man was eagerly thrusting into the small torso, groaning in anticipation of his release. Ahravan blinked, he just…How could anyone… He had never anticipated something like this, not at all. The man tensed up and roared in delight, the body shuddering. Ahravan started to breathe again, he felt a surge of white hot rage and sorrow burst through him and he hooted twice, knew that his warriors would hear him. He couldn't stand it, couldn't stand seeing this. He did draw his blade and with a swift move he did slide forth, kicked the jerking man off the tiny body and rammed his blade down through the man's chest. The man let out a sort of hoarse roar and trembled before he went limp and Ahravan felt like throwing up.

The warriors did reveal themselves and grasped onto the five other men, swiftly subduing them with ropes. Ahravan looked down, it was the small boy who laid there, the body didn't move and Ahravan felt tears stinging his eyes. He rolled him over gently, trying not to look at the bloody thighs and the visual evidence of what had been done to him. The eyes were open and stared straight up, empty and frozen in an expression of horrified confusion. It made Ahravan whimper in horror, the boy was still breathing but judging by the amount of blood there he was fading fast.

Erabhan came running, he stopped when he saw his son and let out the most horrible sound Ahravan had ever heard in his life, a terrible piercing wail he never would have been able to believe that an elf was capable of. The male fell to his knees and grasped the body of his son, rocked it back and forth, screaming in agony and sorrow. Ahravan felt cold, as if his bones had turned to ice and he walked over to the other warriors. They were pale and the rage was visible on their faces. "Where is the girl?"

The men didn't answer, one of them did spit and Ahravan nodded to the warriors, two disappeared into the darkness to go looking and before long they returned. One of them carried the body, covered with his cloak. The warrior was crying. "She…she lay by their horses….My lord…"

Ahravan waved his hand at one of the elves. "Siarhan, you are a healer, what are her injuries"

Siarhan nodded and used the cloak to hide the body as he examined it swiftly. When he was done he was pale as ash and his face wet from his tears. "My lord, they have…She is torn apart, must have bled out"

One of the men spat on the ground and grinned. "They say elven cunt is the best and I must say that both the cunt and the ass was nice indeed"

Ahravan was breathing heavily and Erabhan was wailing still, some of the warriors wrapped the two bodies into their cloaks and lead him away, he needed to calm down. Ahravan felt how white hot anger filled his entire body, he would show no mercy now. "So, you kidnapped two children just to sate your own perverted lust."

One of them men whimpered. "We saw them outside of that camp, heading for the river. It was easy"

Ahravan closed his eyes, his heart was beating like a war drum. "I have faced evil before, but nothing like this. You are to be punished by our laws, here and now!"

The men did struggle against their bonds but elven rope is extremely strong, they didn't stand a chance. The warriors were shocked and disgusted and in disbelief and they still heard Erabhan crying, he hadn't been sedated and they didn't know how to deal with this at all. Ahravan turned to two of the elves, he felt how his voice was tense and harsh. "We need spears, five of them"

The two warriors just nodded and took off towards where the horses were hidden, they had brought their long spears for they could be handy if they came across wild boar or other animals. Most carried one and they were usually very well made and rather heavy. The human warriors carried spears of less length than their elven counterparts but Ahravan had asked for the elven type now. They were almost four meters tall and more like a lance than a spear really. The small group of outlaws hadn't yet realized what they were up for, they were cussing and trying to get away from the elves still and Ahravan stared at them with hard eyes. They were scum, less than that. He had never believed that anyone could be that wicked. He had seen evil enough but that had been of a different type, the monsters were created that way, they didn't chose to be a terrible threat to everything and everyone. It was their nature. This on the other hand…He couldn't even start to comprehend what it was all about.

After a while the two came back with spears and Ahravan told them to remove the metal blades at the end but shape the wood into blunt points. The leader was staring at them with narrow eyes, he didn't understand how these spears could be useful for anything without a spear head and Ahravan walked over to where the man was sitting, the guy did stink and his tunic was so dirty it could have stood on its own. Ahravan kicked the man over, the anger was still seething within him and he needed to get some of it out. He did notice something which hung around the man's neck, a sort of medallion. He bent down and snapped the rawhide string it was attached to, the medallion did look rather primitive but it was made from bronze and he recognized the symbol on it, a sort of disk with several arms coming out of it. It as a symbol connected to the monsters, to the old magic and those who had been on the side of evil back then. He hissed and hid the medallion in his pocket, it was a wicked thing. "Where did you get that, answer me!"

The man just growled. "From your mother!"

Ahravan kicked the man again, under the chin and he spat blood and broken teeth and shook his head. "Speak, or I will make sure that your death is the slowest and most agonizing one you can imagine."

The man growled. "I found it, in a cave near the white mountains"

Ahravan felt a surge of nervous energy, the White Mountains was in the direction where the monsters had come from the first time they entered this world and some said that it was where the centre of the power had been. The medallion could be very important then, a relic of some sorts. He bent down and stared the man in the eyes. "So, you found it in a cave, what else was in there?"

The man looked down. "Some dead bodies, had been dead for decades, some sorts of priests judging by the clothes. And a small crate with coins. Nothing else"

Ahravan stored it in his memory, for some reason it made him feel unwell. He got back up and nodded to his men. "We will start with that one over there, he is the largest of them"

They pulled the man forth and he screamed and fought but to no prevail. Ahravan's warriors did strip him down to his skin and the human was a pathetic sight, the body soft and hairy and the legs spindly and weak. Ahravan growled. "I follow the law of my people as I punish you for murder, you will die as you have killed"

The man stared at them, wide eyed and confused until they bent him down over a rock and got the spear ready. Then he started to scream and struggle even more and Ahravan didn't feel any sort of sympathy at all, they had all abused the children, no mercy would be given. The warriors did push the blunt point into the man's rear and his screams became desperate screeches of agony and fear. The other four started to realize what their fate would be and begged for mercy but Ahravan did close his ears completely. They didn't deserve mercy at all. When the spear was lodged in the man's ass two of the elves did flip the spear up and since the man had his arms tied behind his back he could do nothing. His own weight made sure that he was slowly being impaled upon the spear and he was jerking and kicking and wailing as the shaft slid deeper and deeper into the body and pierced its way through tissue and organs.

They made sure that the spear wouldn't tip over and then they grasped the next one. It was the same procedure and Ahravan stood there with a face made from stone and just watched as the men were impaled one by one, their screams could be heard all over the plains. Erabhan came over when it was the leaders turn, his tears had dried and now Ahravan saw black hatred in the elf's eyes. "Let me do it, I need to do it"

Ahravan swallowed and nodded "Of course, it is your privilege"

The grieving father grasped the last spear and weighed it in his hands, the others did strip the leader and he was bawling with fear now. The man had pissed himself and Ahravan saw that he was far from being brave now that he faced the end. The others were still alive, it took time to die this way and it was a terrible agony they had to endure but it was the law.

Erabhan did didn't just jab the spear inn, like it had been done with the others. He did push the spear end against the man's rectum almost gently, slowly pushing inn and then pulling out again and the man wailed and tried to resist but that was hopeless. Erabhan was growling. "Does this give you pleasure human? The same pleasure you took from raping my children?"

The man was gaping as the elf pushed the spear inn, Erabhan was strong and Ahravan hadn't believed that he could get that much of it inn all on his own. The leader's eyes were bulging and his mouth was wide open, he was making some ghastly choking sounds. Erabhan nodded at the others. "Raise the spear, but at an angle, let it be slow!"

The warriors did raise the spear and unlike the other it didn't point straight up, they aimed it somewhat lower so it would take more time before the man died. Ahravan didn't say anything, he just stood there, watching. The men were writhing in agony, blood seeping down the spear shafts and he knew that sooner or later the spears would pierce something vital and kill them. Ahravan turned to the warriors. "Five of you, bring Erabhan and the bodies back home, the rest stays here with me until these pieces of filth are dead"

Five of the riders immediately obeyed and Ahravan felt tired. The shock of what he had seen lingered still, he hadn't truly believed that humans could be that cruel. But now he knew and he did miss Rhawan even more than before, he forced himself to remain calm, to think straight. It was beyond him how anyone could be this cruel and without remorse, had these men had sick minds? No elf would ever do anything like this, it was simply impossible. Oh he had encountered crime before, some really nasty ones in fact but nothing had ever been as terrible as this. He just stood there like a statue, motionless and cold until the last of the men did draw his final breath. Then he went over to his horse again and found some wine in a flask from the saddle bags, he took some quick sips, just to wet his tongue. This had turned his mouth dry. The warriors were waiting for his orders and he got up onto the horse with a grimace.

"Let the bodies hang, they do not deserve a grave. Let the wolves and the vultures feast"

He turned the horse and let it trot towards the camp again, he didn't look back even once, now he had to reassure his people that they were safe and that nothing like this could happen again. He had a heavy lump in his gut though, telling him that maybe this wasn't the end, but the start of something really truly bad.

Wenja did wake up with a feeling of being made from lead, she stretched and yawned and noticed that she was alone in the bed, Sefa was already up and judging by the light which seeped in through the windows she had slept for many hours. It was already bright daylight outside and she swore a bit and got up, she felt silly still. How was she to face Rhawan now? She got dressed and washed herself and then she exited the wagon only to see that everybody were busy breaking camp. The wagon she was in was the only one not hitched up to the horses yet and she blushed when she realized that she had delayed them by oversleeping. Guards and drivers were scurrying around and Wenja hurried over to the camp fire where Imh was holding out a bowl of porridge for her. She took it with gratitude, her stomach was growling and she felt hollow from hunger. The activities of the night before had certainly worn her out and made her so very hungry. Imh smiled and found some fresh goat milk too and Wenja did swallow it down, feeling parched as well. Theka came over, she was frowning and her face was a bit red, she grasped a kettle of warm water and Imh did look at her with questions written all over her face. "What is the matter dear?"

Theka growled. "That silly girl, such an idiot!"

Wenja blinked. "Prina?"

Theka nodded. "Oh yes, an idiot. She cannot continue like this, she simply can't"

Wenja finished her porridge, it was delicious as always. "What has she done now?"

Theka sighed and made a gesture of slight despair. "She refuses to eat, thinks she is getting fat! She is pregnant, by the gods, she needs to eat! But no, she refuses to see the truth"

Imh did look down. "She has suffered too much Theka, her mind did shatter. She is not capable of accepting the truth so do not try to force it onto her. That may cause her to go insane completely"

Theka smacked her lips together, she still looked angry. "I know that but there is a baby, she has to consider the safety of her child don't you think?"

Wenja did clear her throat. "She isn't capable of understanding that there is a child growing in her womb, accepting that means accepting what was done to her and she prefers to ignore it"

Imh scoffed. "Like a horse wearing blinkers, heading into disaster! Oh sweet gods, someone has to do something soon. She will most certainly snap whence the baby has to be born"

Wenja frowned. "Can the healers do something to help her?"

Theka shrugged. "They can heal the body, but hardly the mind. The shamans on the other hand, now they know a few tricks."

Wenja felt a surge of hope. "That is wonderful, what sorts of tricks?"

Theka did look uncertain all of a sudden. "I don't know, but I think it involves drugs, and meditation and some techniques they keep to themselves. But they do sometimes work miracles, I have seen it. At least they should be able to help her come to terms with it all, she will harm herself and the child if she doesn't start to use her head"

Wenja bit her lower lip. "Is it really that bad?"

Theka nodded. "Yes, there are things you should stay away from when you are expecting and she doesn't, and there are also things you should do which she refuses to even think about. I pray we reach the city soon, she is getting closer to her due day by each sunset, soon she cannot lie to herself anymore"

Wenja remembered Prina as she had been back in the village, a mere shadow of a person and she couldn't really imagine anyone being worse than that but maybe that was possible. There had been a glimpse of madness in Prina's eyes at times, when she faced challenges. Wenja got back to the wagon just as Sefa came sauntering, she was grinning and had her hair gathered in a high bun on top of her head and her arms were bare. She sat down next to Wenja as the wagon started to move. "I had to help the men clean some fish, one was out fishing in the river early this morning and caught quite a lot. I hope I don't stink too bad"

Wenja shook her head. "You smell good, I cannot feel any stench at all"

Sefa just giggled and stretcher herself like a huge cat, she did look very relaxed and Wenja folded her legs up underneath her and tilted her head. "So, is there more I need to know about life on the plains?" Sefa made a grimace. "Like what? "

Wenja shrugged. "The food?"

The dark haired woman grinned. "Ah yes, the food. You have lived in poverty haven't you?"

Wenja nodded and Sefa suddenly looked very important. "You will never have to starve again but I am warning you. Some of the dishes out there can be a bit unusual, or even shocking to some."

Wenja had to raise an eyebrow in astonishment. "Shocking? What can be so shocking about food? I heard what Rhawan said about fish but…"

Sefa gestured outwards. "Yes, that clan does have some odd ways to preserve and serve fish but they aren't the only ones. The plains aren't a rich area Wenja, nobody is farming out there, the soil is too poor and the weather is too unstable. Hunting and gathering is what everybody does to stay alive so the food changes with the areas we enter"

Wenja did lean back against the wall, the wagon was moving a bit around and she had gathered some pillows around herself to avoid getting bruised by the sudden jolts. "Do tell please"

Sefa got into a more comfortable position as well, she straightened her skirts and grinned. "One of the things you will have to get used to is the meat from wild goats and gazelles, that is the most common meat we use. There are also other types of meat but they aren't used that often, like rabbits and wild fowl, and sometimes horse"

Wenja frowned. "Horse?!"

She didn't like the idea of those huge beautiful steeds being transformed to a meal, the very idea made her cringe. Back home nobody ate horse, it was a sacrilege for a horse was so valuable nobody would kill it until it was so old it was inedible.

Sefa nodded. "Aye, I see your expression and don't worry, we do not slaughter our steeds. But there is a species of wild horse living in the wild hills and they are small and stocky and way too wild to be tamed and sometimes we do hunt a few. It is needed, their numbers cannot get too large for then they start to deteriorate in so many ways."

Wenja was confused. "Deteriorate?"

Sefa nodded. "Yes, by inbreeding, the stallions won't let any new males near his mares and thus the herds can become very weak and even deformed. We cull off the worst ones"

Wenja could understand that, inbreeding was a bad thing, every farmer knew that and she remembered how careful her father had been when mating the sheep each winter, he kept lists of which ewe was related to which ram and he never allowed those closely related to breed.

"I guess that is bad, but how bad does it get really?"

Sefa made a grimace. "The worst herd we have come across had been led by the same stud for twenty summers, all of the mares were his own daughters and only a few had been stolen from other herds. We had to shoot five mares and all the new foals that spring, some of the foals were born blind and one lacked both ears and tail"

Wenja gasped and Sefa shrugged again. "But enough of that, horse is eaten very rarely so don't worry about that. We have other dishes which are way more interesting"

Wenja made a grimace. "Such as?"

Sefa smiled. "I will give you an example, it is very delicious and I am quite sure it will be served at your wedding"

Wenja cringed a bit, she had almost forgotten the reason she was there. Sefa giggled "It is always served at weddings because it is said to increase the vigour of the newlyweds. "

Wenja rolled her eyes. "So, what is it?"

Sefa leaned a bit forth. "There is a sort of wild melon which grows in some river valleys, it is rather large and quite rare to come by so it is carefully picked when we do come across ripe ones. It is maybe the length of a grown man and the shape is interesting"

Wenja sighed and rolled her eyes. "Don't tell me it is shaped like…"

Sefa nodded vigorously and with a huge grin on her face. "Like a huge cock, yes! It was almost sacred to the old tribes"

Wenja had to snicker. "So, the huge melon which looks like a phallus is eaten?"

Sefa shook her head. "Oh no, not just like that. You cannot eat it as it is, that tastes just ghastly and it will give a very bad case of stomach trouble. No, it has to be fermented first, and then fried in oil"

Wenja blinked. "Really? Melon fried in oil?!"

Sefa nodded. "Yes, an oil made from a sort of nuts which is quite common here on the plains. The meat is green and a bit stringy but after that it becomes very tender and sweet and then it is rolled in spices and dried for a week"

Wenja was intrigued, back at home nobody spent that much time preparing a meal, food was to be eaten there and then, easy as that. "Dried?"

Sefa nodded. "Yes, then the whole thing is drenched in a mixture of honey, water and juice and baked into a sort of thin pastry, rolled in syrup made from maple juice and baked in an oven very slowly for half a day. The result is to die for"

Wenja had to think about the best meals Sina had made, roasted lamb with hardly any other spices than what their poor mountain farm could provide and the results had been tasty but lean and there had never been more than a mere taste for everybody. She just hoped that they would be better off now and that they didn't have to go to bed hungry again. "You have tried it?"

Sefa nodded with starry eyes. "Oh yes, many times, and believe me, it is so good it is sinful."

Wenja saw that the wagon had changed course, now they were following a narrow river and the terrain was relatively flat. She heard the guards chatting and the horses were moving relatively fast. It was as if they sensed that the journey was getting shorter by the day. "Do you fry things a lot?"

Sefa grinned. "Yes, the dwarves did teach us that art, they have these clay ovens which can be taken apart for transport and they are ingenious. Some stuff is baked in them while much is fried in oil too. There is a container on top of each oven to pour the oil into, thus you can both bake and fry stuff at the same time"

Wenja found the subject intriguing. "What about vegetables? Do you use that?"

She had never been used to vegetables, they were a rare luxury but one she did love. "We have lots of wild vegetables yes, roots and herbs and berries, and of course nuts and stuff. And some sorts of bulbs too"

Wenja frowned. "Bulbs?"

Sefa drew a huge round shape in the air with her hands. "Yes, and one is popular in particular, it is a type which grows only a few places though"

Wenja had never seen bulbs before, only roots and she was curious. "It is edible?"

Sefa nodded. "Yes, and very large, like one of the wagons. It grows for many years under ground and then it sends forth a stem with a single flower and the flower does smell like a rotting carcass by the way. That is how we discover them. Then we have to hurry and dig it up for the moment the flower starts to wither the bulb dies too and it rots very fast. But whence it is dug up we cut it into pieces and it is so good. It tasted like strawberries and honey and we can dry it too and ground it up into a sort of flour. The juice is also used, it is fermented into a sort of wine which does have quite a kick."

Wenja made a grimace. "You seem to be fond of fermented stuff"

Sefa laughed. "Oh yes, you will have to get used to it too. The juice of that bulb is also seen as sacred in some ways, it is rather similar to certain male bodily fluids in appearance"

Wenja had to think for a second before she understood, then she blushed and Sefa giggled. "In the very start of the twelve clans brides would be rubbed down with that juice before their wedding night, to become fertile. It is a sticky mess so be glad you don't have to endure that"

Wenja had to laugh. "I guess I have a lot to be grateful for"

Sefa nodded. "So, tell me about the cuisine of your home, I bet it was mostly mutton, mutton and more mutton?"

Wenja felt a sudden urge to giggle violently. "Oh yes. And mostly old and dry rams!"

Sefa got into another position on the bed. "Go on, tell me more"

The three men Mjorr had hired were former mercenaries and such were normally in short scum and cutthroats who gladly would have murdered their own mother for a few coins. Mjorr had met them in a barn during a snowstorm and he had bought their loyalty with some nice wine and some pieces of gold too. All three were older than Mjorr, none of them were below forty and they had lived long and somewhat hard lives, they knew the character of a man by watching him and this guy was as bad as any mercenary were, or worse. But he was also a bit mad and they had learned never to trust crazy people at all. He had described his sister well and also given them pretty strict orders. They were to kill the wench the moment they found her, not hesitate or waste time by raping her or anything. They could fuck her corpse if they felt the need, but she was to die and that was not negotiable. The three men were not stupid, if they had been none of them would have survived for as long as they had. No, they realized that Mjorr was hiding something from his father and if Mjorr was rich Dagar was so much richer, and with way greater influence. It could perhaps pay off to keep their heads cool and wait. If this secret of Mjorr was juicy enough there could be a chance there, a chance to milk this cow for more than just a few coins of gold. If they earned enough it could be their shortcut to retirement. They had ridden fast along the trading routes and they had realized that the caravan had taken a different route, they should have caught up with them by now and one of the men did remember the old dwarven tunnels.

This meant that they had to travel even faster if they were to catch up with the caravan but they didn't mind. They had bought some very good horses and had spare animals too and they rested for a couple of hours each night but not more than that. Their life in the army had hardened them and they didn't need much rest at all. All three were wearing light armour and solid but somewhat worn clothes, there was little doubt about their profession but they did take some pride in not looking like complete savages. They knew that people lied when they were scared. Buying the truth with sweet talk and wine was a way better method, and nobody would be chasing them afterwards trying to avenge some unfortunate victim. Since they all were aging and no longer filled with the confidence of youth they used common sense instead of violence, they may have been bad once upon a time but now they tried to stay alive by using their heads instead of their blades. It was way better that way and could perhaps ensure a peaceful retirement, or at least an honourable death.

They had reached the steep path leading down to the plains now and they were grateful that there wasn't that much snow there for one couldn't ride down if it was icy. That would be suicide and the three spent the last night before the descent in a small inn which lay precariously close to the edge. All three knew how to act so that nobody got suspicious or hostile, they were smiling as much as they could, they even bought some pints for some of the elderly men who had gathered in a corner and before everybody were chatting away. The men remembered that the caravan had entered the inland at this place, the city of the twelve clans had not been that far away then and the old men spoke of the horses the eternal did ride with starry eyes and shivering hands. The three had encountered elves before and knew one thing for sure, if they were to do this and escape alive they couldn't let themselves be caught, nor allow anybody to suspect that their intentions weren't anything but peaceful. But they had been given quite a lot of gold by Mjorr and they managed to convince these men that they were out to buy a stallion of the lithe long legged breed some of the clans did breed. Their master wanted to breed faster horses and needed a good one.

The elderly men told them that the eternal never sold their horses but the humans which were a part of the twelve clans could perhaps be persuaded to sell them an untried colt, even one which was below their desired standard would be exquisite in the eyes of the mountain people. They pretended to be pleased by this and the old men did speak of the long friendship they had enjoyed with the twelve clans and their warriors. The village had been plagued by some rather pesky earth bears some years earlier and the eternal had managed to chase them away without losing even one of their own. The mercenaries knew that elves are superior warriors and they had no intention of testing those skills themselves. But they did manage to find out where the city could be at the moment, and they had to accept that getting there could be tough. At least before the caravan did, when the elves did reach the plains they would move very fast, and catching up with them would be almost impossible.

The three were a bit disheartened when they happened to notice that one of the men there mentioned travelling by boat along the large river which came from the north. He was a tradesman and was heading towards the city to sell some cloth and other things the inhabitants of the plains couldn't make themselves and the three saw their chance. The boats used were rather fast since the river was wide and rather slow and with sails they could travel way faster than on horseback. The youngest of the three managed to convince the salesman of the wisdom of accepting some extra passengers, just in case and they felt a surge of hope. If they could reach the city and find out what it was Mjorr was hiding they had the upper hand. For all they knew the wench knew something important and killing her right away was out of the question then, they had to make her speak first. As they found a place to sleep that night all three were convinced that this would become profitable indeed.

Bagir and Igkhan had left the tribe early, and Bagir was glad to see that the young hunter in fact did own a horse of his own. It was a very stocky animal with a long dense coat and it seemed to have a rather stubborn temper but he guessed it was normal for that breed. The horses bred for the mountains had to be tough in every manner to survive. Igkhan carried a rather broad short sword and also a short spear plus a bow made for riders. He appeared to be very glad they were on their way and Bagir was very glad he now had a guide who knew the mountains. The high passes were dangerous and Bagir had never come this way before, he had heard the tales other told of the right paths but hearing about them wasn't the same as wandering them oneself. Bagir rode behind Igkhan with his spare horse behind him and they made good speed at first. There wasn't that much snow in this valley, the wind swept it away but Igkhan did warn him that this would change when they reached the lower areas.

210

Bagir was nervous, he had no idea of how far Mjorr and Dagar had come and he was afraid of getting there too late. He felt like hurrying but knew that such an impulse could be lethal in this terrain, he had to let Igkhan who knew the paths be in command now.

It soon became rather apparent that Bagir probably never would have been able to cross if he had been alone, he was used to the mountains for sure, just not these mountains. Igkhan did explain the route to the herder, making simple maps in the snow. The path they had to follow to get to the plains early enough to be able to intercept the nomadic tribes was a rather hidden one and it was dangerous since it was both steep and went through some pretty hazardous terrain. More so, it did cross the areas most inhabited by orcs and Igkhan had already warned Bagir that if they did encounter orcs he was to do all the talking. He knew how to deal with these creatures to avoid any trouble.

They had travelled for a few days when they suddenly realized that trouble maybe was heading their way no matter what they were doing. They had ridden down a very narrow ridge and Bagir was wet with perspiration, both from the stress of clinging to the saddle and sheer fear, if the horse lost its footing they would both fall to their death. Igkhan had changed the shoes of Bagir's horses into some the mountain tribes uses at this time of the year, shoes with a sort of spikes in them and the horse didn't slip even once but Bagir felt how his stomach was lurching with each move the animal did. When they finally reached ground which was a bit more horizontal he was breathing a huge sigh of relief and hoped that they could catch a small break for his legs felt like jelly. Igkhan did stop his horse and his face was suddenly sharp, his eyes narrow. "Up ahead, ravens and crows. Something is dead"

Bagir didn't have the youth's sharp eyes. "Could it be a dead sheep? Some wild animal?"

Igkhan did kick the horse into a rocking trot. "No, it is a huge flock"

He didn't say any more and Bagir did ride after him. They entered a small canyon and Bagir swallowed hard. There were orcs there, about five of them and they were intimidating and huge. The dark skin and visible tusks made them look very alien and all of them wore thick fur clothes and carried weapons, axes and spears. Igkhan held his hands up so they were visible and Bagir did the same. There were several dead bodies in the snow, a very grotesque sight and Bagir did see that they were orcs. Blood and entrails had frozen in place and made the place of slaughter look like a sort of painting but it was real.

One of the orcs did step forth, he was taller than the others and he was old, the thick black hair had streaks of grey and the tusks were obviously worn. He had one blind eye and was scarred and hunched over, he had seen a hard life for sure. Bagir did bow his head since he saw that Igkhan did the same and the young hunter did keep his hands visible. "I am Igkhan son of Arrath, what has happened here?"

The old orc stared at the two men and his one seeing eye was narrow and dark. The creature did smell, a very rancid smell which reminded Bagir of old billy goats and the thing had to have lice and fleas. "I have heard of you brother of the cat, they say you are brave"

Igkhan didn't smile, he just cocked his head. "Brave I may be, but the brothers of the bear are strong and fierce"

The orc sneered. "A human with a tongue of honey, we are mourning our dead"

The hunter nodded slowly. "The halls of the forefathers are surely welcoming them"

The orc spat in the snow and cocked his head. "Maybe, but they didn't die in a battle, they were killed like mute beasts, like sheep"

Igkhan did frown. "Nobody is stronger than the orcs, you are like the foundations of this world"

The old male scoffed. "Like I said, a honeyed tongue. Yes, we are strong, stronger than all and yet four of our warriors and three of our females were slain"

Igkhan didn't reveal how shocked he was, the loss of a female to the orcs was way worse than the loss of a male, females were rare and they were treasured. "I cry with you old one, such horrible loss"

The old orc sighed and his shoulders slumped forwards. "Monsters did this, terrible beasts who came out from the darkness. Our shaman saw it"

Igkhan did wet his lips. "Your seers are wise old one, what did they see?"

The orc turned towards the dead, his face told of grief. "Of a horrible danger to us all, of evil unleashed. They are coming"

Bagir swallowed hard. "Old and honoured one, what is coming?"

The orc stared at him, the face was without expressions. "Death, demons. A forgotten scourge upon the earth. "

Igkhan was staring at the bodies, the other orcs there was trying to get them out of the snow and the corpses were frozen stiff. "What could have killed four of your fine warriors so easily?"

The old male sighed and stared down. "The shamans says the gates have been forced open, only the one born twice may stop this."

Bagir frowned. "The one born twice? That is impossible?"

The old orc shrugged. "The shamans said what they said, their words are the truth"

Bagir threw a glance at Igkhan, they had to start moving again. The hunter cleared his voice. "We are heading for the plains o honoured one, are there dangers in our path?"

The old orc turned around, his one seeing eye was revealing something which reminded them of relief. "The plains? Our shamans told us to send one of our own to the plains, the reason would be revealed by the child of stone they said"

Bagir swallowed. "You will send someone?"

The orc nodded. "Aye, one of our young warriors, the shamans have chosen her"

Igkhan raised an eyebrow. A female warrior? That was most unusual among the orcs, females were so few that most had to take the role as child bearers whether they liked to or not. The old orc grinned, a rather stiff smile. "She may travel with you, you weak humans will need her protection. Resh'kha is strong, a daughter of our chieftain."

Igkhan made a little grimace. "If she doesn't find our company too boring and insignificant we would be honoured."

The old orc just grumbled. "Three travels better than two!"

Bagir saw that Igkhan was nervous and he believed that he understood why. If something indeed had killed that many orcs they were not safe there, and one more warrior could really mean the difference between life and death. The old orc did whistle and a figure appeared from behind some tall rocks, wearing a thick leather cloak and some furs. Bagir had never seen a female orc up close and certainly not a young one. She was….well, he wouldn't call her beautiful but there was a firm strength in her face and the long black hair had been braided back into a firm braid. She had some tattoos on her face and her tusks had been filed down a bit. She did look fierce but also like a person who has some ability to think instead of just rushing into action like a headless chicken. She did look at them with dark piercing eyes and Igkhan did swallow hard. "We are most blessed to have you among us daughter of the bear"

Resh'kha sighed and shook her head. "Two Adahkhi? Well, they would be better off in their huts, I will not wait for them"

Bagir knew that the word Adahkh meant human male and it could be translatable as weak one. He would have been offended if someone else called him weak but he guessed that the orcs viewed everyone not themselves as flawed. The female did grasp the forearm of the old orc and whispered something, then she threw a quick glance at the two men and made a gesture. "Come Adakhi, we cannot wait. We need to get out of here before sunset"

Igkhan saw she was armed and she was moving through the snow with a sort of flowing grace, she was more than two meters tall and her shoulders were wide, the difference between female and male was very little among orcs. He waited until they had come some distance from the other orcs. "She is an outcast, they wouldn't have sent her otherwise!"

Bagir frowned and made sure that he didn't look at the tall female orc. "What makes you say that? The shamans chose her?"

Igkhan made a grimace. "Yes, because she is expendable, I bet she has done something wrong, or perhaps there is something wrong with her, physically. Orcs are very gender oriented"

Bagir blinked. "But there is hardly any difference to be spotted when they have clothes on?!"

Igkhan sort of scoffed. "Yeah, but whence the clothes come off the difference is there, believe me. I recon we will find out why she is the one they send, sooner or later"

The female orc was trotting down the path with a speed the horses had problems keeping up with and she appeared to be angry, there was something about her body language which spoke of tension and she was speaking to herself, or rather whispering. Bagir stared at Igkhan who just nodded and whispered. "Don't talk to her unless she speaks to you, it is considered rude to speak to a female."

Bagir made a swift grimace and tried to keep his eyes on the surrounding mountains instead, Igkhan was clearing his voice again. "I wonder what wounds the dead had? The method of killing can tell a lot of the perpetrator."

Resh'kha turned her head a wee bit. "They were torn apart, ripped limb from limb."

Her voice was gruff and Bagir had a feeling that she wasn't too happy about having to leave her tribe. Igkhan shuddered, something able to rip orcs apart? He would prefer not to meet that creature, or creatures. "Did anyone see the thing which did it?"

The female orc didn't turn her head this time. "Only tracks in the snow, odd tracks."

Bagir knew the mountains since he had spent his entire life herding sheep and he had seen all the animals which lived up there. He had even encountered one of the very rare earth bears once and he had seen the foot prints of the wild giants some said lived in the caves way above the treeline. But if an orc said odd tracks then it had to be odd tracks indeed.

They kept riding in silence for quite a while, they entered a shallow vale with a frozen lake in the middle and now it was getting dark soon so the female did lead them towards some cliffs. Bagir didn't protest, this was orc territory, she probably knew every rock there. There was a sort of fire pit carved into the rocks and some firewood and if you attached some furs to hooks in the rock you could create a sort of shelter. They did and Resh'kha did sneer at them before she sat down with a small bag which probably contained food. It wasn't much, some black bread and what had to be dried meat. Igkhan did stare at her with some pity in his eyes, but he didn't say anything. She ate in silence, the meat had to be very tough for she struggled to chew and the hunter whispered to Bagir. "It is meat from wild dogs, it is unclean. Orcs never touch it normally, she is an outcast for sure"

Bagir just nodded and leaned back, tried to get a conversation going, about something else than their current situation. "So, your sister, what was she like?"

Igkhan sighed. "The sweetest child imaginable, so trusting and kind. She always thought about others before she thought of herself and she was the jewel of our mother's eye"

Bagir nodded slowly. "Do you have more siblings?"

He smiled and threw a piece of sausage over to Bagir. "Two sisters and a younger brother, the girls are already married but my brother is going to be a shaman, he doesn't want to marry but to listen to the gods instead"

Bagir saw that Resh'kha was listening. "I see."

Igkhan was chewing on his food, very slowly. "I am the only hunter in our family so it is my duty to avenge my sister"

Resh'kha did turn her head and stared at them. "Your sister is dead?"

Igkhan did nod. "Yes, a man raped and killed her, we are on our way to warn the eternal that he is heading their way, dead set on having his way with a woman sent off to marry one of them"

The orc tensed up, her eyes got narrow and her skin seemed to darken. "I see, he deserve death then."

Bagir tilted his head. "Yes, he does. The girl he raped was just a child, and he has done the same thing many times before"

The orc growled. "None of us does such things, it angers the Goddess, makes bad luck. I will help you, vengeance is good"

Igkhan did frown. "That is very kind of you, but you do have your own mission?"

She nodded. "Help each other, good right?"

Igkhan nodded. "Yes, yes that is very good indeed. You are most welcome"

Bagir felt a bit conflicted, having an orc on their side was of course wonderful when one considered the fact that she was a superior warrior and way stronger than the both of them combined. The orcs were feared by most creatures, but if this new enemy was something out of this world? Bagir felt a chill running down his spine, things had changed and not for the better, his simple mission had just changed into something different and unexpected. The orc just sat there and Bagir had the time now to really look at her. The face wasn't exactly feminine, there was indeed little difference between male and female when it came to facial features but he did see that her hair was a wee bit softer looking that the hair of the males and her hands were more narrow, more elegant. Also, her skin appeared to be a bit lighter and her shoulders weren't quite as wide as those of the warriors he had seen. She finished her meal in silence and then she just lay down on the cold ground, wrapped her fur cloak around herself and went to sleep. Bagir shrugged. "I will take first watch, we all need some rest now I think"

Bagir agreed and laid down, his blankets were thick and warm and he wondered how tough the orcs really were, surviving in the wild mountains wasn't easy.

The next morning there was strong wind and snow flew between the cliffs, they ate some more and Resh'kha was impatient and also in a way resigned. Had she perhaps hoped that she would be called back, that she didn't have to go after all?

As they rode on Bagir kept staring at the broad back and she seemed even more sad as they entered one of the valleys which lead towards the plains. There was probably no turning back for her now, whatever the reason was for her mission. As they tried to get down the slopes they saw old ruins, hidden underneath the snow. Bagir nodded towards them. "Dwarven ruins, they are very old. And they are sacred to the dwarves. An old city I believe"

Bagir saw that the buildings had to have been massive, and probably very impressive too, there were stones so huge he couldn't understand how they had been moved into place. Resh'kha hadn't said anything to them at all earlier that day, now she spat in the snow and grunted. "Dwarven stronghold. The city of silver delight. Fell a long time ago"

Bagir tried to be polite. "Forgive me for asking, but do you know the story of this place?"

The female orc grunted again. "We all do, old tale. It is in our blood. A warning of times which were"

She walked around the fallen rocks with some sort of reverence. "Dwarves and orcs worked together back then, we were brothers. Things were…different"

She didn't say anything more and Igkhan made a grimace. "Well, I bet it was the dwarven greed which lead to its demise"

Resh'kha shook her head but didn't look at them. "Nay, it was magic. Old magic, bad magic. It made them go mad"

She walked on and Bagir just shrugged, the orc wasn't exactly informative.

That evening they reached a river which proved to be very difficult to cross, there weren't any safe crossings for mile and so they spent many hours in vain until Resh'kha finally found a spot where the horses could get over without any danger of falling. The next couple of days were uneventful, they were getting low on food now and Bagir was getting a bit nervous, they had to eat to keep up their strength and the little grass the horses managed to find under the snow wasn't very nutritious. The oats he had brought would be gone in a few days.

They were camping in a sort of cave when the orc suddenly got up, it was clear that she heard something they didn't and she got pale. "Make the horses lay down, make sure they are silent"

The two men did what they were told to do, made the animals lay down and placed blankets over their heads, the animals were well trained, they would understand that this meant that they had to stay down and be silent. Resh'kha was breathing in a funny manner, her eyes huge. "It is them, it is demons!"

Bagir did peek forth from behind her, they hadn't lit any fires and the cave was well hidden so he didn't fear being seen if this was some sort of natural enemy. If it weren't well then they were screwed anyhow. What he did see almost made him pee his pants, he saw three overly tall figures wandering slowly through the snow, as if their legs were too heavy to move. They were glowing, a sort of orange glow which was rather unpleasant, it seemed…unnatural. The creatures were almost transparent, you could see the skeleton inside of them and they were humanoid in shape but there were just too many bones, it seemed as if each one was made from several others, merged together. Yet they moved and there was a sort of chilling determination within the way they moved. The heads was the worst part though, the shape was completely obscured by the glow, but you could see their eyes for they weren't glowing, they were like black blotches on a sheet, deep black and bottomless, just cold and dead and filled with a terrible evil. They had more than two eyes, he could count at least five on the one closest to them and Resh'kha was trembling all over.

Bagir was glad there was some distance between them, the creatures just kept moving without seeing them but he was aware of the fact that they all would have been dead if they had been discovered. He let out a sigh when they disappeared from view, he had been holding his breath and Igkhan was pale. "Oh by every God."

Resh'kha was moaning. "The goddess was with us, praised be"

Bagir had to sit down. "Was this what your shamans saw?"

Resh'kha did nod, there were tears in her eyes and Bagir frowned. "Are you alright?"

He knew he shouldn't talk directly to her but she did appear to be devastated. The female orc let out a thin wail, filled with sorrow and despair. "It is my fault, I did this!"

Igkhan raised his eyebrows and it made him look rather peculiar indeed. "Ah, that you will have to explain to us?"

She sobbed. "I did something terrible, that is why I have been sent."

Igkhan did send Bagir a warning glance, none of them ought to say anything just yet. Resh'kha hid her face behind her hands, she was trembling slightly. "I used magic, forbidden magic. I lured them to us, I am sure I did."

Bagir frowned, orcs aren't known for their magical proves, as a matter of fact they usually shun magic completely since they believe that the use of such forces makes one weak. To them it is much more honest to solve problems with steel in hand. Igkhan did tilt his head, he didn't look at her at all. "That is just a guess, you cannot be sure!"

Resh'kha gasped, she did seem to be utterly distraught. "The shamans said it is my fault, the monsters, they can smell magic, they are drawn to it, and I…"

She shuddered. "I wanted this one male for myself, I was so jealous of his woman and when I heard she was expecting I went mad, I have no idea what came over me,"

Igkhan still looked down. "You are young, your wisdom is still growing"

Resh'kha snorted. "What wisdom? I did something illegal, unspeakable. I put a spell on that woman to make her lose her child"

Igkhan's voice was dry. "Did she?"

Resh'kha shook her head. "No, but she died in the attack, as did he."

Bagir suddenly realized that the orcs were smarter than he had believed earlier. They knew how the mind works and he felt a renewed respect for them. Resh'kha did feel guilty and guilt, whether real or not, can eat at you like a cancer. Resh'kha felt that she needed to be punished and so she was, but in a different manner than what she would have preferred. Igkhan sighed. "Resh'kha, I don't know your customs and I don't know you, but I do strongly doubt that the magic you used had anything to do with this, you are no mage are you?"

She shook her head and did still look devastated. "No, I am not"

The hunter did nod. "They are attracted to magic you said, it could be that those who died owned something with magical powers, like an amulet or something. That doesn't make you responsible for their deaths at all"

She trembled visibly. "But what I did was wrong!! One should never interfere the way I wanted to do!"

Igkhan nodded slowly. "That is correct Resh'kha, but like I said, you are young. I am sure the shamans meant well, you will find the truth eventually"

She didn't speak again, just huddled together and Bagir took a deep breath before he sat down at the back of the cave. He felt a bit shocked for he had never believed that orc females could be that passionate but why not. They were a strong people, strong feelings ought to be normal then. Igkhan was making a grimace. "They wanted to punish her, for having stepped out of line and yet they also wanted to help her, they have wisdom, it is just not seen that often"

Bagir nodded. "I have reached the same conclusion."

220

Igkhan found his blankets. "We have to be careful from now on, if such horrors roam the land we have to warn everybody we meet"

Bagir supressed a shudder" Alright, how long until we reach the plains?"

Igkhan shrugged. "We have travelled fast but still we won't be there for yet another week or a week and a half. These valleys are long, and the terrain becomes more treacherous as we reach the edge"

Bagir knew that the area where the mountains met the plains was called the edge by everybody, it was a very steep region which surrounded the entire mountain area. He wasn't looking forwards to that part of the trip. Not even a wee bit, he had heard the stories of terrible falls and accidents.

Mjorr and Dagar had travelled for way too long the way Mjorr saw it, he was getting impatient. At the beginning he had been eager, and he had enjoyed it immensely but now he didn't see the fun in it anymore. It wasn't that their journey was a hard one, his father did have money so he could get good meals and good beds and he even enjoyed some luxuries like warm baths and clean clothes but they hadn't gotten any closer to their targets and Mjorr had his problem still. The guards had known medicine which could take care of it, they surely did and they didn't even try to hide their schadenfreude when he told about the fact that he was pissing fire. The medicine they did recommend wasn't that hard to come by, it was a herbal tincture which was sold in almost every village since it was very sought after. Most believed that it could cure almost everything.

Mjorr did buy two flasks from a man who sold such remedies in one of the villages they dropped by and he immediately tried it. The label said that you should drink some and also wash the troubled body part with some of the liquid. He had done that, it had burned like hell but the problem hadn't gone away, if anything, it had gotten worse. So his mood had plummeted and he was acting like a bear with a severe toothache. Dagar had understood that something was off with his son but he hadn't said anything, he had a strong suspicion though and he couldn't help but gloat a wee bit. Mjorr had to learn that every action has consequences and this was one wonderful lesson.

As the days went by Mjorr got more and more cranky and he also got problems riding. His balls were aching and his cock too and he didn't drink anymore since pissing had become a horrible ordeal. At the end Dagar had to take action, none of them managed to be in the same room as Mjorr since he was whimpering and complaining the entire time. They had stopped in a rather large village by a lake and Dagar found an inn and asked the owner if there were any doctors in this area. The owner did see that this man was rich so he did answer willingly enough, they did have a doctor, a rather good one too and he was probably able to heal whatever ailments they were struggling with. Dagar got a room, then he ordered the owner to send for the doctor and told Mjorr that he had had enough of the sour mood and the constant complaints. Mjorr was mortified, he had been sure he had been able to hide the misery but alas, his father wasn't born yesterday and now there was no point in protests. Maybe the doctor really could heal him? Then he would roll the man in gold for sure.

The doctor came after dark, it was a very small skinny man who wore old but good clothes and he did carry with him a faint scent of herbs and something slightly spicy. Dagar did like the man immediately, he was clean and spoke with respect and he did also reveal that he actually knew what he was doing. The man's name was Olof and he was from the larger cities to the south of the plains, had studied there but fell in love with a mountain girl and moved to her home. Mjorr was not really that fond of letting any man see him naked, and the idea of being touched by a male was enough to make him cringe. But now there was no way out, he had to drop his pants in front of the fireplace and the elderly man did nod his head and put on some soft gloves made from fine leather. He did examine Mjorr's pride and joy with narrow eyes and asked a lot of very embarrassing questions Mjorr just had to mumble the answers to. Dagar was a bit worried for his son's health, after all, he wanted grandchildren but at the same time he was glad Mjorr finally had to face the consequences of his actions.

Olof did straighten his back and made a smacking sound with his lips. "The tincture you tried didn't work because this is a very rare disease, and it is very hard to get rid of. You need a totally different cure"

Mjorr was moaning and Dagar was frowning. "He will get rid of it?"

Olof nodded. "Yes, but he has suffered for way too long, this may leave after effects and those cannot be helped I am afraid. But time will see, he is young and strong"

The doctor opened his bag and pulled out several remedies and a huge box of pills. "He need to take one such pill with each meal for at least two weeks. And no alcohol at all in this time, only water or milk."

Mjorr moaned as if he was being run through and the doctor couldn't hide a wry glimpse within his eyes. "There there young man, it isn't too bad. It could have been worse, remember, one night with Venus can become a lifetime with Mercury."

He found a sort of thin straw and cocked his head. "This will hurt, I am warning you in advance."

He grasped Mjorr's pride again and pushed the thin tube into the urethra and Mjorr wailed like a baby. Dagar didn't know whether or not he ought to feel sorry for the lad or gloat even more. But he did know that Mjorr had been bedding some women who were little more than whores and this was the result of that. He waited until Olof was done injecting some sort of greenish liquid into Mjorr's bladder and telling the young man to drink a lot of water for a few days. Then he grasped Mjorr by the shoulders and declared that when they got back home there was no way back, he would make sure that Mjorr got properly married and also that he did stay true to his wife to be, or else he would make sure that Mjorr from that day on could titulate himself as "a gelding". Mjorr paled and tried to protest and Dagar simply slapped him around the ears, he wouldn't accept his son's silly behaviour any longer. From now on it was the end of acting like a moron and chasing skirts, he would keep Mjorr on a tight leash and Mjorr suddenly felt more irate than ever before.

He blamed it all on that goddamn wench, his sister would have to pay for having escaped but she would be dead when they reached the city of the nomads. Wenja on the other hand, she had escaped as well and Mjorr felt an unholy rage, so his father would turn him into a loser? Into a meek pathetic marionette? No way, he would make sure that he got his vengeance, and teach everybody that nobody went against his will once and for all. Dagar could go to hell, he would rule his own life, and Dagar wasn't immortal now was he? Dagar didn't know how rebellious his son truly was and he had no idea of why Mjorr had been so eager to join him on this journey in the first place. Had he known Mjorr would have been in way more trouble than he was. Olof left pills and some ointments and left after having received a generous payment from Dagar, Mjorr just stood there looking more sour than a jug of vinegar and Dagar slapped him over the head once more. "You have been allowed to roam freely for too long, it is time you learn to be a man, not a boy. The first lesson starts today. You are to sleep in the same room as me, no fucking around from now on"

Mjorr just nodded but in his thoughts he was fuming. Oh there would be fucking for sure, he would ruin that redheaded slut for her husband forever, then he would make sure that he did return as his father's heir, the entire village would have to kneel to him, and only him. It was a sacred promise for sure.

The caravan was making good progress now, the riders had spread out and made sure that the wagons didn't encounter any problems for here there were no roads, just tracks and some were very uneven since they were made by animals. Wenja was fascinated, she had overcome her fear of the wide open skies and now she was constantly asking questions which Sefa had a hard time finding answers to. Imh and Theka did tell her about the different plants and herbs they did see along the road and Floth'bha did try to teach her how to use a bow but that ended in a complete failure for the girl just wasn't strong enough to pull it. Ehbrial and Khirhien said that they would find a children's bow for her when they reached the city, just so she could learn the basics with a bow she was able to pull. The mood was good for now they were closing in on the city with every day which went by but still there was a problem and that problem was Prina. The girl had been doing well when they crossed the mountains, she had learned a lot and she had thawed up but now she became more and more withdrawn and quiet and Theka was sure that it was because she had understood her own situation and what it truly meant to her. Before she had acted as if she didn't really accept the truth but now she probably had and it had made her feel even more terrible than when she ran off from home. Wenja tried to talk to her but Prina didn't answer, she was obviously too scared to speak and now she was showing rather well too. Her belly couldn't be hidden anymore and Theka tried to make her eat better and prepare for what was to come but she acted like a fool in so many ways.

After some days they came to a small lake and it wasn't frozen, the water was in fact warm and Rhawan said it was because there was a hot spring underneath it. The lake was perhaps a few hundred meters across and it wasn't very deep but the water wasn't too hot to bathe in and so they all had a long anticipated bath there. Wenja was enjoying it immensely, she felt grimy after the journey and everybody had brought soap and other things they needed too. It made her feel like a new person and Sefa did giggle and promised her some fun later on. Wenja knew that she had to learn even more than she previously had but Rhawan had been so busy lately with finding the right path and he hadn't had the energy to come to any of them. Ahnriel was worried about Prina's health, she had recovered well before but now she was losing weight and that wasn't good, they didn't want to force feed the girl but that could be the result. Wenja did hope that the shamans of the twelve clans really could do something to help the girl. Imh or Theka was with her all the time, nobody left her alone even for a moment and Wenja had a creeping suspicion that Prina was going to use the baby she carried as a substitute for her brother and focus her hatred onto it. For it was no doubt that her anger and hatred had grown during the recent weeks, it had changed from fear to anger and from anger to something Wenja never had seen before. Sefa said it was true hatred, and Prina was using it as a crutch sort of, to strengthen herself. If she only felt hatred then she couldn't feel guilt and it was logical and yet far from the right path to take. Prina had no guilt in what had happened to her and yet she felt that she did, that was how twisted her mind had become from her brother's evil words.

Theka said she often had terrible nightmares and they too contributed to her gradual breakdown. Wenja was shocked to see how changed Prina had become, and she didn't quite understand why she had started to change this much now and not earlier. Sefa said it was because she had started to feel safe, earlier all she could think about was getting away from Mjorr and she hadn't really thought about her future at all. Now she was safe from him but that meant that she could start to think again and that was when the bad thoughts came. Wenja could understand that, and yet not. They still had quite a way to go before they reached Ohtanar and she knew that Theka and Imh were worried.

That night Sefa came to sleep in the wagon with Wenja, it was rather cold there and the fires were kept burning the entire night. The horses were tied up to the wagons and the Zahar was the only animal allowed to run free. There was always a risk of wolf packs near this lake since it did attract so many animals and Rhawan sent some of the riders out as guards. The camp was very peaceful and before bedtime Ehbrial did entertain them all with his flute. The elves did love music and they had a peculiar style to it which Wenja did find fascinating. It was the type of music which flows and meanders like a slow river and yet it had both rhythm and energy. Sefa did show Wenja some moves, they were way more sensual than the dancing Wenja had seen before, it was all about moving one's body in different and very elegant moves and it had to be done so the moves did correspond with the ebb and flow of the music. Wenja found that she loved it, it was way more risqué than anything she had seen before but who cared? Here that type of dancing was normal.

She was tired when she got to bed and Sefa had allowed her to drink a couple of glasses of strong wine, it was a type they didn't have that much of but it was so very good and could make someone very drunk rather fast. Rhawan had been talking a bit with the women and he had revealed that the did miss Ahravan a lot, and that he was longing to get back to the city. Wenja knew that the two were close but she hadn't really considered the nature of the relationship before. They were closer than brothers for sure and Sefa just grinned when Wenja asked if they in fact were lovers. She just hoped that she wouldn't create any problems between them, that would be too bad.

Wenja was fast asleep when she was brutally yanked out of the realm of dreams, Sefa was shaking her rather violently, and in the light from the window it was very obvious that the woman was pale. "Wenja, you need to get up!"

Wenja yawned and felt confused, it wasn't quite morning yet and she had slept like a log. "What is happening?"

Sefa did appear to be a wee bit hysterical, she was shaking all over. "It is Prina, she has tried to kill herself"

Wenja gasped and sat up so fast she did almost head-butt Sefa who was leaning over her. "What?"

Sefa nodded and helped Wenja get out of the bed. "One of the guards saw her laying on the shore, in her shift only. She reeks of wine and we think she has tried to drown herself"

Wenja did throw a robe over herself and they ran out of the wagon. Ahnriel and Imh were kneeling by a figure laying on the grass and Ahnriel was chanting and glowing slightly. Wenja let out a loud gasp of horror, Prina did look terrible and she sank to her knees. "Will she make it?"

Theka was weeping. "Oh gods, we do hope for that yes."

Imh was swearing in dwarfish. "She drank a whole bottle of strong wine, and went into the lake but she haven't drowned. Why we don't know, but she must have been floating"

Rhawan came running, he was wild eyed and when they told him what had happened he stared at Theka and Imh. "You didn't stop her?"

Theka sniffed. "We were asleep, I think she must have poured something into our wine, neither of us woke up. She must have been very determined"

Ahnriel moaned and got up, she was shaking with fatigue. "She will live, with a horrible headache I bet but she is alright. I think the baby is alright too, but I cannot be too sure"

Theka let out a huge sigh of relief and started crying again and Imh closed her eyes for a moment "She has got some serious issues that one, what is she thinking?!"

Rhawan shrugged. "My guess is as good as anyone's I guess. But from now on we need someone watching her all the time, even when she sleeps."

Ehbrial did nod. "I can do that, I am not burdened by other tasks and I do not need that much sleep. I can watch her when the others need to rest"

Rhawan did pet his shoulder. "Good, that is wonderful my friend. This makes me very worried"

Ahnriel and Imh did carry Prina back to the wagon where she slept normally and they had started to look less frightened and more angry. Wenja understood them well, but she couldn't really wrap her head around the way Prina had to be thinking. They would have to ask her when she woke up again. Wenja didn't sleep that well the rest of the night and Sefa was awake and sat there, staring out at the plains through the window. When they broke camp she told Wenja that suicide was a taboo among the tribes, nobody did that. It was unthinkable and if this became well known many would believe that Prina was mad or possessed. Wenja felt even more sorry for Prina now, she couldn't really fathom the level of her despair, the very idea of ending oneself was something Wenja just couldn't wrap her head around. When they reached the city they would have to shield Prina as much as possible.

Prina did wake up again later that day, she refused to talk and she just sat there with a dead gaze and looked like a doll. She had obviously given up and Imh was beside herself with worry. Ahnriel did mention that it was the child which caused this, the very existence of a proof of Mjorr's evil deed. Prina probably felt trapped and had tried to find a way out. But this didn't make things any better at all.

They had travelled for yet a couple of days when they first met others, it was a band of travelling merchants heading west and they could tell the caravan that a village at the edge of the plains had been completely destroyed by some unknown force. Also, a huge herd of bison had been found dead and there were rumours spreading of monsters on the move. Rhawan just shrugged but the men swore there was truth in it. He didn't appear to bother that much with it but Sefa did say that he was worried. He just didn't show it to everybody. Sefa did decide that it was time for another lesson and oddly enough Rhawan didn't protest at all, his mind was on something else and she said that he needed to relax a bit and just enjoy himself.

He did come to the wagon when they made camp that evening and Sefa did prepare him rather well and made sure that they wouldn't be disturbed at all. Wenja was nervous and didn't quite want to do it but Sefa did as usual persuade her. Rhawan was obviously very eager and tried to make Wenja feel as if she did master the situation and Sefa did

228

show her all the spots on a male body which can give pleasure. Some of the things Sefa did show her shocked her a bit but she was getting eager to learn and she did dare to go rather far this time. She dared to use her mouth and tongue on Rhawan and he came hard, shouting her name and covering her breasts with his seed. For some reason she felt much more bold now than she had the last time and she wasn't that nervous about her coming wedding at all. Rhawan did take Sefa again before he left the wagon, Wenja felt a sort of envy now, she saw the immense pleasure joining gave her friend and she wanted to experience it too. Sefa giggled and told her that Ahravan most certainly would give her the night of her life when they finally were wedded and Wenja blushed and had to admit that she was looking forward to it. She had heard only good things about Ahravan and she trusted Rhawan when he said that his sworn brother would cherish her and never let anything negative befall her as long as she was alive.

Rhawan had satisfied Wenja with his tongue also this time and she went to bed feeling slightly swollen and tender, it was a good feeling though and she had to giggle when Sefa said that Ahravan probably would keep her in bed the first days after the ceremony.

Prina on the other hand refused to leave the wagon now, she refused to wash and she refused to talk to anyone. She didn't seem to have suffered any effects of what she had done and that was a miracle in itself for that much alcohol could have killed her and the baby alike, not to mention the bath she had taken. Why she hadn't drowned was a mystery.

Rhawan was very eager now, they were getting closer to Ohtanar and he did spend the evenings with Wenja and Sefa, explaining the life on the plains in great detail. Wenja felt as though she knew everybody now and she was looking forward to ending this journey. She was getting really tired of it.

The city had been in mourning after the death of the children and Ahravan had to explain everything over and over again, most had a hard time believing that anyone could be that mean and horrible and his warriors had to back him up. The parents of the two slain children were of course those who mourned the most and Ahravan made sure that they got help from the shamans and that they were freed from every duty. The atmosphere was a tense one, few could believe that humans could be so bold and kidnap and kill elven children and Ahravan was worried too. It spoke of either ignorance or an evil influence he had started to fear. The stinging demons they had found, these humans, the rumours which spread across the plains, it all made him feel very concerned. He could only hope that his Si'ish didn't encounter any problems on the way. He had a feeling that Rhawan wasn't all that far away now and he did long to see him again, he felt better when he had his sworn brother by his side. The strain of being the leader felt less taxing when Rhawan was there to keep his mood up. Ahravan didn't have all that much to do now when the city was stationary, he could concentrate on gathering information and since the city did attract people he soon learned of a lot which made him even more worried. Huge herds of animals which had been killed, villages which had disappeared and people who had died mysteriously. The monsters they had fought for ages was one thing, they knew them and they knew how to fight them but this was something new and it made Ahravan very worried indeed. The shaman hadn't said anything new and he sent his best warriors out to check the nearby villages and gather more intelligence. If the days of old were to return they needed to be prepared but how did they do that?

He did have one good news though, in the early morning light two of his warriors came riding back to the camp and proclaimed that they had seen men coming with the Da'ith he had asked for. They had ridden like mad to reach the city this fast for it was a vast distance between the land of the breeders and these northern plains but some said that this tribe knew of magic which allowed them to slow time when they were travelling and thus cover much more distance than others. Whether this was true or not was anybody's guess, but they had heeded his words and he was very glad. A Da'ith would be just what his bride to be needed and in these times more than ever. He prepared to receive the riders and they did reach the city late in the evening. They were four men each with four extra horses and then there was the stallion he had asked for. The animal was impressive, he felt a surge of excitement when he saw the huge horse, they were rare and most people would never see one and the city was suddenly buzzing. Everybody came to behold this wonder of equine power and Ahravan had to shoo people away. There would be plenty of time to admire the beast later on.

The leader of the four came forth and kneeled down, he was a tiny man with long black hair gathered in a tight braid and his face was weather worn and dark, he wore leather clothing embroidered with bright colours and most of the embroideries had something to do with horses. "Greetings great Ath'ir, I am Uruthan, son of Aghran, we bring you this Da'ith as you requested. We are honoured to serve our Ath'ir"

Ahravan smiled, he saw that the four were staring at him and the other elves present with a huge dose of reverence and almost religious awe, they weren't used to his race at all. "I am honoured to receive him, your people are blessed to have such among you"

The man was blushing slightly, to receive praise from the Ath'ir himself was probably the very highlight of his life. Ahravan bowed his head. "The horse is magnificent, a prince among beasts. I have never seen one better"

Now all the four riders were blushing like mad and almost giggling like young maidens, there was sheer joy on their faces. "He is bred from the best bloodline we have, and trained by our master trainer. He is the best we have"

Ahravan nodded. "I don't doubt that. He is for my wife to be, she is on her way here now, escorted by my Si'ish."

Uruthan bowed his head. "Then may she be blessed above all other women and may her days be plentiful and fruitful. There is no greater gift for a husband to give"

Ahravan walked over to the horse, he wasn't bound in any way and stood there, watching them with an eerie intelligence within the huge eyes. This breed was very different from the one's most people did ride, it wasn't bred for that purpose at all. The animal was very tall, the tallest horse anyone had ever seen and it was way above twenty hands in height with a tall arched neck and long hard legs. His coat was dark grey like a thundercloud and his mane and tail a bit lighter. The horse had white socks on his front legs and a small blaze and the eyes were very dark grey. Ahravan petted him on the mighty flank, very reverently. Uruthan smiled. "We have brought his things, and he is ready to do his duty. He has been blessed by our priests too"

Ahravan sent the men a swift smile and bowed his head in gratitude. "He is exquisite. Does he have a name?"

Uruthan was beaming with pride. "We have called him Flint, because of the colour"

Ahravan let a hand glide over the arched neck and the horse nickered softly. "Flint, a good name, well chosen"

He went over to Laupir who stood there and almost shook with eager energy, his eyes were huge and Ahravan had to laugh. He had never seen his friend this excited and he did pet the man on his back. "Easy there, you are drooling like a hungry dog"

Laupir did wipe his mouth with a crestfallen expression and Ahravan had to laugh and pet him on the back again. "I was just kidding friend, but I can see that you like him. Do you have their payment ready?"

Laupir nodded and turned around, retrieved two bags from a table and handed them over to Uruthan who took them with a polite bow. "This is the blood of the earth, you will find that they are perfect"

Uruthan opened one of the bags and peeked into it, a soft red glow could be seen. It was rubies, each one the size of the thumbnail of a grown man and perfectly cut. The dwarves knew that art to perfection. The small man gasped and put a hand up over his heart. "We are most grateful oh wise one, this is way more than he is worth"

Ahravan shook his head. "No my friend, no price is too great to pay to keep my spouse safe"

Uruthan smiled widely. "True words, no value can be put on a good wife for she is priceless"

Ahravan raised his hands. "Now, rest and eat and know that you are most welcome to stay for as long as you like. We are very grateful you have come"

Uruthan did lick his lips. "Some food and wine would be good, we are hungry"

Ahravan chuckled and one of the women who was responsible for the cooking there came forth. "Then follow Aila here and she will make sure that your bellies are filled once more"

232

The four did grin and followed the woman while they sang something joyful sounding and Ahravan was standing there next to Flint and felt overwhelmed. The horse was staring at him with calm eyes and he scratched the wide chest and hummed softly. These animals were different from other horses and he walked in front of the stallion to his own corral. He didn't need to put a halter on the horse and he did enter the corral freely. Ahravan was looking forwards to meeting his wife to be, he truly was. He would regard this as a challenge of some sort and he was sure that Rhawan would tell him all about what her personality was like. They needed something positive now, something which could take everybody's mind away from the death of those children and the many dark omens. The seamstresses were busy preparing a new wardrobe and the dwarves too had been given tasks, she was to be the Eth'ir, she had to look like a queen and he would make sure that she never would lack anything. He just prayed that she wasn't some hard hearted and greedy thing only interested in his title, like his first wife had been.

The three former mercenaries had been in luck indeed, the river boat was a very fast one and the merchant was a friendly and jolly fellow who didn't suspect that the three had far from honest intentions. They did try to act as if they truly were honest men out to buy horses and they didn't mind helping out at all. The great river did meander through the landscape in a huge half circle and everybody said it would bring them rather close to where the nomadic tribes were right now so they kept their fingers crossed and hoped that they would get there in time, before Mjorr did. If they were to earn from this that was crucial and they were pretty confident that they were weeks ahead of him now. The boat was the type most used, it was wide with a rather flat bottom and two masts with large sails. The river was flowing from the north towards the south and that was the opposite direction of where they were heading but since the river was slow and wide the sails did push the boat up against the current just fine. The distance they would have to travel was naturally way larger than the route across land but the boat was a way faster alternative than riding since they didn't know the area and the terrain and it was way more comfortable too.

The river was used a lot by merchants and travellers and they saw many boats as the ship made its way upstream. The captain knew the river like the back of his own hand and he kept telling them small stories of the things he had seen in his years sailing the river and since they helped him very willingly he did tell them many things they did find very useful. That the woman the eternal had been sent to bring back home with them was to be the new Eth'ir was something Mjorr had failed to inform them about, it was something everybody on the plains now knew and the three knew that you didn't mess with the eternal. If that girl was harmed in any way they could kiss their asses' goodbye, they were trained warriors but none of them would stand a chance against an elf in open combat. They all knew this and so they kept wondering why Mjorr had sent them to assassinate his own sister. They had understood that she was his own sister for he wasn't that good at telling lies and since his father too was eager to get to her they did put two and two together and understood that she had run away from her family. So, that was just a family matter, no big deal and not enough of a reason to send someone ahead to kill the wench.

As they made their way northwards they kept debating between themselves what it was that she eventually knew, or had done. They would have to find out about this eventually, if they just caught up with the caravan. The captain of the ship was a person they did like so they didn't want him to get involved if this went south, he had been helping them so their honour commanded that he was rewarded. They had been sailing for almost two weeks when they finally reached the area where the clans lived, and the journey had been easy without any incidents. All of them felt a sting of eager energy and as soon as they saw someone out in a boat they asked if the fishermen knew where the city of the eternal was at the moment. The answer was a very promising one, just a few days ride to the northeast and they bade the captain a fond farewell and paid him for his kindness. The man was almost a bit overwhelmed by their generosity and promised to pray for their good luck.

They bought a horse each from some herders who lived by the river and then they rode off, if this girl did know something which could prove valuable it would be just silly to kill the goose which laid the golden eggs. The landscape here was beautiful and yet in a manner naked and open and they felt a sort of nervous energy as they rode on. Now they had to play well, and make everybody believe that their mission was a real one. Each of them had toned down their warrior like behaviour and they had even managed to change their clothing and their weapons by trading the different garments for new ones during the journey. Now they did look like ordinary men, not poor but not wealthy in any way and obviously sent by someone with both wealth and determination. They had ridden for two days when they suddenly came across something which told them that the plains were far from a safe place to be. They had been looking for a place to camp for the night when the horses suddenly started to act up, whinnying and rearing and it was obvious that something scared them.

They were used to horses and tried to calm the animals down, believing that the steeds had caught the scent of wolves or some other predator but they soon found out that this was no mere wolf pack. In the dusk they saw a vague shimmering blue light and saw something which made them whimper and give the horses free reins while spurring them desperately. It did look like skeletons, but they were way taller and larger than any person and they did glow from within, as if the body was there but transparent. They felt a foul stench on the wind and heard odd hollow sounds and they just knew it, if these apparitions did catch up with them they were dead. So they rode for their lives and the poor horses were already tired but the fear did invigorate them. The three men rode in the direction they hoped was the right one, there had to be someone out there, someone capable of warding off these nightmares.

The horses had started to stumble when they saw light up ahead and they didn't know if the horrible monsters did chase them or not but they didn't dare to stop and investigate. Instead they just rode for their lives and all three almost fell of their horses in shock when they suddenly found themselves surrounded by a group of riders on sleek long-legged steeds.

Some were elves and some were humans and it was no doubt that they were guards. Arrows were aimed at the three and they gasped and tried to catch their breath, the horses almost collapsed underneath them and yet the animals refused to stop so they had to really pull at the reins to make them stand still.

One of the riders came forth. "Who are you and what are you doing here? And why the hurry?!"

The man who saw himself as the leader of the three bowed his head, he was pale and shivering and so were the other two as well. "I…I am Geir, of Highvale, this is my brother in law Than and his friend Osbord, we have been sent by our village master Thelian of Highvale to ask if we may humbly buy a couple of good stallions"

The rider frowned. "Why the hurry then?"

Geir gasped. "Monsters, horrible…apparition. We have ridden like this for almost an hour, they were glowing! Huge figures!"

The rider did tense up. "Where? "

Geir wiped sweat from his brow. "We were going to make camp for the night by a cliff surrounded by high bushes and some trees, by a small pond. They just appeared out of nowhere but the horses did panic and the monsters did stink"

The riders did look at each other. "What did these monsters look like?"

Geir explained with a slight tremble within his voice and the riders did look at each other. "The rumours are true, the gates have been opened"

The leader sent Geir a swift glance. "Come with us, the Ath'ir need to hear this"

Geir was trembling still, he had never encountered anything that terrifying and he didn't refuse, after all, the city was right there in front of them and they would be safe there right? The horses could barely walk but managed that final stretch just fine. They were good animals and very well trained.

The city was huge, larger than any of them had anticipated and they saw people and elves everywhere. The two others did stare with awe at the horses and the beautiful eternal, Geir had seen many elves before but he had to admit that seeing so many of them gathered like this was a wee bit humbling. They were guided towards a huge hut and Geir had never seen this type of construction before and was intrigued by the marvellous technique needed to build something which was so solid and yet movable. There were several elven warriors there, all sat on pillows on the floor and Geir was a bit nervous, his legs just didn't bend that way anymore, he was too old and too brittle for this the way he saw it. The elves all wore arms, swords and daggers or bows and in the middle was a sort of dais and upon it sat an elf all three immediately realized had to be the Ath'ir. He was taller than the others by several inches and he had an air of dignity and power to him.

Geir bowed deeply, he couldn't afford to act haughty now, they all had to be humble and demure and then maybe their mission would be a success. The elf got up, Geir wondered how anyone could be so frigging beautiful and yet so masculine. The Ath'ir reminded him of a huge lion or another type of big cat, elegant and strong and aware of it too. "You were chased by some sort of apparition?"

The voice was deep but soft and they bowed their heads. "Yes honoured one, we were."

Ahravan nodded slowly. "Describe them"

Geir wetted his lips and repeated what he had said and the elves started to talk with each other, he didn't understand the language at all. Ahravan did turn to the three. "You were lucky, some of the herders have seen such too, and found many dead animals in their path."

Geir did shudder. "Indeed we were guarded by the gods, our horses did run like the wind"

Ahravan sighed. "We have seen many dark omens lately, and heard of many strange happenings. We fear that this could be the start of something rather bad."

Geir didn't say anything, he just hoped that his comrades didn't do anything silly which could blow their cover. One of the elves came forth and made a gesture towards the three. "These men ask to buy horses, stallions?"

Ahravan stared at the three men, all were above their first youth and they looked as if they had lived hard lives but there was strength in them, and he didn't have time to interrogate them now. He had to send out riders and make sure that the city was safe. "We cannot answer your question right now, you will have to wait until we have assessed the danger."

Geir bowed his head deeply. "We are glad just to be here honoured one, take your time"

Ahravan waved to one of the servants. "Give them a tent and make sure that they have food and a bath. We will get back to you as soon as things calm down."

Geir felt a surge of relief rush through him, they were safe! And if luck still was on their side they would emerge from this as rich men. "We are deeply honoured to be here, we will of course wait"

The servant did guide them towards a rather large tent on the outskirts of the city and it had both beds and a fireplace. It was a very nice place and Geir sat down with a groan. He was still shaken from what he had seen and the other two were pale as well. Than did swallow some wine with obvious relief. "What in the name of every hell were those things?"

Geir shrugged. "I have no idea but I fear we may have stumbled into something nasty"

Osbord tilted his head and took the wine flagon from Than. "As long as they are busy with the monsters we ought to have a chance right? They won't bother with three horse traders if there are such demons wandering about"

Geir nodded. "You are right, it will provide us with a chance. All we have to do is wait for that caravan to arrive, they cannot be too far away now."

Than grinned and sat down, pulling his shoes off. "And while we wait we can enjoy the hospitality of the twelve clans, I must say this place is grand. Way better than any village we have visited before"

Geir sighed and sat down to. "Yes, but remember, keep your mouths shut. We cannot afford any slip of the tongue. If we are to succeed we have to make them believe that we are just humble servants. Remember that"

Than made a grimace. "Got it, take it easy, I won't make any mistakes"

Geir smiled, a very stiff smile "You better not, they are very bloodthirsty when they punish people, believe me!"

Wenja had been fairly relaxed for a few days but now they said that Ohtanar was only a couple of days away and even though she was glad the travelling was done for now she was getting nervous again. Nefhriel hadn't really been that much in contact with her for a while but now the elf did start to give Wenja lessons again, in how to act and what to say during the wedding ceremonies. Wenja was convinced that she would forget everything the moment she arrived but Sefa promised that she would help the bride to be remember the most essential things. Prina had gone into hiding in her wagon, she didn't come out and she didn't speak to anyone and she was kept under guard the entire time. Imh feared that she would try to kill herself or the baby again and so they never left her alone even for a moment. Wenja was shocked by the darkness she saw in the girl's eyes and she didn't really understand how Prina had changed so much. It was as if she had become worse than she had been when they found her hiding in that wagon at the start of the journey. Wenja wished that she could have helped but she had to focus on her own life now, and the wedding which was only days ahead. Sefa made her bathe and wash every day and she got massaged and rubbed with sweet smelling oils and Rhawan did visit the wagon each night and she was rather familiar with the male body now. She wasn't disgusted or shocked by anything about it anymore and Rhawan did willingly teach her about his Si'ish and his preferences.

They travelled fast now for the people they did meet told of strange and worrying things and Rhawan did force the caravan to move even at night. They had to reach Ohtanar fast and Wenja wasn't told of what he feared but she understood that it was serious. Rhawan sent some fast riders ahead of them and they were to prepare Ahravan for their arrival. It was very obvious now that the city was nearby for they saw people all the time, herders taking care of their animals, some hunters and some young ones who were just out joyriding. Wenja felt a bit shy now, why she didn't know but they were strangers and she had gotten so used to everybody in the caravan she no longer had any problems with them. Rhawan was talking to everybody and it seemed as if there were monsters on the move again and they were different from before too. Nobody had bothered explaining that danger to Wenja, she hadn't asked again and now she did regret that but there wasn't time for it now. She had to get ready for the wedding. There were guards placed around the caravan all the time and they even met a group of warriors who decided to join them and help keeping everybody safe. One of them was a friend of Rhawan and he said they had found a whole group of people dead just the day before, all had seemingly been burned from the inside out. The shamans had put spells on the city to keep it safe and many were nervous. Rhawan didn't like those news at all, they didn't need such worries now.

The last night before they reached Ohtanar they stopped by a huge cliff where the river did dive into a deep pool, they washed their clothes and equipment, rubbed down the horses and the wagons and had a small feast. There was fish in the river and Wenja was shocked to see how large they were. The trout they caught in the high mountain rivers back home had been rather tiny and rare and these fish were half the length of a grown man and very tasty. Nefhriel did show her how to remove the scales before one fried them and Imh had some sauces ready which made the tender white meat even tastier than before. Sefa and Theka did warm some water and gave Wenja a bath and they even washed Prina even if she was squealing like a stuck pig. The girl appeared to have gotten right out of her mind now and her eyes were wild and distant. Wenja did pity her and the others tried very hard to treat her with respect but it was very hard when she didn't try to listen at all.

Rhawan came to the wagon that night, he did look a bit sad or rather melancholic and Wenja did understand why, she had accepted the fact that he had fallen in love with her now and she didn't really know what her own feelings were. He had asked Sefa to leave the wagon for just a few moments and he was staring at the floor constantly, obviously trying to gather the courage to speak out loud. When he finally did speak his voice did shiver. "I wish I was Ahravan, for the first time in my life. Tomorrow we arrive and then you will be his wife, I just pray that you still will have a place in your heart for me too"

Wenja felt a bit moved by his honesty. "I swear I will, don't worry about that. You have become very dear to me during this journey"

Rhawan sent her a swift almost shy grin. "I didn't expect to fall in love with the bride of my own Si'ish, but I have. If the gods smile at us then our union will be blessed by your presence"

Wenja did blush, she knew that Rhawan and Ahravan were more than just sworn brothers, Sefa had explained this custom to her and she would probably end up as the third person in a marriage triage. It didn't bother her anymore, Sefa had taught her well for sure. Rhawan did kiss her on the forehead and whispered a short prayer before he left, Wenja was left feeling humble, and also a bit nervous. Who was to say what the next days would bring?

Chapter 7: In bliss and in sorrow.

Ahravan had felt a surge of almost explosive relief when he was told that the caravan was approaching the city, he had to sit down and thank every deity he knew of. Rhawan would be there soon, he wouldn't be alone anymore. He started shouting orders, everything was to be prepared and he had to make sure that his bride to be was welcomed in the best manner possible. The shamans started preparing the wedding ceremonies and the cooks started to prepare food for the great days to come, the entire city had become a buzz of activity. Ahravan felt a bit uncertain, he was looking forward to seeing Rhawan again, he had missed his sworn brother a lot and he just prayed that the journey had been an uneventful one. He would speak to Rhawan as soon as they arrived and find out more about his bride to be. He felt a bit like he was about to take a dive into dark waters without knowing how deep it was, it wasn't a good feeling at all. He made sure that a hut was ready for the girl and then he tried to focus upon his normal duties but found that it was very hard. In just a few days' time he would be a husband again, the question was whether or not she would be a good wife.

The riders said the caravan would reach the city the next day and he ordered the ceremony to start the day after that, there was no point in delaying anything and he wanted this over with, so he could go on with his job. The rumours and the strange deaths had truly upset him and he wondered if this somehow could mean that more trouble was coming. The shamans had placed spells around the city now and they did make people feel more safe but they couldn't all just huddle together within its perimeter Things had to be done and he didn't want to risk the lives of his people.

He wouldn't be allowed to see his bride the last day before the wedding according to the customs and this meant that he wasn't going to meet her until their wedding. It didn't really matter that much for he wouldn't be able to change his mind and this was inevitable so why worry about it? He didn't get much sleep that night, not that he needed to sleep but the last days had been stressful and he had a nagging feeling of something being wrong. The three humans who had arrived had been less than honest, he just felt it and he wanted to find out what they were hiding but how? He couldn't push them into telling him anything and he just hoped that their secret wasn't a dark one.

He did wake up to a city which was in the middle of the preparations, people were running around everywhere and the atmosphere was joyful. He managed to smile as he met Laupir outside of his hut, the man did bow his head and he was grinning from one ear to the other. "She is gonna arrive today"

Ahravan did nod and swallowed hard, it had finally become real to him, the fact that he was to get married yet again. His gut felt heavy and he wished that he could run away, seek shelter somewhere. But the oracle had spoken and he knew that there was no way around it. The caravan wouldn't arrive until late in the afternoon so he went and took one of his horses for a swift ride before he sat down and discussed the situation with the clan leaders. Some said that the monsters had been seen coming down from the mountains again and the sightings of demons did make many scared. But the wedding did raise people's spirits a lot and Ahravan was glad that was the case, everybody needed something good to think about now, something which could make them forget the fears for a while. He had prepared the gifts he was to give his new wife and the seamstresses were ready too, she would be treated like a queen for sure. The day felt like a year, it was so long and when the first shouts were heard Ahravan had almost fallen asleep due to sheer boredom. The caravan was approaching the city and he went out of the hut and made sure that he was properly clad and that he was ready to receive the group he had sent out months ago.

Rhawan came riding towards him at the front of the group, he was smiling from one ear to the next and Ahravan let out a sigh of relief, his Si'ish was alright, then things were good. He had truly missed Rhawan's odd humour and mischief and he saw that the wagons were many and the people he had sent out were all there. Good, they hadn't encountered any dangers then. Rhawan did dismount the horse he rode and went over, with calm dignity but Ahravan could see that his eyes were shining. Rhawan did hug him, a swift but fierce hug which said a lot and Ahravan whispered. "Oh by the deities, I have missed you!"

Rhawan did grin, he was clearly moved. "I have missed you too, but now I am back, and I have so much to tell you!"

Ahravan did put a hand behind Rhawan's strong back and guided him into the hut, the others there would help the women place the girl in her hut and prepare for the next day. "Come, tell me everything"

Rhawan did seem eager. "Oh Ahravan, it has been a strange journey for sure but we did find the girl and we have brought her with us. She is ready to be your wife brother, and she has been prepared well"

Ahravan did nod. "Her family didn't protest?"

Rhawan shook his head. "No, but we did encounter some problems, a local man also wanted her and tried to kill her. We feared that he would try to pursue her. A girl from the village did join us, fleeing from the same man, her brother. He had committed a most horrendous crime and now she is being guarded by Ahnriel and Nefhriel and Floth'bha"

Ahravan did frown. "What crime are you talking about?"

Rhawan did take a deep breath. "She is with child brother, and her own brother is the father. He did rape her"

Ahravan had to blink twice. "Are you serious?"

Rhawan did nod. "Yes, she is…very traumatized but we all hope the shamans can help her overcome it. "

Ahravan did almost growl. "Well, if that so called brother does show up here his life is mine, I do not accept such violence against females"

Rhawan did smile, his eyes were soft. "I know you don't my brother"

Ahravan did pour some wine and let Rhawan have one of the cups. "So, what is she like? My wife to be?"

Rhawan did wet his lips. "She…her name is Wenja, and she is a shepherd's daughter. She is sweet and gentle and very innocent, knows little of the world. We have tried to teach her as much as possible during our journey"

Ahravan did hear the tremble in Rhawan's voice, saw that his Si'ish did look down and he immediately realized what it was about. "Oh Rhawan, you have fallen for her?"

Rhawan did bite his lower lip. "I…I cannot lie to you brother, I…I love her!"

He stared at Ahravan with wild eyes. "But I haven't dishonoured you, she is untouched, I swear. You are the one to claim her maidenhead."

Ahravan had to smile, a somewhat sad smile. "Oh Rhawan, I would never distrust you, and believe me, her innocence means little to me. What does she feel?"

Rhawan swallowed hard. "I don't know, she likes me, but…she haven't opened her heart to me, as far as I know"

Ahravan did sigh. "So she is sweet, and beautiful I guess?"

Rhawan would have blushed if it hadn't been for his dark skin. "Like the sun and the moon brother, you will…you will find her beauty to be irresistible."

Ahravan pulled Rhawan closer again. "And you have made sure that she is ready for this?"

Rhawan did nod vigorously. "Sefa has done a good job, she is ready for you"

The Ath'ir did cock his head. "And what about you? Does she know what we share? Is she ready for you as well?"

Rhawan did look down at the floor. "Yes, I think so, if you…if you are willing to share her then….my heart would soar knowing she can be mine as well"

Ahravan did push some stray locks of dark hair out of Rhawan's eyes. "I am willing to share her brother, the first nights are mine but then I will allow you to join us, if she accepts you that is"

Rhawan swallowed hard. "I…thank you!"

Ahravan leaned in closer. "I have missed you so much, will you stay with me tonight?"

Rhawan did nod and his eyes got softer. "Yes, whatever you say, I am yours and you know it"

Ahravan smiled and the smile was a teasing one. The world suddenly felt good again, his Si'ish was there and the girl was apparently a gem. He felt that some of his worries did dissipate there and then. "Then go and have a bath and return to me soon, I have hungered for your touch"

Rhawan did shudder visibly. "And I for your, I will hurry"

Ahravan did kiss Rhawan gently and the dark skinned warrior did answer the kiss with glowing passion, he was almost panting when they broke apart. Ahravan was glad Rhawan had agreed, he didn't want to spend this night alone.

Wenja had been shocked by the size of Ohtanar, she had sort of imagined a small village, like the one she came from but this was indeed a city. There were literally hundreds of huts and tents and people everywhere and she felt nervous right away. What if people here didn't like her? Sefa told her to stay in the wagon until she was told to leave it and they drove up to a very large and new hut which had to have been built recently. Sefa did beam with joy. "This hut is gonna be yours from now on, your private home."

The others had gathered too and Imh had already carried several crates of stuff into the hut. Sefa did throw a thick veil over Wenja. "Come now, it isn't custom for the people to see their new queen until the ceremony starts tomorrow"

Wenja did cringe. "Already?"

Sefa did nod. "Yes, no point in waiting is there? Oh this is gonna be so wonderful"

Wenja felt nervous again and she kept her head low as Sefa did open the door, the hut was large and divided into several rooms and Theka and Nefhriel had already started to pour water into a huge tub placed in one of them. Wenja felt a bit sweaty so a bath would be wonderful. Imh was preparing a meal and as Wenja sat there and felt more and more as if reality finally was sinking in a couple of women entered the hut and they did bow deeply. "We are your seamstresses my lady, we are here to take your measurements"

Wenja had to stand up as the women swiftly did measure her body and they were smiling and seemed to be very friendly so she felt a wee bit better. It was very clear that she would be properly clad when she was to meet her husband to be the next day. Prina had been placed in a room of her own, she just laid on the bed and acted like a doll and Theka was forcing her to eat some, the old woman could be very adamant when she wanted to. Wenja didn't know what would happen to Prina now, Nefhriel would speak to the shamans the next day, everybody hoped that they could help her come to her senses again.

Wenja was bathed and Sefa did massage her with oils and now her hair was wrapped in linen soaked with ointments and when it was washed out Nefhriel did braid her hair in many tiny braids to give it a wavy look. Her nails were filed and her entire body checked for excess body hair and then Sefa did paint her feet and hands with some sort of thick paste which would leave delicate patterns in her skin when it dried. Sefa did leave the hut for a short while and returned with some boxes she proclaimed contained the jewellery Wenja was to wear the next day and Wenja felt overwhelmed. It was really happening and she sort of longed to go back to before, to the journey. She had gotten used to that, now everything changed once more and she was so agitated Sefa did give her something to sleep on. Without it she would spend the night awake and writhing around and everybody said she had to sleep now, and gather her strength for the next day. After all, it would be the first of three wedding days and among the most important days of her life.

Ahravan and Rhawan ended up in Ahravan's bedroom rather fast, they had missed each other and before long they were naked and giving in to their longing. The bond between them was very strong and Rhawan was only submissive when with Ahravan, he would never allow another male to mount him but he did trust Ahravan and loved him dearly. He was gasping with both pleasure and pain and Ahravan panted and knew he wouldn't last very long this time. He had waited for too long for his Si'ish touch and as he reached his climax he heard Rhawan groan and felt him shudder in the same rhythm as himself. It sent surges of bliss through him, they were together again, Ahravan felt much stronger already, more confident. Rhawan did collapse with Ahravan on top of him and both were covered with sweat and other fluids. Ahravan did kiss Rhawan's sweaty neck lovingly and slid off the bed, he felt so much better now, like he was ready to do anything really. Rhawan did sigh and his eyelids did look heavy, he was ready to go to sleep and Ahravan did kiss him on the shoulder. "Just sleep my light, I will go for a swift walk. I need some air"

Rhawan did just mumble and his eyes did slide shut, he was asleep right away and Ahravan felt a surge of intense tenderness and love. Rhawan was more dear to him than anyone else and he did doubt that this girl would be able to take his place in any way. But he was curious and he got some clothes on again and sauntered out of the hut. He hesitated for a moment, then he did walk towards the hut where his future wife was kept and he knew that she had to be asleep by now. He did enter quietly and Sefa was sitting there working on some garments, she gasped and got up when he came inn, curtsied and kept her eyes on the ground. "You don't have to do that for me dear, you know that."

Sefa nodded. "You are here to see her? It is against the customs but…"

Ahravan nodded. "I know, but I need to see her just once, why I don't know"

Sefa smiled and he saw that Theka and Nefhriel were sitting on the floor, both asleep. Imh was nowhere to be seen and neither were Floth'bha. The dark haired girl was whispering. "She is very nervous my lord, but she is strong, and she will be a good spouse for you. I have trained her well, she won't try to resist you in any way"

Ahravan made a grimace. "Why would she try to resist me?"

Sefa shrugged. "She is a village girl, from the inner valleys. To her marriage was something only men enjoy until we came. Rhawan has showed her how to enjoy a male body and I have taught her all I know. She is a maiden still but no longer ignorant"

Ahravan guessed that this was good. "There was a girl coming with her?"

Sefa nodded. "Yes, Prina, a poor young thing, we are worried for her sanity, and the wellbeing of her and her child"

248

Ahravan sighed. "Make sure she has all the care she needs, such things are tragic."

Sefa did get up, gracefully. "Yes my lord. If you will follow me?"

They entered the room where Wenja slept on a rather large bed and Ahravan did blink in disbelief. She was…he couldn't compare her with any other woman he had met before, such elegance and such a radiant being. Her hair was very long and so shiny and the colour…Like ripe berries, dark and full and he suddenly longed to run his hands through it, to feel its silky weight. He thought to himself that this wouldn't be so bad after all, she was ravishing and knowing that Rhawan did love her told him she was worthy of his affection. The wedding night would be a hot one for sure, he saw the shape of her under the blankets and suddenly he felt that he could have taken her there and then, even if he had been with Rhawan just moments ago. The idea of those long strong legs wrapped around his waist did send his heart racing and he swallowed and smiled at Sefa. "I am very glad you have prepared her, she is gorgeous and the dream of any male for sure. The seamstresses will bring her clothes at dawn, the ceremony starts when the sun reached zenith so make sure she has eaten well and is ready for a long day"

Sefa nodded and grinned. "We all love her Ahravan, she is such a kind soul. You will soon discover that too"

He nodded and turned around, there was little doubt that Rhawan had fallen like a ton of bricks for Ahravan did feel the attraction too. He was so tightly bonded to his Si'ish some feelings were bound to pour over no matter what they did. He returned to the hut and went to bed after having washed and eaten some bread. The next day would be one of splendour for sure, and excitement. For the first time in a long while he did look forward to waking up to a new day.

Wenja did wake up in a state of confusion, for the last days she had slept in a wagon which was on the move so this hut which didn't move felt just odd for some reason. Then she did realize what was going on and she felt her heart starting to race and her palms became sweaty. It was the day, the day she had both dreaded and looked forwards to for such a long time. Sefa was already up, she had gotten the fire going and the huge stone oven did send out a pleasant heat already. Imh was busy making a huge breakfast and Theka and Nefhriel was in Prina's room, trying to prepare her for the day. Wenja had slept way longer than normal and felt a bit dizzy due to this but her sleepiness did dissipate as Sefa did hand her a cup of something very warm. It was some sort of blackish liquid and it had a pleasant but strong odour. "What is this?"

Sefa grinned. "Something few can afford, it is made from the crushed beans of a plant which grows far off to the south, it does invigorate you and keeps you awake. The Ath'ir loves it by the way"

Wenja did sniff the drink, it did look a bit mysterious but she did take a small sip and the taste did surprise her, it was a bit bitter but not bad at all and she did feel a pleasant warmth spreading through her body. Imh had made her a bowl of porridge and some bread with cheese and Wenja sat down by the table to eat. She saw now that all the furniture there could be taken apart for transport rather easily, even the bed and the stove and the walls of the hut were thin and almost transparent in the daylight. Light entered the hut through windows in the roof, and they did appear to be some sort of thin membrane. Sefa saw her look of wonder and grinned. "It is the bag foals and other animals are born in, we gather it after the birth and dry it and then several are stitched together. It is very strong material whence it is dry"

Wenja nodded and admired the embroideries which decorated almost everything there, this people was very fond of colours for sure, and abstract patterns. When she had finished eating she got a huge glass of milk and Sefa did pour some wine into a small glass and grinned at her. "Here, for good luck. They will soon come to make you pretty"

Wenja did take a deep breath and tossed the wine back, it was strong and burned her throat but it did make her feel a wee bit more bold. After all, her husband to be wasn't allowed to sleep with her until the last night and she just prayed that she would like him and that he would accept her as she was. Theka and Sefa started unbraiding her hair and they did brush it very gently so the curls and waves didn't go out, then they started rebraiding some locks and gathered it all with ribbons made from what had to be velvet in a deep green colour. They then added gold chain and gems to it and Wenja did feel a bit odd, she wasn't used to such luxury at all. The women from the night before entered again, carrying huge bags and now Wenja was told to stand on a low box while she was being dressed. The entire outfit did take half an hour to put on, much because the two women couldn't agree on which dress she was to wear, and how to decorate it. But at the end she was put into a dress made from sheer green silk with golden embroideries and it was rather simple in shape and yet not for there were just so many tiny details on it. Wenja felt very self-conscious, she had never worn anything that elaborate before and she wished that Sina and her father could have seen her now, she had changed so much during these weeks on the road.

The women did carry a huge mirror into the tent and Wenja was shocked, with the dress and the hair and all the gold and some makeup she did look…like something out of a fairy-tale. It wasn't her, not really. She got a pair of high heeled boots on and Sefa did attach several small amulets to her underskirts. It was supposed to ward off evil spirits, Wenja could recall having heard of a similar custom back home so that wasn't all that strange at all. Theka was a bit disappointed, Prina refused to leave the hut and even though that fact didn't surprise them at all it still didn't sit well with Theka. Prina had to get out there eventually and start living again, being hidden inside for the rest of her pregnancy would only harm her. Sefa told Theka to forget about it for these three days, they could worry about Prina afterwards, now it was Wenja's grand days and they shouldn't be ruined by Prina, no matter how tragic her case was.

They heard that people were gathering outside and Wenja felt a lump in her throat, created by sheer nervousness. She had to really fight her instinctive need to hide and Sefa did sigh and gave her even more wine to calm her nerves. Finally everything was ready, Sefa was to walk beside her and Nefhriel and Theka would follow suit, it made her feel a wee bit more brave. They were to walk through the city to a place near the centre of it where the shamans would be waiting to give their blessings and then there would be partying and feasting for the rest of the day. Wenja was afraid she would make a fool of herself, she had learned a lot about the language now and she did regard herself as relatively fluent but yet she had her doubts. Her vocabulary wasn't that large and she knew that Ahravan didn't speak the language she had grown up with at all. It was gonna be a challenge. One of Ahravan's warriors did enter the hut and nodded with a wide smile. "It is ready, we are awaiting our new Eth'ir."

Sefa did pet Wenja on her cheek. "Go on dear, hold your head up high, smile. You will win their hearts for sure"

Wenja managed to lift her head but her lips felt stiff and then Sefa did tickle her mercilessly under her armpits where she was very ticklish. That made her laugh and then Sefa just pushed her out of the door. The bright light did stun her for a moment but Sefa did sort of guide her forth and she yipped and had to walk, one step after the other until the small group were heading in the right direction. She felt like an animal at an auction, there were eyes on her everywhere. Everybody seemed to have put on their finery and the kids were peeping out from behind their parents in wide eyes curiosity. Wenja was panting, only Sefa's warm hand did prevent her from bolting like a frightened horse and she could hear her heart thundering like a herd of horses over a plain. They walked in silent dignity towards the ceremonial plaza and everywhere the citizens of Ohtanar did throw some sorts of seeds onto the group. Some did also place pieces of cloth on the ground in front of Wenja so she had to step on them and she tried to do as she had been told, hold her head up high and smile.

Everybody there were so pretty, so healthy and their clothes were so nice. She felt less like an over bedazzled piece of jewellery and more like a person when she did realize that she wasn't wearing anything the other women weren't using as well. The open area was approaching and there were seats places everywhere, and a sort of alter with several people standing there in silent patience. It had to be shamans for they all wore these very elaborate costumes made from animal hide and their skin was covered with paint and tattoos. They did look wild and even the friendly expressions within their eyes didn't change her nervous reaction to seeing them.

Then she did spot Rhawan, he did stand next to one of the shamans and he was wearing this lovely bright blue outfit which made him look so dark and so gorgeous. Sefa let out a sigh of admiration and Wenja had to admit that he did look stunning. But he wasn't her groom and she held her breath as Sefa did guide her the last stretch up to the altar. Ahravan would come when she was in place and now they heard the sound of several voices cheering and some were hollering and shouting like mad. It was tradition, the groom was taken to the altar by his best friends and they would make a racket to spook off any evil spirits. Wenja had to gasp, he was really taller than Rhawan. Not by very much but so much it was very noticeable and she felt faint for a second. Ahravan was very different from Rhawan, the dark skinned eternal was boyish and beautiful and he had a sort of youthful energy which was so charming. Ahravan was older, his energy was one of wisdom and strength and he was also beautiful but in a slightly more masculine manner, He did look a bit more rough than Rhawan, his features were not as even and his body stockier and more muscular and yet he was also elegant and slender. Majestic was a word which did describe him very well, and domineering. She held her breath, his skin was dark like she had been told, but not black like Rhawan's. It was more like dark leather and his eyes were so green it did look unnatural, it was a piercing colour and it made his gaze hypnotic. The hair was long as on all the males there and reached his knees and it had a wonderful deep golden tone with a hint of red in it. She had to admit that he did look angelic, and also a bit intimidating. He simply wasn't human and now she really did notice the differences between the eternal and the humans there.

Ahravan could be seen moving his lips a bit, as if he was whispering something and his eyes got large as he saw her, he raised his right hand and placed it above his heart, bowed his head. Sefa did push Wenja forwards a bit so she stood next to him and Wenja had to wet her lips. She was so much shorter than him, she barely reached the middle of his chest! Oh by every God, this was awkward to say the least. Sefa did wink at her and stepped back and now Wenja had to remember it all, and try to remain calm. Ahravan did bow even deeper and she shuddered when she heard his voice, deep and soft. "I am most honoured Wenja, and you are an amazingly brave woman"

She just managed to smile but felt terrified again, what if she did screw this up. There were hundreds of people watching her and even though most seemed to be very friendly and even a bit taken by her appearance she felt insecure. She stared straight ahead as the shamans started to chant their initial blessings, she didn't understand a word they were saying and it did sound very archaic but the crowd was chanting along and she felt the hypnotic rhythm of the chant. Now Ahravan took her hand, it almost disappeared completely within his large worn one and she was a bit surprised by how warm his skin was and how gently he held her. The shamans kept chanting for a while, then they grasped these small pots of wine and water and poured it out around the two, slowly in circles. Ahravan was smiling at her, his eyes were gentle, calmer than those of Rhawan and they held a sort of melancholy she now knew was because of his great age. He had seen so much and for a moment she did pity him, why she didn't really know.

One of the shamans, a woman, tied a sort of string around their hands and now they had to walk around in a circle, not letting go of each other at all. Ahravan was very careful not to move to fast and she was allowed to find her natural pace so she managed to do this without losing her dignity at all. Then another of the shamans did pour wine over the string before he cut it and threw it onto an open fire. Everybody cheered and Wenja knew that this was it, the first part of the wedding ceremony was done. The shaman did grin from one ear to the other and clapped. "Be blessed and be fruitful, now you may kiss your bride my liege"

Wenja swallowed hard as Ahravan did bow down very slowly and planted a gentle kiss on her lips, it made her toes curl up in her shoes for she felt it, by every God how she felt it. She happened to catch a glimpse of Rhawan though, he was standing there looking a bit sad and she felt almost guilty. Somehow she had wanted him to be a part of this too. Ahravan took her hand and they walked to where several tables had been built and placed in neat rows. They sat down at the one on front, facing the crowd and the people were chanting again and again, Wenja did understand that they were praising her as their new Eth'ir and she blushed to the roots of her hair and tried to smile.

Some of the warriors did silence the crowd with huge arm movements and some women came running into the open area, all wearing some very tiny skirts and a sort of top and nothing more. They started to dance to the sound of a flute and Wenja realized that there would be some entertainment first. Ahravan did hold her hand, it felt safe and she did instinctively seek his protection from all these new things, even if he was a stranger. She did dare to look at him, he wore a similar set of clothes to Rhawan but his was in black and very elaborate and it did make him look stunning since it did contrast his hair. She could see the outline of well-defined muscles through the fabric and she realized that he was a warrior as well as a leader. Some of the servants came carrying jugs of wine and the dancers were outdoing themselves for a while. Then some singers did enter the open area and some of the songs made people laugh out loud so they had to be funny.

The entertainment did last for a while, there were jugglers and some did tricks on horseback while a girl wearing nothing but a pair of small panties did show everybody how she was able to twist her body into seemingly impossible positions. Wenja did almost forget why she was there in the first place. Then the space was cleared again and Rhawan did walk to the middle of it. "Our Ath'ir is honoured by your presence, and delighted by your heartfelt welcome of his new wife. Now it is time for the blessing of gifts"

Wenja had already been told that he would give her things, to show his appreciation of her. She had believed this to be just some small things though, like back home. But now some warriors came carrying caskets with clothes and other things she would need. Some smaller crates did contain jewellery and hair ornaments and there were even woven blankets and bed spreads. Then a man came with two huge long legged dogs on a leash, they were hers from now on and they wagged their tails and did lick her hands. Wenja weren't that used to dogs but they did seem friendly so she dared to pet them. A good hunting dog was essential if one was to go hunting for food alone.

The next thing which was presented to her was four cows and some ewes and a ram, she had never seen sheep that large and this gift did excite her since she was used to sheep. Her father would have loved to own such sheep, their wool looked so thick and silky and they were swift on their feet and yet larger than the ones back home. The cows had huge horns and she saw that they had been decorated with beautiful patterns carved into the very horn itself. Then a herd of horses was being driven into the open space. It was five mares and some geldings and a tall white stallion which did look as if he knew exactly how gorgeous he was. Wenja was overwhelmed, such horses were so very expensive. Ahravan did see that she loved what she saw and his smile got wider, she was such a wonderful sight and her childlike joy made his heart swell in his chest.

Then the horses were taken away and now Laupir came with Flint, the giant horse did nicker and dance and Wenja did gasp. She had never even believed that a horse could get that large, it was enormous and terrifying. Ahravan smiled and pointed at the beast. "He is Flint, he is a Da'ith, a warhorse. He will keep you safe"

Wenja did frown. "I am not to ride him?"

Ahravan shook his head. "No, he will run next to your horse and protect you both"

Rhawan had told Ahravan about the Zahar and the Ath'ir was a bit intrigued as to why the animal still was following them, now he was grazing with Rhawan's own horses and Ahravan couldn't help but feel that he had something to do with Wenja. Flint did bow his mighty head and sniffed Wenja's hands and Laupir was smiling widely. "He likes you, soon we will make sure he bonds with you."

Wenja could only nod, she was overwhelmed and Ahravan did push a lock of her hair out of her face. "We will make sure that you are safe, always. Forget all worries now, here you will truly be treasured"

Wenja swallowed hard and Ahravan grasped her hand, kissed it reverently. "I am nothing but your humble servant from now on my lady, and rest assure that everybody here will adore you like I do, and like my Si'ish does."

Wenja did blush, so Rhawan had revealed what he felt to Ahravan, well, she hadn't expected otherwise. Not truly anyhow. Food was being brought inn and now she did realize that she was hungry, where had the time gone?

The three men who had arrived some days earlier had stayed near their tent the whole time, trying to lay low and be ignored. They had been fed and they had even been given some wine and the leader had taken some walks through the camp, staring at the horses as if he truly was there to buy some. When the caravan arrived they pretended as if they didn't care at all, they showed some curiosity because that would be normal and expected but nothing more than that. But they didn't see the girl Mjorr had sent them to kill at all and Geir started to really believe that something was off. There was most definitely something the man hadn't told them and they hated surprises. Now they were hiding at the back of the crowd as the Ath'ir was being married to that village girl and they had to admit that she was stunning, a very rare beauty and probably a very good wife to be. But the wagon she had arrived in was taken away and the other girl had to be in the hut Wenja had been given so they sort of sauntered towards it, hoping to catch a glimpse of their target.

They pretended as if they were just stretching their legs, talking about horses and as they walked slowly past the tent Osbord did nod towards the entrance. "Someone is coming, don't look"

They stopped and started discussing some colts grazing in a corral near them and Geir kept his gaze hidden as he did throw a swift glance at the people leaving the hut. It was an elderly dwarven lady and a huge woman who could only be a half orc, between them they were supporting a thin blonde girl who just had to be the one Mjorr wanted dead. She was his sister beyond doubt, it was the same blue eyes and the same slender shape but Geir saw something disturbing as the two women helped the girl sit down on a bench in the sun. She was with child, rather heavily with child too and Geir walked on not looking at her even once more. He dragged the two others back to their tent and whence inside he sat down and stared at them. Killing her was out of the question, first of all, they would never murder a pregnant woman for in their belief that would most certainly condemn their souls to eternal damnation and second of all, this was something they could use. Did Mjorr know that his sister was with child? Was that why he wanted her dead? In that case, why? Who was the father? Was Mjorr trying to protect someone? That he wanted the girl dead before he and his father reached the city told them all that the girl knew something Dagar just couldn't find out about and Geir had a terrible suspicion. Than tilted his head, he was a bit worn and his hair and beard had started to turn grey, he had seen a lot and his eyes were dark. "He is the father, by every God, I am sure"

Geir clenched his teeth together, he nodded slowly. "We cannot be sure of it, but I wouldn't be surprised if he is no."

Osbord closed his eyes slowly, there was sheer disgust on his face. "Every God there is should curse him, if he has…if he has lain with his own sister, there is no greater sin!!"

Their tribe had a very strict taboo against incest and such a vile act would endanger everybody, the Gods would strike down upon the entire tribe in wrath. Seeing that pale shivering figure Geir was rather sure that Mjorr had forced himself onto the girl and they did also despise rapists. It was unmanly, and cowardly. They were mercenaries but there is a difference between killing in battle and killing to cover up someone else's foul deeds. They felt used and betrayed and Than hit the table so hard it jumped. "We won't do anything until he arrives, if we can confirm that he…that the child is his…then he is to bear the full brunt of what he has done. The gods will strike down upon us if we don't act upon our knowledge"

Geir nodded. "Aye, we stay, and we protect the girl. If anything she is innocent in this, Mjorr is gonna pay for having sent us off to do this, we could have faced damnation"

They all shuddered and all were a bit pale. Being in danger of losing the favour of their gods was terrifying, yes, Mjorr would have to pay for his sin, and pay a lot!

The feasting and dancing did last for hours and now food was being brought forth in huge amounts. Wenja had never seen such dishes before and she was glad Theka did sit close to her and Sefa wasn't that far away neither. Both whispered to her what it was that was brought to the table and she realized that she was to just take a small taste of each dish. Nobody could eat a lot of each unless they had the stomach of a troll. Wenja did recognize the grilled lamb and the fried fish but some of the other dishes were alien to her. She had never had a sort of meat pudding with spices in it, and the dried smoked melon was delicious as Sefa had promised. There was wine to go with the food and mead too and she soon felt tipsy. Ahravan had to stop the ones serving the food from giving her too much. Small cakes and other desserts were presented to the party goers after the main dishes and now the kids were everywhere, begging for treats. Wenja did see that the children there looked very happy and protected and she liked that, in many families where she was from children were regarded as work force and nothing more.

Now the dances started and Wenja realized that she had to dance with Ahravan at least once, it was expected and she felt stiff as a board as he got up and offered her his hand. She took it with a stiff grin and let him lead her forth until they reached the open area in front of the tables. The music was slow and almost hypnotic and yet it was joyful and light hearted and she liked it a lot. The dance was simple enough, just wandering small steps round in circles while circling each other and they did sometimes change direction and Ahravan's hand was supporting her back the whole time, it made her feel much better and she started to enjoy this. The dance became more vigorous, now the males were to spin their partners around and even lift her every now and then and being tipsy that really made Wenja feel somewhat odd, but it was fun and Ahravan was so very strong and yet gentle. Some did sing very loudly and Wenja didn't understand much but she started to realize that some of the songs were rather obscene in nature for some of the lead singers did exchange some words with very tell-tale body movements and everybody were laughing and mimicking them.

She did even dance with Rhawan and he did whisper endearments to her and she felt herself blush, she remembered what she had seen him and Sefa do and knew that it wouldn't be long before she too was to do these things. It was odd to think about.

The evening became late afternoon and it was getting darker and Wenja did realize that she was tired and her head did feel heavy. She had been drinking too much and she needed the chamber pot and the dress felt heavy now. Sefa did walk over and she did wink at Ahravan. "She is tired my lord, and ready for a good night sleep, I will take her back to the hut if that is alright with you"

Ahravan nodded and bent over, did kiss Wenja on her forehead. "It is, I will join you soon"

Wenja did remember that they were sleep in the same tent now but nothing would happen yet, it was somewhat comforting to know. Sefa did show her the latrines which had been dug in an area of the city meant for this and Wenja found them to be rather smart. There was little smell because they were being covered with dirt very fast and she realized that everybody there were very concerned about hygiene. It was probably just to expect, so many people living together would mean that disease could break out easily if such matters weren't paid attention to. The hut had been rearranged a bit, now there was a small room in front of where Wenja's bed was placed and a bedroll had been placed on the floor there. She realized that Ahravan was to sleep there and she found that a bit odd, he was the Ath'ir after all.

Sefa just grinned. "It is tradition, he will be watching you for these two first nights and then on the third night he is allowed to touch you"

Wenja did shudder ever so slightly. He was so much larger than her, and rather intimidating in spite of his obvious kindness, she wondered if they could do it at all. Sefa did help her get rid of the dress and the jewellery and then she washed Wenja and put her into her nightgown. The bed was very comfortable and soft and the covers made from softly woven blankets and some very silky furs. Wenja did feel that it indeed had been a very long day although it had been over so quickly, there had been so much happening and Sefa did grin. "Over the next days you will receive gifts also from the other citizens of the city, it is tradition. It may not be much but I can assure you that everything is heartfelt."

Wenja did blush. "I did receive such rich gifts today, from Ahravan. I cannot even start to imagine how I can thank him"

Sefa grinned and tucked her inn. "Be a joy to him and that will be more than enough, I can promise that everything was given freely"

Wenja managed to grin. "I think he did like me"

Sefa giggled. "Oh dear, he did more than like you. Everybody with eyes could see that, he is soon as infatuated as Rhawan."

Wenja did actually like that idea, it was…comforting. Sefa did blow out the lamp and Wenja laid there for a while, tired but to wired up to really relax until she heard someone approaching the bedroll. She heard him lay down and sigh when he relaxed into the covers and she couldn't see him but she did smell him, a rather masculine scent which was different from Rhawan's. He whispered. "Are you awake?"

Wenja nodded. "I am"

Ahravan could be heard moving slightly. "You did well today, I am very proud of you. Sleep now, tomorrow is gonna be a long day too"

She remembered that it included baths in some sacred springs and she was starting to look forward to it, she hadn't really had time to get to know him at all. She had seen enough to recognize that he was dearly loved by his peers and that the entire people did obey him out of respect and trust. She smiled to herself. "Good night"

He whispered back, his voice deep and calming. "And a good night to you too my lady"

Wenja found that she finally could relax enough to sleep.

The next morning she was awakened by Sefa who did look very excited, she was almost jumping up and down and Wenja did rub her eyes and yawned. She was still a wee bit tired but the fresh air did awaken her and Sefa did find some clothes for her to wear. Wenja was shocked to see that she was to wear some sort of odd garment which resembled a mix of pants and skirts and Sefa winked and helped her getting the garment on. "You'll need this today, you will be riding a lot"

Wenja blinked. "Ah…I don't know how to…"

Sefa giggled. "You will be riding with Ahravan of course, he will keep you safe."

Wenja nodded slowly. "Are the springs far away?"

Sefa shrugged. "No, not terribly so. It is gonna be a good ride I think, and you will see a lot"

Wenja got the rest of the clothes on and Sefa did braid her hair and placed some rings on her fingers and she did also give her some new boots which were higher and stiffer than the ones she had been used to using. Then she got served a huge breakfast and she realized that Ahravan had gotten up way earlier than herself and that he and some others were waiting for her. That made her feel slightly guilty. She ate and got some milk and then Sefa did follow her outside. She saw Ahravan standing next to a very tall black horse with golden mane and tail and Rhawan and some others were there too, they smiled when they saw her and Wenja felt like some foolish child for she had no idea of how to greet them. She lifted her hand. "Uh, good day?"

Ahravan bowed his head. "A good day to you too, are you ready?"

Wenja nodded and she saw that a tall human warrior did lead forth a smaller grey mare which Sefa did mount with admirable elegance. Ahravan did grasp Wenja by her waist and before she really knew what was happening she was on top of the tall horse and Ahravan did mount up behind her. "Hang onto the saddle horn if you feel insecure but I ensure you, I will never let you fall off"

Wenja tried not to look down, this horse was the tallest she had ever sat on and she saw that the huge horse named Flint was running along the group. Some shamans had joined them and the group did gallop out of the city at great speed. The area was gorgeous, rolling hills and rivers and small lakes and here and there holts of trees. They rode on a well-used track and made great speed and she found that she did enjoy it, after a while that was. Ahravan was very warm and solid behind her back and he held her around her waist with one arm as the other held the reins. She had noticed that the eternal didn't use bits on their horses, just a sort of lose halter and still the animals seemed to obey perfectly. She felt that she had to break the silence. "What is his name? The horse I mean?"

Ahravan was steering the horse with his legs, she realized that now. "His name is Ayr'esh, he is my favourite steed"

Wenja didn't find that hard to believe. "He is very large"

Ahravan chuckled. "Yes, and he has many sons and daughters. He is our best stud, and very precious"

Wenja did admire the shiny coat and the silky mane and then she did notice that Ahravan had let go of the reins and were running his hands through her hair, she blushed. "Do you like it?"

Ahravan nodded. "It is lovely, such a wonderful colour, who did you get that from?"

Wenja felt her face burn again, she felt the warmth of his hand against her skin and the caresses against her scalp were amazing. She had always loved having her head massaged. "My real mother, she died when I was very little and her brother raised me like his own child"

Ahravan stroked her hair slowly. "Rhawan told me about this man who wanted you?"

Wenja nodded. "Yes, Mjorr, he hates everything he cannot have, so he tried to kill me"

Ahravan sighed. "But you are mine now, and if that man comes to this place my warriors will catch him and he will die terribly"

Wenja did shudder and Ahravan sighed again, his arm tightening around her. "Did I overstep some boundaries there? I am honest Wenja, I am telling the truth always. He will be killed if he comes to this city, Rhawan told me what he had done to his sister"

Wenja sighed and leaned a bit back towards him, seeking safety. "I know, but…I prefer not to talk about him now"

Ahravan gathered her hair and planted a kiss on her neck, very gently. "That is alright, do you have a large family?"

Wenja took a deep breath and started telling about her home and her kin and Ahravan did listen and made small comments every now and then, just to encourage her. She relaxed again and he understood that she was used to hardship and toil and not at all spoiled. She had suffered a lot and his heart did soar, knowing he could make her life so much better. The ride took them across some rivers and he did tell her small anecdotes about life on the plains and she was as curious as a child. He did find that to be adorable but he was also a bit worried. There was so much she didn't know and he would have to teach her much before she could be a part of the society of the plains completely.

The sacred grove with the springs was placed at the foot of a very steep cliff and it did look like a huge needle someone had thrust into the very ground itself back in the far past. The cliff was impressive but the grove was even more so with huge ancient trees. They did dismount outside of a makeshift fence made by ropes, they did span the entire grove and showed that this was a sacred site. Wenja felt a bit awestruck, she felt that this was a special place and the trees filled her with a sense of wonder. They did seem like timeless relics from some forgotten world and Ahravan saw her awe and smiled. She did honour nature, that was good. Sefa grasped her hand. "This place is the birthplace of the twelve clans, where the first chieftains did gather to form their union. Everybody does honour this sacred site"

Wenja was dragged off towards a sort of altar and the shamans were preparing for the next part of the rituals. She felt a bit uncertain but Ahravan did smile at her and Rhawan was there too in the background. They had been riding for some hours and Wenja felt that in her thighs, she was glad Ahravan had done the job of steering the horse. When the shamans were done preparing she and Ahravan was brought in front of the altar and the shamans did chant something while circling the two with bundles of burning sage. Then Sefa did make a small cut in Wenja's little finger and Rhawan did the same to Ahravan and the blood drops from the tiny wounds were gathered on the surface of the altar. Sefa did give Wenja a dagger which she in turn gave Ahravan and he gave her a needle and a piece of cloth in return. Then the shaman did cut some hair from them both and burned it over the altar and Wenja almost sneezed from the smell.

Apparently that was it for there wasn't any more chanting and Sefa grinned at her. "Now comes the funny part, follow me"

She followed the dark haired girl through the grove until they reached a sort of entrance into the cliff itself. The warm air which seeped through the entrance told Wenja that this were hot springs and they entered a smaller room where you could get undressed. Wenja did look forward to a warm bath but she still felt shy. Sefa did help her get rid of the clothes and she grinned widely. "You are to enjoy this alone with him, none other are allowed to enter until sunset. From then on you are to avoid food and drink only water for the rest of the night."

Wenja nodded and she felt herself blush and shudder ever so slightly. "But he cannot…you know?"

Sefa shook her head. "No, no penetration at least, he may try to please you a bit otherwise but you cannot consummate the marriage until tomorrow evening, at the sacred mother tree"

Wenja took a deep breath. "Great"

Sefa did smack her across the butt. "Go now, get into the pool. He will join you soon"

Wenja did gasp and Sefa did open the door. The room behind the one she had been in was huge, a cathedral of stone and water and she had to gasp and just stare. Huge columns carried the roof and the pool was a strange blue colour she had never seen before. It was huge too, filled the entire cave but there were different depts. and some parts were sealed off with some sort of wooden contraptions. The place had an intense earthy scent and she had to take a huge breath of air and just force herself to get used to it. The pool had a beautifully carved stair leading down into it and there were benches carved into the rock along the edge and the columns. She walked towards the stair and was a bit nervous, just how hot was this water? She got down the first steps and put a toe into the water, it was warm but not unpleasantly so and she dared to walk down until it reached her knees. There she had to stop to get used to it before descending any further.

But the water felt wonderful whence she got used to it and she walked inn until she was submerged to her shoulders. She had been taught how to swim by her father when she was a mere child for he did deem it as a very useful skill. And now it did all come back to her and she felt rather safe in the water, the odd smell did go away after a short time and she enjoyed the warmth. This pool had room for hundreds of people and she did understand that it was a sacred spot, it sort of created a sense of great awe within people and she admired the way nature was merged with artificial shapes in a manner which made it all seem as if it had been there since the beginning of time itself. She was busy trying to determine if the columns were natural or not when she heard splashing and turned her head around to see Ahravan enter the pool, he was already in over his waist and she blushed and felt silly again. He did smile and waded towards her, extending a hand towards her and she took it hesitantly. She saw that his hair had been braided into one thick braid and it did look like a massive chain of gold as it did hang down his back.

"I trust that you are comfortable?"

His voice was soft and she nodded. "The water is just perfect yes."

Ahravan did smile and gestured towards some of the benches. They sat down and the water did reach Wenja's shoulders but it was barely reaching his chest. She had to stare, he was more muscular than Rhawan, but just as chiselled and the physique was flawless, she didn't have other words to describe him. He did see that she was staring and smirked. "Do you like what you see?"

She winced and blushed all the way up to the roots of her hair. "Ah…hmm"

Ahravan caught a lock of her hair and let it slide between his fingers. "There is no shame in admiring what the gods have created."

Wenja had to swallow hard. "I…I am not used to…"

Ahravan sighed and leaned back into his seat, the water was rather dark and did obscure his lower body and she was glad it did. "Do explain please, I wish to learn more about you, after all we are almost wedded already"

Wenja felt trapped and she felt her face burn with embarrassment. "Uh, back where I am from…"

He reached out and caressed her shoulders gently. "Go on please"

She gathered her courage. "Only a shameless woman would admire a man, she would be seen as…as a whore"

Ahravan sighed and his hand rested against her back for a moment. "Wenja, here things are very different, we appreciate the gifts we have been given, our bodies give us great joy and not accepting this is like…well, not accepting the fact that we have been created. It is…blasphemous."

She nodded and looked down" I know, Sefa and Rhawan has taught me that. "

Ahravan smiled. "Rhawan, you like him?"

She took a deep breath. "Yes, I…I know him, sort of. I feel safe with him"

Ahravan did smile and the smile was a very loving one. "Good, you do know we are more than just friend's right?"

Wenja nodded again, feeling a bit silly yet again, she felt as if she knew nothing compared with him, as if she was a mere child. And perhaps she was, compared with the ageless wisdom she saw within those intense green eyes. "Yes, you are bonded"

Ahravan caressed her back again. "We are, will you accept also Rhawan as you spouse?"

She swallowed, feeling a hint of a strange and very unfamiliar excitement. "I…I will"

Ahravan lifted her hand and kissed it gently. "That is good, nobody ought to suffer because of love. Our people have understood that for ages, too bad humans are a bit slow to accept such fundamental truths."

Wenja just blushed again and Ahravan leaned a bit closer. "Rhawan has shown you pleasure haven't he? I trust that he and Sefa has done their job well"

Wenja felt her heart speeding up. "Ah….Yes"

Ahravan chuckled. "Do not be shy my sweet, and do not be afraid. I will never do you harm, all I want to do is teach you how good one can be to each other."

She yipped and tried to smile and he kissed her hand. "Relax, I will not go all the way, we cannot truly bond until tomorrow night, but I want to explore, learn to know you also in this manner"

Wenja could only nod with huge eyes and he smiled and kissed her hand again, very gently before he turned it around and kissed her palm, very slowly and with a hint of tongue. And then he did lick her palm and she gasped, the intense green eyes didn't leave her face even once as he did it again, and now he did suck her middle finger into his mouth and let his tongue swirl around it. Wenja suddenly had a hard time breathing, and the water had become so much hotter or so it seemed. He let go of her finger and his eyes did sparkle. "You are sensitive, wonderful"

His husky voice sent shivers down her spine and she remembered what she had done in the wagon with Rhawan and Sefa, she had to squeeze her thighs together to alleviate the sudden surge of heat. He chuckled and grasped her by the waist, hoisted her up so she stood on the seat of the bench. Now she was slightly taller than him and he leaned inn and kissed her neck, let his tongue slide over her skin and she felt as if she was on fire. The strong hands did support her and she felt completely safe, and suddenly she desired this more than anything she had ever wanted before. Ahravan felt the change in her, she did submit and he smiled to himself and returned to the long slender neck. Her skin was like velvet and the scent of her intoxicating. He moved forth, now it was her breasts which got his attention and they were perfect, such wonderful and firm half domes which fit perfectly into his hands and the nipples were erect and begging for his attention. He leaned forth, sucked them gently, the left first and then the right and Wenja yelped and her hands did paw at his shoulders, he found that he enjoyed the feeling a lot.

Wenja felt hollow, unfulfilled and incomplete and she felt how a surge of wetness made her slick and ready, he was so good at this and his constant teasing was almost unbearable. It was odd though, she had only felt like this with Rhawan and now she was all alight for Ahravan even though she didn't really know him at all. But he did make her feel so safe and treasured and his hands did cup her ass and he let out a groan and he was breathing hard now. She felt her heart thundering in her chest and she dared to lean forth and kiss him shyly. Ahravan smiled, a warm smile, then he answered the kiss and turned it into a real one. With tongue. It made Wenja's knees turn into jelly and she had to cling onto him to remain on her feet and he chuckled and kissed her neck again. "Oh by the Goddess, you are so ready for me aren't you, so eager."

Wenja could only squeal, she was aching and her body was trembling, The scent of him was making her mad and she arched and let him kiss her throat again. Ahravan almost growled. "This is not going to end well unless I get back in control, I am so tempted right now, I want to fuck you against this column and not stop until we are both spent."

The very words made Wenja quiver all the way to her toes, she wanted him to do it, wanted to wrap her legs around him, let him claim her completely and she didn't care if it would hurt. She felt as if all common sense had left her, all that remained was this overwhelming need to just follow her basic instinct and feel him inside her, feel him complete her. Ahravan grasped her by the waist and lifted her again, held her against his own body as he waded swiftly back towards the edge of the pool. The edge was some inches above the water line and very smooth, carved so that nobody would get hurt if they were to bump into it. He placed her on it and Wenja realized what he was about to do. She whimpered his name and laid back, let him spread her legs and she gasped as he kissed her mound like Rhawan used to do and then started exploring her very gently.

Ahravan was more patient than Rhawan, she realized this rather fast. He wasn't racing along towards the goal but tried to make the journey the goal. Wenja was aching and writhing and he was playing her with the instinctive understanding of a true master. Ahravan was older and more mature than Rhawan and he did manage to control himself so much better than Rhawan would, he managed to forget his own burning need in order to satisfy her and he did hold her at the very edge for much longer than Wenja had believed it to be possible. When he did finally send her over she was sure she was going to pass out, the sensation rushing through her entire body so strong it was like an explosion. She screamed his name and Ahravan groaned and had an expression of almost agony on his face. "Oh by every deity, you are so wonderful, so filled with fire"

He pushed himself up onto the edge of the pool and she saw his entire body for the first time. He was just as exquisite from his waist down and she had to swallow hard as she let her gaze drift down to his crotch. Rhawan was right, Ahravan was larger, not much but noticeably and she felt a surge of nervous energy yet again. How could that fit inside of her? How could it fit inside of anyone for that matter? But she remembered having seen Rhawan fuck Sefa and she hadn't complained even once about his size and this wasn't that much bigger, at least it didn't seem that way. Ahravan was breathing hard. "My sweet, I have to…"

He grasped her and pulled her closer, she was pressed against his chest and he lifted a leg and caught hers with it. "I am not gonna take you, I can't from this angle but I need to come"

She felt him push against her body and shuddered, he was so very hard and so very warm and she felt how slick he was. Ahravan did place his hardness between her thighs, holding them together with his own legs and Wenja did gasp as he started to slide back and forth. She did react out of instinct, pushing her legs harder together to make it better for him and he moaned and his hand on her hip did shiver.

Wenja wanted to push her hips backwards, to bend her body so he could enter her but he held her in place and the feeling of him there made her so over sensitive and so wired up. She was gasping and tried to meet his thrusts and Ahravan groaned. "Yes!"

He pushed his hips even further forwards and now he was sliding back and forth along her slit, the head of his cock did push against her clit with each thrust and Wenja started to keen, to strain against him. The feeling rose in her again, she couldn't resist and Ahravan was groaning with each move, fighting hard to remain in control of himself. All it would take would be a small move and he would be in the right angle to take her from behind but he didn't want to break the rules. He had to stay in control of himself. The others would surely understand if he gave inn and consummated the marriage there and then but he would feel guilty if he did. He just kept sliding between her silky thighs and the feeling was enough to push him towards his release. She was so warm and the slick from her body and his own made it effortless and by the gods how good it felt. Wenja turned her head around, watched him. His face was contorted by pleasure and the sheer effort of it and he was gasping for air, eyes huge and dark and the sight was the final drop. She felt that explosion again, racing through her body. She arched and screamed and Ahravan did push her even closer to his own body as he felt the tension reach its maximum, roared as it found its release and kept roaring as the orgasm raced through him, heard her squeal his name and shudder against him in the same rhythm he felt inside.

Wenja felt the thick hardness pulse as it pressed against her own trembling core and warm wetness did spurt out all over her thighs and her slit. She mewled, her body shaking out of control and she wondered how that would feel when it happened inside of her, not on the outside. Ahravan moaned her name and she felt him get soft again, felt him relax against her back and his hand let go of her hip. "Thank you my beautiful, I...I needed that"

His voice was hoarse and almost weak, he kissed the back of her neck lovingly and she had to giggle. She felt wonderful and so filled with energy and yet she was aching, in a strange and very frustrating manner.

Ahravan did kiss her shoulder and managed to get up, he smiled down at her. "Tomorrow night, how I long for that. I will make you scream my name again, and I swear to you, if you start to swell with child there will be no joy on earth greater than the one I then will feel"

Wenja did swallow hard, she suddenly wanted that too. Even if she was to die of old age before her children were even adults she wanted that, to carry his heirs. She managed to smile and sat up too, she was swollen and over sensitive down there as before but now she knew that her remaining life as a virgin could be counted in hours. She had to giggle and take a swift peek at his cock once more, the idea of it sliding inside of her made her tremble ever so slightly. She bit her lower lip. "I would be honoured to"

Ahravan grasped her hand and kissed it and there was pure affection in his eyes as he stared her into her eyes. "The honour would be all mine"

Wenja blinked, looked down. "Your first wife didn't give you any children?"

He sat up completely and pulled her closer, held her tight. "No, she was…she would have become a terrible mother and she was too convinced of her own magnificence to bother with such things as children. I didn't try to make her pregnant at all"

Wenja had to grin. "She sounds despicable. "

Ahravan grinned too. "Yes, she was. She tried to mess up the relationship between me and Rhawan too, she was jealous I guess"

Wenja did cock her head. "So he didn't offer to…you know?"

Ahravan laughed out loud, a full and very warm laughter, it felt good hearing him laugh, it made Wenja's heart soar. "No, heavens forbid. He hated her, if she had demanded that he got in bed with her he would have done his very best to fuck her do death I bet, a human cannot keep up with the endurance of one of us. He would have been way too much for her"

Wenja giggled and then she too had to laugh. "Then it was good she never did"

Ahravan smiled at her and kissed her brow. "Yes, but he would have done it for me, to free me from that harpy"

Wenja did lean into him, feeling slightly sleepy but at peace, relaxed and safe. "Rhawan told me you tried to make her happy, in spite of it all"

Ahravan nodded. "Yes, we do honour women here, and she wasn't really to blame for her own personality. Her father was, he had spoiled her and the idea of becoming the Eth'ir was what tipped her over into slight madness I guess. Some people cannot handle power, it consumes them. She was fond of trinkets and pretty things and so I gave her trinkets and pretty things and that kept her satisfied"

Wenja scoffed. "So she wasn't fond of your skills in bed?"

Ahravan laughed again. "Heck no! Oh she did enjoy it but pretended not to, just to live up to the ideal of her own tribe. She always kept telling everybody of how she had to "endure" my advances but in truth she was very willing. It didn't take long before I wasn't though"

Wenja had to giggle and hid her face behind her hands, a bit shocked by his confession. "So you preferred to keep away from her?"

Ahravan nodded solemnly. "She was…how do I say it, a hypocrite? Yes, that is the word"

Wenja was very glad Sefa and the others had taught her so much about the language they used here on the plains, she did understand him and only a few words were difficult but she felt that she would be fluent soon enough. "I bet"

Ahravan turned his head towards her. "But you…I will never be tired of you my sweet, you are everything a male could possibly desire"

She felt herself blush again. "You mean it?"

He nodded solemnly and kissed the back of her hand. "Yes, to us you are…incredible"

She bit her lower lip, felt almost giddy and bolder than usual. "How come?"

He tilted his head, let a hand run through her long locks. "Your hair, the colour is so rich, so pure. We never see such colour here. You are so shapely, your curves a mysterious landscape a man would die to explore"

He kissed her shoulder slowly. "Your eyes like pools of emerald water, so deep it could drown me. Your lips so rosy and so kissable, begging for my touch"

Wenja did blush even worse than ever before, here he was describing her using sheer poetry, she was indeed blessed. He let a hand run down her chest, kneaded a breast lightly and she had to hiss and then moan as he rubbed the nipple between his fingers. "And these, oh by the Goddess, no she elf does possess something like this"

He leaned fort and caught the nipple with his lips and Wenja felt her heart speeding up again. What was he doing? He let go, his eyes dark again with desire and she could see that he was hard again. "Your waist, I bet I could grasp around it if you let me try"

He suddenly flipped her over so she laid on her stomach across his thighs. "That rear of yours, perfect halves of a whole, so soft and firm and your skin is like that of a peach."

He did stroke her ass slowly and Wenja had to gasp, she hadn't really known that this part of her body could be so sensitive. He was caressing, no, worshiping each square inch of it and she was panting, feeling how the rough skin of his hands made her own skin burn. She pushed her hips up and he smiled, a warm smile. "Eager for me again little one?"

She nodded and he gave her butt a small smack. She yipped, it didn't hurt, it just felt…tantalizing. "A man could dream of licking and biting into this, and spill himself just touching it"

Wenja shuddered, his voice was low and dark and hoarse and she imagined what that would feel like, the very idea sent her into a fit of shuddering. He let his hand slide down between her thighs. "Wet again for me? I long to dive into that passage of yours, to do more than just taste its sweetness. I long to feel it caress me, embrace me, to fill it with my essence and know that our union is truly blessed"

He let a finger slide between her nether lips and Wenja gasped and rocked her hips against him. He chuckled and let a finger enter her, she had to squeal, the sensation was so intense and new and she was heaving for air before long. "Oh please"

Ahravan was almost humming. "Please what?"

Wenja shivered. "Please do it"

Ahravan chuckled but she felt him tremble ever so slightly. "I cannot, not yet. But I will show you a bit more"

He used a finger on her clit and now his thumb did slide into her and it felt…Wenja could only close her eyes and let go of her ability to think. He was using his hand with slow determination and she laid there across his thighs and moaned as if she was in agony. It didn't take long, she tensed up and he felt it and pushed two fingers inside as she started to pulse and come and she screamed, the feeling of being fuller than ever before was insane. Ahravan was breathing very hard now. "Oh Goddess, you are so tight, and so strong. Tomorrow I won't be able to last if you squeeze me like that"

He held his fingers in place until she was done, then he pulled them out and licked her juices of them, very slowly and deliberately. The sight sent shivers down her spine. He got her up, placed her sitting across his thighs and facing him. She saw that his cock was fully hard again and he grasped onto himself with a hand, stroked it slowly and deliberately. "Would you dare to help me?"

Wenja nodded, she felt brave and she wanted to explore him as well. She let her own hand join his and he did show her the rhythm, he wanted. Her fingers didn't meet at all but she did get a good grip still and he whimpered and closed his eyes. "Yes, like that. Just…continue…"

Wenja did, he was very hard and she felt his pulse and she wanted to please him, almost desperately. He had closed his eyes and his mouth was half open as he leaned back onto his elbows and just let her do the job. She did speed up a bit when she felt him tense up and he opened his eyes again, they were dark and blurred and out of focus and he managed to croak a few words. "I am…coming"

Wenja did look down as the hard length went completely rigid and then pulsed in her grip. She gasped as she saw it spurting out of him, the thick ropes of sticky white liquid landed on his upper belly and chest and he moaned so wonderfully. To Wenja it was like the most lovely music she had ever heard and she giggled and felt strangely humble, she had given him this pleasure and it made her heart swell with a new sensation. He calmed down, panting for a few minutes and then he got up, smiling. "I think we'd better get a bath again, we are both sticky and smelly and we are to fast and pray this night to come. I know what I will pray for, there is no doubt in my mind about it"

Wenja giggled and got up too, she didn't feel shy at all and they walked to the pool and got inn again, she was looking forwards to the next day, and she too knew what she would pray for. Yes, she was sure.

Bagir had never believed that he'd ever slide down a steep slope on the back of a horse but now he was, the edge was a dangerous area but apparently the raving mad orc they had the misfortune of travelling with had come up with an idea of how to get down fast and Igkhan had agreed! They were all doomed. They were heading down a long narrow valley, more of a ravine really and it ended up down at the plains which were rather level at this point. The last days had been spent trying to avoid any dangers and now they were frustrated from not making enough headway but this was over the top. Resh'kha had remembered that they used to inflate the carcass of a sheep in order to slide down the wintery slopes when she was a kid and it had been great fun. So this very steep and very dangerous part of the journey could be done in the same fast and festive manner, according to her.

A part of Bagir did find the idea to be bold, and also smart, for riding down there would most certainly make them stuck completely. The snow was way too deep for the horses to wade through but this was not even an ounce less dangerous. The ravine was filled with snowdrifts and he was just waiting for that tell-tale boom which would signal a deadly avalanche. They had tied the horses' legs together and did cling onto the harnesses as they and their steeds did rush down the hillside. Resh'kha was hanging onto one of the pack horses and the animals were petrified but since they had long thick fur they wouldn't get hurt unless they hit something solid. Resh'kha said they wouldn't, she said she knew how to slide down the slopes on a dead animal but these weren't dead and Bagir was convinced that this was about to end anytime.

Igkhan was hollering like a madman as they skid downwards, covered with snow and with a speed that was terrifying in itself. Bagir had enjoyed sledding just as much as the other kids when he was little but this? Oh by every God known to mankind, it was madness. Resh'kha was in fact steering a bit with her legs, she could break a little by pushing her legs down and she used it to keep the horse she was hanging onto on the right track, the animal was on its side with its legs almost sticking up in the air and it was covered with snow too. They all looked like snow monsters.

The snow did not last all the way down to the plains though, there were a long stretch of land which was free from the snow and they had to stop before they reached that. No reason to worry just yet though, they still had some miles to go. Bagir spat snow and tried to keep it out of his eyes, right, they did save many days by doing it this way and taking this seemingly impossible route but the risk! Resh'kha let out a huge shout, probably to gather her courage and she was smiling, that insane orc was showing off all her huge teeth. She had been silent for days but now she seemed to warm up to them again and she was beyond any doubt the one who was in charge of this little expedition. And Bagir wondered if the orcs were aware of the fact that they owed their insane courage to their females. No human woman would ever risk her life like this.

The area without snow did appear closer now, and Resh'kha did slow down. She waved her arms and they all started to break, Bagir did push his feet into the snow and here the snow was fluffy and they came to a stop relatively fast. They hurried untying the horses legs and the animals got up, shaking themselves vigorously and throwing angry glances at the humans and the orc who had humiliated them thus. But they had all gotten down unscathed and Bagir did sigh and shake his head at the huge grin on Resh'kha's face, she had found the whole thing to be exhilarating. They rode down after having had some food and he knew that they would have to hunt soon, they were out of provisions and the horses were starving. It did take most of the day to reach the plains properly but whence they did they did put up camp to let the horses graze and Resh'kha did produce a sort of map meant to show where they were compared with the city of the twelve clans. It was still a great distance left to cross, first northwards and then west wards and south and Igkhan did recon that they would use weeks to get there. Here there were grass and the horses were eating like mad even though it was dry and rather tasteless. It had to contain some nutrients still and Bagir sent Igkhan out hunting. The young man did return after some hours with several Coney's, a sort of grouse and two huge flightless birds which did resemble overly fat chickens.

Resh'kha was obviously excited about the catch and she told Igkhan how to cook the birds in detail, it was obvious that they were a fundamental part of the diet of her people. Bagir did try to make himself useful by making beds for them all from the thick moss which covered the ground here and there. It was nice to sleep inn and way better than the hard stony ground. That night went by relatively easily and the food gave them new strength and new energy, the next day they all were more positive and even the horses seemed to have shaken off the feeling of depression. Igkhan did tell them that they had to stay close to the mountains and Resh'kha did agree, it would shorten the journey and it would also be easier to find shelter and since the terrain was a bit rocky they could hide more easily if they should encounter anything hostile. Bagir didn't believe that anything did live in this rather barren land but after a few days of travel they did in fact encounter something which was very hostile and they hadn't expected it at all. It was Resh'kha who saw them first, a small group of orcs way ahead of them. It couldn't be more than three or perhaps four of them and they did move along very slowly, as if they were lost and not quite sure of where to go. Resh'kha was excited at first, the orc clans did greet each other with politeness when they were few, even if the two clans should be at war with each other. She was curious to who they were and from where they had come for normally orcs rarely left the high mountains.

She did call out to them and they should answer that call but they ignored it and kept walking, with that same slow almost sluggish style. Bagir felt an odd sensation building up inside, something was warning him and Igkhan had pulled out his bow and he was swearing to himself. The three orcs, for now they saw that they were three, did not stop, they just kept moving and now they could feel a peculiar smell and Resh'kha was frowning. "What is wrong with them? They ought to answer?"

She waved her arm and they didn't respond. "They are impolite, rude"

Igkhan did shake his head. "No, look at them, they are ill, or something even worse. Come on, let us ride"

Resh'kha did wave again. "But...they are kin?! Why don't they respond?"

By now they weren't that far from the three and Resh'kha let out a sort of moan and then she turned around and grasped the pack horse by the reins, she obviously wanted them all to get out of the way there and then. Bagir did spur his horse and Igkhan did the same but now the three did move with sudden speed and that speed was astonishing. They burst forth like shot out of catapults and Bagir had time to see that the one closest to him had a pair of huge black eyes and a maw with blackened rotten teeth, obviously trying to bite onto anything which moved. Resh'kha did shout. "Ride!"

She had drawn her blade and cut the arm of one of them trying to grasp onto her and Igkhan did simply ride straight at the other, knocking the orc over. Bagir felt the stench from them and Resh'kha did run after the two riders, and she was fast. The three figures didn't try to pursue them at all and after a while the travellers did slow down, reluctantly. Resh'kha was gasping for air, leaning over and panting. "Are you alright?"

Bagir nodded but Igkhan was a bit pale. "The one I rode down did scratch me, I think"

He showed them his leg, there was blood on the leather pants and Resh'kha made a sort of cussing Bagir had never even imagined before. She ran over and lifted him off the horse, then she ripped the pants and they saw a thin scratch down the man's calf. It wasn't a serious wound but she did look at it as if it was life threatening. Bagir got a bad feeling. "What was those three?"

Resh'kha found her flint and steel and some dry moss, she started a small fire and didn't answer. Igkhan did look very nervous. "What are you doing?"

She just hissed. "Saving you, have you a steel knife?"

Bagir did hand over his own and she stared at the blade. "Strong, good, must be warm"

Igkhan did blink. "Ah, are you going to burn the wound?!"

She nodded. "Yes, or else you will rot, like they are"

Igkhan became even more pale and Resh'kha did snarl. "Bad disease, very rare. It is almost forgotten but mother did tell me of it, once when I was a child. You go mad, try to bite everything and the bite transfer the disease"

Igkhan was sweating. "Damn it, I wasn't bitten, I was scratched only!"

Resh'kha just stared at him. "Same thing!"

278

Bagir moaned. "We cannot linger here, we need to move on"

Resh'kha nodded and put the blade into the flames. "Yes, but first clean wound"

She let the blade lay there until it was almost glowing, then she did press it against the wound without even warning Igkhan and he roared with pain and flinched. Resh'kha did wrap some fabric around the leg and put the trousers back down into his boots. "Better hurt than dead"

Bagir got a feeling that she hadn't told the whole truth about those three sick orcs. Like, how did they catch the disease and why hadn't he heard of it ever before? But she would perhaps tell in her own time, now they had to move and move fast.

Igkhan was lifted onto his horse again and Resh'kha stared at him with very dark eyes. "If you feel fever let me know, right away"

Bagir bit his lower lip. He had of course heard of rabid animals and he had in fact encountered some too, the disease wasn't common but feared and everybody knew what signs to look for and where the disease was known to exist but that didn't cause that sort of bodily degradation they had seen in those three orcs. Resh'kha kept them going for some hours and it got dark. She found a place to camp in a small canyon, some very thick but short trees did grow there and the branches did in fact form a sort of roof. She unpacked the horses and looked a bit frantic, constantly staring at Igkhan and mumbling to herself. Bagir prepared some dried meat for dinner and Resh'kha was tugging at her hair and looked more and more upset. She hadn't acted thus before, even when they saw those demons. Bagir sat down next to her, he wouldn't back down until he had a straight answer. "Resh'kha, I have lived my entire life in the mountains and yet I have never encountered a disease like that. What is it?"

The she orc did swallow and she threw a swift glance at Igkhan again, as if to check that he was okay. "It is…"

She did blink and made a grimace. "It is a disease created by darkness, an evil thing. It is harbinger of bad things to come"

Bagir frowned. "It is a disease? Nothing supernatural?"

Resh'kha shook her head. "So speaks silly human, knows naught. Disease made by bad magic ages ago, to kill the brave. If back means so is bad magic"

Bagir tilted his head, "Do explain to me"

Resh'kha hesitated, then she sort of turned her back to Igkhan. "Disease eats the soul, makes the sick into….not alive"

She had trouble finding the right words in the common tongue, some words were of the orcs own language and Bagir had to guess their meaning. "First seen back when the darkness came and monsters arrived"

Bagir nodded. "When the clans gathered?"

Resh'kha nodded. "Yes, to keep the lands safe. Orcs didn't join, we don't need help, we are strong, we are fierce. Orcs never bow"

Bagir nodded. "I know, the orc clans are independent."

She smiled, showed all her teeth. "Yes, good, it is very good. But twelve clans keep monsters at bay, keep them north. Wasn't always so"

Bagir frowned again. "The disease came with the monsters, is that what you are trying to say?"

She nodded firmly, a glimpse of pride in her eyes. "Yes, disease means monsters back, bad magic back, someone trying to bring darkness back"

Bagir felt a cold chill running down his spine, he swallowed hard. "Could there be more infected orcs around here?"

Resh'kha shook her head. "I don't think so. No clan in area, those were…what do you say…outlaws?"

Bagir nodded. "Outcasts perhaps?"

She smiled widely. "Exactly, I saw marks, they had brands. Done bad things then"

Bagir winced, he knew that orcs would brand criminals to let everybody see that the individual had broken the unwritten laws of orc society. Some of the brands were horrible and Resh'kha put out her tongue. "Branded tongue, told lies. Branded ear, broken oath."

Bagir tilted his head. "The third one?"

Resh'kha grunted. "No brand but bad orc, I think maybe coward?"

Bagir also knew that among orcs cowardice was regarded as a crime so it had been a bunch of losers. The very bottom layer of orc society. He leaned forth. "How do you think they caught the disease? They will die of it right?"

Resh'kha shrugged. "Me no idea, one carried pouch, could be meeting traders"

Bagir stared at the she orc. "Pouch? I don't understand?"

Resh'kha made a nasty grimace. "Yes, pouch of powder, very popular among rebellious ones. Makes one think one is stronger than everybody, makes men insane. Very addictive"

Bagir gasped. He had heard about such substances but would an orc really stoop so low? "Ah, really? Were they addicted?"

Resh'kha made a grunt again. "Don't know, cannot tell. But possibly, traders sell it, very expensive but many crave it"

Bagir remembered a man from the valley, he had made a living making reed baskets and they were very good and sought after too. But he had developed a sort of gout and to alleviate the pain he started using and within six months he was dead, and everything he had worked so hard to achieve gone. It was a most horrible thing and Bagir would never touch it with a ten foot pole, even to save his own life.

"Do you think there are traders anywhere near us now?"

Resh'kha shook her head. "No, far from trading route, longer east. Maybe trappers, none others"

Bagir sighed and saw that Igkhan changed the bandage on the wound, it did look rather nice now, not too swollen or anything and Bagir was rather sure that the quick actions of Resh'kha had prevented any sort of infection.

Resh'kha refused to speak anymore and went to sleep and Bagir remained there awake for a while, he was so very afraid of being too late, the gods alone knew what Mjorr was up to and he would probably travel fast, and also, he would travel light. When Bagir finally managed to get to sleep he dreamt of racing along a long flat plain on a pale grey horse but no matter how fast the horse ran the end of the plain didn't seem to get any closer. It was very frustrating.

The next day came with cold wind and sleet and the horses were huddling together with their tails towards the wind, they didn't look very happy at all. Resh'kha got them tacked up in record time and Bagir felt stiff and sore. He wasn't a young man anymore and this did take its toll of him. He would of course never admit it but he did envy Igkhan his youth and energy. Igkhan did seem okay, he was whistling as he went to relieve himself and he got in the saddle all by himself too. The landscape was very flat and relatively boring and Resh'kha did sing as she jogged along the two riders, she had a very hoarse voice but it wasn't unpleasant and the songs did seem rather sweet too. Bagir was surprised, he hadn't expected orcs to be able to make music that was pleasant at all. He would have expected something aggressive with lots of growls and roars and a heavy rhythm. Resh'kha did toss her hair back and bared her tusks. "When male wants to woo me, I expect sweet songs, I want him praise me."

Bagir smiled and had to hide a small gasp of disbelief. "So you want him to sing you a serenade?"

She nodded. "All she orcs do, male with sweet voice and good words is good mate. Gentle in bed, me wants to be his flower, his sweet honey, his heart"

Bagir grinned. "Then you aren't that different from other females I think, it is very romantic"

Resh'kha raised her chin and looked proud. "I want strong male, not afraid of saying feelings"

Bagir did find that a bit surprising but it did make sense. Being brave means being honest and hiding your true feelings is not very honest at all, and also not very brave. It was just natural that she orcs would prefer males who weren't shy about their true emotions. They rode on until they met a river, they had to ride along it for a while to find a crossing and Bagir did notice something odd. He was sure he saw smoke on the horizon but every so often it was gone again and he wasn't sure if it was smoke or just mist, or a bit of rain even. He stared at it and couldn't make up his mind. They were heading in that direction and Resh'kha spat and nodded. "Smoke, not mist. Trappers"

Bagir sat on his horse and felt cold and he did notice that Igkhan did shiver a bit, he did whistle and seemed to be in a good mood but he didn't say much and Bagir started to feel a bit nervous as the day went by. Something was off, he was sure of it. It was getting dark when they stopped for the night and Igkhan tried to dismount and fell, as if his legs had turned into jelly. Bagir cussed and Resh'kha gasped and ran over, lifted him up. "You burning, silly man, should have said before"

Bagir felt his forehead and it was hot enough to fry eggs or so it seemed. And he did smell, a sort of unpleasant odour Bagir found very nasty. Resh'kha did smell it too and her grimace was a bad one. "Not good, infection, was too late with blade"

She carried him towards their bedrolls and put him down onto one. Then she removed the bandage and Bagir cringed. The leg did look terrible, in just a few hours the small wound had turned into a gaping crater, oozing puss and blood and the colour was dreadful, an odd purple and red discolouration which made Bagir back off. Resh'kha had a small flask in her belt and she opened it. Bagir frowned. "I don't think water will help?"

She shook her head. "Not water, grog!"

Bagir had heard of orcish grog, it was said to be strong enough to burn the hairs of a horse and have a taste which lasted for weeks. She poured some drops into the wound and Igkhan yelled, a sharp shout of pain. He stared at her with huge eyes as she assessed the injury and she smacked her lips and shook her head. "He needs real medicine"

Bagir tried to think. "Okay, where can we get that?"

Resh'kha shrugged. "Maybe trappers have medicine? I don't know, is serious"

Bagir frowned and tried not to look at the wound. How could a seemingly small scratch turn into that horrific sore so fast? "How serious?"

Resh'kha shrugged. «Two days"

Bagir tilted his head. "What do you mean two days?"

Resh'kha did wipe the puss away from the wound. "Two days and dead"

Bagir swallowed hard. "Seriously? What can we do?"

Resh'kha did look at him with a sort of tired expression. "I said that, find medicine. Good medicine"

Bagir tried to remain calm. "And what exactly do you mean by that? Good medicine?"

The she orc put the bandage back on. "A powder made from some types of bark, very good. Kills infection"

He closed his eyes. "Could the trappers have some of it?"

She nodded and put Igkhan's pants back on. "Possibly"

Bagir bit his lower lip and stared out at the falling darkness. "Could we continue? If we reach those trappers fast?"

The she orc shook her head. "Too dangerous, have to stay for the night. Ride hard tomorrow"

Bagir sighed but he knew she was right. Igkhan tried to smile but he was very pale and sweaty. "She is right you know, nobody knows what is out there"

Bagir felt terrified, the disease was obviously a terrible one and he didn't want to see Igkhan die, he had started to like the young hunter and would hate it if he was robbed of his vengeance by a mere disease. Resh'kha did wrap Igkhan up like a sweet roll and the poor fellow could barely move in all those blankets. He was sweating profusely and she grinned. "Sweat good, heals. Purge the filth"

Bagir knew that many believed this to be true and maybe it was, he was no doctor. Resh'kha caught some fish in a small stream and they ate them raw, Bagir wasn't used to this practice but they didn't dare to make fire now. Bagir had laid down to sleep, convinced that he wouldn't be able to find any rest at all but surprisingly he dozed off almost immediately and woke up suddenly because Resh'kha was kicking him gently. He got up, Igkhan was trembling and appeared to be almost delirious and Resh'kha did look worried. They broke camp very fast and Igkhan was tied to the saddle since he was unable to stay upright. Resh'kha did run very fast, she was tireless and fast as a horse in this terrain and Bagir was glad she was there. She did know this land to some degree and knew what to look out for. Bagir saw that the trapper camp had to be placed within a river valley and it was in the right direction so they wouldn't lose any time while trying to find it. He just prayed that the trappers had some of the medicine Resh'kha spoke of. Igkhan was really ill and Bagir did believe what the she orc had said about his chances of survival.

The area was tundra, no trees and just some low bushes here and there and rocks and sand and gravel as far as the eye could see. Bagir knew that this land was way more fertile than anyone could guess but winter did turn it into a seemingly dead desert. They stopped a few times to rest the horses and Bagir did see that the smoke still was there but it was less of it and he did find that odd. Resh'kha did also react to this, she stared at the thin column of smoke every so often and her face was stoic but he knew her now, she was nervous. They did travel fast and as the sun started to head towards the horizon they realized that something truly was off. Bagir saw a huge flock of ravens and vultures in the distance and Resh'kha swore with her teeth clenched together. She did look intense and Bagir made his horse run even a bit faster than before.

The trapper camp wasn't a large one, it was a few very primitive huts made from hides stretched over a sort of web of interwoven twigs and there was a fireplace and some poles which were used to hang the catch so it could be skinned and gutted efficiently. Now the camp was silent, some dead dogs lay there and also a couple of horses. Resh'kha was a bit green in the face, and Bagir felt his guts sink as he saw that the entire camp had been raided. There didn't seem to be anything left of value and they did find the trappers in one of the huts. All had been tied up and had their throats cut. Whoever did it, it had been a ruthless and brutal murder and Resh'kha did search through the clothes of the dead with desperation. They did stink but the cold nights had prevented them from decomposing very much. She lifted a small leather pouch out from a pocket and checked it, made a small yip of relief. "Here, medicine!"

Bagir swallowed hard. "Who did this? And why?"

Resh'kha did run over to the fireplace, there were still embers in it and the smoke they had seen came from this pit of ashes and coal. "Bad men, from north. See tracks?"

Bagir frowned and looked down, there were footprints there and they were oddly shaped. He realized that the people who had made them had been wearing boots made from fur and he made a grimace. "But why?"

The she orc shrugged. "Bad year? Outcasts? Not know"

She found some dry grass and got the fire started and then she found a clay pot which was whole and started mixing powder and water. Bagir saw that this camp had been a small one with no apparent wealth so killing and raiding here had to be an act born out of either desperation or sheer malice. It had to have happened one or two days earlier and the culprits could still be in the vicinity.

The she orc boiled up a sort of dreadful concoction and then she smeared it into the oozing wound and she did also make Igkhan drink some of it. He was spitting and cussing and complaining but it went down. She smiled. "Good, no longer dying."

Bagir didn't look too convinced. "This will save him?"

She nodded and put the remaining concoction into a small box she had found. "But weak, very weak. Like baby. Need to get to Ohtanar fast"

Bagir sighed loudly. "You don't need to tell me that"

Resh'kha did point to the northwest. "Soon turn west, along the mountains. We are getting there"

Bagir felt exposed and looked at her with some discomfort. "Should we stay here for the night? The ones who killed the trappers could still be in the area?"

She nodded. "They are, left this morning. I smell them. But they have no horses, on foot. Four men"

Bagir cringed, did they have a chance if they had to fight four men? Resh'kha smiled. "Not worry, I am strong, I can fight trolls!"

Somehow Bagir didn't doubt that at all, he just hoped that it wouldn't come to it.

Mjorr was steaming with annoyance and anger, his father was treating him as if he was some mindless dimwit and worse of all, he was kept under constant surveillance. He couldn't even go to the privy on his own and the three men who followed them were laughing behind his back. He hadn't been this humiliated in a very long time. The disease had luckily disappeared and he was glad that was done with but now he was truly struggling. He wanted to get away from his father but it was hard to fool the old man, Dagar was no idiot and Mjorr didn't want to risk being denounced. Dagar didn't have any other heirs but he did always move in his own mysterious ways and everybody knew that a man could adopt someone and turn that person into a legal heir.

They had reached the plains now and they travelled with a small group of merchants who were heading north towards the city. Dagar was trying to charm these men and they did understand that he was somebody of importance and were polite and very respectful. Mjorr on the other hand was being ignored and that pissed him off, he had never been treated thus before, ever! He had to get away from his father, he had to reach the city first so he could avenge all of this. He didn't care how he did it, he just had to make sure that the bitch who rejected him never would attract another male again. He was planning it in detail and the ideas kept his blood boiling the whole time. Here on the plains they could travel relatively fast but in his eyes they moved at a snail's pace. He needed good horses with speed and somebody who could show him the way. That was all he wanted and he tried to get in contact with somebody who could work as a guide every day. But he couldn't let Dagar know and it was a very different balancing act indeed, Dagar had eyes like a hawk and was watching his son constantly.

Mjorr didn't have any money, he didn't have anything except the clothes on his back and the three guards had been paid extra to ensure that he was being obedient. He had been dragged back to the camp once already, by the scruff of his neck so to speak and it had almost made him go ballistic. He was a grown man, not some toddler. Dagar did all the talking and Mjorr could only stand there like some brooding child, he used to be the one everybody listened to and looked up to with admiration and now his father denied him this. The merchants did stop rather often, there were small groups of nomads travelling around who weren't following the city and they often wanted to trade for things they couldn't themselves produce. Mjorr tried to get in contact with them each time, to see if he could find someone who could help him get away. But it didn't work at all, Dagar didn't let him be alone with anyone and it was enough to make him pull at his hair and grind his teeth.

He had given up when they were approached by a relatively large group of nomads, they were looking for something specific, silk ribbons in a particular red colour and the merchants did show them all they had of ribbons. Mjorr did notice a young man who stood there holding a horse by the reins and he didn't look as well-groomed as the others. His clothes were worn and old and he did have a sort of empty expression on his face. He was rather tall though, and fit, but Mjorr had seen people like that before, they did lack something.

Mjorr saw that Dagar was busy with their guards, the merchants had told them that they wanted to take a longer route and Dagar didn't like that. He wanted to go to Ohtanar along the swiftest path and was trying to get somebody to travel with them. Mjorr saw that the young man was keeping his head tilted in a particular manner which usually indicated bad hearing. Great, Mjorr saw his chance and he did take it. The horse the lad held was a tall long legged mare and probably very fast and she carried saddle bags and some blankets too. A curved sword was attached to the saddle on the right side and the lad was probably holding the horse for one of the nomads. Mjorr saw that Dagar was gesticulating and arguing and he sauntered off, he had to get even closer to them to get to the horse but he pretended as if he was truly trying to hear everything which was being said.

The mare was very tall indeed, the breed the twelve clans favoured and Mjorr wasn't used to such large beasts but he was sure he could subdue it, whence he was in the saddle. He walked by the animal as if he was heading towards his father and the three guards, then he grasped onto the saddle and swung himself up with a powerful move. The horse jolted and he grasped the reins from the young lad who almost lost his balance and fell. Mjorr gave the mare of his spurs and the horse broke into gallop right away, he turned her away from the group and the other horses there whinnied and started running too. Mjorr was grinning, he gave the mare a few good whacks from his whip and pushed her forth. She was very fast and Mjorr did find the merchant road and rode as fast as he possibly could. He didn't fear being caught, he would outride anyone and reach the city way ahead of Dagar

The merchants and the nomads stood there in shock for a few seconds, Dagar just gaped and the three guards ran towards their horses but a shout stopped them. The leader of the nomads raised a hand. "You won't catch up with him, that mare is our fastest horse"

Dagar was cussing and swearing and the leader turned to him. "That is your son? Why do something so stupid? He will be caught and when that happens we will punish him"

Dagar was red in the face, anger was boiling within him. "He is insane, has lost his mind. I swear to the gods, if I catch him I will punish him myself!"

The leader was a very stocky man with a shaved head and several tattoos. He tilted his head. "Why did he do this? Why not travel with you?"

Dagar sighed. "Mjorr believes that he can reach the city and harm the woman the Ath'ir is to marry. She rejected him and I do now realize that my son is a raving lunatic."

The nomad leader frowned. "Yes, I agree. Only a mad man would try something that stupid. He won't be able to get anywhere near that woman, and if he tries he will be killed"

Dagar felt conflicted, he closed his eyes. Mjorr had become a great disappointment to him, but he was still Dagar's only son and he straightened his back and clenched his teeth together. "Please, don't pursue him. Allow me to catch him. I will punish him harshly but I do not wish to see him dead"

The leader frowned. "The laws do demand his punishment but okay, we won't chase him but you have to swear that you will deliver him to the Ath'ir for judgement. To steal a horse here is a very serious offense."

Dagar swallowed hard. "I swear, and I do not swear lightly believe me. He has humiliated me and our family name, trust me, I will never let him get away with this"

The leader nodded and raised a hand. "Then you must travel light, and the horses you ride are not very fast. Chose one man to follow you and one of us will guide you"

Dagar felt a bit overwhelmed and bowed deeply. "I am very grateful"

The leader just nodded. "If your son does hurt the Eth'ir he will be killed, no man deserves to see his own child suffer that fate, no matter who he is"

Dagar swallowed hard. "I hear your wisdom my friend, thank you"

He waved his hand at the smallest of the guards and two of the nomads came with some tall horses. A lanky looking young man rode forth on a very nice looking gelding and Dagar gathered his belongings and then they were off. Mjorr had gotten far already and if they were to catch up with him they couldn't wait. The lad who was to guide them was called Hana and he was a hunter and knew the land very well. Dagar had told the other guards to follow the merchants, he would have to make due with just one and when they caught Mjorr Dagar swore to whip the very skin off his back. This degree of disobedience could not be accepted, never! Hana told them that they could keep riding also at night as long as they stayed on the track and Dagar wasn't used to riding far nor fast but for the sake of catching Mjorr he was willing to endure whatever discomfort was thrown at him.

Wenja and Ahravan had finished bathing and both had put on bath robes and they had been fed a small meal before they were to start their fast. Wenja did enjoy his company a lot, he did make her feel safe and more than that, he didn't at all make her feel inferior in any manner. She was used to being a simple village girl, her level of knowledge was very low and yet he made her feel smart and valued. They were shown into a separate chamber by Sefa and there were two beds there separated by a screen. Ahravan did kiss her forehead. "We are to stay silent now and pray, I wish for you to have a good night my sweet"
Wenja did blush but she nodded and went to the left side, there was a sort of mural painted onto the wall and she saw that Ahravan had knelt down in front of the one in his small room so she took a deep breath and did the same. She had never been religious, her father had always regarded religion as something which could be nice but not something you absolutely had to have. He believed that spiritual matters were something which was private and Wenja tried to focus her thoughts and pray properly but it was very difficult. In the end she just sat there and allowed her mind to drift. She wondered how things were back home, had Sina given birth? Had her sister started to get better? Not knowing was hard but she hoped that she one day would find out and she knew that the wealth they had received had transformed their lives forever. She was

290

proud that she was the cause of that, it made the longing a bit easier to accept. She sat there remembering everything, the winter nights when the storms made the house creak and moan like a living being and the stifling hot summer days when nobody were able to do anything at all. She remembered the birth of her siblings and she remembered the exhausted expression on Sina's face, her lack of energy and the many times when joy was replaced by despair. She was indeed blessed since that never would be her fate. In the end she became too tired to stay awake and crawled into the bed. She wasn't able to sit there for many hours and it was acceptable for her to fall asleep. It didn't take long before she was drifting away into the land of dreams and she dreamt of riding a horse of silver along an endless green field.

The next morning she was awakened by Sefa who was wearing a very nice dress. Wenja felt a bit dizzy and she did also feel as if she was in some sort of dream. She was placed in a chair and got her hair brushed and Ahravan was nowhere to be seen, he was being prepared too, somewhere else. Sefa put her into an amazing dress in deep bronze with embroideries everywhere and it was so lovely Wenja felt overwhelmed. Her hair was put up, she got jewellery put on, some make up too and Sefa was beaming with pride. "There has never been a more lovely bride within the twelve clans, I can guarantee it."

Wenja had to giggle and Sefa finished with her hair. Outside there was a real crowd now, many had arrived for this the final day of celebration and the sacred grove was decorated with colourful garlands and even lamps. Wenja felt a sting of nervous energy, she didn't really know what to expect of this day. Sefa had brought some food and they had a light meal and Sefa sat down and took her hand. "When this is over with you will be a wife, and my job will basically be over but I do hope that we still can be friends?"

Wenja nodded. "Of course, you have been a most wonderful friend to me on the journey and of course I want you to remain that way"

Sefa hugged her. "Good, it has been such a privilege to watch you come out of your shell."

She helped Wenja get up and made sure that the dress did look perfect. "They are all ready for you Wenja, so let's go!"

She took a deep breath and entered the clearing where the final parts of the ceremony were to be held. Ahravan was waiting there and so were Theka and Imh and the others. All were dressed in their finery and Wenja saw that Ahravan stared at her, his eyes were soft but held promises. The two were brought in front of the altar again and the shamans kept chanting as sage was being burned and water from a sacred spring sprinkled all around them. Then some odd packets made from large fresh leaves were thrown into the fire and presented as a sacrifice to the gods and one of the female shamans did step forth and tied Ahravan's and Wenja's hands together. They would not be untied for the rest of the day.

They got seated by a collapsible table, most sat on the ground and then food was being served, drinks too and the atmosphere became joyful and way less formal than on the first day. Some were singing and others dancing and Wenja and Ahravan had to get up and dance many times. Most left small gifts in front of the table, and Wenja was deeply moved. Almost everything was handmade, from knitted stockings to hair pins and it was such sweet gifts. The food was actually more treats than real food and Wenja tasted some of it with childish joy. It was things like nuts dipped in honey and dried and sweetened berries and she enjoyed it all. Everybody came to offer their congratulations and even Floth'bha had made her a little something. It was a pocket knife which was camouflaged as a buckle and Wenja did thank the half orc profusely. It was a very nice example of good workmanship.

It seemed as if the entire city was there and some kids were playing games while others just relaxed together and Wenja saw that there were games also for the adults. Some had brought some huge barrels and now some of the males tried to stand on top of them and make them roll a certain distance without falling off. It wasn't as easy as it seemed and several made a swan dive and landed on the ground with a grunt after just a few feet. Merry music was being played and Wenja discovered that sitting there with a hand tied to another person was far from easy. They tried to cooperate as much as possible and so they didn't do any real mistakes.

More food was brought forth, some bards did step up and sang or told stories and Wenja had a really good time. She forgot to be nervous and laughed and clapped, or tried to, whenever someone said something funny or delivered a good performance. Some of the humans had made a sort of play where they re-enacted some famous battles from history and it made many clap and whistle and another group did entertain them all with a story about a very stupid man and his way too lovely and attractive wife. It was the sort of story which makes people roll over with laughter and Wenja did laugh too. Ahravan was almost crying and she could see that Rhawan was standing by a tree, clutching his middle and heaving for air.

Fires were lit and there was more dancing and as the evening went the kids were sent off to the tents to sleep. More mead and wine was found and the music wasn't as jolly anymore. Now it was slower and more sensual and she felt that Ahravan was caressing her hand gently. She started feeling very warm indeed.

Still the party lasted for many hours more and she almost started when Sefa laid a hand on her shoulder. "Wenja, it is time to get you ready"

Wenja swallowed and stared at Ahravan who just smiled and winked at her. The shaman came and cut the thin cord between their hands and gave them a small cup if wine from which they both had to drink. "From tonight on you will never again be separated."

Wenja saw that Rhawan and some other males did tug Ahravan away and she was taken by Sefa and Theka. There was a tent there and she was lead inside where they removed the dress and the jewellery and everything. She was left naked and then they gave her a cloak made from some soft green material. Her hair was brushed out and Sefa did spray her with some perfume. "Are you ready?"

Wenja did feel her chin tremble ever so little. "Ah…I guess so, I am a bit nervous though"

Sefa embraced her. "Aw, don't be dearest, you have nothing to fear remember? This will be a night to remember"

Theka did take her hands into her own. "Be blessed Wenja, may your nights be many and fruitful and may your days bring naught but joy"

Wenja had to blush yet again and Sefa smacked her gently across her ass. "Believe me, before long you will be begging him for more"

Wenja didn't know what to say, she just felt her ears burn and her cheeks had to look like beets by now. They had to wait for a few moments and Wenja felt how her stomach got tight with tension and she was shivering ever so slightly. One of the shamans came for her and she followed the painted male without a word, there was a path between the trees, lit by torches and it lead into the grove. The path wasn't very long but Wenja had time to feel cold and she shivered again as they arrived at a small clearing. In the middle was the most massive tree she had ever seen, it was so thick it looked like a large cabin and the canopy did spread out above her like a table top. You would need a large crowd to be able to reach around that oak and she did see that there indeed was a door there. Ahravan waited there, also wearing a green cloak and he smiled at her. Some of her nervousness did dissipate at the sight of that smile.

The shaman grinned and put their hands together. "As one, from now and until forever"

He nodded and lit a torch which Ahravan was given. "Go now, for three nights this will be your home"

Wenja swallowed hard as Ahravan lifted the torch and the shaman did remove the cloaks from them both. Wenja blushed from her head to her feet but the awkward feeling didn't last that long, they went in through the door which was made from sickles of raw hide and entered the room inside of the oak. It was surprisingly large and Ahravan did use the torch to light the lamps there. It was lovely, a sort of closet had been carved into the tree in one corner and it contained food and drink and the floor was made from soft white sand. The lamps did throw a very mild light over everything and Wenja saw that bed shaped pit in the floor and blushed again. There were pillows and blankets neatly folded in one corner and she did see that there was a small alcove which was divided from the rest of the room by a sort of curtain. Ahravan did grin. "It is a privy"

Wenja swallowed fast. "We really aren't to leave her for three whole nights?"

He nodded and took her hand. "Yes, that is so."

She felt her heart beating fast and tried to remember all she had learned and all she had experienced but it wasn't that easy. He was there and this was real and …she let out a small whimper and Ahravan sighed and let a hand run through her hair. "Are you afraid little one?"

His voice was soft and soothing and she nodded, eyes on the floor. He did lift her chin. "Don't be, remember yesterday in the pool? We can do the same thing and then we'll just see how it goes?"

She nodded and he walked with her over to the bed. The thick layers of silky furs were so soft and Ahravan knelt down in front of her and smiled. "Just relax and enjoy"

He kissed her neck and let his tongue slide over her skin and she hissed and threw her head back, gave him access to it. She yearned for the same feeling as the day before and when he kissed her on the mouth she did participate. It felt wonderful and here nobody would disturb them, it felt safe and good. He kept whispering soothing words as he started to worship every inch of skin, he kissed and licked and nipped at her and she was writhing before long. Now she remembered what she had seen and it made her blood boil.

Ahravan did spend a lot of time kissing her nipples and playing with them and she felt how it almost brought her to the brink but not quite over it. She was so wet she could feel it on her inner thighs and Ahravan was panting and his eyes were dark. "Your passion is so wonderful to behold my dear"

He kissed her hipbones and then her navel and he did raise his gaze and grinned wickedly as he did slide even further down her body. Wenja mewled, she couldn't resist this at all and she opened her legs longingly. He licked his lips almost in a provocative manner, then he went to work and the sensation of that slick smooth tongue on her clit was enough now. She tensed up and shook as it rushed through her, making her yell and writhe. Ahravan moaned. "Yes my flower, just like that. Don't hold back, don't ever hold back"

He turned her onto her side like he had the day before and repeated what he had done by the pool, she was gasping and started to thrust back against him and he had a plan. He didn't want her to feel trapped by his bodyweight and he didn't want to cause her unnecessary pain so he would take her without warning, as she was coming. Wenja panted, he was using everything he knew and by every deity, it was obvious. She was shaking all over, so sensitive and so eager and she felt his cock slide back and forth against her slick folds and the feeling was insane. She kept pushing back against him and he growled and kissed her shoulder, nipped at her neck and used a hand to hold her in position.

He had to fight a hard battle against his own burning need now, he really truly needed to come, and his body was aching but this was about her and he would not give up on his plan, at all. He pushed himself a wee bit higher so the pressure from his cock got stronger against her sensitive parts and she moaned and tossed her head back and he lifted her upper leg a bit. She didn't protest and he kept going, kept aiming for that little pearl of nerves and she started to make wailing sounds. Her nipples were rock hard and he leaned over her for a moment and suckled the nearest one gently. That made her cry out and shudder and he knew she was so very close now.

Wenja was floating in a sea of pleasure, each move sent more and more of it over her like it was waves reaching a shore and she felt that the final sensation was building up yet again. She groaned and leaned back against his body, he was slick with sweat already and she wasn't afraid of him at all now. She trusted him and knew that he only wanted what was best for her. It came crashing over her, she started to shudder all over and she barely managed to groan his name, the world had changed into bright light and sheer sensation and she was completely overwhelmed by it.

Ahravan felt how she started to come and swiftly he did lift her leg a bit higher as he changed the angle of their hips, she was writhing in spasms and he didn't hesitate. He felt the head of his cock slide into her entrance and then he did thrust once, a deep hard thrust which left him sheathed completely within her tight passage. Wenja heaved for air, her mouth wide open, her eyes too. The yell she heard couldn't possibly come from her? Ahravan grunted and held still, felt how her inner walls grasped onto him, pushed against his flesh and it felt insane. He was on the brink of coming and had to fight hard to hold back. Wenja felt as if time itself suddenly had stopped, as if all the sensation she had in her body had gathered down there. It was all she could focus upon, the completely alien feeling of being filled and stretched. It didn't really hurt, it was just so very weird and new and she yelled his name and felt him twitch within her. How could she stretch that far? It felt right, not too much at all and Ahravan moaned her name and caressed her breast. She felt his hot breath against her ear. "Tell me if I am hurting you my dearest"

She whimpered. "You aren't, it is just..,"

He pulled back, very slowly and Wenja yelped, she could really feel it, how that thick cock did slide inside of her and it sort of pushed her over a sort of precipice. She gasped for air and as he pushed back inn she met the thrust with her own hips and the sensation was insane. It was so smooth, so good and she panted again. "Yes, oh yes!"

Ahravan was relieved, he hadn't hurt her at all, she had been well prepared indeed and he started moving a bit faster, changed his position a little bit so he could use a finger on her clit as he fucked her. Wenja was seeing sparks, she felt how she was being pushed back and forth on the soft furs and now she knew why Sefa was so loud for this was so wonderful there wasn't words to describe it. She met his rhythm frantically and he felt her tense up once more, so wet it was gushing out of her with each thrust and he groaned and swore and fought to hold back until she came.

Wenja screamed his name, arched back, clenching onto him in short powerful bursts and he roared and let himself come. It was like an explosion and he kept coming and held onto her twitching hips just to stay in place. It had never been this good before with any other female he had fucked. Wenja felt it, felt how surges of something wet filled her and she screamed again in wild abandon and shook with the force of their shared climax. Ahravan gasped for air and felt how he slowly came down from his high, it had been amazing and oddly enough he could feel her mind now, the way he could feel Rhawan. They had truly bonded when they came together, even if she was a mortal human being. That was most unusual and he felt rather humble. Wenja felt heavy like a stone, and so relieved she was almost silly. It hadn't really hurt at all, it had been just amazing and she giggled and had to hide her face behind her hands. She felt a bit embarrassed by her own zeal but Ahravan removed her hands and kissed them. He hadn't pulled out yet and was still hard and he wanted to fuck her more before the morning came but they shouldn't overdo it. After all, it was her first time.

He nuzzled her neck. "How do you feel my sweet?"

Wenja bit her lower lip. "Amazing, but a bit tired?"

Ahravan chuckled. "Have I exhausted you already?"

Wenja giggled and moved a bit, felt him inside of her and the giggle became a gasp. "No, not completely"

Ahravan growled, his voice low and dark. "Good, for I have so much to teach you"

He made a shallow move and she winced and gasped, good, she wasn't completely spent yet. He pulled out slowly and Wenja let out a small disappointed sigh, she suddenly felt oddly empty like some part of her suddenly went missing. He leaned forth and kissed her on the mouth and she answered it, rather greedily. "First lesson, a different position"

Wenja nodded and sat up, she felt how slick wetness was dribbling out of her and it made her wince, the furs would be completely soaked before they were through. Ahravan caressed her neck and shoulders, licked her nipples again. "So, how do you want me this time?"

Wenja blushed, she bit her lip and stared down. Her eyes got drawn to his cock immediately, it was so long and thick and it was hard to imagine that it had been inside of her already, and it hadn't even hurt. "Ah, there is one thing…"

Ahravan leaned forth and nipped at her earlobe. "Yes my lovely one?"

She decided to be bold. "I saw Rhawan fuck Sefa, from behind, could you?"

Ahravan chuckled. "Do the same to you? Most certainly my lady, but I think we may modify that position a wee bit, or else you may become very sore come the morrow"

He grasped onto some pillows and arranged them and then he made her lay down on top of them so her hips were raised. "Like that, spread your legs a bit"

She obeyed and held her breath as she felt him take his position over her with his arms held straight. He slid straight inn, no hesitation and Wenja let out a wail, he felt even bigger like this and hit something inside of her which sent sparks along her every nerve. She arched her back and it became even better and before she knew it she was moaning and gasping and howling his name as he groaned and grunted and thrusted in a slow steady rhythm. She clawed at the furs, trying to push herself even closer to him and he was panting and gasping. "Oh fuck Wenja, you are so…hnnnnnng…tight, oh this feels so good!"

She couldn't help it, she screamed from the top of her lungs and Ahravan was barely able to speak. "Turn….turn your head around…look at me!"

She obeyed, pupils dilated and mouth open, her expression one of utter ecstasy. It was enough, he pushed in as far as he could physically come and then he roared as he filled her again, it felt as if he just couldn't stop coming and he was completely worn out when he pulled her down onto her side and laid her next to him. He kissed her lovingly and knew that Rhawan was right, she was a rare gem and he would never let her go, ever! "Wanting more?"

His voice was filled with mischief but she yawned and shook her head. "Not yet no, I am so tired"

He nodded and kissed her. "So am I little one, you can probably make a dead man come back to life but you can almost kill one too"

She giggled and yawned again and he pulled a blanket over them. "Sleep tight my sweet, know that you are loved"

She just smiled sweetly and drifted off and Ahravan felt how his heart seemed to swell with a warm sensation he knew was love. She had captured his heart for sure and he didn't regret any of it now. He was sure she would make him the luckiest male alive. He put an arm around her and allowed himself to fall asleep. Suddenly he was looking forward to the days to come.

Chapter 8: The face of thine enemy

Bagir had never spent a night at a place like this, he was very nervous for he didn't like the fact that the murderers could be nearby. The skies were so large there and so open and it did remind him of some jewel studded dome over his head. The stars looked as if they were close enough to touch but he did recognize the constellations and that was comforting. Resh'kha was chewing away at some dry meat and she did look very relaxed. Igkhan was sleeping, it was obvious that the medicine did work for his fever had gone down considerably and he wasn't delirious anymore. Bagir tried to sleep, but he was too wired up and he just kept staring at the stars. Resh'kha sighed and shook out her blankets, then she too stared at the stars and Bagir didn't really know if he should say anything. She did point at one of the constellation. "We call that pattern "the maiden", others call it the hunter. We think it is a maiden who was denied the one she did love and when she died the gods put her up there"

Bagir had to frown. "Really? You orcs aren't renowned for being the romantic type?"

Resh'kha did chuckle. "But we are, it is just never shown to you weak ones, to find a good mate is crucial. That was where I made my mistake, I didn't think"

Bagir felt a bit insecure but he did dare to answer. "You have started to see things differently?"

She did nod. "Yes, I was…stupid. Not worth it, not good male at all"

She made a gesture. "Big and strong but not wise, wise male would not have chosen that woman, but me"

300

Bagir had to grin. "Yes, I don't think you and her could be compared, judging by what I now know about you"

Resh'kha made an odd sound, it did almost sound like giggling, could an orc even giggle?!

"Thank you Bagir, you smart man, for weak one"

She fell silent again and Bagir laid back down and tried to sleep but it did evade him. He was trying to at least doze off when he heard something in the distance, it was some sort of distant rumble and he did tense up and Resh'kha got up, her eyes narrow. "A herd of wild antelope"

Bagir took a deep breath. "Are they dangerous?"

Resh'kha shook her head. "No, of course not, why fear deer?! But shouldn't run now, in the dark"

Bagir felt cold, she was right. Pack animals wouldn't normally run at night unless something had startled them. He got up too and grasped for his blade. Resh'kha did tilt her head, she closed her eyes. "Big herd, many many feet. Perhaps Athi?"

Bagir knew that the orcs didn't have a real way of telling large numbers, everything over a hundred became Athi, and if there were very many it became Ad-athi. It was a large herd of antelope then. Resh'kha did raise her head. "No wild wolves, haven't heard any. No bears here, cats maybe?"

Bagir knew of the many species of big cats which roamed the plains but somehow he didn't think that this was a herd chased off by a predator. The wild animals didn't waste energy by running for a long time, a lion or other predators would give chase and either catch a prey or fail and the herd would stop running very fast. These antelopes were running hard, and they were heading their way. Resh'kha did cuss. "Take horses, hold them"

Bagir did walk over to where the horses were tethered, he did calm them down and took the reins and tied the animals to a huge boulder. It wasn't a moment too early, suddenly ghostly figures seemed to almost fly by, the thunder of hooves was almost deafening and Resh'kha did drag Igkhan in under a log to protect him. There were antelope running everywhere, the animals did see them but didn't veer off at all. Something had to have startled them to such a degree that the sight of some humans didn't even matter anymore. The poor animals were gasping for air and their eyes were wide and white rimmed, speaking of dread. Bagir had to struggle to keep the horses under control, they wanted to run too and he had never seen this many antelope at one time. Resh'kha did use her axe to kill one which collided with a rock and she pulled the body closer to protect it. "Meat, we need meat"

The herd passed by, a cloud of dust hang in the air after them and Bagir did cough and wheeze, the sky was gone for a while and the animals probably kept running until they collapsed. Resh'kha did shake her head. "What wrong? Mad beasts!"

Bagir wanted to say that this could be a case of panic in the herd when they both heard something else, a loud scream coming from some distance, followed by more and they told of agony and dread. Resh'kha did gasp and sort of fell into a combat position and she hissed. "The attackers, they are being attacked"

Bagir felt a chill running down his back. "By what?"

Resh'kha did grind her teeth. "Not know, hurry, we hide"

She gestured for him to pull the horses with him closer to the steep embankment by their camp and she did look very scared. "Maybe monsters, what the clans did keep out. I can smell something"

Bagir did turn his nose to the wind but felt nothing, then again, orcs do have better noses than humans by far. Resh'kha did pack up everything and her eyes were dark. "If need come we ride, even if dark"

Bagir nodded and they fell silent. She was leaning against the rocks and her eyes were closed but Bagir knew that she was feeling for vibrations in the ground, for anything approaching them. He felt terribly scared but he had to keep calm and Resh'kha did not move for several hours. Finally the sun did rise and she got up and her eyes were still rather dark. "Come, we move on"

They woke up Igkhan who did feel better but he was very weak and Bagir saw that the wound was looking a lot better. He got more medicine and some grog and a piece of meat and he did eat it even if it was raw. Resh'kha did gut the antelope and cut it into pieces and placed the pieces on the pack horse. She was impatient and they moved the moment Igkhan and Bagir were in the saddle. She ran and that forced the horses to trot to keep up with her, she seemed to be fed by some sort of frenzy. They did travel for a couple of hours and Bagir was stunned, they did find dead antelope in a wide track left behind by the herd. It was animals which had quite literally run themselves to death and she was taking them towards the source of the stampede.

Bagir didn't protest, they had to find out the cause of the panic and soon they saw something which weren't antelope. It was dead horses and Bagir did see that it was about five small stocky horses with long coats. The animals were more or less ripped apart and he felt nauseous. Igkhan was wide eyed and shocked and Bagir knew that horses to him were almost sacred. A good horse was so expensive nobody could afford to kill one unless the animal was injured beyond healing or so old it was bound to die anyhow. A few hundred yards from the dead horses they did find the owners, men who looked just like their steeds, ripped to shreds. There were body parts everywhere and putting the bodies back together for burial was impossible, it was like somebody had taken several jigsaw puzzles and just mixed them into one huge pile.

Resh'kha did spit. "It is monsters, no doubt. Bad, very bad"

Bagir did look at her with worry. "So? What do we do?"

Resh'kha did grunt. "Hurry, even more. I need steed"

Bagir did frown. "Ah, are there horses here?"

Resh'kha did shake her head. "No, orcs ride different beast"

She did turn around and her eyes were distant. "Wait here, must do ritual, call one to me"

Bagir felt a bit confused but nodded, he couldn't protest. She did run off into the terrain and disappeared and Bagir did feel alone and lost. He did trust her with his life and Igkhan did cough and tried to grin. "Don't worry, she won't be gone for long. She will come back soon."

Bagir shrugged. "So, what sort of steed is she talking about?"

Igkhan chuckled, he was still pale and he did shiver a lot. "The very best for an orc, believe me"

They sat there for a while and Igkhan did cough again, he was really very weak. Bagir did ride closer to him and he saw that his friend was trembling. "How do you feel?"

Igkhan tried to grin but it became something of a snarl. "Terrible, my head hurts and I feel weak like a piece of wet string but I am gonna make it. I want my revenge, nothing is gonna stop me from achieving my goal."

Bagir smiled. "That is good, you will avenge her most certainly"

Suddenly they heard hooves and Bagir turned his horse to see Resh'kha coming along a river on a most peculiar animal. It was a buffalo. A huge black buffalo with fierce looking horns and a long and thick coat. He had to shake his head in disbelief, but the two did fit together, it was truly a perfect steed for an orc and Resh'kha was grinning from one ear to the next as she stopped next to them. "He listened and he did accept my call. Now he will carry me for as long as I like"

Bagir blinked twice. "He is impressive, truly. What is his name?"

Resh'kha did scratch the enormous animal behind its hump. "He is Steelhoof, he will trample our enemies. Now, let us make haste"

She just steered the beast with her legs and took off and the two men had to spur their horses in order to keep up. Bagir had to stare at the peculiar sight, buffalo aren't exactly made to be ridden and it had to be completely horrible to ride one without a saddle or any tack at all, but Resh'kha didn't seem to bother with it at all. She just looked proud and Bagir knew that the orcs did have a rather strong connection to nature, it was just not as deep as that of the elves. The buffalo had to be Resh'kha's totem or something, it would explain the connection. As they rode on Bagir started to notice tracks, and they were unusual. He had never seen animals with feet like those and Resh'kha did stare at them with a narrow gaze. "Monsters!"

Her voice was calm but Bagir did notice the tense tone and her obvious fear.

They kept riding hard, resting only sporadically to spare the horses and Resh'kha did keep pushing on even after it got dark. She didn't like it and Bagir did see this clearly but she didn't allow them to stop until they reached a cliff where they could seek refuge above the level of the plains. She didn't allow any open fire and she kept watch. Her eyes were better in the darkness than those of a human being and Bagir was so tired he fell asleep like a log even if he was hurting everywhere. The horses too were exhausted and he knew that they couldn't continue this wild ride for much longer. The animals were being worn out completely. There wasn't much good feed there on the plains at this time of the year and they were out of oats. Igkhan was still trembling and Resh'kha did give him more medicine and some meat. He did eat willingly but he did look a bit pale still.

The next morning Resh'kha did chase them out of their beds before sunrise and she did look if not eager then tense. She pointed at the mountains in the distance. "We are turning west soon, on the right route."

Bagir did nod and felt his body creak, he wasn't a young man anymore and now he did truly feel it too. He wasn't exactly in the shape of his life anymore. When he was young this would have been a piece of cake but now his body did complain, a lot! Resh'kha did decide the pace now and it was punishing to say the least. The terrain was more ragged here towards the north and it did slow them down. They had to cross canyons and rivers and here and there were dense areas covered with a sort of bush which almost made it impossible to move forth. The horse's legs did snag all the time and even the buffalo did struggle.

They did ride on for several days in this terrain and Bagir was getting very tired indeed. Igkhan did regain some strength but Bagir was getting worries for their steeds. The horses weren't bred for such endeavours and their strength was coming to its end quickly. The mare Bagir preferred to ride was stumbling all the time and Igkhan's mountain horse was lame and struggled to keep up.

Bagir was thus very relieved when they saw what could only be a camp in the distance, it wasn't Ohtanar but it had to be the camp of one of the twelve clans, those who were stationary and didn't follow the annual migration. Resh'kha did look relieved too, she did ride on with zeal now and Bagir saw that riders appeared and they were heading in their direction. Resh'kha did stop the buffalo and she waited patiently. Bagir saw that the approaching riders were all human, wearing some thick clothes and they rode tall long legged horses without any bridle. Resh'kha did look relaxed and Bagir did ride forth a bit and raised a hand in a greeting. The first rider was a slender fellow who wore his hair in a long thick braid and he had a goatee and wore a sword at his side. He did look curious but also friendly and Bagir did bow his head and smiled.

Igkhan did also bow his head and Resh'kha put a hand over her heart in a greeting. The man did stop his tall gelding and tilted his head. "Travelers at this time of the year? "

Bagir did nod and Resh'kha did point towards the direction from whence they came. "Yes, have to reach Ohtanar, Beasts roam the plain, we saw dead men, bad men. And…disease is there"

The man did frown. "Disease?"

Resh'kha nodded solemnly. "The bad one, leaves men like dead yet not"

The man did go pale. "Oh Gods, we have seen…and monsters? We have seen dead animals, and our shaman…Do follow us, please, we need to talk!"

A while after all three of them were ushered into a huge hut and an elderly woman with lots of jewellery sat there and looked a bit shocked by their arrival. The man who met them did bow deeply. "Honoured mother, we have met these travellers and they tell us about monsters and a horrible disease, I think it is…"

She got up, her eyes were dark and she stared at Resh'kha with obvious worry. "Is it the illness which makes you rot and takes away your spirit and yet you keep wander and attack everything?"

Resh'kha nodded. "Yes, bad omen, bad magic back"

The woman nodded and stared at Igkhan. "He is ill?"

Resh'kha did look proud. "Got scratched by ill orc, but I know medicine, he okay"

The woman did tilt her head, there was respect in her face. "Very good, you are no healer young one but you are wise for your age"

Resh'kha did blush and hid her face and Bagir remembered that someone had once said that older wise women were held in very high regard among the orcs. To be praised by one like that had to be very flattering for the orc female. The woman did turn to Bagir. "I sense a strong determination within you, a purpose. What may that be?"

Bagir did take a deep breath. "We have to reach the Ath'ir and warn him of a danger, a man is going to try to harm his new wife, a man from my village who is mad with jealousy and greed"

Igkhan coughed. "He did rape and murder my sister who was just a child and he is a wicked and evil person. It is my duty to avenge her sweet soul"

The woman did stare at them, her eyes were burning. "I see, and you have encountered monsters?"

Resh'kha nodded. "And demons, they killed men and women of my tribe, we saw them, glowing horrors"

The woman did nod. "There have been sightings yes, and warnings have been felt in the air. Yes, the Ath'ir has to be warned."

She made a shrill sound which made Bagir jump and some of the men of this tribe did enter the hut. They did all bow their heads and Bagir realized that this woman was very powerful indeed. Like a chief or shaman, probably the last. She did stare at the men. "Get good horses for these men, and equipment. Make sure they reach Ohtanar fast, this has to be known all over the plains"

Bagir did frown. "Pardon me for asking but the disease, you have encountered it?"

The woman nodded and waved the men off, they just left without a word and she did sit down again. She gestured for them to join her on the mats and they did, Resh'kha did look as if she was overwhelmed somehow, being this close to a shaman had to be special to her. The woman did take a deep breath and stared straight at them. "A moon ago hunters from our tribe came across a man from one of the nomadic free tribes, he was wounded and very ill and they took him inn and tried to heal him. But he only got worse and suddenly it was as if his spirit was gone and he tried to attack them. They had to kill him and they burned the body. Then they saw a young girl who walked around naked and bloody and she tried to attack their dogs, they shot her with many arrows and that body they burned too"

Resh'kha did move her lips and her eyes were large. "The illness."

The woman nodded slowly. "Yes, and animals have been behaving strangely. The darkness has come again I fear, and with it deviltry we have not seen for ages. "

Bagir did wet his lips. "I see, is there anything which can be done"

The woman did smile, a wry grin. "Maybe, there are old prophecies which speak of such a time but nobody can tell for sure whether or not they are true. "

Bagir just sighed and Igkhan did cough again. The woman looked at him. "You will rest here tonight, there will be food and you young man will spend some time in the sweat hut. It will do you good"

Bagir felt grateful, food did sound wonderful and he wanted to rest in a safe location. The woman did nod towards the door and another woman did enter, she was younger and rather pretty with a very elaborately embroidered skirt. "Follow Akha, she will make sure that your stay is pleasant. "

Bagir did bow deeply. "Thank you from the bottom of our hearts"

Resh'kha did start to walk immediately and Bagir and Igkhan did follow, both were hungry and Akha did lead them to another hut where several women were busy cooking. They were placed by a huge table and plates placed before them. Igkhan and Bagir got some sort of stew and bread and cheese to go with it but Resh'kha got a whole side of lamb which had been carefully grilled. She did almost drool from the smell alone and didn't hesitate attacking the meat. Bagir knew that orcs preferred meat and these people did probably know this. The stew was delicious and Bagir did eat until he felt stuffed. Igkhan was taken away by some young men, they were probably healers and Bagir was shown to a bathhouse, it was a hut where they kept several tubs and he did enjoy the warm soak immensely. It was heavenly to just rest and feel warm again. He did almost fall asleep in the water and the one tending to the bathhouse did shake him gently, chuckling while he did it. Bagir got some new clothes on and also some he could bring for later on, he felt immensely grateful and realized that these people indeed were very generous. They had taken the news Bagir and Igkhan brought seriously indeed. Bagir was given a bed in a smaller hut which had to be used for guests and after a while Igkhan did join him there, the young man was wet and he did look very tired but he wasn't as pale and he did sit down on the bed and grinned. "They do know how to get nastiness out of you, that is for sure. The wound looks normal now, and it is itching"

Bagir nodded. "That means it is healing alright, what did they do?"

Igkhan did lay down. "Chant, a lot, and I had to breathe inn all sorts of odd smoke, and they rubbed me with some oils while I was sweating. I feel odd but better, definitely better"

Bagir smiled. "That is good. You will reach Ohtanar and you will avenge your sister"

Igkhan did close his eyes. "Yes, I cannot stop thinking about her, she was so sweet and innocent and she never anticipated anything bad from anyone. We did even encounter orcs who treated her as if she was the most divine thing ever. Imagine? Old gnarly orcs, sitting there sweet talking to a kid, letting her braid their hair or decorate them with flowers."

Bagir had to swallow. "She must have been a wonderful person"

Igkhan did sigh. "Aye, she was like innocence incarnate. I hate Mjorr Bagir, so much it hurts. She should never have suffered such a horrible fate, she wasn't able to understand at all."

Bagir felt a bit sad again. "I know, but Mjorr will be punished Igkhan, believe me. And we will stop him from hurting anyone else."

Igkhan did yawn. "Yes, good night, I am so very tired now"

Bagir did lay down too. "Me too, sleep well my friend"

Wenja and Ahravan did sleep for quite long and she did crawl very close to him, he found that to be adorable and he did like it. To wake up with her resting almost on top of him, hungry for skin contact and as clingy as a kitten was so sweet and he just loved it. He didn't move until he had to use the privy and then he did extract himself from her arms and legs with great care. She slept on and he had to lean over and kiss her shoulder before he got up and sauntered off to do what he had to do. Afterwards he did wash and returned to the bed, somebody had been there and left some food on the table in one corner and he did feel his stomach rumble but he didn't want to eat until she was awake again. The warm furs were like caresses and he did find a good position and closed his eyes again. He dozed for a while, feeling more content and happy than ever before. He could feel Rhawan touch his mind and he opened his bond and allowed his Si'ish to share the memories of the previous hours.

A feeling of joy mingled with slight envy did return and Ahravan had to chuckle. "You are welcome to join us this evening brother"

The answer was a burst of anticipation and love and Ahravan closed the bond link with a grin, he was looking forward to this too. He did run his fingers through Wenja's long hair, the colour of deep dark wine and he remembered the dream he had had while waiting for them to return. The woman in that dream had to be Wenja, he couldn't remember the face of that dream figure but he was sure, it had been the same hair. What had the dream been about? He didn't care now, all that mattered was that his brother was there and safe and that he now had a new love in his life. For it was love he felt, he was old enough to know what the feeling was. It was odd for he wasn't one to fall in love easily but he had to analyse the emotion and he knew that he wasn't as much in love as he did love, unconditionally and completely, already!

It was nothing of that flighty floating madness of his youth when he did fall in love with oh so many for a few decades, this was solid and real and he couldn't deny it in any manner. Wenja was already a part of who he was and he kissed her forehead with reverence. He would do whatever he could to keep her safe and happy and the idea of losing her was like being stabbed in the chest, repeatedly. No, that couldn't happen, ever. He would die too, he was sure. There was something about her, something so special and pure and wonderful and she was not meant to be gone from this world, not if he could prevent it. He of course knew that she would age much more slowly now that she was married to him, and he swore to himself that he would do his outmost go keep her young, even if that would wear him out. He had to snicker, Rhawan would do his fair share of that job for sure, he was eager, Ahravan had felt that through their bond. The other women of the clans would mourn this day, he doubted that his Si'ish would look at other women with the same amount of lust as he had used to.

Wenja didn't stir for yet some time and when she did wake up she did yawn and stretch and then she blushed and giggled and to Ahravan it was the sweetest thing ever. He did take her hand and kissed it and helped her sit up. "How do you feel?"

Wenja did check herself, she felt a bit tender here and there but nothing bad and she smiled. "I feel good, I truly do. I am not afraid anymore"

Ahravan had to grin. "That is wonderful my sweet, are you hungry?"

She nodded and he pointed at the table. "We have food, and then I think it is time for a thorough cleaning."

Wenja could feel how sticky she was in some places and cringed. "Oh yes, no doubt"

Ahravan did grin and helped her up, they sat down by the table and Wenja found that she didn't feel bothered by their nakedness at all. She felt that it was natural and she did attack the food with fervour. It was cheese and bread and some dried meat and then something which had to be scrambled eggs mixed with pieces of fried bacon. She hadn't seen pigs there and Ahravan saw her confusion and grinned. "It is wild boar, there are some herds by the rivers. We hunt them every now and then, just to keep the numbers down"

Wenja did nod. "We kept a pig back home, we got a new one each spring and it got slaughtered in the autumn. Father would send us kids away when it was done, but we heard it and we cried every time."

Ahravan tilted his head. "I understand, we are like that with our horses. They do grow old eventually and if you don't want the animal to suffer it has to be put down."

Wenja did wince. "Oh, I haven't thought of that, I thought that your horses…"

Ahravan did smile. "What?"

She shrugged. "I don't know, lived for as long as you do?"

Ahravan did sigh. "I am sorry, they don't. Elven bred horses can live to be a hundred but nothing more than that. Eventually we have to say goodbye"

She swallowed. "That is too bad, they are so lovely. What…how do you do it?"

Ahravan did sigh. "The horse is put out onto the pastures unless it is injured or sick, and when it is grazing and expect no danger it is shot with a strong bow, straight through the skull. It is instantaneous and they don't have time to feel anything"

Wenja did try to smile. "That is good, I have…"

Ahravan caressed her hand and refilled her cup with wine. "You have seen something bad?"

Wenja did sigh and took a deep sigh. "Ah, yes, when I was little more than a kid. I was following my father to the village for a ceremony and when we did exit the temple some of the men of the village had to put down an old horse which had collapsed. It was…ghastly"

Ahravan did put a hand around her shoulder and leaned his chin on top of her head, he felt her sorrow and knew that the life she had lived had been brutal in many ways. "I am sorry"

Wenja did shiver. "They cut its throat, and it struggled, it struggled for so long and the screams and the trashing and the smell. I had nightmares for weeks afterwards"

Ahravan did sigh again. "Children should never see such displays of horror Wenja, believe me, here children are protected"

Wenja did nod. "That is great"

Ahravan wanted to lead the conversation over to something more cheerful. "So, tonight Rhawan will join us if you agree on it?"

She blushed. "Oh is it morning already, I had no idea we have slept for so long"

Ahravan did grin. "The tree doesn't let light in so it is natural to be a bit confused. What do you say?"

Wenja felt a jolt go through her body at the idea of having Rhawan there with them, it made her lick her lips. "I agree, I want that."

Ahravan did kiss her hand. "Wonderful, he is looking forward to being here with us both"

She did giggle. "I remember what he and Sefa did show me and …am I being bold to say that I want him?"

Ahravan did shake his head, there was joy in his eyes. "No, not at all. I am glad you do, we share so much Wenja and I can feel all that he feels through our bond, he does love you Wenja and among our people love is sacred and shouldn't be restricted in any manner. If you love someone then you have the right to be with that person, even if they already have a spouse. Keeping people apart does never bring anything good if the feelings are true"

312

Wenja smiled softly. "Yes, your people are wise, we humans…not always so much"

Ahravan did have some wine and there was mirth in his eyes. "Yes, you have some odd quirks which we find intriguing at times."

Wenja did tilt her head. "Such as?"

Ahravan did take a piece of cheese and did bite into it, his gaze was distant. "Ah, you do seem to prefer that the male in a relationship is older than the female? Often by a lot! But a young male are vigorous and a mature woman can handle that, a mature man cannot always keep up with a young bride"

Wenja had to blush. "I know, it is weird but…some seem to think that a woman is only valuable as a maiden, or as a mother"

Ahravan did scoff. "They should have seen our women then, healers, warriors, lovers and wives of male's way younger than themselves. They would have gotten a nasty shock"

Wenja did remember weddings at the village where the bride was a mere child and the groom old enough to be her father, in some cases old enough to be the grandfather. It made her cringe. Ahravan did caress her hair. "You are blessed Wenja, and I am twice blessed to have you"

She giggled and had some more cheese and they sat and ate for a while, the food was wonderful and Wenja found some vegetables in the basket which she did find extremely tasty. They were green with a white centre and the taste was so fresh and sweet. Ahravan did smile when he saw how eagerly she devoured them. "You like those?"

She nodded and finished one of the crunchy stalks. "Yes, what are they?"

Ahravan did grasp one too, before she ate all of them. "A very luxurious food, they are rare and grown only in the sacred grooves but they are so wonderfully sweet and it is food reserved for newlyweds and pregnant women"

He did hold the stalk in a suggestive manner. "See? It is said to make one very vigorous and it is also said to make a woman stay strong during pregnancy"

Wenja did giggle and took the last one. "So they are not common?"

He did shake his head. "No, not at all. Getting them out of season is almost impossible"

Wenja did take a taste and grinned. "Can they be stored?"

Ahravan nodded. "Yes, they are peeled and put into a huge jar which is filled with strong wine and then sealed. It is safe to eat them but of course you get drunk if you do"

Wenja nodded and finished the stalk, she did look sad that it was all gone. "You do have much wine?"

Ahravan nodded. "Yes, we make wine from many things, and we do also trade for wine from the south. The cities in the south crave furs and gems and our dwarven friends do dig for gems and we provide them with food and protection."

Wenja smiled and stretched her legs, she had such a natural elegance and Ahravan couldn't tear his eyes away from her. "That sounds great, cooperation I mean"

Ahravan nodded and took some more cheese. "Yes, we do depend upon that Wenja, we cannot make everything we need here and thus we need to get it from elsewhere."

Wenja did cringe. "You mentioned washing?"

Ahravan did smile. "Yes, one moment and there will be water available"

He did get up and sauntered off towards the door and he did stick his head outside for a moment and shouted something. He came back in and sat down again. "They will bring a tub soon."

Wenja did look forward to a bath, she felt as if her entire body was covered with dried fluids and she did smell too. They finished eating and put the basket with the remaining food away and now an elf did stick his head in the door and smiled. He did pull a sort of tub behind him, it was placed on wheels and made from wood and it was very large. Wenja did cover herself up with some furs but Ahravan didn't bother at all. The elf did place the tub in the middle of the floor and then he went outside and started returning with buckets of hot water, it did take some buckets to fill the tub and he did also leave towels and what had to be soaps and shampoo and then he did wave goodbye and left and Wenja felt relieved that they were alone again.

314

Ahravan did put a finger into the water. "Ah, it is warm, but not too warm. Come here my sweet, let me wash you"

Wenja did walk over and he helped her over into the tub and she felt that the water indeed was warm but not uncomfortably so. He did pick up a sponge and started to wash her gently, not leaving a square inch of skin untouched and she did enjoy the attention fully. He made her feel worshipped and special and it was wonderful. He used some sweet smelling soap and it made her skin feel like velvet and then he made her sit down and washed her hair with slow gentle movements. Wenja had never felt thus before, as if she was a goddess being tended to by devoted believers.

Mjorr had been riding hard the entire day and he kept riding most of the night until the mare he rode collapsed. He didn't bother with the dying horse, he ran off and before long he did see lights in the distance. He was dead set on reaching the city, and he did almost regret that he hadn't told the men he hired to kill Wenja too but then again, he wanted to do that himself. He wanted to ruin her thoroughly and absolutely. He found a small camp with herders and stole a horse from a pen not far from the huts. The dogs did bark but he didn't care, he just took the horse and rode off and before long he was miles away from the camp. He clenched his teeth together, he wouldn't let anything stop him, no way. He was rather sure that he would reach Ohtanar without any problems, his father was probably in hot pursuit but who cared? He would get there first and then the problem would be solved. He did ride the smaller gelding until way past midday, then he ditched that horse for a very tall bay stallion which was grazing among a herd of other horses and it wore a halter so it was probably saddle broken. Mjorr didn't even think about the punishment for horse theft, he took what he needed and that was that. He had no idea of how far it was before he reached the goddamn city but he would get there eventually, it was for certain.

Bagir and Igkhan did sleep for a long time and when they were woken up both of them felt dizzy and heavy headed. They weren't used to sleeping for this long but their bodies had needed it. Igkhan did look a lot better now, and he whistled as they got dressed. The new clothes did fit them well and then they were fed. Resh'kha did show up and she too did look well rested and she smiled at them. "Ah, you look good, not tired, that is good"

Bagir nodded. "Yes, so do you"

Resh'kha did throw her braids back and sniffed the air. "We are making way, today we ride fast"

Bagir smiled but he felt worried still. "Yes, we have to. I fear that Mjorr is nearby, he and his father didn't have wagons. They have travelled light and even if they started a week after the caravan they can catch up with it."

Resh'kha tilted her head. "Caravan in Ohtanar by now, I feel it"

Bagir did look puzzled. "How do you feel that?"

Resh'kha just shrugged. "I just know"

Igkhan did pull on a jacket and put his belt on. He did smile. "I am ready, I feel a lot stronger already"

Bagir petted him on his back. "That is good."

They left the hut and saw that some men were standing there ready, they held horses and Bagir did see that they were all the overly tall elegant horses the elves did breed. Two of them had saddles and he realized that they were for him and Igkhan. The animals were both dapple grey and the eyes did watch the two men with calm intelligence. The men did see them and smiled. "We are to follow you to Ohtanar, we will ride now for there is no time to waste"

Bagir nodded. "That is true, our things?"

The man did point at one of the horses, it carried a huge pack instead of a rider and the man did bow his head and touched his chest. "I am Churul, I am one of the hunters within this clan. It is a honour to escort you"

Bagir did bow back. "We are honoured to be escorted by you Churul. What are the names of these steeds?"

Churul did smile. "The gelding is Ashstorm and the mare is Dove"

Bagir did get Dove and got up onto the tall mare with some difficulties. Igkhan did look very eager to ride Ashstorm, he had probably never been on a horse that fast before. The group did take off without any more chat and Bagir saw that the old woman stood in the doorway to her hut and stared at them. The horses did run lightly and the buffalo did look peculiar compared to them but it did keep up just fine and Resh'kha did look almost jolly this day. She had been afraid, Bagir did suddenly realize this. She felt responsible for them all and now with several warriors by their side she felt safer and protected. It was obvious that Resh'kha was the type of a person who tries her best all the time and sees it as a complete failure if she doesn't succeed in whatever task she has agreed upon doing. Bagir did ride next to Churul. "How long will it be before we reach Ohtanar?"

The hunter pointed towards the horizon. "Four days, if things go well"

Bagir did take a deep sigh of relief, four days, that wasn't much at all. What could possibly happen in just four days?

In the city everybody were celebrating still, a wedding was a grand event and nobody wanted to end the festive atmosphere. Sefa and Imh were sitting by a table watching one of the young girls of the clans dance. It was a dance which was reserved for such moments since it was a bit risqué and very sensual. Sefa did sigh, she felt somewhat conflicted and Imh did stare at her. "Why the long face pretty one?"

Sefa did shrug. "I guess I won't be enjoying Rhawan that often from now on, if at all. He will join his Si'ish and their new bride tonight and if I interpret his behaviour right he will favour her over everybody else for a long time"

Imh just chuckled. "Oh but Sefa, there are plenty of other fish in this pond, and some of them are grand indeed. "

Sefa did laugh. "Yes, of course. But I sort of like Rhawan, he is so very good at what he is doing"

Imh chuckled. "Oh you remind me of myself after I got married, me and my husband did stay in bed for weeks. We couldn't keep our hands off each other"

Sefa smiled widely. "I can imagine, you are still a very pretty dwarrowdam Imh"

Imh did blush and gave Sefa's hand a tiny smack, just to prove a point. "Thank you pretty one, if I wasn't this old I would seek a new husband, there are many strong and vigorous young males out there, with a core of stone if you catch my drift?”

Sefa had to giggle, the dwarves were often very direct when it came to such matters, even more so than the elves but they did wrap everything up in euphemisms which everybody knew. Imh did look serious again. “I just wish that Prina would leave the hut and see this, she locks herself away from everything”

Sefa did cringe. “How is she doing?”

Imh shrugged. “Badly, I must admit that she is a bloody nuisance, if she just could open her eyes and start acting like a mature woman. I know what happened to her and I do understand but by every God, she is endangering both herself and her baby. She is over five months on the way now, she is showing and she should start to prepare herself for what is to come eventually”

Sefa sighed. “She cannot accept it Imh, her mind has locked itself.”

Imh nodded and crossed her arms over the substantial chest. “I know, I hope the shamans can help her become free from what happened to her. “

Sefa smiled. “When is that to happen?”

Imh pulled her shawl tighter around her shoulders. “The day after tomorrow, they are finished with all the ceremonies then. I have spoken to one of them and she is optimistic. They have treated people with such illness before, the mind is a fragile thing and it can shatter like glass, they will make sure that this doesn’t happen to Prina”

Sefa did take a look at the party goers. She snickered. “Wenja has started a new fashion trend, I haven’t seen this many redheads here before”

Imh nodded. “Yes, henna has suddenly become sought after, everybody wants to copy her hair. I think the tribes already love her, they saw her sweetness and innocence and took her inn right away”

Sefa nodded. “Indeed, she will be a good Eth’ir, the best I bet”

Imh got up. “I got to go now, I have to check inn on Prina again, Theka is with her but she does need some breaks”

Sefa did tilt her head. “Ehbrial has agreed upon watching her, has he?”

Imh nodded. "Yes, quite often too, he does manage to get through to her, has made her eat and drink and she even smiles when he is telling stories. If there wasn't for her past I would hope for a union there but as it is? I don't think so"

Sefa grunted. "No, that creep which is her brother has ruined her, she may never seek a man's touch again. Bloody bastard!"

Imh nodded. "Yes, I agree fully to that statement."

She did take off and Sefa did relax against the table, she was a bit tipsy and she felt good. The celebration had been a grand one so far and she didn't doubt even for a second that Wenja was having a good time now. Several nights in the holy tree with not one but two gorgeous males? Sefa was envious and couldn't deny it. She wondered if she should join in on the dancing? Yes, Khirhien had often shown some interest and she wouldn't mind a tumble again, she was rather sure that he would be just as satisfying as Rhawan. Yes, some seductive dancing and then a very pleasant night indeed, it was a plan.

Wenja and Ahravan spent the day laying in the bed just chatting and getting to know each other and as the night fell Ahravan did send for Rhawan through their bond. The dark skinned elf did appear just before the moon did rise, he had taken a bath and his hair was still wet. He did enter with his eyes on the ground and he did look almost nervous but Wenja saw that he was very eager and his eyes did shine. Ahravan did reach out towards him and Rhawan did take his hand and allowed Ahravan to pull him down next to them. Rhawan did bite his lower lip and Ahravan did take Wenja's hand. "I ask you again, do you accept also Rhawan here as your spouse?"

Wenja did nod and smiled, she felt very self-assure right there and then, Ahravan did that to her, made her feel empowered and strong. "I do"

Ahravan did kiss her forehead. "Then let it be, we are one as three, and three as one"

He did remove the cloak Rhawan had worn and he was naked underneath it, and already fully erect. Wenja had to giggle, she felt warm all of sudden. Rhawan did hesitate for a second until Ahravan did give him a silent nod, then he leaned inn and kissed Wenja for real, and she did answer the kiss eagerly. Rhawan was suddenly frantic, almost feverish, as if he wanted to possess everything she was at once. He was kissing and licking and touching and almost sobbing with need and Wenja felt herself getting ready for him, she did truly want him now. Rhawan did push her over onto her back and she did lift her legs and locked them around him as he got into position. He did cry out as he did take her and Wenja had to gasp, there wasn't that much difference between having him in her or Ahravan, it felt rather similar but it was good and the position was amazing. She felt his every move and he moaned her name and appeared to be completely consumed by bliss and awe.

Ahravan did lay next to them and his eyes were dark with desire, watching his bond brother fuck their wife was so arousing he had a hard time containing himself. He wanted to get in behind Rhawan and take him as he took Wenja but that would have to wait for later on. Wenja did whimper with pleasure and Rhawan did groan and grunt and he did push himself up so he held himself up with his arms straight, he stared down at where their bodies met and his black skin against her light one was such a stunning contrast, he held his breath and rolled his eyes and Ahravan smiled, almost panting too. "Yes brother, don't hold back"

Rhawan could feel that Wenja was coming, and it was the most wonderful feeling ever, he did scream as his own climax overcame him and he shuddered and ejaculated forcefully, sensing how her strong inner muscles did caress him. He did almost pass out but as he did come down from the high he did notice that he now did feel her mind. Ahravan did smile. "You bonded too? Wonderful, I expected that"

Rhawan fell onto his side next to Wenja who was heaving for air and smiling from one ear to the next. She did kiss him and she smiled and stretched herself like a cat. Ahravan was dark eyed and breathing hard and she did turn towards him and wriggled her hips invitingly. Ahravan didn't hesitate, he did pull her butt towards his groin and spooned her, he did slide inn with one forceful thrust and Wenja did moan with pleasure and tried to meet his thrusts with movements of her own. Rhawan did stare at it, he was almost gaping at how fast she had become wanton and unafraid. It was amazing, and he saw how Ahravan did fuck her from behind with a slow and steady rhythm which made her yell and whimper. It was the most erotic thing he had ever seen, and he was becoming aroused again. Ahravan did change his speed, to fast smooth thrusts without any pause between them and Wenja did scream and writhe as she came again, her body taut like a bowstring and her face contorted by ecstasy. Ahravan did roar and spilled, knowing that his seed and that of his bond brother now mixed in her was a strange thought but it was somewhat reassuring. Also this they would share and he hoped that Wenja one day would bear them both children.

Rhawan was panting again and he sent Ahravan an apologetic grin. "I want it brother, so much but we shouldn't wear her out"

Ahravan did send him a quick grin filled with mirth and he flipped Rhawan over onto his back, the dark skinned one did yelp and then Wenja saw how Ahravan did hold him down and started to go down on him. She hadn't really imagined that two males could do that to each other but seeing it was very enticing. Ahravan was obviously good at it too for Rhawan was moaning and gasping and sweat made his skin look like oiled obsidian, every muscle visible and she did let a hand glide over his chest and just out of curiosity she pinched one hardened little nipple slightly. It made Rhawan jerk and cry out and she giggled, so that was his weak spot? Good to know. Ahravan was using tongue and lips for all they were worth and before long Rhawan did scream again and arched off the bed, clawing at the furs as Ahravan did swallow and afterwards cleaned off him with his tongue. There was a devious glimpse within his eyes and Rhawan did pant as if he had been running hard for a long time. "Gods Ahravan, you did almost kill me there!"

Ahravan did shake his head and laid down next to them. "No way, nobody has died from too much pleasure. You owe me this one"

Rhawan did grin and closed his eyes, he appeared to be close to tears out of sheer bliss and Wenja did lay down and embraced him. Ahravan did the same from the other side and since they all were rather spent they did drift off into sleep rather fast. Happy and content and filled with a sensation of love and peace.

Bagir and Igkhan got to know the riders pretty well, they rode in a tight formation and the long legged horses made the miles fly by as if it was no effort at all. Bagir had never ridden that fast before and he did feel nervous at first but then he did relax and let the horse find its own path and before long he did enjoy it a lot. Churul and the others were talkative guys and Bagir had to listen to several rather rowdy tales and also some stories about the fights they had had against the monsters from the north. Strangely enough nobody did brag about their exploits when it came to those fights, they did openly admit to being scared shitless by the beasts and Bagir was glad they hadn't met any of those during the journey.

They didn't stop that much, just short rests to eat and take a piss and let the horses rest and Bagir felt how his age really did bother him now. He wasn't as strong as the others. Resh'kha did enjoy the journey a lot, she did actually warm up to the riders and showed them some orcish fighting tricks and they did in fact flirt a bit with her, very discretely but it was enough to make the tall she orc blush and stutter.

Bagir knew that Resh'kha in fact could be very sweet behind that rough orcish brutishness she so openly displayed. You just had to get inn under it to see the true personality of the intimidating she orc. They had been given provisions and Bagir had to taste some types of food for the first time. He had never had dried fish before and it did remind him of salted old shoe soles but at least it did hold some nutrition and did fill you up. The cakes made from fat and berries and ground up beef were good, he loved those but the wine these riders drank was horrible. It was sour and acidic and left a dreadful taste on your tongue. Igkhan did drink it though and so did Resh'kha, with delight.

As the days went by Bagir fell into the rhythm of the plains and the riders did show them things they otherwise never would have seen. Dens where foxes used to live, bushes which could provide some food in times of need, the leaves were edible. They showed the mountainfolk's how to find water in seemingly dried out riverbeds and also how to cook using a piece of rawhide and warm rocks. Bagir did learn a lot but he did think about Wenja all the time and he was afraid for her. They didn't encounter any dangers, the nights went by without any incidents at all and one morning they saw smoke on the horizon and Churul did grin. "Ohtanar, just a couple of hours away"

Bagir did take a deep deep sigh of relief, he did feel tired and sore and Igkhan did snarl. "If Mjorr isn't already captured and killed I will have his head"

Bagir nodded. "Yes, we will see"

They rode on and before long they were met by guards, some were elves and Bagir did swallow, he could never really get over how inhumanly beautiful and majestic these creatures were. Churul did explain why they were there and the leader of the guards did gasp and his eyes got huge "Our Ath'ir did marry his wife a week ago, they did move into their common hut just a few days ago. He is sharing her with his Si'ish."

Bagir did blink, sharing her? With Rhawan? He remembered the tall dark skinned eternal and remembered how gentle he had been to Wenja, perhaps that was a good thing but the idea of one woman and two husbands was unusual. But here it was perhaps just natural. The riders did speed up and rode hard towards the city and Bagir did feel his heart speeding up, he was longing to see her again, badly, and he wanted to make sure that she was safe. She had been like a beloved niece to him and he hated the idea of her being in any form of danger.

The city was impressive, huge felt huts and so many people and elves and Bagir felt overwhelmed right away. Many did stare at Resh'kha and her unusual mount but nobody did question her right to be there and she did her own fair amount of staring. They did stop in front of a huge hut and the lead guard did dismount and went inside. Bagir did hold his breath, he had to fight to control his feelings. Rhawan did exit the hut and then came an even taller eternal who was extremely majestic and masculine looking and behind them…Bagir couldn't contain a gasp, it was Wenja but she was so changed! She was radiant, her hair did shine like rubies and her skin was clear and smooth and she had put on weight and she was probably the most beautiful woman Bagir had ever seen. She saw him and let out a shrill cry of shock and joy and he got off Dove and ran towards her, embraced her with a sense of profound joy. "Oh sweetheart, I am so so glad to see you again, you look wonderful, are you happy?”

Wenja did hug him back, there was some true strength in her arms and she did almost sob. “I am, I am so happy I cannot express it, but why are you here now? Is something wrong back home?”

Her voice was thin and he shook his head. “No, not at all. Everybody is fine Wenja, or at least, they were fine when I left, but we have come because of Mjorr”

Wenja did hiss, her eyes did shoot lightening and Rhawan did frown. “Mjorr? What has that creep done now? Do you know that Prina is here with us? She did sneak into one of our wagons when we left your valley”

Bagir did blink. “What? We know she went missing but Dagar did never tell that…oh gods, then she is in danger too! Dagar and Mjorr left the valley a week or so after you left, we think Mjorr is after you Wenja and if Prina is here then Dagar wants to punish her for having disobeyed him”

Ahravan had been silent but his face told everybody of his feelings, he was fuming with rage. “Mjorr did rape her, his own sister. She is kept safe her, and is expecting his child in some months”

This time Bagir had to gape, he felt faint. Rape? Mjorr had raped his own sister? There weren’t words for such a horrible crime, no concept for it. It was….he was panting and his eyes got huge. “Then guard her by every God, Mjorr won’t let his father find out about that, the shame will be too much”

Igkhan did growl and his eyes were dark with disgust. “I am Igkhan of the mountains, I have come to avenge my sister too. Mjorr raped and killed her and she was just a child, it is my right to seek justice on her behalf”

Ahravan did stare at the young human and he did nod. “And justice you shall have. We will send out guards and if Mjorr does come near this city he will be caught and he will be punished according to his crime. You young man may claim his life”

Wenja was pale and she did breathe hard, Rhawan did embrace her and Bagir was comforted by the obvious love he saw in Rhawan’s golden eyes. It was very clear that Wenja was happy and taken well care off and

Bagir felt relieved, as if a huge load had come off his shoulders. Resh'kha had just stood there next to her buffalo and Ahravan did nod his head. "And you sister orc, why are you here?"

Resh'kha did take a deep breath. "Ath'ir, I have come because of our shamans. I did…I did a foul deed and I was sent here. I was gonna find my truth here on the plains, and pay for my sin"

Ahravan did look intrigued. "Your shamans are strong sister orc, we put trust in their words. You are welcome here among us and I pray you will find what you seek"

Resh'kha did blush and lowered her eyes to the ground in submission. Bagir stared at Ahravan, he was impressive and beautiful and he did guess that any woman would be very happy to be his spouse. Heck, even many men wouldn't have said no to a night with somebody like that.

Wenja did take Bagir's hand and she smiled. "Ahravan will organize the guards, now, let us celebrate, I am so glad to see you Bagir, you have travelled very far and very fast too. It is a deed which must be appreciated, and rewarded"

Suddenly there was a flurry of activity, tables and chairs were found and orders were shouted and the horses were lead away and Bagir did sink into a chair for the first time in many weeks and it felt wonderful. Wenja did smile, her eyes were shining. "How is Halda doing? And mom?"

Bagir did smile and felt how the fatigue did sink away. "Halda is sitting upright now, without any support and she is getting stronger by the day. Sina is doing fine too, she hadn't given birth yet when I left but it was just days away for sure"

Wenja did sigh. "Oh I wish I could have been there for her, but alas, here I am. But I am not complaining, I have never been so pampered before and everybody here is so nice."

Bagir did take a deep breath. "I don't see Prina here anywhere?"

Wenja did nod. "You won't. Her mind…her mind has crumbled, she isn't well. She was doing so good at first but then she started to feel safe and then the memories came back and she became lethargic and ill. The shamans have tried to heal her but to no prevail, she has sort of locked herself away within herself"

Bagir did sigh. "Why am I not surprised, that poor child. Nobody in the village liked the way she was being treated but this…Oh Gods, if people find out…"

Wenja nodded and made a grimace. "Yes, Prina is being guarded all the time, she has already tried to kill herself once"

Bagir moaned and closed his eyes. "If they catch Mjorr, what will they do to him? I hope they do torture the beast for he doesn't deserve a nice clean quick death!"

Wenja swallowed hard and took his hand. "A man who has raped will be raped in return, and strangled as it happens. It will be slow and terrible and painful"

Bagir raised his head and his eyes met those of Rhawan. "Good, he deserves that"

Ahravan did smile but the smile was hard and he did nod at Wenja and wandered off, probably to give orders. Resh'kha did bow her head before Rhawan. "We have seen demons, shiny ones, transparent"

Rhawan did sigh. "They have been sighted here too, and other calamities as well. Bad times are coming I fear"

Resh'kha did put a hand in front of her chest. "I am strong, I can fight. Let me be with the warriors"

Rhawan did smile at her, a very pleased smile and he did put a hand on her shoulder. They were of equal height but Resh'kha was way more stocky than him and did probably weigh twice as much as the elegant elf. "And that you shall, one more strong arm is welcome now. I will see to it, you will be given a tent and weapons and everything you need"

Resh'kha did beam, her grin was wide and her eyes were shining. To her this had to be absolutely wonderful. A chance to redeem herself and prove her worth, she was almost shivering with zeal.

Food was being served and Bagir and Igkhan did eat as slowly as they could, but they were hungry and this was better than the stuff they had had on the journey by far. The main dish this day was grilled antelope and the use of spice was masterful. Bagir had never tasted meat that tender and tasty before. Igkhan became almost lyrical as he did brag about the skills of the cook and Wenja did giggle and had some too. She did look relaxed and at peace and Bagir did burp and tilted his head. "So, I take it that they do treat you well here?"

Wenja nodded. "Oh yes, I have been given so many presents and everybody is so polite and kind, I am the luckiest woman alive I am sure"

Bagir sent her a wry grin. "So you are pleased with having two husbands? That is rather odd for us but I guess it is nothing out of the ordinary here?"

Wenja did nod. "I am always guarded, and taken care off, I do not need to ask for anything and they are so considerate. Since Rhawan is Ahravan's Si'ish they do share everything, and it is just natural for them to share a wife too"

Bagir chuckled. "And they aren't wearing you out sweet pea? I mean, two such studs?"

Wenja did blush and giggle, hiding her face. "No, like I said, they are considerate and kind and yes, I do enjoy being with them, immensely, but they do never demand that I bed them, and they do always think of me first and themselves last"

Bagir sighed. "A most glorious way of seeing things. I wish the people of the valleys were as enlightened as this. But alas, they are not."

Wenja did take a piece of venison and ate it slowly, she did enjoy the food a lot and Bagir did lift an eyebrow. "So, I have heard that these people are different than men, but there will be babies in the future?"

Wenja did scoff. "Of course, I do long to give them heirs but not yet, we can wait and I am young still"

Bagir nodded and had some wine, it was like honey compared to the wine the riders had offered on the last leg of the journey. He did grin and petted her hand. "That is good, I bet your parents will be overjoyed to become grandparents."

Wenja did chuckle. "So, what has happened back home since I left, have they moved?"

Bagir did start to tell of everything which had changed and Rhawan went off to meet with Ahravan. He had just sent out groups of scouts to be on the lookout for Mjorr and he had also sent some of the fastest riders south towards the trading routes to see if they could gather any information. If Mjorr and his father were heading their way somebody were bound to have seen them. Rhawan did take Ahravan by the arm and lead him away from the others, concern was written all over his face. "I do not like this at all"

Ahravan nodded sternly. "Neither do I my brother, I feel fear. We have to be careful, if this Mjorr is fanatical enough he may try to sneak inn and Wenja is too visible, she cannot just sit and hide in a tent all day long. She will fade."

The days since they had moved into the main hut had been blessed and peaceful and they had sort of fallen into a routine by now. Each night the three of them would share Ahravan's huge bed and the bonds between them grew stronger and more true each day. Wenja was already loved by the entire city for her gentle nature and kind disposition and she was still being given gifts. Rhawan did sigh. "I should have killed that piece of filth back at the village, it would have saved us much trouble"

Ahravan did give him a swift hug. "You couldn't have foreseen what Mjorr would do, we just have to make sure we find him before he find us"

Rhawan took a deep breath. "Yes, there are guards everywhere now, getting through will be close to impossible"

Ahravan smiled. "Yes, we will never leave her side just to be on the safe side but the city is well guarded."

Rhawan shrugged. "The other things are also worrying, the monsters and the demons and the things Bagir told about, the disease in special, we haven't heard of anything like that for ages"

Ahravan nodded slowly and they walked towards the corral where their horses were kept. Flint was there too and Wenja had visited the huge stallion each day and their bond was getting strong, the horse knew her now and knew that she was the person he was to protect at any cost. The Zahar had also stayed there, and it did graze among the other horses, Ahravan was puzzled by the fact that it liked Wenja so much, he had no idea of why. Zahars didn't bond with others at all, they were solitary animals and would stay away from cities and villages. There had to be some sort of explanation but he hadn't found it, yet.

Bagir and Igkhan were shown to a hut which was to be theirs for their stay there, it wasn't large but very nice and Bagir did look forward to some days and weeks with luxury. Soon Ohtanar had to be moved again and he was looking forward to witnessing that too, it had to be quite the operation. Igkhan was tired and went to bed but Bagir went for a walk before he rested, he wanted to see more of the city and he was impressed by how elegant every possible problem was solved. The latrines were something he never had seen the likes off before and also the huge amount of extra material for huts was impressive. They thought of every possibility and that was wise.

There was some more food brought forth and Bagir had some bread before he went to bed, also some thin wine. He had a feeling that his stay there would be pleasant and he knew he couldn't return home until Mjorr was caught and punished. He had to see that this threat was gone forever.

Wenja did talk a lot that evening, she laid in bed speaking of all the things Bagir had told her when she was a kid and what he had taught her about the mountains and Ahravan did understand that he had been almost like an uncle to her, and a person who she did trust completely. That Bagir had helped keeping her safe made Ahravan very appreciative of the man and Rhawan did also like him a lot. He was a hardened person, well used to a rough life and yet he had a kindness and a good heart which was rare these days. He had endured a tough existence within the steep valleys but it had transformed him into a person of generosity and understanding, the elves did admire that. Bagir would be well respected there, and also appreciated.

The next day Wenja did show Bagir more of the city and Igkhan was already out with the young warriors, testing his skills and flirting shamelessly with the young females. He did enjoy himself a lot and told them about his injury and got a lot of sympathy, which he used for all it was worth. Resh'kha had ridden out and Wenja was impressed by the huge orc. Floth'bha had also joined that group and Wenja hoped that the two could become friends, Floth'bha needed someone like herself.

For the next day's Bagir spent his time getting to know the daily routines of the city, he did try to make himself useful by helping with the sheep and he did soon gain a reputation as someone who knew sheep very well. These animals were way larger than the ones he was used to and they had long legs and were fast like weasels but sheep will always be sheep and he did know how to deal with them. That earned him some respect from the herders and he became a part of their group and was invited to join them for meals and some light partying. That was when Bagir did notice three men who clearly weren't members of the clans, they did look as if they came from the mountains and Rhawan said they were servants of some lord to the south who had wanted to buy some stallions. Unfortunately there hadn't been time to deal with them yet and they were patient and didn't complain at all. Bagir couldn't help it, he felt a bit nervous, he couldn't think of anyone who would send people out there just to buy a horse. It was a thin story and he promised himself to keep an eye on them, just in case. The city was surrounded by guards now and also dogs and Bagir had seen the enormous long legged hounds the elves did breed and knew that Mjorr was in for a nasty surprise if he tried to sneak by the guards. The dogs would attack and they were trained to bite and bite hard.

The fast riders Ahravan had sent out were indeed fast, they had horses of the long legged breed which was used for such missions and they had several spare horses each and rode with great technique. They knew how to make the horse run in rhythm with its own breath and thus stay strong for a very long time and after some days they did meet a tiny group of riders heading towards Ohtanar. They were shocked to learn that this was Dagar, Mjorr's father and that Mjorr had run off and was ahead of them somewhere. They didn't tell Dagar what they now knew, Prina wasn't mentioned at all but they did understand that the elderly man was trying to stop his son from doing something incredibly wicked and stupid and they did also understand that telling him the truth about Mjorr's sudden escape would break him. They just turned around to ride hard back home and told him and his entourage to just take their time. They would reach Ohtanar before it was moved, there was no need to rush it. Dagar was in despair, if Mjorr didn't surrender he would be killed for sure and he wasn't stupid, these men and elves knew something Dagar didn't and it did concern Mjorr. He could only guess what it was but it couldn't be good at all. Dagar realized that he very well could be losing his son, and as the days had gone by he had returned to the faith of his youth and kept praying to every God he knew of to save his son and their family from utter ruin.

The days were cold now and very windy and the herds were kept close to the city, Ahravan did ride out frequently to check on the horses and Laupir didn't leave the herds at all now, he was worried about monsters and also wolves. The foals born the previous spring were becoming independent and would leave their mothers and they were vulnerable in oh so many ways. Bagir had been there a week when one of the scouts did return in a hurry, he did look excited and stopped his horse right in front of Ahravan who was trying to teach Wenja how to ride on a small pony. She did enjoy it but she had some problems with her balance and she did also struggle with giving the right signals. Ahravan did promise her that she would become a good rider soon but she had a hard time believing it. The previous day she had gone with Ahravan and Rhawan to a grove of trees some miles from the city to check for rabbits, the cooks wanted rabbit for some stew and the two elves did catch quite a lot of the small animals in no time at all, or so it seemed. And when they took a small break some cuddling had escalated into them both taking her, Rhawan had even fucked her while riding and it had been odd but delightful as ever. She felt as if she just couldn't get enough of them and they were the same, ready whenever she was and very eager. Wenja knew she was so very lucky and thanked the gods every day for her blessings. Now Ahravan did stop the pony and stared at the scout who bowed his head . "Ath'ir, there is a huge group of people heading in our direction, hundreds, and they bring herds and equipment"

Ahravan frowned. "What? It is too early for the clans to make the spring migration? Who is it?"

Wenja had learned that there were clans who had decided not to join the alliance and were free roaming so to speak, they did interact with the twelve clans rather often but had preferred to be independent and they were often few in numbers and had no territory of their own. The scout did shrug. "I don't know really, the distance was too great, but they were moving forth slowly and I have no doubt that Ohtanar is their destination. They came from the north"

Ahravan did tense up. "From the north? None of the clans are supposed to be north of us at this time of the year? There is nothing to live off there now?"

He did turn to Wenja. "Sweetheart, I think the riding lesson is over for now, I am sorry. I have to check this out"

Wenja did nod, she was just happy to stop for she was a bit tender in some places from the day before and riding wasn't all that comfortable. Ahravan did whistle for one of the guards and ordered him to get Ayr'esh for him. He did smile at Wenja. "Do you want to join me?"

Wenja frowned, "It isn't dangerous?"

Ahravan shook his head, "No, they bring their herds and everything, that is not an act of hostility, whoever they are. I think they may be needing help"

Wenja did nod, she was getting curious and she felt safe with Ahravan. He did send the guard to get Rhawan too and before long Wenja was lifted up onto the tall golden maned black stallion in front of Ahravan. Rhawan did ride his white stallion and did look eager and they gathered a small group of warriors and took off. Wenja did sit sideways across Ahravan's thighs and he had wrapped his cloak around her so she was warm and comfortable. They rode fast but not overly so and she enjoyed the landscape and the things Ahravan did tell her about the things they saw.

After a while they did see a line on the horizon and it was apparent that it was a caravan of people and animals and it was long. Ahravan did hold the horse inn, he did stare with narrow eyes. "I don't believe it..."

He did spur Ayr'esh again and the stallion did spring forth and Rhawan was right behind as they rode hard towards the front of the caravan. Wenja did understand that Ahravan had recognized these people and that it shocked him a lot. As they got closer Wenja realized that these were elves, all of them and that something had to be very wrong for Ahravan had tensed up a lot and Rhawan was cussing. Wenja did swallow. "What is wrong?"

Ahravan did caress her shoulder gently. "Oh dear, they should be many more, I fear that something horrible has happened"

They met the first riders of the caravan, and they were riding tall stocky horses with a thick long coat and heavy heads. All wore fur and Wenja did see that they had no wagons but dragged things behind them on some sort of primitive sled. Ahravan did raise a hand in greeting and the first riders did let out some shrill cries which had to be both relief and joy. "Hail Snowbear clan, what brings you south?"

The first riders did stop their horses and Wenja did see many horses which ran around and also some small long furred cows with enormous horns and brown colours. There were riders who had kids on their laps and some youngsters did keep an eye on the animals but Wenja did notice something odd. There were few men there, too few and she understood what Ahravan had meant. The riders did split into two groups and a horse was brought forth, it did pull a sled behind it and someone was placed on it. Ahravan did let out a small gasp and Rhawan let out a sort of wail. Rhawan and Ahravan did dismount and helped Wenja down too and two people did pull aside furs to reveal the person on the sled. It was a male, and he was very pale, in fact he was white as snow and his eyes were a light piercing grey. He was beautiful but clearly sick or injured and Ahravan did kneel next to the sled and his eyes were huge and revealed shock. The elf on the sled did groan and Wenja did see bandages under the furs, he had to be very weak and the injuries severe. "Fhailar, what has happened?!"

The pale elf stared at Ahravan with a sort of faint smile. "The gods are wrathful my brother, the enemy is back, stronger than ever. They came with the morning and these are all that is left of our clan"

Ahravan did blink in disbelief and Rhawan did moan, he stared at the group with disbelief. "How is that possible? You were…"

Fhailar did sigh. "More than ten times a hundred yes, and our warriors are brave and strong. But it was no use, we had to flee."

He made a grimace and Ahravan did take his hand. "You are here now, we will welcome you all"

Fhailar tried to smile. "Good, they are your people now Ath'ir, I am clan chief no more"

Ahravan did gasp. "What? But…"

Fhailar did groan. "I am dying Ahravan, I have managed to stay alive just to see that my clan makes it to Ohtanar safely. I am at my end Ahravan"

Wenja saw that Ahravan was deeply moved and Rhawan was close to tears. "We have good healers…"

Fhailar did nod slowly. "And so do we Ahravan, some more days and I will meet the ancestors, I am not afraid brother, I know you will look after my kin"

A female did step forth, she was covered with furs and pulled her hood back, Wenja had to stare. She too was very pale with white hair and grey eyes and she had some odd tattoos around her eyes and along her jaw line. She bowed her head. "I am Yahlen, I am his bond mate"

Ahravan did place a hand over his chest. "I am most pleased to meet you"

Yahlen did sigh and there was deep sorrow in her eyes. "Likewise, my husband has told so much about you."

Fhailar did cough and Yahlen did pull the furs back over him. "I am gonna lose him, like I have lost our sons. My heart is heavy Ath'ir, but I want to fight, I want to avenge what I have lost"

Ahravan was pale. "Your sons?"

Yahlen did nod, her face was stern but Wenja sensed the bottomless grief within her, she was showing a hard and cool façade but it was just a lie. She was ready to shatter, like a thin crystal vase. "Three sons I gave him Ath'ir and three I have lost. The monsters killed most of our warriors, the rest of us could only flee. I have a daughter left, that is all"

Ahravan did moan. "Gods, that is…"

Yahlen did stare at him. "I am spent, as he is. I have nothing for which to live now, except vengeance. I demand to fight among your warriors for the beasts will come, sooner or later"

Ahravan did swallow hard. "You are of course welcome to fight my lady, it is your privilege"

She nodded and Wenja felt so terribly sorry for her, three sons? And her husband too? Wenja couldn't even imagine such sorrow and she did wish she could do anything to help the woman.

Ahravan did get a grasp of himself and he did take Wenja by the hand. "This is my mate Wenja, we wed just little over a week ago"

Yahlen did tilt her head, there was admiration in her eyes. "Such delicate beauty, my congratulations. Do enjoy your honey days, they do rarely return"

Rhawan did stare at the group. "How many are you?"

Yahlen sent him a sad grin. "Three hundred and fifty two, most women and children"

Ahravan did close his eyes, he did look tired somehow. "Then do start moving again, we have got to get everybody to Ohtanar. There are dangers on the plains now"

He didn't say anything more and Yahlen did nod and returned to her horse. The caravan started to move again and Wenja was lifted back onto the stallion and they rode along the front riders. Wenja was curious but she felt the sorrow coming from Ahravan and didn't want to disturb him. He did sigh and leaned his chin on top of her head. "You want to know more don't you?"

She had to nod and he wrapped his arms around her. "This clan used to live way northwest, by the eternal ice, north of the mountains. We have rarely heard from them but they were many and strong and we did keep in contact every now and then. Fhailar has been their chief for many long ages and he has always been the strongest among warriors and the best of chieftains."

Wenja swallowed. "You grieve…"

Ahravan did nod. "Of course, we elves regard everybody as family, as kin. We are not that many you know, the loss of so many is horrible"

She did hesitate, then she dared to put words to her feelings. "Will…will the beasts truly come our way too?"

Ahravan was silent, he just held her, and she felt a tremor going through him. "Yes, I am sorry Wenja, they will. And we will have to fight them. If they have decimated a whole clan the mountains won't stop them, they are out for blood, like the last time the gate was opened"

She leaned back against his hard body and felt a shiver of fear running through her. "Can you beat them?"

Ahravan did kiss the top of her head. "We will try, that is all I can say. We have no idea of how they will attack"

She closed her eyes, remembered the dark sorrow in Yahlen's eyes and knew that if something happened to Ahravan or Rhawan she would die on the inside.

They rode in silence for long and when the city was visible it was getting dark. Ahravan shouted orders and the clan of the snow bear did set up camp next to Ohtanar. When the furs came off it was obvious that most there were females or young males and children and the citizens of Ohtanar did react with shock and visible grief. Wails of sorrow was heard and many did smear ashes on their face to express their sorrow.

Wenja was returned to her hut by Rhawan and Sefa did drop by, she was crying and Wenja did cry with her. The bonfires were lit and many did dance to honour the dead, food was being prepared but this was no feast like those held just weeks ago. This was a wake and Ahravan did follow Fhailar into the healers hut. The healers did remove the furs and Ahravan did groan, the smell coming from the bandages told it all and Fhailar did try to smile. "I am in little pain believe it or not, I am alive because I cannot die yet, but my body is beyond healing"

Ahravan did bite his lower lip. "You are the most skilled of warriors, how could this happen?"

Fhailar did grunt and the healers did cut away the soiled bandages. The body of the chief appeared to have been run through with some sort of huge blade and there were several wounds, he had been stabbed several times. It was a miracle that he was alive still. "I was surrounded and one of them had a spear, I have never seen them using weapons but this one did, I am sorry my brother, I fear that the monsters this time are beyond us all"

Ahravan took his hand. "The clans are strong, we will not give up"

Fhailar did wave his hand at one of the women who were present. "Oh, that reminds me, get it Khiba"

The female named Khiba did leave the hut and returned with something wrapped in cloth. "This is yours now Ath'ir. Your symbol of power, of your right to rule"

Ahravan did remove the cloth, it was Fhailar's legendary war hammer, a weapon forged by the dwarves and it was a wonderful piece of art and also a very powerful weapon, capable of crushing the skull of a rhino with one blow. Ahravan did gasp. "I cannot take this?"

Fhailar closed his eyes. "I do not take no for an answer Ahravan. My oldest son was supposed to have this, but both he and his brothers did perish in the fight. You are the only one worthy of this weapon. Wield it wisely, it has great powers"

Ahravan did nod. "I know brother, I know"

The healers did work on Fhailar and Ahnriel did make a grimace, her green hair was unkempt and she did look very dishevelled. "He has just mere days left, if he does last that long"

Ahravan felt a tear running down his cheek and Fhailar tried to smile. "Do not weep for me, I am old, I have lived well. Had my sons made it I would have faced the guardian with a grin, now I will meet them again."

Ahravan did swallow hard. "Your burial will be one to remember"

Fhailar did nod. "Do not waste resources on me Ahravan, you will need everything you have now. Bury me with just one horse and a spear, that is all I need to reach the other side"

Ahravan did lower his head. "As you wish my brother"

Wenja saw that both Rhawan and Ahravan were beside themselves with grief that night and she did hold them both close as they went to bed, nobody spoke but no words were needed, emotions did flow like a river between them now, unchecked and unbridled. When Wenja did wake up that morning the camp was quiet, black smoke did rise from the bonfires and many had put on dark clothes too. Fhailar was on the last stretch of his journey, he was barely conscious and he had asked for Ahravan to be present. It was an honour but one with a bitter aftertaste, Ahravan had always seen Fhailar as an idol and seeing him die was not something he ever had expected to happen. His one remaining child was there, a young female with her father's stern chin and beautiful grey eyes and Ahravan did just hope that she would get over the loss eventually. Yahlen was there, she was clad in a black dress and her paleness was made even more evident by this. All the elves of this clan were almost white in colour and they had grey or blue eyes but none had the same piercing gaze as

Fhailar. Ahravan would miss having a strong ally to the north, without the clan of the Snowbear the north was open and he didn't like that at all. Fhailar had been given something which removed his pain and he was dozing, Yahlen was holding his hand and he did make a weak gesture towards Ahravan. "My brother, remember, the one born twice may close the gate"

He did take a deep breath and then he sighed and fell silent and the hut was so quiet you could have heard a pin drop for a moment, then Yahlen made a thin wailing cry and fell to her knees and their daughter did the same. Ahravan was shaken, he had to leave the hut to give the two room to grieve but he felt like crying to. What now? If the monsters did came, what chances did they have?

The rituals concerning a burial were strict, the body had to be burned within a day of the death and already the funeral pyre was being prepared. There wasn't much wood to be found but in these cases they did allow for dead branches to be burned and the heap was already large. The funeral would be when the moon did rise and he went back to his hut slowly, with heavy steps. He had the responsibility for a whole extra clan now and few of them were warriors. It was giving him a headache. But he tried to appear strong to Wenja and he did order for hot water to be brought to the hut so they could bathe and prepare for the funeral. He heard that the members of the Snowbear clan were screaming and wailing out their grief, and he just hoped that he would be worthy of the trust Fhailar had put in him.

The city was a chaos now but the guards were still there doing their job and the herds the newcomers had brought were taken to good pastures and the horses were also taken care off. Many had wounds or were lame and the farriers had a lot of work to do. The people of the plains were used to handling loss and grief but they had never encountered it at such a monumental scale before. It did leave them all in a state of shock. Many gathered in groups to pray and some brought forth gifts which were to be placed alongside the dead chief to go with him to the afterlife.

Wenja was sad, she felt sorry for them all and both Rhawan and Ahravan tried to cheer her up by making jokes and playing silly. It didn't work very well, she just felt a bit annoyed. The meals this day were meagre, it was tradition when there was a funeral and Wenja did eat her porridge without complaints but Rhawan did make grimaces and did look as if they were trying to poison him. That did make Wenja grin though, and when they did bathe Ahravan became very affectionate and cuddly. She realized that it was his way of draining himself of the grief and so she let him take her in the tub. Afterwards Rhawan was so turned on he too begged her for some attention and she allowed him too to do it, at least she had some joy this sombre day.

The ritual was started in the afternoon, the body of the deceased was washed and dressed in furs and many came by and said their prayers, most of the citizens of Ohtanar did know who Fhailar had been and their respect and sorrow was heartfelt. Yahlen did stand by her dead husband's body, she didn't weep and her gaze was stiff, as if the grief had turned her into a statue. As the sun set gifts were brought forth and the bonfire was to be prepared. They had chosen an open spot near the outskirts of the city and the entire population did gather there. The traditions were rather clear on how the funeral was to be done, one of the few surviving warriors of the clan did lead forth a horse from Fhailar's own herd. It was one of his favourites, an old gelding and the horse wore full tack. They did lead the horse in between the four rocks which did mark the corners of the bonfire and the warrior did give the horse some salt on a rock. As the animal did lick up the treat one of the other warriors did strike it on the forehead with a pickaxe and the horse did drop immediately. Then all the adult members of the clan did bring forth a piece of wood and also the gifts which were placed in the bonfire with several jars of oil and when the fire was built as tall as they could the body was carefully placed on top of it. Yahlen did kiss her husband one last time and she started to sing, a very piercing and wailing song which did express her grief to everybody who could hear. She kept singing until the moon did rise, then Ahravan did hand her a lit torch and Yahlen did shudder and wail but she didn't hesitate, she did throw the torch unto the bonfire and flames began to dance immediately. It was a good sign and the entire tribe did walk around the bonfire with the sun, it went slowly, and they were all chanting and Wenja felt that it was beautiful even if it was very sad indeed. They kept walking until the fire had burned down and in the morning the ashes would be gathered and placed in a box which was given the widow. She would pour the ashes out into the river and into the wind, to be spread out over the nature which had nurtured them all.

After the fire burned down there were groups gathering, singing and drinking and commemorating the dead and Wenja and Ahravan and Rhawan did return to the hut. Prina had been in her hut with Imh and Ehbrial the entire time and Wenja did pity her. The ritual had been so profound and real and she refused to think of the enemy which had slain so many brave warriors. The twelve clans were strong and they could fight, she didn't want to worry.

The darkness was dense and the smoke did hang thick over the entire city now, people were still singing and mourning and the wind did change a bit and threw the thick smoke out over the plains.

None did see the dark figure which crept forward on his belly and knees. He wore a sheep hide he had stolen from some herders and he had left his horse behind, the animal had been almost dead and he didn't need it now. He was going to get his revenge and that was all he could think off. He was tired and hungry and shaking all over but the anger he felt had burned so hot within him he forgot about all this. He would punish the whore who had put him through this. There were dogs there but the smoke did disturb their noses and Mjorr did grin. The gods were with him, the barbarians were celebrating something, he was sure he would find her and then she would be his as she should have been to begin with. Afterwards nobody would wish to touch her with a ten foot pole.

Mjorr did barely move, he did use the small bushes and rocks for all they were worth and he had managed to get to the border of the city. He did seek cover behind a stack of dried cow piles and kept a keen eye on everybody. He didn't see her anywhere, damn, where could she be? He couldn't enter the city, he would be detected for sure and if she was with her husband Mjorr knew he was chanceless. He remembered how that overly tall eternal had thrown him through the crowd as a ragdoll. The humiliation did still sting in his mind still. He sneered, sooner or later she would appear, he was sure of it.

Mjorr was not aware of the fact that this was a funeral and it wouldn't have mattered to him if he had known. He was looking for a woman with

340

dark red hair and he almost yelled when he saw her, a tall slender figure dressed in a black robe. He was shivering with excitement, she was there and the Gods did indeed favour him. He did sneak forwards, he didn't see her face in the darkness but he didn't have to. That hair was so special there couldn't be two women with it. He did pounce on her and hit her in the back of the head with a stone, she went down and he did drag her with him into some bushes behind one of the huts. Now he was filled with eager energy, with zeal! He would indeed get his revenge. He did flip the girl over and tore the cloak up. She wore skirts but he got them out of the way and he was already very ready, almost trembling with need. The idea of fucking that goddamn wench who had tricked him of her virtue was truly arousing. Never mind that her husband had ploughed the land first, after Mjorr was done with her she would never attract a man again. He did use the cloak to tie her arms together behind her back and then he went to work. He did grunt and moan but managed to keep it down as he did plunge into her, he had never felt such joy when he fucked a female, she was so tight and good and he came rather fast. But he wasn't sated, far from it, he just waited for a few minutes before he was fully hard again and this time he did her ass instead, he felt as if he never would lose his power, as if this did ensure that he would remain hard forever.

He did cut her clothes away and growled with desire, finally he was going to fulfil all his fantasies and he did pull the cloak up around her head and cut away at the darn red hair. It was so dark he didn't really see her face at all but it didn't matter, he remembered it all too well. When he had cut the hair away he did fuck her again and as he did that he did cut away at her tits, he would mar her face as the last treat he would give himself. He did empty himself in her several times and when he was so spent he had nothing more to give he did use the knife to cut away her nether lips and clit, he did even thrust the knife into that offensive passage which had rejected him.

The blood loss was already fatal, but he wouldn't quit just yet, he was still feverish with sadistic glee and he did use the knife on her arms and legs too. She would be unrecognizable whence he was done with her.

Igkhan had slept soundly for the last nights, he had regained his strength and he was glad to be there for he learned so much new every day, he did wish to return home as a much wiser man and he did almost devour all new information with glee. This night was a sad one, he had participated in the funeral and he and Bagir had retreated to their hut to sleep but he couldn't relax. Something kept him awake so he did sit by the oven instead and worked on the carvings on a knife blade. He had almost dozed off when he suddenly felt a cold chill and jerked, raised his head. He saw someone standing in the doorway and he saw the door through the figure, and he knew who it was. He gasped. "Sister? Little one?"

She just winked at him as if to ask him to follow and Igkhan did grasp a knife and followed the ghost with a hammering heart and a feeling of utter shock and disbelief. He did stop whence he was outside, she was fading away but pointed at some of the huts which were farthest away from the main part of the city. Igkhan did nod. "I…I will go…"

She smiled and was gone and Igkhan did clench the knife and walked on. It was very dark and he heard nothing but he saw that Resh'kha and Floth'bha were walking through the camp, they had become good friends and they were chatting away in the orcish language. Igkhan did wave a hand and held a finger over his lips and both fell silent and did walk over to him, "What is it?"

Floth'bha wasn't as huge and buff as Resh'kha, she was more slender and almost pretty even the way a human saw it. Igkhan did whisper. "My dead sister, she appeared to me, as a ghost. She wants me to go towards those huts!"

Floth'bha did frown. "They are empty?"

Igkhan did sneer. "I sense something, something bad. She wouldn't have appeared like that for nothing"

Resh'kha did pull out her axe «Go on, we follow»

The three did sneak forth, they used the darkness and Igkhan did feel the smell of blood and then he did hear someone cuss and saw movements. Resh'kha did hiss and Floth'bha did grasp her sword. They did sneak forth, Igkhan had a sinking feeling in his gut, this was something horrible and he knew it already.

Mjorr had been so sure that this was Wenja but when he did uncover the face to disfigure it he found that this was a woman of greater age then

342

the slut and also, she had a much rougher face and way less beauty than Wenja. At first he did fume with rage, he should have checked but then again, he had enjoyed a good rehearsal now hadn't he? It was a good thing to practice and he did swear a bit and cleaned his knife on the robe before he got up to get his pants back in order. He did take two steps and then a huge hand did fall down onto his shoulder and another was placed around his neck. Mjorr didn't scream, he just whimpered as he stared straight at two huge beasts, he had never seen an orc and had no idea of what they were. Then a voice could be heard. "So, you are still in the raping business? Be glad I will follow the laws for if I wasn't I would gut you here and now!"

Mjorr stared at a young man with some odd tattoos and filed teeth and he did blink and tried to wriggle free. "What have I done to you? Let me go"

Igkhan did snarl. "What you have done to me? Remember that one time you visited the mountains and saw this very sweet little girl? The one who was on her way to the healers? The one you raped and killed? That was my sister you bastard and I will claim your life, as it is my right to do"

Mjorr did wet his lips, he did a twist and managed to break free from the grip, he started to run but didn't come far, he was suddenly tackled by a huge dog which grasped onto his leg and shook him and his scream could be heard all over the city.

It did take less than a minute before Mjorr was tied down by several guards and the dead body was discovered and only the fact that Ahravan did show up prevented Mjorr from being torn limb from limb there and then. Ahravan did stare at the human and at the mutilated corpse of one of the city women. The very idea of this being done to Wenja made him freeze to the very marrow and he stared at the man with sheer hatred. "So, you are the creep who wanted to marry the woman who now is my wife? The cowardly bastard who tried to kill her, and now has killed an innocent woman?"

Mjorr cringed, he was furious and terrified and realized that he had done a huge blunder. Was that huge eternal Wenja's husband? He was the most terrifying sight Mjorr had ever seen and now Rhawan did show up too, he did stare at Mjorr and his eyes were filled with something akin to sheer madness. "Has he hurt anyone?"

Ahravan did sigh. "See for yourself, behind the hut"

Rhawan did go to see and he came back almost in tears. "Oh Gods, that is…"

Ahravan raised his voice. "This man has broken our laws, he has maimed and killed and he has raped. He is no longer a living human being, his life has been forfeit. He will be kept until we have decided the manner of execution"

Everybody were shouting and crying out and the dead woman had a husband and parents and their screams and cries were terrible to listen to. Ahravan did make sure that Mjorr was tied up like a ham before he did order that the man was to be placed in a hut and put under heavy guard. Resh'kha and Igkhan did volunteer and so did some of the elves too. Mjorr wouldn't stand a chance at escaping this.

Ahnriel did check the body of the woman and the injuries were horrifying, she was in tears when she reported everything to Ahravan and he did cringe and felt that the world suddenly had turned into a horror story. Rhawan was crying and the grief everybody had felt had suddenly turned into wrath.

Wenja was told what had happened and she became terrified and then she got furious and she did almost demand that she would be allowed to geld the bastard with a blunt blade. Ahravan held her and kissed her and calmed her down and eventually she was thinking again, Mjorr couldn't harm her anymore but she did pity the woman he had attacked and her family. It was really horrible.

Bagir knew that Dagar had followed Mjorr, he too had to be out there somewhere and they decided that they would wait for some days before they decided what to do with Mjorr. They wanted his father to be there, it could be that he could shed some light on the case.

Wenja wasn't allowed near Mjorr, and neither was anybody else. Only Ahravan and Rhawan was allowed into the hut and nobody did mention that Prina was there. Mjorr was almost mad with rage and he did swear and scream and holler insults the whole time but nobody bothered with it.

He could yell all he wanted, his fate was sealed, the only question was when the doom would be put into action.

Ahravan was busy helping the newcomers settling inn and they did send out scouts all the time to look out for monsters. They couldn't use time on that deranged piece of filth. They had to prepare for a war and Sefa did keep Wenja busy with weaving and other things she liked to do. Prina wasn't told that her brother was there, she was still apathic and silent and Imh was very worried that she would succumb to her weakness when the baby was born. She was too weak soon, refused to eat and refused to do anything at all.

The three men had settled inn with the others there, they didn't attract any attention and did also work a little with the horses and they had listened to the rumours which were spreading through the city, they did confirm what they had suspected. Prina had been raped by her own brother and the mere idea of having been used to hide such a hideous deed made them all nauseous. That Mjorr was heading their way was something they were aware off but they forgot about it when the strangers did arrive and they were busy helping out making huts for this northern clan. Being a part of a city like this did in fact feel good and they had thought about maybe staying, after all, they weren't getting younger and here they could do something good with their skills. Geir was a good carpenter and Than was not bad on a drum, Osbord had been good at making ropes in his youth and it was all skills which were sought after.

They too were rudely awakened by the noise made when Mjorr was captured and they did feel very angry when they heard about his latest crime, it was a cowards deed and Geir did decide there and then that they would come clean and tell everybody the truth of their mission there. If it lead to them being punished then be it, they didn't want to stand there and keep the truth hidden anymore. If Dagar did arrive he did deserve the right to hear the truth about his son's devious plans. Now they could only wait for the right moment to tell everybody the truth and Geir wouldn't hold anything back.

The entire city was in an atmosphere of tension now, both the arrival of the heavily decimated Snowbear clan and the death of their chief and the murder and rape of that poor woman had contributed to making people on edge. Ahravan was trying very hard to prepare the city for war, and the warriors did prepare their weapons and horses for battle. But the shaman did warn them, they couldn't fight the demons Resh'kha and the strangers had seen, they were too powerful and lethal to everybody, the only way to fight them was to avoid them completely. Ahravan had made a decision, they wouldn't follow the normal path to their winter grazing grounds on the east side of the mountains, they would be heading straight for the mountains and seek shelter against their flanks. With their backs to the steep barrier they could hold on for a long time, there were caves they knew off where the women and children could hide and if the monsters were as they had been earlier they wouldn't bother with the herds that much. Not all did like this but they did agree, out on the plains everybody were vulnerable and Ahravan and Rhawan did spend a lot of time with the older members of the clans to see if they could map a route which was easy and fast and also as safe as possible.

Wenja was nervous and she was also feeling a sort of intense anger, Mjorr was alive still and she would not breathe freely until he was no more, he didn't deserve to draw breath one day longer than his victims. Igkhan had told her of his sister and Wenja had forgotten her own fear and instead she was feeling wrath on behalf of the many women he had abused and hurt.

After some days Dagar did arrive, with some of Ahravan's scouts. The man was tired and in a bad shape and he did stumble as he did come off his horse, he was no longer the haughty and arrogant leader he had once been, now he was just an old man who had failed in so many ways and were at the edge of his strength and hope.

Ahravan did go out to meet him, Wenja had told him about Dagar and Ahravan did see that this man was broken, the journey had perhaps started as an act of anger, to punish someone who had disobeyed him but over the length of it he had learned the truth of his own son and he had also seen the truth about himself. And it was humbling. Dagar did shiver and fell to his knees. "Please, my son…"

Ahravan did sigh, he did pity the man, even if he had been a complete asshole like his son, he had at least not murdered anyone and he was old, age did demand respect there even if Dagar was a mere babe compared with even the youngest of the eternal. Rhawan did sneer. "Mjorr is here yes, he did rape and murder a woman, and he has done that before, a child! He is awaiting judgement but know that he is going to die"

Dagar did let out a thin wail, he seemed to break down completely. "Oh Gods, I never knew…I have failed, by every God I have failed both him and our name. Please, I beg you, the fault is mine, I am the one who ought to suffer for this"

Ahravan felt sad. "No old man, he did make his own choices, even if you did fail in raising him. He is an adult, he does know right from wrong, He is to be punished, there is no way around that. I am sorry"

Dagar did let out a new wail and Ahravan did wave his hand at some of the warriors. They did pick the man up and carried him off to a hut, he was wailing like a child and Rhawan did stare at Ahravan. "We cannot wait for much longer, it has to be done"

Ahravan did sigh deeply. "Aye, it has to be done, tomorrow morning, the trial is to be held at sunrise."

There was silence around them, most did look very pleased. They had to get this done and get over with it.

Wenja did wait for Ahravan and Rhawan to return to the hut, the cooks had prepared food and she was hungry and also strangely on edge. She felt agitated, as if she had too much energy and she had no idea of how to release it all. Both Ahravan and Rhawan were ravenous when they returned and all three sat down to eat in silence and Wenja did wolf down a lot, she had grown used to eating now and didn't feel guilty when she was full. Afterwards they did take a small break and laid down to rest and Wenja did toss around like a puppy with fleas the whole time. Rhawan did catch her and held her still, his beautiful face did reveal his worry. "What is the matter my sweet? You are all over the place"

Wenja did sigh and tried to relax. "It is just…I feel on edge, nervous, stressed out. I cannot rest until I know that Mjorr is dead"

Ahravan did place a hand on her hip, it was a soothing gesture. "I know my dear, but do not worry. Mjorr has hours left now, he won't escape and his faith is sealed."

Wenja did turn around, there was an almost predatory glimpse within her gaze. "I want to see him die! I deserve it"

Ahravan did raise an eyebrow. "Whoa there Wenja, why the sudden bloodthirst? It will be very unpleasant to watch"

She did almost hiss. "Not as unpleasant as living under his shadow for years. I will not take no for an answer, I demand to watch"

Rhawan did kiss the top of her head. "Then you will be there but remember, you have been warned. It will most likely be extremely nasty"

Wenja did nod. "So much better then!"

Ahravan let his hand slide over her curves, his eyes were a bit sad. "I am so sorry you had to suffer because of that piece of filth"

Wenja did just shrug. "I did live in fear yes, but what about Prina? What he did to her can never be undone. And Igkhan's poor sister? The woman he killed here? The countless others he has forced himself onto, the bastards born without a father? He ought to die a thousand times for what he has done"

Rhawan did grin. "You do have a little warrior in you Wenja, you sound like some vengeful veteran of many battles. I like that, you are strong"

Wenja did blush and Ahravan did send Rhawan a silent glance. They had to get her thoughts over onto something more positive. Rhawan did understand and since she lay there facing him he did slide down a bit and kissed her with both tenderness and hunger. Wenja did yelp and then she did answered the kiss, she had learned so much over these last days and how to kiss properly was one of them. She did feel how Ahravan did slide her clothes off of her and she giggled as she felt how he did tear off his own garments. Rhawan did the same, she was always in awe of the differences between them as well as the similarities. Ahravan was larger in build than Rhawan, more muscular and stocky but Rhawan wasn't exactly petite either, he was just more sinewy and slender and she had seen how very strong he was first hand.

Rhawan did turn her against him and he started to pay homage to her bosom, licking and sucking her nipples while Rhawan did the same to the back of her neck. It made her go half mad and she whimpered and let every conscious though fly for the wind, all she could do now was to feel and need and want and before long they both were busy giving her everything she needed and more.

The next morning came with sleet and sour winds and it was just appropriate. The entire city was up and about but the children were ushered away and the trial was to be held outside the Ath'ir's hut. Some benches had been brought forth but most of the spectators and the people present there had to stand on their own feet. Dagar had been kept under watch and he was forced to be there and tell his side of the story. Ahravan had decided that Prina was to be kept away from the trial, she would be told of the execution afterwards, she didn't need to be made more agitated than she already was. Ehbrial was watching her with Imh and she had been told that Mjorr had been captured but she hadn't reacted to the news. It was as if she didn't really understand and her eyes were blank and empty.

The crowd was silent and the atmosphere was tense and eerie. Ahravan had put on his armour and so had Rhawan and Wenja was wearing a black cloak made from fur and velvet, she did look like a queen this day and many did stare at her with obvious admiration. Dagar was given a seat, he was deteriorating fast now, he had nothing left now and he would be forced to accept the full truth of his son's nature. He was a hard man, harsh and greedy and fond of power but he had never been mad and Mjorr had acted like a mad man, like an animal. The shame did weight down on him like a thousand heavy stones and Wenja was shocked when she saw Dagar. She did barely recognize him, he had aged a lot and the spiteful and arrogant glimpse within his eyes was gone and replaced by a deep agony and despair.

Ahravan was the war chief but the one with the power in such cases was the shaman and some of the elders and they did sit down and did look very sombre and their faces were hard. The shaman did raise her hand and she did stare at the crowd. "The Gods will speak here today, through us all. Justice will be served, and their will be done. No living being here may doubt that or their wisdom"

Everybody was mumbling and fell silent again as Mjorr was dragged forth. He was wearing chains and a thin tunic which was very long. He did also wear pants and boots but nothing else and he was cussing and swearing. His uncouth looks did turn him into a Wildman and many did shake their heads in disgust. He did see Wenja and his eyes got huge, then he sort of exploded. "You feckin' cunt, goddamn whore! I am gonna get you, I am gonna get you and when I am done with you not even those pointy eared freaks are gonna bother with that dirty snatch of yours!"

The crowd did gasp in unison and their eyes got ice cold. Ahravan did raise a hand. "Honoured ones, I do plead you to add whiplashes to the punishment, for slandering the name of our beloved Eth'ir"

The shaman did grin, the grin was vicious. "Granted"

Mjorr was howling with anger and struggling against the chains but Resh'kha and Floth'bha plus a couple of elven warriors did hold them and he didn't stand a chance. Resh'kha did look as if she really did enjoy this.

Dagar did stare at Mjorr and there were tears in his eyes. He did shake and then he did speak. "My son, please, do apologize, do beg them for forgiveness. Do not let this happen to you"

Mjorr got aware of his father and his eyes widened, he did snarl at Dagar. "You are here? You idiot, I could have dealt with this on my own but no, you had to interfere, I spit on your name, and that of our kin, do you hear? You are worthless old man, just food for the vultures"

This time the crowd almost lost it and screams and cries in disgust were heard, speaking like that to your father was unheard of, it was horrible. A crime unlike few others. Mjorr was suddenly hit by several wet cow piles and rotten fruit.

The shaman did raise a hand and everybody did shut up, her eyes were shooting lightning and she stared at Mjorr with a gaze so cold it could have frozen the great river solid. "If anybody has anything to say now do it please, we do accept those who wish to bear witness if there is anything they do know"

Ahravan did frown when the leader of the three men did step forth. He did look down and his face was pale but he did walk forth with steady steps and Mjorr saw him and his face contorted with rage. It was obvious that he knew the man and Geir did take a deep breath. "Honoured ones, I and my two friends did arrive here some weeks ago, but our mission isn't

350

what we told everybody it was. We have lied and for that we are very sorry. We are mercenaries, or rather, we were mercenaries. Old age is catching up with us and we accepted a job we never should have taken just out of desperation. This man here, Mjorr son of Dagar, did hire us to travel ahead of him and his father and kill his sister."

Dagar did gape, his eyes were filled with disbelief and he did go very pale indeed. He had not known anything about this, how devious was Mjorr really? Ahravan tilted his head. "You are telling us this because?"

Geir did raise his head again, there was some pride in his gaze. "Because we realized that Mjorr was trying to hide something terrible, and when we did reach the city we found out what it was. We would never murder a woman my lord, and especially not one who is expecting. Mjorr is a beast, a monster and a coward, we spit on his name and shit on his honour. He did rape his own sister and for that we hate him, we are mercenaries but we do have honour, he doesn't have any at all"

Dagar did gasp, he did look faint and two of the guards had to hold him up or else he would have collapsed. He let out a thin wail. "NO! please, don't tell me that is the truth? It cannot be…NO!"

Ahravan did sigh. "I am sorry old man, it is the truth."

Dagar screamed. "I cannot believe it, I refuse to believe it"

Rhawan did nod to two of the guards and they went off and after a while they did return with Prina, they had originally meant to keep her hidden but this did require that she was there. They needed the evidence.

Prina was being supported on either side by Ehbrial and Imh and she did waddle, her huge belly very visible for she wore only a thin dress and her long hair was unbraided and greasy. Her eyes were empty as before and Wenja did cringe at the sight. Ahravan did point at her. "Here she is Dagar, your daughter! She is with child, her brother's child!"

Dagar stared again, his eyes were enormous and he was pale as snow, trembling. The shock and the shame were beyond anything he could ever have imagined, and he stared at Mjorr and couldn't even speak. His mouth was moving but not a sound was being heard. Both rape and incest were among the absolute taboos of their people and those two combined?

That was when Prina lifted her head and there was life in her eyes again, black hatred. She stared at Mjorr and bared her teeth. Hissed like a snake, pointed at him. "There he is, the snake, the filth, the evil doer. There he is, the evil one who took me in our barn, forced himself onto me and took the only thing I had of value. The father of my child, the bringer of my doom!"

She screamed the last words and Mjorr stared at her belly with obvious shock, he hadn't known that he had knocked her up and he didn't really know what to say.

Geir did swallow hard. "We saw that she was pregnant and swore that we would make sure that Mjorr was punished"

Mjorr did laugh, a wild laughter filled with evil mirth. "Oh but why is she complaining? She wanted cock so I gave her some, and I cannot help being a potent and fertile man, she should thank me. Nobody else wanted to touch that dry little cunt with a ten foot pole!"

Prina did scream, a wild piercing cry and she did a sudden move and managed to knock Ehbrial out of balance. She had grasped his belt knife and Wenja did almost scream as Prina did tear the dress away from her belly and showed it to Mjorr. "Here it is, your offspring, your seed! Do not think that your line will continue, it ends now!"

Ehbrial tried to grasp her but he was too late, she was incredibly fast as she plunged the knife into her own belly with a sore scream and made a deep long cut from which blood did gush immediately. Wenja did scream, many there did faint and Mjorr did stare at the grotesque scene with disbelief. Dagar did pass out and Ahnriel and other healers did descend upon Prina like a flock of hungry ravens. Prina did reach into the wound and she did pull forth something which wriggled slightly. "Behold your son Mjorr, may he join you in hell!"

Then she did collapse and the healers did cover her up and carried her off, blood was raining from the stretcher and Ahravan was pale. Rhawan was just staring and Wenja did weep. Rhawan did embrace her lovingly and Mjorr was laughing, it did sound like a hyena.

The shaman was visibly shaken. "A bad omen, an invitation for evil."

She turned to Geir. "You could have told us of this when you arrived but we blame you not, you did come clean after all and you have proved yourselves to be good men deep down. You are welcome to stay, we need every fighter we can get our hands on from now on"

Geir did nod and bowed his head. "We are very thankful. Mjorr deserves a very long and slow death"

Ahravan did clear his voice. "And that he will be given"

The shaman did stare at the elders and they all nodded. "Mjorr son of Dagar, you have lost the right to live among decent beings, your crimes are unmentionable and your name will be cursed forever. The punishment starts now"

Mjorr let out a wail of protest and one of the warriors did tear the tunic off him and another one did step forth with one of the long whips they used to control the herds of cattle. It was made from rawhide and the warrior did shake it out with great care, as if to make sure that Mjorr saw it. The shaman did nod. "Twenty lashes, make them bite well"

Wenja did shiver, seeing what Prina had done had left her in shock and she did cry. Rhawan was rocking her in his arms and he too was visibly shaken up. The healers were good but Wenja suspected that Prina didn't want to live anymore.

The warrior did swing the whip over Mjorr's back and the technique was wonderful. The elven warriors were so good with a whip they could snatch a fly from a cows ear twenty feet away without the cow feeling it and the whip did tear into the flesh and skin without overlapping even once. When Mjorr felt the first hit he did squeal like a girl and he kept cussing and screaming insults the whole time. When the warrior was done Mjorr's back was covered with parallel wounds and they did bleed but not too much. Mjorr was gasping with pain but far from broken and Ahravan did raise an arm. "It is time for the last part of the punishment. Those of you who wish to leave do it now!"

Some did leave but most did stay and the atmosphere was one of intense hatred, Mjorr had truly become someone they all hated now. Two of the elves did carry a sort of bench forth, it was rather simple and yet sturdy and Resh'kha did grin and held Mjorr as Floth'bha did tear off the rest of his clothes. He did scream and wriggle but to no prevail, the half orc was way stronger than him. When he was naked they forced him down over the bench, his arms were tied up straight out to his sides and his chest did rest on the top of it but the rest of the torso was free. The feet were chained to the bottom of the bench, spread far apart. It started to dawn on him what this was about and he started to plead and beg but nobody did listen. He was strapped to the contraption and couldn't move at all and a rope was fastened around his neck and threaded through a hole in the solid wood. It could be tightened by someone standing next to the condemned and the shaman did stare at Mjorr with no amount of pity. "A man who has repented his crimes and truly regrets them may be given some mercy, but for you there will be none."

She stared at the people present and a few figures did step forth, they all wore black cloaks which covered even the face but their eyes were visible. All were female and all wore a sort of attachable phallus, placed at their groin. Mjorr did let out a wail of denial, this was so below his dignity he had a hard time believing it to be true. To be taken by a man was bad enough, but to have a woman fuck his ass? That was just unbelievable, it couldn't be true. He started to scream the worst insults anybody had ever heard and many more did leave. They didn't want to listen to him anymore. The shaman did smile at the five women, three were human and two were elves and the tools they were to use were rather grotesque with ridges and bulbs and odd shapes. These were made to create agony instead of pleasure and Floth'bha did take the rope and she nodded at the shaman. She was the one to do the first part of the choking. Igkhan did wait behind her, he was to end Mjorr, after what hopefully would be a long struggle. The shaman bowed her head. "Proceed sisters, but make him last until sunset, we want his agony to last"

Wenja did turn around as the first of the executioners did grasp Mjorr by the hips and forced the wooden phallus inside. Mjorr wasn't a large man, he was slender and yet his body was soft and pale and not at all very attractive, he fought with all his strength but it wasn't enough by far. His scream of pain did not make anybody feel sorry for him. The woman did thrust vigorously and he did wail and cry and scream and oddly enough he did get an erection from it, it was probably because of the stimulance and not pleasure.

It did look obscene and he was gasping for air and shivering with the force of the thrusts. After a while one of the other women did take over for the first one and blood was dribbling down his legs now. They kept going and Floth'bha did tighten the rope a wee bit with each hour. The day went by and now very few were present, Wenja did stay there though, she felt ice-cold on the inside and now Mjorr was whimpering and gasping for air. She felt no pity, she would have pitied a rabid dog, not this man.

As the day turned towards the evening Mjorr didn't have the strength to struggle anymore, he just hung there, gasping and gargling and he was torn open and bleeding rather profusely. The pain had to be horrible but nobody did even think of showing him any mercy.

Dagar had been taken away and Wenja did blame Mjorr also for Prina's mad action at the trial, he was guilty of so much hurt and as the sun did head towards the horizon Floth'bha did tighten the rope so much Mjorr had real problems breathing. He was just gargling now and his eyes were rolling in his head. His tongue did stick out and it was dark and spit did run down his chin. The shaman did nod as the sun did sink beneath the horizon. "His spirit will be lost in darkness, condemned to walk behind the shadows forever. His name will be cursed and forgotten, his death one of the unclean"

She raised a hand and Igkhan did take the rope from Floth'bha. He did grasp it with firm hands and stared at Mjorr, the man was only half conscious now from blood loss, pain and strangulation. "You killed my sister, my sweet precious little sister who knew no evil and were innocent as a new-born babe. I do claim your life for hers, may your soul burn forever!"

He did pull, Mjorr did tremble, the body fighting death and rasping sounds could be heard as the lungs fought for air. Igkhan did pull harder and harder and Mjorr was blue now, shaking and trembling. One of the women did grasp the phallus she had used and stuffed it into the trembling man, to the very hilt. It was very obvious what she felt about him.

Igkhan did hold the rope taut until Mjorr no longer moved, blood dripped from the mouth and the eyes were empty and glazed. Ahravan did give Igkhan a sword and the young hunter did bring the blade up and cut the head off the man with one mighty blow. He did grasp it by the hair and held it up with a roar of triumph and sorrow and Wenja felt that she did weep. Not for Mjorr, but for all his victims.

The body was being taken away from the city to be thrown to the wolves and Wenja did follow Ahravan and Rhawan to the healers hut. She felt her heart beating fast, she was faint and felt as if this day had been some bizarre and horrible dream but it had been real. Ahravan did enter and he did look sombre when he came out. "The baby is dead naturally enough, she stabbed it, and it was too early for it to be taken from the womb. She will not make it!"

He didn't say anything more and Wenja did sob and Rhawan did lift her and carried her back to the hut, she was trembling in his arms and the three of them did huddle together on the bed, seeking comfort and safety among those they loved.

Dagar had been taken to a hut and he just laid there, in shock and grief. He knew how his son was to die and the shame was burning in him like an open flame. He had lost everything, his name and his honour and there was just one thing he could do to erase this guilt. His son had done the unspeakable crime, if he returned to the valley he would be shunned, a pariah, an unclean person. A filthy pig would be more revered than him and his money and wealth wouldn't matter, they would spit at him and use his name as a swearword. Dagar did sit there like a statue, there were two guards in the hut and they were discussing something in their own language. Dagar did get up slowly, there was a lamp on the table, a large one filled with fat and it burned well. Dagar did pick it up and the guards saw him and shouted out but he didn't even look at them. He did lift the lamp and poured the fat over himself, let the burning wick fall onto his body and there was a boof and the old man was covered with flames. The two guards did cry out and they tried to cover him with blankets but the old man ran out through the door and collapsed outside of the hut, like a living torch. He didn't scream, he just burned and nobody dared to get any closer, the fat did burn very hot and it didn't take long before he was dead and the body became fuel to a rather fiery blaze. Everybody was silent, they understood his last deed, it had been the only choice for him, the only way to regain at least some honour. This way he paid for his shortcomings and the blame would forever be on Mjorr. They let the body burn into ashes undisturbed. There was nothing else to do.

Wenja did wake up with a headache, she felt horrible and Rhawan had slept so close to her they both were sweaty and sticky. Ahravan wasn't that clingy when he was sleeping but even he had sought physical contact this night. He had crawled low on the bed and lay with his head on Wenja's stomach and his feet almost dangling off the edge. It was a good thing his bed was massive, there was space there even for that sort of manoeuvring.

Wenja didn't want to get up, she was warm and safe and it felt so good being held by her two husbands like that. But she had to pee and her head hurt and she was thirsty.

Rhawan did get up first and shouted for someone to bring warm water. Then he shouted for some food to be brought and helped Wenja get up. There was some hot water in the hut but it was just enough for tea and Ahravan did brew some which could alleviate a headache. Wenja drank a whole cup, even if it did taste like crap. She remembered the remedies Sina had used whenever one of the family felt ill and compared to that this was downright delicious. Rhawan too had some and when water was carried inn they all had a swift bath. Wenja felt a lot better when she got cleaned off, Ahravan loved to wash her with his bare hands and Rhawan too enjoyed that and before long she was ready for the day, clean and rubbed with sweet smelling ointments and all.

The food came just afterwards, some women did carry inn some baskets and Ahravan did thank them profusely and opened the baskets to find bread, cheese and some ham. Some of the clans were experts at making dried ham and Wenja did already love the slightly salted meat with its unusual consistency. The hams she had tasted previously had been tough as old boots and did taste and smell of old ram and these were the opposite. They did almost melt on your tongue and they didn't smell much at all. Wenja had some with the traditional flat bread the women of the clans did make, she had never learned that art and was looking forwards to seeing how it was done.

Rhawan and Ahravan were silently discussing the plans as they ate, the moving of the city had to be done soon and the route was decided but they still had to decide how to protect everybody as they were moving. The caravan was huge and so was the number of people and not all were warriors. With the arrival of the Snowbear clan they suddenly had even more women and children to look out for and it was very hard on Ahravan to have this responsibility. For most of his reign he had dealt with minor packs of monsters, and they could be easy to beat and were months and even years apart. This however called for something much more drastic and he wondered if they had enough warriors to make it. The monsters weren't immortal, they were animals but hard to kill and if the ancient evil which had controlled them was back it would be even harder to get rid of this threat.

Wenja was done eating when Sefa did ask for permission to enter, she came in with Imh and Theka and it was obvious that they were crying, Imh was sobbing and Theka did look like seven sorrows moulded into one.

Ahravan did sigh. "It is Prina?!"

Sefa sat down and wiped off her eyes. "Yes, she died this morning, they couldn't save her. Too much blood loss and no will to live"

Imh gasped for air. "The poor darling, she never really had a chance now did she? That bastard did ruin her completely"

Wenja felt her heart sink and she felt a lump form in her throat, Rhawan did embrace her and Ahravan did kiss the top of her head, there was grief in his eyes. "It is tragic, that brute did claim yet another life, after his own death."

Imh did nod. "At least she is at peace now, with her little one"

Wenja sobbed. "When is the funeral?"

Sefa took a deep breath. "This evening, no point in waiting. She has no kin here and there is no reason for the body to be kept. "

Wenja sighed and buried her face against Ahravan's wide chest. "I want to attend, to show her my respects."

Ahravan did stroke her long burgundy hair and his eyes were distant. "We will all be there, she was a victim and the whole city knows that. "

Wenja closed her eyes and let Ahravan continue stroking her hair, it did soothe her and felt so very good. "Aye, everybody knows"

Chapter 9: Gathering darkness

Prina's funeral was a very quiet one, some did bring gifts and others did chant and sing but the tragedy of this death did make most there silent. Wenja didn't really speak at all, she just stood there until the fire had burned down and Ahravan did caress her hand while Rhawan had a hand on her shoulders the whole time. Sefa did weep and so did the others, Ehbrial did stand there and he did look crushed, Prina had used his knife to cut herself open and he felt guilty, besides, he had both liked her and felt sorry for her and Ahravan did walk over and whispered a few words of comfort to the heart stricken eternal.

The sunset was very red that evening and Wenja knew that some thought that to be a bad omen, they were to move the city in just a few days and already the first preparations were on the way. Horses were gathered and checked for injuries, the tack was being oiled and prepared. The wagons were being checked too and Wenja did like the sudden liveliness there but at the same time, the cause for it wasn't the normal joyful one. She was being more or less forced to ride everyday now, she had been given a small brown mare and she did handle the horse pretty well but it did still feel a bit nerve-wracking to be riding on her own. Ahravan was busy all the time now and Rhawan did also spent a lot of time away from Wenja but he did try to show her his affection whenever they were together and many did laugh and make jokes at his obvious admiration and rather lustful behaviours. Ahravan wasn't any different but he was more discreet if in no way less passionate. He was the most enduring of them and Wenja did some times believe that she would be the first in history to die of pleasure. He could keep going for an unholy amount of time and she usually ended up so wired up and sensitive the smallest touch made her cum screaming.

The scouts were out the whole time now, changing three times a day and Resh'kha and Floth'bha did usually go out on patrol together. The two had become great friends and Ahravan did joke a bit about it. Resh'kha had been exiled from her tribe because of a male but perhaps females was what she truly did desire?

Yahlen of the Snowbearclan was also riding around watching out, she was consumed by anger and grief and Wenja felt unease whenever she was around. The elven woman was so intense and she had such darkness in her eyes. Ahravan said that she would die avenging her husband, it was her right to do so but he didn't like it. A person like that could drag others down with them, they did no longer care about life or death, just vengeance. Wenja felt that it was tragic but she guessed that the loss of a life mate was so traumatic to an elf that it almost drove them insane. After all, elves aren't supposed to die at all.

The day of the moving was approaching fast and Ahravan was everywhere at once or so it seemed, the routines had to be changed a lot and the dwarves which followed the city had been busy making weapons for weeks. Wenja did get a sword from Rhawan, it was not very long but very slender and extremely sharp and clearly made for a woman. She had no idea of how to use it but she was grateful nonetheless. At least she had something more intimidating than a butter knife.

The day before the move was to begin the scouts returned with a small group of people, they were survivors from a group which had lived to the west of the city and they had been attacked some days ago. Bagir and Igkhan were shocked to see the injuries they had suffered and they hadn't brought anything except their horses and the clothes on their back. They were twenty in all, youngsters who had been out herding goats when the attack came and their swift horses the only reason why they did escape in the first place. Bagir had been deeply shocked by what Prina had done and he had sort of retreated into his own mind for a few days, refusing to speak to anyone. Igkhan had been shocked too but he had understood her desperation and her choice, to a woman from his tribe such an action would have been downright normal. Bagir did sit with Wenja quite often after the funeral, he did talk about relatively insignificant things but Wenja knew that he just needed to get a distance between himself and the death of Prina. He hadn't known her but he had known that she suffered a lot. It was a shame in that but Dagar had been one they all feared and nobody had dared to help the poor girl.

The ones who were injured were tended to by the healers and Ahravan did interrogate the others for a long time. Wenja realized that these creatures were something which simply didn't belong in this world, that it was something unnatural and wicked and that the clans in truth did exist to protect everybody else from this danger. Rhawan had told her that the monsters were of many different types but common for them all was that they were driven by a common bloodthirst and desire to kill and destroy. That evening they all went to rest early, the moving day was a hectic one and they all needed to be in good shape and well rested. Wenja was a bit ashamed, she had started her moon days again and she felt that it was embarrassing but neither Ahravan nor Rhawan did see anything odd or disgusting in that. They just accepted it and for the first time she did see Ahravan take Rhawan, she had of course known that they sometimes were that intimate but they hadn't done it until now and she was fascinated and also strangely humbled by the obvious tenderness and care between the two.

It wasn't as straight forward as when they had sex with her, Ahravan did prepare Rhawan first and they needed some oil and also time but when they finally got there it was obvious that Rhawan did enjoy it, even if there was some pain initially. Afterwards they all just laid there cuddling and Wenja hoped that the next days would go well.

The morning came with clear skies and cold air and it was ideal really. The scouts were out already and the huts were taken apart as soon as everybody were up. The content put on the wagons and then the walls and roof and floor was rolled up and put on the larger wagons. Some of the walls were placed on sleds too and the huge long haired cows did pull those. Everybody had a job to do and Wenja did help Sefa pack all their belongings onto one wagon. It was exciting and Sefa made sure that Wenja was dressed well, the air was cold and it was easy to get frostbite if one wasn't aware of this.

The children were scooped up and out onto the wagons and the horses and cattle knew where to go and didn't need drivers. Wenja was impressed, when the wagons were packed there was nothing left. The fire pits were covered with rocks and soil and the latrine pits had been covered already. The landscape did almost look as if nobody had ever been there.

The first part of the journey was along the path they normally followed, they had to go by the river for some hours before they could cross it and from then on they would take a new course which lead towards the mountains.

Wenja sat with Imh on one of the wagons and they did discuss the different ways the dwarves did show social status and wealth. She had never known that you could tell that much from just a few braids but Imh did explain that everything about a dwarf's appearance told something about that person. She did show Wenja her own braids to make it clear, since she wore three beads in each braid it was a sign that she was a widow, not after a new husband and that she had children. Her beard had beads in it too and they told that she was rather wealthy and also that she was independent. Wenja almost got confused by all this information.

The river was very wide where they arrived to cross, but it was shallow and the bottom was sandy and easy to cross for the wagons. The sleds were a problem though and needed help but they did manage to get everything across in one piece. The herds did follow the caravan from a distance and Wenja saw that the people kept a keen eye on the animals. The herds would warn them if something did approach them.

Resh'kha was riding near the caravan, she was on guard the whole time and she did look very determined and ready for a fight. She had settled down rather well and loved being there and she became more open and jolly by the day. The dwarves who followed the clans had their own wagons and rode small ponies and they were armed and Wenja knew that they were exceptional fighters. They had turned onto the new path and now things became more difficult for they didn't know this terrain that well. They sent front riders forth to find the best path, the plains were relatively flat but there were rocks and hidden holes here and there which could crack a wheel.

Wenja did see huge areas covered with what appeared to be small mounds of dirt and Sefa did explain that it was the burrows of a type of animal, a bit like a rabbit but minus the long ears and they could undermine the ground completely. They had to stay clear of these cities and their inhabitants. Wenja wondered if the animals were dangerous but Sefa told that they were harmless in themselves but they could carry some nasty diseases and also parasites. They tended to have the flea infestation from hell and Sefa did explain that you usually could see the fleas move in the fur. Wenja did cringe and Sefa got eager and started to describe the parasites of the plain animals in great detail.

The meals now were simple, nothing hot but Wenja didn't mind, the bread and cheese was enough for her and as the day reached its end they drove the wagons into huge circles and placed guards around them. Wenja did sleep in a tent that night with Ahravan. Rhawan was out on guard duty and sometime during the night he returned and Ahravan took his place. Wenja was glad she was so protected , it allowed her to enjoy the different things she did see. Here and there they had seen huge piles of rocks and everybody would throw a pebble onto the heap when they passed by, it was to ward off evil spirits. They did also see some huge standing stones which had been painted in bright colours and nobody knew why they did it but every year when they passed by these rocks someone would freshen up the colour.

Wenja had been aware of Yahlen's daughter since the clan did join theirs, the girl was a quiet one and kept to herself but Wenja felt that she perhaps ought to do something to lighten her up. She had lost her father and her mother seemed to be obsessed with vengeance and if that didn't mess with you she had no idea of what did.

The elven girl was young, in human years she was several centuries already but Wenja did recognize a vulnerability within her which was almost familiar. She did remind Wenja of Halda and Wenja saw her chance as they did rest by a small brook. The elven girl was watering her horse and Wenja did saunter by, looking at the stocky animal. It was unusual in that it had several dark patches and most of the elven horses weren't born with that sort of colouration at all. They could be dapples but hardly paint. "He is unusual, does he have a name?"

The elven girl did twitch and managed to smile, a very faint smile, there was such pain in her eyes and Wenja felt how the compassion did fill her soul. "Ah, Darkice, he was…he was my fiancé's horse"

Wenja blinked. "Oh, I am so sorry, I didn't know…"

The girl sighed. "It is alright, how could you know?"

Wenja gathered her courage. "Still, I hurt you there, and for that I do apologize, you were close?"

The elf looked down. "Very, we were to get married come the spring. I mourn him every hour but mother…"

Wenja did reach out and took her hand. "Your mother is blind to your pain and feels only the grief of losing your father right?"

The elf nodded, her eyes blurred. "Mother seeks death, I cannot express it otherwise. She wants to fight. Her spirit is broken and…"

She sniffled and hid her face and Wenja did embrace her, it was awkward for the elf was taller than Wenja but she did hold her the way she had held Halda and the elf shivered slightly. "I am so sorry to hear that, grief can do horrible things to people. What is your name?"

The elf swallowed. "I am Yalaih, it means swallow"

Wenja smiled. "And I am Wenja"

Yalaih did tilt her head. "The Eth'ir. And human. You are blessed Wenja, the Gods have smiled at you, two strong males to protect you"

Wenja did blush. "Ah I didn't feel all that blessed to begin with, believe me. I agreed only so that Ahnriel could heal my sister"

Yalaih did frown, there was a glimpse of curiosity within her eyes. "She was ill? Forgive me but our tribe has so little to do with humans. When we came here I had barely even seen a human"

Wenja did sit down on a rock and Yalaih did join her, a bit hesitant. "She had injured her back and couldn't walk and her lungs were failing too. Ahnriel did fix her though"

Yalaih did think about that for a moment. "How odd, one of us would heal from such injuries rather fast, you seem so fragile and yet…you are stronger than we are in many ways"

Wenja had to stare at the elf. "How come?"

Yalaih shrugged. "Your souls, you face so much grief and yet you go on, as if nothing has happened. You can lose a spouse and just…you don't give in to the sorrow."

Wenja did sigh. "I know. My mother lost many children over the years and I guess you get used to loss, somehow"

Yalaih did open her eyes wide. "What? Children? How?"

It was rather apparent that this young female knew close to nothing about humans. Wenja shrugged. "At birth? Or some days or weeks after? It was normal where I am from, if you had ten children perhaps three would survive to grow up"

Yalaih did stare, her eyes huge with shock. "Oh Goddess, at birth? Oh have mercy, it sounds so horrible"

Wenja did nod. "Aye, it always is. But most women would have more children if they survived, it was just the way it is back there"

The elf swallowed hard. "I was too young for us to bond and have children, I do regret that we didn't now. But then again, I wouldn't want my son or daughter to grow up without knowing his or her father."

Wenja smiled. "Yes, that is understandable"

Yalaih did lower her voice. "Mother has gone mad, and I fear for her. I feel as if I am a tiny boat adrift on the great river, and I have no idea of where the current will lead me. They say that I may find a new love but I don't feel as if I ever can"

Wenja sighed and tilted her head. "I didn't think I would find love at all, but here I am, with two husbands"

Yalaih did giggle. "I know, so, how…I mean, two?"

Wenja had to laugh. "I am kept very satisfied if that is what you mean, I was so afraid when I was chosen but now I cannot get enough of them"

Yalaih had a confused expression on her face. "Afraid? Of what?"

Wenja felt embarrassed. "Uh, back where I am from the idea of enjoying ah..sex…was seen as a man's privilege. Us women were to endure and obey"

Yalaih did gasp, her jaw did almost hit her chest. "What? That is…oh goddess, blasphemy!"

Wenja nodded. "I have learned that now yes, my parents were more enlightened but still, the general attitude of the society did get its dirty claws into me. Mjorr was perhaps also to blame for that"

Yalaih did nod and her eyes became hard. "Ah yes, the murderer. He did die very well deserved, my clan couldn't even understand what his problem was"

Wenja did pull her knees up and stared out into nothing. "I think the problem was that he was his father's only son and back in the valleys sons are regarded as valuable while daughters are not. He got spoiled and used to having his way no matter what and Dagar did solve all problems for him, he did even cover up his crimes"

Yalaih shake her head. "We would never do that, favour one child over the others. And daughters and sons are just as welcome. "

Wenja smiled. "As it should be"

The horse did nicker and Yalaih did grin. "Know what, talking to you has been enlightening and also relaxing and I thank you. I better get going now"

Wenja did shake her skirts. "Yes, we are to move again."

Yalaih did take her hand. "Thank you, you took my mind off my grief for a while"

Wenja just nodded and felt a feeling of wonder, she was also rather humble there and then. Being able to help others was after all such a gift.

She did return to the wagon and they did start moving again, the animals had been fed and watered and this was the last stretch of the day before they would have to stop for the night. Wenja did relax and got busy with some embroidery, she had been given some thread and a needle and some nice cloth by Theka and now she was planning on making a nice hairband for Rhawan. The colour of the cloth would fit his dark hair perfectly. She was sitting there when they heard sounds and some of the warriors did ride by at breakneck speed, then another group came racing too and the caravan did stop. The drivers did place the wagons close to each other and the herders did gather the animals and chased the huge long horned cattle forth so they formed a sort of barrier around the wagons. Wenja knew why, the cattle was lethal with those horns and they wouldn't hesitate using them. Resh'kha came riding on her buffalo, she did wield her axe and her eyes were huge and dark and she was clearly very excited.

More shouts and calls could be heard from afar and Sefa came running, she was pale. "Wenja, get into the wagon, now!"

Wenja did obey, she trusted Sefa and knew that if she said something she meant it. They got into one of the wagons and peeked out through the openings. There was a cloud of dust in the distance and the sounds came from that direction but Wenja saw that something was moving towards them at huge speed. Sefa did gasp and covered her mouth. "Oh no, some have escaped the warriors"

Wenja stared, she had never imagined that anything could look thus. The creatures which were storming towards the wagons were something out of a nightmare, they had long powerful front legs and did resemble a huge ape in body shape but the hind legs were tiny and short and almost crippled, they ran on their front legs. The upper torso was extremely muscular and strong and then there was the heads. Wenja stared, she couldn't do anything else. It did look as if somebody had mixed a huge crocodile with a shark and then put the head onto these odd bodies. The jaws were long and narrow and filled with teeth and Sefa did move her lips but she didn't make a sound. It wasn't a huge group, perhaps ten in all but they were huge and fast and the front legs had horrible claws.

They heard a roar and Resh'kha did ride straight at them, she and the buffalo did hit the oncoming attack like an avalanche and the buffalo did send one of the beasts flying sky high. Resh'kha did swing the axe and took the head off one of the beasts with a powerful swing and now there were other shouts heard and Floth'bha and some other riders did join inn. And the cattle did roar and ran at the attackers in a living wall of swinging horns. Wenja saw that beasts were being impaled and trampled, the warriors did cut away at their arms and legs and when they were crippled the next in line did decapitate them and it was efficient and bloody and terrible to watch.

The battle did last for a while, the beasts were strong and could survive a lot but not a counterattack like this one. Finally the last one fell and Resh'kha did raise her voice in a roar of joy. Wenja realized that she had held her breath for a very long time and she had to gasp for air and try to breathe once more. Sefa did roll her eyes. "They were too close, it has to be a huge group, I do so hope that everybody is okay"

Wenja suddenly feared for Ahravan and Rhawan and she sat there in the wagon like a bundle of anxiety until the dust cleared and the warriors did return to the caravan. She did see both Ahravan and Rhawan there and they were unharmed, some were wounded but none had been killed, these monsters had been relatively easy to beat since they were very stupid and easy to deceive. Ahravan was roaring orders and the caravan started moving again, this place wasn't safe at all and Rhawan was riding ahead with the scouts to prepare a camp site.

Ahravan did seek out Wenja when the worst of the organizing was done, he did sit down on the wagon seat next to her and he was covered with dust, blood and sweat. He did look terrible but he was alright and that was the most important thing.

She saw that he was hard pressed and nervous and also that he was tired, there were shadows within his gaze and she saw that there were some lines on his face which hadn't been visible before. She took his hand and he sighed and squeezed her hand slightly. "Bless you my sweet, how are you doing?"

Wenja scoffed. "How I am doing? I am fine you big oaf, what about you and Rhawan? Were they many?"

Ahravan sighed again and leaned back against the seat, he nodded. "A substantial pack yes, maybe fifty or sixty, there weren't time to count believe me."

She swallowed hard and he put an arm around her shoulders. "Worry not my dear, we are gonna keep you safe. We did win easily enough"

Wenja took a deep breath. "The beasts, they were so unnatural, and these are just one of the different versions?"

Ahravan nodded and he kissed her cheek, almost as if he suddenly was shy. "Yes, but like I said, you should not worry. Nobody here will ever let you come to harm"

Wenja did stare at the carcasses, they did stink and they were just leaving them behind. Ahravan kissed her again, very sweetly. "They are nasty but mortal, we can fight them, all the types."

Wenja had a sinking feeling in her gut. "What if there is something new this time?"

Ahravan frowned. "What makes you say that?"

She shrugged. "I don't know, a feeling I guess?"

Ahravan pulled her close. "I am sure that whatever they throw at us we will cope just fine, this has happened before and we did win back then"

Wenja leaned her head against his shoulder, not bothering with the fact that her hair did look awful due to the amount of dirt she picked up from him."

"How did you win? Were you there?"

Ahravan did snicker and shook his head. "No, I wasn't born for yet a few thousand years the last time the gates were open but I have learned about it. The shamans and magicians did manage to close them and the few slips which happens every now and then are just due to residual magic. Some beasts get through from time to time but the gates are in truth shut."

Wenja raised an eyebrow. "Then how do they get through?"

Ahravan took a deep breath. "Basically they are late, they have been caught in between their world and this one and when the gates were shut they couldn't return and after a while they do slowly move towards our dimension and are eventually pushed out into it."

Wenja was confused, magic and such thing were way above her head. "So the monsters you have fought until now are remnants of that ancient battle?"

Ahravan nodded. "That is correct yes."

Wenja took a deep breath. "But the beasts you have encountered now, and the demons and everything are a sign that the gate has opened again?"

Ahravan bit his lower lip- "Yes. Most likely."

She stared at him. "And what can you do with the gates now? Are there shamans that strong and magicians available?"

Ahravan took her hand. "Yes, we have many people among us who are very skilled and the disturbance in the magical force will tell every magician there is that the dimensions are disturbed, there will be help coming from every tribe and every city."

Wenja didn't want to say it but she did anyhow. "And if there isn't any help to be found?"

Ahravan hesitated. "Then we do have a problem"

Wenja looked down. "Yes, I may be naïve but I am not stupid. You can fight herds like the one we just encountered but not even you can fight thousands of beasts. Something must be done"

Ahravan took her hand and his smile was a bit sad. "You are of course right, we will have a meeting soon, the shamans and the seers and the leaders. We have to find out what's going on and what we can do to stop it."

He remembered the men they had impaled and their wickedness and also the small demons which had spawned in those dead villagers, there was a chill running down his spine. "Wenja my dearest, it will be alright, I am sure it will. The Gods are not cruel"

Wenja leaned inn against him again. "Yes, they may not be cruel but who says that this has anything to do with them? If they are from somewhere outside of our world then who is to tell if the Gods can truly intervene with this problem at all?"

Ahravan did stare at her with a puzzled expression, she was young and yet so wise, she saw beyond the easy explanations and sought the core of the problem and he was a bit awestruck by the calm determination within her eyes. "We are not sure, as I said, there will be a meeting"

Wenja smiled and held his hand. She wanted to attend to that meeting, somehow she felt that it was something she had to do. Ahravan did kiss her again and jumped off the wagon. "I have to get back to work, the camp needs to be safe for everybody come the darkness"

He whistled for his horse and rode off and Wenja felt alone, she wrapped her cloak around her and stared out over the plains. She had no knowledge about magic and to be frank it freaked her out but she was practical. She was a shepherd's daughter after all and when there is a herd of something it usually comes from somewhere right? And if you want to prevent them from coming any closer building a fence could be a good idea? Or making them think that entering is a bad idea to begin with?

The caravan did enter a small valley where the warriors were preparing the night camp. They drove the wagons close together again and everybody who had the possibility to do it ran out to gather dry cow dung to burn. They made a ring around the entire camp and it would be set on fire of anybody did spot something out of the ordinary. The wagons were so tightly parked that you could walk between them without touching the ground and she was told that she was to stay in the wagon she had arrived at Ohtanar in. Either Ahravan or Rhawan would join her there and she felt nervous again. Like there was something she had forgotten about and couldn't remember no matter how hard she tried.

Imh came carrying a tray of food and she and Sefa did sit down to have a quick meal and a chat. Sefa had laid her eyes on Khirhien now and was trying to sneak her way into his bed and she was very enthusiastic when she told Wenja about her attempts at making him notice her. Wenja had no doubt that he already knew she was interested, he was just trying to play hard to catch and Sefa was interrogating Wenja about her married life. It ended with giggling and laughter and Sefa had left when Rhawan did enter the wagon to rest. He had washed off but he hadn't bathed so he did still smell and his clothes were stained. He did remove them swiftly before crawling down next to Wenja. He did sniff her hair and cuddled up next to her and she felt how tired he was. She could sense their mood now, and how they felt and he was exhausted even if he tried to hide it. She held his hand as he drifted off into sleep and laid there playing with his hair, the dark blue colour did look black in the faint light and he was like a shadow to look at, all black but she didn't fear him. The thing to fear was out there somewhere.

Wenja did fall asleep and the guards were awake and alert, they switched every second hour and Ahravan were riding around looking for danger the whole time. Resh'kha had killed several beasts and she was still caught in the euphoria of victory, Ahravan had to grin when looking at her brilliant grin and shiny eyes. The female orc was a formidable warrior and he was glad she was there. As daylight slowly started to return one of the guards did sound the alarm, he pointed out towards the plain and they saw that something was moving. It was a type of beasts Ahravan had only heard of, wolf like and extremely long legged but instead of fur they only had thick scaly skin and the heads were oddly small but mostly jaw and the teeth were ghastly, like saws. It was a huge pack and Ahravan took a deep breath and tried to calm himself, these were fast and vicious and also way smarter than the monsters they had encountered the day before and the way they moved told of determination. The warriors gathered and Resh'kha did roar a few times, to sort of boost her aggression.

Ahravan knew that these beasts would be hard to stop and he feared the worst but suddenly something very unexpected happened. There was a shadow flying in before the sun and as they looked up an enormous flock of birds did fly overhead, heading towards the beasts. It was all sorts of birds, from the tiny yellow ones which were hardly the size of a fingernail to the enormous black winged eagles which preyed on sheep or even wolves. They were so many they did blot out the sun and Ahravan couldn't believe what he was seeing, neither could the others. The beasts did hesitate, then they stopped and that was when the birds descended upon them like a thick living mass of feathers and claws.

There was a sound like a distant waterfall, mixed with the shrieking and crying of a million beaks and the beasts did try to defend themselves But the birds were small, and many, and they were fast and flew and the bigger raptors went for the eyes of the enemy and tore them out. Hawks and owls did blind beasts by the dozen and the monsters did run off in a fit of panic. And that was when the biggest surprise appeared, the ground seemed to open underneath the trampling feet and they fell and tumbled and when they went down hundreds of tiny bodies did cover them immediately, gnawing and biting and entering cavities. The screams and roars were horrible and the humans and elves could only stand and watch in horrid fascination as the birds and rodents and other smaller beasts did pick the beasts clean to the bone, one tiny piece at a time.

Ahravan was panting, the sight was unreal, when the cloud of birds did take to the wing only bones were left, bloody and grotesque and completely stripped of tissue. The ground was torn open and transformed into a sandpit and everybody stared at each other. "What in the name of every God was that?"

Laupir was pale and wide eyed and Ahravan shook his head. "I have no idea, but I think the shamans will have the answer. I have never heard of anything like that before."

There were thick heaps of dead birds there and also dead mice and voles and some rats too and as they approached the area Ahravan did signal for the others to hold back. He did ride forth and Ayr'esh did snort and the horse did tremble a bit. He didn't like this at all. Ahravan stared at the dead beasts, they hadn't had a chance and it was ironic, these huge monsters had been killed by something this tiny. Ahravan had never been very sensitive, he was a fighter, not a shaman and he felt nothing out of the ordinary there but the sight of the slaughter did make him shiver a bit. What sort of power was it that had protected them?

He returned to the camp and saw that Rhawan and Wenja had gotten up and approached him, he tried to smile but his face felt stiff, and unnatural. "My light, it seems as if the Gods do smile upon us after all"

Wenja was pale and Rhawan did ride out to see for himself, Ahravan did embrace his wife and felt her tremble. "I heard horrible sounds and I got so scared, so very scared"

Ahravan kissed her and held her close. "No wonder, even I was afraid. We have to move on, there is still a long way to go"

Wenja sighed and then she leaned up as far as she could and pulled his chin down, kissed him gently. "I know"

The caravan started to move but everybody were shocked by the incident and many were frightened, Yahlen and the rest of her clan were visibly upset and speculations and theories were flying everywhere like runaway darts. They had to cross two rivers that day and everybody was helping out. There was a shout of alarm when they reached the second river, dust could be seen on the horizon. Earlier some small groups of people had joined them, survivors from attacks and nomads who didn't dare to be on their own anymore, but this wasn't people. The warriors did look nervous but it was animals. The wild herds of the plains seemed to have gathered and now they followed the caravan from a distance and Ahravan saw both the huge round horned sheep which usually were very hard to come by and wild cattle. There were buffalo as well, antelope and even wild horses and they were heading in the same direction.

That night Ahravan did spend the night with Wenja as Rhawan was out on guard duty and he held her tight the entire night. Two more days went by and they didn't see any more of the monsters but they did come across a small group of nomads who had been killed by something which had drained them completely of fluids. It was a horrible sight and Ahravan knew what those demons did now, it couldn't be anything else or could it? Then they reached a sacred grove and the meeting was to be held in a few days, shamans were gathering there now and they had to wait for a few who were late. Ahravan and Rhawan didn't like that, but if they were to find the truth the presence of all of those blessed was needed.

It was a much needed break for everybody and Wenja was glad that they didn't move now. She felt that the stress was hard on her husbands and since she was done with the moon days she did welcome them both back into her arms. There was something akin to desperation in their love making now, a sort of burning need to forget about the problems within the blaze of passion and she was glad she didn't have to ride, she would have had to sit sideways.

She learned something new each day now and gladly too and they became closer for each night that went by. With her and Rhawan Ahravan could jest and laugh and be just silly and she did see beyond his title as Ath'ir now and saw him for the person he truly was.

The meeting could finally begin, the last shamans had arrived and they gathered in the grove and started a very complicated ritual which hopefully would lead them to the truth. The ritual would last for days and five of the strongest were to do the real job while the others were there to support and strengthen the five. They would have to enter the realm of the spirits to do this and it could take a lot out of them. Wenja was curious and Ahravan was trying to explain everything but he didn't really know what it was about neither. There was constant chanting being heard for days, and drums too and the huge herd of animals had sort of surrounded the camp site. Resh'kha was in awe, she saw this as a sign of them being blessed by the Gods and Floth'bha was also a bit shaken by it all. The last night before the ritual was to end Ahravan did ride out for a while and when he did return he had a sort of packet with him, wrapped in leathers. Wenja got curious and she tried to see what it was but the packet was not very large and the shape was odd. Rhawan did look puzzled as well and Ahravan didn't say a word about it until they had eaten that evening. Wenja felt a bit drowsy after the meal and wanted to lay down for a while but Ahravan did stop her and he did open the window of the wagon to let light inn. The packet was brought forth and he did unwrap it. It was a sort of odd contraption Wenja never had seen before, she couldn't identify it at all. What she did see was that it was made from wood and the material was so smooth and silky as satin. She cocked her head. "It is lovely but what is it?"

Ahravan did grin. "Let me show you"

He did lift the strange thing and now she saw that it was meant to be worn, like a necklace but it was stiff and covered the shoulders like a piece of armour. But there was no protection in some thin wooden rods and it did remind her of the sort of rack some women used to hang their skirts on when they were drying after a wash. Ahravan did fasten the thing at her back and took a step back. "Right, it does fit you"

Wenja sighed and rolled her eyes. "Yes, but again, what is it?"

Rhawan did laugh. "A symbol of authority, an Ath'ir doesn't wear a crown, he is a person who is chosen for the job. But the Eth'ir is something else, you are the leader of the women of these clans now and that is your way of showing it."

Wenja frowned. "I am?"

Ahravan nodded "Yes, you are counted among the blessed now, and thus you may be present tomorrow when the results from the ritual are being told. You are more important than me my light for I am only an authority when it comes to troubled times. You are an authority when it comes to the things which truly matters, home and family and the wellbeing of us all"

Wenja did blush and let her hand run over the wood. It felt almost alive and she turned her head and stared at Ahravan. "Where did you get it?"

He smiled. "The grove, I went to the sacred tree and asked for a token and this was what I got"

Wenja had to swallow, the tree had given him this? For her? That was odd. She kissed his cheek gently. "I thank you, so I better wear this if I am to push my will forth?"

Rhawan chuckled. "Well, if your will is an unpopular one at least. But I doubt that you will need it, everybody knows you now Wenja and they know that you only want what's best for everybody."

She managed to lift the thing off without breaking it, it was as if it had been formed for her and she placed it in one of the closets gently. "I don't really know what to say"

Ahravan smiled and kissed her hand. "You don't need to say anything Wenja, you aren't like my first wife who always interfered, because she believed that she knew more than everybody else. When she really didn't."

Wenja had to giggle and Rhawan did grasp her by her waist and lifted her up, carried her off to the bed and left her standing on it. Wenja did raise an eyebrow in slight confusion, there was no doubt about his intentions if she was to judge the look in his eyes but what was he planning? Rhawan grinned. "You are very flexible my dear, let us see what we can do"

He pulled forth a small chair and sat down on it, right in front of her. Wenja was still confused and Ahravan did grin too and pulled his boots off. He got up on the bed behind her and she turned her head in confusion.

Rhawan did open her belt and then he pulled her skirts down and Ahravan did pull the tunic off of her so she was naked and then he did get rid of his own clothes too. Rhawan too stripped swiftly and grasped her by the hips, made her stand on the edge of the bed with her legs spread. Then he did lean forth and she gasped as his tongue found its way to her most sensitive areas. It sent jolts of pleasure through her and Ahravan did place a hand on her back and pushed her forwards gently. "Lean over him, don't worry, we won't let you fall"

She felt her heart beating faster and faster by the second and she had to gasp as Rhawan hit that sweet spot again at a very good angle. She leaned a bit forward and Ahravan did grasp her again, in a different manner. He got down on his knees on the bed and his hands did hold her thighs apart and they did also hold her up so she laid back against this body. Rhawan did lean forth and continued using his tongue and she screamed as Ahravan adjusted his hips and then entered her fully with one precise thrust. The pleasure exploded in her, the thrusts did push her pelvis forwards towards Rhawan and he did hold her hips too so she didn't feel as if she could fall at all. She placed her hands on Rhawan's shoulders and it was so good she could have died. Ahravan did fill her to the point of it almost becoming too much but not quite and Rhawan knew just what rhythm he should use and how to hold her on the very brink of ecstasy. In the end she couldn't hold back and she came, yelling something unintelligible and probably soaking them both with her juices. Ahravan groaned and fell out of rhythm, feeling her contract around him brought him to the brink too and he came hard, gasping for air and trying not to roar.

Rhawan had been stroking himself every now and then when he had a hand free, now he did nod at Ahravan who let Wenja slide down until she laid on the bed and Rhawan did pull her bottom to the edge of it and then he got down on his knees and placed her legs around his waist before he plunged into her with a smooth movement. Wenja couldn't help but cry out, the pleasure was so intense and Rhawan did fuck her fast and rather hard, she could take it now since she had already come once and was relaxed and he growled and moaned and kept going until she came again, squirting all over his front and screaming his name. Rhawan did thrust three more times and then he did burst too and shuddered violently until it let go off him and he let himself slide out and laid down next to Wenja on the bed. Ahravan did place himself on the other side of her and they just laid there and relaxed for a while.

Wenja turned her head and stared at Ahravan, he was breathing slowly but he wasn't asleep and he was so relaxed, they had needed this for sure. He opened one green eye and smiled "What are you thinking about?"

Wenja giggled. "I am not so sure if I should tell you"

Ahravan did raise himself up on an elbow. "Oh? Do tell, don't be shy?"

Wenja let a hand slide down his chest, he was so very powerful and yet so elegant and she had never known that such perfection did exist until she met him and Rhawan. "Ah, who was your first?"

Ahravan did laugh. "Why? Are you jealous?"

She shook her head. "No, just curious"

Ahravan did snicker and tickled her belly. "If I do tell promise me not to tell anybody else for it is embarrassing."

She grinned. "I swear"

Rhawan chuckled. "Oh I have heard that story before but do go on"

Wenja had to giggle. "Now I am really curious!"

Ahravan sighed and laid down again, he did look a bit flustered. "Well, we elves do reach puberty when we are about fifty years of age, and it is traumatic. Believe me, you humans have it easy, just a few years and then it is over with. We have problems for decades before our bodies do calm down."

Wenja had to gape. "What? Several decades? Oh Goddess!"

Ahravan did nod, there was a pained expression on his face. "Yes, it isn't as much physical as mental you see, we do grow and develop and all that and our voices do change and also our strength and coordination but the major change is in our behaviour"

Wenja frowned. "Meaning?"

Rhawan giggled. "He means that most elves spend at least three decades hornier than a field full of bunnies. It is really horrible, the hormones are running absolutely haywire. I remember that I was ready to fuck anything with a pulse, and I mean anything, two legs, four legs, it didn't matter"

Ahravan rolled his eyes. "You are exaggerating Rhawan, don't let him fool you Wenja, nobody would fuck anything with four legs"

Rhawan did scoff. "Talk for yourself oh great and wise Ath'ir"

Ahravan did look a bit tired. "Look, when our bodies are physically grown the level of sexual need can be unbearable so there is a sort of tradition within the clans. Young males who are entering that stage are being taken care off by older more experienced females or males if that is their preference. I was so bad I couldn't even think straight for more than five minutes and so I was taken to a hut where one of the volunteers was waiting for me"

Rhawan let out a high frequency giggle. "Oh just wait for it"

Wenja did almost shove him away, she was having fun and this was interesting too. "And?"

Ahravan sighed, a very deep sigh. "The female was very attractive, with an impressive set of tits, not as nice as yours I may say but to somebody at my age back then they were magnificent. She did bend down to unfasten my belt and pull my pants down and the moment I was free I…came"

Rhawan did roar with laughter. "Came? You gave her a faceful of cum, that was what you did, and passed out!"

Ahravan sighed. "Yes, you are right, I came all over her face and collapsed and when I woke up she was a bit angry and also a bit impressed."

Wenja giggled. "Oh dear, but you did …you know?"

Ahravan laid a hand under his neck. "Ah yes, we did fuck, like wild beasts and I kept visiting her hut for at least a couple of years, sometimes as much as three times a day. I was desperate but she did teach me a lot and I am grateful"

Wenja nodded. "So much better than back where I am from. Some have no idea of what to do when they get married, I heard a tale once of an elderly man who complained to the healer that none of his five wives were fertile, he had never had any kids at all. Turned out he had taken them in the wrong place his whole life"

Rhawan laughed. "Darn, that is bad. Doing it back there has its advantages but there will be no babies from it, at all"

Wenja did blush and Ahravan did ruffle her hair. "You look uncomfortable?"

Wenja nodded. "I knew that you males do it that way, but I didn't really think that females would allow that, at all. That old guy must have been terribly cruel the way I saw it back then, and still see it"

Ahravan chuckled and kissed her cheek. "Oh but many females like it, it can be pleasurable but of course you will need some preparation first and it has to be done very gently."

She blushed even deeper. "I don't think I am up for that sort of thing thank you very much, it holds no allure to me"

Rhawan grinned and gave her butt a gentle slap. "Too bad, but it is of course up to you. You decide what to allow or not, remember that"

She nodded. "Rhawan, I know Sefa said that you males feel great pleasure from it but it has to do with something you have and females don't right?"

He nodded and turned to face her, his face was serious. "Yes, it is a gland, and for some it can be very nice to have it stimulated. For others that sort of activity never becomes anything but unpleasant. "

She felt her face burn. "But you do like it right?"

Rhawan nodded again and kissed her shoulder. "Yes, but I only allow Ahravan to take me, nobody else. He is the only one I trust"

She had seen that there had been some pain when those two were together so she could understand. Ahravan did pet her on her back and yawned. "Let's get some sleep shall we?"

He grasped the covers and pulled them over them and Wenja did sigh, no baths now, unless you wanted to bathe in some ice cold river. And she didn't truly wish for that. So for the next days she would stink and since she wasn't the only one it didn't matter that much.

Wenja fell asleep right away and she slept like a log.

The next morning the skies were grey and low and the visibility low too, the fog hugged the ground and Ahravan did put his best cloak on and grunted. It was rather cold and the air was raw and felt unpleasantly heavy. The meeting was to be held in the grove and Wenja got on a good dress and warm outerwear and she rode with Ahravan. They had enjoyed a swift breakfast for they were in a hurry. The grove wasn't as large as the one back where they came from now, it was just trees but also here they had a mother tree and outside of it a small wooden hall had been erected. Only the important people were allowed to enter now, due to the lack of space. The shamans and seers were there and so were the chiefs and leaders of the clans. Ahravan and Rhawan were of course expected to be there and so were Wenja. The room was crowded but a small space was left open in the middle and one of the shamans did ask for silence and order. She was elderly and her face covered with tattoos, she did also have hundreds of small amulets hanging from her neck and some did hang from her hair too. The dress was sewn from tiny pieces of leather in different colours, in the dead grass outside she would be very hard to spot.

Wenja didn't know what to think of this, she felt like a stranger still and she tried to hide behind Rhawan but he did push her forth so she stood in front of him. The elderly woman did chant something and she did sprinkle some sort of white powder onto the ground, she was walking very slowly and her face was solemn. When everybody became quiet she did shake the stick she carried a few times, a dried out pumpkin was attached to the end and it still held its seeds so there was a rustling sound coming from it. "Listen my brothers and sisters, listen friends from afar, listen blood of man and elf."

She raised her hands over her head. "The seers have seen, the words have been spoken and the truth has been unveiled. Our words are not lies and our tongues knows no deceit, as it was seen it shall be"

Everybody mumbled and nodded and the woman closed her eyes. "I have been chosen to tell you all what we have found, I am the voice this time and the voice is sacred. It is not to be questioned"

Wenja realized that nobody could doubt the things this woman said, that she was going to tell only the truth and that nothing would be hidden.

The woman stood still for a moment, her arms still raised and her eyes closed. Then she opened them and they seemed to shine with an eerie light. "The voice speaks, the voice is forever, the voice cannot be silenced so listen to its words"

She turned around her own axis a few times and pointed at the four directions. "From the north it comes, from the east it comes, from the south it comes and from the west it comes. I am the truth, I am destiny."

She sat down with the ease of a young maid and crossed her legs, her voice was suddenly very strong. "The darkness has been awakened, wicked minds have helped the gate to open once more. Souls betrayed by their own lust for power and might, renegade wizards, lost souls"

She took a deep breath. "They came to the mountains years ago, and tried to copy the past but the magic was too strong, it killed them, And yet the damage was done, the wheels set in motion and the gates has been forced open anew by the forced of darkness, born outside of the world"

Ahravan remembered what that human being had said before they impaled him, about the dead priests and the amulet he carried. It had to have been those wizards, meddling with something they no longer had the knowledge to meddle with. The shaman did lift her head again. "They did more than just open the gate again, they did bring back something which had been gone from our world from the last time the gates were opened, and it seeks to redo everything which was done back then, to bring the full power of the darkness back into this world!"

There was some whispering heard, people did stare at each other with horror in their eyes. Ahravan did clear his throat and everybody did fall silent. "So, what can be done to prevent this from happening?"

The shaman did look down, her eyes dark and distant. "We have seen, but we do not truly understand what we saw. The cliff of Arothay, it is important in some manner."

Ahravan frowned, his face was robbed of emotion or so it seemed. "The cliff of Arothay? That is a sacred site yes, but it has been abandoned for a very long time, it is…very dangerous to venture near that area"

The shaman nodded. "Yes, it was forbidden ground back then and still is, but somehow its role haven't been completely erased from the pages of history."

Ahravan did take a deep breath. "Somebody has to go there right?"

The shaman nodded, her eyes on the ground again. "Yes, we have seen it, but it…it will be very dangerous indeed. Something…is waiting there"

Ahravan stared at the crowd and his heart felt heavy. "We may lose many if we go, but we will lose many more if we don't. If the enemy can be stopped it will be worth it"

The shaman did nod and she pointed at Ahravan and Rhawan. "Yes, it is your only chance, but only the one born twice can close the gate"

Ahravan groaned. "So we have heard many times and still, we haven't got a clue about what that means"

The woman sort of smiled. "Neither do we, but we know that the meaning will reveal itself"

Ahravan saw that Wenja was a bit pale. "What about my wife? Who will look after her when we are gone?"

The shaman smiled. "She will be going with you, there isn't even a chance of you doing this without her, if she isn't there you will fail"

Ahravan gaped and Wenja felt a bit cold, as if somebody had opened a door and let the draft inn. "I…"

The shaman stared at her. "Wenja, you are our Eth'ir, you are the one to represent the women of the twelve clans, you have great power girl, powers you yet haven't discovered. In you the past may come alive again, the forgotten gifts will awaken anew."

Wenja blinked and Rhawan sort of whispered. "The cave, and the dying troll, the fire spirit"

The shaman nodded slowly, her eyes almost eerie. "Yes son of the plains, she is special, she is chosen."

Ahravan tried to find head and tail of this whole thing. "So we go to the cliff, and then?"

The shaman shrugged. "You may find the key to shutting the gate, once and for all. But it will not be easy, I can promise you that. I see death, and horror"

Ahravan tried to smile. "We have some experience with both"

The shaman did grin, it wasn't a pretty smile at all, more of a sneer. "You think so, you will be proven wrong o brave leader"

Rhawan took a deep breath. "Are we to leave right away? It is far, very far"

The shaman shook her head. "No, when the moon has been full and then a crescent, then you go, not before"

Ahravan did look puzzled. "Why not?"

She did tilt her head. "We don't know, but it seems as if the danger would be much greater if you go too early."

One of the other leaders there, a man who was leading one of the free groups of humans who hadn't decided to join the clans stepped forth and he did look nervous but there was a proud expression upon his face and he didn't cower at all before all the eternal. "I have seen, I have the gift carried by my kin for ages unknown. I know why they have to wait"

The shaman did frown. "Do tell Bharuu, what has your gift shown you?"

The man did step into the middle of the room, he took a deep breath and closed his eyes. "Someone will lure the monsters away, be bait. They are gathering as we speak, the hordes are unleashed upon the plains and yet those aren't the worst ones, they are waiting. And they have to be stopped and lured away, unless the travellers be killed before they reach the cliff"

Ahravan gasped and the entire hut was silent, so silent you could hear a pin drop. "You are sure?"

The shaman's voice was low and trembling, she did look as if she was in a state of shock. The man nodded. "Aye, I am sure, they must lead away, to the woods of Ghaingar"

There was a gasp heard from everybody and Wenja felt that the atmosphere within the hut suddenly had changed, now everybody were scared. "What…why are everybody scared?"

Her voice was thin and weak and she hadn't really wanted to speak out loud.

Ahravan did answer, his voice was shaking. "That forest is cursed, a horrible place. Nobody dares to go near it"

Wenja swallowed hard and the shaman did look as if she was in pain. "When the gates were opened so long ago something escaped that dark world with the monsters but it wasn't ruled by their masters, it was…a spirit of some sorts. And it did settle in those woods and from that day on the forest has been lethal."

Wenja did wet her lips. "So the monsters are to be lead there? Why?"

The man who was named Bharuu did made a small gesture. "The forest will destroy them, or so I hope"

Ahravan took a deep breath. "It may be worth the try, but who would dare to go there? It is an extremely unpleasant area, whatever it was which possessed the forest, it has turned a huge part of the land into…something different"

Everybody did stare at each other and nobody did speak until a gruff voice could be heard. "I will go!"

It was Resh'kha and Floth'bha did also raise her hand. "And so will I!"

Rhawan and Ahravan did stare at each other, they did make grimaces. "That is all well and good, but why on earth would the monsters follow two female orcs? You aren't really much of a bait the way we see it"

The shaman was silent and everybody mumbled. Ahravan was right, the monsters would go for the great groups of people, not two warriors. That was when the door opened and three dwarves did enter the hut, it was three of the masons who was responsible for the ovens used in the huts and they were if not old then at least over their first youth and very experienced. One of them wore a dark red cloak as a sign of being a chosen leader and he did bow his head. "We will follow too, and we do know how to lure the monsters away from their intended path"

Ahravan frowned. "How?"

It was a demand and the dwarf did bow his head even deeper than before. "We have something they will seek, they will be drawn to it like a dog to a bitch in heat"

Rhawan did look curious and Ahravan stared at the dwarf with narrow eyes. "Explain please?"

The dwarf nodded and lifted a small velvet sack, he did open the drawstring and took a deep breath. "I will, this is old, it is from the ages before the gate was opened for the first time and its magic is extremely strong. It will attract everything evil, believe me"

He did open the bag and a strong light could be seen, he did lift it up and it was a gem, the size of a large orange and its colour was intense and almost sky blue, it was as if you were staring straight at a star. Everybody gasped. "A heart stone?!"

Ahravan's voice was hoarse and the dwarf nodded, there was pride in his voice. "Yes, the heart stone of the fallen city of Krimbadar. I am its guardian, and I have been waiting for its power to be unleashed once more"

Wenja whispered to Rhawan. "What is a heart stone?"

The black skinned eternal did whisper back. "They say that back in the ancient days there were dragons, huge ones. The heart stones are what is left when they die, the last drops of blood to pass through their mighty hearts, transformed by the magic they harbour"

Wenja stared at the stone, it was so breathtakingly beautiful and she couldn't understand how it could attract the forces of evil, it was beautiful. The dwarf saw her expression of wonder and smiled. "Do not think that it is just a pretty rock lovely one, it has powers, great powers. With it you can awaken a dragon from the ground, a power mightier than anybody can imagine. A power which is neither good nor bad, just there. Anybody can claim it for their own if they have the courage"

Wenja nodded. "I thought dragons were just legends?"

The dwarf did chuckle. "These days yes, there haven't been dragons for many ages, nobody alive today can remember the time when they did fly. The world has changed since then I think, it has become like a new world in oh so many ways"

Ahravan did raise his voice. "You have heard what has been said, are there more men willing to join in this perilous quest?"

The mercenaries Mjorr had hired had been outside of the hut but now Geir did enter the hut, his hat in his hand. "We will go, we wish to do good, just for once, and prove ourselves"

Ahravan smiled. "So it shall be. When do you leave?"

The dwarf made a gesture. "As soon as possible?"

Ahravan smiled, a somewhat sad smile. "What do you need?"

The dwarf did think for a second or two. "Fast ponies, food and tents and weapons. We can deal with the rest"

Ahravan placed a hand over his heart. "Consider it done brave dwarf"

The shaman had been silent and she did smile, a tired smile. "Still it will be very hazardous, darkness is waiting."

Ahravan just looked down and the shaman did clap her hands. "So you have listened, now be warned, the plains will be swarming with filth soon, everybody must do their job to prevent things from getting worse."

There was mumbling again and people started to leave the hut, slowly and in a sort of order. Wenja did hold Ahravan's hand, she felt confused and scared and Rhawan did stare at Ahravan with huge eyes. "Is there no way around it?"

Ahravan sighed. "No, she has to come, the seer was rather adamant when it came to that. We have to prepare well"

Rhawan did sigh and he did hang his head.

The sunlight outside was almost a shock, as if she had expected it to be dark. They hadn't been inside for all that long and yet it did somehow feel like a whole lifetime, she didn't let go of Ahravan's hand and he didn't try to make her let go. He did understand and he did wave at Rhawan and made him go give the right orders.

Wenja did see that the caravan had been surrounded by even more animals now, deer and antelope and buffalo, and even a couple of packs of wolves. They did look like grey shadows, lurking at the outskirts of the great assembly of living creatures and she made huge eyes when she also saw a huge cat out there. Ahravan did blink a few times, in sheer disbelief. "Are they coming for protection or to protect?"

The elves did look relatively calm but the humans did look nervous, that many huge predators assembled at once wasn't normal at all. They placed Wenja in the wagon again and they did prepare the camp to be moved again, the wagons were checked and prepared and Wenja did feel a sudden urge to get moving, to get away from this place. She felt exposed somehow, almost naked. The caravan was in a way a shield, she became anonymous among the enormous mass of people and animals.

Sefa did come to her and they sat there discussing the situation as the wagon was hitched up and started to move. The mountains were still far away and Wenja wanted to know where this cliff was and how they were to get there. The dwarves were preparing too, gathering ponies and equipment and apparently just three would be going together with the two orcs and the mercenaries. It was a ragged bunch for sure but Wenja couldn't help but feeling some admiration and also a sense of slight fear. They were heading into grave danger and yet they did act as if this was going to be a mere stroll in the park. Resh'kha did stroll around looking proud and Floth'bha was packing her horse with enough weapons to keep an army armed.

Ahravan was distributing tasks among the warriors, and now they did all witness something rather odd. The Zahar seemed to gather the predators around it, wolves, great cats and even some of the small dense but very fierce wolverines seemed to be drawn to its presence and people did stay clear of the group which seemed to grow by the hour. At first Ahravan didn't think much of it until one of the warriors came running looking as if he had seen a ghost. When Ahravan went to investigate he did stare with huge eyes for a while, among the huge pack of predators he did see some very large and powerful creatures which were so rare he hadn't seen any for centuries. They did look like wolves but were three times the size of a normal grey wolf and extremely powerful. They were capable of biting off the leg of a buffalo in one go and could run for days upon end. Also, he did spot a giant cat among the felines, an almost mythic creature he hadn't seen even once in his long life. It was a S'haga and it was the size of a huge horse, what was really going on here?

But the animals didn't attack the livestock and seemed to be guarding the caravan and Ahravan was of course grateful but also a bit nervous. What if the beasts decided to turn on them, and what on earth had drawn them there in the first place? The caravan was moving again, slowly. The front riders did try to make a safe path for the wagons to follow and the rhythm of travelling was yet again the normal one but now they were followed by literally thousands of wild beasts.

The wagons didn't stop for the night now, they just drove out to the side to change horses and kept going, even in the darkness of night. Torches gave light and Wenja and Sefa were used to sleeping while moving, they didn't bother with it at all. They had to get to the mountains as fast as possible. Ahravan came to sleep in the wagon and Sefa did leave, Wenja didn't even wake up and slept on, she had been exhausted by all the things which had happened. Ahravan had to get up before she woke up and he did kiss her gently on the cheek before he left the wagon, he felt that they had to make sure that Wenja was happy and safe, it meant more to him than anything else in the world right now.

That day the caravan did come to a halt, the front riders didn't find a safe path at all, they were heading into a valley and there were cliffs everywhere, they had to turn and drive back for a few hours before they could descend into the valley. A narrow river did meander along the bottom of the valley and now they did see the mountains and everybody felt relief. The caves ought to be easy to find and the atmosphere became more optimistic again. Getting the wagons down wasn't easy, several did fall apart, a couple did topple over and one did break apart in the middle as if it had been cleaved by a huge axe. They made it to the river before sunset and now they couldn't move on at all, they had to wait for the morning.

Wenja did sleep with both Ahravan and Rhawan that night, it was very cold and they huddled together underneath the covers and she did reap the benefits of their high body temperature . Each of them was like a stove and she was sandwiched between them and felt as if she was in a sauna. The morning came with clear blue skies and no wind strangely enough and now the drivers and everybody else started the tedious task of making a path up from the river. The valley was steep on the other side and the terrain was covered with huge flat rocks and smaller sharp ones which could ruin a wheel within the blink of an eye so they had to clear the way completely and the front riders did try to change the direction a few times to find easier paths. Ahravan and Rhawan did mount their horses and Wenja did feel bored and managed to nag enough for Ahravan to allow her to sit up with him.

They rode up from the valley and Wenja did see that the plains ahead of them was a flat stretch of land with few details visible. It was just flat dry land with some snow and dead greyish ochre grasses. But there was a row of cliffs to the south of where they were and Ahravan did turn the horse in that direction. They wouldn't manage to get further than those cliffs that day and it could be an alright place for a night camp. Rhawan was humming to himself and they rode relatively fast. They were caught up with by a group of warriors and Wenja did recognize Yahlen, she was riding a tall mare and her face was painted, the eyes hard and distant and she didn't even raise her hand in a greeting as she rode by. Ahravan did sigh. "She is a soulless now, we say that when somebody is too consumed by grief to think about the good things in life."

Wenja swallowed hard. "She is tragic, she still has a daughter alive?"

Ahravan sighed. "Yes, but that matters little to her now, she wants vengeance, more than anything else"

Wenja saw that the huge stallion had broken out of the herd of horses and were running right behind them, Flint did keep up with them just fine and she did admire the powerful moves. The cliff was ochre too, sandstone with some spots which had to be some other type of rock and as they got closer they saw that the cliff was rather large and wide. The group of warriors were riding around checking the terrain and some of the animals were following them, Wenja did see a huge pack of the huge wolf like beasts and also a couple of lions. They did stop to admire the view and plan the route ahead and Wenja sat there and looked at the cliff. The stone did look naked from afar but there were areas which were relatively flat and some bushes and grasses had managed to grow there, now there wasn't much colour to be seen though and Wenja wondered of this seemingly boring area ever did bloom.

The warriors did gather around them to receive orders and Ahravan did discuss what they had seen with everybody, it was easy to see why he was such a good leader for he did listen to everybody and didn't try to belittle anybody, even if their suggestions were stupid. Wenja suddenly saw that the wolves did gather closer to them, the animals were raising their fur and snarling and they all stared towards the cliff and Ahravan did see it too and he did shout to the others. Something was wrong, the horses started to snort and dance and Flint did place himself in front of Wenja and Ahravan. The huge stallion was pawing the ground and whinnying and Ahravan did stare at the naked landscape ahead of them. "What is wrong boy?"

He didn't get an answer for suddenly the sand seemed to explode as several strange bodies did burst forth from it and Wenja did scream. It was something which did look a bit like scorpions but they were enormous and the tails snake like and armed with several thin spikes. They were everywhere, as if the sand gave birth to the horrors and Ahravan did roar orders and the warriors did gather in tight circles. He grasped Wenja by her waist and lifted her over onto Rhawan's horse. "Keep her safe!"

He did pull his long sword and Wenja saw that the scorpion beasts did run towards them, making a clattering sound. The wolves did attack, with astonishing speed and agility and she did see that they cooperated and worked as one. They would attack the head and as the beast tried to get the attackers with its pinchers two or three would attack the tail and simply tear it apart.

The riders did shout to each other and grasped their long spears and now she did see why they used such long spears, they could skewer their opponent before the enemy could reach them. Ahravan did fight like a demon, astride the huge dark stallion he could move like lightning and the power of the horse helped him skewer several of the beasts. Rhawan just sat there holding Wenja close and Flint was snorting and grunting, getting ready for a fight. The warriors had to spread out and one of the monsters did head in their direction. The grey horse did spring forth and it did jump, as if to clear a fence. It landed front hooves first on the head of the beast and Wenja heard a crushing sound, then the horse spun around and kicked out with the hind legs, practically reducing the ugly head to a pulp. There were beasts everywhere, and some riders went down, it was mayhem and Rhawan was swearing, he wanted to fight but he couldn't, not while protecting Wenja.

Ahravan came back to them, Ayr'esh was covered with sweat and wild eyed and Ahravan did almost snarl. "Ride back to the caravan, we need reinforcements, they are too many!"

Rhawan was shaking. "I cannot leave you brother, I can't…"

Ahravan bared his teeth. "You have to, think of Wenja, she is your responsibility now, follow Flint!"

Rhawan did hesitate, torn between his love for his Si'ish and his need to protect Wenja, he was shaking all over. "I…"

Ahravan did push his horse around them, gave Rhawan's white stallion a slap over the ass. "Go! I will be okay, ride now!"

The horse did spring forth and Flint did place itself in front of them, clearing a path. Suddenly there were wolves there too, helping keeping the beasts at bay and Wenja saw how Flint used its steel hard hooves as battle hammers, crushing the beasts. Neither of them managed to hit the massive horse, he was too fast and knew how to fight. Rhawan did only cling to the saddle and Wenja and she felt cold to the core. What if something happened to Ahravan? She couldn't bear the thought, no, she would rather die than letting him get hurt. She didn't know how or why but suddenly the ground came alive again but now it was not animals but ants, and termites. The sand seemed to open up and the ants did attack the huge scorpions, climbing inn underneath their armour and the beasts went frantic and Wenja did cheer for them as they rode towards the camp. The first wagons had reached the plains and Wenja saw that the massive herd of animals did emerge from the valley like a flood of living tissue, unstoppable and powerful. She felt something in her mind, like a scream, a prayer or a desperate wish. "Keep him safe, please!"

The herd was led by Frostfoot and the Zahar made a screeching sound as it passed them by, heading towards the melee. Rhawan did hold Wenja close. "Do not worry my sweet. Ahravan will be alright, he is the best fighter there is"

Wenja wished that she could believe him, his voice did tremble and those horrible creatures were so powerful and wicked. She just closed her eyes and hoped with all her might.

Ahravan and the others did fight with a wild fury, they couldn't allow these monsters to reach the caravan with females and children and Ahravan did push the feeling of despair aside. They were too few, the scorpions were so strong and even if you did skewer one it didn't die unless you did hit something vital and they were so goddamn fast. He did use his spear for all it was worth and he did kill many but the horse was getting tired and they were being pushed forth against the cliff itself. He did see that the plains were alive with animals now, heading their way but they wouldn't reach them yet and the scorpions were attacking without rest.

Yahlen fought like a demon and didn't listen to Ahravan's orders at all, she was going berserk and Ahravan could only hope that this wouldn't be the end of her.

He saw that one of the riders went down, hit by the tail of a beast and he turned Ayr'esh and cut the tail of the beast with a swing of the blade. The wounded warrior did scream in agony and the scorpions seemed to ignore him completely now that the man was down. Ahravan was about to charge at a particularly large one when Ayr'esh did jolt underneath him, the horse moaned and then he fell, so fast that Ahravan barely managed to get his feet out of the stirrups before the horse hit the sand. Ahravan rolled and got back onto his feet, the dark stallion did thrash around, trying to get back up but it couldn't and the reason was easy to see. One of the beasts had managed to snap its left hind leg clean off.

Ahravan did gasp in horror and sorrow and the stallion did roar, head thrown back and front legs fighting to bring it back up. There was just one thing to do, the brave horse couldn't be saved, Ahravan grasped the spear and ran forth, as the horse lowered its head to try and lift itself off the sand again he did thrust the sharp blade into the neck right behind the ears and severed the spine with one precise cut. The horse collapsed, dead in an instant and Ahravan felt a sense of shock. He had loved Ayr'esh like a brother and he saw that the scorpions were getting closer again. He had to fight on foot and he sneered and gave it his all. Several had fallen now and the huge herd of animals were getting closer by the moment. He did drive the spear into the head of one of the scorpions but without the combined weight of horse and man even an elf wasn't strong enough to get the blade deep into the body. The scorpion almost reared up and Ahravan was thrown off his feet and before he had time to get back up one of them did strike him with its tail. The sharp stinger did enter Ahravan's thigh above the knee and the pain was unbelievable, like liquid fire and he screamed and felt nauseous right away. He tried to get back up but his legs didn't carry him and he thought faintly that Rhawan would make a good leader, and would take care of Wenja. It was just so very tragic to die now, when he had found love.

One of the scorpions did scurry towards him, hissing in something which seemed like glee, and Ahravan grasped his spear and tried to aim it at the beast but it used its pinchers to simply snap it in half. So this was it, the end. Ahravan had never really considered death before but now that it was right there, before him in all its naked and terrifying dark glory he wasn't ready, not at all. That was when a shadow seemed to fly over him and he gasped. It was Yahlen and her horse did fly over him and landed right in front of the beast, colliding with it. The shock made the scorpion rear back and Yahlen was in the air, her spear raised and her eyes ablaze in something which looked like sheer madness. She drove the spear into the beast's eye, deep, so deep most of the shaft did disappear and the scorpion did screech and swung its spiked tail at her. Several of the spines did hit her but she didn't even seem to care, she just tore the spear out again with a shriek and threw herself forth again, attacking yet another scorpion. Now the ants and termites had started to reach the inner group of beasts and they stopped and tried to get rid of the biting and gnawing menace but the ants were simply too small and Ahravan did see that the huge group of animals did reach the cliff.

And he would never forget the sight, in front came a huge herd of buffalo and also some of the spear noses and the heavily built beasts were surprisingly agile. They ran alongside each other, heads down and the long horns which did protrude from the front of their heads did pierce the scorpions or fling them over and the buffalo did throw them in the air and trampled them.

Ahravan did moan, his vision was getting blurred and he knew that the poison from such beast could be fatal even to an elf, he wanted to scream from the agony for it was getting worse by the moment. Around him wolves did tear the beasts into shreds, the big cats did pounce upon their heads, massive paws tearing into their eyes and blinding them, it was a bloodbath. Ahravan just wished that Wenja could see this, it was frightening and also in a way awe-inspiring, mother nature showing her wrath. He was fading and didn't want to go, he wanted to see Wenja again and hold her and tell her how much he did love her, he wanted to see their children being born and grow up. He just hoped that she would understand that he had done this to save her and the others.

His last sight was the underbelly of a wolf which took position above him to protect him from the remaining scorpions.

Chapter 10: Warrior soul

Wenja was trembling by the time they reached the caravan, the warriors were gathering to form a shield wall and the wagons were driven together into concentrically rings. Rhawan did drop her off onto the wagon she lived inn and Sefa did come running, obviously upset. Wenja was crying and Rhawan did yell at Flint which was running around in circles still. "Stay with her!"

The grey stallion did nicker and started circling the wagon, Sefa grasped Wenja by her wrist and pulled her inside. "What happened?"

Wenja gasped and sobbed. "There are beasts out there, huge monsters! I..."

Sefa had seen that Ahravan wasn't with them and she knew how to put two and two together. "He will be alright, do not worry my sweet, please!"

Wenja just gasped and Sefa did stick her head outside of the wagon and yelled for Imh and some soothing tea. Before long they had managed to get a whole cup into her and Wenja was so upset the brew made her pass out like a candle in the wind. Imh and Sefa remained by her side, both were scared and Sefa did sigh and ran her fingers through the long burgundy locks. "The dwarves and the two orcs are to leave tomorrow, I just hope that this won't disturb their plans"

Imh shook her head. "I know Balgar Stonecarver and the two others, they are nothing if not stubborn, and strong. They will do their job no matter what, believe me"

Sefa sighed and stared out of the window. "I just pray that it will be enough"

The warriors did not need to protect the caravan for long, the Zahar and the other predators had turned the entire pack of scorpion monsters into pulp and the warriors who still stood had seen how the Zahar did lead the animals like a general leads his army. The huge S'haga had crushed scorpions and the massive wolves tore the legs off the beasts. A group of warriors from the caravan did reach the battle field and started to gather the wounded and dead, the sight filled them all with dread.

Rhawan had been staying by the wagons to organize the defence in case more monsters did show up and his heart was hammering like a drum within his chest. He was sweating and shivering and he had to really fight his urge to ride back to check upon Ahravan. The women were preparing to receive wounded warriors and the wagons had been placed like a veritable fortress now. The animals did return, some were hurt but not many and Rhawan did see that Frostfoot did run by Wenja's wagon, as if to check that she was there. Could she be the cause for this? He remembered the incident with the troll yet again and his soul did feel a sort of wonder at the idea.

After a while a huge row of warriors did return, also carrying wounded with them, some were placed upon stretchers which had been attached between horses and Rhawan did stare at the line, trying to see the huge dark stallion and its rider but saw neither and dread did fill his heart. He gasped and ran forth, one of the front riders was a friend of his and the elf did turn his eyes towards the ground as Rhawan did approach him. Rhawan was panting. "Ahravan?!"

The tall eternal made a grimace. "Alive, with the wounded at the back, but he is in a bad state"

Rhawan let out a whimper and ran, he ran so fast his feet barely touched the ground and he did see that some of the healers were working on several of the wounded. He did see that some stretchers were covered with blankets and his heart felt like lead, they had lost many, too many. Ahravan was in a stretcher, unconscious and very pale and one of the healers were standing by his side, trying to counteract the effect of the scorpion poison. Rhawan wailed and grasped onto Ahravan's hand, held it tight. It was cold and clammy and he could barely feel a pulse at all. The healer was making a grimace. "We are trying but do not put too much faith in hope, he got stung pretty bad!"

Rhawan did lift the blanket, the sting was in his thigh and the wound was ghastly, black and oozing and horrible to look at. He flinched and the healer tried to cover the leg again. "He fought well Rhawan, if his horse hadn't been felled…"

Rhawan felt tears running down his cheek and suddenly Ahnriel was there, adding her healing powers to those of the other healer. "Rhawan, find Wenja. She has to know, if this goes the wrong way…"

Rhawan couldn't bear the thought but he nodded and told one of the warriors riding by that he had to go fetch the Eth'ir. Ahnriel was chanting, her voice trembling with the effort and Rhawan sank to his knees, one of the other warriors did run by, his face rather pale. "We lost Yahlen, and twenty more"

Rhawan did sob, what could they truly do against this horror? This darkness unleashed? He just sat there, praying like never before and he heard a scream and realized that it was Wenja, she came running with her skirts lifted up over her knees and her eyes were wild. He tried to grasp onto her but she was too fast, grasped onto Ahravan's hand and she wailed, a wild piercing cry everybody could hear. Tears were flowing down her face and there was something akin to madness in the lovely eyes. Rhawan tried to speak. "They are trying to do all they can"

His voice did sound hollow and fake, as if he was spewing forth nothing but lies and yet it was all that he could do. Wenja screamed again, her hand squeezing the bloody hand of her husband and then something truly strange did happen, something which made everybody step back in shock. The ground started to shake, as if in an earthquake and Wenja's eyes started to glow, a sort of intense green glow which was almost eerie. She was pushing her bare feet into the sand, face turned upwards and body rigid as if in spasms, she was calling out but nobody knew the language. Light danced around her, swirling shades of different colours and Ahnriel did gasp. "The spirits of the land itself, she does summon them?! How?!"

Rhawan couldn't answer, he just stared, eyes wide open. The light and the shapes seemed to gather around Ahravan before they looked as if they were sucked into the body, and Wenja did tremble and strange patterns of light were visible under her skin, like glowing tattoos. Ahravan did shudder, then he did gasp and the healer had removed the blanket and they did see how the horrible black wound did change. The black goo did flow out of the wound and with it puss and blood and the horrible discolouration of the skin disappeared too. The swelling did go down so fast they could see it and then there was just a clean red wound and it started to close up, as if pulled together by invisible strings. Wenja was panting, her eyes closed still and her voice was strained and yet strong, yet demanding.

Ahnriel was pale. "Nobody does possess such powers, to control the very spirits themselves and make them do their bidding? It is impossible?!!"

Wenja did sigh and let go, and collapsed into a heap, like a ragdoll. Rhawan did grasp her and lifted her, she was breathing but was very pale and Ahnriel shook her head. "She has used too much of her strength, silly girl, and very brave"

Ahravan was breathing well now, the colour did return to his face and Rhawan couldn't believe it, Wenja had saved him, she had saved his Si'ish and his gratitude was endless. He did kiss her and then he did kiss Ahravan's hand, trembling from head to foot. Ahnriel did smile, a smile filled with a sort of disbelief. "Go, take her to the wagon and we will bring Ahravan over too, he just needs sleep now. He is out of danger"

Rhawan was crying in gratitude, not ashamed to show the world his relief and joy and he did carry Wenja gently to the wagon. Some of the warriors did carry Ahravan and they placed them on the bed, Rhawan was beside himself now, shaking like a leaf all over. Sefa did burst into the wagon and her face was worth a study in itself, a million emotions were being expressed there and then. "What has happened?!"

Rhawan heaved for air. "She saved him, she called forth the spirits of the land and they healed him…she…"

Sefa gaped, she did look like a fish on dry land. "Oh Gods"

Rhawan did pull at the blankets and she helped him get them up to cover the two. "I have never seen anything like it, never! I have no idea how it is possible"

Sefa did bite her lower lip. "Rhawan, I think the Gods have spoken, they chose her when they sent the prophecy. Do never doubt her my friend, they are leading her foot and strengthening her hand"

Rhawan did nod and Sefa made a grimace. "We lost many didn't we?"

Rhawan did look down, sorrow in his eyes. "Yes, including Yahlen. But we expected that, she was heading for death, one way or the other"

Sefa sighed and took his hand. "Lay down, rest. You need it, the others can take care of the caravan now, you have many skilled men out there"

Rhawan suddenly felt tired, like never before, like he had been fighting for days, he could barely stay on his feet. She did push him down onto the bed next to Wenja and did lift his feet onto the bed after pulling his boots off. "Sleep, I will make sure that food is ready when you wake up."

Rhawan did only manage to whisper something incoherently before he gave in to the emotional stress and fell asleep, Sefa did sigh and made sure that he was comfortable before leaving the wagon. There would be funerals and mourning but also rejoicing. Wenja was more than the Eth'ir, she was their hope now. Nobody could convince Sefa that the animals had come of their own free will, Wenja had drawn them inn, subconsciously, or else they could call Sefa a cow!

Outside the wagon the whole group was in a state of light shock, their Eth'ir had done the impossible and if the people had liked Wenja before they now were ready to worship her like a goddess. She had saved their Ath'ir and nobody did question her worthiness nor her right to walk among them. The wagons were guarded still in case of further attacks and as the twelve clans did regain their composure the smaller group which were to leave for the forest did gather to say their goodbyes. The three dwarves had mounted their ponies and Resh'kha had her buffalo while Floth'bha had a strong horse and she was ready beyond doubt. The three men had gotten new horses and weapons and clothes and they were very determined to make up for previous sins. One of Ahravan's officers were to send them off, they had to leave now and many did gather around them. Bagir and Igkhan had been in the camp during the attack, neither was a warrior and Bagir had been rather shocked by what Wenja had revealed about herself. But he was proud and he was certain that she was stronger than anybody could have guessed. Igkhan was impressed by the vast herds of animals which were gathering still, he had never seen that many living beings in one place before and the fact that none of them seemed to be afraid of the people puzzled him. Normally the gazelle and the deer would be gone within the blink of an eye if they caught the scent of a human being but now they were grazing between the wagons and didn't even bother moving aside if somebody came running by them.

The dwarves seemed to be very calm and collected and they all knew of the dangers they were to face, the plains were dangerous in themselves now, and the forest was far away. Floth'bha and Resh'kha did seem as if they were excited and eager to go, both were strong and fierce and capable warriors and everybody had seen how the friendship between the two had made Resh'kha flourish and become jolly and more open minded. They could only pray that she would survive this quest. The healers had prepared packs of things they could be in need of and with all the weapons they brought they should be able to fight just about anything. The shamans did pull Floth'bha aside before they left, she didn't say what they had been talking about but she had a packet in her hand as she returned and she hid it in her saddle pack right away.

The small group left with the first morning light, and the three former mercenaries did trail behind as they had no clue as to where they were going, Ahravan and Rhawan were still asleep so they were blessed by the shamans and officers and Balgar did turn his pony to the northwest and the others did follow. Only the gods themselves knew if they would even reach their goal.

Wenja did awaken when the sun did reach the highest point of its route that day, she just jerked and sat up with a small yelp and Sefa who had been sitting on the floor, half asleep almost toppled over with the shock. She got up and raced over, the two males were still sleeping and Wenja blinked and Sefa did gasp. Wenja's eyes had changed, now there were sparling points of light within the irises, like small green gems. Wenja grasped her throat and Sefa grasped a cup and poured some water into it, she gave it to the redhead and Wenja did drain it in one go, gasping for air afterwards. "Thank you, I was so dry…What happened?"

Sefa frowned. "You don't remember? You saved Ahravan, you made the very spirits of the land heal his wound"

Wenja stared at her two sleeping husbands and her face was blank. "I…I cannot remember. I remember returning to the camp and staying in the wagon and then…nothing?"

Sefa did sit down very gently as if not to wake up the two males. "That is odd, but you used too much strength and passed out, how do you feel?"

Wenja took a deep breath. "Ah…I am not sure? Tired? My head hurts a bit, and I feel dizzy"

Sefa took her hand. "I can understand that"

Wenja did sigh. "I was so scared Sefa, if I had lost one of them…I cannot even imagine what that would do to me"

Sefa nodded. "I would be too, but are you hungry? We need to start moving again soon, the caravan cannot stay here for much longer, there isn't enough food for the animals"

Wenja made a grimace. "Know what? I feel as if I haven't eaten in weeks? My stomach feels empty as few times before"

Sefa got back up again and grinned. "I will get Imh, I am sure she has something delicious ready for you"

Wenja nodded and wrapped the blankets tighter around herself, not remembering was terrifying but she had realized that Ahravan had been very near death and that she had somehow rescued him. Right now he slept next to her and he was covered with dust and blood and didn't look very good at all. He did stink, that was for sure. Rhawan was on the other side of her, and he didn't look that much better. Wenja did slither out of the bed but Rhawan did wake up and a strong arm did pull her down again, very abruptly. "Thank you, from the very core of my being"

His voice was gruff and raw and she smiled and tried to be calm and composed but it was very hard. "I cannot even remember what happened so please, don't thank me"

Rhawan did press his face against her neck. "But I have to, Ahravan would have died without you, you did the impossible"

Wenja felt odd, empty almost. Here she was being praised for having rescued her husband and yet she had no idea of how and why she had been able to do it. It was as if there had been somebody else there, using her body. And it was an unpleasant thought in many ways. Rhawan did kiss her gently and rocked her in his arms. "How long have we slept?"

Wenja did make a nasty grimace. "Too long, my head hurts, and Sefa has gone to get us some food"

Rhawan did release her and sat up, he did look as if he had tried to run through a tornado, his hair was filled with sand and knots and the sheets were a mess. He did look at Ahravan who was stirring, making some faint movements and groaning before he opened his eyes with a yelp. Rhawan did take his hand. "Ahravan? It is me, how…how do you feel?"

Ahravan did blink and groaned, trying to supress some real pain. "Horrible, oh gods, I got stung, I was dying?"

Rhawan nodded, tears in his eyes. «Yes, but Wenja did save you, she called forth the spirits and they healed you"

Ahravan just stared at Rhawan with a blank stare. "That is impossible?"

Rhawan nodded. "Yes, and yet she did it. You would have perished for sure"

Ahravan stared at Wenja who was blushing slightly, his eyes were filled with wonder and gratitude and also some shock. "You…not even the shamans can command the spirits Wenja, I don't know what to say…"

Wenja opened her mouth to speak but closed it again, the door did fling open and Sefa entered with Imh hot at her heels, carrying trays of food. "Here, you need to eat, all of you."

She did put down a huge mug filled with ale and Ahravan grasped it with obvious desperation and started to drain it, straight from the jug. He was obviously terribly thirsty and Sefa did shake her head. "Ah, I anticipated that, I have two more outside."

Ahravan shook his head. "Whoa, I feel so strange"

Imh shook her finger at him. "No wonder, you were at deaths door yesterday, the poison almost got you, but Wenja here is a god send for sure"

Ahravan reached out and caressed her hand. "No doubt"

402

Sefa placed the trays between them, it was grilled fish and some sort of pudding and Rhawan did tear into the food with obvious appetite. Wenja too seemed to forget all about table manners, she just ripped apart pieces of fish and since the sheets already were soiled she didn't bother with spilling. All three ate and Sefa grinned. "I will inform the others that we can start moving again, we can make some way before darkness falls again. "

Ahravan just nodded and mumbled something which was impossible to interpret due to the fact that his mouth was full of fish.

Imh was proud that her food was being devoured so fast, all three were on a veritable food frenzy and before long they were laying there again, moaning as they had been overeating. Rhawan did stroke his belly and groaned, and Wenja did giggle and the she too made a moan, her stomach hurt her. Rhawan did get up again after a little and left the wagon to organize things and Ahravan did sit on the bed and tried to finger comb his hair, with no luck. It had been a terrible experience and he felt nauseous thinking about it now, he did have to think ahead and he sighed and realized that he was rather weak in spite of having been healed. He would need at least a week to recuperate and that would be a week spent in the wagon for sure. Ahnriel wouldn't allow him any sort of exertion and he bit his lower lip and sighed. He had lost his favourite horse and also a good friend and something which was akin to raging hatred did ignite within his chest. He had to stop these monsters, he had to protect his land and his people and those who couldn't protect themselves further inland. He kissed Wenja's hands and smiled at her. "From now on you are as much a leader as me, I bet people will listen to you and deem your words as wise"

Wenja just squirmed, unused to all the praise.

They just laid there for a while and Rhawan did return after having spoken to the officers and other leaders and Wenja did feel as if her skin was crawling, she wanted a bath desperately but there was no way to heat water now. But Rhawan did promise her that there would be some chance for baths when they reached the caves and she couldn't wait. They started to move the wagons once more, Wenja was used to the motion but Ahravan had to lay down and he did stare at the roof and looked uneasy.

Wenja did pack her skirts together around her legs since it was rather cold there now and she tilted her head. "The cliff we are going to, where is it?"

Ahravan sighed. "To the far north east, it will take a lot to get there, I am not going to lie to you"

Wenja frowned. "Tell me more about it, please?"

Ahravan shrugged and placed an arm behind his neck, stretched out. "Well, it is a sacred site but nobody remember why. It is a cliff which looks…strange"

Wenja did move a bit closer and Rhawan did place himself on a low chair, he didn't have anything to do right now. "How can a cliff look strange?"

Ahravan did made a vague gesture. "They say that its shape is a bit like that of a huge skull, not human though, some animal? But it is very large and they say that the very ground in that area is filled with some sort of very dangerous magic"

Wenja swallowed. "How long does it take to get there?"

Ahravan shrugged. "I don't know, weeks? And it is winter, it is hard enough to travel here on the plains but we will have to cross some areas which are uncharted."

Wenja was confused. "Uncharted? Haven't anybody been there?"

Rhawan tilted his head. "Oh, there has been people there for sure but it is so long ago that even the elves have forgotten. Now it is all reduced to legends"

Wenja nodded. "That sounds like a very long time indeed?"

Ahravan grunted. "Fifteen thousand years, or more. We have no idea of what we may find up there. The free clans have never ventured into that area, and it has always been odd, like some piece of another world, dropped into this"

Wenja leaned back against the wall. "How come?"

Ahravan took a deep breath. "Well, there are rumours of a huge swamp north of the cliff? It is said to span for many days of travel and it is said to have creatures not found anywhere else. But it is very strange for there are no swamps that far north normally."

Wenja nodded slowly. "There were bogs where I am from?"

404

Rhawan grinned. "Yes, but a bog and a swamp isn't the same thing, swamps have huge trees and are rather warm, a bog is…just soggy grass and moss and mud, and there are no trees"

Wenja made a small apologetic grimace. "Oh, I see"

Ahravan took a deep breath. "So we will have to worry about a swamp, high mountain passes in winter and also all sorts of wicked creatures. There are goblins in those mountains they say, at least there were goblins there"

Wenja felt nervous. "So I guess that we have to be very careful?"

Rhawan nodded. "And even more so with the monsters on the loose, the area they came from the last time aren't that far away from that cliff. They say the gate was next to the cliff, opened because of the magic it did harbour"

Wenja tried to smile. "Let us hope that the dwarves and the two orcs manage to draw them away then"

Ahravan smiled, a sort of melancholic smile. "Yes, they are brave, the forest isn't a safe destination at all, they say that shadows lurk within its depts., shadows from another world."

Wenja felt a shiver running down her spine and Rhawan did caress her leg gently. "Don't worry Wenja, we will make it, because we have to"

She managed to smile, but it was a very faint smile.

For the next day and a half the caravan did move forth with as much speed as possible and the warriors were mounted all the time, keeping their eyes out for any sign of danger. The mountains were getting nearer by the hour and the dwarves were excited and eager. There were many cave systems in the mountain range which had been discovered by that race and usually they were in good condition and able to house people right away. Imh did entertain Ahravan and Wenja with stories from her youth and the animals did follow the caravan the whole time. Frostfoot seemed to be a leader and the people did notice that birds seemed to gather and then fly out over the plains repeatedly. Rhawan was sure that they were scouts, looking for the monsters and Wenja didn't disagree. It was very strange indeed.

The plains had looked even beyond the cliff where the scorpion monsters attacked but the terrain proved to be very tricky, with a sort of worn look. Everywhere they saw pits, small and large and the flat areas between them were narrow. It became a struggle to find a suitable path and the caravan did move very slowly. They sent forth some riders to find suitable caves and the dwarves sent some of their best stone experts. A dwarf can almost smell a cave from a great distance and there should be a good chance that they could find something useable very fast. Wenja did ride now, she used one of the small mares she had gotten when she got married and Sefa did keep her company. Now everybody acted as if she was some sort of deity and it made her slightly embarrassed. Ahravan was still weak but he did feel trapped in the wagon and Wenja had to use all her wits to keep him from getting very bored. Playing cards did take up most of the time and telling stories and she learned to know him in a whole new manner now.

Then they reached the mountains and the scouts had indeed found somewhere to stay, a huge cave system turned into a city which in fact was rather famous among the dwarves. It had been abandoned ages ago but it was still useable and Wenja felt relieved when she learned that it could be defended rather easily. The dwarves knew how to build things which kept enemies on the outside and the entrance could be sealed off rather easily. The mountains were steep there, and they drove into a narrow valley, at the end was a vertical wall which seemed to stretch into the skies themselves and a sort of triangular opening which looked almost natural. The dwarves did ride in front now, beaming with pride and Imh was riding next to Wenja, her eyes were shining. "Oh I have heard so much about these caves, they are called the caves of green light and they say that they harbour great wonders."

Wenja nodded. "Has it been a city?"

Imh nodded. "Yes, ages ago, it was home to a clan which is gone now, but they were many and they were good diggers. I bet this is a very nice place to stay until the danger is over"

The wagons did enter a long corridor and Wenja was reminded of the dwarven roads they had used on her journey to the plains but this corridor did end rather fast and was replaced by an enormous hall with a flat floor and many poles which were made by stone. It had to be the foundations for some sort of fences. Countless doors did lead out from the great hall, and stairs did lead up to more floors above the first one. The great cave got light from an opening up on the front wall and it didn't look bad at all. The air was fresh and calm and it wasn't that cold in there. The dwarves started to attach ropes to the poles to create corrals for the horses which had pulled the wagons and the huge bulls and mules too. The wagons got parked along the wall, it was as if everybody knew exactly what to do yet again and Sefa grasped Wenja by the arm, giggling. "Come, let's get out of the way, the huts will be put back up again in no time at all. "

Wenja frowned but she did see that the wagons and sleds were being emptied as they entered the cave and some were driven back outside again to make room for more. There were people running around everywhere, the huge wall sections for the huts were pulled up the stairs by teams of small ponies and the dwarves were scurrying around everywhere, obviously very busy and very happy too. She saw huge grins and everybody were chatting and laughing and obviously having a good time. The level of noise within the cave was rather large and Sefa and Wenja did go outside again, the entrance was in fact hard to see if one didn't arrive at the right angle, if you didn't you would only see a sleep rock wall and Wenja was yet again stunned by how clever the dwarves were when it came to rock and stone. They seemed to understand it as if it was a part of themselves.

Wenja and Sefa did sit down on some rocks and Wenja enjoyed the faint sunlight and the feeling of being safe there. She saw that the entire caravan was entering the cave, one wagon at the time, and the speed with which they were unloaded was amazing. "I wonder how the dwarves can live in such cities. Where do they get the food from?"

Sefa arranged her skirts and grinned. "Oh, they do hunt, dwarves are good hunters and there are plenty of game up in the mountains, even when one wouldn't believe that anything could live up there. And they do grow stuff too, in vast halls, lighted by glowing crystals"

Wenja frowned. "Grow things? What sort of things?"

Sefa just shrugged. "Mushrooms? All sorts of them, I have tasted a dish made from cave mushrooms once and if they hadn't told me what it was I would have guessed that it was meat, very good meat even"

Wenja stared at the people who were running by, as if their pants were on fire. "I see, I am glad we are here now"

Sefa nodded. "So am I, now I will have all the time in the world to have fun, the warriors won't have to be out there all the time, the rock does protect us from attack"

Wenja had to make a wry grin. "So you have got your aim straight?"

Sefa did nod and fluttered her eyelashes. "Oh yes. Khirhien is not uninterested and I do have some other suitors too"

Wenja had to shake her head. "Sefa, you are amazing, and I bet you will test everything out before you make a choice?"

Sefa laughed out loud. "Oh yes, of course! I will not settle for anything less than perfection"

Wenja giggled and the two remained sitting there for a while, just relaxing and talking.

The last wagon was emptied just before sunset and now there was light everywhere, Huge crystals had come to life and glowed with a soft and pleasant light, and Wenja did discover that the huts had been erected within halls on the second level. Here there were no roofs needed, just thin fabric and the poles which held the walls up were secured with rope attached to hooks embedded in the rock above. Thus the huts were stable and the ovens were being attached to a system of holes drilled through the rock, like chimneys. When Wenja found her way to her hut Ahravan had already entered and was resting on the bed, the hut was just like before, the roof was the only difference and there was some distance between each hut so there could be some privacy. The dwarven city had room for the whole group and then some and there were stables on the first level and also storage rooms.

Wenja did slump down next to Ahravan, he did smile and caressed her hair, seemingly in a very good mood. "Here our people are safe"

Wenja nodded and closed her eyes, the familiar scent of their own blankets and their own bed was soothing. "I know. I look forward to exploring this place."

Ahravan nodded. "So do I, old dwarven cities are usually very grand indeed. And very impressive. We will see wonders for sure"

Wenja sighed and curled up next to him, she was already tired by all the new impressions and she knew that Imh would come with food sooner or later so she could allow herself a wee nap. Yes, that would be nice, a quick nap and then food. Ahravan placed his large hand on her hip and yawned and she fell asleep rather fast, feeling utterly safe. ¨

The group heading for the infamous forest had come far over just the span of a couple of days and it was thanks to the fact that they hadn't encountered any sorts of problems at all. They had seen no monsters or demons of any kind and since they did follow an old riverbed it was easy to just let the horses and ponies run as fast as they wanted to. The dwarves weren't that eager to speak, they kept to themselves but as they prepared a camp for the night Balgar came over to Geir and sat down, he did nod at Osbord and Than and removed a flask from his belt, offering them all a quick sip. "Here, it gives courage"

Geir did taste the liquor with some suspicion, it did burn and the taste was intense, like burned wheat and rye. He coughed and managed to wheeze forth. "You expect us to need it?"

Balgar did nod solemnly. "Yes, unfortunately. The forest itself is dangerous but tomorrow I will awaken the heart stone, every creature of evil will sense us then"

Than did frown. "Is that really wise?"

The dwarf did lean forth and flattened some of the sand with his foot, then he did find a straw and started to draw a crude map in the sand. "We are here now, see? And the forest is to the west and south, it is very far. What we are gonna do is ride straight to the west until we reach the white river, there we will make rafts and ride the river southwards."

Osbord tilted his head. "I think I have heard somebody claim that evil creatures can't cross running water?"

The dwarf did raise a finger triumphantly. "Indeed, you are right. The river will protect us and bring us to an area very close to the forest. But we have to stay on the river the whole time, we will be vulnerable if we make landfall."

Geir and Than did stare at each other, they started to realize that this could be a very strange mission indeed. "So we will be safe on the water?"

The dwarf shrugged. "Well, from the monsters yes, maybe not so much from the natural dangers the river does contain. "

Floth'bha and Resh'kha did shudder, orcs aren't that fond of water at all and travelling on a river on a simple raft wasn't that tempting. Geir stared at Balgar. "You said you would awaken the heart stone, how do you do that?"

The dwarf smiled. "Through an ancient dwarven ritual, very sacred and secret"

Geir frowned and Balgar did laugh out loud, clapping the man in the shoulder. "I am pulling your leg young one, nothing fancy. I will cut a finger and let some blood fall onto it. That is all that it takes."

Geir did smile, he had long since realized that the dwarves loved to make jokes and that they were surprisingly light hearted. Resh'kha did frown and her face was serious. "So when you have done that, the monsters see us?"

Balgar did nod slowly. "They do see us already sister orc, if there were any here. But they will feel us from afar and be drawn towards us, we will need luck, and skill, to avoid them"

Floth'bha made a grimace. "We are few, perhaps that is a good thing now, not so easy to spot right?"

Balgar did grin. "Yes, and we dwarves has magic, great magic in some ways. I am no magician but I do know a trick or two which will make us harder even to find"

Resh'kha did stare at the dwarf with some respect. "Good, that is good"

The two other dwarves, Dharan Granitehand and Kulkar Hammerstone mumbled and smiled, both were very powerfully built and wore a sort of armour. Their clans had been warriors in the days of old and they still had some warrior skills. Geir was nervous for he remembered what they had seen before they reached Ohtanar and he was afraid of facing something like that again.

That night they didn't start a fire and it was a cold and dark night but they did sleep, wrapped in the thick dwarven carpets. The dwarven females had a special technique and could turn even the roughest wool into something almost as silky as satin. The morning light did come with low clouds and a sour wind, everybody wore good clothing and it was not that cold but Geir and the other men did shiver a bit, they weren't that used to staying outdoors at this time of the year. Balgar didn't hesitate, he did take the heart stone out of the bag and he did prick a finger with his knife and then he did drip some blood onto the stone. It immediately started to glow even stronger and the colour changed to a bright purple, there was a shuddering feeling going through them all and Resh'kha did stare at it with respect. "Great magic, old one"

Balgar nodded and packed the stone onto the bag again, hung it from his belt. "Yes, very old magic. But do not worry, we are not in danger yet"

Geir managed to grin but he had a feeling that the safety wouldn't last very long.

That day they rode due west towards a low hill and it was easy terrain, very smooth with few obstacles and everybody did relax and enjoy the scenery, that was until Balgar did stop his pony with a shout and pointed towards the horizon. Geir stared, he recognized the odd transparent figures with glowing darkness instead of eyes and Resh'kha did whimper and she got pale. Balgar grunted. "The gods be cursed, that was fast I must say, but never mind. I will shield us"

Resh'kha did tremble. "They have spoken of such, I have seen such, demons! What are they really?"

Dharan did loosen his axe from the saddle. "We dwarves know of this sort of monster, we call them Khalak-ushryd, soul eaters. They do devour the soul of living beings, horrible things, they tear people apart"

Floth'bha had huge eyes and Geir felt rather nervous. Balgar did grasp something from his saddle bag and then he did spit onto it and mumbled something before hanging it from the mane of his pony. The monsters seemed to hesitate and they started to drift off course, as if they were tracking dogs which have lost the trail. Geir was hoarse. "Can we stop and rest now? With those things around?"

Balgar grunted and his face was a bit sombre. "No, just short stops now, until we reach the river. I didn't expect them to pick up the scent this fast"

The other two dwarves did look a bit nervous too and Geir realized that things had become more complicated than they had planned for. The ponies and horses were sturdy and strong and could keep a rather brisk pace for days but not if they had to trot or gallop. Balgar made his pony walk on. "Come on, we cannot linger any further"

They rode on and the demons did seem to be stuck to the place where they had first spotted them. Geir rode next to Balgar. "Are they unable to follow us?"

The dwarf nodded. "I hope so yes, at least for a while."

Geir did bite his teeth together, he had been in many a tricky situation over the years but this? Oh he had never encountered anything like this and he was rather sure that now was the moment when he and his friends would show their true metal or perish trying. He just prayed that his courage would hold, without it he wouldn't stand a chance.

As the small group rode westwards things started to happen all over the plains. The groups of monsters did stir, their instincts told them to move westwards, that there was something there which they did crave. They gave up the pursuit of humans and elves and started to move, slowly at first and from the mountains to the north a command came, making their minds turn to catching this something instead of killing. Huge packs of beasts had been waiting in the wild valleys and now they were unleashed, impatiently trampling the ground as their feet carried them to the southwest. Demons and monsters alike, they all knew that they had to obey that voice they heard in their minds and keep it satisfied and happy and it wanted that thing which was pulling at them. And so they went, clambering over cliffs and valleys, crossing rivers and gorges. It was a burning need, the voice wanted it, and wanted it bad. The horde wouldn't stop until it was found for it was just what the voice needed, the missing piece to the puzzle, a source of great power.

The huge herd of animals had sort of stopped and now it surrounded the area with the cave. It was an odd sight but everybody felt safer with them there and Ahravan told everybody that they were to treat the beasts with respect. They did find racoons in the storage rooms and some badgers did decide that the stable was a perfect place to live but the animals were accepted, as long as they didn't ruin anything. The cooks had gathered and now a huge room was turned into a kitchen, it had ovens and open hearths too, and the smell of food could be sensed from afar. Imh and the others were working hard to keep everybody fed and they sent out riders to gather herbs and bulbs which were edible. Igkhan joined such a group, he had learned a lot about edible plants and he did in fact manage to teach them a few new things. Wenja was spending time with some of the other women there, they were weaving using some sort of primitive but very efficient weaves and Wenja wanted to learn. She was very eager to make herself useful and Rhawan and Ahravan was glad she wasn't the type of person who demand that others do everything for them. Ahravan was recovering fast but he still couldn't do much, he got dizzy and felt weak and Rhawan did tease him a bit, although with a friendly tone.

They too had to prepare and Ahravan did sit down with the tribes and the leaders to listen to their tales and try to figure out what they really knew and what was just old superstition.

There were few maps available there, few knew how to read and write and if something was to be kept for the future it had to be remembered. But some did come with useful information and Ahravan did remember it all.

The dead had been buried and the grieving was over now and the life within the mountain became rather interesting. Wenja had gotten used to the routines of the city but this was yet again different. There were unwritten laws and rules and now she did see how they did work in perfect detail. The huge dwarven stronghold was enormous and so complex you easily could get lost if you weren't a dwarf and thus the children were under constant supervision. There were always somebody following the young ones, and making sure that they didn't enter the dangerous tunnels. Wenja had already seen the baths, they were a wonder and she had been stunned. The cave in which she and Ahravan had bathed before the wedding had been wonderful but it was very natural, not much had been done to it. The bathing pools here were very intricate, and the enormous cave they were placed within had been carved so that it did resemble a forest, caught in stone. The water did run from one pool to the next in what appeared to be natural little creeks and everywhere there were carved trees and benches and the dwarves had used different minerals when they made the trees so the canopies did glitter and sparkle in different colours.

The water came from springs and it was very hot when it emerged from the bowels of the earth, some were lead off towards the kitchen where it was used to heat food, some did also circulate within the walls of the living quarters, making it pleasantly hot the whole time and then the majority was lead from one pool to the next. The natural cooling did assure that the pools held different temperatures. Most of the time the baths were open to everybody and she was a bit shocked to find out that everybody did bathe together without being shy at all. Some of the members of the clans didn't bathe like that though, the female dwarves always kept to themselves and had some days and times reserved when they were the only ones allowed inside of the baths. Wenja realized that this was done because of their culture, not because they were shy. Imh told her that female dwarves were very proud of their bodies and were also very eager to show them off but since females were few and sought after they had to avoid becoming too tempting. There were countless stories of brides being kidnapped and Imh did tell Wenja that one dwarven noble in fact had tried to kidnap Imh when she was a young maiden, luckily she did know how to swing a hammer.

Ahravan did spend some time in the baths to swim and stay in shape. The water did help him stretch and strengthen the injured thigh and Wenja was very glad that he was getting better. She still had a hard time believing that she had saved him. He often asked her to join him and a few times Rhawan too spent time with her and one of the women of the clans was a very good masseuse and used oils and ointments that made Wenja's skin even softer than before. Ahravan would bring wine and fruit and then they would just relax by the pool and Wenja was never disappointed when it came to receiving attention. Both Ahravan and

Rhawan did their very best to keep her happy and she grew fond of the baths very fast.

But she was curious about the city and one day Imh did take her on a tour of the city, some other dwarves did join them and Wenja was in awe of all the work which had been done there and she realized that the part of the city they now inhabited was just a small part of it, not even worth mentioning. It was like an entrance shed, nothing more.

Imh did allow her to enter the real city and it was breath-taking, huge halls with details and an architecture which was stunning. Somewhere huge gaps in the rocks had been turned into venting shafts and she realized that there were hundreds of levels here. Perhaps even more. Dwarves do dig and dig well and Imh did tell her that this city once had been famous for its emeralds. They had dug deeply into the earth and uncovered huge gems, the size of boulders. But eventually the wealth had run out and the city had lost its important status and became abandoned after some centuries.

Wenja was a bit stunned by that fact, the dwarves seemed to have been a very industrious people and yet there were empty cities and abandoned roads. Imh did seem sad and she didn't really look as if she wanted to speak but one of the other dwarven females did tell Wenja about the fall of the dwarves. They were few now, too few to be a power to be reckoned with, earlier the dwarves had been the most powerful of all the races, they had been many and strong and everybody did depend on their smithing craft and their ingenuity. It had all ended some centuries earlier, with a disaster so horrible most dwarves still refused to even mention it. Wenja didn't want to pry but the dwarf did take her aside and told of what had been known as the golden plague.

It had started in a city to the far south, at first it didn't raise any alarms for just a few dwarves were ill and it wasn't even serious, just some sniffling and aches. Then the disease suddenly took a turn for the worse and it was a terrible and horrifying development. All of a sudden entire cities became infected and sick overnight, and the vague symptoms had transformed to something out of a nightmare. Many had believed that the gods were punishing them for having been too greedy and many dwarves did abandon their homes and their entire lifestyle and culture to make amends.

Wenja was deeply shocked by what she was told. At first the sick dwarves became unable to drink and eat, then their skin felt as if it was on fire, they burned with a vicious fever and the skin started to fall off in huge pieces, having turned all golden in colour. They would vomit blood and bile and then in the end the bodies became all rigid and stiff and would stink horribly. By then the sick person usually only had a few hours left of life and it was gruesome hours for he or she would still be conscious but barely able to breathe.

The dwarf did tell Wenja that the normal thing to do by then was to give the sick person a swift death, in order to prevent prolonged suffering. There was no cure and no hope and just a few dwarves had survived here and there. Some cities had been spared and thus a once great nation was reduced to a mere ghost of what it once had been.

Wenja was deeply moved by this and she understood why Imh refused to talk of it, it had to be an eternal sorrow they never could fully forget.

As they walked through the city Wenja saw wonders she never would have been able to imagine, the huge gardens where food had been produced, the forges where precious metal had been melted into incredible works of art. She even saw one of the sacred sites of the dwarves, they weren't that religious but they did have some gods and here there were statues of them all. The main god was called Ordnidar, and he was the God of smiths and was depicted as a huge strong dwarf holding a forge hammer in his hand. The statue was so lifelike it was scary.

Wenja did see something in a corner of the sacred room which did puzzle her, it was a statue which was sort of placed there as if it was just stored there but not to be displayed. It was a huge one too, and as she got closer Imh did make a small sound of shock. "By my father's beard, I didn't know they had one of those here?"

The other female dwarves did mumble too and Wenja got closer. In the torchlight the statue seemed to be alive, and she was very impressed by the incredible work which had been put into it. It was a giant cat, like the one who now followed Frostfoot and it was even larger and the stoneworker had carved it from what had to be solid obsidian. It was so black it seemed to swallow all light and she could see every hair in its coat and she could swear she felt the smell of a wild beast. Imh did look as if she was truly shocked and the other dwarves did stay back, as if they were afraid of the statue. Wenja did walk around it, the cat was taller than a huge horse and the body was powerful and elegant and also oddly alien. She had no idea of how somebody had been able to carve it and she did reach out and touched one of the massive paws. For a second she was sure she heard a big cat roar in the distance and a shudder went through her.

Imh did wet her lips. "That is the steed of one of the ancient gods, a goddess we dwarves did worship in ages long lost. She was the mother of beasts, the goddess of the earth, the creator of all life. We did honour her for a long time but I guess things did change with the ages and the belief was forgotten."

Wenja stared at the huge statue. It did seem alive, as if it would awaken at any time and pounce from the pedestal it was placed upon. "What was the name of the goddess?"

Imh sighed. "Suravay, daughter of the full moon. She was a goddess of contrast, forgiving and nurturing but also wild and cruel, just like nature"

Wenja nodded and threw a last glance at the statue, it did almost seem as if the huge carved pupils did follow her as they left the room.

As the days went by the plains seemed to come alive with unexpected survivors, all heading for the dwarven stronghold. Often the leaders would claim to be led by packs of animals and the city could house thousands of people. The survivors would tell of horrors which made even Ahravan cringe and many had fallen victim to both the small insect like demons and the huge transparent type. The other more mundane types had also killed many and Ahravan could only pray that the group they had sent off was able to do their job. If not even the idea of trying to get to the cliff would be suicide.

Some said they had seen huge packs of monsters heading due west, that could mean that the dwarves and the two orcs and the men had started their task and Wenja was worried about Floth'bha and the others.

Bagir would often sit and talk to her to keep her mind away from the journey ahead of them and she was grateful. He was like a piece of home, of something safe and well known and Ahravan knew that Bagir would protect Wenja no matter what. Ahravan was rather busy now and Rhawan was always by his side to make sure that he didn't push himself too hard. Ahravan was glad he had his Si'ish there but sometimes the continuous worry was annoying, Rhawan knew that Ahravan was healed by now.

Ahravan had lost his favourite horse and now he had to pick a new one from the herd, he didn't want a young steed which was untried and potentially unsuited for such an important mission. He was wandering through the herds of horses and Laupir was by his side, he knew every horse they had there and could determine whether or not the animal was good enough for the Ath'ir. Neither of Ayr'esh sons were old enough nor trained enough for this and Ahravan did own several excellent horses but none did stand out the way Ayr'esh had. He was tempted at giving up when he was approached by Yalaih, the young elven maiden did wear a sort of thin veil over her face as a sign of grief and she walked with a sort of heaviness which was rather unusual to elves. Ahravan knew that the grief of having lost her family could kill her, as easily as any sword. Yalaih did bow her head. "Ath'ir. My mother is dead, and my father would have wanted you to take care of his belongings now that she isn't here."

Ahravan just shrugged. "I got his weapon?"

Yalaih nodded. "Yes, but there is more. Follow me"

Ahravan and Rhawan did follow her to the herd of horses which belonged to the snow bear clan, it wasn't large but the animals were tough and strong and rather different in both build and temper from what the other elven clans preferred. Yalaih did stop and put a finger in her mouth, she did whistle and Ahravan heard the sound of a horse approaching. Both he and Rhawan did stare with rather obvious shock, the animal which came trotting towards Yalaih was no ordinary animal, it was a so called Gorheg, a unicorn species which lived only in the high mountains. It was a stallion, almost as tall as Flint and the broken horn and scarred hide told Ahravan that this was a warrior. The animal did snort and lowered its head, sniffing Yalaih's hands and she did feed it a

418

piece of wild carrot. "He is father's favourite, old now but still strong and he is wise and cunning. Father would have wanted you to ride him to save us all"

Ahravan swallowed. "Will he accept me? They do usually only allow one person to ride them?"

She nodded. "He will accept you, for you are strong, like father. He will protect you, he has faced darkness before"

Ahravan did reach out and the massive muzzle did touch his fingers gently, the animal was pitch black all over but it had a sort of white line going from between its ears to between its wide nostrils. The broken horn was encased in gold, as if its master had tried to embezzle the remains of the unicorn's most prominent feature. "What is his name?"

Yalaih did smile, she let her fingers glide through the long black mane. "Khor'ath, it means silver spear"

Ahravan nodded and petted the mighty chest, he didn't reach higher than its flank and he felt impressed and shocked by the power of the beast. A unicorn is not like a horse, they will react very differently and their innate magic can be very strong. "Will you carry me brother?"

The unicorn did snort, then it did touch Ahravan's chest with the end of the broken horn and Ahravan smiled, a swift almost shy grin. "Thank you brother"

Rhawan was still just staring. "Gods, that is…amazing"

Ahravan nodded . "I do not need a new steed after all, this will do perfectly well"

Rhawan did pat him on the back. "I am becoming envious brother, but I doubt that any creature of darkness will fight Khor'ath willingly"

Ahravan smiled back. "Exactly!"

Out on the plains Balgar and the others had the great river in sight and it wasn't an hour too early. Over the last days monsters had seemed to sprout out of the ground and they were surrounded on all fronts except straight forward. The dwarf had lead them well, he did keep the demons and monsters away with his magic and it had worked so far but now they were at a critical phase. They had to make rafts, or find boats. Somehow they had to get to safety out on the running waters and here there were no settlements. There were few trees too and everybody was desperately searching for anything they could use. Balgar had lost weight and he did look as if he had aged several decades over just a few days and Geir did realize that the magic did take a terrible toll of the one wielding it. Dwarves aren't that fond of magic normally but they do have powers and they are great, although rarely displayed. Balgar was a dwarven shaman and thus his status within the clans was high, and he was respected and everybody listened to what he did say. But this was really not something he nor anybody else had ever attempted before and he knew that they had to reach the river fast, or else he wouldn't be able to keep the shields up.

The river was rather wide and slow flowing at this place, it was not very deep but too deep to cross and there weren't really a tree in sight. Usually there would be driftwood on the beach and as they spurred their steeds towards the water they did use their eyes and tried to see if there were any logs left by the spring floods. But there weren't any and Balgar did start to look a bit desperate. Neither of them was capable of keeping the monsters at bay now, there were huge packs of them everywhere and if the shields did fail he estimated that they would be dead within minutes. The ghastly transparent demons were constantly sniffing as if they were about to catch the scent of living prey and the massive ape like monsters weren't much better, he had to stay strong.

They rode along the river, as fast as they could, the ponies were exhausted and even Resh'kha's buffalo did show signs of exhaustion. Geir and the other men were terrified by now and regretted having volunteered for the mission but now there was no way back. They were losing hope, the ice had scoured the beaches and left nothing but rock and sand and if they did ride into the water the steeds wouldn't survive for long, the water was too cold and the animals very warm due to the harsh tempo. That was when Floth'bha did call out, she pointed at a small island in the river, barely more than just a few huge rocks which had been pushed together by currents and ice and against them something was lodged. It was a boat, and not just any sort of boat, it was a ferry. The type people use to transport goods over the river. Balgar did gasp at the sight and Resh'kha did cheer but the two other dwarves did look rather uncertain. "It may be ruined?"

Geir and Than did dismount and walked to the water's edge. "It does look as if it is in one piece, if we can get it lose it may still be floating"

Balgar coughed, he was so very tired now. The spells he used did draw power from his spirit and body and he was close to being spent. "Somebody has to get out there, but the current is so strong"

Geir did smile, there was yet again hope in his eyes. "Not necessarily no, we do have rope don't we?"

He did find a roll of strong rope from his saddle and made a noose at the end of it, the dwarves did frown. "Don't tell me you think you can hit it from here?"

Geir nodded. "I can, we used to rope wild horses when I was a lad, I bet I can get the rope onto the stern from here"

Balgar did roll his eyes and the two orcs did hold their breaths as Geir waded into the water and arranged the lasso. He did aim carefully and Balgar was pale and shivering. The ground did shiver now, the monsters were so very near. Geir did throw, the first attempt was a grand miss, he didn't even make it as far as to the boat but he tried again and this time the noose did land on the stern rather elegantly. He did grasp the end of the rope and turned to Resh'kha. "Can you make your buffalo pull?"

Resh'kha did snort but she did attach the rope to the animal's horn and strangely enough the massive beast seemed to understand what this was about. It turned around and started to put its weight into it and there was a creaking sound coming from the boat. There was a risk that they would tear it open like this but they had to try. The buffalo did use all its strength and suddenly the ferry did come loose, everybody grasped at the rope and with the help of the animal they did manage to pull it to the shore. It was in good shape, no boards were broken and it was dry on the inside but the rudder was bent and the mast broken and it was not exactly made for long journeys. Such ferries were usually attached to a pulley system and dragged back and forth across a river so it didn't need to be very complicated and this was a primitive one. But it did float and Floth'bha and Resh'kha did step onto the ferry and managed to lower it a bit on the side close to the beach. Balgar was close to fainting now, and the air around them seemed to shiver as if on a warm day. Geir did smack the horses across the arse and the animals did jump on board. The ponies were a little harder to get on board but they did manage with the help of a huge rock. The buffalo was the hardest to get on board, but Resh'kha did speak to the beast and finally he did jump, surprisingly high and with an elegance nobody would have anticipated. The ferry was heavily loaded now, and Resh'kha and Floth'bha did use all their strength to push the ferry back into the stream. It wasn't even a second too early for suddenly the shields did fall as Balgar did pass out and they heard an unholy roar as the monsters did see them. A wild horde of beasts did storm towards them but the water did stop them and Geir did take a deep breath of relief. The other dwarves did take care of Balgar and Resh'kha did kneel down by his side. The ferry had no cabin or anything, it was just a flat boat deck and they tied the animals to the remains of the mast. It was barely room to move around them and the dwarves did look uncomfortable. Resh'kha did stare at Dharan and Kulkar and her eyes were a bit nervous. "Will he wake up again?"

The two did shrug. "Yes, but it may take time"

Resh'kha did make a grimace and she did point towards the horizon. "The river won't be this slow and wide everywhere, and this ferry is already too full. We risk capsizing"

The dwarves did shudder, dwarves are not fond of water at all since they are incapable of swimming due to their heavy build and body shape. "We just have to stay in the middle of the river at all times, it shouldn't be too hard?"

Floth'bha did sigh. "The rudder is ruined, she is pulling to the left all the time and I think the keel has a damage too, it wants to spin around its own axis. We have to do something, there is still a long way to go"

Dharan shrugged. "What do you suggest? We aren't boat makers!"

Geir had to smile, those words were the truth for sure, dwarves and boats just didn't go well together. "You have to find something to replace the rudder, break the darn thing off, it will only cause problems"

Resh'kha did stare at the remains with narrow eyes. "No, I have a better idea, we can use the wood, all we need is a strong pole"

They all did look at the remains of the mast but it wasn't long enough and Floth'bha did keep an eye on the banks, the monsters did follow them, howling with anticipation and anger. They had to fix the rudder fast, or else they may drift ashore. Osbord had taken a seat at the bow of the ferry and he was staring down at the water. "There could be something in the water, everybody, do keep your eyes open!"

Resh'kha did shiver, the beasts were horrible this close up and here they didn't have a huge group of warriors to fight with them. They were on their own and the beasts did try to enter the water again and again but it looked as if the water did burn them somehow and they did retreat with howls of disappointment and rage. The ferry wasn't moving the way it should, the weight of all the horses and ponies and the people did make it sluggish and the damage to the keel made it spin every so often. The dwarves were a bit green in the face and Floth'bha did look as if she was suffering but they did stay by the bow and kept their eyes fixed on the waters, hoping to find something useful.

Resh'kha knew that they had many days of travel ahead of them and she just hoped that they could ditch the crippled ferry eventually. The river did a wide half circle and at the bottom of the turn they saw what they had been hoping for, several long branches stuck between the boulders which made the river bank at the site. Geir did use the lasso again and after a while the men had managed to create something which could function as a rudder but it wasn't very efficient nor very elegant. They had just tied it to the remains of the old rudder attachments and it did take a heck of a lot of strength to control the ferry this way.

But it did take them to the middle of the river and now they did see that there were monsters also on the other side of the river, drawn to them by the heart stone. Balgar was still unconscious and everybody was dead tired since they had been awake for days now. The ponies and the horses had laid down and Resh'kha did shrug and sat down by the new rudder. "I can steer for a while, the rest of you, get some sleep. We need it, I don't think the river will change much for several hours yet"

Floth'bha did grin at her and caressed her cheek swiftly. "Good idea, we need some food too, I will try to prepare some"

Geir and the other men were almost asleep on their feet and as fast as they had managed to eat some dry bread and cheese they laid down to sleep. There was barely room for them there but if they laid down next to their steeds the animals did help keeping them warm. Resh'kha did dread the night though, it would be very hard to see anything and the ferry was as easy to manoeuvre as a sheet of spilled oil.

They did enjoy the peace for a few hours, then Floth'bha did take over the rudder to let Resh'kha rest and now the banks were teeming with all sorts of bizarre beasts. There would be no chance at making landfall and they had little feed for the horses and Geir suggested that they found some string and started to catch some fish for themselves, and perhaps river grass for the animals.

The men immediately got busy doing that and the dwarves did help them, Balgar was still not awake and Resh'kha was worried for him. They would need his skills later, if they were to leave the river at all the shields had to be put up again. The river was getting more narrow and wilder and now both Resh'kha and Floth'bha had to stay by the rudder, it was getting darker and they had to keep an eye on the river all the time to avoid rocks. Kulkar had taken up seat at the bow now and he was shouting orders for the two orcs to tell them where to steer the boat. It was back breaking work, the boat was fighting them at every turn and it was so heavy and sluggish every manoeuvre had to be started way ahead of the actual turn. The three men wanted to help but realized that they simply weren't strong enough for this. Only the two female orcs had the immense strength needed to be able to control the vehicle.

The men did fish instead and caught some fish and by using the small iron anchor which still was in place they managed to pull some river grass up onto the deck. The horses were hungry and ate it without complaints and thus everybody was busy. But after yet an hour or two it was pitch black and now the river was turning into rapids. And worse even, it was getting so narrow the monsters had no problems seeing them, which was bad for some of the more humanoid shaped nasties had started tossing rocks at them.

The horses got scared and rocked the boat quite literally and Resh'kha was getting desperate. Balgar had to wake up now, they needed his help and she did shake the dwarf but he did only moan and he was a bit grey in the face. Resh'kha started to worry that he was dying, that he had used too much of his life-force keeping them safe so far. The two other dwarves did share her opinion, they didn't say so but she saw it in their eyes, a certain hopelessness and she could only pray that the beasts didn't hit the ferry with something large.

Geir and the other two men had brought their bows and now they used them for all that they were worth but the arrows did little damage and if anything they only made the beasts more angry. The darkness didn't bother them at all and Floth'bha didn't have much strength left, the ferry was leaning more and more to the side and the situation was dire. Resh'kha did shout to Kulkar and asked the dwarf to look out for huge rocks, if need be they had to run the ferry aground again, in the middle of the river. She was leaning over the shaman when he suddenly opened his eyes and she squealed and tried to back away but he grasped her by her ears and pulled her head down with amazing strength. Suddenly the aging dwarf kissed her, Resh'kha did freeze and didn't manage to push him away and suddenly she felt how a surge of sheer energy raced through her, she gasped and the dwarf did let go, he smiled faintly and his eyes did glow, a weak light which was dying as she watched it. "It is yours now sister, use it well"

Then Balgar did take a deep breath, held it and let go and went limp. Resh'kha did sit up, like hit by lightning, she felt odd, light headed and confused and she almost screamed. She saw colours surrounding everything around her, bright transparent bands of colour like thin veils and they danced around everyone and everything. It was both beautiful and terrifying and Dharan came rushing to her, grasping her shoulder. "I was afraid of that, he spent all that he had didn't he? But you are the one to lead us now, he gave you his strength and his abilities"

Resh'kha did swallow hard. "Why? Why me?!"

The dwarf shrugged. "You are strong sister orc, and you are brave and a pure soul. Not many of those around these days, he saw that you were worthy. You may hide us now!"

Resh'kha just blinked, feeling utterly lost. A female shaman? There were many female shamans among the orcs but they were trained from birth and were never just tossed into it. She felt herself tremble. "I don't know how?!"

Dharan tilted his head. "Use your heart, listen to what it tells you. It will guide you"

Resh'kha heard the hard crack of a rock hitting the side of the ferry and she did bite her teeth together, the beasts were all that intelligent were they? She closed her eyes, listen to your heart? That wasn't all that easy now was it? She had to shield them, what had Balgar done? He had carried a sort of amulet hadn't he?

She did open his shirt and yes, there was an amulet there. She picked it up with shivering hands and to her astonishment it felt warm in her hand, like it was alive. "I have no idea of what you are, but hide us, please!"

The amulet glowed slightly, then a sort of glowing dome did spread from it and it did cover the entire ferry. But strangely enough the monsters seemed to lose sight of them and disappointed roars could be heard all over the banks. Resh'kha did hang onto the amulet as if it was a lifeline and she felt a tingling in her hands and arms, as if it was draining also her. Floth'bha did fight with the rudder and she was sweating. "Brilliant, we can steer differently now, but the ferry is not going to make it much longer"

Resh'kha did get up, the horses and ponies were stomping and her buffalo was snorting. "You are right, but I think we may be approaching a small lake, there could be islands there"

Geir did stare at her with awe. "Let us hope so, we need to rest, we all do. And we need to go over the plans again, without Balgar I am not so sure that we can follow the original one. Not to sound harsh Resh'kha but you are untrained and that jewel is very dangerous now"

Resh'kha did nod. "I know, I know damn it. But what else can we do? We have to lure as many monsters as possible into that forest, and there is no other manner but by land or river"

Geir did frown, his eyes were distant. "I wonder…"

The river was mostly rapids now and the old ferry did barely hand together, the twisting and turning made it spring several leaks and it was getting heavier by the minute. Even if they were shielded they couldn't go ashore, the beasts weren't that stupid and everybody was pale and terrified. The ferry did spin and swing and turn and Than and Osbord did hang over the side puking their guts out, or so it seemed. But suddenly the river did turn rather abruptly and what lay ahead of them was indeed a lake, it was long and rather narrow but a lake and lo and behold, there was an island there, a bit ahead. Floth'bha did almost roar. "Grasp whatever you can find and row!"

Everybody grasped planks and buckets and whatever they had which could be used and the ferry did slowly oh so slowly head towards the island. Resh'kha felt a desperate hope, the water had to carry them to the island and suddenly the ferry did jerk and shot forth again, picking up speed as if something had grasped it and towed it towards the shore. Resh'kha felt hot, as if there was fire burning nearby and she gasped and shuddered. The ferry did hit the beach with a crunch and then it did give up its spirit, the vehicle did dissolve itself into its original materials, planks and boards and they all jumped into the shore as the entire thing was reduced to a pile of rubble. Resh'kha did stare at the sad remains of the ferry, they weren't that far from land here and it was shallow so they could cross but first of all, warmth and food and rest.

The island wasn't large, perhaps five hundred meters long and a couple of hundred meters wide at its largest and it was covered with boulders and a patch of dense and low forest, most likely an almost impenetrable shrubbery with thorns and whatnot. The men grasped what they could salvage from the ferry and started building a fire and the dwarves did carry Balgar's body to the edge of the small forest. They did sing the whole time, something low and sad and very sombre and Resh'kha wished that she did understand the words. They treated their deceased brother with a lot of respect and Resh'kha did walk over, carefully to make sure that she didn't break any taboos. Dharan did smile at her, he did wash Balgar's face and rebraided the hair and the beard. "He knew he wouldn't make it, even when we left Ohtanar"

Resh'kha did frown. "How come?"

The dwarf did fold Balgar's hands over his chest. "He was sick, not even the elven healers could fix it. But he had to go, he was the only one with the strength to awaken the heart stone. Only an experienced shaman is capable of doing that"

Resh'kha did feel a surge of intense sorrow. "Oh, I didn't know…I…"

Dharan tilted his head, the long braids of his beard did clink since there were beads attached to them. "Do not mourn sister orc, he lived well and he did die well. The ancestors will welcome him to their halls for sure. We have to finish what he started"

Resh'kha did nod. "But what was ailing him?"

Dharan did lift Balgar's tunic and Resh'kha did gasp, the skin she did see covering the dwarf's abdomen was almost like stone, hard and grey and odd in texture and blood was oozing through cracks. "It is a curse, one that lays on our race and none other. We come from the womb of the mother earth and sometimes she bids us return to her embrace. This is the result, we turn into…stone"

Resh'kha did wet her lips. "But…how is that even possible?"

Dharan made a grimace. "We do not know, and it strikes very randomly and is very rare but there is no cure for it, if you get it you will eventually die"

Resh'kha did swallow. "I am…so sorry"

Dharan just smiled. "Don't be, we will lay him here, cover him with rocks and let nature reclaim his body. It is as it should be"

Resh'kha did nod and returned to the now warm fire. The men had tied up the ponies and horses and Resh'kha stared at the western bank, it was filled with beasts and she felt them now, cold souls, devoid of feelings except hunger and hatred and she shuddered. There was as if she did feel a voice in the wind, a sweet and seemingly beautiful voice but she could sense the venom in it, like poison hidden in rich honey. There was something out there, and it was after the jewel, and it wouldn't stop at anything to gain it. She closed her eyes, fighting the urge to just leave, she had a mission now and a meaning and she couldn't abandon it, even if she felt like it.

The mountains were a formidable barrier, forming a wall from west to east far north and few if any knew exactly what was beyond this very tall mountain range. The area in which the cliff was supposedly positioned was almost in the middle of the mountain range, but it was in itself surrounded by wilderness. Here deep canyons did cut their way through a naked and very barren landscape mostly dominated by rocks and ice and snow. Few signs of life could be seen here and yet it wasn't desolate. Life did exist here and always had. To the west of the valleys which were

428

known by the people to the south there was an area hidden between two almost vertical mountains. From a distance they did look as one and the same and the deep valley they hid couldn't be spotted unless you came really close to it. The valley had once been carved by ice, slowly and steadily digging into the very bedrock, tearing out chunks of the earth's bones like some giant relentless mole. It had left a huge u shaped valley which was very deep and very dark and it didn't look very inviting at all. Here the sun rarely shone and waterfalls did make the naked rock glisten with moisture.

It was open in one end, the other blocked by an enormous scree and a narrow lake lay in the middle, its waters black like tar. One should imagine that such a foreboding place would be devoid of life but it wasn't. On the eastern bank of the lake several huts were erected, rocks were used as their base and the ribs of enormous beasts carried the roofs, made from hides covered with peat and heather. The huts were hard to see from a distance and thin ropes of smoke did stretch towards the skies. The small village was surrounded by a circle of tall standing rocks, they did look ancient and they were. The centre of the village was a very large hut, the hides forming the roof was kept up not by ribs but by wooden rafters and skulls and bones and other objects did adorn the outside of it. The stench of rotted meat, faeces and unwashed bodies was strong there, and some skinny dogs did scurry around, desperate for a scrap of food.

Inside of the great hut several figures were gathered, hunched together over the oozing bonfires, it was hard to see in there for there was little light and the wood used for heating rather raw, it gave sour smoke and little more than that. A discussion was happening, harsh barking words were being growled across the fires and many a hand lay on primitive weapons made from bone and flint. Only a few there owned things of metal and these objects were revered as if they were a godsend. The people within the hut weren't human, their origin lost in the mists of time. They were short and stocky and yet not of dwarven descent, their bodies covered with thick hair and their limbs thick and powerful. All wore little clothing if any and the faces were dominated by heavy brows and a very large nose. Some were decorated with tattoos and others had used paint and they all wore small amulets woven into their hair.

These were leaders, and they were the strongest of males.

The discussion was heated, shouts were heard and some did make threatening gestures but they didn't attack each other, it was against the laws and would be seen as a loss of all honour. The cause of the discussion was one of them, the leader of the largest of the clans of the people which called themselves Akk'u. He was not the tallest of them but he was strong and relatively young and his arms and legs bulging with muscle. He did look very angry but he didn't say anything, it wasn't his time to speak. He had said what he had to say, now the others would make the final decision.

The oldest among them was the leader of the Rk'ha clan, they were not many but strong and fierce and good hunters and they received great respect. The old male was covered with tattoos and his hair was thin and white but the deep brown eyes were sharp and piercing and he raised a hand. The others did fall silent immediately. "We have heard your voice Bothal,. And you have spoken well. Your tale has been tested among us"

Bothal was looking down at the ground, his heart was beating fast and his jaw were clenched. He had been so sure of himself, the spirit had spoken to him often, told of great things, of great power. If they did what the voice said there would be things of metal for them, and much game and riches. They would never have to starve again.

Old Ch'ka shook his head. "You speak of a spirit, of a voice asking us to do things which we never before have considered. A spirit which bids us to leave the lands of our fathers and kill those who are different."

Bothal did nod. "Yes old one, we will be richly rewarded"

The old male did stare at the younger one with narrow eyes. "And your men, have the spirit spoken to them? Have they seen signs?"

He swallowed hard, shook his head. "No Ch'ka, it is only I"

The old leader turned around and his face was stern, almost angry. "Our people belong here, the mountains are our land and in our blood. The spirits we know, all of them. This spirit of yours is false, an evil force"

Bothal did hiss. "Nay, it is salvation, it is help"

Ch'ka frowned. "So you say but our hunters have seen terrible beasts, moving to the sun lands, and the land is trembling. You have been fooled young one, there is no such force, no such spirit. Beware of the voices in the night for they speak naught but evil. If we do as it bids our people will die"

Bothal growled. "You are fools"

Ch'ka crossed his arms over his chest. "We have spoken, you have heard. No such thing will happen, go back to your tribe, tell them to stop listening to these lies. You will be exiled should you come here again"

Bothal spat on the floor. "You are a fool old man, the voice is stronger than all of us"

The old leader caught his eyes with his own gaze. "We are sons of the mountains, our ways are set, there will be no change"

Bothal did run out of the hut and kicked aside one of the dogs, rage was visible within his face. He hadn't expected to be treated thus, like a mere cub. No, they would pay for this, the voice would make sure that he would be chief of all the clans. Ch'ka did leave the hut, the younger male could be seen walking up the path away from the village and he mumbled to himself. Bothal was young and fiery and stupid like a muskox in heat. Nothing good would come from listening to him, he was strong in body but not in mind and Ch'ka would talk to the shaman, if there were evil spirits in the mountains they would sacrifice blood and meat to the gods and beg for their protection.

The village did become quiet as the day turned to night, their people had very good night vision and an excellent sense of smell and the huts had very little lighting. They used some hollowed out stones in which they poured fat but otherwise from that the hearths were dead at night. Burning a fire at night was a bad omen and not something they would do. The smallest hut was in the end of the village, it was solid and well-made but not very remarkable. It was the women's hut and this very evening one of the females was busy. She was gathering hides and her short flint spear and also some small bags with herbs. It was dark soon and she had to be gone before the sun was completely gone.

She didn't speak to the others there, they ignored her as they ought to and she made a grimace and crawled out of the hut on her knees. Unta was in her twenty fourth summer and she had yet to carry a cub, the others there saw her as cursed. Most had several by the age of ten and seven and she had never born a new life at all. But the moon did make her bleed each month and this time it had come earlier than normal, her spirit was too strong they said, it fought the spirits of unborn children and forced them to leave her womb. She couldn't stay there as she bled, it was a bad omen and she had to go to the hidden hut where the women lived when the moon days were upon them. She sighed and found her way through the rocks and bushes, she was light of foot and rather lithe in build, her heavy forehead furrowed with worry and her dark eyes filled with sorrow. She had mated with many males and yet nothing did ever happen, she was too fierce they said, or too weak. One of the other, she wasn't sure. She did see in the darkness and found the hidden path. The men didn't know where the hut was, it was forbidden to them to even speak to a woman during her moon days for everybody knew that the woman's spirit was so strong during these days that it could devour that of a man and make him no man anymore.

Unta grunted, she had last lain with Kruad, he was a strong warrior and hunter and handsome, he had sired many cubs and he had been good, very good. Unta did grin thinking of it, a male who pleased the females was blessed by the gods, and would leave many offspring. But Unta didn't bear cubs and nobody respected her, even if she was a good tanner and good with the spear.

The hut was simply a small room underneath a heap of peat, invisible unless you knew of it and it was only the grown females who knew of its existence. No male was allowed near it, and if a man did happen to enter it the spirits would make his manhood rot and fall off. Unta knew of several males who deserved that fate.

She rolled out her pelts and put on the belt holding her rags in place, they made some soft rags from the bog cotton which grew on the large marshes, they were to be buried after the moon days were over and no man could even see them. Unta was in pain, her cramps had gotten worse over the last years and she knew that she soon would bleed no more, she was an elderly woman and as a childless one she would receive little respect. Her fate was to grow weak and frail while being ridiculed by everybody. It was a harsh fate and she had grown bitter and angry as a result of this, it was her only defence.

The darkness was complete and she did fall asleep, at least she was better at making soft pelts than anybody else there. She slept soundly but suddenly she woke up, a sound had disturbed her rest, a horrible sound which made her curl up in fear. It was screams, bellows and roars and she trembled and grasped her amulet with a trembling hand. What was this? She was trembling but pressed her face against the cracks in the door, it was made from hides and covered with grass, the cracks were few and narrow but she saw. She saw fire raging towards the skies and dark figures running around, horrible screeches were heard and her heart did almost stop. Her people was being murdered! And the murderers were others like them? She bit into her thumb to stop herself from screaming, if anybody saw her she would die too. The huts were burning, oh the spirits would be furious, you never used fire at night, it would scare the ancestors away and leave you unprotected. There were evil forces out there, drawn to blood and death. She curled up in her furs, not daring to move, clutching her tiny amulet so hard her fingers were almost on the verge of breaking, she had no concept of what she had just seen. The screams did stop, now she only heard distant voices, triumphant. She heard the huts collapsing and her eyes were surprisingly dry, she found that she was unable to cry.

Unta did lay there shaking with fear for several hours and she didn't dare to peek out again until daylight did pierce the door.

Unta didn't know what to do, she was alone and confused and frightened but she had to see if there were others down there, alive. She had survived fights before, males would often fight over women or a kill or between the clans but they did never kill females and cubs. It wasn't right, it would make the ancestors mad at you. She gathered her courage and left the hut, instinct did fight her upbringing, she wasn't really to leave the hut until she had stopped bleeding but this was not a normal situation. She grasped her pack of food and water and gathered her courage. She did sneak her way back to the village, there was just ashes left of the huts, and dead bodies, some burned and others just slain. She saw their chief with his chest pierced by a spear and she recognized the patterns on it, it was made by somebody of Bothal's clan.

Everybody were dead, even the dogs were slain and the women had been caught within the hut and had burned alive. Unta did wail, a thin piercing sound which shocked her for she hadn't known that her throat could make such noise. She felt the taste of ashes in her mouth and she fell to her knees, what now? She had nowhere to go, her clan was gone! She could just as well let the lake drown her for she was not going to make it on her own. She wept until the ground around her was wet and she was trembling. Nothing like this had ever happened in the history of her people. She managed to get up onto her feet, she had to leave before the killers returned. But where was she to go? What reason did she have to live?

She jerked when she heard a sound, it came from the large hut and she was convinced that it was an evil spirit, out to eat her soul. But the sound came again, a sort of strangled cry and she walked over, very slowly and with a cooking rock in her hand. Behind the ruins there was a small pit used to prepare hides and something moved underneath the scorched hides it did contain.

Unta did swallow hard, poked at it with a stick and a grunt could be heard. It was no spirit, it was somebody under there and she grasped the hides and pulled them aside. It was old Ch'ka and he was horribly burned. The skin of his face almost gone and both eyes were ruined, the teeth naked since the lips were burned away and yet the old male was alive. Unta did whimper, the sight made her want to retch but her stomach was empty. The old male did gasp. "Who?"

The voice was garbled, the mouth and throat damaged and yet he managed to speak. "Unta"

The old leader moaned. "Good, you are a strong woman"

He did heave for air. "Go south, warn eternal. Evil is waiting, the goddess daughter must use the…path of the leopard"

Unta felt her heart racing. "I…I am but one…no warrior I…"

The old male did gasp and exhaled and went limp and Unta did realize that he had kept himself alive just so he could say this. Unta fell to her knees, hiding her face within her hands. She tried to make sense of it all but it was impossible. In the end she realized that he was right, she had to go south and she got up and started to salvage anything she found which could be useful. Ch'ka had a metal knife and she took it, trembling. Normally a woman wasn't allowed to touch metal at all, it was said to scare away the spirits of her unborn children. But Unta was barren and so it didn't matter now did it. She did find the pits where they stored food, flat cakes made from ground up dried meat mixed with fat and berries. She did fill a sack and she found some clothes which had been hung out to dry. Her mind was numb but as long as she did act she didn't have to think about anything.

An hour later she was on her way out of the valley, following paths only her tribe knew of and she didn't look back even once, the valley was cursed now. Innocent blood had been shed there and she didn't want to attract angry ghosts. Unta was used to hunting, to following the males so she was light on her feet and fast and she knew the hunting area of the tribe as the back of her own hand. But south? She had to go east to get south due to the mountains and she knew of what Ch'ka had spoken earlier that day, the valleys to the east had become filled with darkness. She was terrified but she knew she had to do what Ch'ka had asked of her.

She did caress her amulet, the tiny goddess figurine was old and followed through her bloodline for a long time, passed from mother to daughter. The wide hips and enormous breasts a symbol of the power of women, if the goddess indeed had a daughter it was Unta's duty to help, it was a sacred calling. She grasped a stick and picked up her pace. She had no idea of how far it was, of the dangers she may encounter but she was determined. She was dead to her people now, her clan destroyed and her blood would die with her. She didn't have anything to lose, no, nothing at all.

Chapter 11: Land of the lost

Ahravan had grown impatient, the hordes of beasts had been drawn away for now and they knew that they would have to travel very fast in order to reach their goal. Everything was prepared and now they only waited for the moon to be in its right position. Wenja was nervous, she knew that this would be dangerous and she had no idea of what they really were to do. Everybody knew of the prophecy, only the one born twice can close the gate. Who was it about? They had to try even if they didn't know and she had started to feel as if the caves were indeed a safe haven.

Ahravan had been moody, he was determined and yet reluctant to speak much of what he did feel. He had chosen two elven warriors to follow them and also two humans and they too did prepare. One was Khirhien who Wenja knew from her long journey and the other one was a rather stocky built male with very pale skin and hair the colour of autumn leaves. His name was Ayhrandur and he was among Ahravan's best warriors. The two humans were brothers and they did very much alike with long dark hair in a thin braid and the sides of their heads shaved but covered in tattoos. Wenja learned that they were very brave and good riders and they did serve Ahravan since he had once saved their father's life. Their names were Gochil and Darush and they were about thirty years of age and experienced warriors.

The last day before they were to leave was very sombre, Wenja had Sefa helping her preparing things to bring, she couldn't take much and she knew the journey would be challenging no matter what. Sefa was in tears and begged Wenja to return in one piece and Wenja could make no such promises. She was scared and not afraid to admit it. That evening Ahravan and Rhawan did take her to the baths since it would be their last chance to bathe before they left and on the journey they did doubt that anybody of them would have the time to wash themselves. Ahravan had arranged for the baths to be empty and Wenja soon realized why. It wasn't only bathing the two males had on their minds for also this they would have to put aside during the journey. Wenja hadn't even had time to shed her heavy coat before Ahravan was kissing her desperately, holding her close as if he was afraid that she would disappear. Rhawan did embrace her from behind and she was almost feeling a bit squashed by the two powerful males. Ahravan did kiss her with a hunger she hadn't experienced from him before and Rhawan was opening her clothes with nimble fingers, exposing her skin to their eyes. Wenja did gasp as Rhawan did nip at the sensitive skin of her neck and Ahravan started to lick his way down her throat and he pulled down her tunic and started to pay full attention to her breasts. She had realized that he found those parts of her specially enticing since elven women were flat chested and she had to gasp as he lifted her up. He held her close and continued to lick and suck and Rhawan did knead her bottom with long dexterous fingers.

He did arrange her with her legs around Ahravan's waist and she had to cling to Ahravan's shoulders as Rhawan did caress her with slow and determined hands.

Wenja felt as if she was on fire, the constant stimulation and the feeling of safety made her let loose and just forget about the world and Ahravan did hold her up. Rhawan did grasp her too and she had to let out a short yell of bliss as Rhawan did enter her from behind, she was so ready and wanted them both so much and didn't last very long at all. She came with a scream, soaking Ahravan with her juices and Rhawan did groan and gave some hard thrusts before he too came. It made her tremble almost violently and she felt boneless and floating. Rhawan did grasp her and held her up against his own body and now Ahravan did take her, slowly and with a steady rhythm which had her mewling and gasping before much time had passed by. She had to trust that Rhawan was able to hold her up and he was obviously not tired for he held her steady so his Si'ish could pleasure her too.

Ahravan did place a hand under her ass and held her in place and she felt herself clench onto him, not worrying if anybody heard her shouts.

The baths were deserted and they had the whole night if they wanted to. In the end all three of them ended up on the benches next to the pools, exhausted and cuddling up to each other, lost in the moment. Wenja almost wished that the morning wouldn't come but she knew what was at stake. She had to go, and so did the others, the monsters had to be stopped. She couldn't imagine what would happen if the beasts did reach the inland, small isolated villages would have no chance at defending themselves and none of them were used to fighting. Finally they did return to the hut and went to bed and Wenja already knew that she would need some time before she could ride on her own, she was stiff and sore and was rather sure that she had been in some positions this day which weren't believed to be humanly possible.

Resh'kha was very nervous, they couldn't stay on the island very much longer, they had rested and recuperated and they were ready to go but she had no idea of how to shield them yet. She had Balgar's amulet and the power he had given her but she was untrained and she had always seen herself as a warrior, not a shaman. The island didn't provide them with food nor much shelter and it was cold there, and windy. If the wind shifted and brought rain they would freeze and the lake was in itself a threat. So they had to leave, cross the shallow inlet and get going but the banks were packed with beasts which seemed to know that there were living beings out there, warm flesh to devour.

How was she to get them past this wall of twisted and evil creatures? She wasn't Balgar, he would have managed to make them invisible relatively easy. The others did rely on her now and she had already made a startling discovery regarding herself. She was a coward at heart, she had always tried to take the path of least resistance and avoid standing up for anything and maybe that was why the shaman of her tribe had ordered her to leave. She had to find her own purpose and it was a hard truth to digest.   But her philosophical ramblings had to wait, they had to get away from there somehow.

Floth'bha laid a hand on her shoulder, giving it a gentle squeeze. "Just relax sister, let the magic be your guide"

438

Resh'kha did sigh. "Easier said than done, I have no idea of how to use such power"

Kulkar did walk over and he did lower his voice a bit. "Use the amulet, it could perhaps show you what to do?"

Resh'kha nodded and grasped the tiny thing with her hand, she felt the power within it and tried to concentrate. There had to be something she could do to help them all? The amulet felt cold in her hand, and then it became warmer and she got a strong and very odd sensation, like somebody was talking to her but out of her hearing range. Resh'kha did whisper to the thing. "Show me what to do, please"

Suddenly there was a flash of light, the winds seemed to disappear and it got cold, terribly cold but at the same time a sort of glowing orb formed above them, giving off a horribly sharp bluish light. Resh'kha did lower her gaze to protect her eyes and the dwarves did moan, they eyes were very light sensitive since they were adapted to a life underground. But the effect on the beasts was horrific, they stumbled backwards, collided with each other, fell down, clawed at their eyes and tried to run away and it was rather obvious that the light was doing more than blinding them. Some did appear to be on fire and others simply collapsed.

Kulkar did grunt and mounted his pony. "Now is our chance, if that light does follow us it will keep them at bay"

Resh'kha was trembling, she had no idea of whether or not the light would do just that or if it would extinguish itself. Neither did she know if she would be strong enough for this but she had to try. They did ride out, crossed the shallow waters and the beasts didn't seem to notice them at all, the bright bluish light did apparently shield them well. Kulkar was their guide now and he did lead them in a brisk gallop away from the beach and into the plains again. Here the landscape started to change a bit, the plains became less fertile and the ground was covered with what could only be described as a mixture of gravel and sand.

The hordes of beasts did follow, slowly and with determination and more seemed to come by the hour, drawn inn from near and far. The light kept them at a distance but the urge did drive them on, no matter what. Here there was little grass and Resh'kha did fear for their steeds, her bison could survive for a long time on little food but the horses couldn't and if they lost them it would be hard to get anywhere fast enough to avoid the monsters.

They rode for most of the day and the light did linger but Resh'kha started to feel the effect of using this sort of power. If this was what Balgar had endured she felt that she had gained even more respect for the dwarf. She did hope that Kulkar knew where to lead them for this flat landscape was confusing to say the least. And where could they stop for the night? They had to stop eventually didn't they?

Kulkar did turn his head and stared at Resh'kha. "We cannot stop, not yet. This area is too dangerous but the light will keep us safe if we slow down a bit. There is somewhere we can rest but it is still far off"

Resh'kha did grunt, she didn't doubt that they all were tough enough for this but the ponies were getting tired and so were the horses. The darkness fell and the light did throw a spectacular show for everyone to see, they had to be like a beacon by now, visible from the entire plain. But it did keep the beasts away and Resh'kha was grateful that it didn't fade. She was feeling light headed and strangely weak and it wasn't a good feeling at all but she could cope with it. She ate some dried meat and had a quick sip from her flask, it did help her a bit. They rode on, she had no idea of what Kulkar was using for references but she did suspect that the stars were his guide. They were extremely clear and Resh'kha did admire them, in her mind they were the bonfires lit by the ancestors in the spirit world and this night they were especially clear. Kulkar did point forwards. "There is a cliff ahead, in the middle of a gorge, and a bridge leads onto it. If it haven't fallen that is"

Resh'kha did shudder. "You don't know?"

The dwarf did shrug. "None of my people have been in this region for at least twelve hundred years, the cliff could be gone too but we have to try, it is the only place we can defend for several hundred miles"

Resh'kha sighed and wondered where a cliff could be hidden out there, it was flat as an ironing board and so very boring with not even a bush in sight. But as the sun slowly started to make its presence noticed again Resh'kha became aware of something new, something out in the distance ahead of them. It was something moving and it was several dark spots. Could it be animals? She doubted it, the plains were evacuated or so it seemed, the wild animals did sense danger and fled them. Geir saw it too and the old mercenary did frown. "What do you think?"

Floth'bha did squint and her eyes were sharp, she did hiss. "At least twenty people, but something isn't right. They ought to flee"

Resh'kha got a cold sensation down her back, she could see it too. The small crowd wasn't moving the way people usually does, there was some sort of slow almost helpless motion there, as if they all were impeded somehow. She turned around, the beasts were behind them with several miles but would catch up fast enough if they were delayed and she didn't like this at all. The crowd seemed to be set on intercepting them and as the light grew stronger she saw that there were both humans and orcs among them. Kulkar did pull at his own beard. "Curses, what are those? They ought to run!"

Resh'kha did bite her lower lip, in spite of the strange movements the group was fast and now she did see that many appeared to be hurt. There was clearly blood on some of them and others had visible injuries. She swallowed hard. "They aren't people anymore, we did encounter such on the way to Ohtanar, they are sick, infected!"

Kulkar did frown. "So they are dangerous?"

Resh'kha did nod. "Yes, very. We cannot allow them to get too near. They are a thing of darkness Kulkar, servants of evil. The disease one brought forth by the masters of the monsters back when the gate were open"

The dwarf nodded. "Right, everybody, we need to ride hard now, and stay clear of those then."

They kicked their steeds into gallop again and Resh'kha didn't take her eyes of the small crowd even once, they were suddenly moving with a horrible determination and if she hadn't already realized that these were people no more she would now. Even the wounded did run like an antelope and didn't appear to feel fatigue nor pain at all. Resh'kha yelled to the men. "If you can hit them with arrows do so, but don't expect them to be stopped by it"

Geir had already stringed his short rider's bow and started to shoot. He did hit one of the humans straight in the chest but the person didn't even make a sound. The greyish face with strangely dark empty eyes didn't even wince and Resh'kha did feel very frightened now. The crowd was made up from twenty two humans, all adults and clothed like normal nomads and three male orcs who appeared to be very young. Probably hunters out to test their skills and prove themselves to their tribe.

The crowd did stink, a sort of sour scent of decay and something unnatural and Resh'kha did sneeze, it was overwhelming and even now, as their steeds did run as fast as they could the infected people did keep up with them. It wasn't natural and Resh'kha remembered what she had heard about this from her own mother. It was indeed something born out of darkness and she didn't doubt even for a second that these humans were slaves to the same will which did drive the monsters. Geir did fire again, the arrow hit one of the three orcs straight between the eyes and the male went down, not moving again. "Shoot them in the head!"

Geir did yell at the others and Floth'bha did release an arrow which flew straight through the skull of one of the humans, as if the very bone itself had somehow gone soft. They shot as fast as they could now and did manage to bring down many of the infected people, the dwarves didn't use bows but Dharan did have a crossbow and he did fire bolts with alarming precision and power. The monsters did keep their distance for the bright light did hover above them still, it just didn't ward off this new enemy at all.

Suddenly the horse Osbord rode did fall, suddenly and with a sickening yell, the animal did roll and Osbord did get back onto his feet with surprising agility. Resh'kha did turn her buffalo around and hauled him up behind her, the horses weren't strong enough now to carry two people. The fallen horse had clearly broken a foot and the infected seemed to tear into it the moment they reached the animal. Geir did swear and sent off an arrow to end its sufferings. Kulkar stared at Resh'kha. "Do something lass, and do it now! They are catching up with us, the ponies cannot keep this pace forever"

Resh'kha didn't know what to do, she felt scared and confused and she was full of disgust and also rather weakened by the use of power. The feeling of doom became too much, she just reacted out of sheer instinct, screaming something in her own tongue and the pursuers did suddenly sink into the ground, as if they had stepped into quicksand. They did sink

442

until their hips were on ground level, then the sand seemed to solidity again and they couldn't get anywhere. Resh'kha felt faint and had to cling to the rough pelt of her steed, she needed a rest soon or else she would make a fool out of herself.

They continued to ride hard, and suddenly the seemingly flat plains did reveal a secret, and it was a huge one. A canyon with sides which were like a sword cut into the landscape, vertical and smooth and Resh'kha did yelp when she saw how deep it was. You could barely see the bottom and it was straight as a board and maybe a mile across. You wouldn't see it until you got really close and Kulkar did look intense. "Now, let us see if we can find that cliff"

Resh'kha frowned. "What use do we have of it if we get trapped on it? Is there a bridge on the other side too?"

Kulkar shook his head. "No, but there is something better. According to our tales the cliff is hollow and from the bottom a tunnel will lead us back onto the plains on the other side of the gorge"

Resh'kha did groan, a tunnel. Why in the name of every deity were the dwarves so obsessed with going underground? She sure as heck wasn't! Orcs have never been fond of such and avoid even natural caves since they do believe that evil spirits may reside within such places and Resh'kha had often enough seen how terrified underground dwellings made her people. They were the opposite of dwarves in that matter.

They rode along the canyon and Kulkar did explain that it did end abruptly about fifty miles longer north, but if they were to go that way they would encounter a terrain so horrible nobody would dare to enter it. For some reason the bedrock was scoured clean and somehow melted, turned into thousands upon thousands of sharp spikes about a hand in length and both razor sharps and strong. They called it the porcupine's spine and nobody knew how it had come into being in the first place.

After an hour of quick riding they did find the cliff, it was like a vertical needle placed in the middle of the gorge, tall and thin and strangely ominous looking and Resh'kha didn't like it at all. It was rather large, almost blocking the gorge but just as tall as it and she wondered how it had come into being in the first place. It had to have been something spectacular indeed. Kulkar did mumble to himself as they rode closer, the bridge was there, made from stone and from a distance it did look fragile and spindly and very unstable. There was a faint remain of a path leading towards it, and Resh'kha did realize that nobody had used the path for at least several centuries, how in heck's name was she supposed to do this? It was several hundred feet to the bottom of the gorge, probably close to a thousand feet or more and she was afraid of heights. Kulkar did dismount and walked forth, stopped where the bridge reached the edge of the gorge. "Not good, the edge here is fragile, the rock eroded and the bridge itself is…doubtful"

Resh'kha did see that, cracks everywhere, some pieces of the rock had fallen off, it did look as if it was ready to crumble at any minute and Kulkar did spit. "Borosh dwarves made this, and they were never known for building very solid things, pretty yes, but never built for eternity"

The bridge was pretty, even an orc could appreciate the aesthetics displayed there. The elegant arches, the thin and yet strong support beams, the many intricate details made to look as if the bridge was natural, a sort of rock spider web spun across the open space. But now the impression was of danger and Resh'kha did stare at the two dwarves. "There is no other way?"

Kulkar did shrug and pulled at his beard again, Resh'kha had long understood that this was a symptom of stress to him. "No, not if we doesn't want to spend an extra two weeks before we reach that forest?"

Resh'kha sighed, it sounded like a snort. "Right, so what do we do then?"

Kulkar petted his pony. "We do cross over one by one, lightest first, heaviest at last"

Resh'kha did groan, that meant her and her buffalo. Dharan did go first, he did lead his pony across towards a sort of opening on the other side and he kept a very frisk pace to avoid putting too much stress on the bridge. Then Kulkar did cross running and Geir and Than ran too. Osbord did sprint over and Resh'kha did see that sand and gravel did fall off the bridge, it was trembling ever so little. Floth'bha did lead her horse across and Resh'kha couldn't help but thinking that if something went wrong they would be stuck there. She managed to persuade her buffalo to follow her across the bridge which by now was croaking and groaning and she heard rocks come loose, falling towards the abyss below. She was feeling cold sweat flowing down her back and she almost screamed with relief the moment her feet were on solid ground again. Her buffalo did snort and the bridge did creak like some dry and dying thing before it simply fell off the ledge on the opposite side and disintegrated right before their eyes. A cloud of dust and debris flew out of the canyon and Kulkar did growl. "Amazing, no way back now, let's go and see what we can find in here"

The opening was rather large and very well made, inside they entered a huge chamber with a sort of well in the middle of it. The dwarves did sprint over and checked it but it was dry. The chamber was round and from it another opening could be seen, it did lead into a sort of spiralling stair with very broad steps, it had clearly been made so that animals could walk there without having any problems. In a sort of container by the start of the stair there were torches stored and Kulkar did light up one with his flint and steel. "Let's go, according to what I know there ought to be a sort of restroom lower down"

Resh'kha hoped that he was right, her body felt as if it weighed several tonnes and her head hurt. At least the monsters couldn't follow them now, they would have to wander around the canyon. The stair was not very steep at all, you could walk normally and it was easy for the horses too, the animals were exhausted and hungry and Geir did look worried. "We still have many days left of travel aye? I don't think our steeds will last that long unless there are oats and hay stored in here somewhere"

The cliff did have some openings here and there, tiny windows which let in fresh air and light but as they got further down the light did disappear and the air became raw and a bit mouldy. But they did find the room Kulkar had spoken off, a huge chamber with some primitive bunks and huge troths filled with a sort of mix of grains and some hay. The hay was dry and old but still edible and so were the grains, oddly enough. Resh'kha had expected it all to have gone bad due to moisture and rodents but it was rather fresh. Kulkar did look proud. "Protective spells sister orc, very strong protective spells. The makers of this were experts at just that, conserving stuff for a long time. Too bad they weren't as good at actually building."

The room had been in use, there was no doubt about that. A few pieces of clothing were left hanging on the bunks and a pair of boots stood underneath one of them. Also, there were scribblings on the wall, in the dwarven alphabet. Resh'kha did find it fascinating and Dharan did grin and offered to translate. "There were guards placed here at all times and I bet they got bored."

Resh'kha had to grin. "I can understand that, what does it say?"

Dharan did giggle. "This one here says; Togush loves to ride Bharan. And this one ; Gagesh is the worst arsehole known to dwarvenkind, may his beard catch fire"

Resh'kha laughed. "Must have been an officer perhaps?"

Dharan nodded. "Aye, the name is from the upper class so I bet he was a bit of a bad one"

They did feed the horses and luckily there was water there, in a small well behind the bunks. It wasn't much but enough and everybody sat down to eat and rest. Resh'kha did lay down, her head was spinning and she felt a bit nauseous. Kulkar did sit down next to her. "Rest sister orc, you need it. The powers work through you now, you need to learn how to distribute your strength"

Resh'kha nodded and closed her eyes. Floth'bha did take her hand. "I will sit here, just sleep if you need to"

Resh'kha sighed and allowed herself to drift off, it felt heavenly.

When she did awaken she realized that she had slept for quite a while, the others slept too and just Floth'bha was awake. It was probably nigh time for outside of the tiny window on the wall there was just darkness. Resh'kha did sit up, her headache had dissipated and she felt a lot better. Floth'bha did hand over a bowl with stew. "Here, I made it from dried meat and vegetables, we need something good now"

Resh'kha did eat all of it, it was rather good and very filling and she felt her strength return to her with each mouthful. Floth'bha was whispering not to awaken the others. "We will wait here until the sun rises, we all need the rest and Kulkar is not sure of the state of the tunnels we are to enter. He wants to do it in the daytime"

446

Resh'kha did frown. "What is the difference? It is dark in there no matter what?"

Floth'bha did shrug. "Yes, but there can be dark powers within such places, Kulkar is afraid of trolls, and other beasts"

Resh'kha did swallow. "Other beasts?"

Floth'bha did just shrug. "Don't ask me!"

Resh'kha did sit there awake for some hours so Floth'bha could rest and when the sun did start to rise they prepared to move on. The horses were well rested but now they were lacking one and they did place their supplies on the riding horses so Osbord could take the pack animal. He wasn't too glad for it didn't have a saddle but it was at least rideable. The stair did continue downwards and now they were below the bottom of the gorge, it felt claustrophobic having that much rock over her head but Resh'kha did push on. The stair ended in a sort of wide chamber which was rectangular in shape and not very embellished and a tunnel did lead out of it. Kulkar was grinning. "I told you so, we can get back onto the plains from here"

Geir made a grimace and Resh'kha did understand him very well.

They started to walk and the tunnel did tilt upwards and it was rather steep at times, then it would become almost flat again and Kulkar did explain that it was because of the different layers of rock. Some were harder to get through than others. They had walked for what felt like an eternity when Kulkar stopped and raised his torch a bit. In front of them in the dust was something grey and white and Resh'kha did gasp when she realized that it was the outer shell of a sort of insect. The size of a large pony. It had been dead for a very long time and was so brittle that a mere touch made it fall apart but she didn't want to meet the living version for sure.

They had reached a little higher when they heard something which weren't natural for a tunnel at all, it was a sort of wailing sound and Kulkar did grasp his axe and looked a bit nervous. Resh'kha did walk up to him. "What is it?"

Kulkar frowned and made a grimace. "Troll, that can only be a troll"

Resh'kha did sigh. Brilliant, just what they needed, more danger to slow them down.

The weather had turned against them rather soon, they had barely come more than a few miles away from the city when heavy sleet and strong winds caused problems. Wenja had bid Sefa farewell and gotten several hugs from the others as well and she felt like weeping but knew that she couldn't. She had to stay strong. Around the city the animals were still gathered and it didn't seem as if they would leave, even when she was. Frostfoot did gallop over but didn't do anything except greet them with a loud whinny, then he did run back to lead the other predators and Wenja was almost glad that he would stay and help protect the city.

Their group had left before dawn and with them they brought two pack horses, they had to travel light and Wenja was sitting up with the others. She wasn't trained enough for this sort of trip yet and she just hoped that she wouldn't slow them down.

The terrain was easy to begin with and luckily there weren't that many beasts there now, all had been drawn away by the brave dwarves and their friends and it was a relief but Ahravan didn't trust that there weren't any around. All of them wore good clothing now, warm and solid and Wenja had been persuaded into a set of warm pants underneath her riding skirts. She also wore thick tunics, a warm jacket and a cloak so she shouldn't feel cold but she didn't really like it. They were all armed and she felt relatively safe but she didn't look forward to this journey at all. Flint did run next to them and Ahravan had given the great stallion a sort of armour, a thick leather blanket covered with small metal rings. It would protect the torso and the horse had been trained to wear it so it didn't impede him in any way. Wenja did try to enjoy the landscape but it was hard, she had too many thoughts in her head so she just leaned back against Rhawan and dozed off. Ahravan did ride the huge unicorn and it didn't allow others to mount it so Ahravan had brought a couple of extra horses for the journey, strong geldings and mares which could run for days. Wenja was impressed by the huge animal and knew that it would fight just like Flint if something happened. She did fall asleep after just a little, and she didn't even dream.

Back in the city the people were going on with their everyday lives, they were gathering to talk and gossip and share information and the dwarves had quickly gotten organized into groups. The dwarves were often members of different guilds and right now some of the females were gathering outside of the old temple. They were given the task of remembering important dates and making sure that celebrations and such weren't forgotten and they wanted to prepare the temple for a festival which hadn't been held for the last centuries but were due soon. They entered the temple but stopped right away, staring with huge eyes. The statue of the giant cat was gone, as if it never had been there and they looked at each other with huge eyes. What in the name of every deity was going on? A giant statue doesn't just get up and walk away on its own and there was no way anybody would have been able to get it through the doors. One of the females did wander over to the pedestal where it had stood and stared at it, the dust was gone and the stone smooth and flawless, without even a scratch. But she did see something and did lean inn and took the small pieces of something and lifted it. It was hair, black silky hair from some sort of fur and they all let out a gasp. Whatever had happened in there, they were sure the gods had reached out and done the impossible.

Out on the plains Ahravan and the others kept riding through the night, they only made very short stops to let the horses drink and Ahravan was trying to determine the right direction to take. The mountain range was wild and very tall and they knew little about it. The clan of the snow bear had come from further west and they never ventured that far into the wilderness and thus Ahravan had to trust his instincts on this one. He felt insecure but didn't allow it to show and he just hoped that they would avoid any sort of problems. As they made stops to eat he did use the stars to navigate and one of the older elves there had said that the cliff was said to be in a spot where the great red star was straight north and the constellation of the spider would be due east. That meant that it was rather far north and Ahravan wondered how long it would take them to get there.

They had ridden for two days when Khirhien did turn his horse around and charged backwards, riding very hard. Wenja was shocked but Rhawan did just shrug. "We have been followed for most of the day"

Wenja frowned. "What?!"

The rider did disappear behind a low hill and when he did re-emerge he did tow another rider behind him, holding the reins. Wenja didn't see who it was, the figure was covered with furs and rode a large long coated horse. Ahravan did ride over to greet their pursuer and he did stare at her with narrow eyes. "So, you wasn't happy staying behind?"

Wenja did see who it was now, it was Yalaih and she gaped and blinked. "Yalaih? What…"

The young elven maiden made a grimace. "Listen, I have lost everything, all of my family. I want to be a part of this, I want to help. The monsters killed my parents, it is my right to seek revenge"

Ahravan sighed. "Good, right, so it is, but you do obey orders from now on, is that clear?"

Yalaih did nod and Wenja saw the determined expression on her face and knew that Ahravan couldn't make her turn back. Wenja felt a small spark of relief, she wouldn't be the only female on this expedition after all.

The young elf did ride at the back of the group now, and she had brought lots of equipment which was tied to her horse, she did of course know how to survive within the mountains and thus she could in fact be useful to them. Ahravan had brought the great war hammer he had gotten from Yalaih's father and Wenja knew that he intended on using it if he had to. They hadn't seen any monsters since they left and it was a good thing but they had come across evidence of them having been there. Huge packs of slaughtered animals, torn to shreds. In one place they found the remains of a group of travellers, their bones scattered around like some broken jigsaw puzzle. It made bile rise in Wenja's mouth and she had to look away. Ahravan didn't say anything and Rhawan tried to act as if he didn't feel anything at all, he failed for Wenja knew him now and knew how affected he was.

But they did finally find a place to rest and it was a cave not far from a river. They had reached the outskirts of the mountains by now, rolling hills with some steeper smaller cliffs and Wenja saw the silhouette of the mountains and felt terribly small and terribly insignificant. This part of the mountain range was dominated by very steep mountains with narrow valleys in between and also some very fast flowing rivers. In the summer

450

the rivers were very dangerous since they could suddenly swell due to rain elsewhere and nobody wanted to get caught by a flash flood. The cave they had found wasn't very large and it was more of an overhang than a cave but it did provide them with shelter. Wenja was feeling a bit tired, she wasn't used to sitting on a horse for that long and her legs felt like jelly each time she had to dismount. Ahravan did keep watch as Rhawan did cook and the others did prepare the camp for the night. Yalaih had brought her own sleeping pelts and laid them out, she too appeared to be very sleepy and Wenja did smile at her. "Why did you follow us?"

Yalaih did sigh. "I had to, I have lost everything and I want to make myself useful, and maybe avenge my family."

Wenja frowned. "Only that?"

Yalaih did look down. "Yes, well, I had a dream…It was strange but…I saw them all again, my brothers and my mother and father and…"

Yalaih did bite her lower lip. "We see such dreams as bad omens, to see those who has died in dreams mean that they are calling for you to join them. "

Wenja gasped. "Yalaih, you shouldn't have come then, this journey is dangerous!"

The she elf just shook her head. "I have no choice Wenja, if death calls for me I cannot escape, no matter where I am. Better do something important and maybe make a difference"

Wenja couldn't argue with that, she just sent Yalaih a faint grin and nodded at Rhawan who came with some food. The porridge he had cooked wasn't too bad but it wasn't exactly gourmet cuisine either, bland was what described it best. All ate though and with some appetite too. Wenja did crawl into her sleeping furs and Ahravan did join her, he wasn't to stay awake and guard them until later and so he did curl up next to her and fell asleep fast. She felt comforted by his warmth and huge frame so close to her and Wenja did sleep too. She didn't even notice when Ahravan did get up and Rhawan did take his place after some hours.

The next morning they broke camp and rode on as soon as the sun got up. Wenja was sitting up with Ahravan who rode one of the spare horses now to let the unicorn run free. The animal could sense danger and he did trust the old battle scarred stallion to warn them if anything did approach them. But after just a short while they found something odd, and it was worrisome. A dead goblin which was laying over some bare rocks, obviously crushed by some unknown force and also torn apart. The goblin was rather large, the size of a human and it wore what could only be war paint. The body covered with odd patterns in a dark green tone and it had carried a sort of primitive weapon too. An axe made from stone with a wooden handle, the stone head had been attached to the wood with sinews and glue and it laid next to the body. Khirhien did pick up the axe and stared at it with narrow eyes. "This is poor work, but goblins here?"

Ahravan did frown. "Not normal, they usually stay within their cities and hate daylight."

Wenja hissed at the sight, the goblin was greyish green in colour with thin dark hair and a face only a mother could love. The features were oddly sharp and bony and the eyes were small and beady. It did remind her a bit of a giant rat if she was to be absolutely honest with herself. Gochil did check the body. "He was attacked by something, something huge. These are claw marks, it could be a S'haga but the size of the marks? If it is then it is a giant one"

Ayhrandur had lifted his bow and the elf did look intense. "There could be such cats here, do you think it can cause us problems?"

He looked at Ahravan who shook his head. "No, we are many and armed, these predators are smart, they go for easy prey and a single goblin isn't even a challenge. Odd thing it didn't eat him though, but maybe he was too smelly even for a S'haga"

Rhawan did chuckle. "Yes, the carcass does stink, I do wonder what he was doing here though, alone in the valleys"

Ahravan made his horse move again. "Most likely gotten lost and ended up wandering around."

Rhawan did toss one last glance at the dead body, he didn't like the idea of goblins, none of them did. Wenja did ride with him now and she turned her head. "I have never seen a goblin before, I didn't think they were that large?"

Rhawan did smile. "They are different than gnomes when it comes to size but otherwise they are very similar. Filthy creatures with little intelligence and they are always malicious. They will eat anything they come across and are like magpies when it comes to shiny objects, they will nick everything which isn't bolted down"

Wenja had to grin, she knew how fond those birds were of shiny things. "But are all as large as that one back there?"

Rhawan shrugged. "No, most are smaller, but not as short as a dwarf, often very lanky looking and sickly too. They stay within their cities all the time and don't venture outside unless they have to, direct sunlight does hurt them."

Wenja had to make a grimace. "But what do they eat then?"

Rhawan copied her grimace. "Everything they can get their hands on? There are fish in some of the underground rivers, there are insects too in the cave systems and mushrooms and fungi of different sorts, and then of course other weaker goblins. They will cannibalise those who are too weak. I guess they are heading steadily for their own destruction, inbreeding and lack of sunshine usually takes its toll"

Wenja hissed. "I can understand that, it did look very sickly"

Rhawan did steer his horse after Khirhien's, he did try to make their tracks as hard to spot as possible. "Yes, they aren't very strong but if they come in numbers they are very tenacious. One or two on the other hand will always flee, they will not attack unless they are sure that they are going to win!"

Ahravan did interrupt them. "We will need to get off the horses soon, if I am not wrong we have a steep hill ahead"

Rhawan did shut up and Wenja did see that Yalaih did stare at the landscape ahead, she looked as if she did find the landscape rather intriguing. She was after all used to this sort of nature and she seemed to be at ease much more than the others. They did indeed enter a steep area and it was rather icy and difficult terrain so they dismounted just to be on the safe side. Wenja was allowed to ride though, she did cling to the saddle and missed having Rhawan behind her for he did keep her very warm and safe. The valley did turn eastwards and became even more ragged and Ahravan was a bit worried. Finding the right area was in itself going to be a challenge and getting lost in there wasn't very smart. The wind was howling between the cliffs and brought the temperature down, everybody did cover themselves up rather well.

For the next days they did follow this valley and then another which was leading them north and they did see tracks as if from an army, heading south. It had to be all beasts and they had left remains of prey and muck here and there and Ahravan spat and was glad they had gone. It would have been very hard to do this if the area had been teeming with such monsters, at least in the numbers they had experienced lately.

But the mountains weren't completely deserted after all, one evening they suddenly met a sort of odd six limbed beasts with large square shaped heads and nasty looking teeth and luckily they got too stunned to react before Khirhien and Ayhrandur with the help of Ahravan and his steed killed them all. It was just five in the pack and they were slow and very heavy built and Ahravan guessed that they simply had been left behind since they couldn't keep up with the others. Whoever created these beasts weren't always very smart when it came to design.

But the discovery of monsters lead to them moving differently, now one would ride ahead and keep an eye open and often that task did fell on Yalaih since she was used to such landscapes and very good at detecting movement from a great distance. She did prevent them from being seen several times as they met other packs and worryingly enough the numbers seemed to increase again, as if this was some sort of second wave ready to be unleashed upon the plains.

Yalaih did also hunt and brought fresh meat almost every day and often it was hares or some sort of rather large plump ptarmigan like bird which did taste a bit bitter but not bad. She seemed to flourish and would smile and crack jokes and it seemed as if the fact that she did have a task to do now was what she did need.

Wenja was taken very well care off, Rhawan and Ahravan would make sure she never got too cold and they would also make sure that she got the food she needed and she was very grateful, to her the journey didn't mean much hardship at all. By now they were far into the mountains and Ahravan did guess that they were approaching the right area, the mountains were less steep now and the valleys did seem to tilt northwards. But they couldn't be too sure, they could only pray that luck was on their side.

Then they met the first real obstacle, the narrow valley was blocked by a waterfall and behind it a frozen lake and they had to use axes to create a path they could use up the frozen water. It did take them two days to get up there and the horses were terrified and shaky. Wenja wasn't allowed to ride this time and she didn't want to either, the waterfall wasn't that high but a fall would kill you nonetheless and she did climb up feeling the cold from the ice like something almost touchable. The landscape on the other side of the waterfall was even more ragged than the one they had previously passed through, the valleys canyons and filled with obstacles of all sorts. The river was frozen so they would often have to use it and they did move forth slowly but steadily. The snow was rather deep in places and they saw tracks of packs of what could only be packs of monsters, it seemed as if they had moved through these valleys just days earlier and it was impossible to determine the numbers.

But monsters weren't the only inhabitants of these high passes and early one day they did encounter a small herd of rather large wild sheep, all with impressive horns and Ahravan was a bit shocked by the sight. The animals shouldn't have been this high above the tree line at this time of the year and many of them were visibly weak and starved. Something had most definitely disturbed them and forced them away from the normal grazing areas. The rams were gathering in a wedge formation to protect the ewes if these strangers were predators but Ahravan did manage to calm the animals down. The lead ewe was an old and experienced one and Ahravan got an image of something very dangerous prowling the hills and lower valleys. He did look a bit nervous as he did mount the unicorn once more. "Whatever awaits us at that cliff, it has awakened more than just monsters."

Rhawan did frown. "What do you mean?"

Ahravan sighed. "They have seen fell trolls, I thought they were extinct ages ago!"

Wenja did understand that fell trolls were bad, whatever they were. "Are there any here?"

Her voice was low and Ahravan did shrug. "I have no idea, could be. But they prefer darkness or dusk, they aren't as sensitive to light as other trolls but they don't appreciate direct sunlight at all. I am glad we are many, and have been warned"

Rhawan did nod. "So no nights without guards being set up, and damn it, we ought to burn some wood but we can't, it will attract everything within the area"

Wenja did look confused and Rhawan did smile. "They fear fire"

Ahravan did ride on and Wenja saw the tension within him, the telltale signs of him being nervous. He didn't show it openly but she could read his body language now and he was scared. The group did spread out and when they made camp that night Ahravan did decide that two and two would stand guard. Wenja didn't have to do that and she felt a bit spoiled as she went to bed that night. She had slept for some hours when she suddenly woke up, a sound had jerked her out of her sleep and she sat up. It was a sort of roar, hoarse and strangely guttural. Rhawan was by her side, he was silent and like a shadow in the dark. He whispered. "It is a fell troll"

Wenja felt ice cold. "Is it dangerous to us?"

Rhawan nodded. "Yes, they are way more aggressive than normal trolls, and hard to kill. And very bloodthirsty"

Wenja did shiver, Rhawan helped her get up and she put her cloak on, feeling chilled to the bone. "If it does attack stay behind us, do not leave the camp!"

There was a second roar, it did sound almost triumphant and was followed by several odd burping sounds. Rhawan cussed. "It has smelled us, curses!"

Ahravan was holding the war hammer he had gotten from Yalaih's father and the others had armed themselves too. Rhawan held his bow and had some arrows ready, with very long pointy heads. The roar came once more, and it was close, they heard something massive moving and Ahravan did gesture to the others there, making sure they were ready. "Aim for its eyes, it is the only vulnerable point of the head"

Wenja felt her heart beating wildly and she heard that the horses were moving, nervous and ready to flee. Then there was another roar heard,

456

and a sort of heavy dull sound of something hard hitting flesh and a wail of agony which didn't come from any human throat. There was growling and roars and the sounds of heavy blows and in the end a sort of gargling hiss which did die down. Then there was silence, absolute silence.

Ahravan did hold his breath, they stared at each other. Something had attacked the troll as it was about to attack them and what in the name of every God had it been? Ahravan did nod at Rhawan. "Forth!"

It was an order and Rhawan did disappear into the darkness, he was extremely hard to see due to his colouring and Wenja held her breath. He was gone for several minutes, then they heard a sort of soft whistle and Ahravan did grasp Wenja by the shoulder and allowed her to follow them, surrounded by him and Khirhien. They stopped just hundred meters from the camp, the remains of the troll were spread out over the rocks and Wenja felt nauseous. The stench was awful and Rhawan stood there and tried to avoid retching. Wenja saw pieces of what could only be thick matted fur, it did look black but probably wasn't and she did almost step on a severed hand. It was almost human but extremely elongated with strange hard callouses everywhere. She didn't see as well in the dark as the elves so she had to have things explained to her. Rhawan coughed. "Whatever killed it, it did a heck of a job of it. This place is covered with blood"

Ahravan was impressed. "What in the name of the Goddess can kill such a troll?"

Khirhien shrugged and the others did also look perplexed. "It must have been massive"

Wenja got a strange sensation of being watched, she did turn her head around, slowly. There as only darkness but for a fleeting glimpse she could have sworn that she did see a couple of glowing golden eyes up ahead, very large and very fierce looking.

She swallowed hard. "I didn't know that trolls had fur?"

Ahravan did caress her cheek with a finger, as if to calm her down. "Fell trolls do have thick fur, they are filthy creatures and I have never seen one before."

Wenja cringed, the smell was still very pungent and they did turn around and returned to the camp. "I think something is watching over us, let us hope it does continue"

Rhawan did only throw a swift glance at her but he did nod and Ahravan did sit down. "We rest until sunrise, we have to keep moving, guardian or no guardian!"

Resh'kha was holding her breath, she had never actually seen trolls and had no idea of what to anticipate and the dwarves did look nervous enough to be ready to flee. The wailing sound was heard again and Kulkar tilted his head. "We have to keep moving, heads up and don't let anything take you by surprise."

The tunnel did turn slightly and Floth'bha had stringed her bow and had an arrow knocked, she nodded at Resh'kha who did step forwards, very slowly and silently. The young orc held her axe firmly and peeked forth, the tunnel wasn't completely dark since they carried torches and there were some sort of moss growing in spots which did give off a faint green light. The tunnel was blocked, not by rocks but by bodies. The source of the wailing was the only troll moving, a smaller less stocky creature sitting on the ground. Resh'kha realized that it had to be a female and it was naked and covered with a thick crust of dust and dried mud. It made the body look as if it had been made from mud altogether. The troll was rocking back and forth, holding something within its grasp and Kulkar whispered. "Beware, even females are horribly strong"

Floth'bha did nod and her eyes were narrow. "It is an infant"

Resh'kha did realize that too, the female did hold a deceased infant in her arms and she felt her heart drop. The grief was obviously very strong and very real and it was probably the female's own baby. Dharan did swallow, his beard did move a bit and revealed the movement. "The others are dead, look at them"

Resh'kha did move forth a bit and the troll raised her head and saw them, or rather, noticed them. The eyes were very small and black and it seemed as if the troll used its nose more than its eyes. She made a wail again and bowed forth, hiding the tiny body from sight.

458

Kulkar did move forth a bit, his hands visible and he did stare at the floor the whole time. It was the way you approach a nervous animal. He did almost sneeze. "They have been dead for a couple of days, the bodies are…bloated"

Resh'kha did follow him, the bodies lay in a pile and appeared to have collapsed on top of each other. They were indeed bloated and grotesque with tongues sticking out of the mouths and bulging eyes and the bellies were distended and sickly green. Resh'kha had never seen anything that disgusting. The female let out another wail and shook herself from one side to the other, her pain obvious. She didn't move at all as Kulkar did move past her and got close to the dead trolls, he did poke at a couple of them and made a grimace. "They didn't die from any sort of injury, this must be disease"

Resh'kha remembered what Floth'bha had told her of the journey through the dwarven roads and the half orc was wide eyed and seemed to remember too. "It is the same disease?!"

She did tell Kulkar of the incident and the old dwarf did nod. "Probably, but how?"

The female troll did sob and laid the infant down on the ground in front of her legs, Resh'kha did see that the body was very stocky and yet humanoid in general shape, just very short limbed. She placed her arms around herself and wailed and Kulkar did something odd, he did scratch something into the dust of the floor, a sort of symbol and the female did tilt her head and made a clicking sound. Then she did draw a symbol of her own in the dust. Kulkar answered and Resh'kha realized that the dwarf in fact was communicating with the troll. After a while he did turn around with a faint smile. "She will not leave this place, but she won't hinder us in any way."

Geir and the two other men did cringe. "Won't she die then?"

Kulkar nodded. "Yes, but is her will. She has lost everything. Trolls are primitive but their clan is everything to them, she will succumb to her grief soon enough."

Floth'bha did wet her lips. "How did they become ill?"

Kulkar did sigh. "They found a sort of jewel, it was hollow and they broke it apart and then they all became sick. She is the only one who haven't died yet, why she doesn't know"

Resh'kha did stare at the grieving female, the troll couldn't be that old and her body was strong but Resh'kha felt something strange there. She did touch her amulet and suddenly she saw light swirling around the trolls, as if they were surrounded by a sort of living sentient mist. The light was spinning around the female as if it was frustrated and then it raced around again. Resh'kha did realize what it was, a sort of spirit. Had it made the trolls ill? Was it malicious then? The light did stop, it did hover like glowing mist above the grieving female and Resh'kha got a strong sensation of sorrow, regret. The thing was sentient whatever it was and it didn't mean to harm anyone. It just needed its home back and Resh'kha did whisper to Kulkar. "The heart stone, bring it forth"

Kulkar did look at her with disbelief but opened his bag and held the gem up. The light did suddenly start to pulse and Resh'kha felt a strong sense of relief and gratitude coming from it, then it sort of disappeared into the gem and was gone. There was an audible poof and everybody stared at her. She swallowed. "It was a spirit, a sort of elemental I think. It had lived in the ground and the trolls did disturbed it. It didn't mean to harm anyone but for some reason trolls get sick when in contact with such a spirit."

Kulkar stared at the heart stone. "And now it is within the heart stone? Is it wise?"

Resh'kha did nod. "Yes, it wanted a new home, I can feel that it wishes to help us"

The dwarf frowned but didn't say anything more, he did trust her new abilities. Dharan was more practical. "We do still have a pile of corpses to pass by?"

Floth'bha did scoff. "We have room, let's go, this place gives me the creeps"

The troll female didn't move from her spot but she did suddenly reach out towards Resh'kha, she held something in her hand and Resh'kha did take it hesitantly. It was a very small and very primitive looking bone flute, with just three holes and it did look as if a child had carved it. The

460

troll did make a whining sound and Resh'kha did put the tiny flute into her pocket. "I will take care of it"

The female made a gesture as if she was playing and leaned forth again, drawing something in the dirt. Resh'kha blinked, it was hard to tell but it did look a bit like a sort of snake? With legs? Kulkar did frown. "Centipedes, damn it, I was afraid of something like that"

Resh'kha did grunt. "Centipedes aren't that dangerous?"

Kulkar let out a humourless laughter. "Ah, the type you think of aren't no, smaller than a hand and hiding underneath rocks. But imagine them longer than a grown man and with pincers strong enough to cut through steel"

Resh'kha did gasp and Geir cringed. "Okay, we have been warned, let's go"

They did manage to get their steeds by the dead and the tunnel was relatively straight now, but rather narrow. Floth'bha did pet Resh'kha on her back. "You are coming into your own friend, your powers are waxing"

Resh'kha did blush slightly. "I just…it feels more natural now"

Floth'bha did grin. "Of course, you are here for a reason, I bet this is it, to become a good shaman"

They moved forth and now Resh'kha was allowed to lead. The tunnel was long and winding and some places very wet too. It was unpleasant but she did feel a draft all of a sudden and a sting of cold. The tunnel did turn abruptly and they saw a huge cave in front of them. It was natural, filled with stalagmites and the roof was way up there. A small river did cross it and the tunnel did continue on the other side. Kulkar did take the lead again, he did stare at the walls and the roof and his expression was serious. "This cave is unstable, see those cracks in the ceiling? This is what we dwarves call bad rock"

Geir did touch the wall of the tunnel and the rock was indeed rather soft and fragile, as if it was rotten. The dwarf did wander forth, very carefully. "We have to cross fast, the ones who dug the tunnel must have found this cave by accident, it isn't safe at all. The river is to blame for that, the water dissolves the very rock itself"

They walked on but the cave was surprisingly large and the river was not very deep but freezing cold. They had managed to get across when suddenly Than let out a shriek and he fell down as if struck by something hard. The reason was suddenly very visible, a sort of dark oily thing did protrude from his back and it did in fact lift him up again, swinging him back and forth. The man was screaming in agony and flailing around but then he suddenly went limp and Geir let out a roar and ran forth. He did swing his blade with might and cut through the dark snake with one move, the thing collapsed onto the floor, blood spurting from it and Kulkar was swearing. "Leave him, he is dead. It was a giant leech, this cave is dangerous"

Geir touched Than gently, the face was ghostly pale and Resh'kha felt sick to the gut, the body seemed to have shrunk, as if the leech had managed to suck up all body fluids within a few seconds. It had been laying in waiting behind a rock and Resh'kha did shudder, it was disgusting.

They didn't have time to bury the dead man, they just had to leave him there and Geir didn't like it but there was no way around it. They had to get going. They reached the tunnel on the other side but now Resh'kha did see what Kulkar had meant by giant centipedes, the tunnel was crawling with them. Each one perhaps five foot long and extremely fast and they were heading towards them. The dwarves did gasp and looked petrified and Resh'kha did realize that dwarves do fear these creatures. The horses and ponies did whinny and trample and Resh'kha did remember the flute. She had been given it for a reason and she did find the small instrument and put it to her lips, tried to make a sound. At first she only managed to create some very thin notes and they did make everybody cringe but then she hit the right tones and a sort of harmony could be heard. It was atonal and odd and terribly shrill and yet it was obviously meant to be that way for it did make the centipedes go haywire. The nasty critters did shriek in agony, banging themselves against the walls, attacking each other and tearing into their own flesh with their pincers.

Resh'kha continued to play, the sound was horrible but they endured since it did chase the beasts away. Before long the centipedes were either

462

dead or dying and they did manage to pass them by. Dharan did cut off the pincers of some of them and put them carefully into a small sack. "They are poisonous and can be used as a weapon"

Resh'kha nodded, she felt a bit shocked still, the adrenaline hadn't left her yet. "You are familiar with those beasts?"

Dharan nodded. "Yes, we dwarves hate them, they tend to occupy the cities we build, creeping inn and feeding off our livestock and sometimes our young. We hate them"

Resh'kha did sigh. "Understandable"

Kulkar did smile. "We will soon get out of here, I can smell fresh air"

Resh'kha felt like hugging him, she was so tired of the darkness now.

Kulkar was right, a short half an hour later they did see that the tunnel did end in open air and everybody did speed up. They entered the plains again from a cliff and behind them they could see the canyon in the distance. Kulkar did caress the bag with the heart stone. "It will still draw upon the monsters, they will have to get around the canyon so now we have to get as much distance between us and them as possible"

Geir did sigh, he did mourn Than and Osbord did look gloomy. "We shouldn't have left him, no honour in that, no proper funeral"

Kulkar shrugged. "I am sorry, but it would have been the death of us had we stayed, the cave had more leeches for sure and the roof was very unstable."

Now they had a horse for Osbord since Than was dead and they did ride on, Resh'kha was glad she didn't have to hide them at the moment. The monsters were way behind them but would soon catch up again and they did allow their steeds to eat for a while before heading further westwards.

Kulkar did look very snug, he was pleased with the progress and Resh'kha did admire the landscape. It was flat but here and there grooves of small trees could be seen and in the distance they saw a row of mountains. The dwarf did grin at her. "The forest lay in that direction, within the mountains. It is a hidden valley but we can find it, it is rather…peculiar"

Resh'kha didn't doubt his words at all, if the forest was to destroy the beasts it had to be something spectacular indeed. The distance didn't seem to be that great but Resh'kha knew that the clear air made it seem closer than it was. She was afraid that the monsters would catch up with them soon, but they couldn't push their steeds too hard. Resh'kha felt that she was regaining her strength now that she didn't have to shield them the whole time, it was a good thing but the Gods alone knew for how long it would last.

It didn't last long, the monsters were not creatures which needed rest nor sleep, they were relentless and unstoppable. They had ridden through the night and crossed over a low crested hill when Geir did raise a hand and pointed at the horizon. They saw a dark line followed by dust and Resh'kha did moan. It was the beasts, and there were even more of them than before, thousands! It did look like a giant herd of some sort of animal from a distance, like a herd of buffalo or antelope but these were not natural. Resh'kha saw the speed with which they were moving and she felt a shiver running down her spine. There was no way they would reach the forest in time, the beasts would catch up with them within a mere day's ride. She couldn't hope to shield them from this many monsters, she wasn't trained, she didn't know her new powers and she did doubt herself. What in the name of the Gods was she to do now?

Floth'bha did see the expression within her eyes, she rode over and placed a hand on Resh'kha's knee. "You can do it sister, do not doubt yourself"

Resh'kha did swallow hard. "I don't know how!"

Floth'bha did stare at her, eyes hard. "You are a shaman now, what would Balgar have done?"

Kulkar did ride up to them too, he did nod in the direction of their pursuers. "Remember, nature does abhor these creatures."

Resh'kha did whimper. "Oh Gods, I…"

She did stare at the naked landscape around her, was there anything there at all? The land was locked in the long sleep of winter but…She saw the snowdrifts which had gathered here and there and got an idea. She got down from Steelhoof and grasped some snow in her hand. It was powdery and fluffy and light and she tried to concentrate. The amulet was glowing against her skin and she closed her eyes and took a deep breath. The wind did pick up a bit, was this working? She could only hope that it was, snow started to drift around them and Kulkar did grin. "A snowstorm, it will block us from their view for sure"

Resh'kha was panting, wind was howling over the plains now, lifting a wall of swirling snow and she felt strange, stretched somehow. The snow was very cold and the wall not at all transparent. Kulkar did nod, his beard did almost camouflage the movement. "Good, let us ride. The wall will hide us for a while"

Resh'kha did get up onto her buffalo again and they did ride, it felt better not seeing their pursuers but the snow wouldn't hold them back for very long. Resh'kha did stare ahead, the day was coming to an end soon and it would get dark, she felt a surge of despair. "How far away is the forest?"

Kulkar did grunt. "Three days hard ride, no less"

Resh'kha did make a grimace. "We won't make it, it is impossible. They will catch up with us"

Kulkar did shrug. "They haven't yet, the gods are with us sister orc, do not doubt them. The monsters have to be destroyed, remember that. If they are freed from the pull from the heart stone they will turn around and kill every living soul on the plains, and then the mountain areas will be next. The population of the highlands have no chance, we have to complete our task. No price is too great."

Resh'kha did shiver, she could imagine what would happen if the monsters did find her tribe, it would be slaughter. Orcs are strong and fierce but even they would be no match against such hordes. "The forest, something lives there yes? Something which will destroy the beasts? Do you know what it is?"

Kulkar shook his head. "Only that it is something which was released when the gate was opened the last time, something on the side of good and yet terribly dangerous. It has changed the forest"

Resh'kha had a hard time imagining what could change a forest and how that could happen but alright, she did trust Kulkar. The darkness did fall very fast and they did ride in a line now, Kulkar did hold the lead still and he was very determined. The ponies the dwarves did ride were tough but the animals were getting more and more tired since there wasn't that much food to be found and they couldn't really stop that often. The snowstorm was behind them and Resh'kha didn't believe that it would delay the monsters very much at all, it would most certainly slow them down for a while but it wouldn't stop them at all.

The idea of starting a wild fire did touch her mind but the thin dead grass wasn't going to burn and the snowdrifts would stop any fire very fast. They had ridden for a few hours when they heard distant howls and Resh'kha whimpered. The beasts were close again, and there was yet a long way to go. "Oh gods help us"

She only whispered it and wished that the power had been given someone else than her, she had no idea of what to do with it!

They pushed their steeds to their limits and Resh'kha did try to shield them again but it didn't work, the magic wasn't strong enough at the moment and she was too scared and confused to really be able to concentrate. Kulkar was swearing. "They will catch up with us soon, do something"

Resh'kha was sweating, trying to think. Then a memory suddenly slammed into her head, of herself as a youngling following her father on a hunting trip. He had shown her how to trap animals and told her a lot of tricks and now one of them did come to her mind, but it was a dangerous one and one which would require something almost unthinkable. She took a deep breath, was she strong enough? Could she trust herself enough to do this? She had to! She turned to Kulkar. "There is one thing I can do, but…"

The old dwarf did smile, a somewhat sad smile. "I know young one, I understand. You are right, know your enemy like yourself."

Resh'kha did watch as he did pull the pouch with the heart stone free from his belt. "You have to get to the forest and do not fear what you see there, stay strong, it will respect your strength"

Resh'kha did bite her lower lip. "I am not sure if I am strong enough…!"

Kulkar did grin. "We will find out soon enough won't we? Do it sister orc. We won't all make it to the forest but you have to, it is our only hope"

Resh'kha did turn to Floth'bha. "I will need you with me, to protect my back…"

Floth'bha did nod. "I am ready sister."

Resh'kha did stare at the small group. "I cannot shield us all, but I can camouflage you as beasts, for a while. Until they have passed you by"

Geir sent her a crooked grin. "Very smart young one, it will be dangerous but you are to become bait yourself, are you sure your beast can run fast enough?"

Resh'kha did nod. "He has to, there is no other way. You aren't fast enough and I cannot uphold a shield for several days, but for a few hours I can make the beasts believe that you are other beasts"

They did dismount and Kulkar did lead them to a small cliff, he did grin and told them to tie their ponies and horses to the cliff, then he did take out their tents and he and Dharan did form one large tent from the smaller ones and placed it over them all, both people and horses. The tent was dark and uneven in colour and didn't look that different from the cliff itself. Resh'kha did swallow, Floth'bha had traded her horse for the pack animal which was more rested than the one she had been riding and Resh'kha did gather her thoughts and tried to remember the feeling and scent of the monsters, the way they appeared as something utterly unnatural and terrifying. She then tried to place the same feeling over the tent and its inhabitants and the air did shiver a bit, she did step back and grinned. The tent did look like a piece of the rock now and if somebody got closer it felt as if there were monsters there. Hopefully the real ones wouldn't stop to investigate.

Kulkar did bow his head. "We will follow, when it is safe, have a safe journey sister orc, and may the goddess be with you"

Resh'kha got back up on her buffalo and she took a deep breath. "Stay safe friends, and do not move until the monsters have passed you by."

She put the pouch with the heart stone into her tunic next to the amulet and it felt alive, like a living thinking thing. Floth'bha did spur her horse and Resh'kha did follow her, the buffalo was fast too and they thundered out over the plains, heading for the mysterious forest which was hidden ahead of them.

Unta had walked for days, her feet were sore and her shoes were worn to shreds but it hadn't stopped her so far. She had a mission and she wasn't going to betray her former chief by failing. She had walked outside of the clan's hunting grounds now, and she had discovered that the mountains were changed. The animals were almost gone, there was a sort of eerie silence there which she hadn't encountered before and she saw tracks from strange beasts. There was a presence in the wind, a cold hissing voice and she refused to listen. She was just a female, a weak one who didn't possess any powers and the voice didn't bother with her, she just heard its echo and she knew by now that it was what had possessed the males and made them attack her tribe. She did grit her teeth together, she was not going to let it get away with its crime, that was for sure.

The valleys she followed now did lead her to the east, it felt right and she kept going even when her body felt like lead. Luckily her feet were hard since they didn't use shoes in the winter and she was well used to the cold. Her people were hardy and could survive the long winters very well. She had eaten a little of the provisions she had taken, she had to make sure that it would last so she ate only when her hunger became unbearable and she drank from the rivers when she did come across open water. But she was getting more and more nervous, there were goblins in the mountains here and she didn't like them. The elder did tell that goblins were evil creatures with wicked spirits and they would only serve their own interests. She had never seen a goblin before but the hunters had described them and when she saw a whole pack travelling through a valley she did immediately know what they were. There were perhaps a hundred of them and they were carrying weapons and acted as if they were under somebody's command. Unta didn't like that, goblins weren't supposed to act like that and she knew that they were normally way too egoistical to cooperate.

She had gotten far but she hadn't yet encountered this daughter of the goddess and she wondered when she would. But a sort of inner voice told her to be patient, that she would meet the chosen one soon enough. As Unta did travel along the valleys she used all her skills to avoid being detected by the goblins, she was a daughter of the mountains and knew how to hide and she had strong senses too. She didn't need fire to make food and she didn't need much sleep. The goblins were more active at night so she did always find some well-hidden crevice where she could rest for a couple of hours and she did even make sure to relieve herself on rock so nobody could see urine stains in the snow.

Unta felt that she was heading in the right direction and she did trust the goddess to lead her feet, she did know that her mission was a sacred one. Unta was perhaps not a person of importance in any way but now she had gotten some sort of dignity after all and she would not let go of it. It was better to die doing the right thing than to live doing nothing. She did miss her tribe after all, they had been her people but she had to stop that voice which was corrupting the other clans. Or at least, she had to do whatever she could to help stopping it. The daughter of the goddess would destroy it, she felt it in her heart and she was proud to help.

Unta was crossing a frozen river when she was discovered, it was bad luck for her senses got disturbed by a gust of wind and the goblins came along a narrow gorge she hadn't noticed. They did howl when they saw her and Unta cussed and ran, goblins did eat anything they could get their filthy paws upon and she didn't want to end up as dinner. But they did pursue her with zeal and she was perhaps used to the terrain and strong but her legs were short and she wasn't very fast. These goblins were rather large and strong and she felt the stench from them and her heart was galloping. She would rather stab herself with the blade of her dead chief than letting them get to her alive. There was one among the goblins which were larger than the rest, it was grotesque like them but there was some sort of sinister intelligence within the dark beady eyes. It did wear a sort of amour and it did yell something to the others. They didn't seem to like what he said but they seemed to obey. None of them did try to shoot at Unta with their primitive bows and the weapons weren't wielded. Unta realized that they wanted to capture her alive and the thought sent cold sweat down her back. She fought her way up a steep little hill and tried to make a run for some cliffs but suddenly there were hands grasping onto her clothing and she was thrown down. Unta did scream and she tried to punch at the leering goblins, she did hit one and felt how bone did shatter underneath her hard fist. Her people were extremely strong and she was used to hard work.

The goblins did howl and backed off and the large one did backhand her across the face. Unta was used to being treated with rough discipline, the older women had often hit her to make her obey, it wasn't anything new to her. She spat at it and the goblin did chuckle. Two of the others did hold her arms and the large one did search her clothes but didn't find anything of value except the knife she had taken from the dead chief.

It did say something and then it tore her fur clothes open. Unta realized what it wanted, she was a female and among goblins females are rare, they usually don't last long. She fought her panic, didn't know what to do but an odd calm did descend upon her. She could deal with this, it was all a part of the goddess plan. Unta was no stranger to rape, it was very common among her people that the males did take what they wanted whenever they wanted it, nobody saw anything odd about that at all. Her first time with a male had been like that, one of the young males had fancied her and the very day she had been recognized as an adult female he had attacked her by the lakeshore and taken her.

Unta had expected something like that to happen, it was part of their culture and even if it had hurt and been rather horrible it didn't turn her away from males. It wasn't his fault that he was a complete klutz and not very experienced. She had been forced many times and she had also bedded males out of her own free will many times and enjoyed it. This was no different, she could endure, it was all for a greater cause. The large goblin did get his own clothing out of the way and Unta would have laughed if she had dared to. The cock this creature did present wasn't very impressive at all, as a matter of fact Unta had seen immature lads with larger ones. But the goblin did not hesitate, it did pressed her legs aside and pushed inside and Unta did not try to resist, she realized that she would be safe or at least relatively so as long as she didn't struggle. She could hardly even feel him, it was pathetic and she would have spat at him in disgust if she had been able to. The other goblins stood there leering and drooling and she was only hoping that they wouldn't harm her physically. If they all were as miniscule as their leader she was rather sure she would be okay. The goblin did roar and the nasty face did twitch through his release. The others did chatter, trying to push forth and the large one did bare his teeth and growled. The message was clear, this one is mine!

Unta was thrown over its shoulder like a piece of meat and she managed to grasp her clothes and was carried off. The large one wanted her for himself and the others were growling and it was rather obvious that they were angry and jealous. Unta did use her eyes for all they were worth, they returned to the gorge and before long they entered a cave and Unta realized that this was a goblin fortress. It was a stinky dark place with little light and a stench of unimaginable things. The huge goblin did carry his quarry over his shoulder and Unta did pretend to be unconscious, her hair did hide her face and she did see that this city was rather well organized. She couldn't understand why, goblins weren't renowned for their prowess when it comes to anything except being nasty. The city was in several levels and she started to suspect that it originally had been a dwarven stronghold which had been abandoned before it was even finished. The tunnels she saw did end abruptly and the evenness of the floor and the lack of natural shapes were rather apparent. Her people did know about the dwarves, they did respect them but hadn't interacted with them for ages. Unta saw that the goblins wore armour and carried good weapons and they appeared to be scared of something or someone. What could transform goblins into an army? The large one carried her through some large halls, nobody tried to stop it and many did stare but none did even speak up. The Unta did see it, the reason why these goblins were so different from what she had been told by the elders. They had a leader, a real leader and it wasn't a goblin. It was a sort of orc half breed, a creature with dark skin and an impressive almost majestic stance. It had a thick mane of dark coarse hair and piercing golden eyes and it wore jewellery and nice robes. Unta felt cold, she felt what this was by sheer instinct. A servant of darkness, a follower of the voice, it's thrall.

The large goblin did carry Unta into a sort of dungeon which was closed off with an iron gate and she was dumped unceremoniously onto a layer of dirty straw. She was glad she had her clothes there for it was cold and damp. The goblin did hiss and pushed her down onto the straw, it did force her legs apart again and took her anew, grunting and gasping as it was fucking her fast and hard and it didn't last more than a minute. It did shudder and moan and then it pulled out and left, she heard the gate being closed.

Unta made a grimace of disgust, she felt warm seed dribbling down her thighs and she found some straw and did wipe it off before she got her clothes back on. She was done with her moon days, but she wasn't fertile so there was no chance of her conceiving a half goblin. That would have been a cause for suicide for sure. But as long as the large goblin did fancy her she was safe from the others and she felt that the daughter of the goddess would come her way, one way or the other. She did still have a small pack of food in her cloak and she could survive there for a long time as long as she had water. There was moisture dripping down the walls, she could lick that off the stone if need be. Unta was patient, her task was not done yet. She formed a sort of nest from the straw and sighed. The dungeon was very dark and the air chilly but she remembered that tall half breed and a sort of determination did form within her. That thing had to die, it had a hold of the goblins and without it they would return to their natural state, she was rather sure. If she got the chance to kill the tall leader she would, it was her duty.

Wenja was still shocked by the fact that something had killed that fell troll, but she also sensed that Rhawan was right, they did have something watching over them and it was something very powerful.

Ahravan did stand guard now and Rhawan did come to stay with her, he did crawl into the sleeping furs next to her and Wenja did curl up against him, she wanted the comfort of bodily contact and he did hold her close as they just laid there in silence. After a while she realized that he wanted more than just a little contact, she could feel that he was hard and he was breathing in a funny manner. She did turn her head around, whispering. "Rhawan? I need it too"

He did gasp and she felt his hand sliding up underneath her skirt, it was warm and rough and she got Goosebumps from the sensation, it was wonderful. She wriggled herself into a better position and Rhawan did nibble on her earlobe, breathing fast. "We shouldn't...."

Wenja gasped as his hand did find its way inn between her legs, gently teasing her. "I don't care, oh Rhawan, do it, I need you"

He did struggle with the laces of his pants and was flailing around a bit before he finally did get the garments out of the way. Then he did flip her over onto her stomach and placed some of the furs underneath her hips. Wenja did spread her legs eagerly, she wanted to feel something real again, not just fear and anxiety and worry. She needed to wind down and a good fuck did usually help her do that. She whimpered as he got into position over her, the sensation of his cockhead slowly sliding along her slit, nudging at her passage made her squirm with an almost unbearable need. She did truly hunger for the sensation of being whole yet again and she did bite into her cloak not to scream as he did slide into place with one slow deliberate thrust. It felt so good she could have cried, it had been many long days since they had done this last and she was panting and grasping onto the furs, desperate to just feel, live within the very moment. Rhawan was outdoing himself, he did keep his rhythm and did change the angle of his hips at uneven intervals and she was close to tears from sheer pleasure. Rhawan did groan and pant and suddenly he shifted to a much more vigorous rhythm, he gasped. "I am sorry, I cannot…"

Wenja wasn't able to answer, she came suddenly and so hard she felt something wet and warm gushing out of her, the pleasure was burning through her like wildfire and she arched and would have screamed if she could. Rhawan did bite her shoulder, it was a hard bite but she didn't mind, she felt him coming and he shook and groaned. "Aaah-nngh!"

He did collapse on top of her for a few seconds, she could feel his heartbeat and she felt oddly humble. He kissed her neck lovingly and sighed. "Well, from now on every goblin within the mountains will be able to smell us, I am dead sure"

Wenja did stretch herself and grinned, she felt surprisingly well now and was way more relaxed than before. She heard silent footsteps and looked up, Ahravan did approach her and he did smirk and tsked at them. "I felt it, you couldn't help it now could you?"

Wenja shook her head and Ahravan did kneel down. "Now you two rabbits have turned me on too, may I?"

Wenja nodded and Rhawan did slide out of the furs, he did relace his pants and his eyes were still dark and filled with bliss. "I will go and stand guard"

Ahravan did smirk and opened his belt very slowly and almost teasingly. Wenja saw that he had a playful expression on his face, he wanted to have more than just a quick fuck and she liked that. Ahravan didn't get any closer, he just opened his pants and exposed himself and Wenja did realize that he too needed it now. He was rock hard and he did sit down slowly and leaned back against the rock behind him. Wenja did bite her lip, not sure of what to do and Ahravan did wink at her. "Come here, ride me"

She understood and straddled his lap, her skirts did cover them up and she did reach down and steered him right. She was wet and open and Ahravan did groan as she slid down onto him. He was leaning his head back, eyes closed and mouth open and Wenja did whimper, it felt so amazing yet again and she started to move her hips. She did find a good rhythm and laid her hands on his shoulders for support and before long she was caught in a maelstrom of sensation and need. Ahravan didn't move at all, he did allow her to take the lead completely and she felt it rising within again. He did groan and winked, lifted her skirts so he could see them being as one. Wenja did lean back a bit so he could see better and he did growl and panted. "Faster, I am so….fucking close…."

Wenja did obey, she moved faster and he did cover her mouth with his hand to stifle her scream as she came again, clenching onto him like a vice. Ahravan did press his face inn against her neck and muffled his own roar thus, she felt the hot spurts of seed which left him and it made her shudder again and again. Ahravan did lean his chin onto her forehead and gasped for a while, she felt him relax but he was getting hard again almost immediately. She had gotten used to that by now, he needed more than one go to be satisfied. He did run his fingers through her hair and kissed her, she always felt almost euphoric from his kisses, they made her toes curl and her heart skip a few beats. "Ready for more?"

Wenja did giggle. "Always"

Ahravan did sigh. "You do tell me if it gets too much right? I don't want to harm you in any manner"

Wenja kissed him back. "Do not worry, you are never gonna wear me out. So how do you want it now?"

She did wriggle herself and he closed his eyes and gasped. "You rode me, so how about me doing the work this time?"

Wenja nodded and he did get up and helped her up as well. It was a bit obscene, he was fully clothed except from his groin and Wenja tilted her head. "And now?"

He did push her towards the rock and placed her hands on it. "Hold on"

Ahravan did grasp her hips and lifted her up and she couldn't reach the ground with her feet, he was too tall but she did find a handhold in the rock and held her upper body level thus. Ahravan did slide into her again, he felt so warm and she squealed and closed her eyes in absolute bliss. He did last longer this time and brought her to a shattering climax twice before he let go of all control and came a last time. When he did let her place her feet on the ground they were like jello and she wondered if she could walk at all now. Her inner thighs were slick and she felt sweaty, but most of all very satisfied and very drowsy. Ahravan did kiss her gently and gave her a small pat across the rump. "Thank you beloved, this was absolutely wonderful"

Wenja grinned back. "And I thank you, I needed that"

Ahravan nodded and re-laced his pants. "We all did, I feel much better already"

Wenja made a grimace. "We do stink though"

Ahravan had to laugh. "Yes, but not much worse than before, we could need a bath but no such thing here I fear."

Wenja did shake out her skirts and she did roll out the sleeping furs, they were wet because of her release when Rhawan took her and needed to dry before she could roll them together. Ahravan sighed. "We have to get moving again soon, these mountains have to end soon, I am dead tired of rocks and snow and nothing green at all"

Wenja nodded. "I agree, let us hope that we will reach our goal soon"

Ahravan did kiss her again and returned to the others, Rhawan was smirking. "You were goddamn loud, Khirhien had to take a swift trip in between those boulders to relieve himself of a small problem and

Ayhrandur is still struggling with a hard on. I bet the two humans aren't much better off"

The two young men did stare at each other and both blushed almost violently. Ahravan did blush too, he made a grimace. "Well, take care of it now, before we leave. We cannot have our thoughts muddled whilst out in the valleys"

The two men did get up and sort of wobbled into the darkness and Ayhrandur did grin and made a very suggestive movement with his hand. Ahravan rolled his eyes. "Yes, you too, I can see that you are aroused"

Ayhrandur snickered. "One would have to be dead if one weren't, you are an insanely lucky one, I hope you know that?"

Ahravan nodded. "I know"

Ayhrandur did disappear for a while too and Rhawan did sigh and leaned against the flank of his horse. "How far do we have to travel? I feel as if we have been travelling in a circle, we see just rock and rock and even more rocks"

Ahravan sighed and sat down. "I have no idea, but the tracks do show us we are on the right path. "

Rhawan did look down and his eyes were distant. "I feel danger close by brother, why I do not know"

Ahravan did raise his gaze, stared at his Si'ish with narrow eyes. "So do I"

Yalaih had been sitting on her own wrapped in her furs but now she did get up and she did sniff the air, "There are goblins here in the mountains and they are everywhere, I do feel that something is very wrong"

Ahravan did frown. "How come?"

Yalaih did wrap her cloak tighter around herself. "Back where we are from, near the eternal ice there are goblins too, but they aren't like the one we found and the smell is wrong. Also the tracks I have seen. Goblins are animals and yet, the tracks tell of discipline and order."

Ahravan tilted his head. "You are sure of this?"

Yalaih did nod. "Yes, I know goblins Ath'ir. We have fought them often, father did hate them and with good reason and yet they aren't hard to fight off. But I feel something is different here"

476

Ahravan did nod and he did try to smile. "I trust your instincts Yalaih, if you see something strange do tell us immediately. You have experience we don't"

Yalaih did straighten her back and she did look rather proud all of a sudden. Being praised thus had to be valuable to her.

When the sunlight yet again filled the skies they did move on, and Ahravan did realize that Yalaih was onto something. There were fresh tracks there and it wasn't monsters but definitely goblins and also a huge number of them. Yalaih did study the tracks. "There is a city somewhere, goblins do often use old dwarf mines or natural caves. One can usually smell them from afar."

Ahravan did groan. "So, what do we do?"

Yalaih did make a grimace. "Move on carefully, but without breaks. We have to get away from here as fast as we can, goblins do not like direct sunlight but the valleys are dark and there could be scouts out even now!"

Ahravan swore to himself, it was just what they didn't need. "Alright, everybody keep their eyes open and do not make much noise. If we are spotted we will have to fight"

Everybody did ready their weapons and Rhawan did hold Wenja closer. He didn't like the idea of a fight there at all. They were exposed and vulnerable and it wasn't ideal at all.

Unta had never learned the language of the goblins, all she knew was that of her own people and she felt that she had no chance of learning the nasty guttural words of these creatures. But she wasn't dumb and she did read a lot out of the way they did interact. The goblins there weren't truly followers of that voice, they were simply too dumb. But the huge half orc was and he was in charge there, they did all fear him. She had learned that his name was Gobaz and the goblin who had caught her was named Aghar. Gobaz had killed their previous leader and turned the otherwise savage goblins into an army and that was impressive in itself, a person without the right amount of ruthlessness and strength wouldn't have been able to do that at all. They would have torn him limb from limb.

Unta was being fed, and she got water and even some old furs to sleep inn, apparently she was valuable for there weren't any goblin females there at all. She hadn't seen any and the way the goblins did stare at her told her that they all were starved for female attention. But her own situation had changed a lot within a few days. Apparently Gobaz had discovered that Aghar had a female stacked away for his own pleasure, and he hadn't accepted that. Aghar had been executed in front of the whole city and then Gobaz had claimed her as his own. He enjoyed watching the envy of the others there so he did always fuck her on his throne, for everybody to see. Aghar had been pathetic in oh so many ways but the half orc did make Unta scream and it wasn't always in pain, he was huge and knew how to do this and he wasn't even too brutal with her.

She had realized that he was constantly alert, always anticipating attacks but he didn't expect any danger from her, she was after all just a female and she was in her own way a very sensitive person. To him she was little more than a pet, a thing with which to have fun and he would treat her nicely as long as he saw it fit. He didn't want to break his toy and Unta had realized that he liked it when she seemed to enjoy his advances. It made the others even more envious if she did scream in pleasure and it did boost his male ego too, so Unta did allow herself to feel pleasure when he did take her. Thanks to this she was treated well and she wasn't afraid for her own life as long as she did continue to provide him with what he needed. But she had discovered that the voice indeed was the thing which did control him, there was a huge crystal mounted right in front of the primitive throne and the voice came from it, and once she had seen a sort of shadowy figure within the crystal, as if there was a ghost trapped within it. Gobaz did obey the voice, willingly and with obvious reverence and Unta did understand that the voice came from somewhere else, and that it was evil.

Sometimes though she heard a different voice when she was alone, a female one and she didn't understand the words but she knew the meaning. She had to wait, she had a task to do, she was important.

Then one day the halls seemed to be emptied and Unta knew that something was about to happen, she closed her eyes and prayed to the goddess for strength. The daughter of the goddess would come, and then Unta would deliver the message and kill Gobaz, yes, that was her destiny.

The group had been moving forth for a couple of days now and each morning when they did break camp there were giant tracks around the campsite, feline tracks. The horses didn't react to them and Ahravan did believe that it was some sort of S'haga but unusually large. Yalaih did lead them well, she was an expert at reading the terrain and she did also make sure that they didn't end up in places where they could be ambushed.

The mountains were not as tall and Rhawan had sworn that he had seen flat lands in the distance, it could be their target and Wenja hoped that it was true. She was so tired of the cold now. They were riding along the bottom of a rather narrow and winding valley when something suddenly shot out from behind the rocks surrounding them. They had been prepared for an attack and yet it did shock them for a few seconds. These goblins were fast and wielded primitive weapons made from antlers and bone.

Wenja was riding with Ahravan, she was seated behind him on one of the horses, a brown mare named Blossom and Ahravan did spin the horse around and yelled out loud. The others did react immediately and Flint did whinny and started to fight the goblins. So did Khor'ath, the unicorn did grasp goblins with its jaws and threw them in the air and Wenja saw that the broken horn did glow, as if it still was there. A mere touch of the otherworldly lance did make goblins fall over as they did burst into flames with piercing shrieks.

Ahravan did grasp Wenja by her waist and threw her over to Rhawan, the dark skinned elf did catch her elegantly and placed her in front of himself on the horse before swinging his sword elegantly at the attacking goblins. Ahravan did use the war hammer he had gotten from Fhailar, it was an impressive sight and he did crush the ones he did hit, it was a very good weapon to use from the back of a horse. The others did also fight well, Yalaih was using her two shorter and slimmer blades with the elegance of a cat and Khirhien and Ayhrandur did work as one and cut a bloody path through the attackers. The two men had jumped over onto two boulders and used their short rider's bows with lethal precision, goblins did fall down with arrows protruding from their heads.

Ahravan did try to get an overview of the situation, the goblins seemed to spring out of the ground and the numbers didn't seem to diminish at all. He did push the horse around the boulders and smashed goblins as he went, he did not hesitate even once. Rhawan did fight with great elegance and yet the fact that Wenja was sitting in front of him did hinder him a bit. She did block his left arm and side and Rhawan did want to place her somewhere else but he didn't have time to help her get behind him on the horse before something hit the animal and caused him to stumble. Rhawan did grasp onto Wenja and held her as they did tumble from the horse which fell kicking and screaming. Wenja did squeal and Rhawan did take the impact, he rolled away from the horse with her and the animal got back on its feet, a gash in its chest did bleed a lot and it seemed to have injured a leg too. Rhawan did yell and placed Wenja behind him against a boulder, Gochil was on top of it shooting and the dark skinned elf did fight every goblin which did approach them with savage fury. The goblins weren't warriors, they knew naught about technique and their weapons were no match for such fighters as the elves but they did try.

Flint did trample goblins with its ears flat and teeth bared and Khor'ath did kill goblins too, the animal was moving so fast it was almost hard to believe. Wenja did tremble, the goblins were ghastly and she didn't think she had seen anything uglier before. The numbers did at last seem to dwindle and Ahravan did turn his horse around, the war hammer was dripping with blood and brain matter and Khor'ath did send out a shrill whinny. The goblins did gather for a last attempt at regaining control but suddenly they heard a roar, it was so strong the ground did seem to vibrate from it and the goblins did freeze, then they squealed and ran, obviously terrified. It was no doubt that it had scared them and the goblins did disappear rather fast, only the dead and dying were left. Ahravan did jump down from the mare he rode and grasped onto a wounded goblin, its left shoulder and arm was crushed and it looked as if the back was broken too. He lifted the goblin by the throat and hissed something, words which made the goblin squeal in fear. Elves do have some magic which is inherent and now he used it. His own thoughts did pierce the mind of the goblin and did pull forth all the information he sought from the creature. When he was done he had a splitting headache and the goblin was dead. He did drop the body unceremoniously and spat at it.

Rhawan did look at him with huge eyes and Ahravan did sneer. "They are under control by somebody, just as we expected. A half orc, a servant of evil. The darkness does control him, just as the monsters"

Rhawan did swallow. "I see, so now what?"

Ahravan turned to Yalaih. "You said that there is a city here somewhere?"

The young elf did nod. "Yes, probably very nearby!"

The Ath'ir had never looked this much like a leader. "It has to be destroyed somehow, as long as that orc is their leader they are dangerous. There are many of them, we cannot risk more attacks, they are swarming all over the mountains"

Yalaih did groan. "We are too few, fighting our way in will be impossible. A sneak attack is the only chance we have."

Rhawan did turn around to see of Wenja was alright but she wasn't there and he did gasp, suddenly everyone became aware of the fact that she wasn't there and Rhawan did first gape. He hadn't even noticed that she did move for she had been right behind him the whole time but now there were nobody there. He did run around the rock, nothing. Then he did notice something, a piece of fur on a rock and he did grasp it and the rock moved. It did fall to the side and revealed a narrow tunnel, too small for an adult male but large enough for a goblin. Some thin strands of red hair could be seen and Rhawan did let out a roar of anger and fear, Ahravan did freeze for a second, then he did fall to his knees next to the tunnel and tried to listen. They didn't hear anything and Ahravan did release a wail, he was shaking all over. The goblins had snatched her from right under their noses and it was so devious and so utterly wicked that it was hard to understand how it was even possible.

Yalaih was pale but her face was suddenly very stern, her chin set and her eyes ablaze. "Ahravan, do not let the fear overcome you. Now is the time to act fast, and wisely. They will not harm her yet. She is to be their hostage, to lure you inn."

Ahravan was wild eyed and Rhawan was panting, his fear made it almost impossible for him to think. Khirhien was the one who did gather his thoughts. "So what do you suggest we do?"

Yalaih did stare at them, her eyes dark. "I go, I can find the city and I can sneak my way into it, I know how to avoid detection. You must find a safe spot which to defend until I return with her, the goblins will try to taunt you, to bring you out of balance so they can split you into smaller groups and kill you all"

Ahravan did pant, he was trembling. "You will get yourself killed!"

Yalaih did nod. "Possibly, even most likely but I will find her Ahravan, and I will get her out of there. I know how goblins think Ahravan, we were taught about them from an early age, we are age old enemies of these nasty creatures!"

Rhawan had a hard time talking. "Listen to her brother, she is right you know. Let her go, she can find Wenja!"

Ahravan closed his eyes, he could feel that Wenja was alive, he had to maintain hope. Yalaih did grasp his shoulder and shook him. "They aren't very good at numbers, they won't notice that one of you is missing, they will not anticipate that somebody can find them"

Ahravan sobbed, he was trembling. "Go, go now. Save her, please!"

Yalaih nodded and grasped her blades and a short bow plus some arrows. She did give the others a swift grin before she disappeared among the rocks like a weasel. Now it became a game of seek and find and she was a master at finding stuff. Khirhien did grasp Ahravan by the collar. "Up, we need to find a place to defend ourselves, they will return."

The tall silver haired elf did lead them to a small raised hill which was flat and easy to defend and he did find some dead branches and lichen. "We will start a fire, they fear open flame and from here we can shoot them before they get too close"

Ahravan didn't speak, his fear for Wenja was almost paralyzing him. Rhawan did embrace him, if they did lose her it was very likely that they both would lose the will to live and simply die from grief, elves could do that.

Yalaih did use her nose, it was extremely sensitive and she used it the same way a dog would, she did sneak her way through the maze of boulders and snow drifts and before long her nose did catch a familiar scent. It was goblins and many of them. Yalaih did sneer, they wouldn't expect somebody who knew how to fight them on their own turf. She did glide along the rocks and made no sound, her soft fur boots didn't even leave tracks and she did sniff her way towards the source of the smell. It was an opening which wasn't very large, it wasn't the main entrance for sure but it was useable for her goal. It had probably been a ventilation shaft and now it was filled with garbage and cobwebs but Yalaih didn't fear that. She did crawl inside and moved swiftly, the stench from this garbage dump would camouflage her own scent and she knew that she had to hurry. Wenja was in danger, and the longer the enemy had her the greater the risks.

Yalaih did enter a tunnel which was in little use, there were few tracks in the dust and she was glad her kin did have good eyes for there wasn't much light there, she did sneak forth and after a while she did see a cave up ahead. It was light up and she did crawl closer, peeping over the edge of it. She didn't see Wenja but the goblins were obviously upset, they were scurrying around and she did see the half orc which was their leader. He did look impressive and was probably very intelligent, if the distance hadn't been too great she would have attempted at shooting him but now it was impossible. The creatures were making a lot of racket and Yalaih did sneak along some side tunnels. She stayed where it was dark and got a sort of image of how this city was constructed. It was an old dwarven mine, only a few levels tall and she was rather sure that the dungeons or what they used as dungeons were lower down. She did find a flight of stairs and had to shot a couple of goblins to use them. She fired so fast they both fell seconds apart and she did haul the corpses into a dark corner where it was little chance of them getting found.

The air was thick with the stench of rot and unwashed bodies and it was obvious that everybody there was gathered in the great hall for she didn't see any other goblins. The leader had appeared to be holding a speech for them and Yalaih did bite her teeth together hard. They would return to the valley for a second attack soon and she had to find Wenja fast. The goblins would most likely take something from her to taunt the elves with. The level was obviously where the goblins did live so she did go even deeper down and this time she was in luck. She felt her heart racing, she had to be fast now and when she saw a bolted door she knew she was in the right place.

She did sneak up to it, the bolt was a simple one and she did slide it aside and opened the door slightly. She let out a thin gasp of relief. Wenja was there but she was unconscious and there was someone else in there. Yalaih did not move and a short stocky figure did enter the faint light. At first Yalaih did think it was a dwarrowdam but when the creature got closer she saw that it wasn't. This was one of the people her clan used to call Dhu'rday, the children of the mist. They were almost human but not quite and very strong and adapted to the tough life among the tallest mountains. The female did grunt and sat down, gesticulated towards Yalaih and the elf did not speak many words of their language but she did know a few. The female wanted her closer and Yalaih did obey. The female had to have been a prisoner there for a while but she wasn't injured and did look to be well fed and taken care off.

Yalaih did point at herself. "Yalaih"

The female did grin, her teeth were large and yellow and the protruding forehead and jaw did make her look a bit odd but she wasn't ugly, just different. "Unta"

Unta did point at Wenja, the girl had a lump on her forehead and some blood in her hair but otherwise she appeared to be unharmed. "Child…goddess child…I give message"

Yalaih did tilt her head. "You give message to…goddess child?"

Unta did nod. "Yes, she is…daughter. Must use path of the leopard"

Yalaih did shake her head. "I do not understand?"

Unta did grunt, let a hand slide through Wenja's fiery locks. "She will know, when time is there"

Yalaih did sigh. "I have to get her out, can you help me?"

Unta tilted her head. "I distract, you wait, soon they come for me. I kill leader, you run"

Yalaih did gasp. "What, but…they will kill you?!"

484

Unta grinned. "Yes, but die well. For cause. My clan gone, my future gone. I no woman, no child. Better save goddess child"

Yalaih stared at Unta, they were the same, both had lost everything, she did understand. "What do you need?"

Unta stared at Yalaih. "Hard shiny"

Yalaih did frown, then she did understand and got her knife out of its sheath. It was a narrow dagger like blade and not very elaborate but razor sharp. Unta did grin and attached the blade to the inside of her fur coat. "Good, he die today. Come to me to fuck, I kill"

Yalaih did cringe, so that was why Unta was kept alive, she was a sex toy. Unta did pet Yalaih on her shoulder. "Hide back in room, soon they come, not see you, close door"

Yalaih did trust Unta, the odd female had honour and courage and she did clearly have a plan. The elf maiden did leave the room and bolted the door again, praying that Wenja wasn't severely injured and that she wouldn't wake up until Unta was gone.

Yalaih didn't have to wait for long, suddenly a pair of goblins came running and opened the door, they went inside and came back with Unta, she wore the cloak over her shoulders but were otherwise naked and she did follow them willingly. There was a faint smile on her lips and Yalaih did wait until they were out of hearing range before she raced back to the door and opened it. Wenja was still unconscious, they must have hit her over the head with something hard and Yalaih did hoist the girl up and carried her outside, bolted the door again and started to walk back the way she had come but it was blocked. There were goblins there and she did find another tunnel which was leading in the right direction, she just hoped that Wenja didn't wake up suddenly and made an unwanted noise.

Unta was being lead towards the great hall, she was used to this routine by now, it happened each day at approximately the same time and she had been very sure that today would be no different. She felt content, she had delivered the message, the pretty eternal would deliver the message for her, now she had to finish her mission. She felt proud, without a leader the goblins would scatter like before and return to their natural state, fighting among each other, being no threat to people out there.

Gobaz did look smug, he had apparently done well and he did grin at Unta as she was brought before him. There was a table there next to the throne and he did grasp her and threw her down onto it, it was made from stone and very sturdy and she was familiar with his routine now. She did rearrange the cloak as if to be more comfortable and the huge half orc did grasp her ankles and spread her legs as she laid on the edge of the table. Unta felt oddly excited, almost giddy. She giggled and the half orc did grunt and got his cock out of the robes, it was ready for sure and he did grasp her hips and pushed inside with a groan. Unta did gasp, this time she did in fact like it a lot, she panted and writhed and the goblins which were nearby did stare with envy, some were in fact touching themselves eagerly. Unta was grasping onto the cloak, as if to steady herself, she felt the knife and knew that the moment soon would be near. She knew how to kill, she had learned that early on.

The half orc did thrust with vigour, having captured that woman would make sure that the elves did wander straight into his trap and the voice had been very adamant, the elves had to be stopped. He didn't think that the voice had to fear a few elves but he was obedient and if the master indeed wanted them dead then be it. He had many goblins and if he lost a few hundred it didn't matter much. They were all pawns to him. He had served the voice for more than a year now and his strength had grown for each passing day, he would be a king soon, the voice had promised him everything he wanted, immortality and wealth and he felt that things indeed were going the right way.

Unta gasped and closed her eyes, the pleasure she felt was mounting and she arched and screamed as she came very hard, seeing stars and few things more. Gobaz was pleased, the female they had caught was not pretty but nice to fuck and she did in fact like it too, he didn't have to fight to get his release and that was always a bonus. He grunted with delight and did thrust vigorously into the clenching passage, oh it was wonderful, so good he barely could describe it and his orgasm came like a hammer blow. He grunted and shuddered and his eyes did roll up into his skull as he filled her with his seed, he had rarely felt such pleasure. As usual he did collapse on top of her and felt her contract around him still, it was amazing.

That was when Unta saw her chance, he was half conscious and didn't react when she moved her arms, Unta was very strong compared with a human female her size, her bones dense and her muscles strong, she did know how to aim the sharp blade. The back of the neck was vulnerable on every living creature and she used all her strength as she did push the thin blade in between two vertebrae and severed the half orcs spinal cord. Gobaz didn't even have time to really register what was happening, there was a sudden sting of intense pain at the back of his neck and then everything went dark. His last sensation was that of his cock twitching in pleasure yet again, finding it odd.

Unta did flip the body over, he was twitching and the body was rigid, the wound at the back of his neck was small and didn't bleed much since the heart had stopped and she did straddle him, he was still hard and she pretended to ride the half orc. The others there were busy now, the show had transformed them into lusty beasts and many there were busy fucking each other eagerly. The twitching of the huge half orc did look as if he was coming still and Unta did gather her courage, she knew that they would chase her, it would give Yalaih a chance and she held the dagger against her body as she did jump from the table and started to run.

The goblins didn't immediately realize that their leader was dead, they just saw that the desirable female was fleeing and their first instinct was to pursue her to fuck her too. Then they realized that Gobaz was dead and chaos did erupt. Since they no longer had to fear the wrath and brutality of their boss all discipline did fly out of the window. They were in hot pursuit right away, screaming and screeching. All wanted to be the one to claim the female and Unta did run very fast, praying that Yalaih and the red headed daughter of the goddess did make it out of there. Unta knew exactly where to take the goblins, the goddess had shown her in her dreams and she smiled as she ran. The goblins would no longer pose a threat to the people of the plains.

Yalaih heard the ruckus which erupted from the great hall, she did haul Wenja with her and suddenly Wenja did twitch and Yalaih did lower her to the ground and held a hand over her mouth. Wenja did squeak but the sound was muffled and Yalaih did whisper. "It is I, Yalaih, do not make a sound. I am here to rescue you"

Wenja did grunt and nod and Yalaih did remove the hand. Wenja's eyes were huge and filled with fear and pain and Yalaih did feel her head gently. "Are you hurt"

Wenja did sniff. "I…what happened? Are they okay?"

Yalaih did nod. "Yes, can you walk? We have to get out of here, you are in a goblin city"

Wenja did get up, her feet unsteady. "I can walk, oh Gods!"

Yalaih grasped her by the hand. "Come with me, and stay silent. There was a woman here, of the people of the mist, she was a prisoner here too but she is trying to lure the goblins away. She said that…she said you are a daughter of the goddess and that you must take the path of the leopard, when the time is right"

Wenja did just blink, she didn't understand and Yalaih did almost run. The entrance she had come through wasn't useable now, they would be spotted so Yalaih did aim for another one. It was one which was used more often and they did run through it. Wenja was confused and in pain and scared and she didn't remember anything at all, the last memory she did have was of her standing behind Rhawan, waiting for Ahravan to give orders.

The tunnel was bringing fresh air and Yalaih did speed up, she did look nervous. "Hurry, we have to get out of here before it gets dark"

The opening was like a glimpse of heaven and they ran side by side when the ground underneath their feet suddenly gave inn. Wenja did scream and her hands did manage to grasp onto a sort of log someone had left there. She felt a sharp pain in her leg and looked down, a sort of spear had gone through her calf and she gasped and tried to get free but it was impossible. Yalaih was next to her leg, the young elf was pierced by several spears but still alive. She gasped and reached out, broke the spear which trapped Wenja with a grunt. "Go, Wenja, run towards…the sun. Go now!"

Wenja did haul herself up from the trap, it was a devilish contraption and she let out a wail of agony, the leg was burning and she saw that Yalaih was dead now, there was nothing she could do for the brave elf so she did tear a piece out of her skirts and tied it around her leg to stop the blood. The spear was old and not very clean and the wound it left was nasty indeed, she had to get help right away. Wenja prayed that Yalaih would be reunited with her family, then she did waddle out of the tunnel and did as Yalaih had said, followed the sun.

Unta had been running for a while, the goblins hot at her heels and she felt proud, she would make sure that they didn't cause any more problems. The goddess was with her, she could feel it and she knew where to go. The tunnel was leading upwards and Unta did make sure that the goblins were right behind her, desperate with the need to catch her.

The voice of the goddess did speak to her, told her of destiny, of courage and sacrifice and Unta was ready. She ran into a very dark tunnel, the goblins were hot at her heels and Unta did close her eyes. When she did feel how there suddenly was no ground underneath her for her feet to find she didn't scream. She just smiled and surrendered herself to the goddess, she would live anew in the goddess will, she had been promised this. Unta didn't feel any pain, suddenly she was just flying above the tunnel, seeing the goblins falling to their deaths in the old mining shaft. The floor was slick and since the ones in the back did push forth there was no way to stop and they did all tumble down into the darkness. Unta saw her own body as a glowing orb, and she heard the goddess again. "You did well child, are you ready to serve me?"

Unta did nod, her soul singing with joy, this was a tremendous honour "Yes mother, I am ready"

There was a flash of light and when Unta did open her eyes again she was on a mountain, she felt a new strength and she got up. She suddenly had four legs and a tail and she did lick her lips. This new body was amazing and she shook herself and stretched. The fur was pitch black and she was very large, the she wolf did growl and then she started trotting down the mountain side, she was to stay close to the chosen one and lead the way, and she would do so for as long as the goddess wanted it.

Wenja was fighting her way forth, her leg did burn and she felt dizzy and confused but she was rather sure that she did recognize one of the cliffs ahead, it had a very odd dark colouring at its top. She gasped with pain and whimpered, she wanted Ahravan and Rhawan by her side, she wanted to be safe again, to be protected. She felt like a child, helpless and naïve and she tried to forget what she had seen. Yalaih had given her life to save her, it was such a horrible realization. The mountains were rather quiet and she didn't see any goblins there, it was a bit odd. Then she heard sounds, it was a fight for sure and she tried to hurry but it was hard, her leg did barely carry her and she was getting very worried. The wound was deep and she had lost much blood.

She did get around a boulder and saw that her friends and husbands were gathered on top of a sort of small hill. They did defend themselves against the goblin horde and she did see that Flint did run around, kicking and biting and killing goblins, the unicorn did the same thing and the piles of corpses were high already. There were so many goblins there, and they were rather eager too, they couldn't know that their leader was dead and Wenja saw that the warriors were running out of arrows soon. She felt a surge of despair and leaned forth, tried to see if anybody were hurt. Apparently they were all okay yet but it wouldn't last for long and she bit her lower lip. She needed help soon, and she couldn't get to them. The goblins had to go somehow, but what could she really do? She had saved Ahravan, and she had drawn all the animals to the caravan to keep it safe from the monsters but it hadn't been something she had done as a conscious choice. It had been done out of sheer instinct. Her heart was hammering and sweat did flow down her body, the pain was getting stronger by the minute and something snapped within her. She did press her fingers into the sandy soil between the boulders and shrieked in defiance.

There was a roar coming from the opposite side of the battle ground, a loud sound which made the goblins squeal and then the sand almost turned to a liquid underneath their feet. They did sink inn, screaming and struggling and they did try desperately to pull themselves out but to no prevail. They did sink down into the ground until the sand started to close around their heads. It was a horrible sight, the goblins were screaming in horror and the sand did seep into their mouths and nostrils, slowly suffocating them. Wenja was panting, she was on her knees now, body shaking. She did raise her head and screamed for Ahravan, then the world went black before her eyes and she did pass out.

Ahravan and the others had been defending themselves for quite a while, the next attack had come right after Yalaih had left them and it was a vicious one too, the goblins were determined to kill them all. Ahravan was not going to go down easily, he was fighting like mad and Rhawan did watch his back, they were an excellent team and the other four did fight well too. The two humans did shoot with expert technique but the number of arrows did go down and they would run out soon. Fighting the goblins without archers would be hard and the little bastards were extremely fast and also very sly in their own ways.

Ahravan did just hope that Yalaih did manage to find Wenja, he didn't fear for his own life but he did fear for her. They were about to shift their tactics to a more head on approach when they heard a distant shriek followed by a roar and then the goblins sank into the ground. They could just stand there and stare in disbelief as each and every one of the attackers did slide into the ground as if it was quicksand.

Ahravan blinked and didn't really know what to think, then he heard Wenja screaming his name and everything went blank. He ran, the goblins weren't dangerous anymore and he did run into the maze of boulders and smaller rocks with a trembling heart. He did find her rather fast, she was laying on the ground and he did wail when he did see blood on her skirts. He did pick her up and she was so pale and grey and yet burning hot. There was a wound on her leg, she had tied some cloth around it but it was bleeding still and did look large. Ahravan did carry her back to the others, Rhawan did let out a groan when he saw her and Ahravan felt weak, almost as if he was passing out. They had to stop the blood and help her.

Khirhien did kneel down where they laid her, he was the one among them with the most experience as a healer and he did remove the rag with a swift movement. The wound was worse than what Ahravan had imagined, it was a through and through, something had in fact pierced her calf and the wound ragged and nasty. "Oh gods, this is not good!"

Rhawan did swallow hard. "Yalaih?"

Ahravan did shake his head. "I didn't see her, she wouldn't have let Wenja try to reach us alone with a wound like that"

Rhawan did lower his head, he felt a crushing sense of sorrow. Yet another brave one was dead. Khirhien did groan and grasped his small bag of supplies. "It must have been a sort of spear, but I don't think I have seen a spear wound with this angle before!!"

Ayhrandur did make a grimace. "A trap, goblins do make traps. Pits with spears in them, covered with a thin layer of straw and soil."

They stared at each other, Yalaih had to have helped Wenja get free, it was…Ahravan did grasp Wenja's hand, held it close to his heart. "Wenja? My light? Please, wake up!"

Khirhien did examine the wound with a sort of instrument. "The bleeding is hard to stop, there is just one way to do it. You need to start a fire"

Rhawan did gasp and then he did look horrified. "Are you gonna cauterize the wound?!"

Khirhien nodded. "The only choice I fear, the spear could have been dirty too, the heat will remove impurities"

Ahravan didn't say anything, he just held her upper body close to his own, feeling helpless. What use was he if he couldn't protect her? If he couldn't save her? He may be an excellent warrior but he had failed her. Rhawan did find some dry grass and some branches from bushes and they got a small fire going. Khirhien did heat up a small steel rod and he did stare at Ahravan. "This will hurt, even if she is unconscious. You must hold her"

Ahravan felt like he was about to burst into tears. "I will, oh gods"

Khirhien didn't hesitate, the second Ahravan did put his arms around her Khirhien did plunge the red hot poker into the wound and they heard a hissing sound and felt the stench of burned flesh and Wenja did scream, a horrible unarticulated howl of agony. Ahravan felt tears flowing down his cheeks. Rhawan was trembling and his golden eyes were wide open and filled with horror. "She cannot die, please say she won't die"

Khirhien did growl something incomprehensible. "The wound in itself isn't too bad, it will heal, the muscles and tendons aren't cut that badly, but I fear that the spear have been contaminated, probably with purpose, she is burning with a fever already"

Ahravan felt faint. "Poison, they do poison their traps don't they?"

Ayhrandur did nod, his face like a porcelain mask. The two men did look just as worried as the elves and Ahravan hid his face within the thick wine red hair and keened. They couldn't lose her, not like this. Khirhien did sew up the wound but left a piece of straw to let it drain and he did put a bandage on it. His face was stern and his eyes distant. He did boil some water on the small fire and made a sort of poultice he did smear over the wound and it was made from dried herbs and fat. Then he made another concoction and it was a sort of tea, it would help her replace the blood she had lost. They managed to get some of it into her and Khirhien did look as if he was very sorry. "I wish I could have done more, but I am no healer, just a warrior with some skills"

Ahravan did stroke Wenja's hair, he did sob and held her close and Rhawan too crept closer and grasped her hand, it was very obvious that both males were beside themselves with worry and fear and Ayhrandur sighed. "Let us make camp here, we will keep watch. The goblins are dead and I doubt that more will come, something tells me that attack was the last one."

They did erect a tent around Wenja and her husbands and looked over the horses, then they made a simple meal but neither Ahravan nor Rhawan had any appetite. Wenja was still warm and the wound had stopped bleeding now but Ahravan felt guilty, horribly terribly so. He should have followed Yalaih, he could have prevented this.

They just laid there, next to her, mumbling words of comfort and love and both prayed that she would wake up again soon, that the wound wasn't infected, that she would be okay. They just laid there for hours, the goblins seemed to be gone and Gochil did go hunting and brought back some Coney's and made stew. There were edible roots there which he knew how to find and Khirhien had some herbs which could be used as a sort of spice too. Ahravan and Rhawan did eat a little, but with no appetite and as the night came and slowly swept over the land it became very obvious that the spear indeed had been poisoned. Wenja's temperature did rise even more, ominous ghastly black streaks appeared on her skin leading away from the wound and her breath had become raspy and shallow. Khirhien saw it and he went pale, turning his gaze away from Ahravan. "I…there is nothing we can do, she…."

Ahravan did not manage to speak, his voice didn't obey him, all he could do was make a sort of hoarse croak. Rhawan did whisper. "I cannot go on without her, neither of us can"

Khirhien swallowed and kept his gaze on the ground. "Then we will fail, and darkness envelop the lands. The monsters are just the beginning"

Ahravan did just wail and rocked her in his arms, overcome with grief and fear, he couldn't lose her. He had just learned to love her and now this? The gods were cruel, heartless, sadistic. "Go, leave us alone, we…"

His voice did break and Khirhien did place a hand on Ahravan's shoulder for a few seconds, to show his support. Rhawan was sobbing like a child and crept closer, they both embraced the woman they loved and prayed, hoping for a miracle but knowing that it probably wouldn't be any chance of her surviving this. Goblins use very nasty poisons and even a trained healer wouldn't have been able to do much. They were going to lose her.

Ahravan did collapse, he didn't fall asleep but rather into a sort of trance, elves will do that if they face emotional trauma and he just laid there, apparently awake but not responsive. His mind was wandering and he remembered everything, every minute since he got the message within the sacred cave. Had the seer lied to him? Had she been wrong? Ahravan didn't know and he felt torn apart, his duty was to his people but his spirit wanted to join hers in the afterlife, if she died he wouldn't have anything left to live for. True love among his people could be that intense, that all-consuming. Suddenly he found himself standing on a barren hilltop, just rocks and dead grass around him. The wind was howling and distant mountains did surround him in every direction. Ahravan did gasp, it was a vision, his people did take such things very seriously and he didn't really know what to do. It was cold there but he didn't really feel it, the wind was tearing at him but it felt as if it went straight through, without resistance.

Ahravan heard a wolf howl and turned around, a huge black she wolf was slowly trotting towards him, head low and tail raised, her eyes were deep golden and filled with wisdom. Ahravan did lower his gaze, he felt that he was in the presence of a deity of some sort and suddenly he heard a voice. Where the wolf had been a woman stood instead. She was tall and elegant, clad in furs and her face was calm and looked gentle. "Ahravan, my dear child, it isn't too late."

Ahravan swallowed. "We don't know what to do, she is poisoned, we have no antidote, she is dying!"

The woman nodded. "Yes, but you can save her"

Ahravan gasped, staring at the strange eyes, they were still those of a wolf. "How, please, tell me how? I would give my own life to rescue her, please"

The tall female smiled, the smile of a loving mother. "Follow the she wolf, she will show you, be brave Ahravan, forget about old beliefs and ancient rules. Remember the prophecy"

Ahravan did sit up, so fast he almost lost his balance, eyes wild and heart beating like a drum. He was sweaty all over and he was trembling. Rhawan did wake up too, he blinked and looked very confused and Ahravan grasped him by the shoulder. "Quick, the goddess, she showed me…we can still save her"

Wenja was ghastly pale now and her breath barely there, the leg was swollen and dark and it did stink. Rhawan nodded, he did trust his Si'ish with his life. Ahravan did lift Wenja gently, they exited the tent and saw that the unicorn was standing right in front of it, pawing at the ground. Flint nickered too and Khirhien and Ayhrandur did stare at them with confusion. "My Ath'ir?"

Ahravan swallowed hard. "We have to go, the goddess has shown herself to me, we can still save Wenja, do not follow. We will be back, I swear"

He did turn to Khor'ath. "Will you accept also her?"

The unicorn did nod and Rhawan did hold Wenja as Ahravan did mount the tall animal, then he did lift her up against his body and Rhawan did climb onto Flint with some problems. There was a howl and they saw a black wolf among the rocks, apparently waiting for them. Ahravan leaned forth. "Follow her, follow the goddess wolf, she will lead us right"

The unicorn did whinny and started to run and Flint was right behind it, also running as fast as its mighty legs could carry it.

Resh'kha and Floth'bha was giving all that they had, the heart stone did tug at the monsters with an unbreakable allure and they did follow it without hesitation, even if they by now were being called back by their master's voice. The power which had created them had realized that this was a trap, that the monsters would do no harm as long as they did follow the heart stone but its pull was too great for the beasts to break. The two riders had already managed to put some more distance between them and the beasts chasing them and it was needed. More had joined the huge herd by now and some were indeed monsters. Resh'kha had seen creatures with the horns of a buffalo and the jaws of a shark, beady red eyes and huge arms with clawed hands. But hopefully the dwarves and the two men were safe and Resh'kha didn't dare to think about what these abominations would have done to people if they had been allowed to roam free. The city was easy to protect now but still people did need to get outside to tend to their herds.

The buffalo was still very strong and the horse Floth'bha had chosen was a strong one, yet the animals were slowing down, they hadn't eaten much for days and water too was hard to find there. Resh'kha was hoping that they would be able to reach the mountains before the animals did lose all strength but she realized that both Steelhoof and the horse would collapse long before that. She knew that both she and Floth'bha would be easy prey without their steeds and she kept praying for something to happen which could solve the dilemma. There weren't any wild horses in the area, neither were there buffalo or other large animals. Everything had been chased away by the monsters or instinct had told the herds to seek the outer mountains. The only beasts left were small ones which could hide in burrows in the ground, prairie dogs and rabbits and marmots, and of course mice and rats.

Floth'bha's horse started to limp, it had stepped on a sharp rock and broken off a piece of its hoof. It did slow them down and Resh'kha did try to raise the shield but it didn't work this time. The monsters did see them from afar and did pick up their pace, Resh'kha knew that even if

Steelhoof was strong it wouldn't be able to keep its speed carrying two riders. She was heading towards a tall rock, in hope of finding something which could protect them or a place to defend when she heard an odd sound. Over them they saw a huge black eagle, it was soaring over the plains heading for the valleys behind the first mountains and it was both larger and darker than normal. Resh'kha had never seen an eagle like that, it didn't look natural. Was this another monstrosity? The she remembered something her mother had told her when she was a child, the sister of the moon was the ruler of all beasts and the one shamans would bow to. Her rule would be shown through her servants, beasts of unusual size, usually black.

Resh'kha whispered. "Oh great mother save us!"

Floth'bha had seen the eagle too and her eyes were huge, she too knew about the goddess and most of the races of the plains did worship her in one form or the other. Resh'kha did gasp. "Look, what is that?"

There was something moving ahead of them, heading in their direction, something large. It was two and the figures were very dark and huge and Resh'kha let out a wail of disbelief. As the two creatures got closer it became very clear that these were wolves, but not ordinary ones. These were massive, the size of large horses and both were black. Floth'bha just stared. "I cannot believe it, they were extinct ages ago?"

Resh'kha had her jaw almost touching her chest. "Apparently not!"

The two humongous canines did run next to their steeds now and Resh'kha did hesitate. "Are we to ride them?"

Floth'bha nodded. "I cannot see what else they are here for?"

Resh'kha remembered the stories told about the R'ubray, of times when her people had ridden these giant wolves and bonded spiritually with them. She gathered her courage, the race had been gone for so long they were a mere legend by now and yet, here two of them were. The strength of the orcs had been diminishing since their companions disappeared, they were being lessened by the loss. She did lean over and grasped the long coarse fur, hauled herself over to the back of the wolf. Floth'bha did the same and the wolves did pick up speed the moment they were on. The horse and the buffalo did break off to the side and ran in a different direction, away from their pursuers. It was very unlikely that the monsters would chase them. The buffalo had no tack and would return to its herd and the horse would probably turn back to the ones they left behind.

Resh'kha did swallow, the power she felt from this beast was immense. She felt humble and confused and very grateful too. "Why is the goddess helping us thus?"

Floth'bha did grin. "She doesn't like anything which isn't natural, and the monsters are not of this world, remember that."

Resh'kha did hold on to the scruff of the wolf's neck, it was odd sitting on one but it wasn't truly difficult. The speed was amazing, and they did head in the right direction too. Resh'kha had gotten her hope back, she did grin and enjoyed the wild ride. The night could come, she wasn't afraid of the darkness whilst riding one of the goddess own creatures. Floth'bha did grin too. "What shall we name them?"

Resh'kha did shrug. "I don't know?"

Floth'bha tilted her head. "I have an idea, what about Bloodjaw for your and Redfang for mine?"

Resh'kha nodded. "I know them names, the wolves of the heroes of old"

Floth'bha smirked. "Yes, fitting names wouldn't you say?"

Resh'kha did see that the monsters did follow them still, and the heart stone did feel warm now, as if it was alive. They would be able to reach the valley fast, somehow they felt that this was very important.

The monsters weren't made to be smart, nor to think much on their own. They were tools, no more than that and when the magicians had tried to reopen the gate and disturbed the magic which had kept it closed their masters had managed to break it wide open again. Now the ancient power was trying to gather strength and conquer the lands but first it had to destroy all resistance and the monsters were perfect for the task. It didn't matter if they were slaughtered by the thousands, there were always more to send forth and they did their job with glee. The sheer power of the heart stone had made him forget about tactics for a while, it had been enough to make him turn his attention away from the really important tasks and now the master of the monsters were in despair. The horde was no longer obeying his orders, they were caught by the darn stone and would follow it and he did guess that it was being used as a bait. He did remember what had broken free the last time the gate had been open, what they hadn't been able to restrain and break for their purpose and it wasn't something he wanted to meet again. No, he had to start with the ones he had corrupted, his progress would be slow, but he had patience. He had waited for thousands of years, some years more were nothing.

But he had sensed something, something which caused him true concern. A sort of presence which only meant one thing, a deity had awakened and gotten involved. Each realm of reality has its own gods and goddesses and some were powerful and some were not, but they didn't like that strangers did interfere with the order of things.

The power which had escaped from the gate was perhaps a deity, perhaps just a malevolent spirit but it was strong and here in this world its power was limited and yet great. It could affect others, plant images and ideas in their minds and lead them, use them for its purpose. It had already gotten hold of many of the natives of the high mountains and turned them into mindless beasts, ready to slay their own kin for the sake of his power. He had also ruled the goblins but now his hold of them seemed to have slipped for some reason and he didn't like it at all. He had no idea of why it had happened, his bond with the leader had been broken all of a sudden. Had the half orc really managed to shake himself free? No, the creature wasn't strong enough, not intelligent enough. It had to be dead and was it simply a case of murder due to jealousy or had the deities been involved?

The voice had no idea, and it bugged him, and the presence was getting stronger by the day. He had to prepare for an attack, for a siege. He did let go of the monsters, they were lost anyway and not worth the trouble. No, he had to get ready, he wanted this world, to possess it and slake his thirst for death with countless lives. The peoples of this realm had managed to beat him and his brethren once but not again, there was no power there that strong now, the gate would remain open and he would bring them all and this realm would burn. The elves of which the goblins had spoken were few, even if they did escape his monsters and the goblins they couldn't possibly be much of a threat. He would remember them, but other things were more important now.

Resh'kha was staring at something which was impossible, something which simply couldn't be. The valley ahead of them didn't look real, it was as if some tremendous force had scooped up a part of some other realm and dumped it right there, without caring about what it did look like at all. The valley did start as a rather narrow almost gorge like pit between tall cliffs but then it did widen out and Resh'kha couldn't see its end, it was almost as if they were at the top of a pyramid, looking down at its widening shape. But that wasn't the odd thing, the mountains and the plains were rather barren, dry and wind-blown, not a place for much vegetation. But the valley was covered with forest, a green thick blanket which for a moment did remind Resh'kha of the layers of thick moss covering rocks in dark wet places. It didn't look natural at all, the valley ought to be as naked as the rest of this mountain range and she did shudder. It did send cold shivers down her spine, she was not convinced that this forest wouldn't be dangerous to her and Floth'bha as well as the monsters.

Floth'bha did look pale and Resh'kha was rather sure that she too was paper white, they heard sounds from the forest, it did sound a bit like the noise of teeth against bones, a slow gnawing and the wolves did whimper and refused to move further. Resh'kha just knew it, her courage was to be tested now and she got down from Bloodjaw and took a deep breath. A narrow path did lead down to the green hell in front of them and she felt her heart trembling. She was an orc, not an elf. She had no experience with the woods, her realm was the naked hills and mountains where the winds did howl and only thin grasses did grow. And yet she had to go, Floth'bha did wet her lips. "Sister…."
Resh'kha did nod. "I know, go with the wolves, this…this is my test"
She did take Floth'bha's hand for a swift second, smiled swiftly and then she was on her way down the narrow path. Floth'bha did reach out as if to stop her, then she sighed and turned around, the wolves did walk towards a cave not far from the path and she did follow. This wasn't her

task, she knew that her turn would come but not now. If she was to see Resh'kha again alive was a huge question but she wouldn't intervene with the fate of somebody else. It wasn't the way of the orcs, each person owned their destiny.

Resh'kha was almost panting, the air down there was dense and thick and the scents sent every hair on her body standing up. There was a presence there, ancient and angry and alien, she had never felt anything like that before and it was terrifying. There were eyes everywhere, watching her hungrily and she whispered a prayer as she walked on. The shadows were deep and the trees, by every deity, they were grotesque and odd and the shapes were not like any tree she had seen before. The trunks thick and twisted with thick bark and the roots many and snake like and she could have sworn that she did see them move. The canopy wasn't green from the ground, more red and blue in colour and there weren't any dead leaves on the ground. What was what freaked her out the most, all trees fell their leaves but here there was just soil, thick dark rich soil which was soft to tread upon, as if some farmer had been there turning it with a plow yesterday.

Resh'kha did sneeze, the scent of the forest was musky, not at all that of trees and land but more that of a predator and she knew that this forest was horribly dangerous, whether it was the trees themselves or the thing that they did hide. The land did tilt downwards, not steeply but here and there small trickles of water did show that the land was not flat. Resh'kha had no idea of where to go, she had to follow her gut and she just kept walking. The monster would soon reach the pass and the path to the valley and she did doubt that this would stop them at all. The heart stone was even warmer now and it was heavy, so heavy she had to adjust the leather rope holding the bag rather often so it wouldn't dig into her flesh.

Resh'kha had never been so afraid in her life, but she kept pushing on. Branches seemed to be reaching for her, slimy and dark and she heard voices in the shadows, hissing and hateful, angry at everything which was alive and free. The terrain did flatten out and now it became boggy and wet, dead grass did stick up between the puddles of dark oily water and she knew that this was a very dangerous bog. Here you would sink and drown if you didn't know how to move. Resh'kha did whimper, the idea of sinking into this stinking mud was horrible, it made her legs feel like lead and her skin was slick with sweat. And yet she did walk on, going from one tuft of grey dead grass to the other, ignoring the dark puddles which were like staring dead eyes, watching her constantly. Hoping for her to slip and fall to a slow death.

Her boots were slick, and her body heavy without the almost weightless grace of an elf, and yet she did manage to get across to dry land. It was a sort of island made from solid rock, dark glasslike obsidian and as she did set foot on it the mist did dissipate and revealed a ring of standing stone, seven in all and very ominous looking. Resh'kha felt the magic within it, it made her skin tingle and she was shivering with fear. Here was something so powerful her mind didn't even have the ability to understand it.

She fell to her knees, not really able to think, the air was electric and the feeling of being watched intense. Resh'kha had felt ashamed when the shamans decided to send her away due to her attempt at winning the male she desired through magic, now she knew that they wouldn't have done that if she hadn't in fact had some abilities. They had seen her soul and her shame and knew that she needed to humble herself, or else she would end up badly. They had been wise, she was to learn and she trembled and forced herself to stare at the circle. Behind her she did hear the sound of monsters breaking their way through the forest, the ground did shiver with the weight of them and their roars got closer and closer, more and more excited. She grasped the bag with the heart stone, breathing so fast it felt as if her ribcage was about to explode. The monsters were out to get her, she felt it. She would be torn to shreds if they reached her and yet she didn't move, she just sat there, staring at the circle. Soon they would reach the swamp…

The voice was soft and a bit raspy, it held malice but not aimed at her. "Do not turn around child of the mountains, do not see"

Resh'kha did whimper, the presence was overwhelming, she felt it so strongly. It was female, and it was older than this world, it was waiting. The monsters reached the swamp, she heard the splashing and the slick sounds of mud, grunts as they forced their way forth, mad with bloodlust and the need to get the heart stone. She stared at the stones, her bones shaking and her cheeks wet with tears, all her instincts told her to turn around so she could see and protect herself but she obeyed the voice. She knew that if she did watch she would never return to Floth'bha, her mind would shatter like a badly made ceramic pot. The monsters were in the swamp, she almost expected to feel their warm breath against her skin and then suddenly, everything changed. The eager roars and shrieks were turned into screams of pain and fear and Resh'kha did feel a horrible warmth against her back, strong enough to singe her hair. She wore thick leather, her skin would be okay but the heat was unbearable. And more so, she heard the trees, heard them move, heard the creaking sounds as roots moved and tore into the horde of beasts, as they ripped them apart and threw the parts away. She heard as branches crushed beasts, as monsters were smothered and battered by solid wood. She heard their dying gasps and the horrible sounds of flesh being ripped apart, bones broken and bodies turned into tiny pieces.

Resh'kha did pray, her voice a mere whisper, a plea for her soul to survive this. She was a mere insect compared with the power she sensed there and could be crushed just as easily. The sounds lasted for what felt like an eternity, she squeezed her hands together so hard her fingernails did bite into her palms and she felt the saltiness of her own tears on her tongue. The fight to remain there was intense, her body screaming for her to flee and yet she couldn't. It would be certain death. It did end, not slowly and gradually but from one second to the next, as if the sounds were just switched off, like when a musician drops his instrument. Resh'kha did take a deep breath, what now? What would happen to her after this?

Chapter 12: Hearts and embers

Ahravan and Rhawan did ride hard, letting their steeds decide the path, the black wolf was running ahead of them, always at a distance and it shouldn't have been possible for no wolf is that fast and yet it was. The terrain was no different than before and they saw only rocks and barren sand, if there was some sort of help to find it was surely well hidden. Wenja was barely breathing, her spirit slipping away and Ahravan was panting with emotional distress. Her body was heavy in his arms and he didn't even pay attention to where Khor'ath did run. The valley did turn and suddenly the wolf did head into a sort of narrow gorge where a river once had dug into the bedrock itself. It was very dark and the bottom sandy and Rhawan did see that the wolf didn't leave any tracks, he did shiver. He had never seen his Si'ish like this, so tense and so close to absolute despair. They did ride into the gorge, it was heading uphill and their mighty steeds did struggle but managed to get up there still the same. They reached a plateau and on it was a cliff. It did look rather normal but there was an opening in it, seemingly a normal cave but Ahravan felt magic streaming from it and they felt a sort of shiver running down their spines. For a second the world did shift in front of their eyes and even if things didn't seem to have changed something apparently had still. The wolf stopped in front of the cave and wagged its tail before it suddenly disappeared and Ahravan did slide down from the unicorn and held Wenja close, Rhawan did stare at the opening with huge eyes. "It is dangerous"

Ahravan nodded. "Aye, I feel it to, but we have to!"

The entrance was so low they had to bow down and they carried Wenja between them. The cave wasn't large, and it was natural but in the middle was a pond and a faint light seemed to come from it. The air in there was warm and oddly fresh and reminded them of a sudden spring thaw. Rhawan did wet his lips. "What is this?"

Ahravan stared at the pond, his eyes were dark and his face pale, he realized what this was and why he had to be brave and forget about the past, and the rules. "It is the sacred well, where souls go after death, where the unborn are waiting"

Rhawan gasped. "No?"

Ahravan took a few hesitant steps forth, he did not believe it. It was said to be a mere legend, an old tale from time before time, when the gods did create the peoples who did inhabit these lands. "It is…the core of creation, I do not know why the goddess…"

Ahravan shuddered, they could save Wenja, but the price they would have to pay? Oh Gods, could he truly do this? Rhawan did whimper, the power in the cave was a benign one, one of love and support and yet it was so powerful it was almost painful. "What are we to do?"

Ahravan swallowed hard, he did lay her down onto the floor. "Rhawan, remember the things we have been told. The one born twice may close the gate? I know the meaning now"

Rhawan stared at him and Wenja and the golden eyes were wild. "Ahravan, it is…impossible, it is the deed of gods, not us, we cannot…"

Ahravan did interrupt him. "We have to! She is dying"

Rhawan lowered his gaze. "We may become outcasts, everybody may shun us."

Ahravan nodded. "Yes, but the goddess did lead us here so it will be her will then. And Wenja will be alive!"

Rhawan did look up again, his chin trembling as if he was about to burst into tears. "What do I need to do?"

Ahravan started to tear off the clothes Wenja wore, he was frantic. "The ceremony in itself is simple enough, but it will require all our strength. I have to pull her back Rhawan"

The dark skinned eternal did place a hand on Ahravan's arm, his voice soft. "I will be your anchor then"

Ahravan swallowed hard. "You know what you are risking then?"

Rhawan nodded, there was deep love in the golden eyes. "Yes, if she does die and pull you with her I too will die. But I love her Ahravan, just as you do. I wouldn't want it any other way"

Ahravan nodded and started undressing. This was magic nobody was allowed to attempt, magic which was banned, magic nobody even believed was real. Also Rhawan did get rid of his clothes and they carried Wenja over to the pond. The water was deep blue and glittering and it was warm too, they couldn't see the bottom at all. Ahravan did hesitate for a second, then he took his knife and made a cut in her hand, then in his own. Rhawan did take the knife and repeated the procedure on her other hand and Ahravan did nod. They pressed their wounds to hers and allowed their very blood to mingle. Ahravan was whispering. "Great goddess be with us, help us. Save her"

Both elves felt light headed, dizzy and Ahravan did pick Wenja up, staring at Rhawan. "I love you brother, I will need your strength now"

Rhawan just smiled and nodded and Ahravan did slide into the water with Wenja in his arms. There was no bottom, just emptiness around them and a feeling of slight panic did grasp him. He did attach an iron grip around Wenja, and with his other hand he did grasp Rhawan who held onto the edge of the pool. If he did let go they were all lost now, the contact with the real world through Rhawan's touch the only thing hindering their souls from searching for their release from their bodies and the eternity of the afterlife. Ahravan did gasp, the water did close over his head, this wasn't water you could swim in, nor float. It was not of any substance at all, a spiritual thing like ether and they were in fact in a different dimension altogether. He did hold onto Rhawan and Wenja and the world he knew did disappear in front of his eyes.

Wenja had been walking along a road, it was a place she didn't know and the forest and the lands around it lovely. It was sunny and warm and she felt safe, protected. The smells of summer were there and she wore a lovely light dress. She felt happy, relaxed. There was something nagging at her though, something she had forgotten? She didn't know, but she wanted to walk on, she had a destination and knew it. When she reached

506

it everything would be fine, there would be no pain or sorrow anymore. But why would she want to avoid that? She didn't feel any such thing? She felt confused again and stopped, tried to turn around but it was impossible. There was something dark behind her, something bad? She felt a sort of fear and did speed up, the road was easy to wander and the light ahead did draw her closer. She suddenly saw somebody standing by the road, it was a woman wearing almost the same dress as herself, and she had the same dark auburn hair like good wine. Wenja slowed her pace, blinking. The woman saw her and smiled, a very sad smile and yet one filled with love. "Wenja, my flower!"

Wenja felt confused, swallowed hard. "Mother?"

Her voice was hoarse and the woman nodded. "Yes, you cannot remember me but it is I"

Wenja gasped. "But…"

Rutha did sigh. "Wenja, I am here to tell you something, something not even your father was aware of. Something nobody knew beside myself. And you must listen for everything depends upon the choices you now will make, the wrong one will spell the end for all"

Wenja whispered. "Mother, you are scaring me"

Rutha nodded and her eyes were very deep. "When I met the man who fathered you I started serving the goddess, it was a secret and a thing only a few women did, they would call us witches and chase us off had they known. I did know that you were special Wenja mine, a soul unlike most. I saw the potential within you but unfortunately my life ended and I couldn't teach you the right ways. I am so sorry I wasn't there to watch you grow but now you have become a strong woman and I am so very very proud of you, my blossoming rose"

Wenja didn't know what to say, her head was spinning, why was she there? What was happening? "Mother, am I dead?"

Her voice a raspy gasp and Rutha shook her head. "No, not yet, but you are dying."

Wenja suddenly remembered, Ahravan, and Rhawan. "NO!! I don't want to, I…I have to live, my husbands…"

Rutha did nod. "I know, and that is why I am here. You have to turn back, it will cost you so much but there is no other way. The goddess is with you child, you can still make it back to the land of the living"

Wenja tried to turn around again, it was impossible, as if there wasn't anything behind her at all. "How? And what is the cost?"

Rutha did look down. "Your mortality, you will no longer be human Wenja mine, you will be so much more. The goddess will be within you, lead you. You will become her servant forever"

Wenja trembled. "You make it sound bad…."

Rutha shook her head. "It isn't, but it will require strength, and the change will be horrible. But there will be joy, and peace and you will be happy, if you do her bidding and manage to close the gate"

Wenja felt her mouth going dry. "I…"

Rutha did make a vague gesture and an image seemed to form in front of them, on the grass. Wenja saw herself, running around laughing, chasing a giggling child with black skin and wine red hair, Ahravan was standing not far from her with his hand on the shoulder of a girl, her skin wasn't as dark but her hair was red too and her eyes wolf like and intense. Wenja felt her chest constricting, her heart was hammering. "My children?"

Rutha nodded. "Waiting to be born Wenja mine, If you do what is asked of you it will be your reward and yet a part of the price you must pay"

Wenja couldn't tear her eyes off the scene until it faded away, a possible future, a possible life. "What do you mean?"

Rutha tilted her head. "One of your children will belong to the goddess, be her hand within the world, her sword and her justice."

Wenja was panting, the pull to walk ahead was getting terribly strong but if she did there would be no adorable little dark skinned angel and no beautiful wolf eyed girl. She did whimper. "What can I do mother, how can I turn back?"

Rutha did reach out and touched her, a sort of shock went through her and suddenly she felt a voice calling her name, desperately. "Walk backwards, do not try to turn around, trust them. Trust your beloved ones,

508

do not let anything you see scare you and do not stop whatever you do. Keep walking backwards."

Rutha did kiss her hand. "Go now Wenja, I will probably never meet you again if this ends well, but I am so proud of you."

Wenja heaved for air, then she took one step backwards, it felt like trying to walk through thick mud with lead boots, like trying to push her way through a wooden wall with only her own strength and body as tools. She let out a cry of defiance and pushed on, one step at a time.

She heard the voice again and she knew it was Ahravan calling out for her, she wouldn't let him down, never. She would not allow him to feel the grief of losing her. She bit her teeth together and pushed back, not stopping. Immediately the bright light became dimmed, the surroundings transformed from a lush forest to an eerie dark one with dead trees and horrible pale eyes staring at her from the darkness. Dreadful creatures lurked within those woods, souls condemned to never find peace and she was trembling with fear but kept walking, one backwards step at a time.

Hands tried to grasp onto her, some did look almost normal while others were covered with remains of flesh and skin, some were just bones and she heard their voices, their horrible anger and sorrow and the need to grasp her, keep her there. She was defying the very laws of nature now, breaking every rule there was. If she did fail this would be her final resting place and she wept with fear but kept going. Pain shot through her body with each step, every move more painful than the others. She shrieked in defiance, nothing would hold her back from her beloved, nothing would prevent her from reaching the future she had been shown.

Ahravan was struggling, in life he was powerful and few things could hope to fight him and live but here he wasn't welcome. He was a living soul, entering the realm of the dead and mist surrounded him, made it impossible to see. The air was thick like oil and each step agony but he couldn't stop, not yet. Not until he had reached her for she was ahead of him, in the mist. He felt her light and her life and he felt how Rhawan did pour as much of his own strength into his soul as possible. Ahravan did scream in pain, it felt like being ripped apart, as if thousands of blades did pierce his flesh at ones, as if acid were poured into an open wound. He didn't stop, he kept walking and suddenly he did see her. She was wandering towards him, backwards. Her body struggling with each move and around her he did see horrible apparitions. Wenja did scream, her strength was coming to an end and she wasn't yet back with her husbands, she had to keep going but it was so hard and the ghosts, they were clawing at her and now she did feel their cold touch and they did tear into her, the pain like ice each time. She was crumbling, her knees about to give in. She raised her head, a scream in despair and defiance. "Ahravan, help me!"

The scream gave him that last burst of strength, that last spark of desperate energy. He reached out grasped her shoulder, locking his grasp onto her. "Rhawan, now!"

Rhawan was clinging to the edge of the pool, and Ahravan's hand. Both were under water and Rhawan had never been this afraid in his whole long life. It was blasphemy what they attempted to do, the ultimate sin and yet there wasn't any other choice than to go through with it. He did cling onto Ahravan's hand with all his might and felt the pull, the unnatural cold which was seeping through their souls. He was panting, feeling the pain of his Si'ish and his fear and also that of Wenja, it was horrible and Rhawan was crying like a child but he did hold in, steadfast and brave as always. If this didn't work he would be just as dead as them and their souls separated for ever, and yet it was a price he was ready to pay.

He felt it suddenly, a jolt of energy, a shout within his own soul. "Rhawan, now!"

He heaved for air, started to physically pull. Normally it wouldn't have been hard at all, people do float in water but this wasn't water, and Ahravan and Wenja had become horribly heavy. Rhawan did gasp and pulled, his muscles screaming with the effort, his joints creaking. He did pull against death itself and it wasn't a fight he was about to lose. He was seeing red, his heart hammering like a war drum, his grip so hard it would have shattered the bones of someone human. He did pull, he pulled against darkness, against despair and heartache, he did pull for love and light and a future and slowly, ever so slowly Ahravan did rise to the surface. Rhawan growled, put a last effort into it and Ahravan's head got

510

clear of the water. He gasped desperately and pulled himself closer to the edge of the pond. There he got a grasp if it and Rhawan did reach into the water and together they did grasp onto Wenja and pulled her back with them. She was horribly heavy, death didn't want to let go of its prey, she was marked by his realm and belonged there and yet these two immortal did dare to defy him?

Rhawan and Ahravan used all their strength, all that they had and suddenly the grasp of the other side broke, Wenja became light and shot up to the surface, her body of normal weight. The two males let out a collective groan and lifted her and themselves up onto the ledge, panting and shaking all over.

Wenja had felt the pull of Ahravan and Rhawan, had tried to help them and yet it didn't seem as if it would work, they were not strong enough. She was being dragged back but all of a sudden there was a figure in front of her, a glowing silhouette which did chase the dark spirits away and suddenly it did shrink and disappeared, sunk into her own body and she felt as if she had received an electrical shock. She screamed and the grasp on her did end, the land of death couldn't hold a soul just being brought to life. And thus it couldn't hold Wenja back either, she was pulled back and everything went black as she felt hands tugging at her, bringing her back to the world.

The chamber was quiet, both males lay there half conscious and Wenja laid between them, pale and white and Rhawan did cough and moan. Smoke hang over the pond and Ahravan did try to raise his head but he was too weak. Rhawan managed to get up onto an elbow, his other arm was dislocated and he was shaking like a leaf. "Wenja?"

His voice a mere whimper and he did pull himself closer to her. She did breathe, slowly. Rhawan did help Ahravan get up and they pulled her away from the pond, both so tired and weak they barely could move. Wenja moaned, then she screamed. A wail of agony. The blackness of the leg disappeared, her body was rigid like an iron rod and she was shaking, her eyes rolled back and Rhawan gasped. "What is happening?"

Ahravan sighed. "Our blood, it is mixed now. She...is no longer human"

Wenja made gargling sounds, her previously nice skin became like porcelain, every imperfection was erased and the mark at the back of her neck did start to glow again, this time it would be permanent.

Her ears which had been round became pointed and when it did stop she laid there, gasping for air and her body seemed to glow for a moment before the light from within was dimmed down and she opened her eyes with a shriek. "Ahravan? Rhawan?"

Her voice hoarse and her eyes wild. Ahravan did embrace her, desperately, clinging to her as if she was a life raft. Rhawan did the same, she was almost smothered for a moment. "We are here, you are alive, oh praise the goddess you are alive"

Ahravan burst into tears and Rhawan was already crying and Wenja just sat there, letting the two males hold her until their combined fatigue became too strong and they all collapsed onto the hard rock and fell asleep. It was Ahravan who woke up first, due to the fact that he was cold and shivering in spite of being an elf. The room was truly chilly and they had used all their strength so it was no wonder that they were heavily influenced by their effort. He did drag their clothes over and covered himself and the two others with their cloaks. It wasn't much but it did help. Rhawan was shivering too, moaning in his sleep and Ahravan could see that his left shoulder was swollen and probably badly injured. They had to get away from there but not yet, they had to rest for a while. He did lay down again, Wenja between him and his Si'ish and he couldn't believe that he actually had managed to do what he had. If he started thinking about it too much he would go nuts so he closed his eyes and tried to relax. She had become one of them, it shouldn't have been possible but still, there she was, changed from a mortal human being into one of them. It was a miracle and one of which he would be eternally grateful. The scent of her was still the same, and the feeling of her breathing close to him brought new tears to his eyes.

They lay there for a couple of hours and then Ahravan did wake Rhawan, his Si'ish did look confused for a few seconds, then he sat up and gasped, the pain in his shoulder very apparent. Wenja was still asleep, she needed it, Ahravan just knew that from sheer instinct and he wished that they had been wise enough to bring some food. Rhawan

512

swallowed hard and his eyes were shiny, he did bow down and kissed Wenja's cheek reverently. Ahravan started getting dressed and nodded. "You are hurt, how bad is it?"

Rhawan tried to smile. "Dislocated I think"

Ahravan finished with his clothes and helped Rhawan get up, the shoulder was indeed dislocated and he did fear that muscles and tendons could have been torn too. He did not hesitate but pulled the arm back into the right position, that made Rhawan howl with pain but it was over within a few seconds and afterwards he did help his Si'ish get his clothes back on and made a sort of sling from some cloth. Rhawan was swearing but Ahravan did kiss him with gratitude. "You saved us all, I cannot thank you enough. You were strong for us both you know, if it hadn't been for you we would all have been dead now."

Rhawan managed to smile but he was still in pain and Ahravan did start to redress Wenja. Her sleep was very deep, almost coma like but he didn't find that worrying at all. He just felt that it was to expect, that it was normal if one could use such a word about their situation. He did manage to get her clothes back on and then he did lift her up. "We better return to the others, they are probably very worried by now"

Rhawan nodded and they exited the cave, both Khor'ath and Flint were still there and Ahravan had to make use of a large boulder to be able to mount the unicorn. Rhawan did the same with Flint and now there weren't any wolf showing the way but they did remember the path they had taken and they made good speed.

Ahravan held Wenja close, still feeling an odd sensation of disbelief. He just hoped that her new appearance wouldn't cause them problems later on. The others had been waiting, Khirhien and Ayhrandur did get to their feet as they heard the hooves and the silvery haired eternal did release a howl of relief by seeing them. Ahravan did slow Khor'ath down and he grinned at the two other eternal and the two humans. He remained sitting there until Rhawan had gotten down from Flint and then Khirhien did reach up and Ahravan did allow Wenja to slide into his grasp. Khirhien did gasp, he stared at her face with disbelief and Ahravan did jump down and nodded sternly. "The goddess did lead us, she is saved"

Ayhrandur did blink, his face a mask of confusion and disbelief. "Ath'ir, her spirit…she has become one of us?!"

Ahravan did nod. "As the goddess wanted it, now, make a fire and get some water warmed up. Rhawan needs some help with his arm I think. And we need food"

Khirhien was hoarse. "My lord, what have you done?"

The voice was a mere whisper and Ahravan sighed and looked down. "The unthinkable but believe me, there was no other way. She would have died and then we would have been doomed to failure. She is the one born twice Khirhien, the one who can close the gate"

The silver haired eternal did look shocked and a bit nervous but he did nod. "You did what you had to do Ath'ir. Let us pray that everybody else sees it the same way, this is…necromancy"

Ahravan sighed and sat down, he held her and stroked her long silky hair. Yes, it had been forbidden magic, dark magic. To bring back a dying soul was a terrible crime but the alternative had been just as horrible. He did kiss her brow and hoped that the goddess would keep her hand over them even now. After a little Khirhien came with some bowls of stew, it wasn't much but it was warm and Ahravan felt his guts howl with hunger, he hadn't really realized how hungry he was. Khirhien did look over Rhawan's shoulder, it was still very swollen and he did click his tongue and smeared some ointment onto it, he did also make Rhawan drink some sort of potion meant to ease the pain. It did make Rhawan spit and curse but he did drink all of it and Ahravan did close his eyes in gratitude, his Si'ish had saved them all. It was something which had to be rewarded, one way or the other.

Wenja did wake up when the sun was rising yet again, she made a mewling sound and jerked and then she opened her eyes, staring at Ahravan with confusion. Ahravan did grasp her hand, hoping desperately that she hadn't suffered any ill effects of her ordeal. She did wet her lips and Ahravan found a cup of water and held it up. "Here beloved, drink. You need it"

Wenja did empty the cup, desperately. "What happened?"

Her voice was thin and frail and Ahravan tried to smile. "You don't remember?"

514

Wenja sobbed. "I just remember that I got injured, that Yalaih is dead. I tried to reach you and then everything went black"

Ahravan did draw a deep breath. "You were truly injured my light, you had a poisoned wound, and you…you were close to death. The goddess did lead me and Rhawan to a cure, you are…safe now"

Wenja did blink, her body felt odd, so heavy and in a strange way alien. Her head hurt and her eyes felt as if she had been staring at the sun for too long, the light was just too bright. "Where am I?"

Ahravan did run his hand through her hair, it was trembling. "Back at the campsite, with the others. You have been unconscious for a while. Are you sure you don't remember anything?"

Wenja did nod, why did she feel so strange? "You…healed me?"

Ahravan did throw a quick glance at Rhawan, begging for support. "Ah, yes, we…We did follow the guidance of the goddess. Wenja…you….you have changed, as a result of this"

She saw that both Ahravan and Rhawan were nervous and a bit hesitant and she frowned. "What do you mean by that, changed?"

Ahravan did grasp her hand and kissed it lovingly, then he did lead it to her ear and she did feel how the shape had changed and she let out a yip. Her fingers became frantic, exploring both of her ears. "Ahravan?!"

He did smile, a very thin one. "You are one of us now Wenja, one of the eternal"

At first she didn't understand, her ears couldn't have heard it right? Or? She tried to calm herself, tried to understand what he just had said. "Ahravan? I…I am no longer human?!"

He did nod and Rhawan did nod too, his face a mask of apologetic grief. Wenja swallowed, once, twice, she felt her very being being thrown into turmoil, into questions. Oh gods, was she one of the elves now? How was that even possible?

"How?"

Her voice a mere whisper and Ahravan did look down, there was a nervous twitch around his right eye. "We did…share our blood with you. It is forbidden magic but…you were dying Wenja, and…if you had died I couldn't have borne it…"

Rhawan did stare at her too, eyes huge and pleading. "Neither would I, we would have died from grief, both of us"

She stared at them, her mind racing like a herd of wild horses over the plains. "I…I am immortal??"

Ahravan did nod, his face was in fact a bit sheepish looking and it would have been hilarious if it hadn't been this serious. She felt her heart speeding up, a billion questions racing through her mind and she stared at them both, helplessly. "What…I am still me?"

Ahravan did grasp her hands again. "Yes, yes you are…you are just…improved"

Wenja had no idea of what to think or feel, she wasn't human anymore? Should she be elated or should she feel horrified? She gasped and leaned forwards, hid her face against Ahravan's neck. "I…I don't know what to think…or feel. But the goddess did lead you?"

Ahravan did embrace her, held her close and rocked her in his arms. "Yes, we…we pulled you back from death Wenja, we almost died too but Rhawan here was strong enough to save us all"

Wenja did see the bandage over his shoulder and she gasped. "You were hurt? And how…"

Ahravan did caress her chin with a finger. "He will be alright my light, do not worry about that. Rest now, and have some stew"

She trembled in his grasp, her thoughts still buzzing like a hive of bees and she hid her face yet again. "What are we to do now? The goblins, did they return?"

Rhawan shook his head. "The goblins are gone, I doubt that they will be a threat again. We will wait for the morning and then we will ride on. We have to get to that cliff"

Wenja closed her eyes, they had pulled her back from death? She was grateful, but she felt conflicted. She was an elf now? Oh gods, she would outlive everybody she had known before, her parents, her siblings, everything. And yet…It was too much to think about, she swallowed hard and tried to relax, tried to gather her thoughts and be calm about it but it was hard.

There was some food and she laid down to rest again, still feeling peculiar and she stared at her hands. There were scars there now which hadn't been there before. A thin white line in each palm, barely visible. She guessed that they would fade in time. She did really have no idea of what to say or do now so she decided to just go with the flow.

Ayhrandur did ride out to check the path ahead and he did return telling of a valley ahead which seemed to lead to the right area and Ahravan did hope that it did. But what would they find on the other side of the mountains? What was this thing or being or whatever which had allowed the monsters to roam freely? The gate had to be completely open and Ahravan did know what that did mean. They had to stop this before it was too late, the deities of darkness were not something any of them could hope to stop. Nobody now had that power.

Rhawan did follow the faint marks Wenja had left behind and he did find the entrance to the goblin city. He did also find the body of Yalaih and buried her underneath a small cairn made from stones. That was all that he could do, the goblins were nowhere to be seen now, he had a feeling that they were eradicated somehow.

That night they slept close together and Wenja was very silent, it wasn't like her and Ahravan was worried that she somehow did blame them. She had been a mortal human, now she was something new and nobody knew how this would affect her. What Ahravan had done was seemingly impossible and it would haunt them forever. But none of them could regret it, not when she was there with them, breathing and alive.

The next morning they did leave the camp behind, all were well rested now and Ayhrandur did lead them. Wenja did sit up with Rhawan now and she stared at the landscape around her, stunned by details she hadn't noticed before, the scents which were so much stronger and the odd sensation of having been half asleep for a very long time. Rhawan did kiss her cheek lovingly. "You are awakening to your new senses my light, we have stronger and more acute senses than a human and now you will learn how to use them"

She nodded, the light was so incredibly sharp still and she had noticed that even darkness wasn't completely dark. One part of her felt giddy, the other part horrified. But she had an odd feeling coming from the back of her mind, a sort of silent presence and she couldn't identify it. It was as if she did know where to go and what to expect and she did give Ayhrandur some advice, all were a bit astonished by this.

They did ride through a valley which wasn't that hard to travel through at all, the terrain was even and the ground not too steep nor slippery. They could see a more flat area ahead now, between the mountains and Wenja knew that this was their goal. That night they did stop by a small lake and she was sure she saw a huge figure watching them from one of the carrocks. Earlier it would have terrified them but now it felt reassuring somehow, it was there to watch over them and she hid a small smile. She had indeed changed, she felt it more and more. She felt stronger, more self-assure, as if there was somebody there beside her, giving her advice and showing her the way, proving that she was more than before.

There were old tracks from monsters everywhere, the snow was riddled with them and yet there were few new ones and Ahravan did wonder what that did mean. Rhawan was sure that the gate couldn't let more than a certain number go through at a time, he was sure that one of the elders of his birth tribe had told him that. It was magic which held the gate open and it couldn't be drained too often.

They had been travelling for a few days when the terrain changed again, now they reached the tree line and the path become more steep and yet it wasn't as treacherous as before. This was a real path and Wenja did enjoy seeing trees again. They were few and very scrawny but they were trees and one evening they did find something even better, a hot spring. They did notice that the water in a small brook they did encounter did look warm and when Khirhien did check it out it was very warm indeed. Before long they did find a rather large pond and decided to rest there for the night, it was a very protected spot where they could use fire without it being seen from afar and Gochil did prepare a real meal this time. Wenja did eat until she felt as if she could burst and then Rhawan and Ahravan did follow her to the pond. It wasn't very large but it was relatively deep and the bottom made from small round rocks, she did tear her clothes off and the idea of finally being clean again was like a vision of heaven. She did wade inn, the water wasn't too warm and she did sigh with relief and joy. Her hair was stiff with sweat and filth and her skin had been crawling

518

for days or so it did seem. She was glad Ahravan had brought a small flask with the soap the elves used for hair wash, it did remove all of it and left the hair silky and clean.

Ahravan and Rhawan did enter the pool too, both were scrubbing themselves vigorously and Wenja did wet her lips, suddenly she did want them again, almost desperately. She had gotten accustomed to her new physical self now, at least to some degree and she felt that her desire too felt different. It was more direct, more demanding and raw and she understood now why the elves were such sensual creatures. Touch felt way more real to them, stronger and more profound. She did lean against Ahravan and reached around him, letting her hands slide down to his crotch and he gasped and didn't do anything to stop her. He was already hard and she let her hands explore and tease and he turned his head and stared down at her. His eyes were darkening with desire and Rhawan sat on a rock and tried to comb through his tangled hair and his gaze too did darken. Ahravan did turn around, large calloused hands were caressing her and it felt wonderful. Wenja hadn't lost her voluptuousness and she was glad, it made her feel way more feminine than the female elves and she hoped that she would stay that way. Both Ahravan and Rhawan did love her curves. "Needy my love?"

The voice was husky and dark and she nodded, she was more than ready already and Ahravan did sit down on one of the rocks underneath the water and Wenja did realize what he wanted, she did turn around and sat down, facing away from him. As she did straddle his lap he did push inside her and she had to scream, it felt better than ever before, so good she saw stars and sparks and if this was how it was going to be for the future she was darn glad they had done what they had. Ahravan did groan and held her hips, did thrust eagerly and she mewled and knew she wouldn't last long. Rhawan did get up and walked over to her, he was fully erect and stopped in front of her, there was a silent challenge in his eyes and she felt very brave and daring there and then. She did lean a bit forth and grasped his hips as she started to lick and suck him and he threw his head back and let out a thin wail of sheer pleasure. It was intoxicating, it was wild and wonderful and she couldn't believe that she did this but it was real. She felt herself getting close and Ahravan probably sensed it too for he did speed up a bit and she had to let go of Rhawan's cock and howl as she climaxed, shuddering almost violently. Ahravan did grunt a few times, then he too came and she felt it, she felt it so well and squirmed in delight. Rhawan did gasp and grasped onto himself, stroked his hand up and down a few times and then he too reached his climax, spurting pearlescent fluid over her breasts. It seemed as if the very sight was making him go half mad with sheer lust for he kept coming for a long time.

Wenja did giggle and her legs felt weak as usual, she got up and felt wonderfully relaxed and at peace. Rhawan did lean forth and kissed her with obvious gratitude and Ahravan did smack her over her rear lightly and with a teasing glimpse within his eyes. "Was it good?"

Wenja pouted. "Yes, you must have felt that?"

Ahravan nodded. "Aye, you were like a vice, a wonderful warm and tight one and by the goddess, you can truly make a male lose his mind"

He got up and grinned. "And I feel like I need some more, Rhawan, are you ready for a bit more?"

Rhawan did lick his lips. "Always my Si'ish, I am yours"

Ahravan did grin and Wenja sat back, she knew what he was doing. He was simply rewarding her for her initiative with a bit of a show, he did know that she enjoyed watching him taking Rhawan. Rhawan did lean forwards, resting his elbows on the edge of the pool and Ahravan did find some hair oil and started to prepare his bond brother, he was always gentle doing this and never in a hurry for he didn't want to cause Rhawan any unnecessary pain. When Rhawan was ready he did push inside slowly and Rhawan did gasp and grunt and Wenja could see the mixed pain and pleasure on his face. As Ahravan started to move Rhawan's gasps and moans became sheer pleasure and he was straining against his lover, as if he wanted Ahravan even deeper within his body.

Wenja got an idea, she did get up and slid over, she grinned and pushed herself inn underneath Rhawan, opened her legs and embraced him, now he just had to lean a bit forth to penetrate her and he did, with a wail of desperation. Wenja did shriek, it was the most arousing thing ever, being taken by Rhawan as Rhawan was being fucked by Ahravan and Rhawan was trembling with each thrust, throwing his head up, arching and keening. Ahravan did pant and moved with enough energy to rock them all in a vigorous rhythm and Rhawan tensed up, his eyes did slide shut and he let out a hoarse roar. Wenja felt the pulsing sensation of his release and came too, suddenly and hard and Ahravan groaned and joined them. It was as if she truly felt both her own orgasm and that of her partners and it almost knocked her out. It didn't die down for several minutes, each small movements firing off new fireworks within and she was feeling like lead as Ahravan did drag her onto a pelt they had placed by the pond. She just laid there panting and Ahravan did spoon her, a hand on her hip. Rhawan did lay down in front of her, exhausted and satisfied and they just laid there, allowing the afterglow of their love making to fade away.

Wenja was sure she was about to go to sleep when Ahravan did jerk, his eyes did fly open and he gasped. Wenja opened her eyes again and grunted, what was it now? She had been so wonderfully relaxed even if she did feel a wee bit tender down there. Ahravan was staring at her, his eyes huge and filled with shock. He did slide his hand down over her belly where it stopped, resting for a few seconds and he made an odd mewling sound. "Wenja?!"

His voice told of disbelief and she frowned, feeling more than a little scared. "Is something wrong?"

She felt hysteria beginning to build up, what was this? Ahravan gaped and Rhawan too did lift his upper body, clearly confused. "You….you are with child"

Wenja froze. "WHAT?!"

Ahravan just stared, his eyes like tea cups and his expression one of utter disbelief. "I can feel it, another spirit, inside of you. It is female"

Wenja gaped. "No, that…it isn't….are you sure??!"

Rhawan too did gasp and laid a hand on her and his eyes too got wide with shock. "Oh sweet goddess, I can feel it too!"

Wenja blinked, her mind spinning and Ahravan swallowed visibly. "You aren't used to being an elf yet, if you had been you too would have felt it already. Oh by every deity…"

Rhawan made some incredibly peculiar grimaces. "She must have conceived before she was wounded, back in the high mountains, before… Oh what have we done?!"

Ahravan seemed to be in shock, his expression one of utter disbelief. "Uh…"

Wenja turned to him. "What do you mean? Is something wrong? "

Her voice was thin, she couldn't be pregnant already? Or could she? But … Ahravan was opening and closing his mouth like a fish on dry land, Rhawan was doing the same imitation. "It shouldn't be possible…we didn't try to…and you were almost on the other side?"

Wenja laid a hand on her belly too, she didn't feel any different than before, there had been no symptoms of her being with child. "Could it be dangerous to the baby?"

Ahravan tried to get a grasp on himself. "Oh ah, I have no idea, that is what I am afraid of, the goddess be with us."

Wenja swallowed, her voice pleading. "Sefa said that you can decide whether or not you can impregnate someone?!"

Ahravan nodded. "Yes, and neither of us have tried to do that, even thought about it."

Wenja felt a bit angry, why she didn't know. "So your inborn birth control has failed then? Perfect!"

She didn't want to sound so crass but her voice was rather venomous and Ahravan did cringe. "Oh Gods Wenja, we are so so sorry"

She tried to think and knew that they were right, it had to have been that one time in the mountains for if she had conceived while they were on the plains she would have noticed by now. It was just a few days old and yet they felt it? It was odd but a strange sensation did spread through her, she had always wanted children and somehow she knew that it would be alright, that nothing bad would happen to this baby, even if she had almost died just after it came into being. She sighed. "What is done is done, how long will I have to carry?!"

Ahravan gaped again and Rhawan swallowed, she saw his Adams apple moving up and down a few times. "A year, our women do carry their young for a year, and you are an elf now"

522

She tried to smile. "I won't be bothered by my size for a while then I recon, so what do I need to know? Is there things I should or shouldn't do?"

Ahravan did blink. "You have accepted it?"

Wenja had to laugh, a thin gasping laughter. "What else can I do? It is there, and I don't think elven women are prone to still births and failed pregnancies?"

Rhawan nodded. "You are right, they aren't. Losing a baby is extremely rare among our people, the times it does happen it has to be through some sort of serious physical trauma"

Ahravan did look down. "You shouldn't be here now, you should be in safety among the others in the city, a pregnant woman is valuable beyond description to us"

Wenja could understand that, elves didn't breed very often and she had seen few elven children among the clans. "I have no choice, and I bet that the idea of removing it is out of the question right?"

The gasp which came from both males was answer enough, the very idea was probably taboo to their race. "Even if it was possible it would be a horrible ordeal to you, it would most likely leave you scarred for eternity. The spirit of the baby is linked to yours, it isn't as it is with humans, it isn't a solitary entity yet."

Wenja did sigh, she suddenly felt tired again, as if she was made from stone. "Alright, then I just have to get used to the idea. Do you have any idea who the father is?"

Ahravan sort of gawked and made a grimace but he did place his huge worn hand over her belly yet again and closed his eyes. He was silent for a moment and when he did speak his voice did crack. "It is mine, I can feel its spirit reaching out for me, seeking my strength. Oh goddess, my daughter…"

Wenja got a weird sensation of déjà vu, as if she already had known somehow, but she hadn't. Ahravan did gasp for air, then he did burst into tears and Rhawan did stroke his hair and seemed to be very emotional too. Ahravan embraced her suddenly and violently, shaking all over. "I have longed for a child of my own blood but why now? You are walking towards danger my light"

Wenja felt strong, suddenly she was the one with the peace of mind, the mature one. Women had born children in worse times than this, through war and strife and she did smile. "I will be alright, I am sure the goddess is with me"

She kissed his brow and reached out, took Rhawan's hand too. "I will bear you children too Rhawan, do not think that you will be forgotten"

Rhawan swallowed hard and his eyes were glassy. "Wenja, I would be so honoured"

She relaxed against them, it was both exciting and terrifying and if they had been safe back at the city she would have been ecstatic. But what could she expect. "So, my question?"

Ahravan did wipe his eyes and kissed her, reverently. "There aren't any specific things to avoid yet, only when the time draws near. But you may experience cravings faster than a human mother, and you will become very tired. Elven children crave much more from their parents than human ones."

Wenja had to giggle and the two males did look at her, questioningly. "What is so funny?"

Rhawan's voice was soft and she bit her lower lip. "Cravings, I remember one of the wives from the village where I grew up, she sent her husband out to get her birch sprouts and crushed limestone, in the middle of the winter"

Ahravan had to smile. "Whatever you want Wenja, we will do all we can to get it for you."

She did smile and leaned her head against his shoulder. "There is one thing I do remember from before I and Yalaih did fall into that trap. Yalaih said that there was a woman there, trapped with me. A daughter of the people of the mist, and she would draw the goblins away from us. But I haven't heard of such a people before?"

Ahravan caressed her belly, in a very protective manner, he had already accepted the idea of becoming a father and Rhawan knew that over the next day's his instincts would awaken. Elven males become extremely protective of their mates while they are expecting and there would be changes in his personality. Rhawan did remember one of his friends who had shared the same symptoms as his wife as she carried their son, including morning sickness and aching breasts. They had teased the poor guy mercilessly.

Ahravan nuzzled her cheek. "They are a race of people who live in the high mountains some places, I have never met any of them, they aren't many and they are scattered but we know of them. They are a bit like the dwarves but live in simple huts and hunt with primitive weapons and they have a very secretive culture. Not much is known about them"

Wenja felt sleepy and closed her eyes. "What do they look like?"

Rhawan shrugged and pulled a pelt over them, it was chilly there whence they were out of the water. "Shorter than most people, stocky and hairy and not very pretty the way we see it but they are renowned for being very honourable and good hunters, and they know the land like none others."

Wenja yawned. "Alright, I want to take a nap now, is it alright?"

Ahravan did kiss her. "Sleep my precious, we will watch over you"

Wenja just sighed and fell asleep and Ahravan did stare at Rhawan with huge eyes, his expression still one of disbelief. "I cannot believe it?!"

Rhawan sent him a swift smile. "Neither can I, but it is as it is. We have to take care of her from now on"

Ahravan did grin, a rather wry and swift grin. "Yeah, and do our duty willingly right?"

Rhawan giggled. He did know of the belief among their people, that expecting parents ought to have sex as much as possible up to the birth to make sure that the baby would become a strong one, they said that the strength of the father would pass into the baby that way. "With both of us doing our best that baby will be a fighter for sure"

Rhawan did reach out over Wenja and grasped Ahravan's hand in a firm grip. "I am so happy for you brother, so very happy. This is wonderful news once we get used to it"

Ahravan nodded, his eyes soft. "Yes, yes it is, but it will take some time to get used to the idea. "

Rhawan nodded. "I am here, always. I will help you both. "

Ahravan just kissed his knuckles and closed his eyes. It was with both joy and fear he did consider this. The next months would be strange to him indeed.

Resh'kha didn't know what to expect, what she now would have to face. The monsters were all dead and she felt that the energy of the circle did grow, staying there had become almost unbearable. She stared at the ground, hearing her own heartbeat in her ears and she kept praying. The silence was terrible after the noise of the monsters being destroyed, she didn't want to imagine the end they found. Resh'kha heard footprints, she did hold her breath, looking down. The footprints were rather heavy and they did stop ahead of her, she held her breath and hoped that it wasn't something ready to kill her. "Daughter of the mountains, you have done well"

The voice was hoarse and raspy and oddly flat and yet it was a feminine one. She did heave for air and felt her heart hammering in her chest. "I…."

She didn't manage to say anything more and the voice did chuckle. "You may look at me orc, I mean you no harm. Quite the opposite"

Resh'kha did raise her gaze, what she did see made her tremble to the bone. She had no idea of what this creature was, but it was horrifying and yet majestic, with a sort of odd beauty which was very alien. It was female but it didn't look soft or meek at all, this was a terribly dangerous enemy. The creature was at least three meters tall, with wide shoulders and strong arms and legs. The hands had claws and it was covered with grey skin which did look almost metallic. The head was wide and it had horns and long pointy ears and the eyes…they were black, pitch black over a narrow and snout like nose and a mouth with razor sharp teeth, way too wide and rather cruel looking. The creature did wear a sort of black leather dress and some elegant and oddly shaped jewellery and Resh'kha did sense that it was powerful, and that it was used to being obeyed. The thing had long black hair, formed into elaborate braids and Resh'kha did see that the creature had some spines along its back and it had a tail too. She had no idea of what race this female did belong to at all.

The creature did tilt its head. "You wonder about me don't you? It is nothing wrong with that orc, you are after all an intelligent being."

Resh'kha did nod, feeling slightly faint. The creature was very powerful, the air did crackle around it. "Yes"

The creature grinned, it was a sickening smile, the teeth were just ghastly, like those of a dragon. "I am Gholrae, I used to be a deity, now I am a shadow of what I used to be!"

Resh'kha did wet her lips. "I…don't understand?"

Gholrae clicked her tongue, it was very long and forked like a snakes. The thing was so inhuman in many ways it made Resh'kha feel slightly sick, the monsters had sort of been based upon familiar shapes and traits but this? It was completely alien. "I do not expect you to understand, not without an explanation. "

The creature did raise a clawed hand and Resh'kha did see a sort of image in the air in front of her, a shimmering mirage of something from another age and world. A giant army was gathered on a dark plain under an oddly red sun, it was monsters, millions of them and large dark figures did wander among them, keeping them in line, making sure the groups were under control. "See them? The dark ones, wicked and evil powers, controlled by naught but greed and useless bloodthirst. One of them has come through and wish to do what his forbearers didn't manage to do. Open this world to his brethren"

Resh'kha did pant, the sight was horrible. "Is this…real?"

Her voice a mere whisper, a thin plea and Gholrae did nod. "It is real, they are waiting daughter of the mountains. Soon the dark one will allow these vast armies to enter this realm and it will burn and everything will die."

Resh'kha did shiver. "The gate must be closed"

Gholrae did chuckle. "Oh yes, you are right, it must be closed. It is the only chance you have. If it is closed properly it cannot be reopened and you will be safe forever"

Resh'kha swallowed. "Why are you telling me this?"

Gholrae did grin, sharp teeth did glitter in the light. "Because I want him to fail, I want to avoid the death of this world. My own realm did once fall victim to them, never again."

Resh'kha blinked. "You were a deity?"

Gholrae nodded. "Of the people of that world yes, their goddess, their protector. You can destroy a land little orc, but you cannot destroy its gods, not as long as there still are those who believe and they didn't kill everybody back there. Some are alive, their slaves. So I am here, having followed them through the gate to see if I can cause trouble"

Resh'kha dared to breathe a bit more freely. "You are an enemy of theirs?"

Gholrae did nod. "Yes, very much so. And I have power, I have absorbed power for ages, feeding upon the darkness they did bring"

Resh'kha did swallow again, the forest was terribly dark and she had a feeling that the realm this creature came from had to have been a very terrifying one. "You killed the monsters"

Gholrae nodded, the black eyes did shine. "Yes, the energy of these servants of the darkness has given me what I need to give the dark ones one last boot up their arse"

Resh'kha did gasp, the deity did indeed use a very colourful vocabulary. Gholrae did lean forth. "You are a servant of the goddess, the power which resemble me when I was being worshiped back in my own realm. We are two sides of the same card, a mirror image of each other. We want the same thing little orc, to protect this world"

Resh'kha did look down. "What do you want of me?"

Gholrae did grin and the long tongue did flicker. "The one born twice can close the gate but the dark one is beyond the power of that person to defeat. And there are other servants of darkness there, if she is to succeed she will need help, more help than she has now"

Resh'kha did frown. "I don't understand, do you mean Wenja and the others? They were heading for that cliff, and it is very far away."

Gholrae did tilt her head, the expression was predatory. "Yes, very far and yet very near, for a deity such things are not important. You can help them, by helping me"

Resh'kha did get up, very slowly. "Can I trust you?"

Gholrae did chuckle. "Yes, I have nothing to lose little orc, but all to gain. So do you. The power I have gained, it is all for nothing if it cannot be used for something good"

Resh'kha did feel that the stones did hum with power and she stared at Gholrae. "What must I do?"

Gholrae did smile, the smile was in fact not as inhuman now that Resh'kha had gotten used to the creature. "Such a brave soul, so pure and so determined. The gem you are carrying, it may harbour that power, and whence you reach your destination it may be used against the dark one. His armies must not be unleashed, they must be destroyed before they break free."

Resh'kha felt her heart hammering, this was unreal and yet it did happen. "So?"

Gholrae did make a snake lake gesture with her arm. "I can do that, I can disrupt the control the dark one has of his servants, but I cannot get near the place in person, not as I am now. I am no longer a deity little orc, I am but a mere speck of dust compared with him. With the power I have assembled in the circle I can regain my former power but if I do he will notice me and that will be a very bad thing. I have to wait until I am very close indeed, too close for him to be able to fight me off"

Resh'kha did squint. "What you are saying is?"

Gholrae grinned. "The power will be harboured by your gem and I will hitch a ride within your soul, I am only corporeal now because you wouldn't be able to see me otherwise. I can become invisible when I want to, a mere spirit. Bring me to the cliff, unleash the power and I will destroy the dark one and the one born twice will close the gate."

Resh'kha frowned. "You cannot close the gate? It would ensure that nobody will have to face that danger?"

Gholrae did sigh, her head tilting forwards in sorrow. "Alas no, if I get near the gate it will suck me inn, bring me back to their world. I will be helpless then. No, I have to stay away from the gate but I can fight the dark one. Please, it is the only way"

Resh'kha crossed her arms over her chest. "How am I to get to the cliff? And I have friends I want to bring, I won't leave without them"

Gholrae did nod, her black eyes were bottomless, like dark holes and Resh'kha wondered what sort of world it was which could give birth to such creatures and gods. She didn't trust Gholrae, but she didn't have much of a choice but to obey and do what was asked of her. She had no desire to end up as the monsters had, and she already recognized the emotions which did pour from the former deity, it was hatred, black and thick as tar and those who hate doesn't bother with crushing others in their pursuit of vengeance. "I will make sure that you all go to the hidden vales up north. You will all be needed for sure, valiant warriors are rare and precious"

Resh'kha did stare at the circle of stones. "I have a hard time believing that the heart stone can contain that much power"

Gholrae did grin and her odd face was wry. "But it can, a heart stone can keep an immeasurable amount of energy, believe me. It will be no problem at all."

Resh'kha did still doubt it but Gholrae did point at the circle. "Just enter the circle and place the gem on the ground in the middle."

Resh'kha did look a bit worried. "And it isn't dangerous?"

The deity did grin again. "No, just don't touch it until it is over and all the energy is absorbed."

Resh'kha did take a deep breath and walked forth, the energy was like warm wind against her skin and the moment she did enter the circle it felt as if she was about to be struck by lightning. The gem was so hot now it felt painful touching it and she just dropped it onto the ground. The earth there was seemingly burned and hard but the gem didn't make a sound as it hit it and it did start to glow even stronger than before. There was a sound as if from terribly hard wind and Resh'kha had to whimper. Sparks flew by her, the forest around the circle seemed to crumble, to be reduced to mist and it all seemed to be sucked into the gem. It happened so fast and yet horribly slowly and Resh'kha did close her eyes, it was simply too much. She kept her eyes shut and when it did stop she slowly opened them again. The circle was gone, so was the forest. The entire valley was bare and barren like most of the other mountain valleys of the area and even the bog was gone. The deity which called itself Gholrae did stand there, transparent. She did bow her head. "You are very brave orc, that is good. You will need your courage. I will join with your flesh and then transport you and your friends to the hidden vale. There I will guide you until the time is right and I may destroy the dark one"

Resh'kha did take a deep breath. "Alright"

She picked up the gem and placed it in its bag again and now it did look normal but she felt a sort of presence within it, very vague but it was there. She did remember the spirit she had trapped in it within the tunnels and decided to not tell anybody about it, something told her that this could be wise. Gholrae did tilt her head and raised her arms, a sort of glowing orb of light formed around them and suddenly the world was simply gone from in front of her eyes. Resh'kha did gasp and had trouble staying upright. She heaved for air and there was a puff and Floth'bha was suddenly there too, with the two wolves. And then the two dwarves and the men too appeared with their steeds and Resh'kha saw that they were asleep but Floth'bha wasn't and she did look terrified but she didn't try to move at all. She stood there, with huge eyes and pale skin. Suddenly there was a sort of jerk and the golden orb did disappear. They stood on a grassy hill and around it was a rather flat area and mountains to the south. Gholrae did wink at Resh'kha. "I cannot get any closer like this, but ride south and go fast, time is of the essence. If the one born twice is to do her task the dark one must be distracted. Be that distraction."

Gholrae did disappear and Resh'kha felt a chill running down her spine and she was dizzy for a few seconds. She felt odd, disgusted almost. So this deity was hitching a ride with her? Well, Resh'kha wouldn't change her ways in any ways, stove away or no stove away. The others did wake up and looked utterly confused and Floth'bha was shivering. Resh'kha did sit down, it was gonna be a long explanation and not one she was too happy about but what was there to do? The monsters had been eradicated and the people of the plains saved for now, but they had to make sure that it wouldn't happen again. "Now folks, listen very carefully for there is no way in heck I am gonna tell you this more than once!"

After a while she was done and everybody just stared at her, Floth'bha was swallowing convulsively. "So we have to drag the attention of whatever it is away from the elves?"

Resh'kha sighed and nodded, she had to sit down. "Yes, basically"

Floth'bha did shake her head. "The deity you have chosen to cooperate with? I do not trust her, not even for a second"

Resh'kha had to grin, a sort of sarcastic sneer. "Of course not, neither do I. But my enemy's enemy may be my friend right? Or at least useful for a while"

Geir nodded slowly, his face was thoughtful. "Yes, she did get us here and if she has her own agenda it is the same as ours, at least to a certain degree. I know the art of war, heck, I have fought way too much and Resh'kha is right. We ought to use this for all it is worth"

Kulkar and Dharan did stare at each other and Kulkar did look very proud. "Each race ought to do what they can to help prevent a complete disaster, we are proud to represent the dwarves"

Resh'kha felt touched, he was right, all the peoples of the plains were present and maybe this was as it should be. She saw that the ponies and horses were well rested and there was in fact grass growing there, not fresh but it didn't look too bad. She did sit down and felt how her head still was spinning slightly, the process of being transported thus had been odd indeed. "Let the animals eat and rest for a while, we cannot leave just yet. We have to get some food and prepare ourselves"

Floth'bha did grasp her bow and ran off to find some game and Kulkar and Dharan did arrange a sort of hearth underneath some rocks. The smoke would be spread and not as visible thus and they needed something hot now. Before long Osbord had some tea ready and Floth'bha did return triumphantly with some large birds. The meal was a good one, Resh'kha hadn't realized that she was hungry but she was, ravenous. After they had eaten they did erect a couple of simple tents and rested in shifts and Resh'kha did try to sleep but it was hard. She kept seeing images in her mind, strange and confusing ones which she couldn't identify as her own memories. It had to be Gholrae's memories she saw, a world underneath a blue sun, people with horns and grey skin and strange animals and plants and then fires and death and a feeling of being utterly helpless. If this was how Gholrae did feel Resh'kha could understand her to a degree. Seeing everything you love being ruined thus had to be horrible, and being unable to prevent it even worse. When she finally fell asleep she didn't get much rest at all and woke up still feeling tired.

The morning came with sour wind and the clouds did kiss the ridges, it was dark and cold and Floth'bha did click her tongue and claimed that it was perfect weather. Nobody would want to venture outside in such conditions, not even the enemy. Kulkar did grunt and claimed that the monsters were hairy and probably stayed warm no matter what and they could still be out there. The ones they had lured away from the city couldn't have been the only ones after all, if you are to invade somewhere you need more than just a few packs of foot soldiers. They did leave the camp and Resh'kha felt restless and worried, they didn't have any idea of what they could expect and she just knew that the enemy was "a dark one" and what exactly did that mean? A dark wizard? Most likely, but what type of wizard? She did doubt that it was something even remotely human if it had come from another world, could they hope to understand at all?

Geir was the one she could rely on now, he had been a mercenary and his experience was invaluable. The aging man was a person she had started to respect for his calm ways and his ability to think even in tight situations, it wasn't something she would have believed to be possible just half a year ago. She had regarded humans as weak and flawed and barely more than vermin but her attitudes had changed and she had to admit to herself that it did feel good. She had broadened her horizon and her wisdom did increase.

Geir was thinking about the things she had learned and his face was serious, he was riding next to her and she had noticed that the horses didn't react to the two giant wolves. They were beasts of the goddess and thus not dangerous to the steeds at all. Resh'kha was not surprised by Geir's opinion on their mission, she had come to some of the same conclusions. They were few, and they were ill equipped and that was the good things he could say. It was a suicide mission if the enemy became aware of them, they couldn't hope to fight off hordes of monsters but if they did manage to remain hidden and used all their stealth they did have a chance. The question was how they were to distract the enemy if they had to stay hidden, it was a tricky question for an open attack was bound to end in their deaths.

The mountain area was narrow and there was a broad valley behind the mountains and Resh'kha did feel that it was their destination, where the enemy did stay and where the gate was located. Geir felt that their only chance was to cause some sort of problem, to do something which would disrupt the plans of this dark one, whatever they were. And preferably without being exposed. It wouldn't be easy at all, and Resh'kha felt the gem on her chest and her mouth was dry.

The area they did cross was desolate and naked and they didn't see any life there at all, which did tell Floth'bha and Resh'kha that something indeed was wrong there. Even this far up north there ought to be wild animals other than birds and also, the lack of snow was confusing. These areas should have been covered with many feet of snow and yet it wasn't that much at all. Resh'kha did feel something in the air, a sort of disturbance and the winds didn't feel normal. She did guess that it was the power she had inherited from the old dwarf which told her this, a shaman knows nature like the back of his or her hand and here it was disturbed in a very odd manner. Floth'bha did come up with a reasonable explanation, if the monsters and beasts were taken from a different world it could be that the climate of this one did bother them somehow? Too much snow could perhaps be a problem to them? Kulkar did grin and revealed that he had several gold teeth. "The long fur we have seen on some, I can only imagine what a pain in the neck that is when it is covered with snow."

Dharan did nod. "Aye, it is coarse, not like the fur of the animals of the mountains. Their fur is slick, the snow slide off"

Resh'kha did nod and she did agree, it did tell them something. This dark one was powerful enough to change the weather, that was in itself scary and what could they really do? She did take a look at her little group, two men, two dwarves and two orcs, it wasn't much to brag about but they were all experienced and good fighters and would the enemy anticipate any sort of problems? Not from the north, she was rather sure of that.

They used a few days crossing the mountains and it was a hard part of the journey but nobody did complain and when they reached the other side they realized that it was bad, it was more than bad, Resh'kha felt shocked to the core and she had no idea of what they could do, if anything at all. The area behind the mountains was flat but in the middle of the plain was a huge cliff, it did look like a spire but the shape was strange and other peculiar cliffs were scattered around its base. The distance was so great they couldn't see any details but Resh'kha did get a feeling of something horribly ancient, older than time itself. And she also got a sensation of vertigo, of something trying to suck her inn, tilting everything upside down and tearing the very fabric of space and time apart. The plain was covered with living creatures, it did look like an ant hill seen from above and everybody just stared. This was the main force, and it was probably growing by the day. The dark one had to be bringing inn new beasts each day and Resh'kha felt a surge of sheer terror. If these numbers were unleashed upon the world nobody would be able to resist them. No city, no fortress, no hidden vale could hope to withstand such power, they would be overrun by the sheer numbers for the leader of this probably didn't bother with losses at all.

Resh'kha did stare at the plain, it was both green and lush in some areas and dry and dead in other places and the strange cliffs did confuse her but she couldn't be sitting there admiring the nature now. To the north of the huge cliff there was an area which had a peculiar green tone and it did remind her of the bogs she had seen in the high mountains back home, the ones which usually didn't look all that wet but could be very hazardous.

How were they to make a difference at all? They were six people damn it, two were elderly, so where the dwarves and the two orcs weren't exactly top notch either. Floth'bha was a half breed and thus not as strong as a full orc and Resh'kha, well, she wasn't all that self-confident to be honest. What could they possibly do? They did follow the line of ridges which seemed to follow the shape of the area and stayed out of sight and Resh'kha could feel it, the darkness which was controlling this the way a conductor does control an orchestra. They tried to get an overview of the situation and Resh'kha had no idea of what to do by now, the dark one had a sort of lair somewhere in there, probably near the tall cliff and they couldn't reach it, it was impossible.

It was Kulkar who came up with an idea and it was so audacious it had to work. He had noticed that the plain ahead of them was dry, but not completely and when they did climb up on some of the taller hills they could see river beds. They did seem to be dry but the green surroundings did indicate that some water still did seep through the soil. Kulkar had a suspicion and at first Resh'kha did not want to listen but then she had to. One day they did come across the remains of an old bridge across a narrow gorge and it was beyond any doubt made by dwarves. It was so old the very rock itself was crumbling but there was no doubt about the craftsmanship and the designs. Kulkar did grin and patted one of the rocks with his gloved hand. "See lass? My people have lived here, ages ago. And I am bloody sure there was a city in here somewhere, and where there is a dwarven city this far north there is a reservoir"

Resh'kha did know that this was the truth, at this height water did freeze during the winter and only a deep lake would be a safe source of water. Dwarves do hate water in one way and need it desperately too. The forges need vast amounts of water and so does the kitchens and household. The dwarves had long ago learned how to harness the power of running water and it did drive many of the complicated machines within the mountains, including huge transport systems made from cables and pulleys.

Resh'kha did tilt her head and Dharan did lift an eyebrow. "If there is a reservoir there is a dam, if there is a dam it can be ruptured and a ruptured dam?"

Resh'kha did wet her lips. "Will lead to a horrible flood?"

Kulkar did grin and shook his head. "Right, damn right. The monster won't be able to cause much problem when they are drowning right? And their master will have something else to think about than to increase their numbers for a few days"

Resh'kha did swallow. "What if the dam is in the wrong area? What if the water will drain to the south and not the north?"

Kulkar did shrug. "That we will find out later won't we? We have to get going and find it damn it, time is of the essence isn't it?"

Resh'kha did sigh and she did nod slowly. "Yes, you are right"

Kulkar did pat his axe with a loving gesture. "We are dwarves, we know the earth and her bones like our own, trust me. If there is a dam we will break it down, we have some tricks up our sleeves"

Dharan did giggle. "Oh shush with you, don't listen to him lass. All dwarven dams are made to be collapsible in case of an emergency. All one need to do is find the mechanism which breaks it"

Resh'kha did smirk. "But it isn't that simple now is it?"

Dharan did look down. "Ah, not always no, and if the mechanism is old....Well, it may be a tough job but doable, absolutely doable"

Floth'bha did look eager. "So? We are going right?"

Resh'kha nodded. "Doesn't look as if there is a choice now is there? We have to try"

Kulkar did pump his fist in the air and Dharan did laugh. "Great, we will not use much time finding the city for sure and whence we find that we will find the dam too"

Resh'kha could only hope that the dwarves weren't too self-confident. Something told her that they had to get things started soon.

The huge cliff was the centre of the entire area, for ages it had been a sacred spot and the reason was rather obvious to anybody familiar with the far ancient story of the area. The magic there was strong, terribly so and it could even be seen at times, like a shimmering in the air on a hot day. It had been thus for a very long time and it was the reason why the gate had been opened in this part of the realm. Such strong magic does twist the walls between realms and create weaknesses. Back in the day the gate had been shut off and it had been a job well done too but the magic has a sort of memory in itself, things do not follow the natural order of cause and effect and sometimes the result comes before the deed. The few monsters which had managed to get through every now and then had been trapped in limbo for centuries and millennia, they had been weakened even if it to them had been just a swift moment. Now on the other hand the gate was soon wide open once more, opening it fully from this side was a horribly power consuming task and yet it could be done. The wall between dimensions was already flawed and weak and it couldn't have been done somewhere else. That was a bad thing since the area was so far away from anything but it was also a positive thing since the troops could be brought through unseen. Nothing could threaten them now and when there were enough of the mindless critters they would be sent south to spread a second wave of destruction across the lands.

The dark leader of these beasts was content, things were going well. The fact that something had managed to lure away so many monsters were of little concern now, the spirit which had escaped so long ago couldn't be that dangerous, it hadn't been very powerful and when he did manage to get more of his own kin through it would be sought up and destroyed easily enough. Let it enjoy this puny triumph, it wouldn't last for sure. The dark one had created a palace for himself, it was easy enough for one like him, it did rise from the ground not far from the cliff and it was made from crystal in a gorgeous blue colour. The shapes otherworldly and breath-taking and he was proud of it. He didn't need a physical abode, not really but he had discovered that in many worlds a palace did signal power and status and thus he had created one. The dark one wasn't dependent on a body, he was energy and will and a soul which did lack all feelings except ambition and greed. To him the monsters were nothing but tools and so were all other living beings. His race had evolved into this state way back at the very beginning of their universe and they were powerful like few others. In their own eyes they had no flaws and were superior to all other.

He did finish the rituals required this day, more troops had been brought through, and the energy coming from the cliff did provide him with strength to keep the gate open and even expand it. He would have loved to have that gem he had felt further south, it had tingled with a tantalizing energy and sending his creatures to retrieve it had been a blunder but not one his brethren needed to know about. They didn't do mistakes, just calculated moves with uncertain outcomes. But the cliff itself was all he needed and he could feel it even now, with the walls of the crystal in the way, blocking his view of it. He wouldn't admit it for all the power in the world but it did frighten him. There was something there, something so ancient and strong it did make even him feel tiny and unimportant and it wasn't a feeling he did enjoy at all. But he had no idea of what it was, and since he had no idea of the history of this realm there was no way he could know. There were no creatures living in the area and the ones longer south had no idea. He had come across some of the small and hairy men of the mountains and none of them had provided him with any sort of answers, even under torture.

He had no need for prisoners or slaves, all the living beasts his slaves did encounter were food for them and it was such a wonderful and efficient way of clearing the way for his own people. In the end the monsters would devour each other when there wasn't anything else left and they could take over a world which was free from such insignificant vermin. His people did feed upon the life energy of a world, of its heartbeat and light and they left behind dead worlds which were barren and scorched. This particular one was very promising and he just wished that he could have tapped straight into the power from the cliff, then he could have opened the gate completely and brought his kin through here and now. But the power was too strong for him to approach it and he hadn't yet managed to determine just what it was. It was frustrating and the attempts he had done at connecting to it had only lead him to back away in serious pain. It was as if it was fighting him, some he did manage to absorb and use from a distance but get too close and wham, he was almost flattened by bursts of energy which was almost strong enough to destroy him.

The plains around the cliff were filled with monsters and they were hungry and eager and he wished to move them all to the plains but he wasn't strong enough. It was a shame and nothing he did contemplate but he wasn't the strongest of his kin. He was in fact a runt. His powers limited compared with the great ones and he had been sent forth to clear the way, like a servant. When the gate was reopened he had been forced to fight his way through and establish a bridge head here and he was bitter but also a bit proud. He was doing well and this ought to ensure his ascension to higher status. He did grin to himself, the human wizards which had tried to contact his kin through their worship had been useful fools, their bodies had been drained of energy and the gate had been awakened yet again. It was a last trick of his brethren, a very cunning trick which had been used when they realized that they were about to be forced to return to their own world. The magic left within the gate itself would ensure that it would open again after many millennia and that it would take a minimum of effort to do so. His forbearers had been very wise indeed.

The dark one was perhaps not among the most powerful of his race but compared with the magicians of this world he was of immense strength and knowledge and nobody there was any match to him in any manner. At least that was what he was convinced of and he did slide over to a table and with a flagon of liquid. He didn't need a body and he didn't need sustenance like other living beings but he did need to drink this every so often. He wasn't of this world and his people had early enough discovered that entering strange realms could bring some dangers even to a creature which was almost indestructible. The liquid came from his own world and it was very precious, it did ensure that he did stay strong and of his own realm, that his very energy didn't start to mingle with that of this world for if it did he was screwed. He would never be allowed to return and that was in his mind the worse thing which could happen. He had known of those who had forgotten to undergo this ritual and in one case he had been there when the hapless soul did return to their plane of existence only to be ripped to shreds by the differences in environment. He didn't want such a fate at all.

There was a soft sound coming from the back of the room and he did take a solid form and shuddered. Being flesh was disgusting, he hated it. But this was not anything he could ignore and he did long for the day when they discovered how this could be avoided altogether. It was not very dignified to have to undergo this every second day.

The sound got stronger and a creature did emerge from a doorway, it was very strange with two pairs of long arms and a sort of snake like underbody. The head was wide and flat with two pairs of eyes and the body was covered with a silky short fur. It was a species which had served his kin for ages, they were able to survive in almost all environments and they were needed. He would never admit to it but without these mindless animals they would all be in trouble. He couldn't physically touch anything of this realm, not when he was a physical being and thus this odd being was one each of his brethren did keep. His was bright green and grey in colour and the eyes were red and shiny. This species was servile enough to function as a slave and it could survive anywhere, also, it didn't get sick or injured by the different environments and could touch objects out of the realm they were from without any harm. He could not.

He did click his tongue impatiently and felt how the feeling of being surrounded by flesh did make him shiver in disgust. How pathetic it was to be bound to this form, even if it only was for a few seconds each time. It was nothing really to the immortal but still he hated it. The creature did slide forth over the smooth floor, it did grasp the flagon and a sort of cup made from the same crystal as the palace and it did open the flagon gently and poured some fluid into the cup. He was hissing as it worked. "Faster you worthless beast"

He wanted this over with and the animal did slide next to him and lifted the cup. He did tilt his head backward and the creature did pour the liquid into him and he winced. It did burn each time and he hated the feeling but as soon as it was inside he felt stronger and the sensation of being drained by his work did weaken. He did growl at the creature which did return the cup and the flagon to their place and he did kick it in the sensitive tail area. "Next time move faster or become a carpet!"

The thing didn't make a sound, it was mute and it didn't even look at him. He had nothing but despise for these beings, so weak and so meek. There was no fight in them at all, they would allow you to do whatever you wanted to them. Too bad they were needed, or else he would have enjoyed watching them all be fried like giant sausages. He did remove the physical body again and the creature did slide back to its lair. He didn't see the red eyes and their ominous glow, the expression of intense rage and hatred in them and the way the creature for a few short seconds seemed to almost coil up like a snake ready to strike. He was already busy preparing for the next day.

It had taken exactly two minutes before both Khirhien and Ayhrandur realized that Wenja was expecting and both were staring at her with their jaws almost hitting their chests, their expressions told of utter disbelief and Khirhien did glare at Ahravan. "Are you crazy? Now is not a good time!"

Ahravan did blush, Wenja did see it, his cheeks were burning red. "We didn't plan for this, believe me"

Khirhien did frown. "Really? You could have fooled me!"

Ahravan sighed. "It is the truth Khirhien, somehow…we don't know how it happened"

Ayhrandur did snicker. "Oh I bet you do, we have heard you all, we aren't deaf you know"

Rhawan did seem to shrink and Ahravan did look very sheepish indeed. "Stop teasing, it is serious. We have to take extra good care of her from now on. There is no way around it. "

Ayhrandur did grunt and sent Ahravan a glare. "You know what people will say when we return to the city?"

Ahravan did nod, his eyes on the ground and Wenja did realize that many would think that he and Rhawan had been reckless and selfish for having gotten her in blessed circumstances when it was such a dire situation. "It wasn't their fault, truly! It just happened!"

Khirhien did smile at her. "I hear you my Eth'ir and I believe them but many will not."

Wenja did push her jaw forth. "Then let us deal with it in due time, right now we have to plan the road ahead."

Ayhrandur did wave a clean tunic at them. "I will go have a bath first, if you others are wise so do you, the stink is rather intense"

He did grin and Khirhien sighed and shrugged. "Alright, you two lads too, we need to get rid of some filth"

The two young humans did giggle and followed the two elves to the pond and Ahravan did sit down with a heavy sigh and his eyes were distant. Wenja did kneel down next to him. "Will there be trouble when we get back?"

She didn't put words to her worst fear, that they wouldn't return at all. He did look a bit nervous. "Maybe, oh Wenja I cannot regret this but at the same time, it will cause some problems"

She did reach out and caressed his long silky hair. "We can deal with it right? I will make sure that everybody is told the truth. This must have been the will of the gods, there is little we can do then"

Ahravan did embrace her. "Bless your heart Wenja, it is too big and too pure to be real"

She just giggled and enjoyed the closeness. After a while the others did return from their bath and they settled in for a night in peace and quiet.

The next morning Ayhrandur was up early to make some food and Wenja did feel a bit odd as she got out of the sleeping furs. She could have sworn that she heard somebody calling her name from afar but there was nothing there when she tried to listen. She had some tea and Ahravan did help her getting dressed and then they were off as soon as they had gathered their belongings. They could see the plain ahead now, it was still far away but visible and Wenja did find it strange. It didn't seem natural at all, a flat wide plain like valley in the middle of the mountains like that?

Ayhrandur did tell her that there was an old legend of something which fell from the skies there in ancient times and formed the valley and she had a hard time understanding how that was possible. The forest got thicker as they made their way down towards the lowland ahead and Wenja did enjoy the smells and sights, she felt less worried for some reason when the trees did shield them, no matter how few and low they were. But they started to realize that the greatest danger yet was ahead of them and the elves could feel it in the very earth itself. It was a stench on the wind, a silent wailing they did listen to at night. The land was silent and vacant and they didn't see any larger animals and even the birds were quiet. The monsters had come this way and that could explain a little of it but not everything. Ahravan was very quiet, he was thinking all the time and Rhawan did try to cheer him up but it was a lost case. They just knew that it was hopeless to change his way of thinking now. He was worried about so much and Wenja just wished that they had known something more about the mission they were on.

They reached the lower hills and ridges within a few days and Ahravan did notice the lack of snow and the odd winds, they weren't natural and also, they could feel a sort of vibration within the earth, as if thousands of heavy feet were constantly moving around. And Wenja could feel something new, a sort of cold sensation and it was ominous.

The mist which lay over the land made it close to impossible to spot any details at a distance but in the evening there was a moment when the mist did drift aside and the elves could see that the plain was almost covered with herds of monsters. It made Wenja pale and Ahravan did wonder how the heck they were supposed to do anything at all with all those beasts there. Getting to that cliff would be impossible. The first rule was to avoid detection so they didn't try to get too close to the plain, instead they did follow the mountains on the west side, heading north towards the cliff very slowly. Wenja felt oddly conflicted, she felt that there was something out there, incredibly wicked and dark and yet there was something else there too, way more subtle but in no way less malicious and determined.

When they did stop to rest she was never alone, and she did enjoy the attention fully but she did also feel a bit constricted by it. She wasn't some fragile vase or a piece of thin pottery, she wouldn't break and yet both Ahravan and Rhawan did treat her as if she was gonna crack if she did bump a toe. At night there was plenty love making and she loved it and craved it more and more but it didn't overshadow her feeling of having overlooked something. The plains were teeming with these horrible creatures and if such a huge horde was released upon their people it would be the end, she should think about that and yet she found that she couldn't. Her mind was being steered in another direction, and she felt that the gods were behind this, one way or the other.

They were travelling in the daytime now, and tried to stay hidden at night. The area was huge and Ahravan would often curse the fact that so little was known about it. It had been sacred for as long as anybody could remember and it seemed as if everybody had shunned the area forever. But getting closer to the cliff wasn't easy at all, the terrain was terrible, steep and filled with sudden drops and gorges and the monsters seemed to spread out from the plain, simply because there were so many of them. Ahravan and Rhawan did often ride ahead and more often than not they would return with dark blood dripping from their weapons. Finding a good path wasn't possible anymore, they just had to chance it and hope that they wouldn't be seen. Wenja felt that her job was yet to come, and it made her feel strangely at ease, as if the fact that she had a mission made her more mature and reflected. Ahravan had revealed that the goddess had shown them the way to the sacred pool where they had saved Wenja and she knew that the goddess was with her still, leading her towards her ultimate truth.

At night she did feel that the cliff was calling for her, but there was yet something she needed, something which she had to find before she could close the gate. She accepted this and as the days went by it became clear that they all felt the presence and followed it.

They had to fight each day, the monsters were everywhere and luckily they were little more than mindless beasts for nobody seemed to be notified of their demise. Nobody came to check why monsters kept dying and the sheer number had to be the reason. That, and the fact that they were hostile even against their own. They would often find dead creatures which had been killed by their own, and often they were more or less eaten too.

The cliff wasn't in the exact centre of the plain, they could see now that it was elliptical and that the cliff was closer to the west side than the east and that it was so strange in shape Wenja had a hard time believing it. The distance was too great for them to see details yet and Ahravan just shrugged and was sure they would find the answers soon. But Wenja felt that the goddess was trying to tell them something, the presence was still there and Wenja started to realize that she was more sensitive than the others there, at least when it came to the spirit world and the realm of the deities. She had never had much faith, her father had always said that the gods were crutches made by the minds of weak humans to have somebody to blame when their own incompetence did lead them astray. But the goddess wasn't like that, Wenja knew now that she was real and the elves did have a strong faith in her and the other Gods of their pantheon. But the goddess was the most powerful one and Wenja was finding a new strength in her belief.

She had slept for some hours in the warm furs next to Rhawan when a strange dream did wake her up, she had to sit up, rubbing her forehead and feeling a bit confused. She had seen a very tall and beautiful woman surrounded by black wolves and she had been pointing at the mountains of the other side of the plain. Wenja had seen figures moving and suddenly she did see that it was Resh'kha and the others, minus the old dwarf shaman and one of the men. She felt sad knowing they had to be dead but it was obvious that they had a plan and that the goddess somehow was involved. Also, Resh'kha had a strange glow around her, an alien feeling almost. The goddess was grinning, the smile wasn't pretty. "The dark sister is waiting for her time to strike, they will lead the eye of the dark one away for a while, wait for my sign by the dark waters"

Wenja did shake Rhawan and he did yawn and stretched, looking at her with narrow eyes. "What is it my light?"

Wenja explained about the dream and Rhawan sighed. "The goddess is with you Wenja, you are her servant now I think, a person blessed and also burdened. If Resh'kha and the others truly are in the mountains on the other side of the cliff they are there for a reason. There is no way they could have gotten there on their own"

Wenja nodded. "I get that, the goddess must have moved them!"

Rhawan shrugged. "Yes, possibly. But if they are to divert the attention of the creature responsible for this mess we better obey the goddess. She can see what we cannot"

Wenja did lay down again, next to him, seeking his warmth. "Yes, so we have to find dark water somehow"

Rhawan took a deep breath. "Somehow I doubt that will be a problem"

Wenja had started to feel that her body was changing now, it was very subtle yet and normally she wouldn't have noticed it at all but she was more aware now. Her sensitivity greater than before and she was amazed by how well she started to know her own body. The elves were perhaps more interested in the spirit than the body but their connection to their physical self was way closer than that of a human being. Wenja could feel that her breasts had started to change, it wasn't visible yet and it didn't even hurt but she knew it. And her appetite did change too. She had always preferred light meals but now she suddenly found that she did crave heavier food, and she was given the best meat each time they did manage to make a kill.

The monsters which did fill the plain were worse than the previous flocks, these were larger and more grotesque and way harder to kill. Luckily they were more stupid, brains had probably been exchanged for brawls and being huge and fierce isn't always a good thing. They did look horrible and were strong and fast but not very well protected and the size made them vulnerable. Ahravan had discovered that their muscles were so heavy and strong their sinews and joints were vulnerable and he did use the war hammer with horrible efficiency. Khor'ath did fight well, the horn would start to glow and the magic within the animal did make the monsters drop dead from the smallest touch.

Flint did also fight with violent energy and kept Wenja safe and she was often shocked by how brutal the stallion was. It was so large the monsters did hesitate for a few seconds and that was when the horse did strike. She had never believed that a horse could be that brutal, he did often remind her of a predator more than a peaceful animal and Ahravan did explain that the wild stallions could fight to the death to win a herd of mares. They didn't encounter any more goblins but they did see footprints of something which was almost human and Rhawan was sure it was people from the mountains, the race which did live high within the naked valleys. They usually had no business being down there in the lowlands and Wenja felt that these were creature's lured inn by the evil which did control the monsters. Khirhien and Ayhrandur did often guard her when Ahravan and Rhawan did ride ahead to check the path and she did feel safe with them. The two human hunters were very cheerful and they never failed to stay optimistic and they stayed that way even when they no longer could use open fire.

Wenja was truly shocked when they came closer to the cliff, now they could see some details and it did look very fragile, not like solid rock at all. It had odd holes in it and peculiar shapes and as she did bend over to fix her boot she did look at it from the side and realized what it was. It was a skull. It was a skull of some sort of beast and it was so huge it pierced the clouds and the strange cliffs around it were nothing but bones, turned into stone. The size of the creature was mind blowing and Wenja couldn't really believe it. But who would spend hundreds of years shaping a cliff into the shape of a skull? For what? She was thinking about it for a while and couldn't find any answers at all. Ahravan did remind them of the old legends of something falling from the skies and perhaps this skeleton were the remains of whatever it had been? The idea was tantalizing and Wenja did decide to go with that explanation. It did make sense somehow. But the cliff was enormous and she felt the pull, the urge to get there, and do her task.

She was worried about the gate, she had no idea of what it was and how to close it, she wasn't a magician at all and even with the guidance of the goddess she did doubt that she would do much good but she had to try. Rhawan was sure that the truth would be revealed soon enough and she tried to find comfort in that thought. The constant fighting was taking a toll on them all, every day they had to slaughter their way through packs of beasts and Wenja saw that it was getting more and more difficult to find a good path which wasn't completely overrun. Then one evening when they were crossing a narrow stream a herd of beasts came rushing towards them and Wenja was sure that this was it, that they wouldn't be able to fight them off for these were huge long legged beasts which did look a bit like a crocodile but with shorter heads with sharper teeth. Ahravan and Rhawan did take combat positions and were ready to start fighting and then a giant dark shadow dropped from a ledge above the river and landed almost on top of one of the crocodile monsters. A hit from a massive paw and the beast lay there in its last spasms and the massive cat did lift its head and roared. The other monsters did turn around on a dime and ran off, clearly terrified.

Ahravan was stunned, it was almost like a S'haga but way larger and it was black with odd red markings on its ears and along its back. The eyes were red too, and it was moving with an eerie grace, making little to no sound at all. Wenja did gape and the cat did tilt its head and she knew that this was the one who had been guarding them through the mountains. It did move closer and Khor'ath did snort but didn't try to attack nor run away and Wenja did feel that this was a being sent by the goddess. "You are her steed aren't you? From the temple?"

The cat did nod and sat down to wash its paws, they were the size of large shields and Wenja stared at Ahravan. "I think we are getting closer to something, or else he wouldn't have revealed himself to us"

548

Ahravan nodded and he did stare at the surroundings. "Aye, I feel that way too"

The monster was dead so they did ride on, carefully now and as they did ride through a turn in the narrow valley they did see what the goddess had meant in Wenja's dream, dark water. In front of them lay a lake, it was round and calm and the water did look like polished obsidian, it was completely black and Wenja felt a shiver running down her spine. It would start here, she felt it, and only the gods knew how it would end.

It was Dharan who discovered the entrance, they had searched through the mountains for what felt like weeks but it was just a couple of days. Dwarven cities used to be very well concealed in the old days and it was mostly because of the threat of being plundered. Kulkar did explain that most cities only could be found by those who lived there and the methods which were used to hide the doors could be very intricate. One particularly popular method was to hide the entrance behind a waterfall, most dwarves do hate getting wet and would hesitate going too near running water. Hiding the entrance at seemingly inaccessible places was common, underneath overhangs and within very narrow gorges only a very agile person could squeeze through. Sometimes getting inside would require the help of several mechanical devises to jack up the door itself or lift the visitors up several hundred feet.

The entrance to this particular city was hidden behind a huge boulder which had to be moved to expose it. Luckily the boulder was placed on ball bearings which still worked and pushing it out of the way wasn't that hard, even if it did make a sound which did resemble that of tormented souls. The tunnel behind the boulder was covered with dust, several inches of it and Kulkar did spit and grunted. "This city was abandoned a very long time ago, I can smell it."

Resh'kha could only smell the faint mouldiness of naked rock but the dwarves were scurrying inside with glee. To them this was a wonderful opportunity to explore some of the long forgotten past of their people.

The old city on the plains had been airy and there had been plenty of light, Resh'kha had liked the place a lot. This on the other hand she didn't like at all, she felt that it was horrible and claustrophobic and the walls were dark and wet and the roof very low. Kulkar did grin from one ear to the other. "This wasn't a place to live, I bet it was a mining community. No need for it to be cosy at all. The real city was probably placed longer south"

He did run through the narrow corridors like a ferret through a scree and the two orcs and the men had a hard time keeping up with him. Dwarves are very bound to tradition, when they build something they will use the same ground plan for everything and thus a dwarf from one city can easily find his way through another one where he never have been before. Kulkar did take them down a few levels via very steep stairs which made Resh'kha feel faint. In places there were vertical shafts which did look like black holes going straight down to hell and she realized that dwarves have no idea of what the sight of heights do to other races. They just wandered along the narrow ledges with deadly drops on each side and didn't even flinch. Geir was shocked by it and Dharan did explain that dwarves have a special adaptation which enables them to do this without problems, they have no ability to perceive depth. To them a black void is the same as black floor, they cannot perceive heights.

This city was indeed a mining city, there were shafts everywhere, disappearing into the darkness like starving maws. Kulkar was a bit confused though, the city had a very peculiar layout and the rock wasn't the type which normally contain ore or minerals. He wondered what they had been mining there for they saw no gems and no signs of wealth. Dwarves do enjoy flaunting their riches and this city did look more like a hole than a city. Dharan did go as far as calling it a slum. But they did find the forges and they were if not state of the art pretty impressive and they had to have been well maintained once upon a time. Kulkar was still wondering what this city had been living off and he did run around with remarkable energy. Finally he did find something and did shout out, waving his hands to make the others join him. It was a sort of stone tablet and it was covered with odd looking runes. Dharan did stare with huge eyes and his mouth was an O in the ragged beard. "This is truly ancient, those runes haven't been used for at least ten thousand years!"

Geir did grunt. "Can you read them?"

550

Kulkar did nod, he was very excited. "Yes, at least most of them. They are well carved, those who did this knew their job"

Kulkar did squint and ran his fingers over the tablet, it was perhaps three feet times four feet in size and very thin and made from obsidian. "The city is called "Grehk-Urzab" That means dark fire in the old tongue"

Dharan did frown. "I have never heard of it before?"

Kulkar nodded. "Neither have I, and it is weird really. The place is huge, I can feel it. The rock is riddled with tunnels, like an ant hill"

Resh'kha did feel a bit excited. "So why were they here? If there aren't gold and gems and stuff here?"

Kulkar did scoff and kept reading, torturously slow in the minds of the others since they were very eager to hear more. "There is a sort of poem here, a few lines, let me see"

He did whisper to himself in old dwarfish and tilted his head this way and that, trying to figure out what it said. "On the day of Ghor-me-razkud he fell from the skies, the great one wreathed in flame. The foe of light and stars and the earth shook and smote his body and in his ashes the dark gems were sown"

Dharan did suck on a lock of his beard, his eyes were distant. "That day, it is an ancient day of celebration, to celebrate the return of spring. Whatever it was, it happened in winter then"

Kulkar did nod. "But what fell? Dark gems?"

He did look very curious and Geir did shrug. "If they were digging for something precious here, don't they have a vault of some sorts? A treasury?"

Kulkar did snap his fingers. "Ah, exactly, that is where we may find the answer I bet. I am sure that those dark gems were what they were searching for here but it makes no sense really, if something fell from the skies it ought to be on the surface right? Not deep within the earth"

Dharan did step in one place, looking like an eager horse before a race. "Well then, let's go shall we?"

Kulkar grunted. "Slow yourself brother, the treasury is probably well hidden"

Dharan pouted. "I doubt it, I think they have done a poor job hiding the city so why hide the treasury? Besides, this place cannot have been all that famous, we have never heard of it remember?"

Geir did throw a tired glance at Resh'kha and Osbord did sigh. He didn't like this city at all and would have preferred to stay outside with their steeds but the two wolves would look after the horses and if something happened all hands were needed. They did follow the corridors a bit further down and found some areas which had to have been living quarters. There was a sort of kitchen there and dormitories and also a bath. The city could have housed a few thousand dwarves at the most and it made it small compared to the great cities of old. Dharan and Kulkar did run around for a while, checking doors and they were yelling to each other on their own tongue. Resh'kha did find the lack of decorations there disturbing, there was no beauty there at all. Everything was simple and functional and that was it. It wasn't normal for dwarves at all, the city of the plains had been decorated with frescoes, engravings and even polished rocks walls where gems and crystals could be seen clearly. This was almost like a tomb in comparison, dark and damp and depressive.

Finally Kulkar did shout, a rather loud cry of excitement and they all ran to where he was. A short corridor did end in a very wide door and there were grooves in the floor which did indicate that barrels of something had been transported into the room behind it. Dharan did rub his hands in excitement and Kulkar did caress the door, searching for a way to open it. "If this is opened by using a password we are screwed"

His voice was dry and Dharan did yelp, that idea didn't sit well with him at all. Everybody did hold their breath, the dwarf was sliding his large worn hands over the stone door the way a lover caresses his partner and every now and then he would tap at the rock with his knuckles, eyes shut and ear close to the stone. Resh'kha did barely dare to breathe to make sure she didn't disturb him. Dharan clenched his hands so tightly she could see that his knuckles were white.

Kulkar did knock one final time, then his hands suddenly moved with lightning speed, pressing onto certain places on the door, Resh'kha didn't see anything which indicated that these spots were different from the rest of it but it had an effect immediately. The door did start to roll aside, smoothly and with little sound. Behind the door was a short corridor with the same width as the door and then a huge room. They did follow Kulkar through and he did stop and stared in disbelief. The room was filled with huge shiny pieces of what seemed to be crystal. Each piece was several meters across and shaped like the ace of spades and there were thousands of them. They were stacked in neat rows and the size of some were stunning. They all stared, what in the name of every God there was could this be? No gems have that shape? They were black and seemed to glitter and the dwarves were too stunned to speak. Resh'kha did gulp and Floth'bha did blink and whispered something nobody heard. The room was enormous and the rock itself did seem to have been almost melted once upon a time for the structure was peculiar and Resh'kha let her eyes follow the swirling patterns of different colours and discovered that a couple of the huge black shapes did stick out of the rock itself. Kulkar did scratch his head, Dharan was gaping and it was obvious that neither dwarf had any concept of what this was.

It was Osbord who said it, the quiet man did tilt his head and frowned. "Those are scales"

Geir turned to him. "Huh?!"

Osbord nodded. "Scales, like those on lizards and snakes, can't you see it?"

Resh'kha had to breathe inn deeply, she felt shocked. "Oh Gods!"

The size of the scales indicated that whatever they had belonged to had been...impossibly large. Kulkar whispered something . "My grandmother's beard, you are right. What creature would be mighty enough for something like that?"

The dwarf was hoarse and Floth'bha did whimper. "A dragon?"

Kulkar did look at her and he did snort. "No dragon could be that huge, it would die due to its own weight, it wouldn't be able to breathe and suffocate"

Floth'bha just shrugged. "What do I know? Those are scales, from a God then?"

Dharan did wheeze. "The poem, remember the poem. They were digging for these scales, why?"

Kulkar did take a deep breath. "Right, they must have had some value or else this was in vain and my people aren't fond of doing things in vain. They will always have a purpose"

Osbord did walk forth, very slowly. He stopped by one of the scales, touched it. The thing was at least five meters tall and very rigid looking. "It is like metal, so terribly hard"

The dwarves did scurry over, eagerly and with obvious curiosity. "Aye, it is, like steel"

Kulkar did bang his fist against the scale and it did ring, like a bell. Dharan did frown and pushed against it, very carefully and it did rock, a wee bit. "Know what? It is light, extremely light"

Geir did pull his sword and did strike at the edge and there wasn't even a scratch in the dark material, but the sword did almost break. "Gods, this is strange"

Kulkar did chuckle, dancing from one leg to the other. "I know why they harvested it, oh yes, they were ingenious"

He did bank his hand against it again and his grin was almost silly. "This is both strong and hard, and light at the same time. Imagine using it for weapons? Armour? Tools?"

Everybody looked at each other. "Well, if it is that marvellous of a material why haven't we heard of it before? They haven't exactly spread the word now have they? A discovery like this one should be one which everybody ought to be aware of as it happened a long time ago. The treasury ought to be empty"

Kulkar did frown, Geir's voice was calm and the dwarf spun around his own axis a few times. "You are right, two explanations, either this is useless for some reason or they were prevented from exploiting the resource"

Floth'bha did touch the edge of a scale, it was as thick as her arm and the edge a bit thinner than the middle. "Could it be that they couldn't use it? I mean it is so very hard, could it be that it simply cannot be cut into shape?"

Kulkar did make several odd grimaces, the thought of dwarves not being able to make use of something they found in the mountains was probably a horrible one to him. He did scratch his head and Dharan did

554

wander further into the room. He did pass one row of giant scales and then he did cry out. Kulkar did run over with the others at his heels. Behind the row was an open area with several wooden stands, odd things were leaned up against them and they were shaped from the scales without doubt. It was weapons, some armour in pieces or complete and also some things neither of them could identify. Tools were left there with pieces of scale and Kulkar did touch them reverently. "I wonder who's hands touched these last, the name is lost to time I fear"

Dharan lifted another tool and Kulkar did yell with excitement. "Ah, there we have it, that is how it is cut. It is hard work and takes time but for sure it can be done. They cannot have had the opportunity to spread this around, but why?"

Resh'kha did see that the tool the dwarf held was a sort of saw, it was glittering and she realized that the saw blade was covered with diamonds, thousands of them. So it did require something that hard to cut this material? Dharan grunted. "They must have had many workers available then, this is back breaking. Just a small piece would probably take weeks to cut free"

Floth'bha did walk along the stands and she did stop. "Look here, it is an armour, made for somebody larger than a dwarf for sure"

Resh'kha and Geir did wander over and indeed it was armour, very crude looking and probably just an attempt at making something usable but it was complete with chest plate, paldrouns and everything. The only thing missing was a helmet. Everything was held together with pieces of what did look like leather and surprisingly it was still soft and flexible. "It is huge"

Geir did touch it gently and did look at the two female orcs. "It looks as if it would fit one of you just fine"

Resh'kha did snort but Floth'bha did snicker. "Oh but it would, it would look very good on you Resh'kha, wouldn't you agree? You would look formidable"

Resh'kha had to blush and Floth'bha did giggle. Kulkar came over and stared at the armour, he did frown. "She is right, the armour does fit an orc. They probably made it just to see if it could be done and since this is so stiff I bet large was easier than small"

Resh'kha did stare at the armour, it was ugly. There was nothing of the elegance one usually saw within dwarven armour, and absolutely nothing of the beauty one could expect from an elven one. It was crude and rough looking and yet it had a sort of presence, it did look intimidating. Kulkar did tilt his head. "Go on sister orc, try it on. It does no good hanging here"

Resh'kha did swear to herself but she sighed and started putting the different pieces on and Floth'bha did help her. It did fit. It was a bit tight over the chest due to the fact that Resh'kha did have breasts but otherwise it was perfect and Floth'bha did grin. "You look like some warrior of old, right out of the legends. How do you feel?"

Resh'kha did try some moves and found that the armour in fact was so light she barely felt it was there, also, it didn't hinder her movements at all. She had to grin. "Alright? It is perfect"

Kulkar smiled from one ear to the other, everything said in praise of the skills of his people was like praising him. "Keep it then."

Osbord did look a bit impatient. "Not to be nagging but shouldn't we be looking for that dam?"

Kulkar did snap his fingers again. "Oh yes, of course. Follow me. We have to get back to the forges and follow the water shafts to the source"

Resh'kha felt that it was an odd sensation to have but as a matter of fact she liked the armour, she felt almost invincible with it on and she had always wanted to be a real warrior. Now at least she did look that way.

The forges were arranged in the traditional dwarven way and before long they were running upstairs chasing the pipes leading water to the huge wheels. The bellows and the machinery hadn't been alive for ages but could be started if need be and Resh'kha knew that dwarves indeed made things to last. She had to pick at the armour from time to time and she wondered where the scales came from, what they had been attached to and why they were there, deep inside of the mountains. As they did run up the stairs they all became aware of something new, a sort of scent which made Kulkar slow down a bit and he did turn his head to sniff. "That is odd, it smells of musk, and rot? The mountain is empty so there shouldn't be any scents here now"

Geir did pant, he wasn't exactly young anymore and running did not sit well with him. "Could some animal have made its way down here? It is a perfect place for a winter lair?"

He did look as if he was afraid some bear would jump forth from behind the next corner and Dharan did shake his head. "Our cities are impenetrable for beasts, no such thing could ever happen"

Floth'bha did look down, the torches they did carry were old but did provide good light and she saw something none of the others had noticed. There were tracks in the dust, not many but visible and more so, not very old. Kulkar did gasp and Dharan did yelp. "Are there dwarves here still?"

They did look at each other and Geir did bow down, glad they had stopped. "I doubt it, the feet are too small, and naked. "

Resh'kha did spit. "Goblins? Gnomes?"

Geir frowned. "Nay, I cannot say that I can identify these, I mean, they look…strange"

Kulkar did lower his torch and he grunted. "They look dwarfish, and still there aren't many dwarves who are that small, or run around with bare feet? If there are dwarves here we ought to have met them by now, they would have noticed our presence and come to greet us"

Resh'kha tried. "A child perhaps?'"

Dharan did throw her a rather surprised glance. "Resh'kha, no dwarven female would ever let a child run off barefoot, and there are several of them. I don't understand this"

They kept walking forth, very slowly and suddenly they came around a steep bend and daylight did pierce the darkness. There it was, the dam. They saw only a little piece of it through an opening in the roof but there was indeed a mechanism there made to open the dam and it did look very elegant. Kulkar did rub his hands together. "Ah, very well made. Let us see what this truly is"

There was a stair leading up through the hole and they did step up. They stood on a narrow peak above the dam structure itself and behind the massive dam was a lake, it was so large they couldn't see its end and it seemed to be very deep for the mountain sides on each side were very steep. It was a vast amount of water trapped there and the dam itself was made from huge boulders which had been put together like a jigsaw puzzle. Breaking it would be impossible, but opening the flood gate at the front was possible. Resh'kha had to gasp thinking of all that water suddenly unleashed and Kulkar did almost cheer. "The river runs in the right direction. All this water will head for the plains for sure."

Geir stared at the dark lake and the grey snowy mountains. "Let us hope the mechanism still works"

They went back down and the room was massive, several huge gears and wheels were placed there and they were connected with chains and thick leather cords. Kulkar did look proud and he whistled as he walked around, trying to find the place where the whole thing was controlled. They did find a sort of control desk after a while, in a room next to the great one and it was rather complex with levers and strange symbols and Kulkar did look a bit nervous. "I bet this is how they open the dam but what levers to move?"

He did touch one of the levers and the thing did creak and shudder but didn't move. "Damnation, is it stuck?"

Resh'kha did wet her lips. "If it hasn't been used for ages it is perhaps ruined?"

Dharan did scoff. "Nonsense. We dwarves does not make things which simply break, ages or no ages. "

He did try to but the lever didn't move. Geir was about to give them a hand too when they heard a sort of howling sound and it wasn't mechanical. This was something natural and it didn't sound very friendly. The musky smell became stronger and Resh'kha did frown and turned around, staring towards the corridor where they had entered the room. She saw something which made her scream in shock and the dwarves did see to and both went pale. It did look like a horde of animals at first, hairy and beady eyed and so many they did cover the floors. The light seemed to hold them back though and Kulkar did curse and appeared to be completely stunned.

Resh'kha did groan, these had been dwarves, long time ago. Dwarves do live until they are four to five hundred but with the time gone by many many generations had passed by and with no new blood brought inn the result was horrific. These creatures were beasts, horribly disfigured beasts which were howling and hissing, gnashing sharp teeth together as they tried to find a way around the light from the skies. The faces were flat and the eyes small and red, the jaws very wide and strong and the bodies skinny and hairy and nobody wore clothes. They had turned into mindless animals which now had smelled fresh meat and Resh'kha felt nauseous. They were gruesome to look at, filled with sores and lice and their hands had long claws. "Gods, what has happened here?"

Dharan's voice was thin and Kulkar was grey in the face. "I don't know and I don't care, come on, we have to move the levers"

Geir and Osbord did pull their bows and Resh'kha did see that the light did move across the floor as the skies did move with the wind, it would be dark soon. "Kulkar, Dharan, you have to open the dam, fast!"

Kulkar saw what she had seen and his eyes were huge. The creatures which had been dwarves were clearly out for blood and they were many, probably in the hundreds. "Keep them at bay"

Resh'kha did grasp her axe and Floth'bha did weight her sword in her hands. "We will try"

Geir grunted. "We don't have many arrows"

Floth'bha did bare her teeth. "Then shot the largest ones, and switch to blades. We cannot let them get past us"

Kulkar and Dharan did try the levers and pulled with all their might, they were stuck and Dharan did open the pit which did contain the chains from the controls. The reason why it didn't work was very obvious, the chains had corroded and formed one solid mass. They all stared at each other, this was exactly what they didn't need right now!

The dark lake was surrounded by very vertical cliffs and they did look strange in some places, like they had been half melted. The colours were peculiar too, from light ochre to dark brown or even black and Wenja was a bit confused about them. Ahravan and the others hadn't seen a place like that before and couldn't explain it and the water was so dark it did look like ink. They did make camp by the shores, on the only spot where it was possible and Wenja felt that the air there was loaded somehow. The place was special, in more ways than one. There were no monsters there now, the huge cat did stand guard at the mouth of the valley and Wenja wondered what she was to do, if she was to do anything at all.

They couldn't stay there for too long for there was nothing to eat for the horses and the place was ominous and very cold. They couldn't make fire there and she didn't think that it would be safe to move from the spot at all. But she was right about it being a place where things would start, she had expected dreams again and this time they started off very strange. It was as if she was a bird, soaring way above the mountain valleys but this wasn't these valleys, or at least it didn't look as if it was this area. The landscape she saw way beyond her was rather naked and ragged but it was natural mountains and animals and people lived there. She saw short stocky people clad in hides and she saw huge herds of animals on their annual migrations. It was a peaceful sight and one which brought both serenity and calmness to her mind. Then it changed all of a sudden, there was a glow in the skies and something came crashing down, glowing red and tumbling through the clouds, leaving a wake of red fire and black ash. It did collide with the earth and the earth shook in reply, vast areas were blown to smithereens, glowing red and floating away as even the rock itself had melted. The impact left a plain, flat and strange and the mountains around it looked as if they had been pushed together and tweaked by some giant's hand. The landscape was utterly changed and life eradicated everywhere. It would take centuries before the plain did become habitable. The cliff was there though, a dark twisted shape which slowly got paler and more cliff like. It was truly a great creature which had fallen, so fast and hard it had left nothing but the very bones there at the site of impact.

Wenja found it hard to believe and she also found it hard to believe that the plain really was the place where such a catastrophe had happened but it was true.

Then she saw the lake again, and their tiny camp from above. The huge cat was standing at the beach and staring at the tent where she knew she slept and it did nod its head. In front of it a sort of ice bridge seemed to form and she realized that she was to cross it. The woman did appear again, surrounded by her wolves. "You must let my steed carry you, and you must retrieve the one thing which may destroy the gate forever. It is kept in a temple on top of the peaks and when you find it and bring it back it must be awakened within the sacred circle. Then it must be brought to the gate. You will know what to do child, do trust yourself, and the path you have been given"

Wenja did swallow. "What is the thing I must find?"

The goddess smiled, the teeth those of a wolf. "You will see, if you make it all the way to the temple. His slaves will try to stop you"

The dream did end abruptly and she sighed and opened her eyes. There was no point in trying to deny it, she had to go and if she was to interpret the dream go alone. It was her test, her task and she did peek out of the tent. The giant cat was waiting by the lake, as in the dream and Wenja felt a surge of panic. So fast? Right now? She didn't feel ready at all but what point was there in delaying this? She got up and Rhawan did wake up and reached out for her. "What is it Wenja?"

She took a deep breath. "I have to go, the goddess have shown me that I must leave and find something important."

Rhawan did get up, grasping her almost desperately and Ahravan did approach the tent too, looking worried. "You cannot go alone?! It is dangerous"

She nodded. "Yes, but it is how it must be. I have to try. There is something out there which can close the gate and only I can find it apparently. You must wait here. You were tested when you rescued me, now it is my turn to do something impossible"

Ahravan did look very nervous. "Wenja, are you sure you must do this alone?"

She did nod and smiled. "Yes, there is no way around it. Please, the cat is waiting, he will carry me"

Rhawan did almost sob. "Carry you where?"

Wenja did shrug. "I have no idea, but there is a temple somewhere here. I guess it is my destination"

Ahravan did hug her, his embrace very firm and very warm. "Then go with the goddess my light, we will pray for you until you return to us"

Rhawan did hug her too and the others there did gather, visibly shaken. The cat did yawn and she did walk over to it, she was already well dressed and Rhawan gave her an extra knife and some dried meat. "Come back alive and in one piece, please."

She kissed them both and felt oddly strong, she should have been more scared but found that she wasn't, not much anyhow. Just excited in a new and peculiar manner. The giant cat sniffed her and huffed, it did lower itself onto the ground and she climbed onto the back, it was like sitting on a horse but the fur was long and silky and the moves were different. She did hang on and the cat turned towards the lake and roared. The sound did echo from the cliffs around them and she now knew that the odd shapes was because the very rock had been melted when that thing fell into the ground, and pressed aside.

Ahravan and Rhawan did stand side by side, both terribly nervous on her behalf but they did trust the goddess. She had allowed them to save Wenja and for that they were eternally grateful. Yet they couldn't help but feel fearful, she was their light, their great love and to see her go without being able to follow her was horrible. Ayhrandur did walk over and patted Ahravan on the back. "She will be fine my Ath'ir. I can feel it, she is stronger than us all"

Ahravan did nod but his eyes were distant. "I know, but what is she about to face?"

Chapter 13: Mist and darkness

The two dwarves were staring at the mechanism, it was utterly ruined and despair was written on their faces. The chains which controlled the mechanism were useless, not even with many workers and a week ahead of them would they be able to free the chains from the rust which had encased them. The room was too wet and since nobody had been there to remove that moist air this was the result. The two orcs were watching how the light slowly waned from the opening in the roof and the beasts were hissing and pushing forth, eager to attack. The two dwarves didn't even look at these strange beings, to them it was horrible, knowing that these grotesque beings once had been proud dwarves like themselves. Seeing the faces of their own kin twisted and corrupted thus brought them to tears and they tried to concentrate on the work ahead instead. Kulkar did pull at his beard. "Can we control the mechanisms from somewhere else?"

Dharan did scurry around, trying to understand the complicated system and he did look terrified. The small beasts would soon be unleashed and they had to get this done now! He came back with eyes like dinner plates and his legs did almost shake. "The control cables do lead to a pulley at the end of the pit, we may be able to turn it if we use something as leverage"

Kulkar did run over to where Dharan stood, there was indeed a pulley there, it had to be distributing the movement from the cables to the real mechanism and it was huge. Kulkar did groan, the thing was made from several wheels and chains were threaded over each wheel, giving it tremendous weight. And what wheels to move? That was in itself a mystery. They didn't have time to figure out the mechanism there and then, they just had to try and hope for the best. Kulkar and Dharan did grasp onto one of the chains with their gloved hands and pulled. Dwarves are very strong, much stronger than a human but the chain didn't budge even an inch. "Curses, can this too have rusted?"

Dharan did check the axle but it didn't appear to be damaged, the wheels ought to be able to move just fine. It was just that each wheel in the pulley were heavy and the chains taut. The entire thing did rely on the power from control mechanism to move, it wasn't made to be used otherwise. Dharan started running around again, his eyes wild. "Is there something here we can use to push the wheels around."

Geir did run over to a door at the end of the room, it did lead into a narrow dark room where the dust lay thick. "It may be something here, it looks like a storage."

Resh'kha and Floth'bha did not attack the small monsters, they waited to save their own strength and still there was light. These once dwarves were not fond of sunlight at all, that was very obvious. Resh'kha did hate the fact that she was so tall, it gave no advantages when the opponents were so small. The beasts would burst forth at any moment now and Floth'bha did hiss. "They are nasty, look at those teeth!"

Resh'kha did see it, the beasts had teeth which did resemble those of a bat, thin and needle like and very many of them. It made her shiver to the bone. She tried to think of something she could do to stop these beasts, could the gem help her? It had been silent since they reached the city and felt just dead, no other word could describe it. And the deity which hid within her very being hadn't made its presence known either. Resh'kha did groan, what good did it all do if it was worthless? She did think of the amulet too but it was as if the powers she had gotten from the old dwarf had gone dormant when she entered the city, she didn't feel them at all anymore and it was very strange.

Geir did run forth, he threw something at the two orcs. "Here, go low and knock them over"

It was two lances, the wood was surprisingly strong and there were long narrow blades at the end. Resh'kha did weight the one she caught in her hand. She did see what he was thinking about, they could use the lances the way a gardener uses a sling blade to remove weeds and Floth'bha did sneer. "Yes! This is what I am talking about!"

She did grasp the end of the lance and growled and Resh'kha felt jealous for a moment. Floth'bha had such courage and such a fierce aggression. It was perhaps because she was a half breed and had been fighting her whole life.

Geir had brought more lances and threw them to Kulkar and Dharan. He did shout at Osbord. "You help the ladies, shoot the large ones"

Kulkar did choose one of the wheels and they did attach the lances in the mechanism and started to yank at the chains. There was a distant groaning sound and the chain moved, perhaps half an inch. The entire mechanism was simply too heavy and Kulkar and Dharan did look at each other. "No way they have been able to control this manually. How in the name of the first fathers did they use this monstrosity?"

Geir did step back, the control room wasn't that large, the main mechanism was in the great room in front of it and it had been very massive indeed. "Could they have been using something to power it?"

Kulkar did yip. "Of course, they were advanced, the very mechanism tells me so. They must have used the waterwheels, or something else"

Resh'kha did growl. The square of light on the ground did slowly vanish and the horde was making sounds which did resemble a pack of angry rats. "If you are to do something do it now! We don't have much time!"

The light vanished, suddenly and completely and only the torches and some faint non directional light from the opening did light the room. The small beasts did shriek as one and came rushing forth, teeth bared and claws extended. The madness in the red eyes all too familiar and Floth'bha did swing the lance with horrible strength. The long blade at the end was sharp as a razor and heads did fly, it did look rather peculiar since the momentum of the small monsters did make the heads fly up when cut. The bodies did take several steps before they fell, gushing dark blood over the floors. Resh'kha saw that the technique was effective and did copy it. Her axe returned to her belt and she did swing the lance with all her speed. "Get the dam open damn it, we cannot keep doing this forever"

The two dwarves did run through a door into the main room and Kulkar did swear. Now that they knew that the mechanism needed extra power to work the source was all too obvious. There was a huge metal cylinder at the end of the room, and from it several gears and chains were connected to the mechanism which did open and close the dam sluices. "My sister's moustache! They used steam!"

Geir did look confused and Kulkar shook his head. "It is a boiler, they used steam to move the mechanism. There is a piston in there, it is being pushed up and down by steam, and pulls the chains, making the mechanism move"

Geir didn't understand, few humans had any concept of this but Dharan did cuss so bad Kulkar did cover his ears. "We need the boiler, now!"

Geir did point to a corner beside the metal structure. "Could that be a clue?"

Kulkar did sprint over and opened the hatch, it was a narrow staircase leading down into darkness and the two dwarves didn't hesitate, they plunged inn. Geir did roll his eyes, he didn't like this at all but what the hey. If the dwarves did dare to go he ought to be just as brave.

Resh'kha was swinging the lance desperately. The heap of corpses was getting high and yet they kept coming, it was indeed madness. "How many are there of these bastards?"

Floth'bha did grunt with each swing of the lance. "Too many. Can you hear it? The sound of feet? I bet there are thousands living in this mountain"

Resh'kha did swallow a bout of nausea, the stench was horrible and the blood made the floors slick and dark. "What in the name of everything unholy have they been feeding on then?"

Floth'bha did decapitate yet a handful of these almost goblin like dwarves. "Beats me, each other?"

A surge of monsters did burst through the door leading to the control room and the large room with the mechanism and these were larger than the first ones and they did look horrible, with extended jaws and strange greyish skin. The arms were large and strong and very long and Resh'kha gasped. "These are like warrior ants, goddamn it!"

Floth'bha was panting. "Keep going, don't let them through, we have got to stop them so the others can make the mechanism work."

566

These new horrors did just scoop their smaller brethren aside and made some ghastly cackling sounds as they ran forth. They were so large one swing with the lance was barely enough. Osbord had started firing now, not wanting to waste arrows on the smaller ones. He was a good archer and each arrow made a kill but it didn't make much of a difference. The numbers were just too great.

The dwarves did enter a huge cave, and it did indeed hold a sort of boiler. There was an oven with a huge container on top of it and there were pipes and valves and the air was damp and raw. Geir did sneeze, there was mould growing on the walls and the floor was covered with a knee deep layer of black mud. Kulkar did release a long line of swearwords and fought his way through the mud, the oven was apparently in order and there was water in the container. Also the pipes were whole and alright but there was obvious something which made him very upset. Dharan too did whimper and Geir did blink. The room wasn't that wide but long and the other side of it from where they entered was covered with thick layers of black goo. It had to have been a sort of storage but Geir had no idea of what they had kept there. Kulkar did grunt. "Gods curse it, and devour the souls of those who made this calamity"

Geir frowned. "What is wrong?"

Dharan did roll his eyes and tore at his beard. "What is wrong? What is wrong?! I will tell you what is wrong human! To heat water you need something which burns and here they used coal. And that coal is what we are wading through right now!"

Geir did look down. "The mud?"

Kulkar nodded. "Aye lad, the mud!"

He did scoop up a handful of the goo and threw it at the walls with a yell. "Water has made its way in here, and over the years it has turned the coal to mud, useless wet mud. We cannot use the mechanism after all. We cannot make the chains move at all. We aren't strong enough"

Geir did wet his lips- "Then what do we do?"

Kulkar shrugged. "Try to get away? Try to get outside? The little bastards won't leave the city I am sure"

Dharan sort of whimpered. "But what about our mission then? We need that water to wipe over the plain"

Kulkar sneered. "And how are we to accomplish that ha? The goddamn dam is not going to crumble any time soon, it was made to last for eternity"

They ran back upstairs. The two orcs and Osbord were fighting desperately to keep the beasts at bay and Kulkar yelled at them. "How long can you keep them at bay?"

Osbord shook his head. "Not long, we are soon out of arrows, and they do keep coming"

The heap of bodies was so tall now the attackers had to climb over them but that didn't seem to stop them at all. "We have to get out of here soon or we are screwed"

Resh'kha did cut down one of the attackers with a groan. "We have only one way to go then, up!"

Kulkar sighed. "We cannot open the dam, there is no coal and the mechanism cannot be used without steam. It is impossible to make it move."

Resh'kha moaned. "But we need that water?!"

Dharan did look very sorry "I am very sad, I would have loved to watch the mechanism work, it would have been marvellous to see I am sure. "

Resh'kha looked down, her arms were heavy and she was very tired, they had fought desperately and yet they couldn't quit at all. Floth'bha had a deep cut along her left arm from where one had managed to scratch her and she was trembling with fatigue. "Isn't there anything we can do?"

Geir shook his head. "No, I am sorry. We have to get out of here now, before we are overrun"

Dharan sighed. "Oh blast it, we have failed"

Kulkar did gape. "Blast it? Oh by the forefathers, we can! We can blast it!!"

Resh'kha couldn't turn to look at him. "What are you saying?"

Kulkar spun around himself. "We can blast the dam sluice, I know how to make blasting powder"

Dharan did grasp onto his beard with both hands, he did look terrified. "You do? Oh by my lower beard, but do we have what is needed?"

Kulkar ran towards the storage room where Geir found the lances. "Maybe, such things are usually stored near the places where work is done. If these dwarves knew the art they would have used it for sure"

Dharan did look disturbed, his eyes huge and his skin pale. "Monsters and now this, oh curse this day"

Dharan did return with several jars, his eyes shining. "All I need is here, what I need now is time"

Resh'kha did swear, her arms and legs moving constantly. "No bloody shit! Be fast, these dirty critters are becoming too strong"

She was at the end of her strength. Kulkar had found a huge iron pot and now he was mixing powders and liquids and mumbling as he worked. Dharan did whimper. "Do you know what you are doing?!"

Kulkar did shake his head. "I have seen it done, never done it myself. So this is done by chance"

Dharan did shudder and Geir realized that this was dangerous indeed. "If it goes wrong, what will happen then?"

Kulkar did stick his tongue out. "We all die, in a terrible blast"

Geir was pale. "How comforting"

Resh'kha did pant, she had to move very fast, the door wasn't that large but wide enough to let several through at once and the dead didn't make much of a barrier at all. Floth'bha did rear back with a scream, she had a deep gash across her belly and blood did pour from it. Resh'kha did feel cold, they wouldn't make it! Kulkar did stir the pot eagerly and his eyes were filled with dark joy. "If we go now we go as heroes of legend."

Osbord did release his last arrow and switched to sword, he was pale too. Kulkar did lift the pot. "Now we have to place this in the right position"

Geir did groan, he too had drawn his sword. "And where is that?!"

Kulkar grinned, a grin filled with sheer madness. "Where the sluice is opened of course! We have to cut the chain which holds the counterweights up"

Geir did roll his eyes. "Great. And how do we get there?"

Kulkar did point at the opening in the roof. "I suggest we go up there and take it from the top of the dam. There are always inspection hatches up there"

Resh'kha did shout. "Then go, now! I cannot hold them back much longer!"

Everybody did scurry by her, Geir did support Floth'bha who was oddly pale and her face told of both agony and weakness. Kulkar did carry the pot with a sort of gentleness which told Resh'kha that the content was very volatile and she hissed and fought on. The moon was up now but the moonlight didn't seem to scare the beasts at all.

Wenja had a hard time understanding what she now saw. The lake did freeze over, in a narrow path the cat immediately started to follow. She felt an urge to look back but she didn't, she felt that it would be unwise for it would shatter her resolve. She did cling to the long dark fur and looked ahead and as soon as they were on the beach again the ice disappeared. The valley did rise, becoming a narrow canyon and the cat didn't hesitate at all. It did wander ahead in a steady pace and Wenja saw that the mist had fallen, the day felt like night, it was very dark and the light was dim and oddly flat. She had a feeling of being elsewhere now and the cat did nod, as if it knew her thoughts and wanted to tell her she was right. The canyon did rise for a long time, and she saw naught outside of it, just mist and she was confused. She was way above the level of the mountain passes by now? But the terrain rose and rose and she couldn't understand how it was possible. The cat did nod its head again. "Elsewhere, the goddess own land. Temple here and also there"

Finally they did reach a sort of plateau and Wenja did stare. The mist still lay low, covering the mountain sides and from the flat area several paths could be seen. All steep and all looked as if they had been carved from the rock the day before. There were small statues placed everywhere, depicting animals and natural scenes and Wenja held her breath. "Which one to choose?"

She let the cat walk by each possible path, they did all lead up into the mist and she felt as if she was in a dream yet again, an odd and peculiar one for sure. One of the paths did look very easy and smooth and then the next would look as if not even the cat would be able to climb it. They were different and she knew in her heart that she had to pick the right one, or else this would fail. Then Yalaih's words did emerge from her mind, the path of the leopard. Was there a leopard there? She saw a small statue by one of the paths, a cat and it was sitting peacefully licking its paw. She took a deep breath, "This one, I chose this one!"

The cat did grunt and started climbing the steep stairs, she had to hang onto the fur with all her strength but the cat did move very smoothly and she discovered that she was strong enough to cling on like a burr. She didn't look down at all, only up and the mist seemed to split as she was being brought upwards. The stair like path was oddly shaped and at times she had a feeling of flying and then she felt as if the surroundings were not really there, a mere illusion. She felt dizzy and wanted to close her eyes but found that it wasn't that smart, she had to see where they were going. At times the path was flat and they followed a sort of road, well made and very nice, then the road would become strangely eroded as if it was thousands of years old and if she did look down it sometimes did disintegrate underneath them.

She wondered how this was possible but maybe she wasn't supposed to know at all. The cat did jump over gaps in bridges and one place it did wade across a river with water which was oddly orange in colour. Then the cat did slow down and they entered a valley which did look surprisingly normal. The rocks were rather ordinary, the grass short and ochre in colour and the terrain was actually rather idyllic. There were some trees growing in small grooves and the temperature wasn't that bad at all. The mist did lay over it all though, and the sun couldn't be seen. The cat did walk on, it did appear to know where it was heading and Wenja did feel a tingling sensation within, she felt a nervous tremble in her hands and she knew that there was danger ahead. The valley did dip towards a lake and by the lake was a temple. It was a rather rough looking stone building and it wasn't very elaborate at all. Just four walls and a roof and there wasn't even an open place in front of it. Just grass and bushes. It did look abandoned and yet it wasn't derelict in any manner. It could have been built last month.

The temple wasn't abandoned though, around it she could see people, short stocky men carrying spears and wearing leather clothing which didn't appear to be very elaborate. Just pieces of animal hides stitched together somehow. They were scurrying around and did look upset and confused. The cat did stop and sniffed the air and Wenja felt it too, a smell of unwashed men. She did grunt, she had gotten used to how good the elves did smell by now and these did smell like the goat herders who stayed in the barns the whole winter without ever taking a bath.

She made a grimace and leaned forth a bit, the men were obviously aggressive for some reason and she felt that they were dangerous. There was something odd about them and she didn't really think, she just relaxed and let her thoughts flow and she saw that each man was surrounded by light but it was somehow contaminated. It did look as if something dark and viscous was clinging onto them, and she felt disgusted. The energy around them was just as bad and the cat did tilt his head. "They will kill you if they come near you"

Wenja sighed. She already knew that, it was almost as if she could read their minds, these were people of the mountains, ensnared and seduced by the dark force which did bring in the huge packs of monsters. These were promised power and freedom, status and wealth and yet they hadn't really understood what they were involved inn. They had followed their new leader and Wenja saw images in her head, burning huts and slaughtered females and young ones, chiefs with their heads chopped off and villages where nobody were alive anymore.

It was madness and the goddess was furious, these men had been brought here so they wouldn't do any more harm to their race and Wenja realized that this was a part of her test, to check if she truly was worthy of this. At the moment the mist did hide her and the cat from these people and she knew they would attack if they saw her. Their master wouldn't allow them to escape his clutches and they were loyal to him now, completely his slaves.

She had to free them of the dangerous influence but how?

Wenja remembered the animals which had gathered around the caravan, the Zahar and the other carnivores and she did tilt her head. Their minds were a bit simple, they weren't as logical as humans and

572

their knowledge of the world relatively limited. They knew their own lands and people of course, all they needed to survive there in the mountains. But everything outside of that little sphere was unknown to them or something they didn't care about at all. Wenja was a bit fascinated, they had obviously slaughtered their own kin to please this voice some of them heard, they were obvious very superstitious and it didn't take much to make them scared of the supernatural. Wenja had to make use of that, she didn't want to use violence and she knew that she was being tested in many ways, could she free them without hurting them? The energy was swirling around them, like a dark veil trying to smother their thoughts and it was corrupting them a lot, she sensed it. They would normally never harm one of their own.

Wenja did grin, a slow and vicious grin, she had an idea. The dark energy would get something else to chew upon, something less harmful than these men. She felt the surroundings and felt life everywhere. There were mice and voles and other rodents everywhere, even some larger ones hiding in between the roots of the trees. She gathered her concentration and frowned, in her mind she transferred the dark veil from each of the men and applied it to a rat or vole. It didn't feel as if she was doing anything too hard but it did apparently work for the men did straighten themselves up and they stared at each other as if they were strangers to each other.

Wenja giggled. The rats and voles and other animals did freeze, then they did disappear into the soil again, confused and scared and not mentally able to follow the orders from the dark power. They would simply hide and the men stood there, stunned and confused. Wenja heard voices calling out and some of them appeared to have complete breakdowns. Then the mist did fall down over them and when it was gone so were they. Wenja felt that they had been brought back to their own valleys and their own time. The cat grunted "Well done"

She heard its voice in her head and smiled. She hadn't killed them, that was good. She let the cat carry her down towards the temple and she felt the power from it. She felt the mist rise and saw sunlight for the first time in a while and as they stopped in front of the door she knew that this temple was horribly old but she was there in a different time. It had been destroyed when the creature struck the earth but in this time and place it still existed and the thing she had been sent to retrieve had been hidden there, before the darkness ever entered this world. It was the only place it was safe.

She just felt the truth in her bones, and she slid down from the cat and stopped at the entrance. She heard the voice of the goddess in her head. "Beware daughter of man, what you will see in here will be with you forever."

Wenja nodded. "Why me?"

The goddess was heard chuckling. "You are rare Wenja, a soul with an infinite capacity for love, and believe me when I say that everybody else would have died back at that goblin city. You are the one born twice and with blood of man and elf alike, not fully any of them and yet capable of understanding both. Go now, the moment you leave the temple and awaken the relic the dark one will know of the relic kept here and we all must move fast"

Wenja did nod and stared at the entrance, it was very dark and she didn't really see anything in there. She hesitated, every instinct she had told her that she shouldn't enter this place, something about it felt very dangerous. Wenja thought about Ahravan and Rhawan and the thousands of people who would be in trouble if she failed in this, there wasn't truly a choice. She took a deep breath and stepped inside and the world did go black around her immediately and she got a feeling of falling. She didn't even have time to scream, was this right?

Resh'kha did fight with all her strength, the sheer number of bloodthirsty beasts was incredible and she saw that the smaller ones already were eating their fallen brethren, the sight was grotesque and she fought the urge to spew. The others had managed to get up the stairs to open air and she didn't really know how to get up there safely. The beast would be at her back immediately. Geir was standing at the top of the stairs, he held a torch high. "Resh'kha, now!"

He did toss the torch down and the beasts did run away from the flames. Resh'kha did sprint up the stairs, her legs were shaking with exhaustion and her armour was covered with blood but it had done a marvellous job protecting her so far. There was a huge slab of rock up there, a sort of hatch which probably were made to cover the opening but it was broken in half and not large enough to cover it and also, very heavy. Geir and Osbord did push with all their might and Resh'kha did help. They managed to push the piece of rock over the opening but it did only help a little. There was still room for the small beasts to get up and now there was no sunlight at all. The night was dark and a narrow moon didn't give much light at all. The two dwarves were running along the top of the rock dam, they were in a hurry now. Geir and Osbord did draw their swords, the opening the monsters had to get through was not that large but the critters were agile and still desperate.

Floth'bha did stand closer to the dam, she was clutching her belly and Resh'kha felt a surge of horror, was her friend seriously injured? The two men and the female orc did fight in shifts, the creatures did fall back down the stairs when they died and soon a there was a new heap down on the floors. Resh'kha could only hope that the dwarves did manage to do their job, and that it would work. The other part of the huge stone slate was simply too heavy for them to move and Resh'kha was rather sure that the small monsters would be able to push it out of the way, simply because they were so many.

Kulkar and Dharan did find the inspection hatch, and there was a ladder leading from it down into the dam itself. The opening which could be used to drain the dam was massive and very well made, the gate was made from both rock and wood and they saw the massive weights which would be lowered to raise the gate. They were held up by chains and the mechanism which they hadn't been able to activate would have released those chains and controlled their descent. Kulkar did raise his torch and held the pot with the dangerous mix, he did nod towards the chains. "I have to place the pot just on top of that gear there, it should blast the whole thing to smithereens"

Dharan did gulp, the distance to that place was great and there was a huge dark void underneath them. "How are you gonna get there?"

Kulkar did point. "There is a ladder over there"

Dharan did run over to the wall and did lift the ladder, it was a solid one made from steel and it was long too, getting it over to the gear wasn't easy at all. It was in fact very heavy and Dharan had to use all his strength to manoeuvre the bloody thing over the gap. The gears which held the chains were massive and he did doubt that the pot was enough to even make a dent in the solid metal. Kulkar did look nervous, but he didn't hesitate. The aging dwarf was nothing if not brave and since his race don't have a perception of height it wasn't the fear of falling which did hold him back. It was more the fear of dropping the pot. They could faintly hear how the others did fight the beasts and Kulkar did slowly make his way along the ladder, one step at a time. They didn't have that much time at all and Dharan did take a deep breath of relief as his friend did reach the massive mechanism. The weights hung straight underneath the system, massive blocks made from rock and metal and they had to weight many tens of tons each. It was needed, the gate which held the dam watertight was huge and this power was needed.

Kulkar did swallow hard, he did find a spot near the place where the gears were attached to the roof and placed the jar there. Then he did pull some meters of relatively thin rope out of his pockets and luckily it was dry. He did place the end in the pot and then he did stretch the rope out along the ladder as he slowly made his way back to Dharan who stood there on the edge of the inspection platform, rather pale looking. "Will this work?"

Kulkar tried to smile. "Let us pray that it does."

He did jump down and put Dharan's torch to the rope, it did burn, as a matter of fact it did burn rather well, and fast too! "Run!"

They did climb out of the bowels of the dam as fast as they could and now Kulkar did realize that they had done a blunder, a monumental one. If the dam did blow, where were they to seek cover? They couldn't run across the dam now, they had to go in the opposite direction. Seeking cover within the city was out of the question and beyond the opening they had run up from there was just naked rock, almost vertical. The three who were fighting off the beasts did stare at Kulkar and Dharan who came panting, running like crazy. "We have got to get out of here, it will blow up soon"

Resh'kha did gape and the others stared. "Are you kidding me? You have set it off and we have nowhere to go?!"

576

Kulkar did look sheepish. "Uh, we didn't think that far?"

The monsters did still try to get up to get at them and the screeching and roaring was intense. Floth'bha moaned. "Resh'kha, can you shield us?"

Resh'kha did frown. "What?"

Floth'bha was very pale now. "Like on the plains, for a few moments"

Resh'kha tried to focus. "Uh, I guess so?"

Osbord did smile, it was a very thin smile, almost bitter. "Do it, I will lead them off"

Geir did gasp. "No, it is certain death!"

Osbord smiled, a genuine smile this time. "Yes, this whole mission was certain death and we all knew that when we left, isn't this what we all hoped for? A honourable death, doing a good deed?"

Geir did nod. "Aye, you are right, it is"

Osbord smiled at Resh'kha who was hacking away at the beasts. "They are stupid, they will follow fleeing prey. Don't let this be in vain"

Resh'kha did touch the gem and the amulet and now it felt alive again, like a warm living thing. She did close her eyes and they all ran away from the opening, hiding behind it. The air did shiver and for a few moments the people gathered there were invisible to the beasts, except Osbord. The man waited until the beasts started to pour out of the hole in the ground like ants from an anthill, then he did run. He ran out onto the dam and the beasts did in fact follow him, the instinct so strong and the man was indeed very brave for he knew that the explosion was imminent and nobody knew just how strong it would be.

The stream of beasts did end, all of them which were still able to move were out on the dam now and Kulkar panted. "Get back down there, now!"

A few beasts were still alive though wounded and Resh'kha did end them with her axe, they did scurry down into the opening and Resh'kha was the last one to get in and she turned her head just in time to see the explosion. It was grand, it was so powerful the entire dam for a few seconds seemed to be lifted off its foundations. The top disintegrated since the roof over the mechanism was blown out and the floodgate was lifted in one violent tug as the weights did drop suddenly and without control. The sound did throw echoes between the mountains, it was like violent thunder times a thousand and rocks did fly everywhere. Resh'kha did watch how blocks the size of houses did fly and there was a moan coming from the lake as the water suddenly found a way out.

The explosion had weakened the dam a lot, it was old and even though it was well made water had been burrowing through the foundations and turned solid ground to mud. This was the last straw, the final nail in the coffin. As water did gush out of the open flood gate in a horizontal beam of black other beams of water started to appear along the edge of the dam, where it was connected to the bedrock. There was rumbling and roaring and it was like watching a waterfall mixed with blocks of stone and mud. Resh'kha couldn't look away, she was transfixed upon the incredible sight. The monsters and Osbord had vanished the moment the explosion went off, they had been very close to the inspection hatch and thus they had been reduced to vapour within the blink of an eye. Resh'kha was glad Osbord hadn't had time to suffer, it had been instantaneous.

The dam did simply give up, it was reduced to blocks of stone and disintegrated completely. The whole lake pushed forth and the sound was deafening. Resh'kha did whimper and Geir did pull her with him down into the control room again. The stench of dead monsters was overwhelming and Kulkar stood there shaking like a leaf all over. He was both shocked and in awe and also grasped by a feeling of having done something impossible. "It shouldn't have been that strong, it shouldn't! It was impossible!"

Geir did make a grimace. "Was the room dusty?"

Kulkar did nod. "Yes, very. Not at the bottom I think for water did seep inn but there was a lot of dust there yes, why?"

Geir shrugged. "Ever heard of a dust explosion? The pot did set off a second explosion and I once saw a mill blow itself up, there wasn't anything left of the building at all. Even heavy beams were reduced to toothpicks!"

Dharan nodded slowly. "Ah, that makes sense. But all that water will most certainly have an effect on the plains"

Geir grinned. "It will be an almighty flooding for sure. I don't think those monsters will like getting their feet wet"

Resh'kha did grasp onto Floth'bha. "How are you, is it bad?"

The half orc did grin but there was pain in her eyes. "A deep gash, a bad one."

Kulkar did force himself to breathe slowly, to ease down. "Right, I bet there is a storage of medicinal supplies in here somewhere, or at least bandages. We have to get out of here sooner or later, we cannot linger for there aren't food here and I bet that thing you carry need to get to where the enemy is right?"

Resh'kha did nod. "Yes, yes it does. "

Wenja woke up to a sound she never had heard before, it was a sound so loud she instinctively pressed her hands over her ears, even before she did open her eyes. She felt cold, and she did shiver too. The sound was that of a battle, roars, screams and the thunder of what had to be massive collisions. Slowly she did open her eyes again, she lay on a naked hill, covered with just gravel and sand and around her there was indeed a battle being fought. She got to her feet, discovering that she was naked and that the skies above her were dark and filled with smoke and flames. It was a vision of hell, around her people were fighting monsters and these were nothing like the ones she had seen out on the plains. These were way larger and way more terrifying and they were just so many. The people fighting them were of all races, she saw both humans and elves and dwarves and even some orcs. All wore elaborate armour and fought with a sort of fierce discipline she realized was needed. It was like an elegant and yet deadly dance and it was mesmerizing in its horror.

Some of the largest of the monsters did wield weapons and she could see structures, walls and buildings which did look more or less collapsed, she felt somehow that this once had been a city and a wonderful one too. The remains of architecture told her of great beauty and a sort of serene elegance which now was being ravaged and torn. She did swallow, what was this really? It was a test, she could see that but what was being tested? The thunder of battle didn't seize, both sides suffered great losses and yet none of them did yield or hesitate. The warriors did lunge forth, never cowering before even the most terrible of their opponents. Wenja turned around, it was the same in all directions, slaughter and mayhem and she didn't want to see this much death and destruction but knew she had to.

She started to walk, why she didn't really know. She just walked down from the small hill and realized that nobody could see her. She walked by the monsters and the warriors and she was invisible to them, as if she wasn't there. Maybe she wasn't, maybe this was all an illusion. She felt that she ought to head towards the centre of the city and there were some clues in the ruined buildings as to what direction she was to follow. There were streets and she did find a large one and followed it. Her mind simply stunned by what she did see.

After a while she realized that all there hadn't been warriors, ordinary people had lived there and she had to swallow the taste of bile in her mouth. There were corpses everywhere, people cut down like vermin, brutally killed in manners which were simply mind numbing in their grotesque reality. She saw men and women crushed by rocks, impaled by crude spears. She saw people bitten in half, ripped into shreds. She saw dogs and horses killed by heavy hammer blows, some caught underneath collapsing walls. It was as if there still was a wailing in the air, from spirits too distraught to head for the other side.

She saw a small girl laying in the street, clutching a ragdoll still, her lower body turned into pulp by some unknown force. Wenja had to turn around, retching and gasping for air. She felt sick to the core, torn apart by the fact that there was nothing she could do, nothing she could do to help these people. There were still civilians present, she saw families scurrying around like rats, trying to seek shelter and there were rocks flying through the air, hitting structures or just the streets with heavy thuds. They had to use some sort of siege machines for sure.

She saw that there was structure to the way the warriors fought, a clear strategy and there were officers among them, leading the men and keeping an overview of the situation. She was very confused, was this something which had happened? Was this a vision of the last time the gate had been opened?

She ran through the streets and came upon a sort of city square, the defenders had a sort of command station put up there, and she saw many people who carried signs of having great power. The armours and everything did seem very well made, and even the cloth they wore had bright colours and was woven in a manner she hadn't seen before. If this was the far past then much had been forgotten since then, that was for sure. The fighters were gathering around a huge stone slate, a map had been laid out over it and it was a map of the city. Wenja did see where she was and she did also see symbols placed everywhere which did indicate where the enemy was heading. She had to find something, something important. And it was on the enemy's side of the city for sure. She just knew that this was her goal, that the relic was there and had to be found.

She didn't know what it was, or how to get it since she obviously wasn't even really there but she did walk on. The monsters didn't see her and she didn't fear for her own safety but the things she did see made her shiver to the core. The defenders had suffered heavy losses, most bodies were just left where they fell since retrieval was too dangerous and the smell was unbelievable. They had to have been fighting for days or weeks even. The city was a ruin and she wondered where this was, she hadn't seen much of the world after all. The devastation got worse the farther she went, here there wasn't really much left of the buildings at all, only piles of rubble and everywhere there were monsters. Huge and small and heading in direction of the battle field. Then she sort of got past the monsters, the ruins became quiet, almost eerily so and she felt a horrible presence there, a pressing gnawing ache in her very soul and she slowed down. There were shadows between the ruins, towering dark figures which seemed to be made from just mist and yet they were real, not mirages.

They were darkness incarnate, cold ruthless souls filled with nothing but hatred and greed and she had never felt that scared before. Could they sense her? Was she brave enough to move forth? Whatever she was after, it was behind them and she thought she saw light far ahead, a faint flickering one but it did call to her. The dark ones, she knew what they were, the leaders of the monsters, their masters. And she felt the gate too, like a void pulling on her very soul but she did resist it and focused upon the now. She had to get the relic, so the world could be saved, once and for all. She started to move and the huge figures seemed to sense that something was there, they turned and shifted and moved like fog above water and she was shivering but kept going. She didn't try to sneak, she just walked on. She realized that these horrible apparitions did sense fear more than anything else and so she refused to be scared of them. She walked on and avoided wisps of dark mist and thoughts which did slide by her spirit like the filth covering stagnant ponds. She just wasn't there, she kept thinking about Ahravan and Rhawan, of her future daughter and her friends. They were what was important now.

She got by, they didn't manage to sense her and she went towards the light, it was like a firefly among the dark shadows of a deep wood and yet she saw it. She entered what had been a park, now there were just trunks and burned wood left of it but it had been lovely once. Everybody could see that. There was a figure standing there, a small and frail looking being which did have a physical body. It was bent and apparently very old and yet it had some power left. It lay around it as a cloak, barely noticeable but Wenja did know that this creature was very wise and did possess great knowledge. It did stare at her and she swallowed hard. It was impossible to say what race this was, it was ugly the way humans would see it, wrinkly and grey with a black snout like nose and watering dark eyes covered with cataracts. The hands were thin and the fingers long and skeletal, it did only have three fingers on each hand and the head was relatively long but flat from the sides. It did look odd but Wenja saw a sort of perfection also in this strange being. It had been formed thus by its own world and how was she to deem it bad? She probably looked just as horrid in its eyes.

The being held something packed into cloth and it did lower its eyes to the ground as she did approach. "Daughter of these lands, are you the one I have been waiting for?"

Wenja did nod. "I am"

The creature nodded, slowly and its mouth did move. It didn't have teeth, just bare gums and yet it did smile. "Good, bring this to the sacred circle and awaken it. But beware, the dark one of your time will sense it"

Wenja took a deep breath. "Who are you? Why are you helping me?"

The creature snickered, it was a cackling sound, not from a human throat. "Oh young soul, your world is not the first one these marauders do attack. I am what is left of my race, of my home. I am old and weak and they don't sense those who are thus, they seek power wherever they find it, in every form."

Wenja still didn't understand and the creature did make a gesture as if to embrace everything that they saw. "To them we aren't here, they sense only a shadow of our beings. This is the past, the only safe place to hide the relic. What was done cannot be undone child of this world, but the future is like a great tree with many branches and each branch is a possible outcome. We are trying to make sure the right branch is chosen."

Wenja took a deep breath. "Alright, so, what do I do now?"

The creature did hold the object forth, still wrapped in cloth. "Take it, when the time is right throw it into the gate. It will destroy that magic forever and the gate will never be opened again."

Wenja bit her lower lip. "It won't be easy now will it?"

The creature did shake its ugly head. "No, it may cost you everything young one, but you have to try. There are others too trying to help now, the goddess of your world is like a general, leading her armies into battle. Do heed her orders and her warnings and trust in yourself. Your light is strong"

Wenja tried to smile and took the bundle from the creature. It did wink at her. "The cliff does hold a secret, unleash it if you can and the dark ones will be destroyed"

Wenja felt the weight of the relic, it wasn't large and it wasn't heavy and it was difficult imagining that something this small could possess such power but who was she to doubt this. She held it close and bowed her head. "I thank you"

The creature bowed back. "And I thank you. I have waited here in this moment for a very long time young one, you are brave and not without compassion. A hardened soul cannot awaken the relic"

Wenja frowned. "How am I to…"

There was a jerk, a feeling of falling and she did have time to let out a yell before things went dark again. She opened her eyes with a grunt, feeling rather annoyed and a bit angry. Why did these things always end thus? With more questions than answers? She was in the temple, it was a very small dark room without much decoration and there was just a simple stone pedestal there and on top of it was the bundle of cloth hiding the relic. Wenja got up, she felt rather determined now, as if she had had enough of this prophecy chosen one thing. She walked over and grasped the relic and the cloth did come apart in her hands, as if it had rotted away completely. It was a small glass container, not very special at all. Just made from rough glass, a tiny jar the type some ladies use to store perfume in. There wasn't anything out of the ordinary about it at all and for a moment she did fear that they had been tricked and that this was fake. Then she felt the tingling sensation of magic running up and down her arm and she sighed and placed the tiny jar in her dress.

She turned and walked outside, the cat was there waiting for her and she nodded at it. "It is done, I have the relic. Now what?"

The cat did bow down and she did climb back onto its back, now she started feeling tired and a sensation of dread was clawing its way into her mind. The things she had seen…it would happen again if she didn't manage to close the gate and this time there weren't large armies ready to protect the land. If they couldn't stop the flow of monsters they were all doomed and the horrible deaths she had seen made her tremble. No, she had to do this, she had to make sure that it never came to it, no matter what. The cat started to trot and she closed her eyes and held onto the fur, she was tired and felt almost disconnected. It had been so much, and she was after all just one person, and not a terribly wise one.

She opened her eyes and gasped when she saw that they suddenly were moving along the beach heading towards the little camp. She had just closed her eyes for a few seconds and yet, here they were and she sat up and felt confusion grow within. The cat didn't slow down until they reached the simple tents and Wenja saw that Ahravan and Rhawan already stood here, waiting for them. Wenja felt an intense surge of relief, of joy. She had been afraid she wouldn't see them again and the moment Ahravan did lift her down she did embrace him fiercely. "Oh Ahravan, I am so glad to see you!"

Rhawan too were in tears of relief and she hugged him too, laughing as she did. "I am back, how long was I gone?"

Ahravan did make a grimace. "Not very long, some hours? But it was long enough if you ask me, what happened?"

584

Wenja felt the warmth from the tall male and leaned against him. "I will tell, but I need something warm, and rest. I feel very tired"

Ayhrandur and Khirhien and the two men did also gather around her, very curious and relieved that she was back and Khirhien did manage to warm some water and made tea. Wenja did tell them everything, very slowly and the elves did stare at each other. Ahravan did shrug. "It must have been a grand city you saw being destroyed, too bad I know very little of the past of this realm"

Khirhien was thinking hard. "I think I may have heard about that one, when I was young. It was a mere fairy-tale but one I sort of remember. My grandmother told me about it"

Everybody were staring at him and Khirhien did blush. "It was in the south, along the coast they call the bay of Shenalay. A great city of men and elves and it was famous for its beauty. Mighty kings ruled it for ages and it did harbour many wonders. They called it Khor'thialay, the city of silver"

Rhawan did squint. "Aye, I have heard that name too, long ago. But nobody today know where it was, or if it was even real"

Wenja sighed. "It was real, and what I saw…it has horrible. I cannot even begin to imagine the sufferings those people have gone through. And the monsters, they were way larger and stronger than the ones we have met."

Rhawan did sigh. "Then we do know that we have to get this gate closed, before things like that pass through. The kingdoms of the ancient days are no more, and the twelve clans are not strong enough to stop the beasts, not anymore. We may have been more powerful back in time but now we are too few."

Wenja did touch the relic gently, she still kept it in her pocket for it wasn't that large at all. "Odd really, I would have anticipated this thing to be something grand and amazing, like a powerful weapon or something like that but it is just a tiny glass jar."

Ayhrandur did tilt his head, his eyes were dark. "Do never think that small means weak, I have seen tiny shrews attack animals ten times their size and winning too. It is a mistake done by those who fail to see the truth about things, to only respect what power is visible with the naked eye."

Wenja nodded and leaned against Rhawan, she felt that they had to move on but first she needed rest. A long rest. She was perhaps one of the eternal now but there was still enough human in her to make her require rest rather often. Rhawan did nod at the two human hunters. "We leave the moment she is ready for it, stay alert and keep the horses ready for a swift departure if something happens."

They did nod and Wenja laid down in one of the tents. She closed her eyes and felt that Ahravan did lay down next to her, he did just hold her and it felt good, and safe too. She did fall asleep right away but the sounds of that battle was still ringing in her head and she still felt the stench of death in her nose. The goddess had said that she never would forget, right, then she accepted that price for she had to save her people from suffering the same fate. Wenja did sleep for almost half a day, when she did wake up she was well rested but felt a bit sleepy and she had to wash her face with cold water to really wake up. When she had eaten a bit she was lifted onto Rhawan's horse and they were off yet again. The huge cat was still there though and now it was leading them all, and Wenja did realize that it did know where they were going. She could just hope that they would reach whatever goal the goddess had set for them easily and fast.

The valleys leading towards the plain with the odd cliff were steep and winding and also very narrow at places and the transition from mountains to plain sudden. The plain surrounding the cliff was filled with beasts now and the dark one was frustrated that he couldn't just send them out to the other areas of this world to wreak havoc upon it, he just wasn't strong enough for that and it made him utterly frustrated. If he could have accomplished this on his own, oh the glory and the power he would have gained and the respect, not in the least the respect. He was used to being treated like someone who was inferior and lowly and he hated it. His race knew that art to a T, hatred was something which had been bred into them from the very beginning and he had become a master of it. Now he was working with the expansion of the gate and it was very demanding. His

586

focus was upon that, not the surroundings. The monster he had brought through already had to fend for themselves until everything was ready and the fact that they were that many didn't really bother him.

Now huge packs did roam around, hungry and angry and ready to fight and this plain was very naked and barren. There wasn't much which grew there and it had never held any wildlife to speak off due to that fact so the monsters were not very happy at all. Huge groups did move towards the mountains by sheer instinct, they were looking for food and when they heard a slight rumbling sound none of them did react at all. They didn't have the intelligence to perceive the danger, nor were they smart enough to truly be afraid of anything. The dam had contained a whole lake, very long and very deep and as the valleys below it did split into several wider ones the water did take different routes. Thus the water did arrive at different times and the effect was horrifying. A black wall of liquid did burst from one of the valley openings, it was the valley which did lead directly up to where the dam had been and the water had a very straight path to take. The wave was at least twenty meters tall as it reached the plain, and it was just as much mud as water, mixed with rocks and dead trees. Its speed was tremendous, the front was pushed forth by all the water behind it and the first monsters which saw it didn't realize what it was. There was no concept of such a thing in their tiny brains. Instead they just stood there, staring at the strange dark mass until it was too late. When their instincts did kick in the wave was already within a mile from them and even if they tried to run it was useless.

Then the other valleys did spew forth water too, the waves did meet and congregate and formed a horrible pattern of maelstroms which did grind anything into shreds. The monsters didn't stand a chance, they were huge and tough and made to endure serious injuries but the force of the water and debris mixed with the fact that they couldn't breathe under water did spell doom. The waves did gush out over the flat plain and since there wasn't a single hill or as much as a small valley there nothing did slow it down. The water found only a smooth surface and did slide along with the speed of a swift gazelle.

The dark one was busy with his work when he heard a strange sound, it was a distant whoosh and he couldn't identify it. The palace from which he did work had no windows and he turned from the table he was floating by and felt the earth shake underneath his form. An earthquake? That was strange? He had been trying to give the crystals which did control the gate extra power to increase the speed of which it did open but he hadn't been able to do much of a difference at all and his mood was not good. He made a gesture and a part of the wall became transparent.

He froze, the plain was turning black, something did rush forth towards him and his first instinct was to flee. He was still having memories of a time when they had possessed bodies all the time and his instincts were still there, buried deep within his very soul. He couldn't leave the gate, it would become unstable and he was torn between his duty and his sense of self preservation. It was water, a horrible flood and the monsters he had managed to bring through were being thrown around as in a swirling river and it didn't appear that any of them did manage to get away for where could they go? There was no place which was safe now and he put up a wall of defensive energy around the palace, the gate and the cliff. The dark wave of water and debris did stop abruptly and made the entire crystal building sway but it didn't crumble and he could only watch in disbelief as the water did swipe all over the plain. In fact it did reach the far north of the plain and also the western part. The water did lose much of its speed and power on the way but the wave was still several meters tall and it did move rather fast.

The plain was covered with a several feet thick layer of mud, rocks and dead beasts and the dark one was stunned. No, he was frozen. This couldn't be happening, it wasn't possible?! How could this happen to him! The great ones would blame him for this, not that they didn't have enough monsters to replace the ones who had died but the time it did take to bring them through? The great ones among them didn't like delays at all and he felt small and weak for a few seconds. The idea of fleeing did touch his mind briefly, he could try to find some dimension where he could hide for some ages? No, they would find him, and then the punishment would be horrible indeed. He had to minimize the damage and make sure that this didn't slow them down.

The water did calm down and the plain was turned into a bog now, the only monsters which had survived were the ones who had reached the outskirts of the mountains and had gone high enough to escape the flood. He had only a mere percent of his original army left and it as just dreadful. He had no idea of what to do and spun around himself for a while, trying to figure out how to bring the gate into a more efficient mode. The gates were holes through time and space and their creation as well as their continuing function was horribly power consuming. Was there a way he could make the crystals more efficient. He did stare at the crystal slab into which the crystal were embedded. Could he…?

He would have swallowed hard if he had been in a body there and then, there was one thing he could do but if it went wrong… Was he brave enough? Could he control it? He gathered his focus and laid his hands on the crystals, they were warm to the touch and very pretty but he didn't see the beauty in them. He saw a machinery made to keep the gate open and bringing the entire control over had been a horrible business since it didn't go well with the energy of this world. But he had done it and he was sure he could manage this challenge just fine. He started to move the crystals into a new pattern. Until now they had drawn power from this realm but if he did pull energy also through the very gate itself? It was of course a bit counterproductive since he was to bring their home power, not take it from them but it was a small sacrifice and soon it wouldn't be needed so why not really. It would speed things up, the great ones did appreciate some initiative.

The light surrounding the very gate itself did change, it had been glowing in an odd orange tone of red and now it became slightly green, it didn't look good but he didn't care. It wasn't about how the gate did look, it was about how it did work. The gate did look like a hole in the air, a dark gaping opening which did glow slightly and it was spinning. The spin did increase, and the opening seemed to widen a wee bit. He would have jumped for joy if he had been flesh there and then, it did work. They would forgive the loss of some monsters wouldn't they? It wasn't as if they were valuable and there were plenty back in the home world. He did allow the gate to stabilize itself and then he removed the window, he didn't need to see the misery the wave had left behind. Now he had to focus on bringing through as many new horrors as possible, he knew that some of his brethren who were tasked with creating these things were very creative indeed. They would love to show the great ones how efficient their creations were, yes, he would gain support from those of course. Forget about this tiny setback, it would be alright and he would achieve the influence he did deserve. They would see how clever he was and his fate would change for sure.

Resh'kha and the others had searched through the city, there were no enemies left there which they did see and Kulkar did know where to look for medical supplies. The rooms which were this city's equivalent to a hospital was close to the great air shafts which made the very centre of the city and Kulkar found the closets and storages fast. They were rather well stacked, the city had to have been abandoned or something for nothing had been removed. Most of it was very old and useless but some of the things they did find weren't that ruined at all. Floth'bha was very weak and the gash in her abdomen was indeed nasty, deep and torn and just ugly looking and Kulkar did find some thread and a needle and started sewing the wound. Floth'bha didn't make a sound and Resh'kha did cringe, it didn't look very good at all. Dharan did check the rooms for other things they could use and came back with a sack full of stuff. Geir did frown. "Please tell me there is something edible here?"

Dharan did grunt. "I doubt it, a lot! If there is food left behind it is way too old to be eaten. No, we have to leave the city, this place may be safe now but we cannot live here"

Resh'kha nodded. " Indeed, I have got to get to that cliff, I know I am needed there. The chosen one must close the gate and I have to make sure that she doesn't fail."

Floth'bha did look a bit better, she managed to sit up. "Resh'kha is right, that is our goal"

Resh'kha did place a hand on her shoulder. "I don't think you ought to go sister, it isn't wise. You are wounded after all"

Floth'bha did close her eyes, her face was a bit drawn. "You are right my friend, I cannot follow you to the cliff. I am too weak. But I can move out of here on my own at least"

Kulkar turned to Resh'kha again and his face was very serious. "I will go with you Resh'kha. Geir can protect Floth'bha and we can find a good place where they can stay until this is over. It is only fair that the dwarves do their part of this job.”

Dharan did grunt. “I can help watch Floth’bha too, she did fight well and it would be an honour to watch her until you return”

Floth’bha did look moved. “I…You are willing to stay behind just to make sure I am okay?”

Dharan just shrugged and looked a bit smug. “Of course, besides, if Resh’kha is to reach that cliff I bet two is less visible than three”

Resh’kha felt very troubled, she didn’t want to leave Floth’bha behind, she had come to realize that the half orc was becoming way more than a dear friend and the idea of maybe losing her was terrible. But if they found a safe spot where she could heal until things were alright again? “Then be it, I and Kulkar will go to the cliff, and face whatever deviltry there is out there”

Kulkar had already proved that he was brave, terribly so. Dwarves are often seen as rather reserved and quiet creatures but he did prove that their blood did run hot when it needed to. “Then let’s get out of here and find something edible and a place to stay. Then we will go to face destiny, whatever it may be”

Resh’kha did help Floth’bha and they did make their way out of the dwarven stronghold the same way they entered. The valleys which did lead north from the dam were scoured clean but there were higher ones and Kulkar did lead them into one of those. It had some forest and a small lake and it was rather idyllic. After a few hours he did find a small cave and there was plenty of dry wood too. Dharan and Geir did take off and managed to shot a sort of sheep and the dwarf did find some bulbs in the earth which were edible. Mixed with meat and some herbs Dharan had nicked from the infirmary of the city they managed to make a good meal. Floth’bha did sit down with a groan, the wound had been very long and Resh’kha was afraid it would get infected. The filthy claws which had caused the injury weren’t exactly ideal for preventing infection and since Floth’bha was only half orc she wasn’t as immune to infection as a full orc. Normal orcs hardly ever got that sort of infections Resh’kha did fear, their wounds would close up without problems but she did know that Floth’bha never would admit to being in pain. She was a tough one and

Resh'kha had only fondness for the other female. Floth'bha did eat with good appetite and Kulkar did put some herbs in a cup of water and washed the wound with them.

The two wolves were still there, waiting for them to leave and Resh'kha felt that the deity she carried was starting to make itself known again. She could understand the need for vengeance, heck, to an orc that was second nature of somebody did insult you or your clan but she didn't want to trust Gholrae, the creature had been of a devious nature and the orc didn't like to take chances. She wouldn't obey Gholrae blindly, that was for darn sure. The day was at its end and they couldn't leave in the dark so they had to wait for the morning and Resh'kha did lay down next to Floth'bha and listened to her breathing. She was afraid of putting her feelings into words, she didn't know how to but she hoped that she would get the chance to open her heart later on, when and if they returned. The next morning she and Kulkar did prepare to get going, the dwarf had to ride the wolf Floth'bha had ridden previously as his pony wouldn't be able to keep up and the dwarf did look a bit nervous but the animal did accept him. Resh'kha did hug Floth'bha and crossed her fingers, the wound didn't seem to have gotten infected but such things could change fast and Dharan did swear to keep an eye on it. Resh'kha was suspecting that Floth'bha was weaker than she was showing them, she was proud and strong and didn't want to cause concern among the others and Resh'kha did hug her before they did ride off, still not able to be honest about her feelings.

The two wolves did run very fast down the valleys, everywhere the ground was scoured clean by the rushing water and the air was raw and damp. Here and there the very bedrock seemed to have been torn open as if by a huge can opener and rocks and debris were left in piles here and there. But that was nothing compared with the plains, as soon as they saw the now black surface ahead of them they knew that the monsters were gone. Nothing could have survived this and Resh'kha just prayed that they would be able to get to the cliff without sinking inn.

Kulkar stared at the cliff and his face was stern, he did spit and patted his axe. "I will make sure that we win sister orc, if it is the last thing that I do"

Resh'kha did grin at the dwarf. "I know you will"

The huge cat did lead them down towards the plain again and Wenja remembered that there had been mentions of a sacred circle. Now there weren't that many monsters around since this area was very steep and the valleys more like the steps of a stair than real valleys. It did cause problems here and there but they did manage to move forth without any mishaps. Wenja could feel that something was happening out there, a sort of restless energy which made her wonder and she knew that Resh'kha and her group was out there somewhere too. She hoped that they were okay. She had discovered something odd now, something she hadn't noticed before. Both Rhawan and Ahravan were listening more and more to her, and so were the others too. She was suddenly being respected in a whole new way and it was a peculiar sensation. It wasn't that they hadn't truly respected her before but now they did bow to her will without even questioning it and she felt that it was strange for she had never been used to that sort of responsibility before. Ahravan would just laugh and shrug it off and claim that she after all was the Eth'ir and that they owed it to her. After all, she was being led by the goddess now and she had proved her courage. They did travel down a valley with a small river in it and then they saw what was meant by a sacred circle. It was indeed a circle, made from stones and it was placed at the bottom of a small bowl like indentation in the earth. It did look almost like the pot holes you can find in rivers where rocks have been spun around and gnawed into the bedrock. The circle was made from seven huge stones and they were all very pale and identical. The place was eerie and Wenja felt that the hairs did rise along her neck. "What is that?"

Her voice was hoarse and Ahravan did frown. "I have no idea."

Rhawan shrugged. "Neither do I my dear. I have never seen a site like that."

The cat did saunter over to the circle and sat down, it did look almost smug. Wenja was helped down by Ahravan and she sighed. "I was to awaken the relic here, but I have no idea of how or what is meant by it. Awaken it? It is a glass jar damn it"

Ahravan did walk over to the first stone, it was so smooth it felt like touching well-made glass and the ground between the stones was also very smooth, as if it had been polished. He did make a small yip. "Look here, look at the ground!"

They all gathered and Wenja did stare at the crystalline surface, it was dusty and odd but there seemed to be a sort of pattern in it, probably carefully carved into the stone.

Ayhrandur did run to get some water and they did throw some water skins over the surface and it became very shiny indeed. Like the floors of some palace. There was indeed a pattern there and now that they did wash off the dust it started to glow slightly. It was gorgeous and intricate and yet none of them had any idea of what it did mean. But there was a naked spot in the middle, very small and just the right size to place the glass jar. The group did wander about, staring at the pattern, trying to come up with an explanation to what this meant and what they were supposed to do. The stones stood there like silent sentinels and Gochil did go over and started washing the stones too with a saddle blanket, just to see if there were inscriptions there. The first two rocks were naked, nothing there except from a completely smooth surface. Then on number three he did cry out. "Here, there is something here"

They ran over and Ahravan did stare at a symbol he in fact did recognize. "It is the tree of life, I have seen it before. The shamans use it, to show that all live is one"

Darush was already eagerly wiping off the next rock and there were inscriptions also on that one. This symbol was not as easy to recognize but Khirhien did identify it as a symbol which did mean rebirth and growth. The next stone had a symbol which meant a union of some sort and then there were the two last stones. Wenja did wipe off the surface of the next in line, it was a symbol Rhawan did know, it did mean a spiritual awakening but it could also mean healing of the body through spiritual means. The last symbol was one of protection and they all stood there looking at each other, what did this truly mean?

Wenja did walk over to the naked spot in the middle and placed the glass jar in it, nothing happened but the jar seemed to glow a wee bit, as if it did agree on the position. Rhawan did scratch his head. "Something is missing"

Ahravan nodded and took a stroll around it, staring at the stones. "You are right, something is most definitely missing. Let us summarize what we do know about this thing, it is supposed to close the gate?"

Wenja nodded. "Yes, I am to toss it inn."

Ahravan tried to think logically. "I bet the gate is powerful magic, and powerful magic always dances on a razors edge between success and failure. But it has to be stable enough to last for a long time, I can hardly imagine that a mere glass jar will be enough to throw it off balance enough for it to be ruined."

Rhawan grunted and Khirhien did squint. "You are right, it won't do anything as it is now. It came from another world you say?"

Wenja nodded. "Yes, probably one where the people had been wiped out by the monsters"

The silvery haired eternal did nod and his eyes were distant. "They would want to rid the world of this menace indeed. There has to be more to the relic then. It has to contain something special perhaps?"

The jar was seemingly empty but Gochil did make a small sound. "I think I may have an idea"

Everybody stared at the young human, he did blush like a beet. "I mean, the monsters are deadly, they ruin everything right? And I bet their masters are the same, only after causing destruction"

Ahravan did nod. "That makes sense yes, do continue"

The man did gesture towards the pattern in the floor. "It is completely symmetrical, can't you see that? Perfect! And the symbols of the stones, it all adds up to one thing…"

Wenja did interrupt, her voice very small. "Life, we must fill it with life, but how?"

They looked at each other, eyes a bit large. "What is the life force then, blood?"

The idea of sacrificing blood made them all wince. Darush did let his hand slide along the rock nearest to him, just to move and the wet cloth did remove more dust and filth. There was a symbol there too, almost hidden closer to the ground than the other ones. Almost on floor level as a matter of fact and Ahravan saw it and went red in the face. So did the others too except Wenja who didn't understand. "What?"

Rhawan did bite his lower lips, his eyes were filled with mirth and yet very serious. "What creates life Wenja mine?"

She did frown. "What creates life….OH! Oh my, I see"

The symbol was obviously placed there on purpose and Rhawan did snicker. "We do still use that one at times, we paint it on doors when visitors are to knock instead of just walking straight into a hut."

Wenja felt warm all over. "So it basically means that somebody is…well, busy?"

Ahravan nodded, still looking embarrassed. "Indeed it does."

Wenja stared at the two of them and her face felt a bit stiff. "Uh, does that mean that…hmmm we are to…."

Rhawan was looking at the skies and the others were trying not to look at anyone at all. "Uh yes, I do think that this is the idea. The energy of the act of making love, it is pure Wenja, it is life and it is something I bet the enemy have no concept of, love"

She blinked and felt silly, but she somehow knew that they were right. The jar had to be filled with life, with defiance of the destruction the darkness brought and she realized why she was to be the one to awaken the relic. She was to be in control and it would be through her that the jar was turned into a weapon against the dark forces. She gathered her senses, calmed herself down, tried to be in control of herself but it wasn't easy at all. "Right. We are to…do it, here and now, in the circle. So how do we proceed?"

Ahravan was blushing still, Rhawan did look very embarrassed and it was Khirhien who still was calm enough to think well. "I say we take the horses to the other side of this valley and make camp there. We will be out of sight then, and you can…ah…have fun in peace"

Ayhrandur giggled. "Yes, it isn't as if we haven't heard you before."

Wenja swallowed hard and stared at her two husbands, both did look a bit more serious now and she took a deep breath. "Good, that is…great. Do that"

Khirhien and the others did leave the bowl shaped pit and Wenja took a deep breath. "I have a feeling of knowing how this is to be done, if it is all right with you?"

Ahravan did stare down at her, his eyes were gentle as always and she knew that he would accept anything she did suggest. In this she was the person in charge, it had to be that way. «The goddess is leading you isn't she?"

Wenja did nod, she took a deep breath. "She is I think, I can feel what she wants me to do. And I know there is no other way. We are being lead Ahravan, and all we can do is follow, or else everything will be in vain. Are you ready to submit to my will?"

Ahravan did smile, it was endless trust in his eyes and Rhawan did nod slowly, he did seem to be in awe of the moment and Wenja did close her eyes and felt that this circle was more than just a monument. It had some sort of importance beyond its apparent beauty. "You are to be passive now, until I say otherwise. This is a ceremony to honour the goddess and the life of this realm, you have to accept being used"

Both males did nod and Wenja saw that the others were out of sight now. She felt her heart hammering, it was a solemn moment and she had never had this feeling of reverence before. This spot was sacred, way more than the cliff and it was old, much older. She could feel that the circle was eternal, a place which did exist in all worlds and realms and they were all interconnected and she realized what the goddess wanted to do. It was madness and yet not, perhaps it was the only way. She saw that the rocks around them started to look almost transparent and they did shine, a soft white light. A sort of dome did form around them so the bowl shaped pit became part of an orb and she raised her hands to the skies and everything went quiet. They didn't hear anything, not even the sound of the river which wasn't that far away. This was a world in its own now and the pattern on the floor did seem to pulse and glow, shifting and changing. "I am the tool, I am the chosen, I am the bringer of light. Let me be thy hand, let me be thy heart, let me hear thy song"

Wenja had no idea of where the words came from but she was part of something now, something very ancient and strong, something carried from mother to daughter since the beginning of time and she was no longer a poor shepherd's daughter but the culmination of millennia of hope and prayers. She turned to Ahravan and placed her hand over his heart, her eyes did shine. "You are the earth which strengthens the root and from which it draws its life"

She turned to Rhawan and touched him the same way. "You are the rain, bringing relief to those who thirst and let the roots drink deep."

She raised her hands again. "I am the seed, from which the tree of life starts. It is so, may the great mother bless us all"

She saw that the outside world was invisible now, hidden by the glowing wall and she didn't really care. She started to undress the two males, slowly and with gentle touches and they allowed her to do it, as if they were mere dolls. When they both were naked she removed her own clothes and the mark at the back of her neck did glow intensely and now they did see that it was the same pattern as the one on the floor of the circle. It was all connected and she felt how the life of this realm did flow into her, turning her into an incarnation of the goddess. She had never been more beautiful and she had never been more powerful, more at peace. This was right, this was as it should be and she wasn't afraid at all.

Ahravan suddenly remembered the dream he had had, now Wenja was completely alike the woman in his dream, the green of her eyes had gotten some silvery grey in it too, and she was sheer power. He knew what she had meant, the love of one, the power of the pure spirit which was Wenja, ready to give her all to those she did love. The blood of two, the blood he and Rhawan had shed to save her by the sacred well. The power of three, the power within their union, three bonded together with unbreakable bonds of love and trust. The promise of four, the promise represented by her unborn child, the one who would turn three into four and create a new future for them all. This was a defining moment, the moment of destiny and truth and he did accept it humbly and with an open heart. He did know her now, and knew that she was chosen well, that the goddess had picked her brave caring soul among countless others and known that Wenja was the right one for him and Rhawan, and that she was brave enough to do what she had to do to save her future.

She started to gently caress Rhawan and Ahravan, slowly sliding around them both, following a rhythm dictated by the very earth itself. It was a sensual dance, meant to entice and tease and arouse and she did encourage them to touch her back. There was no hurry, time didn't exist within this orb of light and soon everything was forgotten except the need to fulfil what life asked of them. Bodies did writhe in the ecstasy of touch and who's touch it was didn't matter at all. It was a dance of flesh and desire and love and absolute trust and Wenja did lead them, her intuition the tool which did show them the path to take. It had never been like this before, Wenja had enjoyed their love making immensely but this was on another level, it was spiritual as much as physical and they truly became as one. She didn't really know where she ended and they started and it was divine. She gave them pleasure in every manner she could and they did repay that in full, she was aglow with the joy of being alive and each time one of them did climax the rocks around them did glow brighter and the hum from the earth itself became stronger. Ahravan and Rhawan had shared this many times but it was so much more now, their bonding went deeper than ever and they all knew that this meant that they never would feel the need for a new partner. They were three but one and it was a connection stronger than most other. The pleasure of the flesh became insignificant compared with the pleasure of knowing that they were safe with each other, that nothing now could make them question the feelings they did share or the loyalty of their bond mates. The earth drank from the love they did radiate and she did distil it and sent it back, multiplied and purified, it went back and forth, each time stronger, each time more powerful and more true until they too did glow like the circle itself.

It was building up to something incredible, something beyond this world and she was sure she saw glowing figures within the now almost invisible rocks, dancing and sliding around, sharing her joy. It was the spirits of the land and she did remember having drawn them to her and made them heal Ahravan and she was grateful to them. When the end finally came it was so strong it made them almost pass out, Wenja did see that the top of the stones did burst into beams of light which did congregate at the centre of the circle and she placed the jar there with a howl of ecstasy. It was done, it was fulfilled. The light from the rocks seemed to fill the jar and it burst into light, an intense light which didn't burn their eyes oddly enough. The pattern of the floor did change, and so did the pattern at the back of her neck. Now it was more geometrical and way larger than before, covering the top of her back and it did glow brightly. The light from the pattern did fly forwards and entered the jar too and there was a booming sound and the dome did disappear.

The rocks were as they had been, they felt the cool wind and heard the river and the others were standing on top of the pit, staring and looking awe struck. Wenja kissed Ahravan and Rhawan, both were exhausted and so was she, it had taken so much out of them and she had to grin. The things they had done... But she felt the glowing spark which was the spirit of her unborn child within and knew that her daughter from now on would be something different, something new. The power of the circle had been distilled through that child and it told Wenja that her daughter would be unlike any other living being. It was a humbling thought and yet she couldn't help but worry. But the goddess was with her, it would be alright, she just knew it would.

Ahravan did pant and managed to get up on his knees, his body slick with sweat and Rhawan was just lying there, looking a bit sheepish. "I have never been knocked out by love making before, pardon me Wenja but I am sure you could have offed us both there"

She did giggle and grasped the jar, it was warm to the touch and she smiled. Knowing that they now had the weapon they needed to destroy the enemy.

The dark one had been working like mad to bring through new scores of monsters and he had also managed to send some mental messages to his brethren back in their own dimension. They had brought forth the worst beasts they had managed to create and were very eager to show off their creations. He hadn't asked the great ones for permission but he was sure that it would be alright, after all, the goal was all that mattered. The gate was sucking power from both dimensions and it did still expand and he was convinced that this would continue. The energy he felt from the cliff was annoying, he wished so badly that he could tap into it and use it. It would be enough to open the gate like never before, to let the entire army through at once. He wished that he knew what this energy was and why it was there, but he didn't have the answers and couldn't waste time trying to find out. He was about to revel in the arrival of a huge group of absolutely terrifying beasts when he became aware of something new, a sort of sickening sensation of having forgotten something very important. There was something there, something which did feel like a stinging blade through his very being and he reared back and yelled. It was pain, real pain, real agony and the gate did move, tossing from side to side as if blown by a strong wind. The connection between the worlds was rather long and it did take time to get the creatures through and he hadn't expected to meet any problems now. There was a shriek heard, not in the physical sense but a mental one, from those on the other side. He did whimper, what was happening?

The gate did shrink a lot, the energy it had been drinking from this realm's life force had been cut off, as if by a knife. Now only energy from his home dimension did feed it and it wasn't that stabile, not as strong. The gate would collapse and he felt it, the wrath of the great ones. They would punish him, they would tear his soul into shreds and thrown them into the endless void between dimensions. He had to get the energy back and now! But the earth underneath him felt dead, barren. There was no life in it, or it didn't allow him to feel it and he roared with rage. The palace was shivering and the blue colour did shift to night black for a few seconds. He did hear them calling out to him, accusing him of being useless, a failure and a disappointment. "Zhradhuu, you cannot even oversee this? We knew it, you are not to be trusted"

He did panic, there had to be something he could do! There had to be a way to avoid a disaster. The gate was not closing up any more but it was not going to let anything through as it was. It did look like a slightly open gaping anus and he was trembling, spinning around like a blurry cloud of mist. Then it did strike him, the idea! The solution! He didn't hesitate, he didn't have time to. He had created the crystal palace easily enough, all by himself by using his own innate energy. He could do that again. He would have been panting if he had been flesh and blood, his energy burning black with stress and despair. He did force rocks out of the ground in a long line from the cliff to the gate and then he did transform them into crystal. That was how they did empty worlds of energy, by transforming matter and consuming the very life of the world.

The life of the living was useless, as free energy it could be exploited and thus all the death. He did form a long line of crystal, elevated above the ground on elegant pillars and he did extend the ends, one did dig into the very cliff itself and the other did slip inside of the open gate. The gate did suck energy, and now it did start to drain the energy from the cliff. A little at first, then more and more and the gate did expand once more and started to glow in a bright blue colour. He did yell with glee, he had done it! He was weakened a lot and he didn't really know why and how it did work but that didn't matter. He knew that his hide was saved for this time.

He didn't sit there to rest on his laurels, he had to organize the new arrivals and he was truly not very strong now. He did feel a sting of annoyance and anger, he did need to go physical again and have that drink. He did walk over to the table and sent a mental signal through the palace, not trying to be even a wee bit pleasant. The creature did appear again from its lair, the head lowered and the odd body did sway as it made its way forth. He did kick it to make it speed up and he took shape and the creature did lift the flagon and did pour into the glass again. It did nod its head and he did open his mouth and the creature did pour the silvery liquid into him once more. He did wince and shuddered, it was never anything but unpleasant but needed. He did send it another vicious kick before he went to take a peek at the new arrivals. The creature did put the flagon and the cup back in its place, it didn't make a sound but the eyes did glow again, an ominous and eerie glow of sheer hatred and if it had been able to make what a human would call a smile it would. The flagon was the only thing it had, its sole responsibility and its only chance. These creatures weren't really regarded as anything except tools and their obedience was something which was expected and seen as a guaranteed. The creature did hiss, a very low sound which didn't sound friendly at all. It had the memories of its ancestors, such things were inherited in their race and it knew what had happened to its home world and its brethren. They were patient, one individual didn't matter at all in the long run but their vengeance would come, one way or the other. Time would be on their side and now it had seen its chance. The liquid within the flagon was in fact one made by these creatures, an excretion from a gland in their body and none of the masters knew it but they could change it by changing their own body chemistry. It wasn't easy and it would ultimately kill the creature since it would poison itself but it was a price it was ready to pay. The liquid the dark one had ingested this time would have its effect, soon enough.

Resh'kha and Kulkar did make their way across the plain, it wasn't really easy but they did avoid the most soggy areas and the devastation created by the wave was immense. There were dead beasts everywhere and the smell was overwhelming already. It wasn't as much decay as it was the fact that they had all emptied their guts when they did die. The mud was thick but the wolves did seem to be able to avoid any dangerous spots and Resh'kha did see that there were monsters arriving at the cliff. There were huge packs spreading yet again and she hissed and wondered how they were to do anything at all. If they were detected they wouldn't be able to get anywhere near the gate, whatever it was. Resh'kha could feel that Gholrae was impatient but she did also feel that the deity did guide her and she was clearly told to hide and wait. They had to get ready for the right moment and Resh'kha did agree, if they only knew when that was. Kulkar was eager, his eyes shining and his entire body language spoke of excitement. To a dwarf this had to be a sure path to honour and Resh'kha did wish that she was as confident as him.

The darkness did help them a lot, they did manage to get to the cliff and Resh'kha was in awe of it, she had no idea of what it had been but its might was stunning. The monsters were a problem but they were still on the front side of the cliff and they did arrive from the opposite direction. As they crept forth Resh'kha felt the magic from the cliff and it was staggering, like a pain almost and she did fear it almost as much as the horrible sensation the gate gave her. And the presence of what could only be one of the masters, a sickening sensation of almost touching something utterly vile and nasty. They did see the palace now and was shocked by its fragile beauty but the gate filled them with dread and they saw how it spewed forth more and more beasts, in a long stream of dark and twisted bodies. Resh'kha couldn't even imagine how such beings were possible and yet, there they were and they were alive.

Kulkar did grunt. "See that crystal beam? From the cliff to the gate? I am rather sure that it will be my target"

Resh'kha did nod. "You are right, that will disturb things, a lot. But how are we to get close enough?"

The two wolves did wag their tails and let out some small wuffs, she did stare at them. "You will help us? That is great"

The wolves did sit down and since they were in hiding behind some boulders and debris Resh'kha didn't expect them to be seen yet. But if they got closer to the palace there was no way they could hide. Kulkar did stare at the glowing bridge like structure and his eyes were narrow. "The goddess will show us when to strike, I know she will. All we can do is wait"

Resh'kha tried to smile back. "Yes, and hope that we won't be spotted before we are ready for it"

Wenja and the two others did get dresses, she felt a bit sore and stiff and she was sticky in funny places but she did also feel quite amazing. She did kiss both Rhawan and Ahravan and she put the now glowing jar in her pocket and knew that she soon would have to use it. The others did still stare at them and Wenja felt a bit embarrassed, it was no way the others could have heard them but she did realize that they felt the change in her. She had become more than before, like a part of the goddess and it made her a bit self-conscious. They had to rest for a while and Wenja did eat with good appetite, she didn't really feel the fact that she was with child yet but soon she would and she wondered what Sefa would say when she got the good news. She was sure that her friend would be very excited indeed.

When they did leave the valley with the circle behind she knew that she from now on had to do things right. She had to listen to that voice in her head and make sure that she didn't step out of line, not even once. Their opponent was terrible and clever and also very powerful and not to be underestimated. The huge cat did saunter in front of them and now they saw the cliff clearly. They were in the hills beside it and from a higher elevation they did see the masses which seemed to just appear out of nowhere.

Ahravan did frown. "We have to get you to the gate right? But how are we to get that far? There are monsters everywhere down there "

Rhawan did nod. "The plains looks as if they have been flooded? But the gate is open still"

Wenja did wet her lips, she had to toss the jar into the gate, and she felt that the goddess had a plan. A diversion would be set into motion. The problem was getting close enough, the area was crowded already and the beasts did spread out gradually. Ahravan took a deep breath. "I don't think we will be able to fight our way to the gate. They are too many and these are larger and probably a lot harder to kill than the ones we are used to"

Ayhrandur had a serious expression on his face. "You are right, we cannot hope to get to the gate unseen. And they are indeed horrible, we are only six warriors, and even with good horses we cannot get that far."

Ahravan tried to think, was there some sort of tactics they could use? The plain was bare and wet and there was no way they could use fire to deter the beasts. Gochil and Darush did look a bit scared and Khirhien was staring at the beasts down there with obvious hatred. "They have to be destroyed, all of them"

Wenja did nod. "Yes, but the most important thing now is to get the gate closed off"

Ahravan did grunt. "And to do that you have to get to it, safely!"

They stared at each other, it was a dilemma and one to which they found no answer. That was when Rhawan did point at the plain with a gasp. "What in the name of every deity is that?!"

Resh'kha and Kulkar were waiting and it wasn't exactly what Resh'kha had expected to be doing. Sitting behind some mud covered slimy boulders with a dwarf, waiting for the time to strike. Orcs weren't like that, they preferred to face the opponent openly and show their strength. Such sneaky stealthy business weren't their way at all. It made her feel frustrated and a bit depressed too. Then suddenly she felt a sort of jerk and Gholrae stood there next to them, the strange entity did sneer. "I have things to do, the chosen one must not be hindered and I have been given a task. You will know when to strike Resh'kha, listen to the goddess."

Resh'kha did gape. "Strike what? Gholrae? Wait!"

But the deity was gone as if vanished into thin air and Resh'kha did feel tempted to pull her own hair out in frustration. This didn't tell her much at all. Kulkar did chuckle. "Oh I bet she has a trick or two up her sleeve. She knows them beasts you know, if they did destroy her home I bet she has some ideas for sure."

Out on the plains the new hordes of monsters were running forth, spreading as they came through the gate and these were the ultimate creations of the dark ones. Each one a killing machine with very little brain and a very hungry gut and their instincts were blunted to say the least. They were bred and made to be expendable and they only needed to be smart enough to do what was expected of them. Eradicate all resistance so the dark ones could harvest resources unhindered. It was a tactic the dark ones had started to use ages ago since it meant that they didn't have to waste precious energy on fighting. Accidents can happen even to one who is superior and they eradicated that risk by letting others fight for them instead. It was a clever strategy for sure.

The beasts were created by mixing different species with the help of magic and then simply copied by the thousands, also with the help of magic. It was power consuming but it did assure that they had all the warriors they needed when they needed them and they had huge reserves too. The creators responsible for these new horrors were proud and very sure of their own skills. They had managed to make living beings which were simply too powerful to be destroyed by ordinary weapons. They felt no fear nor hesitation and had no sense of self preservation. They were perfect. Only that they were not. The dark ones had thrown away the cloak of flesh ages ago, they did no longer need a body with all its restrictions and needs and they did look down upon all beings which still needed to be physical. They had forgotten about how it was to be flesh and blood and thus they had no understanding of how it did work. They had simply forgotten.

The beasts were scurrying around, aggressive and hungry and then something did appear in front of them. Odd beings which seemed to rise from the mud and the beasts did stop and stare, confused. The beings did resemble them a bit but were smaller and more elegant and also brighter in colour. The huge beasts seemed to almost freeze, then they all roared and burst forth, eyes fixed on the smaller beings. The dark ones had never had use for females, they created their slaves without such and thus these males had never even felt the scent of one. The dark ones didn't remember how it was to feel desire, they could have created genderless slaves but in their haste they didn't think that far.

The monsters did charge forth, and the females did run too, out over the plains with amazing speed, spreading a trail of scents which did drive the monsters insane. Gholrae did hover above the plain, invisible as her creations did lure the monsters away. It was hard to create this illusion with both sight and smell but needed. If she was to get her vengeance this had to be done and she bared her long teeth and slid back towards the palace. Soon it would be her turn. The two wolves did run ahead of the illusions, spreading the scent which did drive the beasts mad since things made from thin air don't have smell. It was a trick the Goddess did approve of her and thus Gholrae was allowed to borrow the two huge wolves for her purpose. They all had to cooperate now.

Ahravan did gape, the monsters did chase something slightly smaller like they were crazy and Wenja did grin from ear to ear. "A distraction, I knew it."

Ahravan took a deep breath. "Right, we have to move now. Are you ready?"

Wenja did nod and she walked over and embraced him. "I am, I am not afraid Ahravan, I can do this. I have to do this. No matter what happens, I love you both"

Rhawan did hug her and kissed her and she gathered her courage. The cat walked over and she smiled. "Take care, keep them off my back and I will do my part of this"

She did climb onto the back of the animal and they started to move, Gochil and Darush weren't experienced enough to ride out onto the plain to fight so they stayed behind, ready to give aide to anybody who needed it. The monsters were all running away from the gate, towards the creatures on the plain and thus there were few left, mostly weaker and smaller ones which didn't dare to challenge the larger males. Wenja started to glow as she charged forth on the back of the huge cat, she felt no fear now, only determination. It would end this day, one way or the other.

Resh'kha and Kulkar were staring at the running monsters with huge eyes and Kulkar did snicker. "Clever, very clever. Not removing the balls of them beasts was a mistake. By my sister's sideburns, this is one sight to behold."

Resh'kha did shiver, the monsters were naked, they carried clubs and other primitive weapons but no clothing nor armour and the fact that there were females nearby couldn't be hidden. It did look obscene and bizarre at the same time and the males were howling with lust the moment they exited the gate. It did obviously take away even the last remnant of obedience for nothing could stop them now. Resh'kha managed to tear her eyes away from the howling horde and heard a distant voice. "The crystal beam, now!"

Kulkar heard it too and he did run forth, axe ready. It was dangerous for the dark one would most certainly notice this and come to stop them but what else could they do? Resh'kha did gather her courage and joined the dwarf, clenching her teeth together. Nobody was ever gonna say that a dwarf dared when an orc didn't.

The thick beam of crystal was beautiful and apparently very solid and Kulkar did see the energy flowing through it. He did frown. "The gate is drawing power from the cliff somehow, we have to stop that, but how? I doubt that our axes can do much to the crystal , I think it is very solid."

Resh'kha stared at the spot where the crystal beam did join with the cliff. The material was greyish and dark and did resemble very hard bone but she took a deep breath. "It isn't exactly granite. We can surely free some chunks of it"

Kulkar grinned and lifted his axe. "Aye lass, let us see how good our blades are"

They ran over and Kulkar started hacking away at the dark substance around the beam and pieces did fly around their ears. They would be able to at least hinder the flow of energy and Resh'kha did put all her strength into the job.

The dark one had been busy calculating the number of monsters they could get through in one day and he discovered the spectacle by chance. He did look up and since he had a transparent window facing the gate he saw how the monsters started running the moment they left it. He frowned and turned around, opened a new window in the direction they were running and he did gape. What in the name of every dark star?! He just stood there for a few seconds, dumbstruck and confused and then he felt it. A new presence, intense and burning and he realized that it was something powerful, something with the potential to destroy it all. He did roar in rage and prepared to burst forth, protect the gate with all he had and he knew that no being of this realm would be able to fight him and live. He would eradicate this being which did bring such a burning light. Then the gate did shudder and the blue beam of energy did seem to fade. He shrieked and saw that two beings were trying to destroy it and he did panic. If there had been more of the dark ones there it would have been no problem but the monsters were seemingly uncontrollable now and he had to save the gate.

He did rush out from the palace, dead set on dealing with this threat and then the flaming energy.

Wenja did ride in the front, the few monsters which still were scurrying around did try to attack but the light from the jar did blind them and Khor'esh and Flint did tear into them. Suddenly the two enormous black wolves did join them too and Ahravan and Rhawan did use their swords with calculated elegance. The scent the wolves had brought out onto the plain was so spread and strong now they didn't need to carry it further away and thus they could help the chosen one reach the gate. They were large and strong enough to tear into the beasts and a huge black female did also appear out of nowhere and started to fight, her teeth sharp and her will adamant. They would not allow these beasts to stop them, even for a second. Wenja felt the malice ahead, the dark cold from a world which had been destroyed and she saw that the beam of shimmering energy from the cliff did tremble. A distraction indeed, she knew it was Resh'kha and one of the dwarves and she had to smile, a stiff smile. They did put themselves in mortal danger thus. But she remembered the words of the creature which did give her the relic and she took a deep breath and closed her eyes. She did reach out, knowing it was dangerous but it was needed, a part of the goddess plan. She saw the cliff as if it was transparent and deep within the earth, buried for ages she saw the source of the energy the dark one was trying to tap into. She gave out a mental call to Resh'kha.

The female orc had been hacking away at the cliff with all of her determination when she heard the call, she recognized Wenja's voice and rejoiced in the fact that she was alive but the message did puzzle her. "Throw the heart stone into the cliff, do it now! The dark one is coming!"

Resh'kha didn't stop to question Wenja at all, she did as she was told. She did pull the heart stone out of its bag and threw it into the openings in the cliff. Since she was strong it did fly well and landed on the sand with a soft thump.

The dark one saw that the largest of the two figures did a swift move but he didn't see what it was, he just had to stop what they were doing and he did attack with all his fury. Since he wasn't flesh he couldn't harm anything physically but he was energy and both were hit with beams of scolding hot power. Kulkar did fly backwards, he did collide with the cliff but he did wear armour and it did take much of the impact. Resh'kha did discover that the black armour made from scales protected her well. She did barely feel anything and she sneered and without really being aware of it she did activate the gifts she had gotten from the old dwarven shaman.

Wenja did see that the heart stone did land right above the source and she forgot about the gate and the fight which was going on. She reached into the stone and connected its energy with that of the cliff and her voice did ring clear and true. (RISE)

The ground did tremble, the heart stone did burst into an intense red colour and it did sink down, to join the one deep within the earth. The enormous amount of power Gholrae had gathered in her circle was

610

suddenly unleashed, and it was strong enough to rip through the earth and free the power hidden deep within the roots of the mountains.

Resh'kha did swear, the dark entity was not something she could fight since it wasn't physical and she did raise a shield around herself and Kulkar. She screamed to the dwarf. "Keep hacking!"

Kulkar did obey, his axe did resume its work and the dark one did roar and tried to get through the shield, beside himself with rage and fear.

The heart stone had kept one secret, the spirit which Resh'kha had encountered in the tunnels with the dead trolls and now it did awaken and sprang free. It wasn't a very powerful entity, nor was it very wise. It was old yes, but such spirits are usually not very experienced. Yet it did know what to do and it was of the earth after all. It did force a wall of sand up from the ground and it did hinder the blasts the dark one did throw at Resh'kha and Kulkar. Her shields weren't strong enough to withstand more than a few such attacks but this did buy them some time.

Wenja and the huge cat did pick up speed, she did clutch the jar in her hand and now the monsters became aware of her and the light. Most were still drawn away by the female scent but some were obedient and formed a wall to protect the gate. Ahravan and Rhawan were next to her, and now Ahravan did see what he truly had been given in Khor'ath. The unicorn did lower its head, the horn did grow again, a bright lance of piercing light and they ploughed into the monsters like a sledgehammer. The wolves did rip the monsters into shreds, their speed and power terrible to behold and the energy from the gate was scolding hot and so very strong. Wenja did scream, the energy streaming from the gate was horrible, it was tearing into her very soul and trying to devour it but she felt that the spark which was her daughter's soul did protect her and the cat didn't slow down even if the energy did scorch its fur. She kept a steady course, not hesitating, not fearing.

The dark one did feel the energy of yet another entity but couldn't see it and he got distracted, he tried to raise a crystal dome around the two to crush them and felt that it was hindered somehow, the spirit Resh'kha had shielded within the gem was doing its best to shield her. The ground did start to shake and the cliff did disintegrate, it became dust, a massive heap of dust the size of a hill and yet that dust didn't fly out over the plains as it ought to. The alluring females did disappear, the monsters were far from the gate now and the dark one felt how a most unwanted sensation did burst through him. He was shifting to flesh and blood, without wanting to!

The force hidden in the earth did rise, a wave of massive power and will and as it did rise it spread, adding to the power of this realm. Then the soul of that ancient dragon which had fallen from the skies reached the air again and took shape. The dust did raise once more, and its shape was suddenly visible for all to see. Enormous and terrifying and it did lift its head to the stars among which he never would fly again and knew its task. The dust did glow red, the power of the circle and the strange forest did fly freely, adding to the power of the land and around the former cliff a pattern started to glow in a bright green colour, it was the symbol of protection and it did make the very ground shiver. This realm did reject the powers from the other realm, all worlds would do the same now, awakened by Wenja and her mates through the holy circle.

The dark one did scream, he couldn't control his powers like this, he was vulnerable and he tried to flee back to the palace but didn't get that far. A tall and horrible figure did block the way. He had never seen Gholrae but he did recognize the species and he was stunned. He didn't really have time to wonder before she attacked and he felt the first pain in a very long time. He did look down, long claws did tear into his very flesh and cut through bones and tissue, ripping into the beating heart and yanking it out of his chest. His last thought was one of complete confusion.

The great ones had sensed that something was going on and several were on their way through the gate, determined to punish their useless servant. Their sheer energy did expand the gate to let them through but then there was a sort of disturbance and they tried to speed up.

Wenja saw that the tall greyish figure which had killed the dark one did run forth, past her and dove into the gate. The massive dragon did shrink to the size of a man, the energy made it glow with dark light and it too did enter the gate. It was like swimming up a waterfall, getting closer was almost impossible and very painful and the others couldn't get this close. Only Wenja had that power now and she did see dark swirling figures within the gate, saw how the odd female was ripping into them and keeping them back so they couldn't enter this world and Wenja lifted her hand and threw the jar with a scream of sheer defiance. She did throw it and watched it dance through the air, watched it glitter and glow and suddenly it appeared to be sucked inn. The gate did swallow it and instinct told her what to do. She covered her eyes with her arm and the cat did crouch down. The crystal beam did shatter like thin glass and Resh'kha and Kulkar were tossed to the side in a rain of splinters and smoke. The gate did swell, then it did shrink, suddenly and absolutely, from a broad open hole in the air into a pinprick and then with a loud boof and a bright flash of light it was gone. A wave of energy shot over the plain, almost knocking them all over, making the very air shiver and glow and a scent of something burned did sting their noses. Everybody was crouching down, waiting for the energy to calm down.

The dragon and Gholrae rushed through, reaching the other end before the gate did close. The grand ones who had been delayed by Gholrae tried to flee too but it was too late, they were utterly destroyed as the gate did disintegrate. The power within the jar did make contact between the realms impossible and the gate did simply seize to exist. The entire energy of several realms had been gathered within the jar, the life of living beings, of whole planets. Awakened and sanctified by Wenja and against it darkness didn't stand a chance. The energy within the jar was that of a supernova and the very fabric of time and space was rewoven, changed and turned into something new. It was too strong to be torn through now, the great ones would never be able to leave their own realm again for it was sealed off, surrounded by an orb of impenetrable energy. All worlds were now connected, a grid of protection around them and nothing like this could happen again. The circles were everywhere, alert and armed and the Gods and Goddesses ready to defend their realms if the need should arise again.

On the other side the effect was horrible, an explosion of cataclysmic proportions, tearing into the very land itself and flattening the waiting armies, burning them to cinders as if a sun had fallen onto their world from above. The dragon felt the closeness of dark minds and souls hungry only for power and it did resume its full power again, fed by the power of the explosion. Gholrae did laugh, a wild and horrific laughter and here she too could become what she once was. She did retake what was taken from her and as the massive dragon did tear into the delicate structures the dark ones erected for themselves and destroyed them Gholrae did kill all the beasts she could see and she didn't spare any of them. She wouldn't be done before they all were dead and neither would the great dragon. Even the oldest of the great ones stood little chance against the flames of a being created to fly among the very stars themselves. The world was caught in a firestorm, the life energy stolen from dozen of worlds returned to where it came from, this was now a dead world and the great ones did pay the ultimate price for their arrogance.

They were sheer energy, they had thrown their mortal bodies aside and now their strength became their weakness. It was nothing there to keep them assembled, nothing to protect them. Being an ethereal being of power can be the ultimate freedom but also a death sentence and they had been digging their own graves for a long time. There was no unity, no feeling of wanting to protect each other. It was each one for his own and thus there were no attempt at creating a common front against the onslaught. If they had cooperated they could have survived, as it was it became their destruction. The power of the dragon flames did simply devour them and there was no afterlife, no hope left. The race which had been a scourge for so many others was eradicated and only dust remained of their constructions and vast armies.

Gholrae did laugh, her powers as a Goddess fully restored and she did rise above the scorched lands and on her command the crust of the planet started to tear itself apart, volcanoes did erupt violently, the surface was turned inside out and nothing would remain of what once was. This planet would maybe harbour life again, but it would never become a danger to other worlds and it would have limited time since the very sun was growing old. Gholrae did return to her own world now, she would free her people and restore it to its former glory and life would go on, as it was meant to do.

The dragon did leave the spheres of this world and did head out into the void between the stars once more, it had lost some of its might but not all of it and over time it would return to its former strength and power. It

614

had all the time in the world and it would not allow itself to be pulled inn by the forces of gravity again. Its magic would protect it from such a blunder and if it at all thought about the impact it had had upon the world it collided with it didn't allow it to affect it at all.

The blast had thrown everybody off their feet and the plain was trembling, the earth was screaming as the balance was reinstated and Wenja moaned and struggled to get back onto her feet. She felt very dizzy and everything was turning around in front of her eyes. Resh'kha and Kulkar did get up, both were cut in several places by shards of flying crystal but not too badly and they staggered forth. Ahravan and Rhawan ran to Wenja and helped her get up, both were visibly shaken and scared and the huge cat and the wolves did gather around them. Wenja had a ringing sound in her ears and she had to blink, what was going to happen now? The gate was closed, no doubt about that.

Ahravan did kiss her and Wenja did whimper, she felt horrible, as if she had been tossed down a steep hill. Resh'kha did shake herself, she had blood everywhere and she was covered with dust too. She did look terrible. "What now? There are still beasts out there?"

Ahravan did jolt, he did stare out over the plains and Resh'kha was right, the last ones which had passed through the gates were still there, nobody had killed them and they were many and strong, and now the dark one was gone, nothing did control them anymore. Wenja did gasp, she could feel them. They were confused and angry and they felt a sort of pull towards the palace which still stood there. "The palace will pull them inn, we have to get out of here"

Rhawan did whistle for their steeds and he was about to mount up when Ayhrandur and Khirhien came galloping, behind them Gochil and Darush did appear in a cloud of dust. They did look terrified and the reason was obvious. Everything the dark one had dragged into this world over the last days was being pulled back towards the palace, the last remnant of their own world left here. It was calling for them with tremendous force and it was not going to let them get away. The dark one had gathered a lot of his own energy to create the palace and it did still wish for its slaves to do their job. Ahravan did gape, what came down from the hills was fell trolls, hundreds of them, and behind them scores of the transparent demons. All pulled back and all ready to follow the final biddings of their master.

Darush was hollering "They are coming from everywhere!"

He was right, they were truly everywhere and coming from almost all directions. Wenja felt sick, the demons were like dark voids moving towards them, horrible cold minds set only upon killing and they did tear into some of the monsters and trolls as they went, only to get them out of the way. The huge cat did growl and Khor'ath did nicker, the unicorn did paw at the ground and Ahravan did pull himself together with a gasp. "We have to go, now!"

Wenja did stare at the palace. "It is calling them to it, it has to go"

Rhawan did toss her onto the back of the cat. "We have to deal with that later, now we have to get away from them"

Ayhrandur did throw himself onto his horse, the animals were wide eyed and on the verge of going into a fit of panic. "Where to? They are everywhere?!"

Resh'kha did point north. "There is a swamp to the north of where the cliff was, we may be able to evade them there? The flood didn't reach it I think, or if it did it could still be a chance that we can hide there?"

Ahravan did groan. "A swamp?! I have heard about it, I don't think it is safe!"

Resh'kha did growl at him. "Maybe not, but safer than the monsters, Wenja is exhausted and Kulkar is hurt, we don't stand much of a chance"

Rhawan did nod. "She is right, let's go before it is too late!"

They did mount up and Wenja did stare at the palace, it did look otherworldly and it was beautiful but it was an ominous beauty, one with a dark secret. It was harbouring the will of its creator. They did ride towards where the cliff had been and the ground there was uneven and filled with craters. Wenja did turn her head against the palace, the blue crystal was beautiful in itself and she did see that an opening did appear in the wall. A strange creature did emerge, it was like a snake with several arms and an odd flat head and it did look very ill. She felt a strong surge of pain coming from the being, but also pride.

616

She did reach out to the being, sensing that this too was a victim of the dark ones, wishing to help. She did yelp as its memories did pour into her like a flood. "Oh Goddess!"

Rhawan rode next to her, his eyes were huge and he did bleed from some cuts but he wasn't seriously wounded. "What?"

Wenja gasped. "That creature, it did poison the dark one, if it hadn't then we would have been in worse trouble than we were"

Rhawan did turn his head too, the creature did collapse. "What is wrong with him?"

Wenja did cling to the dark fur of the cat. "It is dying, it did poison itself to poison the dark one, it did produce a liquid needed for the dark one to exist in another world than its own. It did sacrifice itself to save us all"

The creature did collapse on the ground and two of the monsters did tear into it immediately. There was a short shriek and then silence and Wenja did cringe. The thing had deserved a way better fate than this, it was tragic. They rode hard and Resh'kha had pulled Kulkar up onto Bloodjaw and held the dwarf tightly, it was clear that he was badly hurt.

The plain behind where the cliff had been was covered with debris but they made good speed and the monsters and the demons and all did follow them driven by their need to kill. Wenja was trying not to be overwhelmed by what she felt, it was a new sensation being able to pick up the emotions of other beings and they were horrible. It made her way more scared than the gate itself and she was shivering. They did see that the landscape did change ahead of them, it became more uneven and they saw a line of green ahead of them. The odd thing was that it hadn't been there before. None of them had seen it except Resh'kha and Kulkar and it Resh'kha did moan. "Oh Goddess, it is like that goddamn forest again!"

Ahravan did stare at her. "Was it that bad?"

The she orc did nod vigorously. "It was worse than you can imagine, it was trees but they weren't trees, not really"

Khirhien did lean forth over the neck of his horse. "Trees and not trees at the same time?"

Resh'kha did roll her eyes. "Yes. They were just shaped like trees but in truth I have no idea of what they really were"

Rhawan did nod. "Better not to know I guess!"

The number of enemies at their heels was staggering and the demons were very fast but the sheer number did slow them down. Resh'kha felt her amulet glow again, it felt warm and alive and she did pull it out of the tunic she wore under the armour. It did glow faintly and she felt that her connection with the land did reawaken. This plain wasn't polluted by the dark ones anymore, it was freed from their influence and she felt that it was angered by the presence of this evil. The plain had been naked and barren but now they were heading into a vast area covered with forest and swampland and it did seem to become more and more vigorous and ancient the further they got, this was truly strange. Had it been there always, just shielded from their eyes or had the circle awakened the forest and brought it there from somewhere else? It was hard to tell really. Wenja did moan, the spirits of the land were visible to her now, she saw them as swirling shadows and she did point forwards. "Ride towards the centre of the swamp, there is something there…"

They did obey her without questions even when the ground became soggy and odd plants did cover the land. It was at first tall grasses, then bushes and slowly trees became a forest. This was sickly and grey and the trees thin and reed like but they grew older as they did push forth. The animals struggling with the wet surface and the mud and Resh'kha did see that the flood hadn't reached this area at all. There had to be some reason why it didn't drain itself but she had no idea of what. But as they did ride forth the surroundings did change, subtly. The forest did look more healthy, the sickly appearance did disappear and Resh'kha could feel that it had been waiting for something.

The beasts did follow them, she had almost expected the trees to destroy them as it had in the forest Gholrae had created but here nothing of that sorts happened. They had to keep going and the amulet did feel heavy now, Resh'kha did feel that it was important. Ahravan too had gotten a weird feeling, as if something was scraping against his skin near his waist and he did grunt and scratched it but it didn't disappear. He hadn't been near any bugs and suddenly his fingers felt warm. He did look down, it was behind the small pocket he had in his belt and he frowned. Something in there was warm? He did steer Khor'ath with his knees and did open the pocket. It was the medallion he had taken from the human who raped the two children, back before Wenja and the others reached the city. He did blink and stared at the thing, it was in fact very hot and he did cussed and put it in the sheath where he kept his daggers. It was thick and did protect him from the warmth. Wenja did turn her head swiftly. "What was that?!"

Ahravan did look sheepish, "A medallion of some sorts, taken from dead dark priests I think"

Wenja did look very shocked, "By the Goddess Ahravan, it is powerful. Can't you feel it? It is darkness, it does attract the beasts too!"

He suddenly felt like tossing it into the mud. "It does? Oh Gods!"

Resh'kha did grimace. "It is very wicked, I can sense it too. But you were meant to have it."

They did enter an area with very wet ground, the animals were wading now and the forest around them had changed to giant trees they hadn't seen from a distance. These had thick roots which did anchor them to the swamp and flat canopied. It was warmer there than it ought to be too and Wenja did wonder. She let the cat find the way and after some time they did notice that it was getting drier again. The ground did rise and now the beasts were just a mere mile behind them. They could hear them roar and grunt and they tried to pick up more speed to put some space between them and their pursuers.

Then suddenly they saw it, the tree. It was the largest any one any of them had ever seen, so massive it was hard to believe that it was actually real. Why they hadn't seen it from the cliff was hard to say but probably due to magic for it did feel as if the very air was alive with power there. The tree was not of any species they knew of, it was made from several trunks and they did twirl around each other like dancers. Enormous branches did reach out like arms and the canopy was surprisingly green in spite of it being winter. Wenja did gape. "The tree of life"

Resh'kha did swallow hard. "We aren't on the plains anymore are we?"

Wenja shook her head. "No, this is the spirit world, the world of the Goddess. It has been made real to us, and it will remain this way now, forever. An oasis of some sorts, for all to see"

The beasts were getting closer and they did ride up the slope towards the massive trunk. Wenja was in awe, she did slide down from the cat and reached out, touched the rough bark. "Please, what are we to do? We cannot hide here"

The tree seemed to shudder and the branches did groan and sway. Ahravan did turn Khor'ath and the beasts were just a few hundred meters from them now, howling with eager bloodthirst. That was when the goddess suddenly did appear in front of them and she did smile at Ahravan. "Toss the medallion in front of you, you will know when"

Then she did disappear again and he did remember what he had been told, when the time is right it is right, not before. He did grasp the medallion and the ground in front of the tree did change, it was water there instead of solid ground and it was deep. It was like staring into a deep gorge and the blue colour was beautiful and tranquil. Wenja was transfixed and Resh'kha did pant. "She wants it back, all that they have taken. They are to be a sacrifice!"

The monsters did run towards them at full speed and the fell trolls and beasts were so close now they could smell them. They all backed away from the edge of the water and the attackers did in fact run on top of it, as if it still was solid ground. To them it probably was and Ahravan did wait with his heart in his throat. The beasts did growl and pant and leered and then he just knew it. The medallion did burn his hand and he did throw it, it did fly in a gorgeous curve through the air and landed among the beasts, it did sink and so did they. Suddenly.

They sank as if they were made of lead and there was some splashing but not much, they didn't even have time to scream. They were pulled down into the deep blue darkness by their own weight and Ahravan did see that they tried to swim but it was impossible. The Goddess wanted their lives in return for the ones they had taken, there was no mercy to be found. But the demons were not flesh, they were something else and did hover over the water, still moving forth. Resh'kha did gasp and she did raise her amulet, it did glow like a star now and she felt how her entire being did scream in disgust. The demons did rush towards them but the light from the amulet did make them stop as if they did meet a wall and Resh'kha did chant something she didn't even understand herself. She did feel how the powers of the land itself were behind her, how she was the spearhead, swords edge, the tool of the light. The demons were clawing towards them, trying to reach them and she knew now that her pathetic attempt at claiming that male for herself had been just silly, it had nothing to do with the fact that he had been murdered by such beings. She did growl and held them at bay and Wenja did join her in the chant. A deep male voice did also ring out over the water, it was rough and deep and Kulkar did cling to the wolf and he was swaying but giving his all. The young hunters did also sing and the air around the demons did shimmer. They did scream, pushing forth and Wenja felt the pressure from their terrible will as something physical, like a cold caress by dead rotting hands, slimy eel grass or something simply not natural. She did heave for air and then she did raise her voice even more.

The demons weren't like their masters, they knew how to cooperate and they knew how to fight the light. They spun a cocoon of darkness around themselves and did move forth a bit, Resh'kha did moan in agony, the unholy beings did try to invade their minds and break their resistance and Ahravan and Rhawan did lay their hands on Wenja, giving of their own strength to her. And Ayhrandur and Khirhien did the same. Wenja did glow now and her voice was like thunder, Resh'kha did glow also and the two females were incarnations of the Goddess at this very moment. The dark entities were cloaked in veils of swirling black energy and they refused to yield. The tree did creak and groan and the ground did move too, as if in pain and repulsion. The two females gave their all, pouring all their hope and light and power into the magic holding these dark enemies back and yet it didn't seem to work. The darkness crept forth, these demons were relics from a world so terrible not even the dark ones had dared to conquer it but they had managed to enslave some of its most dreaded denizens and turn them into their most horrible tools.

Ahravan was sweating and Rhawan was close to passing out, his eyes rolling in his skull. The huge cat did roar and the dwarf was panting for air, the pressure to give inn was horrible and the demons did stare at them with empty black eyes, like dead stars in a sea of life. That was when the unicorn did step forth, and he did roar. It was a sound nobody had heard before and the old stallion did raise its head and suddenly the horn did grow back out, the coat became shiny and sleek and it did glow. The horn was a lance of light and its eyes did shine as well. It did toss its head back and screamed and then it did charge. Across the blue water, as if it was weightless, as if the very winds did carry it. Ahravan did gasp and there was a shrill shriek coming from the beast as it did lower its head and the horn did pierce the cocoon of darkness. The demons howled, the pressure did disappear as they tried to flee but it was too late. Light did flood the cocoon, it did pierce the veils around them and then their very beings.

Awful screams could be heard as they writhed and clawed at the light but it did burn them, devour them and turned them into nothing. Khor'ath did neigh in triumph and reared, it was an amazing sight and the demons let out one last cry and were gone. The water did disappear, it became solid ground again and Khor'ath did throw its head around and bored the horn into the soil. The sand did split and a spring did appear, water flowing out of it and creating a small creek, filled with sparkly clean water.

The tree did creak and roots shot forth, diving into the clean water and the canopy seemed to grow and become more green than before. The air was loaded with energy and Resh'kha did gape, what they just had seen was impossible. The unicorn did look young again, as if it had been rejuvenated and Ahravan did wet his lips. "You were never just an average unicorn now were you?"

The huge animal did shake its head and the horn did glow still, he did paw at the ground, as if he was eager to go. Wenja turned to the tree, its shape seemed to have changed, it did look stronger and more vigorous and she had to smile. "It was returned, everything that the dark ones did steal was returned to our world, to the tree of life"

Rhawan was standing next to Ahravan and he was just staring, his amber eyes were huge. "Is this real?"

Wenja did nod and she went over and dipped her hand in the spring. "It is, we did it. The gate is gone, our world is safe now"

Kulkar did grunt and he appeared to tremble. "Good, that is good"

He did tumble from the back of the wolf and Resh'kha did grasp him. "He is hurt!"

Wenja did nod. "I see, bring me a water bottle"

Khirhien did give her his own and she did fill it with water from the spring. "Remove his clothes, we have to see what is wrong."

Resh'kha did obey, she did gently peel aside the dwarf's clothing and they saw a horrible dark bruise which did cover his entire side, it was where he had landed when the dark one did blast him away from the crystal beam. It was obvious that ribs were broken and it was in fact odd that he was alive. A human being would have been dead as a stone already. Kulkar did moan. "The bastard did get me good now didn't he? Goddamn hudr'akkh"

Resh'kha didn't know the word and the elves did cringe. Wenja did look curious. "What?"

Ahravan did wince. "Uh dear, you don't want to know for sure!"

Wenja did glower and Rhawan did giggle, his eyes filling with tears of mirth. She put out her tongue and he did grin. "Alright, but look here"

She did pour some water from the flask onto the bruise and it did slowly disappear. Kulkar did gasp and he touched his side gently. "It is gone?"

Wenja nodded. "Yes, fill your bottles people, this water will heal anything"

They did obey and Resh'kha did stare at the tree, her eyes were still filled with reverence and awe and she appeared to be almost in a trance. Wenja did lay a hand on her shoulder. "You did well sister orc, you did follow the Goddess and helped save us all"

Resh'kha did smile, her eyes a bit distant. "Yes, but…I wish the others were here, Floth'bha and Dharan and Geir are still in the mountains, Floth'bha was wounded and…Oh Gods!"

She got up and grasped her bottle. "I need to go, I need to go NOW!"

Ahravan did nod to her and Bloodjaw and Redfang did walk over, she did mount Bloodjaw and the giant wolf did take off. The orc did cling to it and shouted. "I will bring them with me back!"

Ahravan did just shake his head and Rhawan did grin, Wenja raised an eyebrow. "What?!"

Ahravan embraced her. "Nothing, I am sure that Floth'bha won't be alone for much longer, a certain female orc shaman has taken a liking to her"

Rhawan tilted his head and nodded solemnly. "More than a liking I think"

Ayhrandur did sit down and the two humans did the same. Khirhien did check everybody for injuries and did wash their cuts and bruises with water from the spring and they did disappear. Wenja laid back, she felt at peace but also oddly wired up. It was over, it was hard to believe. She took a deep breath and closed her eyes. The power of the tree was soothing and gentle, like that of a loving mother and she did smile. "Let us rest, we are safe here"

The horses started to graze and some huge fruits did drop from the tree with soft plods. Rhawan did pick up a couple and sniffed them cautiously. "Are they edible?"

Wenja did nod. "Yes. They are for us"

Each fruit was the size of a child's head and had a very sweet scent and Rhawan did take a bite of one and his expression turned to one of bliss. They all started to eat and Wenja had never tasted anything that sweet and savoury. It was wonderful and she ate until she couldn't room any more. They all just laid there, resting and overly full. Wenja did rest her head on Ahravan's thighs and Rhawan did rest his neck on her thighs, they laid there staring at the skies. It was so very hard to believe that it was over. Ahravan let a hand slide through Wenja's hair and she did almost purr. Things were good again, no more monsters and no more fear. Rhawan did burp and covered his mouth with his hand and Ahravan did grunt and shook his head.

Wenja did lay there for a while, nobody spoke, they had enough with their own thoughts and the place was still warm and pleasant. Kulkar had laid down next to some roots and was snoring like a saw mill and the two young hunters did sleep next to each other, curled up like kittens in a basket. They were all weary and slowly even Ahravan did give inn to his fatigue and fell asleep.

When they did wake up there was a table standing in front of the tree, it hadn't been there when they fell asleep and it was covered with things. As they woke up they did slowly venture over to the table, half of it was filled with food and wine and Rhawan did look very smug when he did find a bottle of his favourite wine there. Wenja did find some cheese and bread and she found that she in fact was hungry yet again. The other half of the table had objects on it, covered with a thin cloth and when they had eaten Ahravan did pull the cloth aside. The first thing they saw was a leather pouch with a delicate embroidery of the great tree on it. It was not very large but it was filled with something and Ahravan did open it hesitantly. It was seeds, huge seeds of different types and there was a small note there. He did read it out loud. "For Wenja, she is the life bringer. May the Eth'ir bring wisdom and peace to the people. Take this and plant these seeds all over the plains, the pouch will never be empty. This is your task now my child"

Wenja did take the pouch with almost religious reverence. It was a gift from the goddess. Ahravan did pull at the cloth again and several weapons were revealed. It was swords which did look almost identical but there were small differences still. It was one for each of the males present even the human ones and the note said that they from now on were the Goddess own knights, her champions. Ahravan did lift one of the blades with reverence. It felt perfect in his hands and had the delicate slightly curved shape the elves did prefer.

The last object on the table was a sort of horn and the sight made Kulkar tremble, he did take it with huge eyes. "The horn of Daradhin the noble. It has been missing for ages"

Wenja did frown. "Really, it is just a horn?"

Kulkar did shake his head. "No, it isn't just a horn my dear, it is a symbol of our people. It may unlock our most ancient secrets. If I blow this horn even hidden cities will be made visible to my eyes. I am to find the old keeps of our people and bring the dwarves back to their forgotten realms. I am the kin seeker now, the bringer of a new age of strength"

He did cry and Wenja had to pet his back, the dwarf was beside himself with joy.

Khirhien did caress the sword he had been given. "Wasn't there any gifts for those not here?"

Wenja did grin. "Oh, I bet there are, they have gotten them already I am sure"

Ahravan did sheath the sword. "I just hope that Floth'bha and the others are alright"

Wenja raised an eyebrow in an enigmatic grimace. "Oh I bet she is, just you wait and see."

Dharan and Geir had been worried, they hadn't shown it openly for they were both proud and they didn't want to cause Floth'bha any extra fear but both knew that her wounds were worse than they appeared. The scratches and bites were the worst, for the odd dwarf creatures had been devoid of anything even resembling hygiene and Floth'bha did have a fever. The half orc was trembling slightly but she didn't reveal her pain at all and Geir had managed to make some stew and she did eat but her appetite was not good. She didn't appear to care about much and Geir had seen such behaviour before. He had been a mercenary for most of his adult life and selling your sword meant that you saw death almost each day, and death wasn't the worst he had seen by far. The cities and kingdoms to the far south had use for such as him and he had been in battles which had lasted for days. He had seen brave men reduced to bawling imbecils, others became lethargic and indifferent and then there were those who became frantic and couldn't settle down again. Those were the ones who most often did end up offing themselves after the war was over.

Floth'bha was in shock, that was the truth. She had probably fought a lot in her life and seen much misery but the fight within the dwarven city had become too much. He hadn't really had time to reflect upon it, and he was after all very experienced but now in retrospective he did realize how bad it had been. The horrible creatures and the explosion and the sheer madness of it all. It was no wonder the half orc was shocked and struggling to come to terms with the whole thing. Geir had cleaned her largest wounds and added herbs but he was afraid of infections and Dharan was also nervous. The female did look pale and her eyes were rather dull and her gaze distant.

Geir did offer her the last drop of liquor they had left and she did accept. The tiny amount of strong liquid did seem to do her good and she did smile. "Thank you"

Geir did nod and sat down next to her. "Believe me, I have seen worse than that fight."

Floth'bha did grunt and leaned back against the roll of blankets behind her back. "I hear you, and I believe you. I thought I was a warrior but…"

Geir shrugged. "You are a warrior Floth'bha. Nobody could have been prepared for what we did experience back there."

Floth'bha did cringe. "I have fought the monsters many times human, I have shed blood, both of beasts and men and also some orcs but I have never…"

She swallowed hard. "Those beings, they were just…wrong! I cannot describe it otherwise"

Geir sighed and crossed his legs, he did feel his age now. "Yes, something which weren't meant to be."

Floth'bha did stare out into nothing. "I have been so proud to be a part of the twelve clans and I have tried so very hard to do my duty. I have never been afraid of being seen as a coward but now…I fear Geir"

The man did tilt his head. "Tell me what you fear Floth'bha, I may be able to help"

The half orc did stare down at the ground. "I fear that Resh'kha will think I am weak"

Geir did snort, he shook his head. "Floth'bha, you are a half orc and you have better senses than me but even this old human can see that she is quite taken by you!"

Floth'bha did blink, her voice was a bit thin. "You think so?"

Geir heard the hope in the voice and nodded. "Yes, when you meet again I bet there will be confessions."

Floth'bha did shudder and bit her lower lip. "I have never truly…"

She turned her face towards Geir and her eyes were shining. "I have never loved anybody, not really. I like both males and females and I have never tried to deny that, but Resh'kha, she is…"

Geir did grin. "A force of nature right? She is impressive"

Floth'bha did embrace herself, there was a vulnerability in her gaze which was very real and profound "Yes, something like that. And she is a servant of the Gods now, a shaman. She is more than me and yet I cannot help but hoping. She did try to make a male prefer her instead of another woman and I thought that for sure she doesn't like me in that way but now…I have to hope, or else…"

Geir did pet her arm. "Do not worry, Resh'kha has realized some truths for sure. I think those wbo sent her off knew her better than she was aware of. Trust me, it will be alright"

The half orc did grunt and nod and Geir did leave her to her own thoughts. He was sure that Resh'kha would tell Floth'bha of her feelings when she did return but he did worry about Floth'bha's health. The wounds were not nice to look at.

The next morning Floth'bha was even worse and she did complain about aches and pains and that told Geir that it was very bad. She wouldn't have let anybody know of her pain if it was anything short of unbearable and her fever had risen too. But to their confusion they did wake up to find a huge bag laying in front of the camp fire. Dharan did dare to approach it and it was leather and very heavy. When he did open it he did find an axe with a very exotic look, a sword and some daggers plus several strange amulets with symbols Geir didn't recognize at all. But Dharan did and he was ecstatic and beside himself. Apparently they had great meaning to dwarves and he did explain that a person carrying one of those had great authority within their community and could function as a sort of ruler for a period of time.

Floth'bha did lay claim to the axe and she was thrilled by it but why had these things come to them and who had brought them? Geir said that one never should check the teeth of a gift horse but Dharan did feel a bit insecure still. Floth'bha said that they would have noticed if anyone had entered the camp at night and Dharan did reluctantly admit that she was right. Geir was a bit shocked by what Kulkar had done, he had never heard of any substance capable of blasting up such amounts of rock. Dharan did explain that it was an ancient secret of the dwarves but not one many knew of and also, not one they were prone to use if they didn't have to. It was volatile stuff and also very unpredictable. You did never know just how strong the explosion would be. But Dharan was sure that the city they had found would be inhabited again, when the problem with the monsters was solved.

Floth'bha was very feverish by the evening and almost in a sort of half-conscious state, she would probably become way worse soon and Dharan didn't think she would make it unless some miracle did occur.

628

The infections she had gotten from the wounds were just too powerful and Geir did go off trying to find some herbs he knew could bring the fever down but they were too high up in the mountains for that. As he was heading back to the camp he did see a giant black wolf running towards it at full speed and Resh'kha was on its back, hanging on like some huge ape. He had to shake his head, there was no doubt about her intentions.

As he did enter the small camp he saw that Resh'kha was giving Floth'bha something from a small bottle and the half orc did appear to get better as they were watching, her colour did return and she did sort of wake up again. Geir did sit down and removed the bandages and lo and behold, the grisly wounds did disappear as if by a touch of the Gods. Resh'kha was beside herself and Dharan did grin and nodded at Geir. "Let us give them some privacy shall we?"

Geir had to snicker and the two males did leave the camp for a while.

When they did return the two females were in a tight embrace whispering endearments to each other and Resh'kha did grin from one ear to the other. "I wasn't too late!"

Geir did nod, he was rather stoical about it all but did ask about what the outcome of the mission had been and Resh'kha did tell them everything. Dharan did gape. "We are very lucky to be alive, the goddess was with us"

Resh'kha nodded and kissed Floth'bha on her forehead. "Yes, we will rest here for a day or two and then we have to go and meet the others"

Geir saw the glow of affection in the eyes of the two and did snicker. "And I guess a congratulation is in order now?"

Floth'bha did blush and Resh'kha did look proud. "Yes, we have agreed…"

Floth'bha did play with one of Resh'kha's ink black braids. "We are getting married, it is the right thing to do."

Dharan did look moved, Geir hadn't believed that it was possible. "Many will be very pleased and happy to hear that. You are a stunning couple."

Resh'kha did blush this time and just mumbled something. Geir got up and started preparing some more food, now Floth'bha had a raging appetite and so did Resh'kha and Dharan had to go out hunting and he did come back with a small deer. The meat didn't get time to hang but was devoured there and then and the atmosphere was one of relaxed joy. Now there wasn't anything left to fear and they could contemplate the things they had been through. Geir did miss Than and Osbord but both had been brave men and he was sure their ancestors would welcome them in the halls of the great beyond. He was still alive and still hale and he was rather sure that he hadn't fought his last battle just yet. The whole thing had had an invigorating effect upon him and he felt stronger than for a long time.

That night he and Dharan did move their bedrolls to a small hollow underneath the roots of a fallen tree. It was very obvious that both Floth'bha and Resh'kha were starved for affection and physical contact and they didn't try to hide it. The outbursts of pleasure and confessions of adoration and love were endearing but also a bit too loud for Geir's liking. It was impossible to sleep thus.

The next morning both the females did look very dishevelled and sheepish but they couldn't keep their hands off each other and Dharan did just laugh at them. Geir was glad they were a part of the twelve clans, he had seen societies where this sort of display would be looked down upon or even outlawed and he had long ago realized that the twelve clans were way ahead of most human societies when it came to acceptance. He had never married, not only because of his dangerous profession but also due to his hearts desires. Where he grew up the truth about what he did long for would have put his life in danger and he did never reveal his true nature to anybody back there. Out in the fields on the other hand? There things did change a lot, there nobody did care who's touch you did seek the night before battle when the fear and the hopelessness became too much to bear on one's own. With no females available it was normal to seek the company of your brothers in arms and he had never looked back.

Floth'bha and Resh'kha were obviously very happy together and he did realize that Resh'kha in fact was very pretty when she did smile and had that light of joy in her eyes. He did hope that they would have a good life together.

Since Floth'bha was healed now they could leave to join the others and Resh'kha did warn them that not all the monsters were dead yet. They had been drawn towards the place of the gate but not all had naturally enough made it there in time for the final extermination by the goddess. There were still beasts roaming the mountains and the areas to the south too, so for many years to come there was a chance that the twelve clans would have to be more busy than ever. The horrors had had the time to spread far and wide. Many had been drawn away by Resh'kha towards the forest of Gholrae but that hadn't been all of them by far, many had been too far off to feel the tug of the heart stone and there had been packs in the mountains, heading south who by now had to have reached the plains. The she orc had seen some packs on her way to the camp but she hadn't tried to engage them and the huge wolf had been so fast the beasts had no chance at catching up with her. Now they did move slowly towards the plains again and the other wolf did suddenly appear so Floth'bha too had something to ride. The small group did leave the mountain valley when the sun was at its highest that day and they did notice that things had started to change immediately. The dry and barren mountains had become way more lively, Resh'kha couldn't describe it otherwise. The air had been odd, flat in a way without the scents one would expect from such an area. Now they did see that the snow was melting, birds were returning and Geir was rather sure that come the summer the plain would be green and lush. The dark energy of the gate was gone and couldn't devour life anymore, this area would return to its natural state.

They did see some beasts and the things did seem to be confused and unable to really do much harm. They were scurrying around and some did look sickly. Dharan was talking about gathering enough dwarves to return to the city and re-inhabit it. It was grand and he was sure that they could find some use for the huge scales besides making armour. Resh'kha was not even paying attention to his long descriptions of plans and hopes, she had more than enough with Floth'bha. She had never really expected herself to open up the way she had now and she had never expected that she would find the touch of another female that much more satisfying than that of a male. Resh'kha was no maiden, she was after all a grown female and she had urges but she had always done what was expected of her, what she always had believed to be right. The males which had tried to woo her had always felt lacking in some way or the other, she had never truly been happy with any of them and now she did know why. She did also know why she had tried to use magic against that one male and his mate. It wasn't that she wanted him, it was that she had been jealous of him, of what he had with his mate. Resh'kha had seen the love between those two and wanted it for herself and her mind had been a bit twisted by her own feelings and the expectations she expected everybody to have for her. Now she knew the truth and she was grateful, she had indeed seen the truth and the future did look light once more. With Floth'bha by her side she would never be alone again and she wouldn't be regarded as somebody not worth mentioning when she was a shaman. From now on she would be a person of importance and so would Floth'bha.

The great tree was like some giant sentinel and now there was a soft breeze making the branches move slightly, the air had changed a lot and the greenery seemed to spread out from this strange oasis. Wenja was rather sure that it from now on would be a part of this plain, visible to all. It was yet again a sacred spot but of a whole new and different reason than before. She was in awe of the life she felt there, the raw unbridled force of nature which seemed to grow by the hour. Ahravan and Rhawan did share her awe and Khirhien felt that the true nature of this place had been hidden away for a very long time. The Goddess hadn't wanted it to be corrupted by the power of the gate. Ahravan was eager to return to the city now but he knew that they would have to wait for Resh'kha and the others. It felt good just resting there and knowing they were safe.

Wenja was listening to the whispering of the leaves and she did see things, things she knew were visions sent by the Goddess. She did see the past, did see how the mighty armies from the south did fail to fight the monsters off completely and how the clans of the north did succeed where they couldn't, because they did cooperate, and did respect the land. She did see how she had been chosen for this task, simply because she was a person with little knowledge of this. A scholar with knowledge of the war of old would have been overwhelmed and would have doubted that anything could be done. She was very humble and was grateful she had been allowed to end this scourge and yet she didn't understand everything just yet. Ahravan did calm her down, explaining that there isn't everything which is to be explained, some mysteries must always endure.

Ayhrandur and the two young humans did hunt and brought them some fowl and there were lots of berries and fruit there, they did eat well and they did go around exploring too. The area was large and held many wonders and Wenja still had this childlike fascination and innocence everybody found very endearing. There was a river running through the forest and it hadn't been there before, but now it did spread over the plain, bringing life with it. Wenja knew that the dry barren plain was a thing of the past now. The tents they had brought were put up near the great tree, and they had made a real camp out of it since they had no idea of how long it would take for Resh'kha to return. Wenja had listened to Kulkar's tale of the dwarven city and its inhabitants and how they did blow up the dam and it made Ahravan look shocked and Rhawan did almost refuse to believe that the dwarf had been able to release all that water.

The river was rather cold but that didn't stop them from bathing and Wenja had started to really feel the differences between who she had been and what she had become. She was not as vulnerable as before, her body could handle cold much better and she didn't get tired the same way. She did bathe with her husbands and although the bath was chilly she didn't really freeze. Way back in the tent Ahravan did rub her skin with some cloth and before long drying off had become something else completely. She was still hungering for their touch and knew that this feeling probably never would disappear. The bond between them was incredibly strong. She had discovered that Rhawan loved it when she did give him small love bites and Ahravan would always become extremely aroused if she was very vocal when she was with Rhawan. The fact that her body could handle all the attention was almost unbelievable but it did and she did crave it. But as the days went by she had started to realize that she was going to have to change even more, she wouldn't show her condition for yet many months but she had started to feel the first unpleasant changes. She had started to feel nauseous in the mornings and it was very early but Ahravan said it was because her body still was transforming. She wasn't fully an elf yet and there would probably always be some part of her which did remain human, at least when it came to her way of viewing the world around her. She had a perspective no elf had and it could prove to be valuable later on. She didn't enjoy the feeling of almost puking when she got up and luckily Ahravan did know a way to make it less intense. He would massage the bottom of her feet and it did always work, she felt way better after a while.

The plain was covered with debris from the flood and now it seemed as if that layer of mud and rocks and other things acted as fertilizer for it was getting green everywhere. When Resh'kha and the others did return they could tell of grass and bushes where none had been just days prior and Wenja felt that it was like a miracle. The news that Resh'kha and Floth'bha now was a couple was received with cheering and congratulations and they did celebrate that evening with some stew Kulkar did prepare dwarven style. After the celebration Ahravan and Rhawan did take Wenja with them to a clearing in the woods they had found and they stayed there most of the night, making love and a level of noise which had even Khirhien raising an eyebrow when they returned in the morning, claiming that they had made more noise than a herd of rutting bucks.

It was time to leave this oasis and the huge cat did still stay there, it appeared as if it was to follow them back to and Khor'ath hadn't left either. Ahravan spoke with Resh'kha and knew that they would come across monsters also on the way back, only some had managed to get to the plains after all and there had been huge herds spread far and wide which now were leaderless and on the prowl. He and his warriors would have quite a job ahead of them. Their animals had been well rested and Wenja did touch the great tree with some sadness. She wanted to stay there for the feeling she got there was amazing, one of peace and acceptance, a sort of silent knowledge that life would go on, no matter what happened.

They rode by the crystal palace on the way back, it was still there, and it did look very alien but there was no energy there now, no danger. The will which had filled it with darkness and evil intent was gone forever and it wouldn't pull on anything again, except those interested in odd architecture. It was simply a huge building with strange shapes and from now on it would be like a silent reminder of what had been. It was standing on the very edge of the forest and everybody who wanted to enter it would pass by it. Even the dark ones had been able to create a thing of beauty, it was something worth remembering.

Chapter 14:The unbroken circle

Wenja felt eager to return to her friends now, she was longing for real baths, for real food and for feminine companionship. Resh'kha and Floth'bha had more enough with each other and couldn't stay away from each other for more than a few hours at a time and Wenja wanted Sefa and her odd humour and practical way of seeing things. Ahravan too saw this and knew that things would change whence they returned. He was ready to carry the consequences of his actions, many would question his right to do what he had to save Wenja and he was rather sure that the humans in special would have a hard time accepting it. But that was not something he was too worried about at the moment, now they had a hard and long journey ahead of them and they soon discovered that the beasts indeed weren't all gone.

The packs were not large, and they didn't act with as much aggression as before but they did try to attack if they saw the travellers and now Ahravan did show why he had been chosen to be the Ath'ir. He was able to read an enemy and place the counter attack right where it needed to be and since they now had more fighters they usually won rather easily and killed all the beasts. Wenja would sit there on the cat and Flint would attack anything which got too close to her and she wasn't afraid anymore. She knew everybody would protect her and that nothing bad would happen to her. Ahravan had become extremely protective of her, often to a degree where it became a bit bothersome but she didn't complain. Rhawan did explain that this was normal and not something he could control, it was a part of their nature and there was nothing Wenja could do to change this. Rhawan too was very aware of her now, in a whole

636

new manner and it felt like having a servant at each hand, always readily available to do her smallest bidding.

The cat did lead them and the wolves would also help them find the best paths. The black she wolf did show up from time to time to warn them of beasts in the area and when they did have the chance to take them by surprise they always did, it was the smartest way. Wenja didn't have to fight at all, but she did see that it was far from easy. The beasts were huge and even without the dark one to control them they were out for blood. She was glad they had several flasks with water from the spring for smaller injuries were impossible to avoid. And oddly enough the flasks didn't seem to get empty at all. During these days she started to get an idea and as they travelled the idea became a decision within her mind. It was one she wouldn't go back on.

They didn't even see a hint of the goblins they had encountered and Wenja felt in her heart that the tribe which had kidnapped her was eradicated somehow. Not that she or anyone else would mourn their demise. Since they didn't have to hide they could use a straighter route and an easier one too and they would make real camps when they rested and cook too. The wolves did keep watch at night and the huge cat did also stay close to the camp and it was rather clear that nothing could get by him unseen. As they got closer to the edge of the mountains they did see that the amount of beasts let through the gate was staggering indeed, they had spread out like locust and their hunger was insatiable. They had driven away all the wildlife and the ground was torn open in many places where they had been digging for rodents and prairie dogs. Even old tree trunks had been ripped apart in the search for something edible and Ahravan was very nervous now. He was thinking about the city and if these beasts started to trek southwards it would be right in their way. Wenja did share his fear now that she did see how bad the problem truly was. There was nothing there which did govern the beasts and they were roaming freely like never before, the threat was worse than ever even if no new ones would show up. So they did hurry, often Rhawan would have to force Ahravan to take breaks and Wenja did feel sorry for him. He was frantic at times, convinced that the city would come under attack soon and she did remind him of all the defenders which had showed up but it didn't calm him at all. So she and Rhawan did their best to distract his mind and it did end with them all being sweaty and sticky and very relaxed, almost every time. Wenja knew her mates now, and they knew her and she had learned what turned them on. Rhawan was very easy to arouse, a glimpse of naked skin, a certain glimpse within an eye and he was ready as ever. Ahravan on the other hand was not as much triggered by sight as by touch. Oh if he did watch Wenja and Rhawan together he would most certainly be turned on but otherwise he was not as easily ignited as Rhawan. He was older and used to having responsibilities which did limit his ability to just let go and have fun but Wenja had discovered his secrets by now.

Even the lightest touch to the tip of his ears would make him harden immediately, a kiss at the back of his neck, a swift caress of his skin anywhere on the body, it was all things which got him going and if Rhawan was like a wildfire racing over the plains untamed and unbridled Ahravan was more like a coal fire deep within the ground. Whence it was set off it would burn and burn and only get hotter. Wenja too had learned what triggered her own desire now and the two males had found out as well. Rhawan would tease her endlessly if she did sit up with him, he knew by now that she would react immediately if he did lick her neck beneath her ear and often he would drive her to madness thus. Often she did end up sopping wet and aching and had to drag him with her into some crevice out of sight so he could finish what he had started. And Ahravan was not much better. He wasn't the type for quickies, not really. He preferred long sessions when he could spend time worshiping every inch of her and she did at times wonder how on earth she did survive the onslaught of pleasure he did create within her.

She did long for the baths back at the city, she felt that she did reek and remembered something Sefa once had told her after one of the sessions with Rhawan during their journey. Humans have a much stronger scent than elves, an elf don't have much body odour at all and are hard to track thus. She had noticed this for Rhawan didn't smell much at all compared to her father and other men, some did reek like old goats and she was used to the fact that men had a rather foul odour at times. Sina had often spent long hours scrubbing her husband's clothing and

638

Wenja had noticed that the scent rarely could be removed completely. But there was one exception and that was the fact that the seed of an elven male did smell a lot more than that of a human male. Wenja had had a hard time believing it when Sefa did tell her of this fact but now she had realized that it was true. The smell was rather pungent and oddly sweet and not at all unpleasant but very noticeable and Wenja knew that she couldn't hide what she had been up to at all when she was around elves, or humans too for that sake. If you didn't wash immediately afterwards the smell was unmistakeable.

Now she was surrounded by the smell of sex all the time and she did see what it did to the other elves in the group. Both Khirhien and Ayhrandur would disappear into the darkness and be gone for a while and if Sefa was right in her assumptions about Khirhien and his supposed interest in her Wenja was rather sure that Sefa would be left unable to walk for some days after their return. Ayhrandur did apparently have a lover back home and the two human warriors had sweethearts too who probably had something to look forwards too as well.

They did reach the plains again without mishaps and not they could truly pick up the pace. They rode hard and did see that some packs of beasts already had reached the grass lands but it was hard to follow the tracks since the spring had come and the snow did disappear.

The thaw was causing the rivers to swell everywhere and it did slow them down since they had to find safe crossings but Ahravan was relentless, he did push forth and they did obey him, knowing that he was right about his need to check that everything was alright.

When they finally saw the inner mountains Wenja was very tired and also oddly driven, like her husband. She felt that her presence was needed somehow and she also knew that many would doubt Ahravan when they learned of what he and Rhawan had done to keep her in their lives. But the goddess had wanted it and she wouldn't sit there and let them be blamed for something which was meant to be.

At every stop they had made she had sown some seeds and the bag didn't empty at all, it was always full and she knew that the trees she left would grow and bring more life to the mountains and plains. There would be fruits and shade and joy and she did her task almost religiously. The goddess had trusted her with this job and she wouldn't fail at it at all.

The last stretch was a tense one, they did see that the herds of animals still did roam the area and protected it but the animals were uneasy and skittish and Wenja realized that they did sense trouble which was brewing. As they got closer they were discovered and met by a group of warriors and as soon as they did recognize the group there were screams and shouts of joy and relief. Laupir was among them and he did hug Ahravan fiercely, almost in tears and everybody wanted to shake their hands and just make sure that they were real. Laupir did not know how to control his own excitement, his eyes were shining and he did almost tremble. "My Ath'ir, things…things are happening"

Ahravan did frown. "Things?"

Laupir did nod. "More monsters, they were gone for a long time but now we have seen packs again, and they seem to be mad. What has happened? Did you close the gate?"

Ahravan did nod. "Yes, Wenja did close the gate and the threat is gone but there are still many monsters left in the northern mountains and they will be drawn south I fear, out of hunger. We need to prepare"

Laupir did stare at Wenja, her hair was down so he didn't see her ears but his eyes did widen and he gasped audibly. "My Eth'ir…you….oh great goddess, you are an eternal now?!"

Wenja knew that she had obtained that odd glow which did show the true nature of the elves, a sort of ethereal quality humans didn't have and she did nod. "Yes, it…it was needed"

One of the other warriors was an elf and he did stare too. "And you are with child? At such a troubled time?!!"

Wenja had to blush and she felt a bit odd but she did hold her head up high. "Yes, that was not intended but happened and we are very happy!"

The elves there stared and she did notice that some had an almost religious reverence in their gaze. This ought to get interesting indeed. Ahravan did make a gesture. "We need to get back to the city now, defences must be planned for the beasts will come, more of them than ever. But if we manage to defeat and eradicate them now there will be no new ones for sure. We will be safe"

The warriors did cheer and they kicked their steeds into gallop again. Resh'kha and Floth'bha did ride their wolves and got some odd looks but nobody did protest and the huge cat too was shown a great deal of respect. Wenja longed for a bath so bad her skin felt as if it was crawling and she let out a small gasp of relief when they saw the entrance. Now there were guards placed there, and somebody had erected as sort of barricade made from the bottom of the wagons plus rocks and tree trunks. Ahravan got a bit pale when he saw it and turned to Laupir. "Have there been attacks?"

Laupir did nod, eyes on the ground. "Yes, two. We fought them off with the help of the animals gathered here and there weren't that many of the monsters but they fought with tenacity. We killed them all but it was hard, very hard"

Ahravan did groan and Khor'ath did whinny and pawed at the ground. "I was afraid of that, we did cut off the source but the numbers were too great and they were too far spread."

Wenja did see that a huge number of people had started to gather and she did see that many showed great relief knowing that the Ath'ir was back. She was staring into the crowd to see her friends and as Rhawan did help her down from the cat she saw that Sefa came running at breakneck speed towards her. Wenja barely had the time to brace for impact before her friend did hug her fiercely. "Oh bless every God there is Wenja, I was so worried for you!!"

Wenja felt moved, she did swallow and hugged Sefa back and realized that it truly felt good being back in oh so many ways. Imh and Theka could be seen waving their hands at her from the crowd too and Ahnriel and some of the warriors who had followed them on the journey to the plains did look just as relieved. Sefa did let go and she did stare at Wenja, her eyes got wide. "What…Oh gods, you have…changed!"

Wenja bit her lower lip and nodded. "Yes, I will tell you all about it but now I need a bath and some food and some rest"

Sefa did look at the giant cat and Wenja did notice that the dwarves in special stared at it with awe. They knew what this was and as the group made their way into the city many began to sing. Ahravan and Rhawan went with the warriors to get an overview of the situation and Resh'kha and Floth'bha did hold hands and were extremely proud of each other. When people became aware of the new couple there were congratulations and expressions of joy and Resh'kha did blush and giggle and some of the women there came with some silky shawls they threw over the two to symbolise a new union. Wenja was promptly dragged off to the kitchen area by Sefa who obviously believed they all had starved half to death during the journey. Being back there felt good and yet oddly confusing. She had gotten used to the company of very few and now she was back here with thousands of people and her new and sharper senses did make her feel stressed out quite often. Sefa had her placed by a table and ran to get some food and the others of the group did also gather there. Kulkar did look as if he was ready to drop dead from starvation judging from the expression of extreme anticipation on his face and Dharan too did rub his hands together, licking his lips.

Geir was more controlled but he too did look forward to real food again and Khirhien and Ayhrandur were already wolfing down a huge portion of stew each. Kulkar got a rather enormous mug of beer and drained it in one go, his eyes were bulging at the end but he didn't stop even once and heaved for air when it was empty. Wenja had to laugh and the dwarf did hiccup and grinned. "The nectar of the gods, I cannot believe I survived for so long without ale".

Sefa did bring Wenja a rather extreme portion of the excellent stew and sat down next to her, her eyes were shining but there was a hint of worry in her expression. "So what is the story? You are different?"

Wenja sighed and pulled her hair away from the ears and Sefa did squeak. "Wenja?! What on earth…No, they cannot have transformed you through intimacy, that much fucking would be lethal to anybody, even them. What has happened?"

Wenja sighed and leaned back, letting her hair fall back and she gathered her courage and started telling about the thing Ahravan and Rhawan did to save her, the Goddess and the well and the fact that she had almost died. Sefa did stare with eyes the size of dinner plates and she did open and close her mouth a few times. "You almost died? And they transformed you into an elf?"

642

Wenja nodded. "Yes, you can say I was reborn in a manner, I am the one born twice. They did it to save me and to follow the biddings of the Goddess"

Sefa did nod slowly. "I did see the cat, her own steed you know. Oh Wenja, you are no longer an ordinary person, they will turn to you now, for guidance and wisdom. You have been touched by the Gods, so what is the price you have had to pay? There is always a downside to these things"

Wenja did swallow hard. "Well, there is this thing…I am pregnant"

Sefa gaped, her jaw almost hitting her chest and her eyes told of disbelief. "Wenja?! Are you insane? Why…"

Wenja took a deep breath. "It wasn't planned, believe me. We think it happened when…when I was almost on the other side, the newly conceived spirit of the child saved me. It is Ahravan's by the way, a girl"

Sefa squeaked, she was a pale. "Oh by the axe of the dwarven Gods, the Gods will claim that baby, there is your price Wenja. Such a favour is never for free"

Wenja looked down. "I know."

Sefa reached out, grasped her hand. "But I hope you are happy? It is early to get pregnant before a year is passed by but you are strong and Ahravan is probably very proud too?"

Wenja had to grin. "He is, he did weep when we found out. You are right, I have dreamed that the goddess will claim my daughter as her servant, that she will be a special person for sure. But I am not afraid, it will be alright"

Sefa smiled, there was wonder in her eyes. "Of course it will."

Rhawan and Ahravan came over, both did look tired and also worried and they did sit down. "The elders will have a meeting at sunrise tomorrow, we need to make plans, and they want to know all that happened. They want you there too Wenja, not all are convinced that we did a good thing when we brought you back, they fear that you may harbour dark things from the other side"

Sefa did scoff. "Pha, idiots. Wenja is sheer light, there is nothing wicked within her, anybody with eyes can see that. "

Ahravan did send her a swift smile. "Yet, a meeting is called for. We have to prepare for more attacks"

Wenja just nodded. "I will be there as long as you are there."

Ahravan just smiled and Rhawan did empty his cup of wine, he did look tired and Wenja did run her hand through his hair. It was matted and dirty and he did grin. "We are off to the baths, I bet you are dying to get there too?"

Wenja nodded, she hadn't had a proper bath for what seemed like years in her mind and she finished her food and the two did follow her to the room where you changed your clothes. There were some simple robes laid out for those who preferred to be clothed until they did reach the water and Wenja saw that there were a few others there but they were gathered by one of the smaller pools at the back of the huge room. She saw that Ahravan did bring jars of everything they needed and she didn't hesitate getting inn. The water was very warm but she loved it and as soon as she did get wet she started scrubbing herself with vigour until the two did step in to help her.

Wenja saw that the water surrounding them became almost grey for a few moments, they became filthier than they had expected from their journey and now the dust and grime said goodbye in huge clouds. Ahravan and Rhawan did scrub her hair and filled it with soap and shampoo and after half an hour it was clean again and she felt like a new person. She did help the other two in turn and Ahravan was dozing as she and Rhawan did comb through his thick golden mane. They all had needed this, just to relax and be themselves and not worry about everything. The dark silk which was Rhawan's hair was harder to get through for it was thinner in structure than Ahravan's and yet very strong. Wenja did admire the lush shine, the dark deep blue colour was black in the light of the baths and he did look like some obsidian statue, like a likeness of a God carved from stone.

She did caress his taut stomach and admired how the muscles did flutter as he did move, almost giggling since he was a bit ticklish. "I have never seen anyone else with skin as dark as yours?"

Rhawan did shrug. "Well, it is more usual among the tribes to the far south"

644

Wenja did frown. "Are you from the south? I thought you were of the twelve clans?"

Rhawan did sit down again and he did make a grimace. "I am, now. But I was born in the far south, from a very small tribe living on the borders of the plains. Many among us were this dark, my father had black skin and black hair, he was like a shadow"

Wenja blinked, a bit fascinated. "Really? And your mother?"

Rhawan smiled. "A beauty with dark blue hair and skin like yours, the best weaver among the tribe's artisans. She was so good at it"

Wenja saw that Ahravan was almost half asleep and they did leave the pool and laid down on the low benches which did surround the pools. "So why are you here then? You have been here for a very long time right?"

Rhawan did nod. "I have, I joined the twelve clan's millennia ago, it is …It is a bit of a troubled story"

Wenja did not know this about Rhawan, he had never spoken much of his past and she saw the echo of pain in his eyes. "What happened?"

Ahravan did open one green eye and mumbled. "Tell her brother, she does deserve to know"

Rhawan sighed and Wenja did take his hand. "It is really a bit nasty, are you sure you want to know my light?"

Wenja did nod and he took a deep breath. "I had barely come of age when I left my home Wenja, I left everything behind, my parents and my tribe and I haven't looked back even once. What happened was…It is hard to explain!"

Ahravan did lift himself up onto an elbow and his face was filled with both compassion and something which told Wenja of ancient wrath. "No it isn't, you were abused and that is not something you ought to hide my dear, it wasn't your fault"

Wenja gasped. "Your parents?!"

Rhawan did shake his head vigorously. "Heavens no! No elven parents would ever hurt their child, in any possible manner. But…"

He did look down. "Listen, I have told you that I only allow Ahravan to…take me right? I trust him, I cannot stand it if other males does try to get that intimate with me. It wasn't my parents, it was a tutor, a human hunter who did live with our tribe and he was going to teach me about the hunting techniques of our people and …I did trust him, at first”

Wenja was stunned and her eyes huge, she had never anticipated something like that from Rhawan and she now remembered how angry he had been when they discovered Prina in the wagon and what she had been through, no wonder if something similar had happened to him. “How old were you?”

Rhawan did shake a bit. “About forty, I had entered puberty but I hadn’t awakened yet, I was innocent and naïve and that piece of shit knew this of course. Oh he did teach me a lot of useful things, it wasn’t all bad but he had this odd habit of touching me when he was praising me”

Wenja swallowed. “Touching?”

Rhawan did shudder in disgust. “Yes, at first there wasn’t anything odd about it, a pat on the back, or on my cheeks. I was after all still a kid, I wanted to be praised and I loved it when he did brag about me. I didn’t anticipate anything bad for how could I? The very idea is alien to us”

Ahravan had been silent but now he did reach out and touched Rhawan’s hand lovingly. “Yes, among our people such is unheard of. “

Rhawan did close his eyes. “The touches became more…sexual…after just a few months, I didn’t really react at first for I saw others touching all the time as is the custom among our people but something about it felt wrong”

Ahravan sighed. “Wenja, your people does regard us elves as very tempting, as very beautiful and many does lust after us, even when they do fear us”

Wenja remembered that from the journey to the plains. “Yes, I know of that”

Rhawan sighed and laid back against the bench. “The hunter was clearly interested in me and he knew that I wasn’t ready for that sort of contact yet and still, he couldn’t help himself. He was in denial of the true nature of our relationship. He was my tutor and one I was supposed to be able to trust him completely”

Wenja bit her lower lip. “What did he do to you Rhawan?”

646

Her voice was low and thin and the dark skinned elf did look down, he did shiver a bit and Ahravan got up and embraced him. "Something awful, something nobody has the right to do"

Rhawan tried to smile. "We were out hunting for antelopes in the steep mountains, we were miles away from the village but thanks to my reluctance to go with him my father had followed us in secret. I had started to act strangely around the man, didn't want to spend time with him like before and father, well, he knew how some humans did regard us eternal. He didn't want to believe that something was off but he wanted evidence so he did sneak after us. I thank the Gods that he did"

Wenja just stared, her heart aching already. "Did he…"

Rhawan let out a sort of sob. "Rape me? Yes, but it did escalate well before that. He didn't pat my back anymore but my ass, he would grope my crotch too, or try to kiss me. He kept saying that I was growing up and needed to learn and I hated it, it wasn't right"

Wenja was aghast. "And your people did allow such a person to live among them?"

Rhawan did nod. "Yes, because they didn't know that some people are sick in the head, remember that I was a child still, growing yes but not at all fully developed. If I had been an adult elf that man would never have been able to subdue me in the first place, I would have torn him to shreds."

Wenja was silent, Rhawan was trembling in the firm grasp of Ahravan who kept stroking his back, making cooing sounds to calm his Si'ish down. "I had gone to bed for the night, I was so very tired for we had been chasing this one antelope for hours and I wasn't yet strong enough to run for an entire night like an adult. I did fall asleep…"

Wenja had to swallow hard, she felt sick to the core and through her bond with Rhawan she did feel his anguish and his sorrow, and a faint echo of agony. Rhawan did hide his face against Ahravan's wide chest. "I woke up with him on top of me, I didn't understand at all and he said he would show me how to make love like an adult. I did panic, but I wasn't strong enough, I didn't manage to get him off of me. He…"

Ahravan did catch Wenja's gaze. "He did indeed rape Rhawan, did fuck him again and again until he passed out from the sheer pain and blood loss. If I had been there I would have ripped that bastard's throat out"

Rhawan did sigh. "It was horrible, I was so helpless and I couldn't believe that it was true, I believed that there had to be something wrong with me, why would a human want to do these things to me otherwise? I wanted to die, I couldn't bare it but he kept doing it, saying that he would tell the others I had fallen into a crevice and that they never would find me."

Wenja gasped. "He wanted to kill you?!"

Rhawan did nod. "Yes, he knew that the others would understand the moment I returned home, he knew that we elves can speak through our minds and he wanted to get as much out of me as he could before he did end me. That was when father did arrive and it wasn't a moment too soon. I was close to dying"

Wenja did hold her breath. "What did your father do?"

Rhawan sighed and looked at her again. "He did pin the bastard to a tree with his spear, then he did cut off his cock and balls and impaled him with his own spear. The man died slowly, as he did deserve"

Wenja swallowed hard. "And then?"

Rhawan tried to smile. "I was nurtured back to health, it did take years before I could stand the touch of somebody I didn't know and I struggled for years when my body started to awaken to its own needs and desires. I felt so filthy but the shamans back home were wise and showed me that I had no guilt, that I wasn't tainted or ruined. But I couldn't allow any male to mount me, until I met Ahravan"

Wenja shivered. "I understand that"

Rhawan took a deep breath. "I left my home early, I couldn't stay there for there were just too many bad memories, too much grief and doubt. I bet my parents still live within the mountains, and I hope they are happy"

Wenja swallowed hard. "Do you miss them?"

Rhawan sighed deeply and embraced her, she felt his warm breath against her neck and returned the embrace with all her love and compassion swelling within. "Of course, I have a sister by the way, younger than me. I left because of her, I feared that…"

He choked on his words. "I feared that I would taint her somehow"

Wenja did stroke the thick dark locks and she knew that these things had happened millennia ago and yet the memory did seem almost fresh to Rhawan. She could sense it through their bond and she wondered how he had managed to overcome the trauma to become the very jolly and easy going person he was now. Elves weren't fond of change, she did know that now and yet he had. Ahravan did smile, a very sad smile. "I saw that hurt in him when we first met, and yet he didn't allow it to break him. I admired that, and I still do"

Rhawan would have blushed if it had been visible. "Ahravan has been my light for many long years now, he helped me overcome the memories"

Wenja smiled, she had sensed the intense feelings the two males did share. "And me, when did you start thinking of me as something else than just Ahravan's future wife?"

Rhawan tilted his head and the boyish glimpse within his eyes did return. "The moment I first laid eyes upon you, you were so different from everybody else there and I think I saw the light within you even then."

Wenja did grasp his hand and kissed it reverently and Ahravan did sit up and embraced Rhawan from behind, kissing his ear and caressing his chest gently. "You did see deep then, and true. I have never regretted trusting you thus"

Rhawan did almost hide his face within his hands in sheer embarrassment over the praise and Wenja did slide her hands up his thighs, slowly and with obvious intentions. "I liked you too you know, even if I was scared of you. You were so different, so powerful"

Rhawan gasped as Wenja started to stroke him gently, he did react immediately and he moaned and leaned back against Ahravan who did continue to kiss and caress slowly and gently. Wenja was always stunned by how completely Rhawan would surrender to Ahravan, how perfectly he did yield to Ahravan's advances and how lovely they were together. It was a love way older than herself and it made her humble to watch it. She was dead set on giving Rhawan as much pleasure as possible and before long she was very busy licking and sucking him. Rhawan was trembling and gasping and Ahravan did hold him in place, mumbling small encouragements to Wenja who tried to outdo herself. When Rhawan did come he arched and panted and Wenja found that she had no problems doing this for him, without any feeling of shame or doubt.

The others had left the baths so they were alone and after just a little they were all eagerly involved in some rather hefty love making, Wenja was glad she had taken a bath and that her muscles were soft and stretched for otherwise she would become very sore indeed very fast. When it was over they just laid there dozing until Wenja started to feel cold and they returned to their hut. The familiar scent of it and the warm bed was like a vision of heaven and Wenja did fall asleep almost the moment she laid down, exhausted and relaxed and feeling very safe and also oddly confident.

The next morning they were awakened by Imh who was banging on something outside of the door, she didn't stop until Ahravan did push the door open and glared at her. It turned out that she was using a ladle to bang on a kettle and she was grinning from one ear to the other. There was little doubt that Sefa had spread the happy news to everybody and Ahravan did sigh. "What?"

Imh grinned even wider. "I have breakfast ready for you all, and extra ale for Wenja, she needs it now"

Ahravan did roll his eyes, the dwarves always insisted that expecting females did need lots of ale and he didn't envy Wenja at all. The ale they did serve those who were blessed thus was a very dark and bitter one and sometimes it was so thick it did look more like tar than ale. Imh did scurry inside and cleared a table before bringing inside all the jars and baskets of food and Rhawan did leave the bed area looking very dishevelled. The thick hair hadn't been braided and he was yawning so wide you could count his molars. Wenja saw that jug of ale and she did almost rear back in shock and Imh started a long speech about how healthy it was and how it would strengthen her baby. Wenja did look as if she'd rather drink horse piss.

Ahravan did go to check upon the situation and he did just wolf down some bread and cheese and left Rhawan and Wenja to the gentle care of Imh who obviously was beside herself with sheer joy. Wenja felt

650

conflicted, she didn't want any extra attention and yet she did realize that she would get just that, in loads and loads.

She did eat and Imh managed to get her to drink a whole cup of the dark ale, it made Wenja shudder from her head to her feet. Ahravan did return and they got dressed, the meeting was to be held early in the day so they had to prepare well. Wenja felt that she really didn't want to be there but knew she had to, she didn't want anybody to say anything bad about Ahravan and Rhawan, they had done what they had to do and screw the eventual consequences. She got on a very nice dress in dark bronze velvet and she did braid her hair loosely. She felt as if she was heading into a battle.

The meeting was to be held in one of the great halls within the city and it wasn't one where she had been before. It was shaped so that everybody could see and hear the ones speaking and she and Sefa did stay behind as the leaders did sum up the situation. There had been several attacks but there didn't seem to be people left out on the plains, at least not this far north. The tribes who weren't a part of the twelve clans had wisely emigrated south or into the inland and thus they had avoided the worst of the problem but there were large packs of monsters on the loose and they were heading south too. Ahravan and Rhawan did try to come up with ideas of how to stop them, and many did fear that the beasts would be drawn to the city first and foremost. Here there were people and the monsters didn't care about wild animal's as much as sentient beings. They were a weapon and the wildlife hadn't been a threat to the dark ones at all.

But the discussions were stuck, nobody had any really good ideas as to how to protect the area and even the shamans did doubt that they could keep the beasts out for any substantial amount of time. The city was easy to defend but they were just so many defending it and the beasts didn't fear for their own life and health at all. All they wanted was to kill. One of the elder there started asking questions about the quest Ahravan and Rhawan had taken and they did answer, the entire thing was explained and there was some commotion among the large crowd which had gathered there. Ahravan didn't try to hide the fact that Wenja had been close to death when they brought her back and he didn't try to hide that they had known what they were doing. The elder were mumbling and so were the shamans and the warriors and many did look as if they were a bit angry or nervous. Wenja didn't know why, but she did sense their thoughts, their intentions. She felt what they were going to say and she walked forth, got up onto the dais where the speakers stood and took her place next to Ahravan and Rhawan. Some did frown, she hadn't been summoned yet but she held her head up high and her eyes were shooting sparks or so it seemed. If they were to slander her husbands she would beat them to it. One of the elders there was an elf who probably was some millennia older than Ahravan and Wenja did sense that this one in fact was jealous of him and his power and popularity. Such feelings were not common among elves but they did exist and she realized that there were more similarities between the eternal and the mortal than she had previously believed.

She stared at the ancient elf with the dignity and pride of a queen as she crossed her arms over her chest. "You all saw the cat who followed us, you have seen that the unicorn Ahravan was given has been returned to his former strength. You have learned that the gate has been closed, once and for all and that the dark ones who opened it in the first place never will bother our world again. It was all because of them! It was all because of the Goddess and her good will and help. I am here because of her, I am her servant now and I speak with her voice."

The shamans did snicker and nod, their eyes revealing a not small amount of smug glee, they knew the truth and would never deny that it had been needed, whatever they had done. The leaders did stare at her, the one who did resent Ahravan did try. "But they broke the laws, one should never try to bring a dying person back with the help of magic!"

Wenja glared at him, she was impressive in this moment, her back straight, her chin raised and her hair did shine in the torch light like flames. "They did what the goddess asked of them. Forget that I am their mate, forget that I am the future mother of their offspring. I am the one to be born twice and they did fulfil that prophecy by saving me. If they hadn't done it the lands would have been overrun by monsters and there would only have been darkness and death left."

The old elf made a grimace. "Still, couldn't the goddess have done something by her own hands, I mean…"

Wenja did interrupt him. "The gods cannot normally interfere directly, you should know that. They work through us, we are their servants, the pieces to be moved on the chessboard of fate. No, she couldn't have saved me for that would have turned me into a deity, which I am not"

Everybody did look down and Wenja did take Ahravan's hand. "I am his spouse, the Eth'ir and my words are not to be questioned in this, is that clear? I will not hear a negative word about his actions and choices"

She fixated the crowd with a strict stare. "What was done was done, now we have to focus on the future, we have to keep ourselves safe until the threat can be eradicated"

There was loud mumbling and voices did call out, suggestions which were more or less smart. "Shut up and listen!"

The voice came from Resh'kha who stood in a corner with Floth'bha resting in her armpit. They were snuggled up together rather nicely. Wenja did throw them a grateful glance and she did lift the bag she had been given by the goddess. "I have an idea, and I am sure it will do the trick rather well. I can sense it"

The shamans did nod and everybody stared at the bag. Wenja did grin. "Sometimes you cannot see the forest because of the trees"

She walked down from the dais and set a course for the entrance of the city. The area in front of it was sandy and dry and the cliff was forming a very long narrow corridor towards the entrance itself. Khor'ath was out there, the dark unicorn did whinny and snorted and Wenja did pet him before she walked out towards the plain. She stopped when she came so far that the cliff no longer protected her flanks. There were others following her, curious and confused and Wenja did feel how the earth itself was waiting underneath her. The goddess had prepared everything well. Wenja opened the bag and Khor'ath did lower his mighty head and poked a hole in the sand with the horn. Wenja dropped a seed into the hole and pushed the sand back over it and then she took a few steps and did the same again. She kept walking, forming a line between the rock walls and everybody just stared. This wasn't fertile ground at all, it was too dry and the sand held little nutrition. As she started the third row back and forth between the cliff walls the seeds she had dropped first started to sprout and the seedlings did stretch out towards the sun like a child reached out for its parent.

The shamans had started to chant and Resh'kha did walk along the rows, shouting blessings in her own language. Wenja did grin at the orc, her magic was more aggressive, more enabling and that was needed now. As they did walk back and forth a veritable wall of thin reed like seedlings did stretch out of the sand and the sand itself got covered with a sort of thick green moss. It did look completely unreal and unnatural and yet it felt surprisingly fitting for the surroundings.

Wenja did stop after twenty rows, the seedlings seemed to spread on their own now, through the roots and the area in front of the city was by now covered by a rapidly growing forest. And it did spread out, along the cliffs, outwards, up the cracks and crevices too. Wenja was very tired now, as if she had worked hard for days and perhaps she truly had spent much of her strength. Ahravan and Rhawan had been standing in the background, stunned by her authority and the way she had subdued the critics. She wasn't a poor shepherd's daughter anymore, that was for sure. Now she was truly a queen, a chosen one and she was a force to be reckoned with.

Wenja turned to the crows. "Go back inside, come the morrow and we will see what the goddess has brought us"

The huge herds of animals were grazing not far from the city and she did see Frostfoot and the Zahar had been seen to kill monsters by the dozen. It had in fact grown a bit taller and she was rather sure that the goddess had brought him their way, it hadn't been a coincidence at all that Rhawan found him. Ahravan did grasp her and kissed her gently as she walked by, he whispered into her ear. "Thank you, you were impressive my light"

Wenja did giggle and closed her eyes in bliss. She felt very content now, she had done a good job. "Oh I needed to do that, that tall brown haired one didn't want to let you off the hook, I think he wanted to create doubt about your suitability as Ath'ir"

Ahravan grunted. "Oh Bhelandir, he is a sour apple and has always been, always convinced that he knows best but if he did he would have been chosen instead of me and he would have been Ath'ir instead of a shoe maker."

Wenja did laugh again and they went back into the city to look at the maps and try to see if there was some way to eradicate the packs before they moved too far inland and southwards.

The rest of the day was spent there, in the storage rooms which had become a sort of operations centre and the warriors did gather there to receive orders. There hadn't been any packs nearby for several days and so most were present and Ahravan did tell them all about the monsters they had seen, the fell trolls and the goblins and how they were to fight if it came to that. Wenja sat there with Sefa discussing clothing and she did notice that Sefa did look very smug indeed. She had apparently spent last night in a very pleasurable manner for she had some hickeys which were revealing to say the least and she had an odd gait. Wenja felt that it was wonderful to have this moment of normality again, just sitting there chatting like ordinary girls do and she watched how Ahravan and Rhawan did demonstrate the best ways to kill the different beasts. Floth'bha and Resh'kha did also enter the hall and sat down and Resh'kha did tell about her experiences. The two dwarves had spent the last hours with their own people and it was rather obvious that Kulkar and Dharan had managed to convince the other dwarves that it would be smart to go north to investigate and explore the city they had found. The two were extremely eager.

There was a small feast that evening with lots of meat and wine and yet nobody had dared to wander outside. The forest was still growing and they could hear odd sounds coming from the entrance. The night was spent sleeping and watching others dance or tell tales and when the morning did come everybody was shocked to the core. It was indeed a forest, and it did look as if it had been there forever. Massive trees, almost the size of the great mother tree up north, thick grooves with smaller slender beeches and birches and massive oaks with ragged bark and thick canopies. And on the ground thick moss and grasses and also row upon row of thorny bushes, now adorned with lovely rose like flowers. The forest covered the entire area in front of the cliff in every direction and for many long miles and Wenja was stunned just like the others. The forest felt as if it was aware, in some strange manner. Walking in among the trees meant you were being watched and everybody felt a bit shocked by the eerie sensation. But nothing did happen and the animals did eat the grass and here and there springs had emerged and fed small rivers.

It was lovely and brought new life to the region for sure but how could it be protection? That question was answered a few days later, some of the scouts returned to the city in a hurry, there was a whole herd of beasts heading in their direction and they were huge and nasty and among them were also swarms of the smaller stinging kind of demon, the type which laid eggs in people. Ahravan did run around giving orders and the entrance to the city was barricaded with rocks and solid timbers. The cliffs were just too vertical to be climbed and there was no way the beasts could enter the city through the light shafts and the ventilation holes, the dwarves had been very smart when they made this place. The beasts were indeed huge and they had probably come down from the mountains just days prior for they were strong and eager. Wenja saw that it was several hundred of them and the animal herds had moved out of the way, as if they knew that this was somebody else's business.

Everybody was prepared for an attack and the monsters did not hesitate. They entered the new forest and now everybody did see what Wenja had created. The trees were indeed sentient and aware of the darkness which did approach them. Suddenly roots and branches were swinging through the air, thorny bushes did transform to whips with long sharp talons and the monsters were stopped immediately. The sight was horrifying, the roots and branches did pierce the beasts and appeared to suck the very juices out of them, only dry husks were left and it went surprisingly fast. Within a few minutes not one of the large beasts was alive and the smaller stinging ones were simply dragged down into the moss and disappeared. When it was over there was an eerie silence and then the trees started moving in the wind again, as if nothing had happened.

Everybody did stare at each other, there was little doubt that this city was a safe place now and for forever, nothing bad could enter it. The forest was a death trap and no creature of darkness could get through.

Wenja was smiling as she walked along the path leading up to the entrance, her people were safe, that was all that mattered.

Ahravan and the other warriors were coming up with a plan, the forest was there for a reason, not just to protect the city but to reclaim what was once taken from this world by the predecessors of these beasts. They had to lure the beasts to them and it did mean that many had to go out there to function as bait. They did light huge bonfires on top of the cliffs and the sight of smoke did draw some beasts towards the city, but the best method was to let them see people and now the very best and fastest riders were sent out. They would drag the carcass of a dead goat after them to create a tempting smell and it did work.

Wenja would stand in the entrance each time one of the riders returned with a pack of monsters at his or her heels. She didn't flinch or retreat even once and she did trust completely in the forest and the power of the goddess. Ahravan was in awe of her courage and many did see that the Ath'ir had gained a wife who was way more than anybody had expected.

For some weeks the city was busy getting rid of the monsters, the riders had to go further and further out and the packs became smaller by the day. Some monsters could be killed where they were and the packs had started to attack each other to get meat. As the spring did bring green grass and new life the sight of monsters became a rare one and the tribes started to return to the plains. Bagir and Igkhan did return to the inland that spring, they had spent months there now and wanted to go back to their homes and Wenja did weep when they said goodbye and Ahravan did make sure that Bagir and Igkhan did get good horses and great riches. Floth'bha and Resh'kha had a very wild and lively wedding and everybody were having a great time. It was amazing.

The plains were safer now than before and the trade picked up again. The twelve clans had decided to stay in the city for a year and move again when the next spring came, they had to be sure that the path was completely safe and Wenja was glad. She didn't want to travel while being pregnant. She was starting to feel a bit bothered by it when the autumn came, she was getting heavier and as she started to show many did treat her as if she was a deity in the flesh. The great cat had disappeared when the monsters did but Frostfoot and the herds were still in the area. It was rather clear that the clans would be protected for many years to come.

Ahravan would spoil her royally and at night he could lay there with his face close to her stomach, humming songs or telling tales and it was truly very sweet. Wenja was sick rather often and didn't eat as much as Imh wanted her to, this lead to her being almost force fed on a daily basis and she did hate it. Sefa did reveal that she too was expecting one day in the early days of winter, she had managed to snare Khirhien and the two were regarded as a married couple by now. Wenja was very happy for Sefa since the other woman was going to be a terrific mother. Sometimes the two males became a bit too much the way Wenja saw it and then it was nice to retreat with Sefa and just be an ordinary girl again. Ahravan and Rhawan did treat Wenja as if she was made from something incredibly fragile and it felt annoying at times. She did also get weird cravings and Imh was a life saver, she did understand what it truly was that Wenja needed and managed to get substitutes for the most insane things. It wasn't always delicious but it did stop the urge rather fast. The warriors were still needed for although there were few monsters left they travelled in small packs now or even alone and that made them hard to spot so everybody were alert and aware of the potential dangers out there. The clans had gotten used to living in one space now but it did feel strange to some, they weren't used to it and longed for the spring when they could travel again.

Sometimes monsters would show up at the forest and they were disposed of very quickly and the forest did grow still but now at a more normal rate. Some of the dwarves did leave for the north, eager to explore and Kulkar and Dharan was among them, they had become people of importance now and many did look to them for advice. The plains were returning to normal now and the herds of wild animals did slowly spread again but some of the predators did stay in the vicinity of the city. Frostfoot and Khor'ath did seem to cooperate at times and the huge wolves and cats did stay there and would often finish any beasts before they even reached the city. But there was an increase in the tiny beasts which laid eggs and they were very hard to find and also showing up at very strange places. One of the warriors swore he had seen one trying to climb a tree in one of the sacred groves and another told about several dead ones he had found by the river banks. They had probably tried to cross the river but drowned.

Wenja was very busy these days, as she got larger and moving about got harder she had to stay in the city most of the time and she had to prepare. She didn't really have to do much for she was given all the stuff she could possibly need and more by the women of the clans. Baby clothes and equipment was delivered at her door almost every day and among the object were quite a few which did confuse her a lot. Somebody had left some rather pretty sea shells there, they were completely smooth and round on the inside and the outside had been carefully carved into delicate patterns. Wenja couldn't understand what they were for but Theka did explain, they were for protecting her nipples when she was nursing her baby. One did fill the inside with ointment and placed them over the nipples and thus one did prevent the fabric of one's dress from chaffing against the sensitive tissue.

Wenja hadn't really thought about that before, when Sina had been nursing it hadn't lasted all that long since she was weakened by the hard work and the lack of decent food but Theka did inform Wenja that she would have to nurse her baby for at least a year. Wenja started to feel as if she was about to become a dairy cow and her chest did grow just as much as her belly. At times it was hard getting out of the bed but she had all the help she could possibly ask for. She was sitting by one of the pools in the baths and enjoying the warmth. Sefa and Theka and some of the other women there were bathing and having a good time, in the winter there wasn't that much to do except sharing gossip and stories and Wenja did like this. It was a sort of safety in it, a familiarity. Everybody would take care of her and protect her and it was such a wonderful safety in it.

Sefa was in the pool explaining how Khirhien usually would spoil her royally and Wenja did giggle and recognized some of the things that were being told. Now that she was getting really large she couldn't sleep in every position she liked anymore, she found that cumbersome but her husbands did his best to make it up to her. They would rub her feet and bring her food and just be there for her even when she felt miserable and accused them of being too protective or enjoying her misery. Theka did work as a midwife from time to time and advised Wenja to keep being active until the very last weeks and she had to blush and admit that yes, she did crave intimacy just as much as before but it was a bit difficult now. And she also had to run off to pee all the time.

Imh had arrived with some dessert she had made and everybody were tasting them and bragging about how delicious they were. Wenja had gotten a huge bowl with a sort of sweet porridge and it was very tasty indeed. She was about to finish the bowl when she felt a sudden kick, the baby had been moving a lot lately but the kick was almost vicious and it made her curl up for a second, in time to see. A small scorpion like creature was scurrying across the floor, heading for her and it did ignore the others there, it was aiming for her and the tail with the long needle like stingers was raised.

Wenja froze, she just knew it, the darkness didn't give inn willingly, it wanted a last go at vengeance and it was going to succeed. The small monster did look as if somebody had mixed scorpion snake and spider and it had small glowing red eyes and it did look just vicious, It wasn't a natural being, it was created by evil and it did move so fast it was hard to believe that it was true. If it did sting her it would kill her, even if she by now was mostly elf. One of the other women there saw it and screamed and Wenja tried to get up but she was too heavy and clumsy. That was when Imh suddenly proved her courage and the toughness of the dwarves. She moved with surprising strength and speed and kicked out, the way a kid does when playing ball. Her foot did make contact with the creature and sent it flying in a wide arch, it did end up in one of the small pools with very hot water and they all heard a terrible shrieking sound as the thing did sink.

Wenja was shivering and trembling and Sefa did embrace her, Theka did yell orders and Imh stood there looking very proud. Now Ahravan and Rhawan would make sure that one of them would be present at all times and it didn't take more than five minutes before Ahravan did arrive, wild eyed and panting. He was lifting her like she was weightless and carried her back to their hut and she was a bit hysterical so Sefa did bring some relaxing herbal tea. Ahravan was pale and trembling too, he had been told how close it had been and it was beyond doubt a last vicious attempt at killing the one responsible for the defeat of the dark ones. He did send all the warriors in the city to search every nook and cranny and they did, with torches and lamps and the dwarves did help them eagerly. The city was searched from top to bottom and no less than five of the small monsters were found, all hiding in areas where there weren't people most of the time. All were killed and burned and the huge hunting dogs were released to run free through the city. They would catch the scent of these little devils and alert people. The ones which had been found had entered through a small side tunnel which had partially collapsed ages ago but still provided a small hole the beasts could use and now it was bricked shut and filled with mortar, nothing would come inn there again.

That night Ahravan held Wenja very tight and she knew how dangerous it had been and how this proved that evil was present still, just not as powerful and visible as before.

She would always be different and her daughter would probably be very powerful, it could be that the darkness knew this and wanted that threat removed, before it was even born. But her child had sensed the presence and warned her and she wondered again about how her life had changed.

The next weeks Wenja wasn't allowed to go anywhere without anybody following her, not even to the privy. Sometimes Resh'kha or Floth'bha did guard her and other times it was one of Ahravan's warriors if he or Rhawan was caught up doing something else. Many did leave the city now, they returned to the old rhythm of their people and headed for the familiar pastures. It was if not completely safe at least safer than before and Wenja was looking forward to travelling again too, but not before she had given birth.

She was getting very tired of being this huge and would compare herself with a bloated balloon, but she didn't really loose her optimism and it was mostly said just in jest. Some of the other women there came there to help her prepare and as her body was becoming more and more elven she discovered that there were differences she needed to learn more about. In the twelve clans the rearing of children was seen as a very personal thing, if somebody wanted many children it was fine, if they didn't want any that was fine too. Everybody was different and of different interests and different skills too so nobody would be mocked because of their choices. Wenja had some long conversations with Theka and Nefhriel and the other friends she had gotten, when she grew up she did see how the expectations of the society did ruin many lives and she was so glad this place was different. In the village a woman had one place and that was in the home as a brood mare and worker. Again she was praising all the Gods she had been chosen to be Ahravan's wife. She wanted kids and always had but only as many as she could handle and not one new one each year until she was a toothless skinny old hag.

She was being treated as if she was a treasure by everybody and the shamans in special did show her great reverence, it made her feel a bit self-conscious but Ahravan did encourage her to talk with them and explore her role.

When they started to move again she would sow seeds at every stop and the plains would change over time, she was glad that she now had a task and one she was proud of. She was in fact sitting there chatting with one of the shamans about the powers of the circle she had seen on the journey north, where they had awakened the relic. The shaman wanted to know as much as possible and she was explaining about it when she got an odd sensation of being wet? She felt mortified, she had in fact peed herself a few times and it was very embarrassing but nobody did really care about it. These things did happen and since she by now had reached the time when the baby could be born any day Theka had prepared her for small mishaps. But as she got up she discovered that this was much more than just a small mishap, liquid was gushing down her legs and she froze completely. The shaman saw what was happening and snickered. "Oh by the Goddess, your little one is on the way Eth'ir. May the Gods smile on the hour of her birth"

Wenja had to take a deep breath, she wasn't ready, no way! She didn't want this! She had been so sure but now she wasn't and Theka came running and grasped her hand. "Easy my dear, she will not arrive just yet."

Theka and another woman helped Wenja return to the hut, they did un-braid her hair and removed every knot from her surroundings and then Wenja was clad in a very loose gown and placed in the bed. She felt terribly vulnerable and alone and the first contractions made her react with panic. Ahravan did arrive, he had been out with the horses and he was very pale. Rhawan too did come running, trying to calm Ahravan down and for a short time it was chaos. Two hysterical males and one even more hysterical mother to be but Theka did manage to calm everybody down. Ahnriel did arrive with one of the elven midwives and the hut became crowded. Sefa did arrive too and Wenja did feel a bit overwhelmed by the sheer number of people present. But soon she had other things to think about. Since she had become an elf in almost every possible manner she would face a slightly different birthing experience than a human woman, her pelvis was still rather wide so it wouldn't be too terrible but full blooded elves did usually spend several days before the baby was born. That piece of information didn't sit well with her.

As her body prepared Imh did bring some food and drink and Ahravan did walk around, as nervous as a squirrel and Rhawan did try to make him sit down for he did make everybody dizzy with his wandering. Theka did order one of the huge bathtubs to be brought inn and it was filled with hot water with some herbs in it and Wenja had learned that giving birth in water was normal there. It was easier for both the mother and the baby. Wenja had learned a lot about the things which were to happen and how to response but the contractions did banish it all from her brain or so it did seem. She hadn't believed that such pain was possible and she was panting and wailing and struggling. Theka did order her to suck it up rather strictly and oddly enough that did work. She didn't want to embarrass herself or Ahravan and remembered that Sina had given birth many times without even a midwife present, and now she was there having several present. She had no reason to complain.

Theka said that her baby was in a hurry, it did progress rather fast and it did only take a few hours before Wenja was told to prepare to push. She was helped over into the tub and everybody who didn't have to be there were shooed outside by Theka who by now had showed that she indeed could be both firm and determined. She had a lot of authority and did commandeer the others around. Wenja was told that she was ready and she had never felt less ready for anything in her whole life.

She was kneeling in the bathtub and Ahravan was told to get in there too to let her support her weight on him. He did step inn, by now Wenja was beside herself with pain and fear and Ahnriel did place her hands on Wenja's back to ease some of the discomfort. Theka did try to take their minds off the process by telling of her own births. When her first was born the midwife was of those who claimed that no pain relief was to be given for it would be ungodly and wrong. Theka had almost torn that woman's hair out in rage. Wenja was also ready to tear things off, namely Ahravan's things. She was never gonna let him or Rhawan near her again, she accused them of being complete bastards who only thought of their own pleasure and she did scream insults. Theka did only grin and Ahravan was in tears, terrified that something bad would happen and regretting that he had gotten her knocked up in the first place. Theka did relatively dryly comment that Wenja would look forward to the day when they could start fucking again, people always did.

But this last stage did take time, Wenja was very strong and young and it did progress very well but did take time. Theka did reassure her that the next time would be way easier and Wenja did almost foam at the mouth proclaiming that she never would let this happen to her again. In the end her instincts did win over her rage and fear and she did start to push as she should but her screams of pain did make Ahravan tremble and Rhawan had to leave the room, he wasn't able to stay in there anymore. Theka had gotten into the tub behind Wenja and Wenja was panting and wailing, on her knees and more or less hanging from Ahravan's shoulders. Theka did grin and winked at Ahravan. "She is a strong one, don't worry. This is an easy birth, I have seen way worse in my days. Come on girl, one more push, with all you have. I can see the head now and my oh my does she have your colour"

Wenja did howl, the agony all she could sense and suddenly she did remember, she remembered the journey through the land on the other side, the meeting with her mother and the vision of her children. She would bear more children and by the Goddess, how in heck's name could she ever become stupid enough to let this happen again? There had to be something fundamentally wrong with women who chose to have many children! But she did push, she felt how her body struggled and strained and then something seemed to come loose and left her and her final scream became a tired sob. Theka did catch the baby with expert technique and lifted it gently out of the water. Two seconds went by and then they heard the healthy howl of a very vigorous infant and Ahravan burst into tears.

Theka was laughing. "No doubt about this one, she has your skin Ahravan, and your eye colour but such peculiar eyes"

Wenja felt so horribly tired but suddenly that didn't matter. She did turn around and grasped for her baby, desperate to hold her and smell her and just protect her. The eyes were indeed odd, the intense green colour of Ahravan's eyes but with a dark ring around the irises and they did look very wolf like. Wenja remembered now, her daughter would be a servant of the Goddess, and she accepted that now. It was perhaps not such a bad price to pay after all for her happiness and survival.

Ahravan kept weeping and Rhawan did return and he wept too and Wenja was convinced that this was the most precious baby ever born and every God ought to protect those who did try to harm her in any way. Theka did make sure that the placenta was whole and that Wenja didn't have any tears and then the little one was washed and wrapped in a blanket and Wenja was completely and utterly in love. Suddenly she wanted more children, dozens of them and Ahravan had to laugh and Theka did giggle and said that this was normal too. But Wenja didn't even notice them now and soon the room was occupied only by the parents and Theka. Wenja needed rest now and she hadn't realized how tired she was until the baby did fall asleep. She wanted to stay awake but it was impossible.

Three days after they did hold the naming ceremony, it was custom that the father did choose a name for the new-born and it did rely on the connection between the two. Ahravan was very proud and so was Wenja, She had recovered amazingly well and was able to be up already the day after the birth. She was stiff and sore and she was aching but it didn't matter that much. The baby was very calm and appeared to evaluate everything she did see with those piercing green eyes and she would nurse and sleep and she did barely cry even once.

Ahravan did present his daughter to the clans and there was a lot of cheering and shouts of joy, every birth was a thing worth celebrating in their eyes and there would be a huge feast that evening. Ahravan did seek the spirit of his daughter and her name came back, he did lift her so everybody could see her and she did coo and grinned. "I present to you my daughter, she is Tanarae, and she is a chosen"

They had already seen it, the faintly glowing patterns in her skin and they were like Wenja's, just larger and more elaborate. One morning when they woke up there was a black she wolf sleeping underneath the crib and Wenja knew that it was meant to be there, it would watch over her daughter for the rest of her life and the huge cat was also spotted again, it too would act as a guardian so Wenja knew that the Goddess did watch over her child. Tanarae was a quiet child but she did seem to have an eerie connection with the land and the animals and Frostfoot and Khor'ath did seem to worship her. The Zahar would even allow the child to sit on his back and Wenja realized that Frostfoot had been for her daughter the whole time, he was to be her steed one day when she was fully grown and so was Khor'ath. Flint did also worship the child but the horse was mortal and he did still protect Wenja but in some years' time he would be allowed to be a breeder instead of a fighter. One day they would discover what Tanarae was all about but not yet, for now Tanarae was Wenja's most precious little bundle of joy and she proved to be an excellent mother. Not that anybody ever had doubted that. Tanarae did mean Child of the woods and there was little doubt about that, the little one had no fear when she started running around exploring her surroundings, and the trees of the forest seemed to react to her and protect her. Wenja was very happy now and very content and as they yet again returned to their nomadic lifestyle she did follow the Goddess orders and planted some seeds at every stop. The city became a sacred place now, a temple to the goddess and the twelve clans would stop there rather often and the shamans and seers would stay there and it also became a place for healing and wisdom among all the races. Even orcs would come there to learn and it became very famous for its beauty and peace. After a few years the last monsters were gone and the threat was gone, people didn't need to fear that problem anymore, thanks to Wenja and her husbands.

The sun was almost near to setting when the large group of travellers did enter the farm yard, the buildings were new and large and warm and the paddocks were filled with good sheep and cattle and some horses. The group was expected, riders had been sent ahead to tell of their arrival and Wenja did hold her breath as she got down from her horse. She rode a huge black mare who was a daughter of Ayr'esh and among the best steeds they had. She bit her lower lip and Ahravan did nod at her, his eyes soft and filled with trust and love and she smiled back, it would be alright for sure.

The door did fly open and Wenja couldn't help it, she let out a small cry of joy. It was Ulfar and Sina and they had changed so much. Both were elderly people now and grey and wrinkled but so much healthier and Wenja did run over and allowed herself to be embraced. Ulfar was close to tears and Sina did cry and Wenja almost choked. "How is everybody?"

Ulfar did wipe his eyes. "See for yourself"

There were several people in the doorway, she saw Bagir at the back of the group, grinning widely. She first saw Surun, he was a young man now, tall and straight and his eyes were clear and filled with silent wisdom, no longer confused and distant as they had been. Idah and Farkur were also there, Farkur was almost an adult and a huge burly fellow already, sporting a long beard and thick braided hair. Idah was a neat girl with dark hair like Sina and a very sweet face, she did look very healthy and happy. Wenja did swallow, staring into the darkness and a figure did appear. It was Halda, and she was a beauty now, tall and golden haired and very elegant and she was no longer crippled at all. She did move like a normal person and she wore her hair braided up, it was clear that she was a married woman now. A slender young man was visible there too and Wenja had to grin, there was little doubt about his identity. Sina did grin and reached out and another girl did emerge from the house, she was also very pretty and rather small and she did stare at Wenja with obvious curiosity. Sina was barely able to speak and she had to gasp for breath a few times. "This is Ildera, she was born after you left"

Wenja did nod and Halda did walk forth, hugged her firmly. "Bagir did bring the bottle of water, and we drank. I am completely healthy now, and so is Surun. It did heal us"

Wenja did take a deep sigh of relief , her plan had worked and Ulfar did turn around and stared at Ahravan, it was obvious that he was impressed by the tall eternal and he did reach out and shook Ahravan's hand. "So this is my law son, I must say that I never expected this to ever happen back then but it has been a blessing, a grand blessing for us all. We are no longer poor and we are all doing well"

Ahravan did bow his head and smiled. "The blessing has been mine, believe me, I am eternally grateful for what you did send me. She is our light and joy"

Wenja did giggle and Sina did stare towards the figures seated in the light wagon, her voice a mere whisper. "Are those?"

Wenja did nod and waved her hand. "They are, come forth children, these are your grandparents"

The children did step forth, since they were elven they did grow slower than a human one and did look much younger than they were. "This is Tanarae, my firstborn, Rhydar who is my second and then the twins, Arathan and Chidlar."

Sina frowned. "Twins?!"

Wenja did grin from one ear to the other. "Yes, with a father each, thus the different skin"

The two boys had been a surprise just like Tanarae had been, suddenly Wenja discovered that she was pregnant again and this time with two. The birth had been terribly hard and she had been afraid of losing them both but Ahnriel had managed to keep them all safe and after that Wenja was convinced that four children were enough for her.

Rhydar was the only of her children she had planned for and Rhawan was his father, thus the almost black skin and golden eyes. Wenja hadn't been in labour for more than four hours to have him and he had been a handful and still was, a very strong willed kid with an eerie ability to spin

668

others around his little finger but there wasn't a mean bone in his body, he was just very good at using every opportunity to his benefit.

Arathan was dark like Ahravan and he had deep golden red hair but Chidlar was black skinned and black haired and his eyes were light grey so he did look rather intense. Both would be excellent warriors and riders and they loved the plains as much as their fathers. Wenja was immensely proud of them all.

They had all fared so well during the long journey back to her birth place and she wanted them to meet their grandparents. She had decided that she didn't want any more children and now her body was completely elven and thus under her complete control. Bagir did come to hug her too and Wenja felt a need to weep. The family had moved from the high valley into the more fertile ground further south and they were well off now. Their future was secure and she felt an intense surge of gratitude. Rhawan did greet Sina and Ulfar with great joy and they did hug him and Sina did drag Wenja aside and asked her how she was able to cope with two such studs. Sina hadn't really changed that much but she told Wenja that after her last daughter was born she had money so she could buy herbs which stopped her from conceiving ever again. Now she was too old anyhow and could look forward to having grandchildren.

Wenja's kids did run all over the place to explore and they sat down to tell the tales of the years which had gone by. Bagir had told everybody of Mjorr and his father and their fates and the village had split their belongings between everybody. Now the village was larger and run by a son of the former leader and it was a good place. Trade had been established with the people of the mountains thanks to Igkhan and the hunter had married a girl from the valley. There had been some warriors following the group and they did camp outside of the farm and Sefa had of course followed Wenja. She had a son with Khirhien who was left back home since he was more interested in being with his father than travelling. Sefa was impressed by the hospitality of Wenja's parents and she did entertain them with telling of the small mistakes Wenja had made on the way to the plains. Resh'kha and Floth'bha had also joined them, the couple had adopted several children from different races and started a sort of orphanage and they were loved by all and did a great job raising strong and independent kids who did merge with the twelve clans and made the clans grow.

Wenja did tell Sina and Ulfar of the trek north, of the tests she had been through and the scars they had left in her mind but also the pride of having defeated darkness. Now the plain of the cliff was a sacred site many did visit and the huge mother tree was seen as an incarnation of the Goddess. That made Ulfar get up and disappear into one of the side rooms, he returned carrying something in his hand and Wenja did gasp. It was a small medallion, in the shape of a wolf's head and it was very pretty and very old. Ulfar had to clear his throat before he was able to talk. "This was your mother's Wenja, it disappeared just after she died and I looked for it for a long time but I was sure it was lost forever so I never mentioned it for you. It was meant for you, she said so. But when we did move we did take the old house apart and under the floorboards this had lain the whole time"

Wenja did grasp the tiny piece of metal and it felt warm and alive and tears did well up within her eyes. Suddenly she felt so much closer to her mother again and remembered the vision she had had as she laid dying. "Thank you mother, wherever you are, I thank you!"

She whispered it and Ahravan did squeeze her hand, smiling since he knew what she was thinking about. Ulfar did reach out and caressed Wenja's cheek. "You have become a true queen now my little one, one of the eternal for sure. I am so very proud of you, you saved us all"

Wenja did blush and Rhawan did kiss her cheek lovingly. She had given him two sons and if Ahravan had been emotional Rhawan had been that much worse, he had been bawling at the birth of each of them and he was an extremely dedicated and caring father, just like Ahravan. She couldn't have loved them more.

Wenja lowered her gaze. "I guess I have come full circle, I wanted my children to see this place, where I was raised. "

Ahravan held her hand. "I was told that marrying Wenja here would bring great joy, I did doubt it in my silliness but now I know better. She has indeed brought great joy, the daughter of the moon was right. The prophecy was the truth, I should never have doubted its power"

670

Ulfar smiled from one ear to the other. "Yes, you have come full circle my daughter, you have returned as a bringer of life and peace and we owe you so much. It was a day of blessing when Ahravan's emissaries did arrive at the village"

Wenja did stare at the gathered crowd, her parents were getting old, one day they would be no more and her siblings would get children and one day they too would be gone but for now she was there and everything was good and the future wasn't set yet. It could hold both joy and sorrow but she was ready for both, she was strong, she was in her heart one of the eternal and the heart of the eternal is forever beating. She would be there for them all, as it was meant to be. She held the hands of her husbands and nodded. "Yes, it was indeed a day of blessing, a day of fate. I owe my happiness to you Ulfar for allowing me to choose and to you Sina for letting me go"

She hugged her parents again and watched as Ildera did show her children the lambs and calves. She had been poor but now she was more than wealthy and she was at peace. No more dark clouds in the form of over eager suitors, no more monsters roaming freely. Now she was the one who sows and it was good that way. Yes, it was indeed a blessed day when she was chosen and so was this day, a day of memory and family. She would make sure that her siblings had everything they needed, and also their offspring and one day some of them would perhaps travel to the plains and they would be very welcome. The clans had returned to their age old traditions and it was good, it was the way of the Goddess. The trees she had planted did grow, leaving a trail of fresh grooves all over the plains and with them came new life and new beauty. Ahravan did kiss her forehead reverently and she giggled, squeezing his hand and Rhawan did wink at her. "The wagon has good springs, when the kids have gone to bed?"

Wenja did giggle again. "Yes, and both of you. I wouldn't have been here if it wasn't for you"

She did pat both her husbands on their firm rears and Rhawan did squeak and Ahravan did grunt and rolled his eyes with mock shock. Wenja placed her arms around their waists as they entered the farm house, the road had been long but indeed, the circle was unbroken, and it would stay that way forever.

The end.